IRVING WALLACE

THE PRIZE

SIMON AND SCHUSTER, NEW YORK

Dedicated
to
My Parents
Bessie and Alex Wallace

"The whole of my remaining realizable estate
shall be dealt with in the following way:
The capital shall be invested by my executors
in safe securities and shall constitute
a fund, the interest on which shall be annually
distributed in the form of prizes to those
who, during the preceding year, shall have
conferred the greatest benefit on mankind.
The said interest shall be divided into five
equal parts . . ."

—ALFRED BERNHARD NOBEL
November 27, 1895

"The honors of this world, what are they but
puff, and emptiness, and peril of falling?"

—SAINT AUGUSTINE
c. 400 A.D.

I   The northern night had come early to Stockholm this day, and
that meant that autumn was almost gone and the dark winter was near at
hand.

For Count Bertil Jacobsson, as he walked slowly through the lamplit Hum-
legården park, his lion-headed brown cane barely brushing the hardened turf,
it was a happy time, his favorite time of the year. He knew the promise of this
cold premature night: the winds would come, and the mists sweep in from
Lake Mälaren, and eventually, the snow and ice; and there would be no
guilts about locking himself in his crowded, comfortable apartment, hibernating among his beloved mementos of a half century, and working on his
encyclopedic Notes.

Emerging from the park, Count Bertil Jacobsson arrived at last on the sidewalk of Sturegatan. The evening's constitutional was over, and the final exciting business of the night—the culmination of ten months of intensive and
abrasive activity—would soon take place. For a moment, almost wistfully,
he turned to look back at the park. To any other man, what had recently been
so lush and green might now seem stark and denuded, the trees stripped of
foliage and outlined grotesquely in the artificial light like gnarled symbols of
life's end in a surrealistic oil. But Jacobsson's peculiar vision transformed the
scene by some special alchemy to a kind of initiation of life, a nativity when
nature was reborn, and the old year at last delivered of first life. Again, he
told himself, his favorite season had arrived, and tonight, this night, would be
a memorable one.

Turning back to the street, automatically glancing to the right and then to
the left, and reassured that the thoroughfare was empty of traffic, Count
Bertil Jacobsson began to cross it almost briskly, swinging his cane in a wide
arc. When he reached the opposite sidewalk, he stood directly before the
narrow six-story building that was Sturegatan 14.

Tugging open one of the two towering metal doors—it had become more
and more a feat of strength in recent years—he entered the Foundation building, and, as ever, felt warm and safe inside the dim hallway that led to his
office, his home, his museum, his life. Moving forward, he heard his leather
footsteps on the marble floor, then paused briefly, as was his habit, before the
giant sculptured bust of Alfred Nobel. Studying the sensitive, craggy, bearded
face, Jacobsson was again unsure. Was this the way the old man had really
looked, the way he remembered his looking, when Nobel was very old and
he was very young? At last, with a sigh, he turned left, moved past the sign

7

on the wall reading NOBELSTIFTELSEN, and with effort climbed the marble staircase to what American visitors persistently misnamed the second floor.

Opening and closing one of the glass-paned doors, Jacobsson again found himself in the reception corridor, with its familiar green carpet and rows of tables and chairs. Proceeding along the corridor, he noticed the bookcases on either side, those on the one side packed with investment journals (to which he constantly objected, no matter how often he was told that the Board's primary job was one of finance), and those on the other side with expensively bound sets of Spanish, French, German and English works of the winners of decades past.

He could see Astrid Steen, his plump secretary, standing at an open file behind the counter of the reception office, her back to him.

"Mrs. Steen—"

She turned quickly, dutifully, and he saw on her face the same sense of excitement that was mounting within him.

"Are the telegrams ready?" he inquired.

"Oh, yes, sir—on your desk."

"Where is everyone?"

"Up in the apartment. They are drinking your whiskey, I'm afraid."

He chuckled. Every year, the same.

"For them, the job is over," Mrs. Steen added.

"Not yet—not yet—"

"The Foreign Office called. An attaché is on his way."

"Good. I shall be in my office."

Count Bertil Jacobsson went into the Executive Director's room, regretting his superior's recent illness, but secretly pleased that as Assistant Director the task was wholly in his hands. He hastened through the small office, and entered his own even smaller office, in the adjacent room.

Removing his felt hat and wool overcoat, and carefully placing his cane in a corner, Jacobsson winked gaily at the portrait of his friend, old King Gustaf V, that hung on the facing wall. He saw the large manila folder on his desk, quickly took it, and then sat down heavily on the soft blue sofa.

With rising anticipation, he opened the manila folder. He was pleased that this year, at his suggestion—he could not remember that it had ever happened before—the Royal Academy of Science, the Caroline Institute, the Swedish Academy, and the Nobel Committee of the Norwegian Storting had all agreed to make their choices known to the world simultaneously. It would provide for greater drama, Jacobsson had argued, and he knew that he would be proved right.

Studying the contents of the open folder in his hand, he suddenly frowned. Quickly, he shuffled the typewritten telegram sheets for the one that was missing, and, then, he remembered. The Norwegian Storting had, just as it had sixteen times in the past, informed the Nobel Foundation that it would not give a peace prize this year. Recollecting the decision that had been transmitted yesterday, again he silently nodded his approval. This was a time for many things, but not for public accolades to peacemakers.

Gingerly, lovingly, he held up the first drafted telegram, and moved his lips as he read it to himself.

IN RECOGNITION OF . . . IN SUPPORT OF HUMANITARIAN IDEALS . . . THE NOBEL FOUNDATION OF STOCKHOLM ON BE-HALF OF THE SWEDISH ACADEMY IS PLEASED TO INFORM YOU THAT YOU HAVE TODAY BEEN VOTED THIS YEARS NOBEL PRIZE . . . DETAILS FOLLOW STOP HEARTIEST CONGRATULATIONS STOP . . .

There was a rap on the door. Jacobsson looked up, as Mrs. Steen put her head in.

"The attaché is here, sir. He is ready for the telegrams."

"Yes—yes—one moment—"

Hastily, Count Bertil Jacobsson counted the telegrams, read and reread them to see that all were in proper order, and at last he rose, and almost reluctantly handed them to Mrs. Steen.

"All right, they can go out now."

After the door had closed, Jacobsson, his fragility accented by the removal of his burden, walked slowly past his desk to the window. He stared down into Sturegatan, saw the chauffeured limousine waiting, and then lifted his gaze to the vacant park again.

November fifteenth, he thought. Indeed, a memorable day. His watch told him that it was 9:10 in the evening. So late for a memorable day to begin, but then, he knew that while it was late in Stockholm, it was earlier, much earlier, in Paris and Rome and Atlanta and Pasadena and that place called Miller's Dam in the state of Wisconsin.

Down below, he saw the chauffeur jump out of the limousine, circle it, and open a rear door. By craning his neck, Jacobsson could see the tall figure of the attaché, carrying a briefcase, approach, bend into the car, and disappear from sight.

In a moment, the limousine engine roared, and the telegrams were on their way to the Swedish Foreign Office on Gustaf Adolfs Torg. Within the hour, they would be delivered to Swedish Embassies in three nations, and then be relayed to the winners themselves.

The winners themselves, Jacobsson thought. He knew their names well now, because he had heard them repeated regularly in the long months after their nominations, through the investigations, debates, haggling, and voting. But who were they really, these men and women he would be meeting in less than four weeks? How would they feel and be affected? What were they doing now, these pregnant hours before the telegrams arrived and before their greatness became public glory and riches?

His mind went back to his Notes, to what others in past years had been doing at the moment of notification: Eugene O'Neill had been sleeping, and been pulled out of bed to hear the news; Jane Addams had been preparing to go under ether for major surgery; Dr. Harold Urey had been lunching with university professors at his faculty club; Albert Einstein had got the word on board a ship from Japan. And the new ones? Where and how would the prize find them? Jacobsson wished that he could go with the telegrams, with each and every one, and see what happened when they reached their destinations.

Ah, the fancies of an old man, he thought at last. *Nog med detta.* Enough of this. He must join his colleagues in the upstairs apartment for a drink to a good job done. Still, it would be something, something indeed, to go along with those telegrams . . .

It was 8:22 in the evening when the telegram from Stockholm reached the Swedish Embassy in Paris. The Ambassador's pink and concave male secretary, still busy typing the notes on the African mediation question, opened the wire routinely. But as he scanned the contents, his eyes widened with awe.

The first portion of the telegram was addressed to the Ambassador: PLEASE DELIVER THE FOLLOWING BY HAND TO THE PARTIES ADDRESSED STOP OFFER PERSONAL CONGRATULATIONS ON THE BEHALF GOVERNMENT STOP

The message trembled in the secretary's grasp as he continued to read. Desperately, he tried to remember where the Ambassador had said that he was going. Not home. Not the Opéra. Not the Palais de Justice. Cocktails— that was it, yes, at the residence of some diplomat, but he had not said which one. And then later he was to be at Lapérouse in the Quai des Grands-Augustins to dine. The secretary recalled making the reservation himself for ten o'clock.

His eyes sought the wall clock. Still an hour and a half before he could inform the Ambassador of the momentous news. For that period, the news, the secret, so important, so desired, was his alone. There was pleasure in this.

He settled back in his chair, like a little boy who had seen St. Nicholas, and began to reread the message that the Ambassador had been charged to convey:

FOR YOUR RESEARCHES IN SPERM STRUCTURE AND YOUR DISCOVERY OF VITRIFICATION OF THE SPERMATOZOON FOR SELECTIVE BREEDING THE NOBEL FOUNDATION OF STOCKHOLM ON BEHALF OF THE ROYAL SWEDISH ACADEMY OF SCIENCE IS PLEASED TO INFORM YOU THAT YOU HAVE TODAY BEEN VOTED THIS YEARS NOBEL PRIZE IN CHEMISTRY STOP THE PRIZE WILL BE A GOLD MEDALLION AND A CHEQUE FOR TWO HUNDRED AND FIFTY ONE THOUSAND FIVE HUNDRED NEW FRANCS STOP THE AWARD CEREMONY WILL TAKE PLACE IN STOCKHOLM ON DECEMBER TENTH STOP DETAILS FOLLOW STOP HEARTIEST CONGRATULATIONS STOP

The message was addressed to DOCTOR CLAUDE MARCEAU AND DOCTOR DENISE MARCEAU SIXTY TWO QUAI DORSAY PARIS FRANCE. . . .

It was only 8:30, and, except for the proprietors and the waiters, they had the restaurant to themselves.

In fact, Dr. Claude Marceau and Gisèle Jordan had already finished their dessert, *gâteau de riz,* or rather Claude had finished, and now watched Gisèle daintily spoon the last of her rice caramel with vanilla sauce. It had been a delicious meal: *soupe de poissons,* followed by the *spécialité* of the evening, *Le Jésu de la Marquise,* which consisted of *saucisson chaud, pistaché, truffé, salade de pommes à l'huile d'olive et romarin,* but the *pommes* sparingly for both.

Claude was distressed at eating this early. It was barbaric. Gisèle and he had never discussed it, but the necessity was understood by both. Neither could afford to be discovered. At this hour, there was less chance of being seen. Even the restaurant, Le Petit Navire, found during a stroll early in their courtship, had been made their place, because it was in that obscure, dark side street, the rue des Fossés-St.-Bernard. While it was occasionally patronized by some of the finest gourmets and restaurant collectors in Paris, its main clientele consisted of the management and better-paid laborers of the Halle aux Vins across the street. None of these customers, Claude and Gisèle were confident, would be likely to recognize a distinguished chemist of the Institut Pasteur or a Balenciaga mannequin.

Gisèle had finished her dessert. Her napkin was at her mouth.

"Café?" Claude asked.

She shook her head. "No. But I will have a cigarette."

He found the thin silver case in his pocket, extracted two English cigarettes, lit one, then lit the second off the first and passed the first to her. She brought it to her lips and inhaled deeply.

"Perfect," she said.

"Because I kissed it first," he said.

She smiled, and impulsively reached her long, tapering hand across the table to touch his hand. He turned his hand, palm up, and encompassed her own.

"I love you, Gisèle."

"I love you," she replied softly, but her face wore its professional public mask of beauty, emotionless, seemingly detached, and it always made him momentarily unsure.

Eager to be reassured, to consume the steps of ritual that would bring him to the exact moment of reassurance, he asked, "Shall we walk?"

"After the cigarette."

"Very well."

They sat in silence, Gisèle toying with the matchbox, looking down at it, inscrutable, and he unable to take his eyes off her public face. It was an incredibly lovely face, he decided again, and now it belonged to him. He studied it in an indulgence of self-congratulation. Her hair was ash-blond and bouffant, the eyebrows penciled dark and high, and the eyes an icy pale blue, set wide apart. Her nose was straight, as in those Grecian statues in the Louvre, and the lips generous, full, soft, and the deepest hue of red. Her cheekbones

11

were high, leaving shadowed hollows beneath them. The large diamond earrings she always wore made her face seem even narrower.

Suddenly, she ground out the remnant of her cigarette, pushed back her chair, and rose. Taking her purse, she said, "I'll be right back. Don't go."

"Never."

His eyes followed her across the room. He saw that the three waiters were observing her, too. She moved like a mannequin, with fluid grace, tall, thin, hips slim, thighs and legs long, all elegant and aloof and slithering. As she walked, her legs, close together, provocative, stretched straight before her, the pointed pumps turned slightly outward, her smooth buttocks undulating in the manner of all practiced mannequins. At last, she pirouetted around a corner and was out of view. Straight out of *Elle* or *L'Officiel*, Claude Marceau thought, all haute couture, clothes, face, figure, all glacial and unruffled and not merely mortal. Perhaps it was this that had attracted him first, the challenge of what was or seemed emotionless and unattainable and too near perfection.

Yes, this had attracted him first, he knew definitely, and what had held him, finally, against all caution and scientist's reason, was not her public presence but her private behavior. From the very first time, she had become a different person. Two weeks ago—when it had stimulated him beyond anything he had ever felt before—she had undressed before him, boldly, almost tauntingly, first slowly, the shoes, the long sheer stockings, the dress, the half-slip, and then faster and faster, the bra and garter belt and pants. Wholly naked to him, she had become a different person. Once stripped of fashion and pretense, once basic white flesh, and breasts considerable in circumference but stylishly flat, these accentuated by her elongated, bony body, she had become pure animal. She shed with her apparel all vanity and studied sophistication. There remained no single artifice. In nudity, she withheld nothing, became the epitome of the French courtesan, displayed desire rawly, and enjoyed the sexual coupling completely without pretending a special gift in giving but revealing a passionate gratefulness in receiving.

Although Claude had possessed her a half-dozen times in the two weeks, the anticipation of it—the transformation—again aroused him more keenly than ever, and he longed for her to return and be off with him. As he called to the waiter for the check, his mind was still on the miracle of their union. He had a certain pride in the affair. It was not only her evident desirability and beauty, which, after all, he could not show the world, but the fact that she enjoyed him.

He was forty-six, and she twenty-seven, and he had been an intellectual and a man of science since his youth. He had been too long devoted to tubes and bottles and counters that smelled of acid, and too devoted to introspections, to regard himself as debonair or attractive, although now, in these last weeks, he had felt attractive. His hair was bushy and graying, his broad face not yet fleshy but regular except for the narrow eyes and beaked French nose, his body inclined to weight and called by one newspaper "heavy-set," but still strong and firm, so that he continued to play tennis once a week and play *boule* in the Bois twice a week. She could have younger men, gayer men, richer men, and certainly unmarried men. Yet she had him and wanted no more. Here was another mystery of chemistry that he and Denise must investigate. He realized, immediately, that he had subconsciously thought of the name of his wife. That was improper, and he erased her name. He would not think of her on this night. He was in no mood for brooding over his culpability.

Again, attempting to see himself through Gisèle's eyes, he tried to weigh his value. Assets: intelligence, sensibility, modest fame. Liabilities: age, a certain stodginess, married.

About to continue his reverie, he saw Gisèle approaching, the bouffant impeccable, the bowed lips wine, the long legs crossing in lazy strides against her tight purple skirt. He tried to rise as youthfully as possible, opening his wallet and counting out the necessary francs and despite *service compris* a generous tip to the serving people who would understand the bribe.

He took up her full-length natural brown mink coat, held it as gallantly as a cloak, and she spun gracefully into it, coolly enwrapped and beauty enhanced.

Outside, in the balmy Parisian night, they stood in the dark, narrow street, her hand in his, gazing at the great fenced Halle aux Vins.

"I should like to go in there some night and sample everything," he said.

"We do not need that," she said, squeezing his hand.

"Still want to walk a little?"

"Oh, yes. The Seine."

There were small dangers in this, he knew, but here was a night in November such as the one during which they had met, really met, in September. So he agreed.

She linked her arm in his, and they strolled leisurely across the rue des Chantiers to the Boulevard St.-Germain, glanced into the corner café to see if there were anyone they might recognize, then crossed and walked the block to the Quai de la Tournelle. They crossed again to the low stone wall above the Seine, passed several closed wooden bookstalls, and halted to survey the placid river. On the river, like a floating chandelier, one of the *bateaux-mouches*, its curious glass dome shining in the half-moon, approached. Beyond it, the lights of the city were spectacular, and to the left, they could see the towering bright mass of Notre-Dame.

He nodded at the sight-seeing boat. "I have never been on a bateau-mouche. Have you?"

"Several times. It is wonderful fun."

"I had always supposed it was for tourists—"

"It is for us first, the way the Seine is."

"Yes. Some night, let us do it. I almost feel like a tourist anyway—everything new—"

They observed the boat again, and then, automatically, without the exchange of a word or pressure of their hands, they resumed walking toward Notre-Dame. The air seemed cooler now, and for Claude, this was evocative, conjuring up the first night that he had met Gisèle. Actually, he had seen her before he had met her. He had seen her in the late summer.

It was a time when his life had become directionless and monotonous, and he had been possessed of a nervous restlessness. The preceding six years had been different, for there had been a luminous goal, and a total dedication to its achievement. Going back the six years, he remembered that the goal had been established by a chance remark Denise had happened to make one noon.

He and Denise had become interested—possibly an unconscious reaction to their own personal inability to conceive offspring—in genetics, in the biological processes of perpetuating the race, and specifically in the effect of chemicals on chromosomes and genes. They had, as so many scientists before them, experimented with the Drosophila fly. They had attempted to induce artificially changes of the genes, as a means of predetermining or controlling the future sex of offspring. This work in mutations had not gone far, and had not been original, and Claude and Denise were discouraged on that fateful day when they joined several fellow workers lunching in the office next to the laboratory. During the repast, someone had mentioned a Russian paper devoted to advances made in transplanting a female ovum, and this had stimulated a heated discussion on heredity and sperms and fertilized eggs. Denise, in one of her infrequent fanciful moods (occurring whenever she was quietly desperate), had remarked playfully, "Suppose it were possible to preserve the living spermatozoon of a Charlemagne or an Erasmus, or the unfertilized egg of a Cleopatra, and implant them today, by modern means, centuries after their donors were dead?" The fancy had been electric. Claude and Denise had continued to speculate upon it, first romantically, and, at last, scientifically.

The first years had been drudge years of collecting facts. From this handful of facts had grown a tentative hypothesis, and then had followed crude experiments with lower animals. During these experiments, they had made a startling discovery, whose validity was soon verified by the statistics from mass experiments. After their joint paper had been read and published, and widely hailed, and popularized in the press, and Claude and Denise had been exposed to a brief burst of publicity, they had suddenly found themselves at a curious dead end of existence.

The six years of absolute concentration on one subject, without any life or social intercourse beyond that of the laboratory and each other and the spermatozoa, had left them mentally and physically debilitated, drained to the marrow, and without resources to interest themselves afresh in anything else. Weary of their work after victory, they had left its routine development to other eager minds around the world. For themselves they had been brought to rest in a vacuum of accomplishment. After discussing, and quickly discarding, several new projects, they had by mutual consent agreed to relax, fulfill workaday demands in connection with their discovery, and wait mystically for another inspiration. For the first time in years, Denise had busied herself about the old apartment, sorting, repairing, replacing, and had caught up on correspondence and relatives and the few friends left. Claude found his own vacuum more difficult to fill: tennis and boule, of course, and lunches on the Right Bank, some speeches, investigation of investments, and effort to catch up on reading long neglected. But it was dull and not man's occupation.

It was at this time, by chance, that several English colleagues had come visiting from Oxford, and since it was late July, and the fifty Paris fashion houses were busy showing their new collections, the English wife of one colleague announced her desire to see such an event. With his recent position of eminence, Claude Marceau had no trouble obtaining the necessary invitations. The invitations were for a Balenciaga collection, to be displayed in the great couturier's rose stone building off the Champs-Élysées, and because he had nothing better to do, Claude had reluctantly accompanied Denise (who had never been to such an affair either) and the English couples to the showing.

Claude had released his invitations to the head *vendeuse* on the third floor, and then had passed, with his wife and guests, into the main salon. Two rows of gold painted wooden chairs were distributed around the showroom. Claude and his party took their places before the large mirror at the far end. The sudden barrage from the overly bright corner ceiling lights and the dozen lights in the recessed center of the ceiling had been the signal for customers to remove their coats, and Claude had gratefully imitated the others.

At once, the showing had begun. Claude had watched with mild interest as the animated mannequins, ten working in unceasing tandem, emerged from behind a curtain opposite, paraded across the floor toward him in their outlandish coats and jackets and dresses, carrying in their right hands cards with their costume numbers, spun before him, returned past the three windows toward their entry, and exited by a side opening.

For Claude, at first, it had been restless and tedious nonsense, and then, without being aware of it, he was erect on the edge of his gold chair. Suddenly, all of his senses were engaged. He found himself staring at a mannequin whose breathtaking beauty, chic, haughty manner dominated the functional modern room. This, he would later learn, was Gisèle Jordan.

She appeared and reappeared, with the nine others, and Claude was mesmerized. Once, perhaps on her twelfth presentation, striding disdainfully before his party, pirouetting before the women, sweeping her furs off her daring cocktail gown, her blue eyes had held on his. They offered no message, only a challenge. Or so he thought. Afterwards, riding home, he had dwelt on the moment, cherished it, and let it play out, but then his factual scientific sensibility had taken over. The moment had been illusion, invented by his need, and he decided with finality that he had been mistaken and foolish.

But two months later, still in the doldrums and taking the crisp air on the Champs-Élysées at dusk, he learned that he had not been foolish. Passing Fouquet's, he had casually glanced at the faces behind the tables, and one of them he recognized at once. What had emboldened him to confront her he would never know. But he had, indeed, halted, made his way to her table, and introduced himself. Her face had reflected immediate recognition—yes, she remembered him from that showing several months ago, and she knew his name through his reputation. She invited him to sit with her, and he did, and she spoke easily. He realized that Balenciaga was nearby, in the Avenue George-V, and that she often came to Fouquet's for a glass of champagne after work and before dinner. Most frequently she came alone, but sometimes she met her agent for fashion magazines, M. Favre, a slight and dandified latent homosexual who loved her possessively and was important to the advancement of her career.

They had talked and talked, and two hours later had dined at Le Taillevent in the rue Lamennais, off the Champs-Élysées, and later walked, starting and stopping often, the length of the Faubourg-St.-Honoré to the Madeleine. It was near midnight when he had put her in a taxi. After that, he had walked the entire distance back to the apartment, his mind boyish and alive and in a turmoil. Denise was listening to the wireless, not at all alarmed by his late return, and he made an unrehearsed excuse quickly and deftly, and was gay and joking with his wife, and for the first time in a year, he had felt no tiredness or depression at all.

In the weeks following, first once a week, then twice, they had met discreetly, with the spontaneity of an accidental encounter, each unsure of the other, and each aware of Denise and M. Favre. But after six weeks, they knew simultaneously, instinctively, that the intimate conversation, the self-revelations, the hand holding, the kissing were not enough. And so she had, at last, given in to the inevitable climax without his urging, and had invited him to her small two-room apartment, exquisitely furnished (the living room pieces were from the best antique shops in the Flea Market), in the rue du Bac, not far from the Boulevard St.-Germain. And there, with little preliminary, she had revealed herself to him, all molten beneath the glacial surface, and that night, he had been stimulated, virile, and attractive again. That night, for the first time in six years, he had not once given a thought to spermatozoa, at least not clinically—or to Denise, his collaborator.

Reliving all of this now, as he strolled along the Seine, had briefly removed him from the present reality. Gisèle's voice, intruding upon him, was a surprise. "Claude," she was saying, "whatever are you brooding about?"

"Brooding? Heavens, no. I was thinking back—how we first met."

She gripped his arm more possessively. "I never think of that. Only of now."

He nodded. "It is best."

Ahead, he could see a taxi disgorging well-dressed men and women into the world of pressed ducks—Tour d'Argent—and he knew that there was the populous danger zone, and that he could continue no farther without risk.

He stopped in his tracks. "Let us go, Gisèle. I want you."

She caught her breath. "Right now?"

"As soon as possible."

"Yes. I would like that."

They waited patiently at the curb, and he signaled the next free taxi leaving the Tour d'Argent, and once inside, they headed for the rue du Bac. She sat apart from him, in her genteel public way, and they held hands on the seat between them.

He stared absently out of the car's window, as the old narrow streets of the Left Bank blurred past, and he wondered what would finally happen to them. It was impossible to imagine a life without her, yet it was equally impossible to imagine divorcing Denise after twelve years. Yet, he asked himself, why not? Denise and he were childless, so that would pose no problem. There was adequate money since the discovery, so that was no problem, either. Denise was self-sufficient, too much so, he often thought. She had the capability to survive and adjust. She was not dangerously *female*—which he interpreted to mean that she was not an emotional hysteric, a leaner, an obsessive neurotic.

Still, why was he so fearful that she might learn of his affair? He examined the question. Was it that he was too sensitive to hurt an old companion? Or—was it because she was more than mere companion and wife? Was it because she was a partner in his work, and thus essential to him? Could Beaumont have been Beaumont without Fletcher? Or Gilbert have been Gilbert without Sullivan? Or Chang survived without Eng? Perhaps, in a dozen years, they had become the Siamese Twins, and to cut one off might mean death to both.

Possibly, divorce was wrong. Why not continue the status quo? Possibly, like Victor Hugo, he could spend his lifetime exactly like this, with a wife in one place and a Juliette Drouet somewhere else. How many years had Hugo openly managed his double life? Claude calculated: Hugo, at thirty-one, had met Juliette in 1833 when she was twenty-seven (Gisèle's very age!), and kept her for mistress all the rest of her life, which was long, for she did not die until 1883. He had kept his mistress for fifty years, and when she had died, he had remarked, "The dead are not absent, but invisible." But was Gisèle a Juliette Drouet? And was Denise a Madame Adèle Hugo? Or would it finally have to be a divorce, a scandal? Did the Curies ever think of divorce? Questions, questions. The devil with them. There was tonight, and Gisèle beside him, and tonight was all and the only reality. He focused his attention through the taxi window. They had turned into the rue du Bac . . .

The moment they were inside Gisèle's living room, Claude took her in his arms, holding her close and kissing her neck, and ear, and hair, and forehead, and lips. Shivering, feeling his imperative desire and her own, she pushed him off and, without a word, hurried into the bedroom.

Claude secured the door, then moved to the cognac decanter on the marble top of the aged wooden commode. He poured a drink, held the glass between his fingers, rolling it gently, warming the amber fluid with his warm palm. Leisurely, then, he sipped the cognac. Doing so, he surveyed the room. It possessed an air of casual elegance. Gisèle's good taste was evident in the antique sycamore writing table inlaid with porcelain plaques, in the Louis XV period lamp bases and ashtrays found in the Flea Market, in the matted illuminated manuscript pages framed on the walls.

He could not help but contrast the charm of this with his own tasteless living room, large, indefinite, disorderly, velvet sofas and chairs clashing with the wallpaper in imitation of the Directoire design, which Denise had furnished. In all fairness, Denise had possessed no more time than he had to devote to furnishings. Like him, she was a full-time scientist. Yet her poor taste extended to the matter of dress. He considered Gisèle's flawless suits and dresses, and could only remember Denise wearing a spotty linen chemist's smock, or at her best, ordinary blouses and loose skirts and flat-heeled shoes that were usually scuffed. Thinking of his wife's attire, he was reminded of Jonathan Swift's description of the woman who wore her clothes as if they had been thrown on her with a pitchfork.

The cognac inspired him to further comparison, odious as this was, and he judged his two women, mistress and wife, side by side in nudity. He tried to be fair. Technically, divested of all clothing, Gisèle was less than perfection. When she was unclad, her lines were too spare, bony, almost skeletal. It was the body required of all mannequins who earned 20,000 francs a week, he knew, for its dimensions were made to display the drape of garments. In full attire, Gisèle was incomparable; in nudity, there was something missing. What made up for her physical deficiencies when disrobed was Gisèle's impatient fever for love, and this Claude understood and appreciated. By comparison, Denise was shorter, fuller, rounder. Her shortcomings were her hair, shingled in a masculine bob, a nose too pugged, hips too wide, thighs too thick. In full dress, she was not *soignée,* and bulged and protruded too much to possess the mannequin chic. Stark naked, she was twice as attractive. And in all fairness, and this Claude admitted to himself even now, there was the advantage of her bosom. Denise had enormous pear-shaped breasts, and to this day, in her forty-second year, they hardly sagged at all. Still, he told himself, he had to admit a preference for Gisèle's flatter breasts, as well as her slat hips and buttocks. They were unpretentious, but more inciting, because Gisèle was more inciting.

Was it caddish to project the comparison into bed? He sipped the cognac. It was wrong, but his mind unreeled the pictures. Sleeping with Denise, so fleshy, so tired, so inert, was like crawling into the womb. It was safe, easy, secure, never unexpected. It was *nicely* pleasurable. But Gisèle, taut, vibrating, aggressive, her magnificent flesh a wild and memorable offering, was—he considered a conservative description befitting a scientist—surfeiting? No. Enthralling? No. Captivating, yes, more, much more—captivating, satiating, and an indescribable ecstasy.

The memory of what would soon be repeated now aroused him. He finished his cognac, then quickly undressed, laying out suit and shorts on a chair, and stuffing his socks into his shoes on the floor. Naked, he went to the closet, found the maroon silk robe Gisèle had recently bought him, and pulled it on, loosely knotting the belt.

As he entered the bedroom, and halted beside the *coiffeuse,* she had just emerged from the bathroom. She was turning down the lights, all but the dim lamp behind the telephone on her bedstand. As she moved, he could see the smooth outlines of her straight hips and thighs through the sheer mauve peignoir. When she turned to him, and saw his face, she smiled and straightened deliberately, her nipples revealed through the transparent chiffon.

She sat on the bed, kicked off her mules, and fell back on the pillows, her arms outstretched toward him. "What are you waiting for, *chéri?*"

He went to the bed, and lowered himself beside her, and as always, could hear his heart, as she also heard it.

She reached across and pulled the cord of his robe. "Darling," she whispered, "my own—" And then, *"Viens vite—"*

Immediately, he slipped out of the robe and pressed against her. Eyes closed, sighing audibly, she parted her peignoir, and showed him herself. He placed his cheek against her breast, and she kissed his hair, and pulled him into her, and thus, in the familiar all-new way, they were joined.

From the bedstand, the telephone shrilly jangled.

They froze in their embrace, as stiff, immobile, marble as satyr and nymph on a Pompeiian wall fresco.

They listened. The telephone rang a second time, louder, and a third time, a thunderclap.

"Let it ring," he whispered.

"No," she said suddenly, "it might be M. Favre—"

She fumbled for the receiver, found it on the fourth ring, and brought it to her flushed face.

"Hello—"

"Mlle Jordan?" It was a woman's voice. "This is Mme Marceau. Let me speak to my husband."

Gisèle lay petrified, gazing with bewilderment at Claude's face above her. The telephone was waiting. She tried to find her voice again. "But—there is no one here—"

"Put him on. This is important!" It was a command.

Gisèle was dumbfounded, helpless. Her poise was gone. She covered the mouthpiece fully, and looked imploringly at Claude. "Your wife—she knows—"

"No, I cannot. Say anything," he begged.

Gisèle would not return to the telephone. "She says it's important—"

The length of their exchange had given them away, and Claude knew it. Miserably, he disengaged his body from Gisèle's, took the prosecuting telephone, and sat up, cross-legged, on the bed.

"Denise? Listen to me—"

"You listen, you rotten pig—you pull your pants on and come home. The press is on its way—we've just won the Nobel Prize!"

It was 5:07 in the afternoon when the telegram from the Swedish Embassy in Washington, D.C. clattered through the electric machine of the telegraph office located on West Peachtree Street in Atlanta, Georgia.

The mousy-haired girl, with thyroid eyes, on the machine at the time, pulled the message out with a rebel yell. "Lookit who won the Nobel Prize!" she shouted. The other two girls came out of their chairs running, and the jubilation even attracted the three delivery boys, who had been shooting dice in the rear.

Eventually, the exclamations and buzz of excitement brought Mr. Yancey, the manager, out of his cozy cubicle. He had been reading the Atlanta *Constitution* and drinking a coke, beside the heater, his favorite occupation on a dirty-gray, rainy afternoon such as this.

He appeared buttoning his trouser top and buckling his belt around his flabby middle, and calling out, "What's up? What's up? What's going on here?"

One of the girls passed the strip of tape to Mr. Yancey, and he read it, and grinned broadly. "Say now, say now, this is a big day for the capital of the South." Although the victor had been born more than three thousand miles from Atlanta, and had only made his home here the last three years, the hero-starved half a million Atlantans considered the great man their own, by adoption. "Biggest thing since old J. S. Pemberton concocted Coca-Cola," said Mr. Yancey. "Biggest thing since Margaret Mitchell."

"Lemme deliver it," one of the young boys piped up.

"Not on your life, son, not on your life," said Mr. Yancey. "This is a solemn occasion. This is somethin' Mr. Yancey does personally."

"Bet you just want to have yourself another look at that Miss Emily," said the mousy-haired girl, daringly.

"Take care, sister," said Mr. Yancey. "This here message is too important. You get it ready now."

He waved the strip of tape. "Man, oh man," he said, and then, before releasing the message, he read it once more.

IN RECOGNITION OF YOUR DISCOVERY AND INVENTION OF A PHOTOCHEMICAL CONVERSION AND STORAGE SYSTEM FOR SOLAR ENERGY AND OF YOUR PRACTICAL APPLICATION OF SOLAR ENERGY TO PRODUCE SYNTHESIZED SOLID ROCKET PROPELLANTS THE NOBEL FOUNDATION OF STOCKHOLM ON BEHALF OF THE ROYAL SWEDISH ACADEMY OF SCIENCE IS PLEASED TO INFORM YOU THAT YOU HAVE TODAY BEEN VOTED THIS YEARS NOBEL PRIZE IN PHYSICS STOP THE PRIZE WILL BE A GOLD MEDALLION AND A CHEQUE FOR FIFTY THOUSAND THREE HUNDRED DOLLARS STOP THE AWARD CEREMONY WILL TAKE PLACE IN STOCKHOLM ON DECEMBER TENTH STOP DETAILS FOLLOW STOP HEARTIEST CONGRATULATIONS STOP

The message was addressed to DOCTOR MAX STRATMAN ONE THOUSAND FORTY FOUR PONCE DE LEON AVENUE ATLANTA GEORGIA. . . .

For Max Stratman, at the age of sixty-two, it was always a pleasure, which few people would understand, to lie on the hard table in the darkened room beside the elaborate electrocardiograph equipment, while an efficient, antiseptic nurse dabbed the paste on his chest, arms, and legs, and then applied the electrodes with their five lead wires—one to his chest, two to his arms, and two to his legs. This experience, in which he engaged twice a year at the behest of the United States government, was soothing, relaxing, and always conducive to clear thinking.

This afternoon, however, as Max Stratman stretched on the table, chest, arms, legs bared, half watching the tall bespectacled, comely nurse attach the cool electrodes to his skin, his pleasure, for the first time in memory, was shadowed faintly by apprehension. He reasoned that the apprehension had entered into the EKG test because today the test was especially important.

In the three years past, since he had accepted the government's offer to join the high-level staff of the Society for Basic Research outside Atlanta, he had attended these checkups, one in January and one in July, as a matter of routine. But now it was only mid-November and the next checkup was not due for two more months, yet here he was supine on the table, teeming with electrodes and wires, not as a matter of routine but as a volunteer.

Max Stratman was as pragmatical as the Teutonic forebears on his father's side of the family. He rarely rationalized any position, but met it head on. He knew exactly why he had telephoned Dr. Fred Ilman yesterday, at Lawson General Hospital, a mile from the Society building, and had requested an immediate appointment. In the first place, there was the surprising and exhilarating offer from Washington, D.C. The offer was critical to Stratman because, projected over the next two years, it might fully solve a personal problem, a certain responsibility, that had been weighing heavily upon him. Yet he had been made to realize that accepting the offer would mean changing his way of life, would put more strain on an old, ill-used, and often reluctant physique. Still, the change was something to be desired, a godsent gift, because it would alleviate his one major worry. The question he had asked himself, after the Defense Department call, was this: could he dare to undertake the change?

There would have been no question at all, had he not recalled the results of his last cardiogram in the summer. At that time, Dr. Ilman had cheerfully informed him, displaying the strip of graph paper that bore the curve of his heartbeat, that a minor irregularity was in evidence. But it was minor, Dr. Ilman emphasized, of no importance, provided that Stratman did not drastically change his habits. If Stratman continued to live like a sloth, without peaks or valleys of excitement, without excessive activities or long hours or pressure, he might continue his doubtful way of life—his erratic diet, daily beer, meerschaum pipe, lack of exercise—and possibly live forever.

"After all, you're not a youngster any more, Max," Fred Ilman had said on that occasion. "If you were a much younger man, and you came up with this minor irregularity, I would suggest a special regime against the future—oh, you know, lighter diet and low fat, no drinking, cut down on smoking, moderate exercises. But you are sixty-two, and to suggest any drastic changes, to rock the boat, could be worse than letting you sail along, at moderate speed, as you are now doing. So go back to your drawing board and your quantum nonsense and your solar sleight-of-hand, and don't bother me until next January. Just stay as sweet as you are, and my regards to Emily."

But now, there was suddenly an urgent necessity to rock the boat, and Max Stratman was having a cardiograph test in November, not January, because the decision must be made by the weekend.

The nurse had finished applying the electrode to the first paste spot on his chest, and now she turned back to the EKG machine. "All right, Professor Stratman," she said, "we'll begin. It'll only be a few minutes."

The machine behind his head began to whir. The strip of graph paper, recording the superficial biography of his physical heart, began to emerge with its coded story. Head turned on the pillow, Stratman watched it a moment, unaccountably pleased that the nurse had referred to him as "Professor," in the old-fashioned European manner, rather than as "Doctor," in the less dignified American style. Herr Professor, it had always been, until 1945, when Walther had gotten him to the Americans, just before the Russian authorities came calling. Still, he had not minded the informality of the Americans, because they compensated for social failings by their genuine friendliness, their appreciation of his small genius, and, above all, because they brought him to a wondrous climate of freedom. Not once, it seemed, since he had been spirited out of Germany, had he glanced back over his shoulder to see who might be listening.

The nurse was manipulating the electrode on his chest, moving it from spot to spot like a chess piece, and Stratman observed her quietly. After a while, he tired of this and stared up at the white ceiling and the glass light fixture. His preoccupation had always been mental, above the shoulders, and hardly ever had he been concerned with his body. Now, he was conscious of his body, that his brain had remained forever young whereas his traitor body had grown old.

Fastening on the last idea, Stratman tried to recollect if he had ever thought of his body as young, that is, young as his brain, and he found it difficult to recollect one instance. Then, at once, he recollected several instances. He had been young that Christmas Day in Frankfurt, when he had skipped through the snow after his father and discovered the new pony shivering behind his father's distillery shed. And he had been young, later, when the family had the frame house in the outskirts of Berlin, and one magical afternoon they all drove in the buggy to a barn, with makeshift chairs inside, where jumpy images were thrown on a screen, and he heard everyone praise the new invention known as cinema. And he had been young that day on the Ku'damm, holding Walther's hand, peeking between the rows of people ahead, when he had caught a glimpse of the resplendent Kaiser astride a white horse, followed by the goose-stepping, steel-helmeted troops.

After that, it seemed, especially in the Gymnasium and at the University of Berlin, he had always been old, and he could never quite remember that he had ever appeared different than he appeared today, to himself, reclining on this table. He peered down his chest at the rest of his body and smiled privately: a beached porpoise, having an EKG.

The numerous photographs of him that appeared in the American newspapers and magazines did not upset him, despite the way they made obvious his ugliness. In fact, it seemed, the Americans rather cherished him this way. He was their image of a German Herr Professor—or Doctor, if you will— of the old school. Max Stratman was five feet seven, but seemed shorter, more diminutive, because he was hunched. His head was massive, too large for his body, and his forehead seemed to recede to infinity because he was bald except for a bristling hedge of gray hair surrounding the extremities of his head. His face was round, red, wrinkled, and his nose perfectly bulbous. He wore thick, steel-rimmed bifocals at his desk, and squinted myopically when he did not wear them. His face was not formidable, but wise and sympathetic, and he was quick to smile, to see the humor of almost anything, himself foremost. He was pudgy and rumpled—"his clothes look like they have been borrowed from a scarecrow three sizes larger," a news magazine had recently remarked.

This was as he saw himself in the University days, and this was as he saw himself today. Apparently, nothing about him had grown older than old, through the decades, except maybe his heart. Maybe. *Ach*, we shall see, he thought.

He heard the nurse's voice behind him. "That's it, Professor Stratman," she said, tearing the graph paper strip from the machine and placing the roll on a small desk.

"Thank you," said Stratman politely.

"It was an honor, Professor," she said, as she removed the electrodes from his chest, arms, legs, and wiped the paste from his body.

He watched her curiously. She had said, so respectfully, that it was an honor. He had thought that he was old hat here. Squinting at her now, he realized that she had not been at Lawson General Hospital, or at least not with Dr. Ilman, when he had been here in the summer. She was new. He admired her tallness, short haircut, pert, intelligent face, trim white uniform. She was not Emily, of course, but still he admired the handsomeness of American young women, and especially the Southern ones.

As she returned to the electrocardiograph machine, he nodded at the instrument. "An interesting and valuable toy, *gnädige Fräulein*," he said. "One day there will be better machines, deeper probing, more sure. But, for its limitations, it is good. It is a fact I knew quite well the man who invented the EKG."

"You actually knew him?" She was as impressed as if he had said that he had known Pasteur.

"Yes—yes. Willem Einthoven, a Hollander. I spent several weeks with him once in Rotterdam. He won many prizes for that gadget—even the Nobel money."

"I bet you've known everyone, Professor. Dr. Ilman says you knew Einstein."

"It is true. Albert, I knew well. I met him first in Berlin—*ach,* what times, what times we had—and then I would see him, occasionally, in Princeton. A terrible loss, not only for science, but for humanity. You know, Fräulein, good men there are not many—most men are good, yes, but always, always, for reasons—but Albert, he was a *good* man, pure and simple, no reasons."

"When he talked, could you understand him?"

"Understand him?" Stratman sat up. "A grammar-school child could understand him, if she listened. I remember, once, somebody, an ordinary person, asked him to explain his theory of relativity, of time, of why all motions of the universe are relative and not absolute, and you know what Albert said? He said, 'My friend, when you sit with a nice girl for an hour, you think it is only a minute—but when you sit on a hot stove for a minute, you think it is an hour. Relativity!' "

Both the nurse and Stratman laughed, and then he requested his pipe and pouch. While the nurse found them in his unpressed jacket, Stratman went on. "I will tell you one Albert Einstein joke for your friends. There was a Mr. Goldberg who wanted to know about the Einstein theory, and when it was explained to him, he nodded. 'I see,' he said, 'and from this he makes a living?' "

The nurse screamed with delight, and Stratman chuckled and was happy. At last, he stood up on his bare feet and began to fill his pipe. "Now, if you please, enough of Albert Einstein. We must devote ourselves to Max Stratman. I will dress."

"No, please, Professor—" She grabbed up the EKG graph paper. "Dr. Ilman must see the results first. He sometimes makes us do it again. Will you please wait, as you are, until I show him this? Excuse me—"

She was gone. Max Stratman shrugged, put a flaring match to his well-seasoned meerschaum, and felt the chill on his feet. Despite her injunction against dressing, he decided to sit down and pull on his socks and shoes. As he did so, slowly, seated on the chair beside the desk, he reviewed with precision the events of yesterday.

The call from Washington had been from the Secretary of Defense. The civilities had been brief. The Secretary had asked him, bluntly, if he would care to undertake a bigger, more vital job, at more than twice the money he was now being paid at the Society. Although Stratman was an international figure of renown, the salary that he received for thinking and speculating at the Society for Basic Research was comparatively modest. The new sum offered him was, by his terms, staggering, and immediately he saw that it would completely cancel his debt to Walther and solve his problem with Emily. He evinced his interest.

"I know you're deeply immersed in further researches on the possibilities of solar energy," the Secretary had said, "and it's all very promising—I've seen your reports—but it's all way off in the future."

Stratman had found that he must come to the defense of basic research in general. "All research is a dream for the future, Mr. Secretary. Rockets were once way off in the future, and nuclear fission, too. And even my work in converting and storing the sun's heat for energy, that was once in the future. Yet, if I had been given no time to think about it a few years ago—"

The Secretary had not wanted to be thus engaged. "I know, Professor Stratman," he said, "we are in sympathy with the way you people work. However, the fact is you have harnessed solar energy. It's a reality. It's one of the big things we have to work with. And we want to move ahead. We want to exploit our gain before our enemies do—"

Stratman had sighed over expediencies, and then remembered the huge sum that he was being offered, and he had not interrupted again.

The Secretary had gone on crisply. There were competent physicists throughout the nation toiling night and day to develop further Stratman's recent discovery. The Defense Department had studied the program, and had felt that it was too scattered, too disjointed, and that lack of direction and cohesion might cause a fatal lag in the work. The facts had been laid before the President, and he, himself, had recommended that Max Stratman be appointed coordinator of the vast program and be well paid out of unassigned Defense Department funds.

Impressed, Stratman had inquired, "What would the job entail?"

"Constant travel around the country. You could headquarter in the Pentagon. But we'd want you in Palo Alto, Boston, Key West, Death Valley, Phoenix, El Paso, out in Libya at Azizia, wherever the solar people are working, to see that they're getting the most out of their time, to see that they're on the right track, to straighten them out when necessary, to show them shortcuts, to give them pep talks, when necessary. You know the kind of men they are, and you know that you are about the only person in the world they'd listen to. It could accelerate our program and be a real contribution to the government. You'd be responsible only to the President, and report to him at monthly intervals."

"How long would you need me?"

"Two years."

Stratman did not like the job. He saw through the subterfuge. It was really a glorified salesman's job, one that might be done as well by a politician or militarist or educator. What the government really wanted was his name, possibly to impress the young men on the project, possibly to extort more money from Congress. They wanted his name, and he wanted—*nein*, he needed—their money. It was a dilemma. It was a dilemma because the work at the Society, which they could not yet understand until it was reality and utilitarian, was far more important. He was on the verge of new breakthroughs in converting solar energy, but he could never give them a date, and so it would have no value to them. Also, capsuled in his office at the Society, he could live on in his old way, undisturbed, free to breathe and think. The new job might demand energy and strength that he did not possess. It was this last that made him remember his summer visit to Dr. Ilman, and at once he knew that his decision would develop not from his wishes but from the oracle that was Dr. Ilman's electrocardiograph machine.

"I will need the remainder of the week to decide," he had finally told the Secretary of Defense.

"We must know by Saturday," the Secretary had said.

"You shall."

"Please keep in mind that it was the President, himself, who suggested you for this job, Professor."

"I am not unaware of it, Mr. Secretary."

When he had hung up the receiver, he had known that he must accept the offer. It was then that he had lifted the receiver off the cradle again and had telephoned Dr. Fred Ilman for an immediate appointment.

Suddenly, he realized that the door beside him had opened, and that the nurse was standing in the doorway.

"You may dress, Professor," she said. "Dr. Ilman will see you now—in his office."

He searched her bland face for an opinion, but there was none. He rose, took his shirt off the hook, and began to dress.

A few minutes later, he entered Dr. Ilman's small, gray office. The physician was hunched over his desk, writing on a sheet of paper. He was hardly taller than Stratman himself, a slender, wiry Missourian in his late forties, with crew haircut and darting eyes and a reputation for candor. Although he was no longer in the army, he worked for the army as an orthopedic surgeon in Lawson General Hospital, one of the major amputee hospitals in the nation, and several days a week he doubled as an M.D. to treat government personnel at the hospital as well as the geniuses at the nearby Society for Basic Research.

No sooner had Stratman come through the door than Dr. Ilman dropped his pen, leaped to his feet, and extended his hand.

"Max—how are you?"

Stratman took his hand cordially. "That is for you to tell me, Fred."

Dr. Ilman waved Stratman to the hard-backed chair across the desk. "Sit down, light up your pipe, and we'll straighten everything out."

Stratman sat down and put a match to his cold pipe, and Dr. Ilman settled into the swivel chair behind the desk.

"I'm curious, Max, extremely curious, about what brought you here today. You weren't due until January. Why the request for a cardiograph today? Didn't you feel well? Did you have chest pains? What?"

"I think I told you on the phone. I wanted a checkup."

"But why? There must be a reason."

Originally, Stratman had not planned to go into his motivations for Dr. Ilman. He did not wish to be forced into explanations and family history and mysteries. Still, Ilman was a friend—he met Ilman and his wife socially at least once a month—and a perceptive and penetrating man, and Stratman saw that it would be time-wasting to be devious.

"I see it is no use to evade you, Fred," he said, at last. "There is a specific reason, yes."

Dr. Ilman waited patiently.

Stratman resumed. "The government has offered me a bigger job, a better one. It will be a management job, and I will have to be exceedingly mobile. The position would require constant travel and, well, certainly an added burden of work and responsibility. I thought I should have a checkup before accepting—"

"Why do you need such a job, Max? You are full of honors—"

"*Ach,* honors. Did you ever have a cooked entree of honors? Money, Fred, there is twice the money I am making, and I need it."

"I had imagined you were comfortable—"

"It is not enough. I am thinking ahead—of Emily."

"In my opinion, you have done nicely by your niece. And when you are no longer here, I'm sure she will do nicely by herself. I would guess she has problems, whatever they may be, but she is competent, attractive—more than attractive—and young enough to manage for herself, when and if it becomes necessary. I can't for the life of me see why any decision you make in the present must be based on her future."

Dr. Ilman waited, but saw that Stratman was not prepared to reply at once. Instead of pressing for an explanation, Dr. Ilman found a cigar in his lower drawer, bit off the end, and made elaborate preparations to smoke it.

Stratman sat meditatively, peering through the shutters, hypnotized by the rain as it splattered against the window, and fanned into rivulets that trickled slowly to the sill. He wondered how he could explain the truth to a physician who was merely a friend and not of his blood.

Could he tell Illman about the events of 1943? Both he and his older brother Walther had considered themselves agnostics, if anything. Although the mother he cherished had been Jewish, Stratman's father had been Lutheran. Stratman had grown up between the two faiths, or, as a compromise, outside them, and consequently he had known as little of Judaism as of Protestantism. As an adult, he had not affiliated himself, or interested himself, in any religion, beyond that of Science. He had not believed in a Maker, a Creator of an orderly universe, but had believed that if the universe were truly orderly, it had been an accident of natural forces. He had felt that to ascribe the beginning of the universe, the planets, earth, man, to Something was merely evidence of man's lack of imagination. Groping mankind had invented words like "beginning." Did there have to be a beginning? Could not the universe have always been here? Could not its existence have been beyond the grasp of man's feeble understanding and semantics? If explanations need be sought, they could only be sought by Science. Meanwhile, let cretin man satisfy himself with his spiritual playthings—holy books, relics, churches, temples, Jehovah, Zeus, Buddha, Quetzalcoatl, Son of Man, Prophet, and all the rest of the tranquilizers.

But in 1943, one aspect of Max Stratman's thinking changed. From pure scientist, he was converted to Scientist-Jew by the fanatics of Hitler's National Socialism. He was found to be tainted, but still valuable to the state, and so he was removed from his teaching position at the University of Berlin and transferred to the Kaiser Wilhelm Institute in the same city. In this Institute, Germany's leading physicists, engineers, chemists were toiling to create fission of uranium. Stratman was assigned to work on heavy water imported from the Norsk Hydro hydrogen electrolysis factory in occupied Rjukan, Norway, with the purpose of constructing a chain-reacting pile. His older brother, Walther, a nuclear engineer less imaginative, more methodical than himself (whose only minor achievement, the result of a youthful avocation, had been a scientific paper on the bubonic plague or Black Death epidemic in history), had been removed from private industry to work on a crude uranium machine—in America, it was being called a nuclear reactor—in the shed behind the Institute. Walther's wife, Rebecca, and his young daughter, Emily, had fared worse, and been deported to Ravensbruck Women's Concentration Camp, which had been built to imprison two thousand enemies of the Reich and now held twenty-five thousand of them. Max Stratman and Walther Stratman had been advised that as long as they cooperated in advancing Germany's atomic program, no harm would come to Rebecca and Emily, and so they had cooperated, minimally, and were rewarded monthly by a brief letter from Rebecca Stratman.

Now, so long after, sitting and blinking at the rain on the window of a Georgia hospital, Stratman wondered if he could tell Ilman about the events of 1945. With Berlin aflame, and Hitler's body drenched with gasoline outside the concrete bunker in the shadow of Brandenburg Gate, advance units of the Russian army were assigned to ferret out and capture German scientists. They had raided the Kaiser Wilhelm Institute and placed its occupants under house arrest in a farm at the outskirts of Berlin, pending arrival of Soviet authorities.

Meanwhile, Walther had made secret contact with a similar advance American unit which went by the code name ALSOS and possessed a file, found in Strasbourg, of every German scientist and his current address. Walther let the members of ALSOS know that neither he nor his more illustrious brother, Max Stratman, wished to carry on their work under a second dictatorship. Immediately, and at great risk, American agents of ALSOS had agreed to rescue the Stratman brothers from their Communist keepers. Max Stratman had been given to understand that there were means to rescue both Walther and himself at the same time—but on the fateful night, at the crucial moment, there had been means to save only one of them. Max Stratman had refused to be that one, but had finally been persuaded to escape after extracting a promise that Walther would follow shortly after. Only later did he learn that there had never been the slightest chance to save Walther, and that Walther had insisted on giving over his place to a brother who he felt had more to offer Science and the free world.

From that moment of Walther's sacrifice, Max Stratman had realized that he was on earth, a liberated man, as his brother's proxy, that his obligation was that of Charles Darnay to Sydney Carton. Thereafter, at his passionate insistence, he had remained in the American-occupied zone of Germany, while the authorities had aided him in the search for Walther's wife Rebecca and his daughter Emily. The Russians, who had overrun Ravensbruck, reported that neither Rebecca nor Emily was there any longer, and Stratman feared the worst. He had continued his search, and in short weeks, Emily, just turned sixteen, surprisingly had been located at Buchenwald—surprisingly because Himmler had earlier ordered Ravensbruck purified and had commanded all Jewish inmates shipped by cattle cars to Auschwitz, the horror compound southwest of Warsaw in Poland. For reasons that Stratman would learn later, Emily had been the sole Jewess to survive the transfer to Auschwitz, and, in the waning days of the war, had been sent south to Buchenwald instead. However, Rebecca Stratman had been less fortunate. Several months before the liberation, with her pink slip of paper, she had been carried off to Auschwitz, and had been one of three million naked women, children, men, to suffer death by gas in the camp's busy extermination chamber.

And so it was young Emily, alone, who had become Max Stratman's charge and his conscience, and the more so because of what Stratman had learned (from an American Army psychiatrist, who had confiscated concentration camp dossiers intact) of her existence in the female hell that was Ravensbruck. Emily had been emotionally damaged beyond repair, Stratman had learned—in a manner that he could not, to this day, revive in his own mind—and she had needed her uncle not only then, but now, just as Stratman had decided that she needed the security that he must offer her following his death.

After recovering his niece, Stratman had been placed, along with other rescued German scientists, in detention quarters, Farm Hall, an old country house not far from Cambridge in England. Here he had learned of his brother Walther's lonely death months before in a Siberian labor camp, where he had been interned after his part in Stratman's escape had been exposed. Today, for Emily, there was only her uncle, Max Stratman knew, only he, himself alone.

The events had occurred long ago. The traumatic results of those past events were ever present.

Only a minute or two had passed, but for Stratman it had been two decades. He turned from the window and met Dr. Ilman's gaze.

"My mind was wandering," he said apologetically. "Perhaps senility. I forget what you asked me, Fred."

Dr. Ilman carefully placed his cigar in a tray. His voice was soft. "I had only inquired—why it was important to change your life—make more money —for Emily's future. But you must have your reasons—"

"I do." He nodded at the coiled graph paper on the physician's desk. "You have not given me the results of the cardiograph, Fred."

"No, I haven't." Dr. Ilman took up the graph paper, unwound it, and passed his eyes over the jagged line. "Max, I'm not going to let you take any new job that requires travel, excitement, worry, no matter how much money is in it." He looked up. "You can still have a long life ahead, and it's my duty to see that you don't throw those years away."

Stratman waved his hand at the graph paper. "Don't give me riddles, Fred.

I'm not one of your old women patients who needs hand holding. What's wrong with me?"

Dr. Ilman straightened in his chair. His tone was now brisk, professional. "There have been changes of T waves in this electrocardiogram—inverted T waves—they clearly indicate an early coronary insufficiency. Do you understand?"

"I think I understand."

"No panic. Behave, and you'll have years enough to discover ten more uses for solar energy. But take that new job, and—listen, Max—I wouldn't give ten to one on your lasting more than a couple of years."

Stratman sat immobile. "I don't need more than two or three years, Fred," he said quietly.

"You need a lifetime, like every human being," Dr. Ilman said sharply. "Believe me, Max, it's more important to Emily to have you alive than to have an inheritance after you are dead."

Stratman shook his head. *"Verzeihung—*Fred, you do not understand, you do not know." He pushed himself out of the chair. "Thank you. Do you see me again?"

"Regularly. Next week to start with."

Stratman smiled faintly and started for the door. At the door, Dr. Ilman's voice caught him.

"Max, about the job, what are you going to do?"

"Think about it."

"Well, just think about being a vegetable, a happy vegetable. Much more fun than being a dead globe-trotter."

Once outside, Stratman hastened through the rain to the parking lot, where the colored driver was waiting in the government car. He ordered the driver to return him to the Society building. As they passed briefly before the seemingly endless array of low-slung, dull, wooden barracks that were the Lawson General Hospital, Stratman thought how strange it was that this was the only place where Emily could have contact with men. She was in her early thirties now, and he had never known her once to go out on a date with a man, not in high school or university or in their years in New York. And certainly not in Atlanta, where she had been more a recluse than ever, with her books, her records, her piano, her sewing, and her television. The more incredible, he decided, because she was so physically lovely and mentally bright.

As they drove through the rain, he tried to picture Walther's Emily, his Emily, as she might appear to others of her own age. Her hair was brunette, glossy, cut back in a bob, semi-shingled, but grown long where it covered half her forehead and curled forward under her cheekbones. Her face had a delicate, exotic, Oriental flavor, the impression reinforced by slightly slanted green eyes, so often cast downward when she spoke to a guest, a small tilted nose, and a pale, ethereal complexion. Her fragility was a rebuke to her German ancestry, and somewhere in the family tree, Stratman was sure, there had been an immigrant Siamese. Her body was slender, but fuller, more substantial than her features promised—the bosom young and deep, and the wasp waist exaggerating the full hips. About her there was an aura of one withdrawn from the turmoils of the world, one unbruised and unmarked by life, with the untouched and unused perfection of a new, life-sized doll. Her mind and wit were original and quick, but she rarely offered her mind, and the wry humor seemed too frightened to surface often. Men, Stratman perceived, were enchanted by her. They desired her. Emily did not desire them. Her defenses were many. When they approached too closely, she skittered off like a fawn. When they spoke too intimately, she retreated into a shell of silence, or sometimes resorted to sarcasm. She was made for men, but men were not made for her.

Her only contact with the opposite sex was at the Lawson General Hospital. Shortly after they had arrived in Atlanta, she had driven her uncle to visit Dr. Ilman. While her uncle was being examined, she had been taken on a tour of the amputee center by the doctor's nurse. Several months later, she had volunteered to do practical nursing at Lawson three times a week, and she did it still. She had learned the language of the amputees—"amps," she came to call them, as they called one another. She had learned that artificial limbs were "prostheses," and an arm was an "upper extremity," and a "BK" was a soldier whose leg had been removed below the knee, and a "syme" was one who had lost his foot but not his heel, and that "guillotining" meant crude, immediate surgery of a limb on the field of battle. She mingled with the young men, with their T shirts, jock shorts, and cumbersome leather and metal prostheses, and worked with them, and conversed solemnly with them, and they adored her, and she adored them and was not repelled. If Emily did not understand her devotion to Lawson, or would not face its true motives, her uncle understood it completely. These were not males, and she was not a female. These were amps—physical cripples—and she was an amp—an emotional cripple—and harmony was natural.

"Here we is, Professor." The chauffeur had spoken, and they had come to a halt before the Society building. Stratman emerged from his reverie, opened the door, and saw that the rain had ceased. He studied the leaden sky briefly, then closed the door, climbed the four stone stairs, and entered the foyer of the Society building.

The moment that he was inside, he heard his name. The switchboard girl removed her earphones. "Professor Stratman—your niece has called three times. She seems terribly anxious to get hold of you."

Stratman felt his heart thump. Emily had called three times. Unusual and ominous. He asked the girl to connect him, and as he started for the telephone booth, he realized that his heart was still hammering and that Dr. Ilman would disapprove, for the T waves had been inverted, and he now had "a condition." Closing himself inside the booth, he removed the receiver and listened. What he heard was a busy signal. He opened the booth and put his head out, questioningly.

The girl shrugged. "Busy."

Stratman left the booth. "Keep trying."

For ten minutes, as Stratman paced the inlaid floor, the operator tried his number, and every time, the response was a busy signal. Stratman's mind worried: she had fainted, and the phone was off the hook; someone was using the phone to summon an ambulance; the police were on the phone ordering all squad cars on the alert.

At last, he could endure the suspense no longer. "Send for my auto," he commanded the operator.

In short minutes, the automobile was waiting for him. The drive from the Society building along Peachtree Road to the five-room bungalow on Ponce de Leon Avenue that he and Emily rented was fifteen miles. To Stratman, it seemed fifty miles, especially since the chauffeur refused to speed over the rain-slicked asphalt highway.

It was twenty-five minutes before he saw the bungalow. Then, as they approached, he saw Emily. She stood on the small porch, a scarf round her head, a leather windbreaker over her blouse and skirt. He felt the knot in his abdomen unwind. She was alive. She was well. Nothing else mattered.

As they drew up before the bungalow, he dismissed the chauffeur. Stepping out of the car, he saw Emily running down the walk toward him.

"Uncle Max—!" she cried.

He slammed the door and waited, again concerned. But he saw that she was beaming, and that was unusual, too.

"Uncle Max!" She reached him breathlessly, and blurted the next. "You won the Nobel Prize!"

He stood, head cocked sideways, uncomprehending. "What? What? I do not—*wiederhole, bitte*—"

"You won! The telegram came an hour ago!" She fished inside the windbreaker and showed it to him.

He held it in both hands, close to his nose, for his spectacles were still in his pocket.

"Oh—Uncle Max—imagine—the Nobel Prize!"

He lowered the telegram and looked at her, dazed.

"I—I cannot believe it," he said.

"But it's true. All the newspapers know. They're all in the living room right now—reporters, photographers—they say it was announced from Stockholm on the news wires."

He tried to focus on the telegram again. "Fifty thousand three hundred dollars," he murmured. *"Gott im Himmel."*

"You're rich—"

"We are rich," he corrected, meticulously. And, at once, he realized that he could call the Secretary of Defense tomorrow and turn down the new job—that it was not necessary any more, that he had won Emily's buffer against life, that Walther would rest in peace, that he could keep his old sedentary cubbyhole with its promise and contentment—and he knew that Dr. Ilman would be pleased.

Suddenly, something occurred to him. "Where do we get this prize? In Stockholm?"

"Oh, yes. You must go. The newspapermen said so. It's a rule you must pick up the money within one year—except if you're sick—or you can't have it. Several Germans couldn't pick it up once, because of Hitler, and later, they couldn't get it."

Stockholm was a long way, Stratman realized. The journey, the activities, the ceremony would be strenuous. By all rights, he should consult Dr. Ilman first. But then he remembered what awaited him in Stockholm, and he saw Emily's enthusiastic face, and he knew that no imminent heart attack or stroke could keep him from the prize that would solve everything.

He took Emily firmly by the elbow and started her toward the house. "Tell me, *liebes Kind,*" he said happily, "what are you going to wear when you curtsy before the King?"

It was 1:51 of a hot, sunny afternoon when the telegram from the Swedish Embassy in Washington, D.C., automatically typed itself out on the tape of the electric receiving machine in the telegraph room located on Colorado Street in Pasadena, California.

The harassed fat girl at the machine hardly read the message, as she snipped it free. Expertly, using the cutter on her finger, she sliced the message into short lines, moistened them, and neatly glued them to the blank. The message formally prepared for delivery, and before her, she suddenly realized the import of its contents.

"Migawd," she said aloud, "twenty-five thousand dollars!"

The two men at the counter overheard her. One, the skinny young man in frayed blue suit who was an employee of the telegraph office, turned away from the penciled words he had been counting and asked, "Who got rich?" The customer, across the counter, a middle-aged man with rimless glasses who resembled a lesser bank executive, also displayed interest.

The fat girl lifted herself from her chair with a grunt. "It says here—somebody in Pasadena—never heard of him—just won the Nobel Prize."

She went to the counter and showed the telegram to her skinny co-worker. As he read it, he whistled. He handed the wire to the customer, who pushed his glasses higher on the bridge of his nose, and said, "If I were you, I would not wait to deliver a message of this importance. I would telephone it to the party concerned." Importantly, he began to read the telegram.

FOR YOUR PART IN THE DISCOVERY OF ANTIREACTIVE SUB-STANCES TO OVERCOME THE IMMUNOLOGICAL BARRIER TO CARDIAC TRANSPLANTATION AND YOUR INTRODUCTION OF SURGICAL TECHNIQUE TO SUCCESSFULLY PERFORM A HETERO-GRAFT OF THE HEART ORGAN INTO THE HUMAN BODY THE NOBEL FOUNDATION OF STOCKHOLM ON BEHALF OF THE ROYAL CAROLINE MEDICO CHIRURGICAL INSTITUTE OF SWE-DEN IS PLEASED TO INFORM YOU THAT YOU HAVE TODAY BEEN VOTED THIS YEARS NOBEL PRIZE IN PHYSIOLOGY AND MEDICINE STOP YOUR SHARE OF THE PRIZE WILL BE A GOLD MEDALLION AND A CHEQUE FOR TWENTY FIVE THOUSAND ONE

HUNDRED AND FIFTY DOLLARS STOP THE AWARD CEREMONY
WILL TAKE PLACE IN STOCKHOLM ON DECEMBER TENTH STOP
DETAILS FOLLOW STOP HEARTIEST CONGRATULATIONS STOP

The message was addressed to DOCTOR JOHN GARRETT NUMBER
FOUR HILLSIDE TERRACE PASADENA CALIFORNIA. . . .

As usual, the drive from Pasadena on the ever-crowded freeways to the
Miracle Mile section of Los Angeles took Dr. John Garrett longer than he
had expected. What made the trip even slower, this early afternoon, was the
fact that Garrett was deeply engaged with his thoughts, with the new speech
that he intended to deliver tonight, and with the rights and wrongs of it.

By the time he had arrived at Western Avenue and Wilshire Boulevard,
and parked the black Jaguar (his first lavish purchase, on payments, after
his sudden ascent to prominence) in the familiar gasoline station, he had
made up his mind (no matter what Dr. Keller advised him) that he would
present the new speech unedited and unexpurgated.

Striding the half block to the seven-story medical building, Garrett observed his reflection several times in shop windows. He was not displeased
with what he saw: an arresting, forceful young man of resolution. He had
almost forgotten his pleasure, a decade before, when Saralee had shown him
an article based on a poll taken by the American Institute of Public Opinion
on the average American male, and he had learned that he conformed almost exactly to the norm. According to the statistics, the average American
man was five feet nine inches tall, weighed one hundred and fifty-eight
pounds, had brown hair, wore spectacles, caught one and one-half colds in
winter, smoked cigarettes, drank liquor socially, preferred brunettes to
blondes, demanded that his wife be a good companion rather than a good
cook, enjoyed baseball above all other spectator sports, liked beefsteak and
French fried potatoes more than any other single dish, awakened at six-thirty
on weekdays and went to bed by ten at night, and would rather live in California than any place on earth. Incredibly, John Garrett had found that these
statistics described him almost exactly—the one exception being that he preferred French fried onion rings to French fried potatoes.

In the past two years, however, John Garrett had taken less pride in regarding himself as average, much to Saralee's bewilderment at the sudden
change of party line. More and more often, Garrett liked to think of himself
as a unique entity, special, nonconforming, and somewhat set apart from
ordinary specimens of *homo Americanus*. Whether or not this personal rebellion against the average was due to his recent renown in professional circles, or due to his liberating sessions with Dr. Keller, Garrett could not say.
On the other hand, his wife Saralee could say, but she said it only to herself:
John deserves to be bigheaded once in a while, because he discovered something that will help "the human community"—the last, she had read in a
magazine—but in her eyes, and most of the time in his own, she suspected,
John Garrett was still five feet nine, one hundred and fifty-eight pounds, and

hair brown as ever at forty-nine, and he was still as unsure and insecure and dependent upon her as ever, thank God.

Having reached the entry arch of his destination, John Garrett quickened his pace, rapidly climbed the single flight of stairs, and found himself face to face with the glass-paned door that bore the black legend, L. D. KELLER, M.D. As before, he wondered why psychoanalysts did not print PSYCHIATRIST instead of M.D. beside their names, and then decided that as long as there remained so much fear and resultant hostility toward analysts, discretion was the better part of honesty.

Opening the door, Garrett stepped into the office, then paused to close the door softly behind him. He moved through the empty blond reception room, and entered the spacious main office as unobtrusively as possible. He could see at once that they were all present, sitting, compulsive and neurotic, in the same chairs as ever, and that the session was in full swing. No one turned to greet Garrett as he tiptoed to his chair, for it was understood that he was always late ("tardiness may often be a resistance to the embarrassment of discussing taboo topics in the presence of others," Dr. Keller had once remarked), but now Dr. Keller, from behind his oak fortification of a desk, acknowledged his arrival with the slightest flicker of his eyes.

Garrett sat stiffly a moment, then consulted his watch. The group therapy session always lasted precisely one hour and twenty minutes. Since Garrett paid ten dollars for his weekly attendance, this meant that he was paying twelve and one-half cents a minute. Because he had been sixteen minutes late, there remained only one hour and four minutes of time. The delay had cost him two dollars. Still, there was eight dollars' worth of time left. He needed part of that time, today, especially today, but there were six others who needed it, too. Perhaps a close search of the faces of his fellow patients, he decided, would tell if their urgency matched his own.

They were seated in a crooked semicircle before Dr. Keller's desk, and Garrett began reading from left to right. On the beige divan to the far left were Mr. Lovato and Mrs. Perrin. Mr. Lovato, a slight, homosexual artist with a growing reputation for painting children in the candy-box style of Thomas Gainsborough, sat with his knees awkwardly crossed. Garrett recalled that when he had first come into group therapy four months ago, Mr. Lovato had always sat with his knees pinched together, like a prim parochial-schoolgirl. But a month ago, apparently somewhat liberated by analysis, he had begun to cross his legs in the more masculine manner. Mrs. Perrin, a top-heavy matron in her fifties with purple gray hair, sat with lips compressed, worrying a small purse with her hands. She was recovering from a nervous breakdown. Although married to a wealthy citizen of Van Nuys, her problem was a neurotic inability to spend a penny, even on the necessities of life, even on laundry or a loaf of bread, without becoming agitated. She rarely spoke, perhaps once in three weeks, but when she did speak, it was about her tiny triumphs in managing a purchase for fifty cents or a dollar.

Garrett shifted his gaze to the next patient, handsome, young Adam Ring, the rising actor, now slumped lazily in the easy chair, monotonously swinging a charm which was a rabbit's foot. Ring, whose bronzed face in profile re-sembled that of a head on a Greek coin, was in therapy because of a sexual difficulty. He spoke of it lightly, jokingly, but Dr. Keller was not deceived. Adam Ring's virility was redoubtable when he seduced young women of foreign race or color—Oriental, Indian, Mexican, Negro—but his virility was questionable and impaired when confronted by a Caucasian.

Directly to Garrett's left, in a straight chair, sat the incredible Mrs. Zane. A plain and freckled housewife in her middle thirties, given to gingham and shirtwaists and a certain helplessness, she had been complaining steadily (at least as long as Garrett had been in the group) of the sexual excesses forced upon her. A Catholic with five youngsters in the lower grades, she had re-vealed that her cross was an economically inept husband, too incompetent to hold a job a month. At last, by chance, this husband had obtained a well-paying job with a garment manufacturer. When it had appeared that he would lose this job, too, Mrs. Zane had desperately tried to prevent the catastrophe by inviting her husband's employer, and his wife, to dinner. The result had been that the employer, long disinterested in his mate and bored with golf and high finance, had been sufficiently moved by Mrs. Zane to make her his extracurricular activity. Instead of being fired, Mr. Zane was promoted to chief salesman, at higher salary, and sent out of the city four times a year on extended trips. In return, although it had never been spelled out in so many words, Mrs. Zane was expected to be receptive to the advances of her hus-band's employer. A pliable and generous young woman, Mrs. Zane had not resisted. For the past year, she had entertained her husband's employer regularly, and because he was insatiable, her view of him was curiously hori-zontal. Her guilts kept the church confessional busy, and her doubts led her to Dr. Keller.

John Garrett enjoyed Mrs. Zane, but today he was in no mood for her. She had the appearance of one who had much on her mind, and was rest-lessly awaiting her turn, and Garrett knew that he would have difficulty obtaining the time that he required. Turning slightly in his chair, he saw Mr. Armstrong, the stocky, beetle-browed compulsive gambler, rocking slowly, lost in his own deep broodings. Garrett always regarded the gambler as an ill-starred Branwell Brontë doomed by circumstance. He liked to consider Mr. Armstrong in soap opera serial terms: Will Armstrong's new roulette system smash the Nevada syndicate tomorrow? Will he save his job in the nick of time? Will he rescue his mortgaged house? Will he win the respect of his complaining wife and children and relatives? Will he ward off debt and destruction? Alone, of all of them, Mr. Armstrong recorded and read aloud his fantastic nocturnal dreams.

Beyond Mr. Armstrong, leaning intently forward, sat Miss Dudzinski, who had a mare's face and a body all unpadded bone, and who chattered on with the rapidity of one who feared to be overtaken by interruption. Miss Dudzinski was in her late twenties, and definitely old-maid material. She lived in a three-room apartment with her frail, hypochondriac mother, who had a worn heart and bad bladder and practiced the savage tyranny of the weak and the old. Miss Dudzinski supported them both by working as stenographer in a large real estate office. She was in group therapy because she was in the midst of a triangle—the dramatis personae consisting of a shy bachelor, who toiled as a drugstore clerk and was sufficiently lonely to consider Miss Dudzinski as beautiful; of Miss Dudzinski, whose entire life had been a search for a shy bachelor who was a drugstore clerk; and of Mrs. Dudzinski, enjoying her fortieth year on the brink of death.

Considering Miss Dudzinski now, and conjuring up the appalling picture of someone wishing to sleep with her, and in action with her, John Garrett suddenly realized that Miss Dudzinski was leaning forward because she was speaking and probably had been speaking for some time. With an effort, for he had his own problem, one less trifling than these, Garrett pretended to listen.

"—well, I tell you, Dr. Keller, I'm at the end of the rope. I don't know which way to turn," Miss Dudzinski was saying, the words tumbling out, each one close on the heels of the last. "It's the horns of a dilemma. Clarence told me plain out last night, he's not going to wait another six months to see if I make up my mind to marry him or not. He was pretty outspoken for somebody who's an introvert. He said if I wouldn't tell him right away—well, he was going to quit his job and go back to Cleveland. He said you've got to choose between your mother and me, or something like that, but that was what he said. I told him it's easy for you to say, but I've still got my responsibilities to Mother, she's human, I can't abandon her just like that to run off and marry and only think of myself. What'll happen to Mother? If she died, I'd never forgive myself. I'd carry it to the grave. But still there's on the other hand—Clarence—"

She looked around the room, almost imploringly, at the others, and before anyone could speak, she resumed, addressing the group as well as Dr. Keller. "You all know me. I don't have to lie. I'm not beautiful and I know it, besides I don't think that's the important thing because spiritual is more important. But we all know men hold more store by looks than anything, and Clarence—I'm not ashamed to admit it—I guess I've told you—he's the first man who ever proposed to me, and besides he's nice and I want to have a respectable husband, too, like everyone." She swallowed. "But what'll I do with Mother?"

She sat back, and eyed the others hopefully. Dr. Keller straightened his bulk, put down his pencil, and pinched his broad nose. "Well, now, Miss Dudzinski, this anxiety—"

Before the analyst could continue, Adam Ring, from deep in his chair, swinging his rabbit's foot still, spoke up. "I'll tell you what to do with Mother," he said. "Drown her."

Miss Dudzinski gasped and Ring was pleased, for he liked to shock. Irreverence was his attention getter and his protective barrier, Dr. Keller had told him several times. Before Miss Dudzinski could protest, Adam Ring went on. "Your old lady's no different than all the rest, Miss D. She's got you by the cord, and she's not letting you cut it. Why should she? You're her meal ticket. You're also her nurse and full-time companion. You listen to me. Blow her off. Stick her in some sanitarium—your husband'll pay to keep her out of his sight. She'll be happier in the end, and you'll have your guy. Look, you said it, kid, you're no Miss V. di Milo. There's at least one guy for every girl on earth. For you, figure that's the limit. Here's the guy. Grab. Hold him like a sweepstakes ticket. Let him go and what have you got left? Mother's Day for the rest of your life."

Mr. Lovato waved his hand in a flutter, and spoke in a gentle, effeminate voice. "Although I think Mr. Ring put it crudely, even threateningly, I concur with his sentiments all the way. As Dr. Keller has often implied, we can't have our cake and eat it, too. I believe you have to approach your decision coldly and logically, Miss Dudzinski. If you leave your mother for your young man, your mother has an alternative. She can find some other elderly woman to live with or move into a sanitarium or busy herself in many ways. Moreover, she's had a full life of her own and need not consume yours, which my mother tried to do, too. On the other hand, if you give up the young man, you may have no alternative. You may remain unwedded for a lifetime. I feel you simply have no choice but to accept your young man's proposal."

Listening, John Garrett determined to add his own opinion, which was no different from the others, only so that he could lead from his opinion into his own problem, and in that way, be sure that he would have his needed time. But before he could speak, Mrs. Zane, to his left, quickly made herself heard.

"I don't think it's as easy as everyone is making out," said Mrs. Zane. "It's all well and good for single men like Mr. Ring and Mr. Lovato to say make Clarence your choice and forget your mother—but Miss Dudzinski's mother *is* a responsibility, a human responsibility, and must be considered. You all know I can speak feelingly of this, because I can see all sides. Miss Dudzinski's problem is an exact parallel to my own. I'm caught between two people, also, and do you think it's easy? Do you think I enjoy being forced to have sexual intercourse with Mr. Zane's boss every night, while Mr. Zane is out of town?"

"Well, cut it down to twice a week," Adam Ring called out cheerfully.

"Oh, please, Mr. Ring," replied Mrs. Zane, "this is no joke. I know you think I'm sexually promiscuous—"

"My only objection is that you don't share the wealth, wonder girl," said Ring with a grin. "You've got me real curious about what's under those panties. I'd like a piece of the action whenever you find time—"

"I wouldn't have you, you impotent egotist!" flared Mrs. Zane. She turned toward the desk. "Dr. Keller, why is he so hostile toward me."

Dr. Keller, eyes hooded, remained imperturbable, and Adam Ring retained his set grin.

Mrs. Zane shook her head. "I know you're thinking that, too, Dr. Keller. You've made it plain I should try to curb my outside actions during my therapy, and you think I'm only increasing my sex life to defy you."

"You know better than to bait me, Mrs. Zane," said the analyst quietly. "Don't try to speak for me. When it is necessary for your good, for what is best for you, when it is necessary for me to articulate for you certain emotions you do not understand, I will be less impersonal, I will speak. Now—you were saying, Mrs. Zane—?"

"I was saying I'm tormented constantly by my situation." She addressed her co-patients imploringly, her temper receding. "You all know what I go through. I have Miss Dudzinski's anxieties. What should I do? What is right? If I stop, Mr. Zane will be fired. I know that. He'll be shattered. If I go on—well, I feel sinful. I lie awake nights, night after night, and ask myself all the questions. Am I being disloyal to Mr. Zane? Or am I truly helping him at great sacrifice? I pray to the Lord, and pray someday He will answer me. Heavens knows, I don't enjoy the act that much. I can see Mr. Ring smirking—but I don't, you all believe me. I'm exhausted. I have five children and a husband, too—and his boss, every night. I'll give you an example. Let me tell you what happened last night—"

John Garrett knew that Mrs. Zane had done what he had intended to do—interrupt so that she might have the floor. His admiration was mingled with annoyance. He was impatient with Mrs. Zane's prolific and perspiring acrobatics, and her secret pleasures and atoning guilts, and he wanted to voice the exigency of his own immediate problem. He glanced at his watch once more. There were thirty-four minutes remaining to the session. He hoped that Mrs. Zane's indulgence of the night before had been brief, silent, hedonistic, but he doubted it.

Waiting his turn, he thought back to how he had got into this damn group thing. It had begun with the increasing periods of depression and the persistent headaches, of course, the pressures against his forehead and the back of his skull coming daily with regularity, intruding on his achievement, and work, and home life. He had seen his physician, and subsequently an ear man, and then a neurologist, and suffered all the tests, but nothing pathological had been indicated. At last, upon the suggestion of his physician, he had reluctantly called upon a psychoanalyst in Pasadena.

There had been three months on the couch, ridiculous and wasted. Then, one morning, the psychoanalyst had recommended analytic group psychotherapy. The reasons given for this suggested change, which Garrett found senseless, were that persons like him, who hated and retreated from social contacts, who performed poorly in social situations, could most benefit by group therapy. Moreover, Garrett learned, his hostility toward the psychoanalyst (an extension of his ancient resentment of his father, whom his mother had worshiped and to whom she had given all her time), made person-to-person therapy difficult. Garrett learned that, attached to a group whose members suffered similar hostilities and anxieties, his anger might be modified, and that more progress might be made. The Pasadena psychoanalyst had then suggested that a Dr. Keller, of Los Angeles, was one of the best men in the field. And so, after an undecided week, Garrett had joined the group.

True, with the months of group psychotherapy, despite his shame at the public exposure, and the frustrations of competing with others for time and Dr. Keller's attention and approval, the head pressures had become more irregular, sometimes disappearing for several days in succession. But the source of the headaches still remained a partial mystery to him. Despite Dr. Keller's occasional remarks to the contrary, Garrett chose to believe that his discomfort had started with the entrance of Dr. Carlo Farelli into his life.

Certainly, in the period before the advent of Farelli, John Garrett had reached a peak of personal happiness, a summit of satisfaction, that he had never dreamed of attaining. Now, daydreaming in Dr. Keller's office, he had no trouble slipping backward into the recent past, to the events that led to his triumph and the event that led to its decline and fall. You pushed a button in memory, and lo, you slid back . . .

He was, he knew (for now he could afford a certain candor with himself), a drab, colorless and withdrawn research workhorse in the Rosenthal Medical Center in Pasadena. He possessed the degrees, and the knowledge and techniques that had earned him the degrees, but he was neither imaginative nor creative. Nothing about him soared. A thousand colleagues would have agreed that his epitaph would one day be one word: competent.

Yet, for some inexplicable emotional reason, he became interested in a dramatic phase of medicine—that which dealt with tissue transplantation, the technique of replacing the missing or damaged parts of a human being's body with new parts. Mulling over old medical journals, Garrett learned that the field was not a new one. Almost two thousand years before, a Hindu surgeon, Suśruta, had used cheek skin to help create new noses for his patients. In more recent times, in 1870 to be exact, Dr. J. L. Reverdin, of Paris, had introduced modern free skin grafting. Early in the twentieth century, Dr. Charles Guthrie, of St. Louis, had successfully grafted the head of a donor dog to join the head of a host dog, thereby fashioning a two-headed canine.

To Garrett, in his earliest enthusiasm, it appeared that anything was possible in this field. But not until he left his reading, and participated in actual experiments, did he fully realize the nature of the obstacle that hindered progress. The obstacle was not in surgery, where advance in techniques had been sufficient to make possible the replacement of an old, dying organ in the human body with a new, living organ. The obstacle was biochemical. As a self-defense against germs, the human body threw up an immunological barrier that not only warded off invading diseases but also destroyed foreign tissues that might be helpful.

Once he perceived the problem, Garrett devoted more and more of his energies and time to studying it. Figuratively, Saralee became a widow, and the children orphans, due to his work. Where colleagues were satisfied with eight hours given to research, Garrett was not satisfied with twelve or fourteen or sixteen hours. The medical laboratory became his *Santa Maria, Pinta, Niña* rolled into one, and he was as single-minded in his exploration as had been their admiral.

Soon, he was sated with knowledge of the human body's rejection or immunity mechanism. This was the reticulo-endothelial system. It consisted of antibodies and powerful white cells known as lymphocytes in the blood that protected man by killing off bacteria, viruses, or any strange or foreign cells that entered the body. This rejection mechanism was everyman's friend, but

40

Garrett came to regard it as his personal enemy. For if the rejection mechanism warded off diseased cells, it also murdered healthy new cells, since it could not tell the difference. This, then, was the difficulty. If a man were dying for want of new kidneys, or small intestines, or lungs, or heart, you could not transplant a fresh vital organ for the old, because the rejection mechanism, antagonistic to foreign tissue, would murder it—and its host.

The rejection mechanism became Garrett's target. And what confirmed his aim were the exceptions to the rule. Toiling side by side with his colleagues in the Medical Center, he found that transplants of pieces of artery, sections of bone, the cornea of the eye were long-practiced grafts that had nothing to do with the rejection mechanism. A new cornea in place of an old one survived because antibodies and assaulting white cells could not get at it. As to transplanted blood vessels and bones, they did not need to survive for they were merely scaffolding across which normal host tissue could grow.

What interested Garrett even more was another exception to the rejection mechanism. There had been case after case of successful organ transplantation in identical twins. Chemically, identical twins were the same person. They emerged from the same fertilized egg. Their tissues were not foreign to each other. A kidney from one identical twin could be grafted into his ailing brother, and it would endure, because the rejection mechanism would not recognize it and would leave it alone. But the moment that the same transplantation was tried on nonidentical human beings, the kidney, or any other organ, would die.

During 1958, in Boston, a risky nonidentical transplantation had been desperately attempted. A young woman from Ohio had lost her only kidney and was dying. A courageous team of physicians had taken the healthy kidney of a four-year-old and grafted it into this young woman. To thwart the rejection mechanism, the physicians had given the young woman massive treatments of X rays. The young woman lived twenty-eight days. The rejection mechanism had, indeed, been neutralized, but the excessive radiation was fatal.

For a brief period, Garrett was discouraged. Then came a major breakthrough. Sir Macfarlane Burnet, of Australia, and Dr. Peter B. Medawar, of England, proved that the rejection mechanism in one human being could be taught to accept tissue transplants from another, under certain circumstances. Experiments with rodents showed that if a mouse embryo were injected with cells from a nonidentical donor mouse, then later, when the embryo was an adult, it could accept skin grafts from the same donor without rejection. For this, Burnet and Medawar won the Nobel Prize in 1960. And, at once, John Garrett, along with hundreds of others in his field, was encouraged to believe that soon it might be possible to make a homograft of legs, kidneys, lungs, and hearts.

In that optimistic period, Dr. Robert A. Good, of the University of Minnesota, was saying, "Though much more basic research is needed, the first successful organ graft between nonidentical human beings could conceivably, with luck, take place tomorrow." And Garrett, one midnight in bed beside

41

Saralee, was telling her, "I believe it, I absolutely believe it—and I'm going to be the one to do it—with a living heart."

The days spun ceaselessly past, and he had no knowledge of date or week or month. It was as if he were on a perpetual hamster's wheel. He isolated himself from his colleagues, because he had no time for small talk or relaxation. He went ahead alone against the enemy, trying to find a weapon to overcome the immunological barrier, the rejection mechanism. He experimented with massive X-ray treatments, with steroids, with nitrogen mustards. Each led to a dead end. No matter how slight or drastic the modifications that he made, these weapons, while they did indeed neutralize the rejection mechanism, also destroyed white cell production, stripped the body of immunity to disease, killed in other ways what he was trying, after all, to save. The problem remained as large as ever: to discover a treatment or serum that was selective, that would not destroy all reactive or immunity mechanisms, that would neutralize whatever it was that rejected a foreign graft, and leave unharmed that which protected the body against disease.

Once, depressed by the impossible maze, Garrett tried to find a path around it. In that time, he fancied that he could simply ignore the rejection mechanism by circumventing it, by inventing a compact artificial heart of plastic material, that could be grafted inside the chest cavity and that would be accepted because it would be nonreactive. For months, the idea excited him. A plastic heart replacing a failing or damaged natural heart inside the human body would give its host—literally—a new lease on life.

Methodically, he studied all the mechanical hearts then in existence. These ranged from the heart pump and oxygenator created by Dr. Clarence Dennis in 1951, to a two-chamber pump run by batteries (it had kept a dog alive nine hours) produced by a team at the University of Illinois. Garrett saw that these mechanical heart-lung devices all had one factor in common— they were used *outside* the patient's body to keep the patient alive during cardiac surgery. What Garrett envisioned was such a device *inside* the body— the natural heart removed, the machine heart substituted—located in exactly the same place: orthotropous transplantation, with an external power pack. But there were question marks here, too, not the least being how to keep the plastic bag, between the two lungs, contracting and relaxing without failure. It might be resolved in the future, Garrett decided, but he preferred to grapple with the present, the probable.

Unhappily, he returned to his maze. He must find his way on the battlefield where the familiar enemy, now so well known to him, was the rejection mechanism that barred his transplantation of a living heart, either animal or human. He abandoned the radiation treatments, the nitrogen mustards, and plunged into unknown byways. And then, it happened, came to him, as simply and undramatically as waking or walking or laughter.

It was late of a morning. He had been toiling over his laboratory specimens—the mice, dogs, calves—checking, noting, noting again, modifying, when he discovered the new substance that apparently—yes, it was clear, plainly evident—neutralized the rejection mechanism but did not, at the same time, destroy all immunity. For a week, Saralee and the children knew not of his existence except on the telephone, and after that week he was almost certain. He had a serum—the serum—and with Lincolnian simplicity and straightforwardness he christened it Antireactive Substance S.

Once he had his serum, and having proved it out on lower mammalian creatures, not yet on man, he gave parallel devotion to surgical techniques of organ grafts. He considered all aspects of the homograft—an organ moved from one human into another human—and vetoed it as too formidable. More logical, more probable, and his skittering mice and tractable dogs and climbing simians supported him, was the heterograft—the transplantation of an animal heart into a living man. Exulting months followed, and by then he had settled upon the heart of a calf, a calf weighing what a potential patient might weigh, as the likeliest possibility for success.

Twice, he grafted calves' hearts into dogs, and one dog died and one lived for a while. More modifications of the serum and the surgical technique, and on a black and forbidding winter's night in Pasadena—he had already telephoned Saralee that he would not be home for dinner, and that she need not wait up for him—he prepared for his third transplantation of the heart of a calf into the chest cavity of a huge dog. He had assistance now, and by eight o'clock all was in readiness. The donor calf's heart was under perfusion and cooling. The host dog had been treated with improved Antireactive Substance S, and was already hooked to the heart-lung bypass machine. What remained was the crucial surgery. But Garrett never accomplished it, not on the dog, at least.

In another room of the Medical Center, in those hours, an elderly truck driver—later to be known in scientific papers as Henry M.—had been rushed to the hospital, suffering a severe coronary occlusion. In emergency surgery, his heart began to fail, and there was no hope of his survival. In those dark minutes, through the influence of the resident surgeon (an admirer of Garrett's) upon the patient's weeping family, John Garrett was encouraged to attempt his transplantation of the calf's heart into this suddenly available human chest, instead of the waiting canine.

The responsibility was staggering. Garrett had never before introduced Antireactive Substance S into a fellow human, let alone attempt a heterograft. But by now, he possessed a fanatic's belief in his as yet only partially proved findings. The nervous impetus that had geared him for the experiment on a canine was now automatically transferred to the unconscious truck driver. The mass of tissues on the table before him might be man or beast, for all Garrett knew. His conscience was in his fingers. Henry M., who hovered on the far edge of death, was injected with Antireactive Substance S. He was hooked to the cardiopulmonary bypass machine. Surgery proceeded. The heterograft, with all its complexity, was made surely and swiftly. And then, the question. Would the patient live?

When the clamps and catheters were being removed, Garrett's mind went to an old paper he had once read. In 1934, the Russian physiologist, Dr. S. S. Briukhonenko, had applied a mechanical heart and lung to a suicide victim, a man who had hanged himself, and the machine had brought the man back to life. The patient had opened his eyes, been aware of the physician and staff surrounding him, and had then closed his eyes forever. Even though this was different, the all-important serum, a mammalian heart, Garrett feared the same pattern when the truck driver, Henry M., opened his eyes at daybreak and blinked his bewilderment and then his gratefulness.

But Henry M.'s eyes stayed open, then and since, and he lived on with his sturdy calf's heart, unaffected by the rejection mechanism, and in medical circles and soon in the press Garrett became the Jesus who raised Lazarus from the dead.

In short months, Garrett would learn that only one cardiac patient in twenty possessed the proper blood and tissue qualifications compatible to accepting the sensational serum that would neutralize the rejection mechanism and allow the body to accept the radical transplantation. Nevertheless, encouraged and supercharged by the case of Henry M., Garrett succeeded in grafting his substitute hearts into seventeen more human beings, whose blood and tissue had been screened beforehand. Every one survived. The implications were fantastic.

When Garrett read his definitive paper on his work at the Western Surgical Association in Denver, he was hailed by scientists throughout the world. Despite the limitations of his discovery, everyone seemed to sense that the first giant step toward longevity, even immortality, had been made. It was as if, in his day, Ponce de Leon had actually found the Fountain of Youth and bottled its waters. From a nonentity with a wild dream, John Garrett had become a savior unique. He held his rarefied position exactly ten days. On the tenth day, he was asked to move over. There was another to share the occupancy of the spotlight with him.

The wire services of America carried the long and dramatic story from Rome, and the newspapers of America paraded it across their front pages. It appeared that Dr. Carlo Farelli, the eminent Italian physician, had just published a brilliant paper claiming and proving the very same discovery that Garrett had made. Farelli had also found a serum that, like Antireactive Substance S, made a heterograft acceptable, and had successfully transplanted resurrecting mammalian hearts into twenty-one persons from Italy, Switzerland, and Austria.

Overnight, Lazarus was multiplied, and Jesus was not one but two.

The world rejoiced. John Garrett was confused. His fame, while no less secure, seemed dimmed because his glory was shared. Colleagues abroad made inquiries not only of Garrett, for further work in the field, but of Farelli. The press quoted not only Garrett but also Farelli, and the Italian was quoted more frequently because he was a colorful showman as well as a great scientist, and better equipped than the reticent John Garrett to communicate his ideas to laymen.

Several months after the advent of Farelli, John Garrett's headaches began.

And here I am, he told himself, conscious once more of his surroundings and that Mrs. Zane's interminable recital of her libidinous history was coming to an end.

"—until at last he fell asleep," Mrs. Zane was saying in a voice become hoarse. "But can you imagine two times in one night? I mean, I wouldn't mind, I'm not that old, but when you're tending five children all day, well, enough is enough. Anyway, I got dressed and took a taxi, but it must've been after midnight when I finally had the dishes cleared away and changed Joanie's bed—she's still wetting—and got to sleep. I'm at wit's end, is what I want to say. I think I'm the most depraved person in the world."

Her voice trailed off on the last, and she settled back in her chair, the sordid saga of infidelity again exorcised, and her features now relaxed as if her tensions had been relieved.

"You'll find your way, Mrs. Zane," Dr. Keller murmured, as he studiously jotted some notes on the pad before him. "You're further advanced than you think."

He peered up from beneath his bushy eyebrows, his enormous chest heaving as he inhaled and exhaled, and he studied his group. No one spoke. It was as if the smash main attraction had been on, and no one wished to follow it with a lesser act.

John Garrett saw that it was now or never. He lifted his right hand, partially, like an uncertain schoolboy. Dr. Keller noticed the gesture, and nodded.

"Well, I guess I have a pressing little matter," said Garrett. He made a deferential bow at Mrs. Zane beside him. "Perhaps it is not as—as emotional —as involving as what we have just listened to, but it is important to me." His eyes met the psychiatrist's again. "As you know, I'm to deliver an address tonight. At the United Forum. I'm told there will be a full house, and that the press will attend. It's a singular opportunity for me to be heard and to express my views on my—my problem. Now, I've written my new speech, as I told you I would. The question remains—should I deliver my new speech—say what I want to say? Or should I settle for the usual one I've been giving—you know—'Hippocrates and the Human Heart'? What do you think?"

"I don't think the decision should be in my hands," said Dr. Keller instantly. "You are acquainted with the analytic process. If I make your decision, you will not gain by it. You must learn to make up your own mind, come to your own conclusions."

Garrett frowned at what he considered a reprimand, although he knew better. The psychiatrist was always saying that people must come to the understanding of themselves, by themselves. He was only a guide, a catalytic agent, sometimes an interpreter. Often, he had once said, he could advise a patient what was wrong with him after two or three visits. But the knowledge would be of no value to the patient, unless the patient found out the same information by himself. This frequently made the route tortuous, but in the end, the repair was more effective and permanent.

"I guess I have made up my mind," said Garrett. "I think it was made up before I came here today. I suppose I wanted to hear what you would say

45

first." He paused. "I've decided to give the new speech. I'm going to blast the hell out of Farelli."

He looked left, and then right, and then at Dr. Keller, for approval. There was interest in his decision, but no obvious support. "Yes," he said, using the affirmation of silence as a prop, "I think I have to do it. I've made a discovery, done one important thing in my life, by myself, all by myself, and I don't think I should lose half the credit for it to some foreign Cagliostro who is indulging in piracy and plagiarism."

"Are you sure that Dr. Farelli indulged in—as you put it—piracy and plagiarism?" Dr. Keller inquired mildly.

"I have evidence. Circumstantial, to be sure. But juries often convict a man on less. As I've told you several times, I had vaguely heard of this Farelli, but knew nothing specific about him. He never published papers, until he published that carbon copy—well, nearly—of my paper. I've since learned he is more of a science promoter than a pure scientist. His greatest discovery has been in finding new means of selling himself. Oh, he created an antireactive serum similar to mine, and performed those heterografts, and had those successes he boasts about. That's all been verified. The question is—how did he come upon his discovery? I'll tell you how. I've learned he has all of my published papers—you know, my progress reports from the earliest period. Furthermore, scientists from abroad who visited my laboratories in Pasadena from time to time then went back to Europe and, purposely or inadvertently, revealed to him precisely what I was doing and how I was doing it. I'll give you an analogy. We invented the atom bomb. Eventually, Russia would have invented one, too. But it might have been much later. What accelerated their work was information that was leaked to them about our work by spies—the Rosenbergs, Fuchs, countless others. In a more blatant way, Farelli must have been learning about my work, putting two and two together, and when I had my findings to tell the world—well, he had his. I contend that is unfair, immoral even, and should be exposed."

He had been addressing himself to Dr. Keller strongly, emotionally, and now he was out of breath. The psychiatrist, tapping his pencil softly on his pad, used the opportunity to comment.

"You may be correct in your assumption, Dr. Garrett. I can't say. At the same time, I do not see any real indicting evidence against Dr. Farelli. You know, as we all know, that, more frequently than not, great scientific discoveries are not made in a sudden, dramatic fashion—in one moment—the Eureka-I-have-found-it type of thing. It occurs, but more often in movies and on television than in real life. Most discoveries are come by slowly, gradually. Dozens of men, through the years, contribute bits and pieces, invaluable findings, and then one day a man or several men, building on the past, integrate the pieces into a useful whole, and the world has a discovery. Many times you, yourself, in this room, have acknowledged the contributions of your predecessors—Briukhonenko, Dennis, Clarke, among others, come to mind in the matter of the heart problem, Medawar, Burnet, Billingham, Brent, Owen, Merrill, Woodruff, the pioneer Guthrie, Shumway, Kaplan,

Nossal, and many others, who've worked on tissue grafts and reactive mechanisms. You had access to the reports of these people. In a sense, they were your silent collaborators, even though you accomplished the big and final task. Isn't it reasonable that Dr. Farelli in Italy also had access to the work of these people, and was steered by them as you were? Isn't it possible?"

"No, it is not possible," said Garrett vehemently. He was shaken and unnerved, and now he was defensive. "I've never claimed that I did it by myself, that I owe no one a thing. Of course I do. We all do, always. But the Farelli matter is different. The coincidence of it stinks, and there are many who agree with me. If he were an artist, he would be labeled a copyist or a forger, and be drummed out of existence. I don't think he should be allowed to graft my mind onto his and win adulation for it."

Dr. Keller remained calm, but surprisingly persistent. "Ever since you began telling us about your obsession with Farelli, I took it upon myself to do some historical reading on science matters. Merely to inform myself." He smiled at Mrs. Zane and Mr. Lovato, and added, "In fact, where I feel I must and can, I do this in most of your cases." He swung back to Garrett. "Consider the discovery of insulin for human diabetes. A profound discovery. In 1923, Frederick Banting and John Macleod were credited with the find and jointly awarded the Nobel Prize. But what were the facts? As far back as 1901, L. V. Sobolev was doing work in the field. Based on his work, Banting and Macleod, as well as C. H. Best and J. B. Collip, pushed the research farther. There you have five men. In 1923, only two of them shared the honors and the money. Was this right? Banting did not think so. He resented Macleod's getting half the credit and cash, when Macleod was not even present at the time the crucial experiment was conducted. To express his disapproval, Banting gave half his money to Best, who had not been honored at all. In recitation, Macleod gave half his money to Collip, who had received no credit either. And no one mentioned Sobolev. Now, this does not parallel your situation exactly, Dr. Garrett, but I'm sure you see what I'm driving at— the business of scientific credit is a Gordian knot—"

"Are you telling me not to make this speech tonight?"

Dr. Keller shook his head and sidestepped the trap. "No. I repeat, that decision is your own. I'm simply trying to open your mind to the ramifications. You may cause an international scandal, with what many may consider faulty evidence. I'm trying to make you be as objective as possible about Farelli, and not use him as a whipping boy for motives and neuroses which may go deeper than mere suspicion of plagiarism. Farelli is not your father, Dr. Garrett."

"You're merely upsetting me—"

"I should hope so," said Dr. Keller blandly. "But I want you to think— think before you act."

"I'm making that speech."

"Very well, then."

Garrett, shaken, became sullen and mute. Dr. Keller glanced about the room. Adam Ring had pulled himself erect in the easy chair, and was beginning to speak.

"I wish all I had to worry about was some wop," said the actor. "Me, I love wops. The gals are built like you know what, and I can go the mile with them. It's those American broads—" He shook his head, clenched his hands, and went on. "Since our last semester, Doctor, I've seen the New York broad I was telling you about. She had the hots for me and I don't have to tell you how I felt. There I was, and there was she, in our birthday suits, and—you guessed it—no score. If it weren't so crazy, I'd laugh. Two hours later, tail between my legs, I went calling on the Japanese singer again. I was terrific. Ask her. It's a riddle, I tell you, and I still don't see where I'm getting any help here. But I was thinking about something you said last week. You called me on that time when I was maybe seven or eight—and the old lady—"

John Garrett hardly heard the deep drone of the actor's voice. He suffered in silence about what he believed had been a reproach from the psychiatrist. He would make the speech, he knew, but momentarily he was less sure of his ground. He tried to sort out the reasons for his resentment of Farelli. Why did this unknown, distant Roman upset him so? At once, he remembered the fragment of something that Keller had once stated, and he was hit by a ray of illumination. His anger was not solely directed at Farelli, but at what Farelli represented. Garrett had never had anything in life alone, all his own. Nine brothers and sisters had shared his remote parents with him. At the university, in the class election, he had tied in the voting with someone else for treasurer and held the office with the other jointly. Even his wife, Saralee, had been married before. When he had been inspired by one moment of genius in his life—how many moments of genius can one man expect in his span?—when he had been so inspired, and deserved all the honors, his greatest achievement had been obscured by a far-off thief in Italy. And the capping blow. When he finally needed help, he had been forced into *group* therapy. As ever, as always, he had been made less than a whole man. The plural analysis he minded least. What rankled the most was Farelli, symbol of Garrett's loss of identity. He was half a man, and there was no justice to it. But this time, he reflected, he would not be overwhelmed or submissive. He would fight back, win credit and identity.

His musings were interrupted by Dr. Keller's voice, loud and clear. "Time is up, I see. This was a fruitful meeting. I hope to meet with all of you next week."

The others were on their feet and leaving. Garrett was the last to rise. He followed the others through the door. As he departed, he heard Dr. Keller's telephone ringing. It always rang when the session ended. Apparently, it was then that his answering service called to relay messages left, messages which Dr. Keller would handle in his free ten minutes.

Outside, on the sidewalk before the building, the members of the group took their leave of each other. Mr. Lovato, Mrs. Zane, and Miss Dudzinski remained huddled together for their good-byes to the rest. They then proceeded, as was their custom in defiance of Dr. Keller's disapproval, down the block to the cafeteria, where they would take coffee and rolls at a table and continue their post-mortem self-analysis together. Mrs. Perrin hastened off to the bus stand, still insufficiently liberated to take the taxi she could well afford. Mr. Armstrong strode off to his chaotic rented bungalow, only two miles away. Adam Ring had his magnificent Aston-Martin parked in the street. "Good luck, tonight," he called to Garrett. "Give the wop hell." Although the expression made Garrett wince, the actor's support restored Garrett's humor. "The same to you," he replied, knowing that Ring had a mulatto girl friend tucked away in a Sunset Boulevard apartment. The actor slid into his imported car, waved, and was gone. Garrett walked slowly toward the gasoline station.

He had reached the curb, and was waiting for the light to change, when he heard his name.

"Oh, Dr. Garrett—!"

He whirled about and saw Dr. Keller trotting toward him. Dr. Keller was a massive man, seemingly somnolent, and it was strange to see him in motion.

When the psychiatrist drew abreast of him, Garrett observed that Dr. Keller's face was as excited as an exclamation mark. "Your wife's on the phone upstairs," he said, panting. "She has marvelous news for you—you've just been awarded the Nobel Prize in medicine!"

Garrett allowed the words to sink in, and he accepted their impact naturally, with hardly any surprise, for he had secretly fantasied this moment for so long. But suddenly the shock of thrill reached his innards, and he felt the goose pimples on his arms and the flush on his cheeks.

"You're sure?" he asked, incredulously.

"Absolutely. Mrs. Garrett has the telegram from the Swedish Embassy." He offered his meaty hand. "May I be the first to congratulate you?"

Garrett took the psychiatrist's hand dumbly, and then released it. "I don't know what to think," he said helplessly. "What does it mean?"

"Your discovery is officially honored. Your fame is now secure."

"The Nobel Prize," he said, half to himself, savoring the words.

"Your wife's on the phone—she's waiting to speak to you."

They started back, making their way swiftly through the women shoppers. Inside the building, ascending the stairs once more, Garrett's methodical mind began to translate the award. There was always money in it, and a trip, and above all—above all else—the international recognition of his work. For the first time, Farelli had been shunted aside. At last, he himself had received the full and exclusive honor that he deserved. His love for those anonymous Swedes, who had been wise enough to see the truth and present it to the world, was boundless.

Upstairs, Dr. Keller pushed Garrett into his office, while he considerately stayed behind in the reception alcove to smoke.

Garrett rushed to the psychiatrist's desk, and brought the free receiver to his face. "Saralee?"

"Darling! Isn't it wonderful?" Her usually mild, modulated voice was pitched out of control.

"There can't be any mistake?"

"No, it's here! The telegraph office called, and I thought it was a joke and demanded they send the wire over. They did right away, and I have it. I tried to get you—but Dr. Keller's service wouldn't put me through until now. It's all true! Two newspapers called from Los Angeles—"

"Read me the telegram."

Apparently she had it in her hand, for she read it immediately. Garrett listened, numbed, and then requested that she read it again, more slowly.

When she had finished, he said, "We'll be going to Stockholm. I'm just wondering about the children—"

"We can leave them with Aunt Mae. John, this is so marvelous! I've dreamt about it so much. I never dared tell you. But you deserve it, and now you have it—forever—a Nobel Prize winner—"

"Yes—"

"Dean Filbrick called. All the faculty at the school and everyone at the hospital knows. They want to have a celebration tonight—impromptu—after your speech—"

Garrett had forgotten the speech. He tried to fasten his mind on it.

He heard Saralee again. "One second, there's someone at the door."

"Skip it—"

But she had gone. He held the receiver and enjoyed the glow of success within him. There would never be another day in his life like this, so entirely his own, so fulfilled.

Saralee had returned. "It's another telegram." He heard the crackle of paper, as she opened it, and then a dead pause, and then her curious voice again. "It's—it's a cable from Rome—Italy—" Her voice faded.

"Who from?" he inquired loudly, to bring her back.

"I'll read it. 'I have just been informed by the Swedish Embassy that we are sharing this year's Nobel Prize in medicine jointly. I am honored our work has been so recognized and doubly honored to receive the award with an American colleague I respect. Please accept my sincerest congratulations. I look forward to seeing my other half in Stockholm. Best wishes.' It is signed, 'Carlo Farelli.' "

Garrett remained very still. There was no anger in him now, no fury, only an overwhelming defeat in this moment of victory. His frustration could not be articulated in language. He knew, finally, that he was being tied to this despicable Italian for life and the hereafter. His mind went back into the baseball lore of his youth—the immortal double-play combination of Tinker to Evers to Chance—how Tinker and Evers hated each other, and would not speak to one another, but were forced to continue their public cooperation and harmony before the world for their entire professional lives.

Saralee's voice came tinnily through the receiver. "John, this shouldn't spoil anything—"

No, he told himself, he would not let this spoil anything. He would go to

Stockholm, for his half moment, and have his confrontation with Farelli, and make the moment whole and his own. Somehow, the Nobel committee and the world would yet know the truth about which was the genius and which the usurper. But not tonight, he realized at last, not on the night of a day like this.

He sighed. The new speech was out. Tonight, again, it would be "Hippocrates and the Human Heart." But there would be a different night, next month, in Sweden, he was sure. . . .

It was exactly 4:30 of a chilly afternoon when the telegram from the Swedish Embassy in Washington, D.C., had arrived in the reconverted notions store, next door to the *Weekly Independent*, that now served as the telegraph office in the rural hamlet of Miller's Dam, Wisconsin.

But that was forty-five minutes ago, and the message, with several others, still lay in the electric receiving machine, unseen by human eyes, untouched by human hands, uncommunicative.

The lone keeper of the office, during the eight day hours, was Eldora Fleischer, eighteen-year-old daughter of a local dairy farmer, who usually divided these hours between original paperback novels and motion picture magazines, or daydreamed of making a sensation in Milwaukee or Chicago, where a wealthy and princely suitor would find her and persuade her to elope. Sometimes, in her more practical moods, the dream took another form. She would be working in the office, when *he* would enter, distraught. Because his Continental had developed engine trouble, he was delayed in this tank town and had to send a wire—probably to the Governor or someone important. He was wealthy and princely, as well as young and handsome, and when he saw Eldora, he no longer wanted to send the wire. Smitten, love at first sight, he begged for her hand. At first haughty and remote, Eldora finally allowed herself to be persuaded. And off they went in the Continental—happily repaired—on their elopement, which would astonish the royalty of the Old World. Prepared, always, for this dream to become reality, Eldora adorned herself for her role. Her long hair was freshly bleached, her mascara artfully applied, her pancake makeup ready for the cameras. She wore her best and tightest and thinnest dresses to work, even on cold days, and the necklines were always plunging. Elodra was short, milky, buxom, definitely aphrodisiac, and patiently she worked and waited.

But at 4:15 this afternoon, she had tired of waiting. The week before, she had made the acquaintance of a new boy who had moved to town. His hair was wavy, and his face not unattractive despite the pimples, and he was impressively tall. He had moved to Miller's Dam from Beloit—a metropolis, after all—and he was twenty-two—along in years and mature—and he was a grocer's clerk and would be more. His first name was Roger. His last name was unpronounceable. His importance was this: when Eldora saw him, she tingled, and liked the feeling.

At 4:15, he had sauntered into the telegraph office. It was his day off. He had made some amusing jokes, really clever, and had invited Eldora to join him in a smoke. Since Eldora did not dare to smoke publicly—one of her father's Baptist friends might see her—she suggested to Roger that they retire to the tiny storage room in the rear. The telegraph office was rarely visited at this hour, and if it was, the bell over the door would ring and warn Eldora.

Now it was 5:15, and Eldora was still in the storage room with Roger. She had smoked two cigarettes, and he had smoked three. Not once had the front doorbell disturbed them. They had talked, and finally he had pulled her down on his lap, rocking precariously on the old swivel chair. He had kissed her neck, and the cleft between her breasts, until she thought that she would die of ecstasy, and now he had slid his hand under her dress.

"Wait," she said, "wait, Roger—"

She jumped off his lap, and ran to the storage room door, closed it, and bolted it from the inside. She would not be able to hear the bell, but there could be excuses if she was reported, and she did not care, anyway. At once, she returned, and settled in Roger's lap, and closed her eyes. More boldly, his hand rubbed under her dress again, over her plump thigh, until his fingers touched the fringe of her pants.

Her eyes were still shut. "Roger," she whispered, "you can do that—but nothing else."

"Aw honey—"

She opened her eyes. "I mean it, Roger. I'm a lady."

"Okay, sweetie—"

He kissed the hollow of her neck, and she closed her eyes once more and hugged him tightly, and his hands moved slowly beneath her pants.

Neither one of them heard the front doorbell.

The front door had been opened, and the bell sounded, by Jake Binninger, the stubby, myopic, eager reporter, rewrite man, clipper of exchange newspapers, and advertising salesman of the *Weekly Independent,* next door.

He always appeared frenetic, but now a new dimension of enthusiastic agitation seemed to have been added. In his hand he carried a tear slip from the teletype machine, which was fed by a national news wire. He searched the room for Eldora, and could see her nowhere.

"Eldora?"

There was no response. He quickly reasoned that she had run out for a cup of coffee. Nevertheless, he was determined not to leave without confirmation of the incredible dispatch in his hand. According to the dispatch, the notification had been sent to Miller's Dam by telegram. There must be a carbon of the telegram. Jake Binninger wanted the confirmation—the story was the biggest thing that had happened to anyone in Miller's Dam since the Pike's Creek murder, a decade ago—and, if true, he wanted the exact contents of that wire.

He circled the desk, found Eldora's list of deliveries—there had been only six this day, and not one the one he sought—and then, almost as an afterthought, he began to read the messages in the machine.

He found it at once, gave an exclamation of pleasure, and speedily brought out his pencil and copied the wording of the wire on the bottom of his tele-type sheet.

IN RECOGNITION OF YOUR POWERFUL AND SIGNIFICANT WRITINGS IN SUPPORT OF HUMANITARIAN IDEALS AND IN ESPECIAL APPRECIATION OF YOUR EPICAL NOVELS THE PER-FECT STATE AND ARMAGEDDON THE NOBEL FOUNDATION OF STOCKHOLM ON BEHALF OF THE SWEDISH ACADEMY IS PLEASED TO INFORM YOU THAT YOU HAVE TODAY BEEN VOTED THIS YEARS NOBEL PRIZE IN LITERATURE STOP THE PRIZE WILL BE A GOLD MEDALLION AND A CHEQUE FOR FIFTY THOUSAND THREE HUNDRED DOLLARS STOP THE AWARD CEREMONY WILL TAKE PLACE IN STOCKHOLM ON DECEMBER TENTH STOP DETAILS FOLLOW STOP HEARTIEST CONGRATU-LATIONS STOP

The message was addressed to MISTER ANDREW CRAIG SEVENTY SEVEN WHEATON ROAD MILLERS DAM WISCONSIN. . . .

It was 5:20, and they had been conversing and playing gin rummy for two hours, when Lucius Mack realized that his companion was about to pass out.

Andrew Craig's long fingers woodenly clamped on to the cards, fanned out erratically, in his hand. Carefully, too carefully, he laid the cards face down, fumbled for the fifth of Scotch, and emptied the last drops in his glass, hitting the rim slightly so that some of the liquor dribbled onto the table. He set the bottle down, then lifted the glass with its inch of liquor, and considered it blankly.

Lucius Mack saw that Craig was too intoxicated to bring the glass to his lips.

"I think I've had about enough, Andrew," said Mack tactfully. "Let's pick up this game tomorrow. I've got to get back to the shop."

Craig lifted his head with effort and tried to focus his glazed eyes on his friend. "Somebody's got to keep—to keep—wheels of industry turning," he said thickly. He managed to swallow the last dregs of his bottle.

Mack pushed back his chair, and rose. "Like to lie down a bit?"

"Like nothing better, Florence Nightingale," said Craig. "No games. I'm stoned, and we both know it, an'—and I like it."

Mack came around the table to Craig, prepared to assist him out of the chair, but in a gesture of self-respect, Craig set his hands on the table and heaved himself upright. Standing, he swayed precariously, and flattened his hand against the wall to keep from falling.

He narrowed his eyes, to find Mack, and then smiled. "You're good, Lucius—good guy." He remembered his duties as a host. "Sure you had enough to drink?"

"Too much, with a night's work ahead."

"Someday I'd like to say jus'—just that—'Too much, with a night's work ahead.' "

"You will, Andrew, believe me."

Craig removed his steadying hand from the wall, and tried to take a step toward the bed, but he staggered. Mack caught his arm firmly, supporting him. Craig conceded defeat. "Got the dizzies. All the juice gone down to my pins."

Mack slowly led the author to the bed, then helped lower him to a sitting position. The instant that he made contact with the mattress, Craig fell back on a portion of the pillow. Easily, efficiently, as he had done so many times in the past, Mack lifted his friend's long legs from the floor and settled them on the bed. Then he removed Craig's leather moccasins and placed them neatly under the night table.

Briefly, he stood over Craig and examined him. The prostrated figure, rangy and surprisingly muscular for one so committed to self-destruction, was clothed in an old, gray sweat shirt and soft corduroy slacks. Mack decided that his friend would be more comfortable this way than in pajamas. Despite the heat blowing in from the floor furnace vent, the autumn chill crept through the window cracks, and Craig would require warmth.

Lucius Mack returned to the table, and set about cleaning it up—Leah, Craig's sister-in-law, downstairs, could not tolerate a mess. Mack gathered the playing cards into a deck and stuffed them into the box. He dropped the empty Scotch bottle beside the other one in the wastebasket. He took the two glasses into the bathroom, rinsed and dried them, and then placed them atop Craig's green file cabinet.

This done, Lucius Mack stood in the center of the room and surveyed it. He liked the narrow, brown, cozy room, beneath the frame house's gable, and it was as much his own as the rooms he kept in the Perkins boarding-house. His eyes took in the rolltop desk, and covered typewriter, so long unused, and the five shelves of books, mostly reference and history, with the uppermost shelf reserved for Craig's own four novels, in the American, English, and odd foreign editions.

Lucius Mack had known the Craigs, or Craig, more than five years, and for more than two of them he had known Craig intimately. It hardly seemed eight years ago when Andrew and Harriet Craig—he so boyish, with only two novels published and a third one planned—had arrived to make their residence in Miller's Dam. They had bought the Hartog place, this place, on Wheaton Road, and renovated it, and in the beginning had kept to themselves, rather like honeymooners. Lucius Mack had met Harriet Craig one morning in the first month of their residence, when she had visited the newspaper to place a classified advertisement for day help. Memory usually dimmed with the years, but Mack still retained what had impressed him then: a dark blonde, quiet and self-possessed, with a pleasing, almost gay Slavic face, all features broad but regular—he had guessed that her antecedents were Lithuanian. She had been of medium height, perhaps more, and only seemed smaller side by side with Craig, whose lanky body went upwards of six feet. She had been generously endowed, the full figure of a woman in every way, with a certain solidity that seemed to settle well against the Wisconsin landscape.

A week later, Mack had written Craig requesting an interview, and almost immediately Craig had come calling in person. At the time, Mack had been the fledgling owner of the *Weekly Independent*. He followed the hard-set rule of all small-town newspapers—mention everyone's name in print at least once during the year and more if possible. This was difficult, since so many members of the community were so dull. The arrival of newcomers from the East, especially a published author of growing reputation, provided an opportunity for Mack to enliven his pages.

What the editor-publisher remembered most about Craig's first visit were his tousled black hair and quick eyes, amused, encompassing, the implied cynicism of his half-smile, and the general impression of elongated, sunken, brooding features. Craig had proved a fine subject, and an easy, disarming talker. He and Harriet had been married five years, and enjoyed a honeymoon trip abroad, from Scandinavia to Italy, and she had suffered a miscarriage in the East, and they had lived on Long Island for five years, where Craig had written the first two novels. Once, on a trip to Madison, where his wife's younger sister, Leah, had been attending the university, they had passed through Miller's Dam. Later both had spoken, in accord, of buying a house in such a small, peaceful town and settling down there, someday, someday when there was an advance large enough. Both had continued living in New York, chafing at the compressed, tumultuous existence—"millions of people being lonesome together," Craig had said, quoting Thoreau—for the Craigs had both been Midwest-born—and then Craig's second book had won sufficient approval from his publisher to guarantee a sizable advance on his third idea. Without a moment's hesitation, Andrew and Harriet Craig had moved to Miller's Dam.

Remembering now that first interview, Lucius Mack recalled that Craig had been a fascinating conversationalist. Most men have one or two specialties, at most a handful of interests, and display vast ignorance of and disinterest in everything else. Not Andrew Craig. He had shown himself to be interested in literally everything, and the custodian of the most bizarre bits of knowledge. In that first interview, in his lively manner, he had discussed the French Jesuits who had sponsored Father Marquette, the trajectory of Three-fingered Brown's curve ball, the sexuality of Alexander Hamilton's mistress, Mrs. Maria Reynolds, the peculiar genius of Charles Fort, the joys of pyramidology, and the reasonableness of Kazentsev's speculations that the meteoric explosion on the Tunguskaia River of Siberia in 1908 had actually been a nuclear explosion from outer space.

Eight years ago, it had been. And now?

Standing in the middle of the room, Lucius Mack gazed down compassionately at the figure of his friend sprawled on the bed, watched the heavy breathing and the deep, deep slumber. Except for the gouged lines of dissipation beneath his eyes and beneath his cheekbones, Craig seemed as he had seemed then, although now he was thirty-nine. Despite the fact that he was sixteen years the author's senior, Mack felt at one with him, felt a contemporary with no bridge of years between them. Perhaps they had found each other good companions, after that first meeting, because they were alike, their minds galloping the earth and the surrounding universe, and unlike the others who were time-bound and narrow earth-bound by the price of hogs and corn and prairie isolationism and *Better Farming*.

Almost weekly, in the early times, Craig had ambled into the newspaper office to have a shot or two with Mack and talk and listen and talk. But after Craig's time of trouble, after the injury, and the breaking down, and the surrender, Mack had taken to calling upon his friend four or five times a week. This was usually in the afternoons, before Craig had become too drunk. They would lounge in the upstairs room, the bottle between them, Mack taking one to Craig's six, and converse as of old, perhaps more recklessly, more fancifully with the heavier drinking. Sometimes, in a desultory way, they would play gin rummy, too. It had been this way for almost three years, and these days ended, during Craig's bad periods, exactly as this day had ended.

Lucius Mack sighed, and collected his pack of cigarettes from beside Craig's blue humidor. He heard Craig stir fitfully on the bed, and watched unconcerned. Craig was on his side now, one lank arm outstretched, his legs curled, and he was sleeping hard. Mack wondered if he dreamed. He hoped not, not now, not these years.

Mack let himself out of the room, noiselessly, and went carefully down the two turnings of wooden stairs. The living room was fully lighted against the bleak day, and Leah Decker, her face pinched in the familiar disapproval she always showed at this hour of the day, sat in a corner of the deep plaid sofa, industriously knitting.

With Mack's entry into the room, she looked up with her eyes. "How is he?"

"Sleeping."

"How much did he drink this afternoon?"

"Oh, a few fingers, no more."

"I bet!"

Patiently, Mack struck a match and put it to the cigarette between his lips. He inhaled and blew out the smoke, and dropped the match in a nearby ceramic tray. "Look, Leah," he said without exasperation, "I've told you time and again—Andrew's had a bad time, been through a bitter time, and this is his way of escaping it. He's not like all other men. He's a creative person, sensitive as can be—"

"That doesn't give him license to behave like Edgar Allan Poe. Even if he'd proved he is Poe. It's wrong—drinking all day, passing out every night—"

"Come now, Leah, you know this thing goes in cycles—"

"It's getting worse," she said flatly. "It used to be two weeks on and two weeks off. Now it's three weeks on and one week off."

"We have to endure it for now. When a man's lost his wife, the shock—"

Leah put her knitting aside. "He killed Harriet with his drinking, and now he's trying to kill himself. I hate being the witness to two murders." She stood

56

up and massaged one hand with the other, turning her back to Mack, and then turning again to face him. "Heavens, Lucius, don't you think I know how it feels? She was my sister—just as much as she was his wife. But you don't see me, or anyone else, carrying on like this, liquoring up day and night, half the time unconscious from that and sedatives and depression. Harriet was a terrible loss for me, too, but after proper mourning, and thinking about it, I found myself. My God, it's been three years. Life goes on. On and on. Life is for the living. There's little enough of it, anyway. We'll all have our turn, you bet." She stopped. "Will you have some coffee?"

They always had coffee together, after his visits to Craig. He bobbed his head. "Yes, sure, if you don't mind."

Leah Decker went into the old-fashioned kitchen, and Mack followed her, finding a chair at the dinette table. He traced the floral design painted on the maple table, and he watched Leah brewing the coffee. She was a handsome woman, he reckoned, by any standard. She might not grow old well, but she was handsome now. She had Harriet's Slavic features, except that they were tighter, more pointed, and her hair, which was brown, not dark blond, was swept back tight and bunned in the back. Her body was taller, straighter than Harriet's had been, and pleasing although more rigid and unyielding. She had none of Harriet's gaiety or humor. She was practical, sensible, and —too often recently—querulous. Mack forgave her the last, because her lot was not an easy one. After the accident, she had come to help out, to bury Harriet and to nurse Craig, and she had simply stayed on. For all her faults, she was selfless in her devotion to Craig, and always softer and more feminine in his presence. Her harder side, her complaints, were reserved for others.

Mack knew that her life here was lonely. Craig was too rarely sober or mobile or sociable. And Mack understood that things could not be easy, financially. By now, Craig's meager savings must have dwindled away, leaving innumerable debts, and there was little hope of salvation. Craig had one hundred pages of a new novel, *Return to Ithaca*, but only a handful of these pages had been added in six months. Briefly, there had been an opportunity for a teaching job at Joliet College, four miles north of Miller's Dam. A solemn, scholarly literature professor at the school, Alex Inglis, a frustrated writer in his fifties deeply devoted to Craig's books, had pulled strings to bring his idol into the college as an instructor. This high hope had dissolved when, to impress the Board of Regents, Inglis had arranged a literary lecture by Craig, at Joliet, and Craig had appeared too drunk to go on.

The Craig household still survived, Mack was certain, because Leah was economical and husbanded what was left of Craig's past. Royalties from paperback editions of the novels, and foreign editions, and television adaptations, dribbled in, and Leah made the most of them. Also, she helped keep alive Craig's limited cult throughout the country, and interest in his old work, by cooperatively corresponding with every fan and critic, by encouraging them to write about Craig, and by bedeviling Craig's despairing agent to press continually for reprints and new editions of his four books. Thus, she maintained Craig—and herself—above water. But for how long?

And why? The last question was the one that interested Lucius Mack. Why had Leah Decker, an eligible woman no more than thirty-four, dedicated herself to this existence? Was it that she was sorry for her brother-in-law? Was it that nearness to a once-promising literary figure enriched a potentially drab life? Was it masochism? Or was it—and Mack had often speculated on this point—that she secretly wanted her sister's husband, the future security and prestige he might provide, even his love? Mack wondered.

"It'll just be a minute," Leah called over her shoulder, as she took the rolls from the oven.

"No hurry."

Watching Leah, Mack wondered about another thing, too. Whenever Mack or other close friends were present, and Craig was not, Leah always decried her brother-in-law's drinking. She played Carrie Nation, and evoked sympathy and admiration. Yet, Mack wondered. Somehow, there were always fresh bottles of Scotch in Craig's room, and Craig did not buy them. Somehow, Craig drank before Mack saw him, and after. Mack wondered if Leah actually, in subtle ways, encouraged Craig's drinking, or at least went along with it, to reduce his potency as a man. In this way, she could have him dependent on her as part nurse, part mother, part wife. Without drink, as once he had been, Craig might leave Miller's Dam, depart from the place and Leah's person, and she would be left without him, in a void and old-maiding. Still, there were arguments against such behavior on Leah's part, such as the fact that his insobriety meant his inactivity as an artist, and this impoverished him and, in turn, Leah. What was the truth about Leah? Mack reveled in these old man's games.

She brought two cups of steaming coffee to the dinette table, and then bringing the heated rolls and butter, she sat down across from Lucius Mack.

Stirring sugar into her coffee with her spoon, she said, "You know, I've tried to talk to him several times these last weeks. I mean, about trying to write a little every day—do something." Her eyes stayed on the spoon. "I wish you'd speak to him sometime. He might listen to you."

Mack poured cream in his coffee, and then sipped his drink. "We've discussed it many times, Leah. What do you think we talk about up there? A good day'll come, I'm positive. Right now he's caught up in this pattern of self-destruction. But at the core, he's too tough to kill himself. He *is* a writer. He *has* a mind. One day, these factors will dominate him. One day, he'll wake up from all of this, and the bottle will be a stranger, and he'll say to himself—Christ, where have I been? And he'll say to himself—it's my turn to live again. And then, he'll be like he used to be."

"Sometimes it never happens. Poe—"

"Nonsense. Forget Poe."

"Well, I'm waiting for that day. Three years is an awfully long time." She pushed the plate of rolls toward Mack. "Have some. You need filling."

As if to punctuate Leah's dietary advice, the wall telephone in the kitchen rang.

There were few calls these days, and Leah was quick to reach the telephone and unhook the receiver. She listened a moment, and, disappointed, told the party to hold on, then held the receiver toward Lucius Mack.

"For you," she said. "Jake Binninger at the office."

Mack got to his feet and went to the telephone. He wedged the receiver between his shoulder and his chin, as was his habit, and listened.

Seated at the table again, Leah, absorbed in her own thoughts, paid no attention. Sipping her coffee, she almost spilled it when she heard Mack's sudden exclamation. She looked up surprised, to see his creased face opened wide and red with pleasure.

"Are you sure, Jake?" he was pleading into the telephone. "It's not a hoax? Read it to me again—the whole thing—slowly—now go ahead."

Only the hum of the refrigerator could be heard, as Lucius Mack pressed against the telephone, and Leah observed him with curiosity.

Mack broke the silence. "All right—that's enough—what a day! Now, look here, Jake, you just drop everything and hop over, and bring all that with you."

He hung up with a bang and spun around.

"Leah, it's sensational—the news just came through—Andrew's gone and won the Nobel Prize for literature!"

Her face was puzzled. "What do you mean? I don't understand—"

Mack took her by the shoulders, half lifting her to her feet, and shaking her in his enthusiasm. "The Nobel Prize—!"

"In Sweden?" she asked blankly.

"The biggest in the world. Over fifty thousand smackers for Andrew Craig!"

"Explain it, Lucius. I don't know. I'm all mixed up."

"You know—you know—the annual award to the best author on earth—and they've just announced it from Stockholm—they've voted it to Andrew."

"Oh, my—my—" She was almost speechless. "Is it true?"

"Jake got it on the Associated Press wire. He checked. The telegram from Stockholm just came into the office on Main Street."

"What do we do?" she asked helplessly.

"We get Andrew on his feet, and damn quick. AP and UPI are flying their men in from Chicago. *Time, Life,* and *Newsweek* are, too. They'll all be here tonight. And the Milwaukee and Madison papers are sending down special correspondents. They've all checked with our office. This is news, Leah—this is big!"

"But Andrew—he can't—"

"He can and will," said Lucius Mack. Grabbing Leah by the elbow, he began to propel her out of the kitchen, when suddenly he halted. "No, wait. You set up gallons of hot, black coffee, while I wake him. We've got to get him partway sober!"

Leah moved her head mechanically in assent, and pointed herself back toward the kitchen. Mack ran through the living room, raced up the staircase, and burst into Craig's bedroom.

Andrew Craig lay flat on his back now, arms stretched wide, filling the bed as if crucified. His respiration was nasal and difficult.

Catching his breath, Mack crossed to him, and sat on the side of the bed. "Andrew—Andrew—"

There was no response. He took Craig by the shoulders and shook him. "Wake up—"

Craig wriggled, and then he opened his bloodshot eyes. He searched Mack's face, trying to orient himself, learning finally who he was, and who was above him, and where he was, and in what condition. He licked his parched lips.

"What going on?" he muttered. "For Chrissakes, leave me alone—"

He turned his head on the pillow, but Mack took his face in his hands and brought it back before him.

"Andrew, this is important—"

"I gotta sleep it off—"

"No, listen—now, listen good, man—we've just got a flash! You've won the Nobel Prize—the real McCoy, I'm not kidding! They cited *The Perfect State* and *Armageddon* and your writings in support of 'humanitarian ideals.' Andrew, it's true, and there's fifty thousand bucks that goes with it!"

Andrew Craig lay unmoved as a cadaver, eyes open, staring past Mack, letting the communication find transmission through his fogged brain.

Mack took his friend by the shoulders again. "Did you hear what I said, Andrew?"

"I heard." He did not budge. "It's a gag, isn't it?"

"Every word true. Jake Binninger's on the way from the office with the telegram and AP lead. In a couple of hours, half the press of the country'll be here!"

"Why me?" Craig asked suddenly. "I haven't had anything out in four years—"

"I don't know why—I don't know how—I only know it's happened. Old Zeus has come down from Olympus and crowned his man. Andrew, do you know what this means—what day this is? This is the day you've become a Nobel Prize winner—joined the rest of the big ones—made the majors!"

"I can't think of what to say."

"You'd better, and fast. You're going to be doing a lot of talking—to the whole world—tonight."

"Lucius, I'm drunk."

"We're going to make you sober. Leah's in the kitchen now."

"What did she say?"

"She lost her faculty of speech."

"I'm glad for her." He tried to prop himself on an elbow, groaned, bringing his hand to his head, and dropped back on the pillow. "Wow. I really hung one on. Lucius, I can't get up. Lemme sleep a little."

"No. Definitely not. You're no more Miller's Dam. Now you belong to the ages. Up."

Mack took Craig's arm and pulled, and Craig pushed, and was abruptly upright, but in agony. He swung his legs off the bed. Mack knelt and slipped the moccasins on Craig's feet. "There."

"Do I have to dress?"

"I don't think so. You're a famous author now. Nobody gives a damn how you dress. Only I want you to look sober. Better throw some water on your face and comb your hair."

Grumbling, Craig managed to stand up, holding his head between his hands as if to keep it screwed on his neck. Setting one foot hesitantly before the other, he tottered forward and disappeared into the bathroom. After a brief sound of running water, he emerged, better groomed, but still in agony.

"I dunno, Lucius. I see three of you, and all look like Simon Legree. The bed is now twin beds, and I want to sleep in both of them." Shakily, he took his brier pipe from the table, and then the worn, half-filled pouch. He considered Mack a moment. "The Nobel Prize, you said. What does that mean?"

"I told you. Over fifty thousand dollars."

"No—that's good, but—what do I have to do?"

"Well, there's the press tonight. And in three weeks, you go to Stockholm—"

"Stockholm? I could never make it."

"Sure you can."

"No. I did it once—but that was with Harriet," he said almost inaudibly. "Now, I'm alone." He made a move to leave the room, but his knees buckled, and he snatched at Mack and held. His grin was sickly. "Guess I need a collaborator, Lucius. Help me down."

They descended the staircase and progressed through the living room slowly, and, finally, they reached the kitchen. Jake Binninger had just arrived, his sheepskin coat wildly misbuttoned. He was wiping the thick lenses of his spectacles, as he watched Leah read the telegram and teletype dispatch he had just delivered to her.

Andrew Craig's entry into the kitchen brought Jake Binninger across the room in two leaps. He grasped Craig's limp hand and pumped it. "Mr. Craig, this is wonderful! I'm proud to know you! A million congratulations!"

"Thank you, Jake."

Leah had held back. As the reporter stepped aside, she came forward. She went up on her toes and brush-kissed Craig on the cheek.

"I'm happy for you," she said.

"Thanks, Lee."

"Here's confirmation." She handed him the telegram and teletype message.

Craig's hand shook as he accepted the sheets, and groped for and found the nearest kitchen chair. He lowered himself carefully into it.

"You smell like a brewery," she said to Craig. "That's not right—in your position. I want you to drink black coffee, lots of it—"

He was reading the telegram. "Not now," he said absently.

"And that getup," she went on. "A Nobel Prize winner in a sweat shirt, cords, and dirty moccasins—they'll be taking your picture—"

Lucius Mack, still in the kitchen entrance, interrupted. "I told him it was all right, Leah. It's what they expect of an author."

"They expect dignity." She turned to Craig and her tone softened. "Please, Andrew—"

"Lee, I couldn't climb those stairs again. And if I could, I'd never come down." He dropped the telegram and teletype message on the dinette table. "I guess it's official. But I don't know about Stockholm." He looked up at his sister-in-law pleadingly. "Lee, I can't get through this evening without some kind of pick-me-up. There's a bottle in the cupboard."

Leah refused to move. "Black coffee," she said.

"Awright, dammit, make it coffee then—anything."

As Leah went to the stove, the wall telephone rang. She had the Silex in her hand, and nodded to Jake Binninger, who jumped to answer the telephone.

It was a long-distance call from Craig's publisher in New York, and this was their first contact in a year. The publisher's congratulations were hearty. He had good news for Craig. Tomorrow, work would begin on a de luxe omnibus containing three of Craig's four novels—"we'll use the old plates, thinner paper, and this time, illustrations"—and it would be called "the Nobel edition" and be expedited to catch the spring list.

The publisher, who had long before written off Craig, the advance on the next novel, and the next novel itself, was now eager to know if Craig had resumed writing. "If you mean, have I stopped drinking, the answer is no," Craig said harshly. The publisher treated his reply as a joke. He reiterated his faith in Craig. Tangible proof of this would be a check going into the mail within a week, an advance against the omnibus and an additional advance on the new novel. He was proud that his house was associated with a Nobel Prize winner. He hoped to see Craig before the Stockholm trip. Craig remained noncommittal and, as soon as possible, hung up. "Bastard," he muttered. Leah admonished Craig. The publisher had every reason to have behaved as he had, before and now. How would Craig have felt, in the publisher's shoes, toward a writer who took money and did not write? Craig's good humor returned briefly. "I revise my comment," he said. "Poor bastard."

Before he could leave the telephone, it rang again. This long-distance call was from Connecticut, and it was Craig's literary agent, with whom he had been out of personal touch for months, but whom Leah constantly wrote. Morosely, Craig listened to the faraway effusions and well-wishes. The agent also had news. There had been three calls from motion picture story departments in New York, tentative feelers on Hollywood jobs after Craig came back from Sweden. Apparently, all of them wanted Craig, but also, they all wanted to know about his health. Craig was more amused than irritated. "Tell them," he said, "I'll work for them for five thousand dollars and five cases of Ballantine's a week." The laughter in Connecticut was uncertain.

Ten minutes later, just as Craig had finished his cup of coffee and Leah was pouring him more, there was a third long-distance call, this one from Boston. Craig took the receiver from Jake Binninger, and found himself connected with the most renowned lecture manager in the business. Unlike the others, he was a brusque and forthright man. "This Nobel Prize," he told

Craig, "makes you a salable commodity, now. We can book you for a year solid—women's clubs—the chicken-à-la-king circuit—at a gross of a hundred thousand dollars. Our commission is half of that. The rest is yours, clear. We pay all expenses, routing you, travel, hotels, food, publicity. It's yours, if you want it, on one condition." Craig's voice was edgy, as he asked the condition. "Women's clubs are touchy," the lecture manager said. "Our deal is we deliver our literary people sober. I heard you're on the booze. Is that true?" Craig decided that he liked this man. "Yes, it's true," he said frankly. The manager was matter-of-fact. "Well, if you stop, let me know. Anyway, congratulations. You're way up there now."

Back at the table, Craig felt as if his last energy had been suctioned out of him. He could not assemble his thoughts. He drank the second cup of hot coffee, as the others watched him.

"How do you feel?" Lucius Mack asked.

"Lousy. Half drunk, half hung over. Do you think this is the way Ulysses S. Grant felt at Appomattox?"

The doorbell chimes sounded. There was someone outside.

Leah wrung her hands nervously, and started for the door. Lucius Mack blocked her way. "Wait a minute." He touched Craig's shoulder. "What do you say, Andrew, if it's the out-of-town reporters? Can you make it?"

"No," said Craig.

"Okay." He spoke to Leah. "If it's the press people, stall them. Say he's got fever, the flu, and maybe they can see him in the morning. Meanwhile, tell them I'll be glad to take them out and give them a fill-in, color, background, et cetera. Have you got it straight?"

"If you've handled Andrew Craig for three years, you can handle anybody," she said briskly, and was gone.

Mack studied Craig for a moment. The author had one hand over his cup of coffee, and he swayed gently in his chair, eyes closed. Mack beckoned Jake Binninger.

"Jake," he said, "this is a big story for us and all the papers we're stringing for. Now, you get yourself down to the library and dig up all the Nobel data you can find, and take it back to the office and bone up fast. Soon's Andrew can talk, I'll get what I need from him. Funny, how long you know a man, and you don't know his vital statistics. I don't even know where he was born."

"Cedar Rapids," said Craig from the table.

"Well, see, I didn't know," said Mack. He returned to his reporter. "Now, you go out the back there and get on it, and I'll catch up with you later."

As Binninger left by the rear door, Mack strained to hear the voice at the front door. He waited apprehensively, and then he heard the pad of footsteps on the carpet. Leah appeared, and she was followed by Alex Inglis, the Joliet College professor. Inglis, his Anglo-Saxon face ruddy from the cold, and his expression frozen into permanent awe, entered the kitchen as he might have entered Count Leo Tolstoi's study at Yasnaya Polyana.

"It wasn't the press at all," Leah was saying to Craig. "It's Alex Inglis, from the college—"

Craig opened his eyes and acknowledged his admirer with a blink. Hastily, awkwardly, in his heavy black overcoat and muffler, Inglis sat in the chair opposite his idol.

"I can't tell you how thrilled we all are," Inglis said with reverence. "The entire campus is agog. Imagine, a Nobel laureate under our very noses—"

"Thank you," Craig murmured.

"So few American authors have been honored," Inglis continued. "Sinclair Lewis, Pearl Buck, Eugene O'Neill, William Faulkner, Ernest Hemingway, Thomas Stearns Eliot—if you would consider him an American—and now, Andrew Craig."

Craig showed no reaction, and Inglis looked up for Leah and Mack to endorse his enthusiasm, and then he continued pedantically, "Think of it. Mr. Craig is now in the Nobel company of Kipling, Rolland, Anatole France, Thomas Mann, Galsworthy, Churchill—"

"An' Gjellerup an' Pontoppidan," muttered Craig. "Know that? Those Joes won it in nineteen—uh—seventeen. Call me Gjellerup an' shake well before pronouncing."

"Please—" said Leah.

Inglis was confused. "Mr. Craig, aren't you well?"

"Professor Inglis, I'm drunk."

"Well, uh, I can't blame you—no, indeed not—the award does call for celebration." He swallowed hard. "I came down here, primarily, to congratulate you—"

"Pardon me," said Craig. "You're a good fellow, Inglis."

"—but also to relay some additional good news. I was with the head of the Board of Regents when all of this happened. I have his permission to tell you this. We have received a sizable endowment to enlarge—immensely enlarge—the Midwestern Historical Society, and it will operate quite independently of the college. This should be completed by summer. There will be an opening for a curator—rather like the position Archibald MacLeish filled in the Library of Congress—and it would be ideal for you, Mr. Craig. It would be ideal, because it would actually be an honorary position, one constituted to give the Society prestige and attract gift collections. The actual workaday tasks would be performed by a staff of librarians. Except for attending one meeting a month—oh, and perhaps making an occasional speech somewhere in our behalf—you would be independent and free to work on your own novels at home. The honorarium would be fifteen thousand per annum. Of course, I know with all that Nobel money—"

"Won't be any Nobel money by the time it's January," said Craig, who had squeezed his eyes to bring Inglis into better focus. "That's a good offer."

"I'm delighted you think so. The Board of Regents is highly favorable to your appointment. They are most impressed with the Nobel matter. Of course—" He hesitated, and Craig, sobering for an instant, eyed his visitor keenly.

"Of course—what?"

"The Board is willing to make the appointment formally after the Nobel

64

Ceremony—I mean, after you've received the honor and made your address."

"Why not now, Inglis? Are they afraid I might disgrace them—have another fiasco—like the time I was supposed to lecture up at the college? I bet those graybeards don't think I'll make the Nobel Ceremony or get on the Stockholm stage sober. They're afraid of a scandal, aren't they?"

Inglis seemed to retreat into his great overcoat, suffused with embarrassment. "It's not that, Mr. Craig—"

"What else can it be, dammit? I'm on probation. Go to Stockholm, Craig, stand up before the world, display academic dignity, show that you are purged, cleansed, reformed—and come back to us, not only with your laurels, but a new man. I'm on probation. That's it, isn't it, Inglis?"

"Stop badgering him, Andrew," said Leah. "He's doing his best. He's on your side, like everyone else. They just expect more of you now, that's all."

"Well, I'm me," he said belligerently. His eyes found Inglis again, and his mood mercurially changed. "It's a good offer, and thank you, and thank them. Maybe I'll earn it—but don't put money on me, don't do that."

"Mr. Craig, I know it will work out. You're a great man. I read *The Perfect State* eight times. I know you won't disappoint anyone in Stockholm."

Craig had closed his eyes, and was rubbing his forehead. He was not listening.

Leah signaled Inglis, and he quietly rose and tiptoed out of the kitchen after her. Mack followed them.

Andrew Craig was alone.

He felt a thousand years tired, and his head felt stuffed and heavy, and his deadened, sodden nerves begged for unconsciousness. He circled his arms on the table, and laid his head in his arms, and tried not to think of the turn of events. But his fatigued brain did not sleep. He thought: I was only trying to die slowly, peacefully, unobtrusively, like a forgotten old plant in the shade. He thought: Why did those Swedes expose and humiliate me by forcing me to die in public? He thought: I'm an immortal now, in the record books, but I'm as sickeningly mortal as I was when I awakened this morning. He remembered George Bernard Shaw's sardonic remark, when he received the Nobel Prize at sixty-nine: "The money is a life belt thrown to a swimmer who has already reached the shore." He thought: Only in my case I'd rewrite it . . . a life belt thrown to a man after he's drowned. He thought: Nothing.

Andrew Craig had passed out.

II

It was a crisp, sunless, silvery early afternoon in Stockholm, the temperature 15° C., this first day in December, when Count Bertil Jacobsson, formal in his silk hat and overcoat, brown cane tucked under his arm, pearl-gray spats on his shoes, emerged from the Nobel Foundation at Sturegatan 14 and walked to the Cadillac limousine awaiting him at the curb.

The Swedish Foreign Office had furnished the limousine for the occasion. Now it stood in splendor, its rear door held open by a blond, liveried chauffeur. As Jacobsson approached, the driver inclined his head respectfully, and saluted. Jacobsson answered with a nod, and entered the car. He settled into the nearest corner of the cushioned rear seat, already amply filled by Ingrid Påhl and Carl Adolf Krantz. On the return trip, he and Krantz would sit in the jump seats and allow their guests to join Ingrid Påhl on the softer rear seat.

"Good afternoon, good afternoon," said Count Bertil Jacobsson. "A lovely day for our beginning."

"Hello. Yes, lovely," said Ingrid Påhl nervously.

Krantz, who always appeared preoccupied, muttered, "Count," in greeting, and no more.

The chauffeur had slammed the front door and was behind the wheel. Jacobsson leaned forward, slid the glass partition open, and said, "Arlanda Airport, please." He consulted his watch. "We are early. You may make this a leisurely drive."

He closed the glass partition, as the car started and moved away from the curb, eased himself back into his corner, and turned his head to his companions.

"Why so solemn, my friends?" he asked. "I always find these first meetings refreshing."

"I never know what to say," said Ingrid Påhl.

"We are privileged," Jacobsson went on. "We have the opportunity to receive, and intimately acquaint ourselves with, the geniuses of the world—"

"Whom we have made famous," Krantz interrupted acidly.

"Not so, Carl, not at all. They have their fame, all of them, before we recognize and crown it." He considered this a moment, objectively, and then revised his judgment. "Well, not always, but usually, often enough." He regarded his companions for a moment. "I hope neither of you regrets participating with me on the reception committee? It was not only my judgment, but the various academies—"

67

"We are honored," said Krantz curtly. He stared out the window a moment, and then he added, "Perhaps I'm still smarting at the vote. Except for Professor Stratman—"

"You're surely not objecting to Dr. Garrett and Dr. Farelli? Their findings electrified the entire world."

"The press, the press," said Krantz. "We were swept away. I think we should be more judicious. Perhaps their heart transplant, limited as it is, may be the great medical discovery of our time. On the other hand, it may be a circus stunt. I think the Caroline committee should have waited another year or two, for more experiments, more results. As to the Marceau team, I am still not impressed. Sperms in cold storage. Who cares? There were a half-dozen more worthy findings to be honored. The literary award to the American, I won't even speak of—"

Ingrid Påhl's chins quivered with indignation. "*Var snäll och*—please, Carl, do not mix in again. You are a physicist, not a literary critic. I am sure you have not even read Mr. Craig's books—"

"I read one. It was enough."

"Well, you simply have no judgment in such matters. I do not meddle when you make your decisions in chemistry and physics, and I do not think you should interfere with those of us in the Swedish Academy. Every year, the same. You made the same comments when we selected Sinclair Lewis, Pearl Buck, Ernest Hemingway. Why is it always the Americans you object to? Why is it that you were only happy when Eucken and Heyse and Hauptmann, your darling Germans, won?"

Krantz's lips were tight. "On this level, I will not discuss the matter further with you."

Krantz turned back to the window. Ingrid Påhl opened her beaded handbag with irritation and sought cigarette and holder for solace. Jacobsson, who had been listening with concern, determined to remain detached.

By the time they had reached the suburbs of northern Stockholm, the first portion of their twenty-two-mile drive to Arlanda behind them, Jacobsson realized that he could not remain detached, at least not within himself. It was his task, as senior head of the Nobel reception committee, to see that they presented a united and gracious front. For ten days, from this afternoon until the Ceremony on the afternoon of December tenth, the three of them would be living together, and living with their distinguished guests who had won the prizes and come long distances to receive them. Any note of discord or dissension among the three of them, before their guests, the press, the public, would be disgraceful. Jacobsson decided that should another such argument occur, he could not remain above it, outside it, but must act to put a stop to it at once.

He blamed himself for influencing the academies to let Krantz and Ingrid Påhl join him on the reception committee. In his absorption with the preparations that had been in his hands the sixteen days since the telegrams had been sent to France, Italy, and America, he had forgotten their antagonism to each other. As always the preparations had been hectic. There had been the detailed letters sent off to the winners. There had been the schedules and programing. There had been the reservations for choice suites at the Grand Hotel. And there had been the reporters.

In the midst of all this activity, it had fallen upon Jacobsson to recommend to the academies two of their members to join with him in receiving the winners. Because there had been no time to give it lengthy consideration, Jacobsson had hurriedly suggested the names of Krantz and Ingrid Påhl. His choices had been automatically approved. At the time, several weeks before, he had thought the choices excellent ones, regarding them as separate individuals, and not as collaborators with one another and himself. Both were eminently qualified in their fields, or so it had seemed.

Now, casting a sidelong glance at his companions, as if to support his earlier judgment, he tried to see them as the foreign guests would see them. Ingrid Påhl, beside him, was puffing away steadily at a John Silver cigarette in the ebony holder. A floral hat covered most of her graying hair. Her enormous face, with flat, fat features, was like a pinkish mound of unkneaded dough. Beneath her loose chins hung many strands of necklaces of varied colored stones. A great pudding of a woman, her shapeless body was encased in a tentlike blue dress. She resembled, Jacobsson often thought, Mme Helena P. Blavatsky, the Russian theosophist with whom his father had been photographed in London near the end of the last century. Although her face was now grim, aggravated still by the disagreement with Krantz, she was ordinarily pleasant, almost bland, exuding naïve Swedish simplicity and sweetness.

Because Jacobsson had wanted one member of his reception committee to be conversant with literature, as a gesture of respect to Andrew Craig, he had selected Ingrid Påhl with no hesitation. Not only was she well-read, but she was also Sweden's only living Nobel Prize winner in literature. This laurel constantly made her a useful showpiece. On the other hand, this same wreath, Jacobsson shrewdly perceived, too often made her shy, even miserable, in the company of notable visiting authors who had been awarded the prize more recently. For Ingrid Påhl, who had been unanimously voted the prize over a decade earlier, had always felt unworthy of it. Her novels, gentle prose poems dedicated to her beloved Sweden, lush word landscapes without people or life, had been honored before more thunderous and memorable works of vitality by international greats. The award, Jacobsson knew, had embarrassed her, and she had never rid herself of the sense that she was being paraded before the world under false pretenses.

The dangers of national nepotism, Jacobsson thought. Sometimes we are unfairly critized, but sometimes quite justly, and then both giver and taker are the victims. In literature, a dozen Scandinavian writers, besides Ingrid Påhl, had received the Nobel Prize—while Marcel Proust, George Meredith, Thomas Hardy, Joseph Conrad lived and did not receive the prize. Poor Ingrid, Jacobsson thought, and now she dreads meeting Andrew Craig, whose creativity she worships and whose cause she so vigorously championed.

Jacobsson shifted his gaze to the third member of their party. Carl Adolf

Krantz was Ingrid Påhl's opposite in every way. Physically, he was a gnome. Mentally, he was a giant. Personally, he was an irritant, grudging, troublesome, disagreeable, contrary, brimming with acerbity, but stimulating, interesting, brilliant. When seated, as now, he seemed more dwarfish than usual. His thin strands of hair, dyed black, greased, lay flat on his squarish head. His eyes were tiny pinholes, his nose a miniature snout, his mouth puckered as if a cork had been pulled from it. His neat brush mustache was black, as was his short pointed goatee. His suits were always too tight, all buttons buttoned, and he wore bow ties at his collar and lifts on his heels.

There was an air faintly stiff and officious, entirely Germanic, about Krantz, which was what he intended, although he had been born in Sigtuna, Sweden. His pride was that his father, a minor government diplomat, had raised and educated him in Germany, a nation and people he admired—through all regimes—beyond words. His happiest memories were of his student days at Göttingen University and Würzburg University. Returning to Sweden with his parents, he had felt alien, a feeling which had never fully left him. After a decade in private industry as a physicist—several of his papers had earned him minor renown abroad—he had been offered a post in the Institute of Theoretical Physics at the University of Uppsala. Eventually, he had begun to teach, and he aspired to the chair of physics at the University. With the advent of Hitler, his mind had turned from physics to politics. His native country's abject neutralism made him ashamed, and he had identified himself with a resurgent Reich. On every pretext, he had visited Berlin, staying at the Kaiserhof Hotel, and mingling socially with Keitel, von Ribbentrop, and Rosenberg. During World War II, in Stockholm, he had preached for and written in favor of the German cause—to countrymen who had not known war in almost a century and a half, and whose survival depended upon neutrality. In those tense years, Carl Adolf Krantz had become a controversial and embarrassing figure to his fellow Swedes. The Reich's fall was, in a way, his own.

In the cooler halls of science Krantz's worth was not damaged. But in higher circles he had fallen into disrepute. During the decade before the war, he had been a member of the Royal Swedish Academy of Science, and had been one of two members with the right to vote for both the Nobel Prize in physics and the Nobel Prize in chemistry. After the war, his roles on the Nobel committees had not been altered. However, at the University, the situation was different. When, finally, the august chair of physics had been open, Carl Adolf Krantz, despite seniority, had been passed over for a younger man. This slap in the face, this public reprimand, he could not forgive. He had resigned from the school at once. And, in the several years since, he had devoted himself part time to the Institute of Radiophysics in Stockholm, and given more and more of his days to his Nobel activities.

Despite Krantz's checkered past and his erratic personality, Jacobsson had settled upon him as the third member of the reception committee because of his breadth of knowledge. Almost singlehandedly, at least at first, Krantz had disregarded political differences to lead the inner fight to get Professor

Max Stratman the Nobel Prize in physics. And although Krantz had opposed an award to the Marceaus, his position as a judge in chemistry made him eligible to converse with them as intelligently as he would with Stratman. Jacobsson had considered requesting the Caroline Institute to offer one of their own staff to the reception committee, but a fourth member would make the group unwieldy, and this seemed unnecessary since Krantz's knowledge spilled over into physiology and medicine, too. And so, finally, it had been Krantz, to join with Påhl and Jacobsson. But observing the crusty and embittered physicist now, Jacobsson had brief misgivings.

With an inaudible sigh, he straightened and saw his own countenance reflected in the glass partition. Examining his shimmering, ghostlike image, he was suddenly aware that he was probably no more qualified than either Krantz or Påhl to represent the will of Alfred Nobel, or, at least, that they were no less qualified than he. Hypnotically, his eyes held on his image, trying to see what the approaching new laureates would see of him. What? A very old man. An outdated aristocratic head. Sensitive scholar features. Face like wrinkled parchment, whitish-bluish, almost transparent. The body's frame less tall now, limbs brittle, swathed in heavy garments to appear fuller, stronger, formidable. "I am a misanthrope, but exceedingly benevolent," Nobel had written of himself. Perhaps, thought Jacobsson, a description of his own self, as well.

Jacobsson closed his eyes, and the image was gone. He had not been young since the previous century, he remembered with surprise. The world of this afternoon was the world of tomorrow's people. Did he belong here now? Yet, truly, who belonged here more? He told himself that he represented continuity. After all, how many alive could bridge the long years, from those first winners in 1901, Roentgen, van't Hoff, Behring, Prudhomme, Dunant, Passy, to this year's winners, Stratman, the Marceaus, Garrett, Farelli, Craig? And who else could quote the spoken words, heard in person, engraved on memory, of Alfred Bernhard Nobel?

As an impressionable adolescent accompanying his father on a royal liaison mission, he had been privileged to be in Alfred Nobel's presence at least a dozen times, first in Paris, and then in the lonely villa at San Remo during 1896, the last year of Nobel's life. In view of the fact that Jacobsson had been blessed with an inherited competence, he had been able to make the Nobel Foundation his vocation since 1900, the year preceding the first awards.

In recent years, because he had begun to place a value on his unique position and because he felt that he owed something to posterity, Jacobsson had begun his Notes. These were his memories of the past, jottings of the present, relating his knowledge of the secret voting sessions of the Nobel academies, impressions and anecdotes and activities of the various laureates, descriptions of the events and ceremonies, in all a priceless grab bag of history. Jacobsson had begun the Notes—there were now seventeen green ledgers filled in his crabbed hand—not many years past. The first entry had been made late the night following that November day when the Swedish Academy, in closed session in the Old Town, had voted the literary prize to an obscure Sardinian authoress, Grazia Deledda, instead of to Gabriele D'Annunzio, because the majority of members had privately objected to D'Annunzio's amorous exploits and to his swindling a Danish widow of her home, Villa Carnacco, in Italy. That had been 1927. Since then, except when he was ill, Jacobsson had entered something, some fact, some gossip, each day. He had always supposed that it would be a book, a large, handsome published book, to justify his life somehow. But in recent years, he had realized that he would never write the book. For him, the contribution of the raw Notes would be enough. Someday, someday, some other would write the book.

Abruptly, Jacobsson shook himself free of self-absorption and re-entered the present moment, again a part of Ingrid Påhl and Carl Adolf Krantz and the limousine. The authoress was dozing lightly beside him. Krantz concentrated on the task of undoing a metal puzzle; he always carried several new ones in his pocket.

Idly, Jacobsson looked out of the car window at the Stockholm suburbs unreeling before his vision. Beyond the highway, the soft sloping hills were defiantly bronze-green despite the cold. Here and there, in sight and then gone, the rural barnlike wooden houses, most of them beige-colored but cheerfully red-roofed. How he enjoyed this land, with its shiny lakes and birch trees and clusters of primeval forest and gaping open spaces filled only by Scandinavia's cerulean sky endlessly welded to the verdant earth. Actually, he thought, this was Ingrid Påhl's dominion. In her slender volumes, she had staked out her possession by adoption and love. Essentially, Jacobsson knew, he was a city being. He left the cocoon of the city only in December, on these occasions, and was forever surprised at the visual wonders of the surrounding countryside and his pleasure in them. Annually, each December, he vowed to return, for an outing, a vacation, but by January all resolve had evaporated and he was part of and one with his metropolis again.

"Bertil." It was Ingrid Påhl's voice that brought him out of his trance.

He swung around, attentive. She was fully awake now, inserting a fresh cigarette in her holder, and then lighting it. He waited.

"Bertil," she repeated, coughing smoke, "here we are, and I do not even know our schedule. Is it strenuous?"

"You mean our receptions? Not at all." He dug inside his overcoat, and then inside his suit coat, and removed a folded sheet of onionskin paper. As he opened it, he saw that Krantz was also interested. "Here it is," said Jacobsson. "Shall I read it aloud?"

"Please," said Ingrid Påhl. "I cannot read in a moving vehicle."

Jacobsson brought the open sheet closer to his face. "December one. That's today. Two twenty-five, afternoon. Dr. Denise Marceau. Dr. Claude Marceau. By Air France at Arlanda Airport. This evening. Seven o'clock. Dr. Carlo Farelli and Mrs. Farelli. By Scandinavian Airlines. Also Arlanda. December two. That's tomorrow. Eight in the morning. Professor Max Stratman and—"

"Eight in the morning," groaned Ingrid Påhl.

72

"He is worth welcoming at any hour," Krantz snapped at her.

"—and his niece," Jacobsson read, hurrying on. "By train from Göteborg. Central Station. Twelve thirty-five tomorrow afternoon. Dr. John Garrett and Mrs. Garrett. By Scandinavian Airlines. Arlanda Airport. On the same flight from Copenhagen, Mr. Andrew Craig and his sister-in-law."

Krantz snorted. "Sister-in-law. Now, we pay for them, too?"

"He is a widower," Ingrid Påhl answered angrily. "Do you want him to come alone?"

"Please," interjected Jacobsson. He studied his sheet, then lowered and folded it. "As I said, Mr. Craig will be on the same flight with the Garretts. That will make all of them. So you see, Ingrid, the reception part of our duties will be done with and over by early afternoon tomorrow." He returned the paper to his inner pocket. "Of course, after that, there will be our other little duties. But I am certain they will be stimulating. And, as usual, the Foreign Office is loaning us several energetic attachés to help out when you and Carl wish to nap."

"The French couple we are going to meet right now, I do not know a thing about them," said Ingrid Påhl. "What should we know, Bertil?"

Jacobsson shrugged. "What is there to know? They are renowned and dedicated chemists. Despite Carl's dissent, their discovery has met with universal acclaim. Except for the cuttings from the Paris newspapers—mostly features and interviews about their work—I know nothing of them personally." He nodded across the seat. "I think that is more Carl's department."

Momentarily, Krantz's stubby fingers ceased working the metal puzzle. "They were proposed last year and this year, among five hundred others. There was the general weeding out, and then our committee of five recommended the Marceaus along with a half-dozen others. I heard the lengthy investigation reports of our chemistry experts, and they were highly favorable, as you know. But there was little in these reports about the personalities of the winners. As far as I have been able to learn, they are both in their forties. He is older by several years. They have been married a dozen years or more. They have been dedicated to the idiot sperm project six or seven years, I think. They work in the Institut Pasteur, although not officially connected with it. They do not seem to have any interests, outside their work—like most of us in science. I would suppose, being married to each other, and their work, they will be inseparable and of the same mind. Somewhat dull, I predict."

"Oh, I wonder about that," said Ingrid Påhl. "I am perfectly fascinated by married couples performing outside their marriage as collaborators. It happens so often in the sciences. I wonder why it does not happen in the arts. Can you imagine a play by Anne and William Shakespeare? Or a novel by Catherine and Charles Dickens? Or a painting by Mette Sophie and Paul Gauguin? I suppose this does not happen because creativity in the arts is more individual."

"Nonsense," said Krantz.

Again, Jacobsson sought to prevent conflict. "No matter what the reasons, the sciences have seemed to produce some remarkable married teams." His mind went back to the Notes. "I think immediately of Madame Marie Curie and Pierre Curie. They shared the physics award in—when was it?—yes, 1903, with Professor Henri Becquerel. That was for their joint researches on radiation phenomena. As I recall, the Curies each got one-quarter of the prize, and Becquerel got one-half. I remember my disappointment when we learned that the Curies were too exhausted from overwork to attend our Ceremony. The French Minister to Sweden picked up their award."

"Is that not against the Code of Statutes?" asked Ingrid Påhl. "I thought you had to attend in person or forfeit—"

"Yes, within ten months—'should the prize winner fail, before the first of October in the calendar year immediately following, to encash the prize awarders' cheque for the amount of the prize in the manner laid down by the Board, then the amount of the prize shall revert to the main fund'—that is the regulation," said Jacobsson. "However, the Curies did appear the following summer for their money, in time to remain eligible. Eight years later, as you know, when Marie Curie was a widow, we gave her a second award, this time in chemistry—I believe she was the only person ever to win two Nobel Prizes."

"Her second winning," said Krantz, "was for the greatest discovery in chemistry since oxygen. It could be said that she gave us the atom, as we know it."

"In any event, this second time, ill as she was, Marie Curie did attend the Ceremony," said Jacobsson. "Do you remember her visit, Carl? No, that was before your time. She was in her forties, a lonely woman, but lovely and devoted to her career. She arrived here with her sister and daughter, and told me that she was most impressed with the Ceremony."

"We gave that daughter a prize, too, did we not?" asked Ingrid Påhl.

"Yes. Actually the daughter and her husband. Irène Curie had married one of her mother's junior assistants at the Institute of Radium, an impoverished young man named Frédéric Joliot, who had graduated from L'École de Paris. There is one more married couple for you. Irène and Frédéric Joliot-Curie. They won the chemistry award in 1935." He paused. "I am trying to recollect if there were any other married couples—"

"The Coris in 1947," said Krantz promptly.

"Ah, yes," Jacobsson agreed. "Gerty and Carl Cori. Medicine. They came from St. Louis in Missouri, and received half the award, and we gave the other half to the Argentinian, Houssay. Something to do with hormones—"

"They discovered how glycogen is catalytically converted," said Krantz with precision.

"At any rate, we do occasionally bless the fruits of marriage," said Jacobsson. "I look forward to meeting the Marceaus."

"I think it is odd," said Ingrid Påhl.

Jacobsson seemed startled. "Odd? What is odd?"

"To be a married couple winning the Nobel Prize," explained Ingrid Påhl. "In fact, to be a married couple winning anything that has to do with work.

It gives marriage only one dimension. The laboratory is the home, and the home is the laboratory. No variety, no change of pace. And too much harmony. Besides, what does this do to the male's role? He has gone out, club in hand, to kill a bear for supper, and bring it to his admiring mate, but instead his mate has been out with him, and deserves as much credit for killing the bear as he. Where does that put him? And her?"

"I am sure the Marceaus never think of such things for a moment," said Jacobsson primly. He considered his watch and then looked out the car window. "We'll be just in time for them. Twenty more minutes."

The three sat in silence now—Krantz who had been wedded and divorced long ago, and Påhl and Jacobsson who had never been wedded at all—thinking their own thoughts about marriage and the prize. . . .

They had hardly exchanged a full sentence or a civil word since they had left Paris for Stockholm.

Reclining in her leather seat beside the blank window, uncomfortable in a black-and-white wool tweed suit, tailored at the last moment to fit her newly trim figure, and unrelaxed because of her enforced proximity to her husband, Denise Marceau let her gaze rove disinterestedly over the airplane's elegant interior. For a while she watched the two young French stewardesses, blond hair swept daringly high, confident in their white blouses and tight blue skirts, treading up and down the aisle among the passengers, followed sometimes by the uniformed steward. Then she was conscious of Claude, slumped low in the seat beside her, legs crossed, smoking a cigarette as he turned the pages of an Émile Gaboriau novel. She did not look at him fully. She could not trust herself to do so. She had not bothered to bring along any reading of her own, because she was too occupied with her seething mind. It was enough.

She extracted an American filtered cigarette from her purse as unobtrusively as possible, for she did not want Claude to light it or want any of his attentions. Hastily, she snapped her lighter and applied it to the cigarette, so maintaining another small victory in her remote independence.

Not many hours ago—three, four, five at most—they had been brought across the smooth highway from Paris to Orly Field by a convoy of Institut colleagues and pompous government officials. They had boarded the Air France jet, Flight 794, at 10:40 in the morning, amid a noisy fanfare and demonstration from their friends and the circle of newspapermen. As they climbed into the plane, there had been shouts below for one last photograph. She had permitted Claude to hold her arm—the possessive façade of marriage—as they posed. The second that they were inside the jet, she had shaken her arm free.

In the noiseless, capsuled period since they were airborn, there had been only monosyllabic exchanges between them. Are you comfortable, Denise? *Oui. Champagne? *Non*. Like one of my books? *Non*. Beautiful plane? *Oui*. The translucent barrier between them, like the one separating two male Siamese fighting fish, was made more bearable by the fact that they were, indeed, in an aquarium, watched, peered at, attended, thankfully not alone. Other passengers, informed of their fame and destination, drifted by to make conversation with Claude. Either a stewardess or the steward seemed to hover constantly, awaiting command. Several times, one of the pilots came back to inquire if they were comfortable.

Now, Denise Marceau was aware that the taller stewardess was addressing them on the intercom. She spoke first in French, then in English. "It is exactly two o'clock," she announced. "We will put down in Stockholm on schedule, in twenty-five minutes. Thank you."

Watching this stewardess, whose small brassière cups were outlined behind her white blouse, Denise was unaccountably enraged. Or accountably, for she associated this anonymous girl with Gisèle Jordan, and hatred of her husband filled her throat. She had almost spoken up in Copenhagen during the brief stopover when they had not left the plane, but had finally sat without progress or purpose. Now her resentment and wrath were even greater. Blindly, she twisted toward Claude.

"Why in the devil do you not put down that goddam book and say something for yourself?" she demanded, fighting to keep her voice low.

Claude recoiled instinctively from the harshness of her sudden outburst, then slowly, controlled, he placed the bookmark between the pages, shut the book, and sat up. "What do you want me to say?" he asked. "I have tried to make conversation a dozen times. But you insist on punishing me with silence."

"I should not have come on this damn trip at all. I do not want to be seen with you. You were with that bitch the night before last, and do not try to deny it."

His composure broke ranks briefly. "What do you mean? Denise—"

"I mean you deliberately went to see her, dined with her, went to someone else's apartment and slept with her."

"You are upset. You are imagining—"

"Stop it, stop it. I *know*."

She would not reveal to him exactly how she knew, even though he had probably already guessed, but still, she would not tell him outright. She would not discuss this part of it or any other details of her humiliation of the three weeks past.

"Your horrible affair was bad enough," she was saying. "How I can even look at you again, I don't know. But to lie to me after—deliberately lie—promise me, pat me on the head—a passing indiscretion, a mistake, no more—and then brazenly resume—"

"Denise," he said with difficulty, glancing off to see if they were being overheard, "nothing more passed between us. I simply had to see her once more to—to tell her—"

"You saw her more than once more, and you slept with her. You have lost all your pride and prudence. You do not give a damn about me, us, our reputations—you are going on headlong—like some schoolboy in the Place Pigalle, in love with a prostitute."

76

She was uncontrolled, he saw, surprisingly wild and capable of anything. He did not wish a scene now or here, especially not here. "Denise, please," he pleaded. "Wait until we get to Stockholm and we are alone. I shall explain everything. This is a problem between us. We will work it out privately."

"No—now—"

"I have tried to speak to you a dozen times in the last weeks," he said with exasperation, "but you were playing the great wounded—the sufferer. I could not get a word from you. Now you want to stage it here, in a crowded plane. Look, people are watching us right now. Where is your sense of respectability—decency? We still have a marriage—"

"Have we?" she demanded. "I love that. Look who speaks of decency—respectability—with a kept whore on the side."

"Denise, I beg of you. Everyone's listening."

This time, his plea reached her. She bit her lip, surreptitiously observed the passengers around them, and then sat back in sullen silence.

"We will find a solution," he added lamely, desperate to placate her. "Soon as this Nobel affair is over with—"

"To hell with Nobel," she said, "and to hell with you." With a violent wrench of her body, she turned her back on him, curling in the seat, arms folded, pretending to sleep.

But Denise Marceau did not sleep. The play in her head was this, and the Chevalier von Sacher-Masoch had lent his name to it: act one, the discovery; act two, the confirmation and confrontation; act three, they lived unhappily ever after.

Act one. She let the players perform. She did not direct them. She was the leading lady. To avoid illusion, to highlight reality, her mind took her from the present and placed her on the stage of the past.

After the reading of their paper had secured their triumph, Claude's restlessness began, and she had understood it for she felt as he did. The cluttered apartment was particularly empty after the busy, crowded years in the laboratory. Yet she adjusted quickly, occupied herself with women's work, and was soon more satisfied.

Claude remained unsociable and moody, and when he took to protracted periods away from the apartment each day, she did not mind. People varied in their needs and ways to find their balance. She was correct in her tolerance, she believed, for soon Claude's natural enthusiasm and vitality returned. Life became tolerable, even fun, again. Although his need for her body was less, she excused him. Six years of exhaustive labors had taken their toll. Moreover, he was affectionate and thoughtful, which was pleasing. One day, she surmised, he would be completely rested, and then be able to give her more. Sometimes, evaluating his returned good humor after evenings at restaurants or the club with other men, she decided that he was weighing a new project, a fresh undertaking, and this she hoped for more than anything else. While she could not articulate it to herself, her instinct told her that in scientific collaboration they succeeded in a union closer, more passionate, more successful, than those of other mortals who had only the lesser union of flesh.

She tried to pick up the slack strands of old friendships more and more, having some of the women whom she had so long neglected to the apartment for cakes and conversation, going shopping with others, and forcing herself to make luncheon dates. She was not surprised, therefore, when a friend, with whom she had long ago attended the Sorbonne and had recently revived old times, telephoned to invite her to tea the following afternoon at Rumpelmayer's in the rue de Rivoli. She had tried to delay the engagement a few days, for she was absorbed in selecting new dining room furniture, but her friend's beseeching insistence forced her to capitulate.

The following afternoon at exactly four o'clock, Denise met her friend, Mme Cecilia Moret, before the sweets counter in the foyer of Rumpelmayer's. Cecilia Moret, an energetic thin woman who wore sunglasses, filled in her pocked cheeks with powder, and carried an introverted miniature white poodle in the crook of one arm, led the way through the tables crowded with stylish French and English matrons, to a relatively isolated corner in the rear. They found an unoccupied table. Cecilia tied the leash of her poodle to a chair leg and fed him a sugar cube and baby talk. Divesting themselves of their coats, lighting cigarettes, they ordered tea and toast for Cecilia and coffee and small éclairs for Denise.

Cecilia carried the conversation, ecstatic about a Bombois oil that she had found in the rue de Seine and handbags she had found for the holidays in the rue La Boétie, and Denise listened dully, wondering why she had neglected her dining room furniture for this. The moment they had been served, and the waitress was out of earshot, Cecilia's tone changed from the frivolous to the conspiratorial.

"What is Claude up to these days?" she inquired, squeezing her lemon peel into the pale tea.

"Nothing much. Trying to dream up a new project, I suspect."

"Are you doing anything together?"

"Not really. I think this is a vacation for both of us, after six years' collaboration. I am catching up with domesticity. He is out a good deal, seeing if he has any men friends left."

"Mmm," said Cecilia Moret, with a subtle skepticism that made Denise, sensitive to semantic nuances, study her with sudden interest.

Cecilia touched her lips with a paper napkin, thoughtfully, and when she dropped the napkin, she removed her dark glasses as if to reveal a nakedly sincere and intimate face.

"Denise, I have something to tell you. No one else will, I am sure. And I feel, in good conscience, I must. It is for your sake, it is you I am thinking about. If I cannot be honest with you, then who can, and what is friendship for anyway?"

Denise crinkled her eyes, puzzled.

Cecilia continued. "Have you any reason to suspect Claude of—of—oh, misbehavior?"

"I haven't the slightest idea what you mean."

"I will be frank with you, because I am not ashamed of being frank about my own problems—well, to you, in this case. Eight years ago, my dependable Gaston, reaching your husband's age, had a—a most shameful affair with a Lido girl. I learned about it in this room, this way, from an older woman who was a friend of mine, and I thank the Lord for her. You can be sure I put an end to the stupid affair immediately. It was not pleasant, I assure you, but today Gaston and I are more in love than ever, and it is as if the other never happened. I owe our present happiness to the fact that I was able to stop his aberration in time, before he went too far." She caught her breath, and then went on. "Now, in your case—"

Denise felt the heat high on her cheeks. "Cecilia, what *are* you saying?"

"I think your Claude is playing it fast and loose. I have reason to believe this—"

"What a terrible thing even to imagine!"

"Hear me out, Denise. Last Friday night, I was burdened with showing some Americans—friends of friends—life on the Left Bank. We decided to walk a good deal, so that they could see more. I was on my way to show them St.-Germain-des-Prés. We were in the rue du Bac, going slowly, chatting. A taxi pulled up across the street, beneath the lamp. I hardly paid attention, until I saw Claude step out of it. He was facing toward me. He did not see me, but I saw him. He was under the light, and there was no mistake. I almost called out to him—but just then someone else emerged from the taxi. A young lady. I could not see her well, except that she was tall, young, extremely smart in her grooming and clothes. Claude paid the taxi, and it left. He put his arm around the girl's waist, and kissed her cheek, and they went into the apartment building. I even noted the address—53 rue du Bac. I cannot tell you how upset I was for the remainder of the evening. It was so difficult to believe—Claude, so conservative, and famous now—taking such risks. And then I thought of you, and what I had been through. I tell you, I had quite a weekend trying to reach a decision. Should I tell Denise? Shall I not? Now you know my decision, and you can act as I once acted."

Denise had sat paralyzed with shock and disbelief throughout the recital. She was still unable to find her voice.

"It was near nine o'clock Friday night," Cecilia added. "Was he out then?"

With uneasiness, Denise peeled back the days. Nine o'clock Friday night. Callaux's wedding stag. No. That was Thursday evening. Nine o'clock Friday night, Friday night. Yes, yes, Pavillon d'Armenonville in the Bois de Boulogne. A late dinner and reunion with a former colleague from Lyon who was doing work in the structure of proteins.

"Yes, he was out then," said Denise, hardly hearing her voice. "He—he had a meeting. With a chemical researcher."

"Well, we must be fair. Maybe this girl I saw him with was the chemical researcher."

"No. His friend is an old man with a beard."

"This friend had no beard, I can tell you."

"I cannot believe it, Cecilia," Denise said brokenly. "Claude's never been like that. We are happy. He—now that he is so well-known—why, there is always loose talk about famous people, that they are adulterers or homosexuals or dope addicts. People have to do that. They cannot stand idols too long. They have to tear the famous ones down to their level."

Cecilia saw that her friend was distraught, and Cecilia was not offended. "Denise," she said levelly, "this is not secondhand gossip. I was a witness. My own eyes saw it."

Denise suddenly pushed her chair back. "Let us go from here. I want some air."

They walked, the poodle preceding them, under the arcades of the rue de Rivoli to the rue de Castiglione, and then turned right and walked the two short blocks to the Place Vendôme. Denise remained unseeing, unhearing, totally unaware of the expensive shops, the pedestrians in the streets, or her friend's monologue about Gaston and the deceit of men in general and the traps of marital life.

In the Place Vendôme, circling toward the Ritz Hotel, Denise felt her legs giving, and knew that she could not continue. She wanted to be alone, in her bedroom, and she wanted to think.

"I had better get home, Cecilia," she said. "It is the maid's day off. I have to make dinner for Claude."

"Well, you just remember the man's name, he's a marvel," said Cecilia. Denise looked at her without comprehension, "What man's name?"

Cecilia shook her head. "You haven't been listening at all. Poor darling. I do not blame you. I remember how I felt that day. I was trying to tell you that before I had it out with Gaston, I got facts and data, so that he would have no comeback. I located this private detective. M. Jean Sarraut. He is off the Étoile in the Boulevard Haussmann. Very discreet and expert. He used to be with the Sûreté Nationale. It is costly, of course. Somewhere about a hundred and fifty new francs a day, as I remember. I hired M. Sarraut for two weeks. The results were a revelation. When I brought out M. Sarraut's portfolio of reports, Gaston was unable to utter a word. I advise you to hire this man, learn the facts, and then confront Claude. You will win, I assure you. A few years from now, you will thank me."

They had reached the taxi stand. "Cecilia, I cannot hire a detective. I mean, it is all right in the cinema—but Claude—he's my husband."

"You do as I say, or perhaps he won't be your husband."

When Denise returned to the apartment, it was cold, and she put on the heat. She was too shaken to cook. For an hour, she moved restlessly around the living room, searching the recent past for clues to support Cecilia's fanciful story, and finding some so circumstantial that she had to reject them. At seven o'clock, after changing her clothes, she determined to start dinner. Before she could proceed, the telephone rang, and it was Claude. He was sweet and apologetic. He told her that he had, by chance, run into an old acquaintance from Toulouse University, and the man was doing some remarkable work in a new area of genetics, and it would be valuable to spend the evening with him. Pretending scientific interest, Denise wondered who this man was, and Claude said that he was someone she had never met, a Dr. Lataste.

Casually as possible, Denise wondered where they would be dining. They were going directly to the Méditerranée, said Claude, where they had a reservation, and then they would retire to Dr. Lataste's hotel suite for further talk. With effort, Denise forced herself to ask what hotel, and Claude replied promptly that it was the California in the rue de Berri.

Denise waited one hour, smoking cigarette after cigarette, and then another half hour to be certain, and then she telephoned the Méditerranée, not at all sure what she would say if Claude was brought to the phone. When someone at the restaurant answered, she inquired if they held a reservation for Dr. Marceau or Dr. Lataste for this evening. She was told there were reservations for neither one. Allowing for a chance of error in the reservation, she requested that Dr. Marceau be paged. She waited. At last, she was informed that no Dr. Marceau was present.

Still, she said to herself, this was not evidence enough. Often, she and Claude, at the very last moment, had changed their minds about the restaurant at which they intended to dine. Now she waited another hour, smoking incessantly, and then, with trembling hand, she lifted the receiver and dialed the California Hotel. She asked to be connected with Dr. Lataste's suite. There was an interminable wait. She listened for the hotel phone to ring the room, tempering her fears. It did not ring. The operator's voice came on shrilly. There was no person named Dr. Lataste registered in the California Hotel. Denise said thank-you dully, and hung up.

Her next act was direct and simple. She took down the telephone book for the eighth arrondissement, leafed through it, returned it to its shelf, and then she dialed M. Sarraut, private investigator, and was not surprised to be put through to him even at this hour. She asked for an appointment in his office the following morning, and it was granted.

All of this took place the day and the evening of November eighth. One week later, almost exactly to the hour, on November fifteenth, M. Sarraut telephoned. He said, in his neutral bass, that he possessed the goods she had ordered and wondered if she was free to accept delivery within the next thirty minutes. With thumping heart, she said that she was quite alone this evening and would eagerly await the delivery.

In twenty minutes, the thin manila envelope, securely gummed and sealed, was delivered by a sallow-faced young man, whom Denise tipped 200 old francs. The moment that he was gone, she shut and latched the front door, made her way unsteadily to the coffee table where her half-finished whiskey waited, sat down on the edge of the sofa and ripped open the detective's envelope. There were three pages of type, neatly single-spaced, terse and ineloquent, yet the raw material of ten thousand novels.

She read, and reread, and reread once more, the pitiless report, rocking silently on the sofa like an old lady suddenly widowed and bereft, until only phrases came up at her like daggers. "Shadowed by four operatives in relays . . . on two occasions in six days met and dined with the same young lady at the restaurant, Le Petit Navire, in the rue des Fossés-St.-Bernard, and on both occasions retired later to the young lady's apartment on the third floor at 53 rue du Bac. . . . The first occasion was November 10. They met inside the restaurant at 7:22 P.M. They emerged at 8:47. They walked on the Boulevard St.-Germain for 17 minutes, holding hands. The man in question summoned a public vehicle. They arrived at the rue du Bac at 9:21. They proceeded inside together. The man in question emerged at 11:43 in the evening. He walked to a kiosk, found it closed, and returned to his dwelling by public vehicle. . . .

"The second occasion was November 12. The man in question arrived at Le Petit Navire at 7:50 P.M. The lady arrived 8 minutes later. They emerged together at 8:59. They talked in the street. He kissed her. They walked, his arm about her waist, to the corner of the Quai de la Tournelle, where they waited four minutes until they found a public vehicle. They arrived at 53 rue du Bac at 9:16. The door was locked. She rang for the concierge. They waited and embraced. They entered the building at 9:19. The man in question emerged alone at 12:04 A.M. Apparently a public vehicle had been summoned by telephone. He waited, and when the vehicle arrived he proceeded directly home. . . .

For future reference, our operatives have superficially investigated the young lady in question. . . . Name: Mlle Gisèle Jordan. Birthplace: Rouen. Age: 27. Occupation: Mannequin. Place of Employment: Balenciaga, Avenue George-V near the Alma. Hair color: Blond. Height: 5 feet, 7 inches. Weight: 112 pounds. Other dimensions: bust—32 inches; waist—23 inches; hips—34 inches. Marital status: Never married. Miscellaneous: Leaves work daily 5:05, takes bus No. 63 from the Pont de l'Alma, departs bus corner of Boulevard St.-Germain and rue du Bac, arrives home generally 5:25. Has long-term lease on flat subdivided from landlady's quarters. Rental 580 new francs per month. Apartment consists of living room, bedroom, one bath, no kitchen. Hot plate on premises. Décor Louis XV. . . . If client wishes more information on lady in question, it can readily be obtained."

The threat of these cold facts froze Denise into a state of stupor. It was as if she had suffered concussion of the brain. Until now, she had gone ahead protected by a safe sense of unreality, somehow certain that it was all a low Gallic comedy of errors, and that in the end all would be well in this best of all possible worlds. But here before her, as vitrified as the sperms that she and Claude had worked upon so long, were the facts. The other person was real, young, glamorous, with dimension. The assignations were real, time, place, with sensual intervals implied. A superior enemy named Gisèle. Her own Claude!

Denise's emotions ran the usual cycle of this unique grief: she was in turn revolted, appalled, horrified, agitated, intimidated. As Denise sat shivering, the cycle had run its course from amazement to mourning to fear. There was not yet self-pity, and so she did not drink. She merely sat in a comatose state, unmoving, unthinking, as stone.

How long she sat, she did not know. Much later, when she realized that the buzzer was sounding, she tried to rally, expecting Claude and preparing defenses. Beyond the door, when she opened it, stood an elderly, well-dressed gentleman—she thought he had worn a pince-nez—carrying a bouquet of red roses and a telegram. He was, he said, the Swedish Ambassador to France. He had come, he said, as the bearer of good tidings.

She found sufficient social instinct to allow him into her living room. She took the telegram and read it, and half heard his profuse congratulations. She remembered little else. The rest would remain a blank to history. Had she replied? Had she offered him a liqueur? Had she shown happiness? All was amnesia. Perhaps he had stayed five minutes. Surely he had mistaken her speechless state for one of ecstasy usually seen in the stigmatic. A proud, kind man, he had disappeared with understanding.

No sooner had he retired than the telephone had begun. *Figaro. France-Soir. Match. New York Herald Tribune.* They were telephoning not for information but to learn if she and her husband were home. They were on their way, a half-dozen or more, reporters and photographers. And she was alone.

The self-possessed Dr. Denise Marceau of the laboratory would never have made the next decision. But she was disoriented, in a home not fortified. She found the telephone book, and in it the hated name. When she heard the other's voice, and identified herself, her sensitivity traveled with the sound waves. She *knew* that he was there. And then his own voice, that of the trapped schoolboy, confirmed his infidelity. . . .

It was a half hour before he appeared. When he arrived, she was in the center of the sofa, sufficiently drunk to make her regal and assured, surrounded by a semicircle of reporters and photographers. She had been mouthing the litany of the laboratory, which required no concentration, but the questions were now getting more personal, more alarming, and her poise teetered. Claude came in time, like the uniformed cavalry in those dreadful American western films, and she was rescued from indiscretion.

She refused to meet her husband's eyes, knowing that he was watching her, anxious to gauge her mood, her probable reactions. She stood still for the nauseating instant his lips brushed her cheek, a salute to their victory for the photographers. Magnetically, he drew all attention to himself, replying to a new outburst of questions with vigor and color. During this exchange, she touched her forehead, murmuring headache, overexcitement, and slipped off to the bedroom. She secured the door from the inside, and an hour later, when he tried it, he found that he was locked out.

She slept not well but soundly, and in the early morning, when she emerged fully clothed in sweater and skirt, she saw that he had had his night on the sofa. She came upon him in the dining room, having brioches and coffee, and prepared with his rehearsed speech. While dressing, she had thought that she could maintain complete control when she saw him, but throughout the short, sharp scene which began immediately upon her entrance, she clung desperately to the civilized line to keep above hysteria. Her accusations reflected her hurt, all infinite shame, and loss of pride. He reduced what had happened to a lapse of good sense, pressed and squashed it down to a minor masculine flaw, an accidental fall. There was little that he could say under the circumstances, yet he said a good deal, self-probing, self-analyzing, his failure, his weakness, and what he said was what she had hoped to hear. But hurt had damaged her deeply. He understood this, and aching at her distress, he blurted the promise that the outer involvement was ended, that it was through this day, that if she believed him, she would not regret it. She had gone to the bedroom, red-eyed, and he had gone out, and the scene was done.

In the following few weeks, it was their Nobel award that made life possible. During the afternoon hours, it seemed, they were never left alone together. Their living room teemed with welcomed guests. One day, their colleagues. The next, government officials. Another, faculty. Another, press. The nights were saved by their deliberate timing. Every night when he returned, she was asleep, drugged with pills. Every morning, when he awakened, she was already out in the city, devoting these early hours to preparations for Stockholm.

For Denise, the report delivered every third day from M. Sarraut was the focal point of existence. There were four such reports in all, before the departure for Stockholm. The first and second showed that Claude had kept to his promise. He had not seen Gisèle. With the third, Denise's hopes swelled. He had still not seen Gisèle. Obviously, it had been a foolish masculine aberration, to use Cecilia's description. And it was over. The fourth and final report was delivered to Denise two evenings before she was to leave for Sweden. This report exploded in her face.

As ever, M. Sarraut's log of infidelity was terse. It left so much between the lines, so much to the imagination, Denise wanted to scream. In the three days past, Claude had broken with asceticism not once, but twice. No longer Le Petit Navire, but two different obscure bistros in Montmartre. No longer 53 rue du Bac, but an apartment borrowed from a friend of the lady in question. In each instance, the man in question had been with the lady in question, in the apartment, over three hours.

If Denise's wound had been healing, it was now ripped savagely open again and lay raw and throbbing with pain. Denise could see clearly through her tears this time: the alcoholic was unable to keep his hand from the bottle, no matter what the consequences. Familiar grief made her reasonable, questioning. Was it sex alone, or sex and love? In either case, the answer provided no consolation. If it was Gisèle's sex alone that drew him—and the vivid pictures this conjured up made her almost ill—then her own inadequacy was heightened, and her failure impossible to surmount. She shuddered at this animal defeat. Yet, it was always said, this was the lesser defeat. Eventually, a male might tire of the act, as it lost its variety, and tire of the actress, and return home chastened.

But the defeat was primitive and deep, nevertheless. If it was love as well as sex that drew him to Gisèle, then Denise knew that she had no armor of resistance at all. If his affair was emotional, encompassing sex as only one part, and including all other affections, she was lost. Did he know which it was? Perhaps not, not yet. She feared his learning. Here she was, and here they were, and what should she do? Challenge him with the threat of immediate divorce? What if he took up the challenge, scandal or no scandal? What if she lost? To abandon so quickly the field of combat, to give him up after all these years, to that young, tall bitch, reinforced her anger. To be left alone, alone, sterile in the damn laboratory, an appendage severed, was impossible to contemplate. Yet to remain like this, wife in name only, pitied by that bitch and by him and by herself, was equally unthinkable. What to do? For the moment, sheer hatred of the two of them sufficed. That, and then added to that, a word that carried limited pleasures of its own—retribution.

Later, sluggishly disrobing for bed, the pills taking their effect, she knew that she was too ineffectual to exact immediate retribution. Somehow, somewhere, something would occur to her. How could this nightmare have come about? They had been so close, worked so well together, day and night, so many years, enjoyed so much, laughed in secret, accomplished such wonders. Imagine, Nobel Prize winners. It had gone wrong because they had run out of work, finished with their thing in common. Where do you climb after Everest's summit? The hidden pitfall had been victory, itself a Pyrrhic victory that meant the end of goal, a sink of inactivity.

Once in bed, drowsy, welcoming the approaching false death of night, she tried to envision the enemy. What had trusty M. Sarraut's first report said? Balenciaga model. Five feet seven. A thirty-two-inch bust. A rail, a board, a thin plank of wood. How could Claude abandon her for *that*? And it was then, before sleep, that she determined to find out for herself.

Claude was still asleep the next morning when she made the arrangement with a friend—not Cecilia, whom she could never bear to face again, but a friend who was extravagant and knew about clothes—to get an invitation to Balenciaga. The friend agreed to assist her in choosing a formal gown there for the Stockholm ceremony. Denise knew that she did not require a gown, since she had recently bought one, but she desperately needed to scrutinize and disparage the enemy.

In her anxiety, Denise arrived ten minutes early for the afternoon appointment. Restlessly, she considered the Indo-Chinese figures, studded with semiprecious stones, in the windows of Balenciaga. To her dismay, they gave what lay ahead an aura of being the mysterious unknown. At last, Denise went inside, wandering among the Empire tables, with their scarves, gloves, hose, explaining to a black-garmented salesgirl that she required nothing from the boutique, that she was waiting for a friend.

The moment that her friend arrived, Denise entered the elegant rose-leather-padded elevator. On the third floor, an elderly, respectful vendeuse, the saleslady assigned to Denise by the house of Balenciaga and evidently aware of her customer's prominence, eagerly greeted the pair, and led them into the showroom, inquiring after Madame's exact wishes. Madame's wishes were for a formal evening gown.

Seated on a gold chair before the large mirror, exactly where she had sat last summer when she had been here with the English visitors, Denise awaited the appearance of the mannequins. The suspense was unbearable. She had lost eleven pounds since her troubles began, and felt more presentable because of it, but still she felt awkward and uncomfortable and increasingly nervous.

She tried to instill within herself the confidence of the mistress of the mansion, who has summoned before her the wretched and erring upstairs maid whom the master had been discovered pinching. But now, as the distant curtains parted, and the exquisite mannequins paraded across the salon toward her—with each one's approach she inquired of the vendeuse, in a whisper, the name and price of the modeled garment and, ever so casually, the name of the celebrated mannequin wearing it—her confidence ebbed.

It was the fourth girl who made a stylish entrance now, and the saleslady's whisper told her that this was Mlle Gisèle Jordan, so popular in the fashion periodicals. Denise stiffened and waited as the tall figure, tiara, skin-tight white satin décolleté, pastel gloves drawn above the elbows, strode nearer and nearer. By some curious trick of vision, Denise saw only the girl's breasts, unbound by any brassière beneath the gown. Perhaps she had unconsciously focused upon this first, because here she felt definite superiority.

From the first day of their marriage, Claude had made much of her breasts —measuring a formidable 38—and she felt that he could not appreciate a flat-chested 32 half so well, not honestly. It surprised her that the nearing, gently shimmying breasts were as large as they seemed. They were extremely large around, and the dimension reported by M. Sarraut had deceived, for it had only reported fullness. The breasts were flat, yes, small in lack of depth, but round and young.

Disconcerted by her loss of this one imagined superiority, ashamed of her focus, Denise concentrated on the entire form of the young creature who gyrated before her. At once, her heart sank. The animal was beautiful. The ash-blond hair, pale blue eyes, high cheekbones, the damn moon breasts, the long thighs and legs, were breath-taking perfection. Before the creature could leave, Denise advised the vendeuse of an interest in the satin gown. Gisèle was ordered to circle the showroom again, and stand before Madame.

Gisèle, too remote for contact, stared coolly above her customer into the mirror, her mind far away. Denise, feeling the blood in her own face, examined her adversary. She tried to be laboratory objective. She had a microscope and before her the living cells. What did Claude see in this microscope? Youth, for one thing. The flesh was taut and young and little used by time. But, Denise told herself, she, too, was young. On several occasions young research assistants had propositioned her. And then, with a twinge, she remembered that those occasions had been fifteen years ago, and that she had not been young for more than a decade. She applied her eye to the microscope once more. The cells swam off. The flesh remained. The specimen was magnificent in every way, and she was not. The specimen was exotic, and she was not. Still, what did the specimen have that she herself lacked? She stared: two arms, two breasts, two legs, one vagina, and as scientist and student of sperms, she knew that the last did not vary much from female to female, differences were technical, minute, infinitesimal. Scientifically speaking, what could this specimen do in bed for Claude that had not already been done? There were only so many words to utter, so many gasps of pleasure, so many movements, so many positions, and finally, it came to the sperm, and she had seen thousands and all different but all the same in the feelings their giving evoked.

Her eyes left the microscope and fastened wholly on what M. Sarraut discreetly termed the lady in question. The mystery of sex, the eternal enigma. Why, Denise asked herself, is her offering better than mine? Because it is younger? Newer? Different in feeling? Or is the seat of captivity her total entity and not localized in her organ? Is she more interesting, more amusing, more vivid, more energetic, more flattering, more passionate?

She stared at the outlines of the lengthy, lovely limbs pressed against the satin sheath of gown, and the hateful image superimposed itself—Claude luxuriating in that superior female body, Claude lost, lost forever. Denise was crushed, routed, and another second of this would be unendurable.

She signaled that she had seen enough of the gown, and she did not bother to watch her conqueror leave.

She heard a voice. It was the vendeuse addressing her. "What does Madame think? Is it not enchanting?"

"Oui," she was saying, "but it is not for me. *Merci."* She felt thick and graceless and old. She felt the unwanted orphan in the rear. She turned to her friend. *"Je ne veux rien acheter maintenant.* Let us go."

Suddenly the painful memory was interrupted, and she realized that she was not in the salon of Balenciaga but in the cabin of a jet headed for Sweden.

The amplifier crackled. A stewardess was speaking, first in French, then in accented English.

"We are landing in five minutes. Please refrain from smoking. Please fasten your seat belts. Please fasten your seat belts. Thank you."

Denise uncurled from her chair, and sat up, patting her suit where it had wrinkled. Outside the window there was no motion. Only a monotonous expanse of iron-grayness, like her mind. She found the belt straps, and after fumbling a moment, she hooked them around her waist.

She saw that Claude had closed his novel—damn him, able to read at a time like this—and was grinding out the butt of his cigarette. Now he, too, locked himself in his seat belt.

He looked at her. "Did you get any sleep?"

"Like an innocent child," she said viciously.

He said no more, but stuffed his book into the Air France bag, zippered it, and pulled it between his feet.

Sitting erect, waiting, she again despised the whole idea of the trip, with its enforced togetherness. A year ago, the honor would have been the greatest event of their lives. Today, this afternoon, the honor was empty—no, not empty, but something that leered and mocked. There would be little more than a week in Stockholm. It would be tolerable, possible, only if they were endlessly occupied. This would keep her from being alone with Claude, and give her time to regain her poise and to think out the immediate future. In two weeks they would be home, and they would be three, and the decision that was her own would have to be made.

She felt the slight lurch of the jet in descent, and felt also momentary panic at what lay ahead. She tried to imagine what would be demanded of them. She wondered if she and Claude would have to undertake all the rituals together. She dreaded the ordeal of their single celebrated face, the required oneness of happy marriage and happy collaboration that the world expected to see. Marie and Pierre Curie were what everyone wanted. The irony was not amusing to her. Marie and Pierre and Gisèle Jordan.

There was a crunching, grating noise, as the jet touched down and began the noisy process of braking to a halt on the 11,000-foot cement runway. Outside the window she saw a streak of forest, of parked airplanes and trucks, of modern buildings, and a hangar with futuristic upswept roofs, of people in dark clusters. It was the people that frightened her the most. They had invented a certain celebrated chemist named Dr. Denise Marceau, cool, detached, dedicated, profound, when really she was entering their lives as a cheated middle-aged wife named Mme Claude Marceau, befuddled, unsettled, angry, broken. Which of them would dream that Nobel could have been erased by Balenciaga? The test would be her reservoir of strength. Could she survive this week of exposure without precipitating a scandal?

"Come on," Claude was saying, "we have arrived."

When they came down the temporary stairs to the runway, they were engulfed at once in a mob of howling people. Claude had her arm, holding her against the crush, and somehow she found a bouquet of flowers in her hand. Indistinctly, she heard the names of the reception committee, Count Something Jacobsson, Ingrid Something, and Something Krantz.

The Count Something Jacobsson was between Claude and herself, saying, "We announced the press conference for tomorrow. We wanted it orderly. But somehow they find out—try to catch you here anyway. You do not have to answer the questions—not now." He was pushing them through the crowd, as cameras, lifted high, captured them, and reporters shouted at them in four tongues.

Hurried along, pressed and guided by the committee, with the pack close behind, she found herself stumbling through the gate toward a limousine. Count Something Jacobsson was speaking in her ear. "Accommodations—Grand Hotel—rest until tomorrow—then—"

Breathless, she reached the open door of the limousine. As she stooped to enter it, she heard one reporter's voice, more raucous than the others. "Dr. Marceau!" he cried out to her. "Do you recommend all married couples have work in common—more in common—more—?"

The voice trailed off as she buried herself in the interior of the car, fighting the urge to weep and scream. Claude was beside her, and Somebody Something beside him, and two Somebody Somethings in the jump seats. The automobile was moving, only to Denise Marceau it did not feel like an automobile but like a ferryboat, the one driven by Charon, across the "Abhorred Styx." . . .

By the time the Nobel reception committee had deposited the Drs. Denise and Claude Marceau in their Grand Hotel suite—"I am sure they were happy to see us go, they seemed so exhausted and nervous," said Ingrid Påhl—and assigned a Foreign Office attaché to attend their wants, there was barely time to dine and return to Arlanda Airport to greet the seven-o'clock Caravelle jet bringing Dr. Carlo Farelli and his wife Margherita from Rome.

The three committee members were finishing their dinner in the Cattelin Restaurant, behind the Royal Palace in the Old Town, but their conversation was not of Farelli.

"What time does Professor Max Stratman's ship arrive in Göteborg to-night?" Carl Adolf Krantz wanted to know.

"I am not certain," Jacobsson now replied. "I know it will be late. In any event, we are to expect him at the Central Station by eight tomorrow morning."

"I hope he had a good crossing," Krantz mused in his beer.

"Why all this fussing about Stratman?" Ingrid Påhl was addressing herself to Krantz. "I have not seen you this excited about a physicist since the year Heisenberg came here from Leipzig." She smiled with malicious innocence. "After all, Stratman is only an American."

Krantz took the bait. "He is a German."

"He is a Jew," said Ingrid Påhl, having a wonderful time.

"He is a German," repeated Krantz doggedly.

"Well, he certainly scurried off to America the first chance he had," said Ingrid Påhl happily.

Krantz frowned. "I see. You are pulling my leg. Personally, I do not care where he is from—only what he is—and he is, today, the world's foremost physicist. Do you have the least idea of what he has done?"

"I read the papers," said Ingrid Påhl. "He has discovered the sun has more uses than giving a suntan."

"You are hopeless." Krantz finished his beer, and devoted himself to Jacobsson. "I hate to think of Professor Stratman arriving in Göteborg without any kind of special reception. After we have dispensed with Farelli, I think I should like to telephone Professor Stratman in Göteborg. Do you have any objection?"

"Whatever you wish," said Jacobsson.

"Yes," said Krantz. "I will welcome him by telephone." He fingered his goatee. "I do hope he had an agreeable crossing."

Later, and for a long time after, Emily Stratman would remember 6:18 of the evening of December 2 as a crucial moment of self-revelation in her mature years. Curiously, whenever she would think of it, she would also remember reading somewhere that most dummy clocks used for advertising by American jewelers were set, or painted in, at about 8:18 in the belief (incorrect) that this was the moment that Abraham Lincoln had died. The persistent association of these two ideas, she would finally decide, was because both had signified the end of life.

But the moment of self-revelation, while near, was not yet at hand. It was slightly past four o'clock of December 2, and the magnificent white vessel of the Swedish-American Line had, an hour ago, left behind the dim coast of Norway and was now cutting through the choppy sea toward the Swedish port of Göteborg. Emily Stratman, a suede jacket over her chartreuse wool shirt, relaxed contentedly in a wicker chair beside the cane table on upper A Deck. Through the glass enclosure, silhouetted against the brooding horizon, she could see a lone fishing yawl with three sails. The sky above was murky and ominous. Despite the threatening weather, she was not yet ready for port. The nine days at sea had been her most glorious experience in years, and she wanted more days, to prove herself.

Inevitably, her mind had turned to Mark Claborn. She expected him. They had made no date, but she was sure that he would come. Still, she wished that they had made an appointment. She had even put off ordering a drink until he appeared.

When she heard footsteps directly behind, she twisted quickly, her face smiling to greet Mark. But her visitor was Uncle Max. Her reaction did not hide the disappointment.

"You were expecting someone younger, *Liebchen?*" asked Professor Max Stratman with a smile.

"Younger, yes. Handsomer, no."

"*Ach,* you are learning the pretty words." He settled in the wicker chair across from her. "I have been speaking to the purser. We are almost there."

"What time do we dock?"

"Ten tonight. The Stockholm train leaves at eleven. There will be plenty of time." He looked off. "Miserable weather. I hear it is raining in Göteborg. Why do they have the Nobel Ceremony in December?"

"The anniversary of Alfred Nobel's death," Emily answered.

"I am glad somebody in this family reads history." He shivered. "Brr. Cold. Will you join me in a drink?"

"We-ll—" She considered, and then decided that she could have another if Mark came. "Yes. Snaps."

"Snaps? I see you are really going the Swedish way. Do you know what it is made of?"

"Yes, alcohol and alcohol—flavored with caraway. Two snaps, and they bury you at sea."

"If my niece can have it, I can, too." He waved until he caught the eye of the deck steward, and then he called out his order.

When the drinks were served, Emily took hers not in a gulp, but gradually, to nurse it. Stratman studied his own glass with a feeling of misconduct. He had seen Dr. Fred Ilman several times before the trip, and Dr. Ilman had been flatly against it. Too much commotion, he had warned, too many people, too much exertion and food and drink. Stratman had explained that a condition for receiving the Nobel money was that you picked it up in person. Dr. Ilman had pointed out that several persons, notably John Galsworthy and André Gide, had got their prize money without traveling to Stockholm, because they were ill. Nevertheless, Stratman had been insistent. For several reasons, he had not wished his heart condition thus made public. News of it would disturb Emily, in a way that might be dangerous. She had suffered enough insecurity without this. Furthermore, the Society for Basic Research might become alarmed, and severely curtail his allotments and assignments. He did not want to be restricted when there was so much to be done. And so, on his honor, he had promised Dr. Ilman that he would behave—no agitations, no galloping about, no drinks.

He lifted his glass. "*Skål,*" he said.

"Half *skål,*" Emily replied, indicating that her own glass was now only partially filled.

They drank, then sat quietly, as they so often did, lulled by the gentle roll and pitch of the ship. Watching Emily in repose, he was pleased with the accomplishments of the sea change. A recluse, she had desired it and feared it, he knew. But somewhere, and at some time, between their arrival at Pier 97 on the North River in New York on the morning of November 24 and their entrance into their adjacent bedrooms on B Deck, Emily had seemed to make some sort of resolution about herself.

Cupping the snaps in his hand, he wondered how she had worded the resolution to herself. He had never tried to find out, never sought to intrude upon her private world, but in nine days at sea, he had observed how she had implemented her decision. Ever since he had rescued her, his brother's only child, from Buchenwald at war's end, she had remained distant from healthy, normal men. He could not recollect a single exception. By his side, she would attempt to be civil with a man, or more often, men in groups, but never once had he known her to be alone with a member of the opposite sex. Knowing the source of her abnormality, Stratman had never tried to correct it. If this defect was to be overcome, Emily would have to overcome it herself. On this Swedish ship, apparently, she had tried to do just that.

From the first night, she had, with effort, refused to confine herself to her cabin. She had been determined to be as social as any of the other 950 passengers. Every morning, she had participated in the ship's run sweepstakes. Every afternoon, she had answered the bugle call to horse racing on the deck, and six times had held winning numbers. Every dinner, she had sat at the Captain's right, to his enchantment, and had the white wine and the red wine and shared the wonders of the portable smorgasbord. Every evening, she had played bingo in the music room or attended the movie in the dining room. Every night, she had joined others in after-dinner coffee on the deck and again, later, at eleven o'clock, for the inevitable smorgasbord.

With enforced gaiety, no less enjoyed, she had celebrated with ship's companions the passing of Cape Sable Island on the third day, the sight of Cape Race, Newfoundland, on the fourth morning, the view of the Orkney Islands and Scotland on the eighth day, and this morning she had enjoyed the outlines of Norway with friends.

For the most, Stratman had observed, his pride and relief mingled with worry, the friends she had made were young men near her own age, early thirties, or somewhat older, early forties. She was nervous with them. She was reserved with them. Yet, bravely, unaccustomed as she was to this stimulation, she stood her ground with them. Not unexpectedly, the males on board pressed her hard for privacy. Her lovely face, with its Far Eastern cast, her fleshy, abundant, tapering breasts beneath tight sweaters, her curved hips, wrought fantasies among the eligible males. Her virginity, although she could not know this, had been widely discussed. Her retiring and shy manner, the being in the crowd but not a part of it, influenced the male consensus strongly. The consensus had been almost unanimous: virgin. And so, her appeal had been greater than ever.

Stratman was proud of his niece's achievement. It might rightly be called, he thought, her coming-out party. He was the ship's celebrity, but she was the ship's success. Perhaps, he thought, from this time on, it will be different.

Now, across the table from her, he sipped his drink, and enjoyed her sweet profile, and decided that Walther and Rebecca would have been gladdened. She was staring out to sea, at the whitecaps and the mist, and he wondered what she was thinking.

Emily's thoughts, this second, were not far removed from her uncle's musings. She, too, had been reviewing her nine days aboard the ship. She was not displeased with the results of her effort to attain some degree of normality. At the same time, she was not entirely satisfied, either.

Her resolution had been to prove to herself, and to anyone, that she was a woman like any other woman alive, a paid-up member of her sex, as normal and as female as her contemporaries. She had succeeded partially, but not wholly, and this was her only source of dissatisfaction. This was why she had come on the deck at this hour, when most of the others were resting or dressing. She wanted to be alone with a man who wanted to be alone with her. To what exact purpose, she did not know. But somehow, the accomplishment would be a mighty one. And again, her mind turned to Mark Claborn.

She had met him, or rather been aware of him, for the first time on the first afternoon at lifeboat drill. Tardy, she had arrived after the opening few minutes of instructions. As she squeezed into line, she tried to adjust her cork jacket properly but became impossibly entangled. The dark young man beside her had laughingly lent a hand, and soon she was prepared against disaster. Only when the drill had ended, and she had seen him walk off, had she realized that he was handsome.

Thereafter, she was frequently aware of him, sometimes playing table tennis or shuffleboard with other young men, sometimes strolling with Swedish and Danish girls, and twice he had nodded to her with courteous indifference. Of the lot aboard, she had decided, he was easily the most attractive. He was of medium height, wavy hair as black as her own, straight features on a square face, with prominent jaw and muscular neck. His shoulders and chest were athletic, narrowing to flat hips. He was given to wearing expensive casual sport shirts and sweaters, with his denim trousers.

She wondered if they would meet, and on the fifth day, they did. She was seated on the deck beside the green horse-racing mat, clutching her tickets, watching the two women passengers shake the dice, one for the number of the wooden horse, the other for the number of moves. Someone gripped the empty chair beside her, and then pulled it into line and sat down.

"Do you mind?" It was he.

She automatically tensed, as she always did, and was less cordial than she had intended. "Public grandstand," she said, indicating the other passengers.

"I'm Mark Claborn," he said. "Attorney-at-law. Chicago."

"How nice."

She considered introducing herself, but before she could, he had solved that problem. "You are Miss Emily Stratman. Atlanta. En route to Stockholm to help your uncle cart off the loot."

"Well, I would hardly put it that way—"

"No, no. I'm kidding. I'm very impressed with your uncle. He's the only authentic genius I've ever seen close up, though once, when I was a boy, someone pointed out Clarence Darrow driving past. But your uncle—I always try to stand near him, when he's surrounded, just to glean a few words of wisdom."

"How did you know my name?"

"I asked the purser. It's a long trip—my first time on a ship, to tell the truth, not counting the Great Lakes cruise I took two years ago. Is this your maiden voyage, too?"

She considered her reply. "In a way, I suppose so. Actually, I was born in Germany—"

"Really? I would never have guessed it."

"Because I was brought to the United States when I was very young." She smiled. "Oh, I'm true-blue American by now. I've been through the Age of Truman, of Tennessee Williams, of Stan Musial—Rodgers and Hammerstein, Dr. Jonas Salk, Rocky Marciano, Joseph McCarthy—you see?"

"You've just passed with an A-plus." He paused. "Where are you going after Stockholm?"

"Home."

His face reflected disappointment. "Too bad. I won't be in Stockholm, but I'll be in Copenhagen, Paris, Rome. Vacation. I was hoping we'd run into each other again."

"I'm afraid not."

He nodded off. "You've lost this race. May I buy you a ticket on the next? What number will it be?"

After that they saw each other regularly, always in the proximity of others, but regularly. They had drinks in the bar. They attended a movie. They toured the ship. They played bingo. They shared the late night smorgasbord. She found him flattering and amusing. He had defects, of course. He had read little outside of Blackstone. He was rarely serious. He lacked depth and sensitivity. But he was attractive, and he was fun. Now, this final day, she wanted to be alone with him.

Across the table, her uncle suddenly gulped the last of his drink, and pushed himself to his feet. "I must fill out papers," he said vaguely.

Intuitively, she sensed the reason for his leaving, and turned to see Mark Claborn approaching.

"You don't have to go, Uncle Max."

"I was only warming the seat for the young man, anyway. See you at dinner." He waved to Mark, and waddled off.

Mark Claborn came around the table and took Stratman's chair. "Hello, Emily. I wondered where you were. What've you been doing?"

"Staring at the ocean, hating to think I must leave the ship. I like it the way it is out there, the way I like rainy days and nighttime."

"You're not exactly a bundle of cheer."

"But I am. I also like winter. Have you ever read Cowper?"

"I'm afraid not."

"He liked winter." She hesitated, then recited, " 'I crown thee king of intimate delights, Fireside enjoyments, home-born happiness' and so forth."

"I'm not with your man. To me winter means nose drops." He looked off. "I took the liberty of ordering drinks for us. What are you drinking?"

"Snaps."

"That's what I ordered."

"Telepathy."

"No. Empathy—despite winter." Then, he added, "Because we're getting in so late, they're having a full-course dinner. There are some extra tables. Think you can join me at one?"

"Why, I don't know. Wouldn't it be rude?"

"The Captain never comes down the last night. You've been eight dinners at that table. Surely you can spend one with me?"

"All right. I'd be delighted."

The deck steward brought the snaps.

Mark Claborn took his glass. "Let's do it the way the Swedes do it. Remember?" She remembered. The bartender had taught them. They solemnly held their glasses rigid before their chests. Mark toasted their next meeting. They looked into each other's eyes, and then swallowed their drinks all at once. They brought their empty glasses down to their chests again, eyes still meeting, and then set the glasses on the table.

"Great custom," he said. "One toast is worth one thousand words."

"Only because it leaves you speechless," said Emily. "Must be a plot of the snaps cartel." She felt the heat of the drink in her temples, and now expanding through her chest and breasts.

In the next hour, they each had two more drinks, and then Emily called a halt.

"I'm not drunk," she said, "but I didn't know you brought along a friend. We'd better call it quits. I don't want you to carry me in to dinner."

"I'd like nothing more."

"I prefer to stand on my own feet."

"I'm sure you do. The question is—can you?" he said teasingly.

"Always," she replied, squinting to see him better. "Watch." She rose, and stood at attention.

"I bow to your sobriety," said Mark, "but not to your independence." He grinned. "Damn the Nineteenth Amendment."

He left several bills on the table, then took her arm. He walked her to her cabin on B Deck. Neither spoke, until they reached the door of the cabin.

"I'll pick you up here at seven," he said.

She leaned against the door, lightheaded. "I suppose I should treat you to something before dinner. Southern hospitality."

"You should indeed."

"I have a bottle of bourbon in the room. Somebody sent it to the boat. Will it mix with snaps?"

"This is the Swedish-American Line."

"Come at six. Will that give you time to change?"

"Too much time."

After Emily had gone into her cabin, she remained uncertainly in the center of the room, feeling the rhythmical heave of the ship beneath her and listening to the creak of the wood. She was not drunk at all, she decided, but then she was not sober. She tried to evaluate her feeling. The feeling was one of well-being and irresponsibility. The feeling was weightlessness, mind and body both. She kicked off her sandals, and threw herself on the bed. Sprawled on the blanket, she tried to tie her mind to a thought. There was not one to grip. She let go and slept.

When she awakened, it was with surprise that she had been asleep at all. She sought the wall clock. Seven minutes to six. In seven minutes, she would not be alone. The logical act was to change quickly into her dinner dress and apply fresh makeup. She felt illogical, defiant of risk, daring. She wanted a shower, and she would have it.

Swinging her weight off the bed, she stood, pulled off her shirt and unzipped her pleated skirt. She unhooked her nylon stockings and rolled them off, and then took off her garter belt and threw it on the chair. She weaved into the bathroom, considered locking the primitive metal latch, decided that was foolish, then went to the bathtub and turned the knobs until the shower was going full force. Next, she undid her brassière, and pulled off her pants and dropped both on the wooden stool. Starting for the bathtub, she saw herself in the full-length mirror of the partially open door. This was not narcissism, as you always read in those novels, she told herself, but a form of reassurance known only to herself. Her nudity was without blemish. Any man, Mark or any, seeing her thus, would have agreed that this was purity.

She stepped into the bathtub, drawing the ringed curtains around her protectively, and then moved all but her head under the powerful spray. She reveled in the punishment of the water, and began to sober.

She did not hear the cabin door open, and she could not hear her name. Mark Claborn had knocked and, receiving no reply, had tried the door and found it open. Emily was nowhere to be seen, except in the evidence of her clothes, which lay in disarray. He called out for her, and there was no reply. And then he heard the shower. He walked to the bathroom door, and peered inside the steamed room. He saw her outline behind the wet curtain, and that was invitation enough.

With a grin, he returned to the bedroom. The clock told him that it was five after six. She had asked him for six. She had promised to treat him to something. The hint had been broad enough. Here was something. The invitation stood. He pulled off his coat, yanked off his tie, and began to unbutton his shirt. He was a young man of considerable experience in novelty. This would be memorable.

Once he had stripped, Mark's excitement accelerated. She was waiting. He pictured her. He then hurried into the bathroom, closed the door, slid the latch, and strode to the bathtub. He could hardly contain himself. He groped for the shower curtain, found the end, and ripped it aside.

Emily stood nude, her back to him, streams of water chasing the soap down her limbs. At the noise, she wheeled around, almost losing her foothold. What she saw, through the steam, petrified her: Mark, his lascivious grin, his huge, hairy chest, the horrible, blatant torso.

"Sa-ay, now, honey," he was saying, "I knew you were beautiful, but—"

She reached to cover her breasts first, and then darted one hand below. She had lost the power of speech. Her eyes widened with disbelief, as he climbed into the bathtub.

Her voice surfaced in a shrill cry. "Are you crazy? Get out!"

"And miss the fun?"

He stepped beneath the shower, reaching for her. With a tremor, she tore away from him, and leaped out of the tub. Landing on the bathroom floor, her wet feet gave way, and she fell on the bath mat. Rolling off it, her slippery body on the tile, she clutched for the mat to cover herself.

As she tried to pull the inadequate mat around her waist, she felt Mark's hand on her shoulder, pinning her to the floor.

"Let go of me!" she cried. "What's got into you?"

"Cut it out—stop the act."

His hands were on her breasts. Horrified, she released the mat and tried to grab his wrists and remove his hands. With ease, he pulled one hand free of her wet fingers, and tore the mat aside and threw it against the wall.

"There now—now—"

Panting, she pressed her thighs together, as he loomed above her.

"Honey," he was saying, "be a good girl, honey. We can't get anywhere with your legs like that. Come on, now, relax, enjoy yourself—"

"No, damn you, I don't want that!"

One hand was on her thighs, as the other fended off her fists. "Sure you want it, sure you do—you wanted it all this trip—you kept telling me without words."

She held his defensive arm, and began to plead. "No, Mark, no—I can't—"

"Listen to you, the way you're breathing—"

"I'm scared!"

"Stop that stuff. You'll love it, I guarantee you, you'll want more. We've got hours—"

96

Suddenly, he freed one arm, slipped it around her back, so that it came around to cup a breast. She snatched at the invading hand, trying to sit up, trying to push herself upright, and as she did so her legs and thighs came apart. In an instant, he rolled between them, above her.

She was exhausted, her heart against her ribs, and the decision was now, relent or fight. She was conscious of the suspended second. To lie back and let the muscular naked body above enter and consume her or to beat off and repel the ugly menace of its offering?

With all her strength, she smashed both fists against his chest. For a moment, he tottered above her, then reeled backwards on his haunches in genuine surprise and bewilderment.

She sat up. "Get out, or I'll scream!" she shouted.

He sat blinking at her a moment, awkward and foolish. "You mean it." It was a flat statement. He climbed to his feet. "You don't have to scream. And stop shaking like a frightened rabbit. Rape isn't my line. But you sure had me fooled. I've never been wrong before—"

"You're wrong now!" She had recovered the bath mat, and, still sitting, shielded her lower parts. "Please go!"

With some remnant of dignity, he turned, unlatched the door, and went into the bedroom.

Trembling, Emily stood up, edged to the door, and held the knob. She could hear him dressing. She started to close the door, when he spoke.

"I still say I wasn't wrong. I just wonder what happened between the time you said yes to yourself and no to me. Something happened."

"Nothing happened," she said through the door. "I was a little drunk, and you—you misinterpreted it."

"Maybe. Honey, tell me one thing. Between us."

She waited.

"Are you a virgin?"

"Yes."

"Well, that explains a little." He paused. "I'm leaving now. I'm sorry for both of us. No hard feelings. See you at smorgasbord."

She heard the door slam, held back, then peered out, and saw that the cabin was empty.

Emotionally spent, she turned off the shower and then dried herself. After tidying the bathroom, she went into the cabin and mechanically dressed in the garments that she had recently discarded. Closing the zipper of her skirt, she felt dizzy. She lowered herself to the bed, and finally fell back on the pillow, hands covering her eyes from the overhead light.

Twenty minutes later, passing to his room, Max Stratman thought that he heard her sobbing. He placed his ear to her door, confirmed his suspicion, and hastily opened it and went inside.

"Emily, *um Himmels willen*, what is the matter?"

"Nothing, Uncle Max, nothing—I swear."

"Why are you crying like this?"

She tried to contain her sobs, and finally reduced them to a soft whimper. "I'm not crying—see?"

He pulled the chair up beside her bed, and perched forward on it, like a kindly country doctor. "Something has happened. We have no secrets."

She rolled on her right side, studying the hedge of hair on his oversized bald head, the worried eyes behind the steel-rimmed bifocals, the concern in his wise old red face. Here was one of the great minds of the world, a genius cherished and honored, and she, a neurotic nobody, was troubling him with her petty problems.

"It's nothing," she repeated without conviction.

"Please tell me. I will not go until you tell me."

She tried to visualize her father, and could not, and suddenly there was only Uncle Max, and she wanted to tell him. Haltingly, avoiding his eyes, she related the events of the past hour or more, from the time Mark had escorted her to the door to the time he had left her nude on the bathroom floor to dress and leave.

"That is all?" asked Stratman, when she had finished. "You are not leaving out anything?"

"He didn't touch me, I swear—"

"No—no assault?"

"Uncle Max, I'd *know.*"

Stratman rose, agitated. "It is terrible, anyway. No one is safe. I will go to the Captain at once—"

"Oh, no!" She sat up and swung her legs off the bed. "I don't want him in trouble—"

"You care for him that much? Is that it?"

"I don't care for him at all," she said vehemently. "He means nothing to me. But I'm just not sure he's all to blame."

"What does that mean?"

"Only—I had too much to drink—I invited him—he misunderstood. It is something that happens every day." She softened her tone. "Let's not make a fuss, Uncle Max. I don't want to go through that. It would embarrass me. It would be easier to forget it. We're almost there. We'll leave the boat soon and not think of it."

"You are sure it is that simple?"

"Oh, yes. I was upset, naturally. But I'm all right, you can see. I don't want an incident, that's all."

He looked at her. "Maybe I can get the ship's doctor. To give you a shot, calm your nerves—"

"No, not even that. Just let me rest, and an hour before we get in, come and get me. I'll be ready." She tried to change the subject. "Do you think there will be a reception when you get to Göteborg?"

"I doubt it. Everything is in Stockholm."

She feigned enthusiasm. "I can't wait. It's really been a marvelous trip."

She dropped back on the pillow. He waited until she was comfortable. "I'll be next door if you need me."

"What about dinner?"

"I'm not hungry. I'll have the steward bring a sandwich. I'll come back soon. You rest."

He went to his cabin, disturbed. In a way that he could not define, he felt that he had failed Walther. What had happened to Emily must never happen again. He had overestimated her. In Stockholm, he would not leave her alone. Pacing past his bed, he heard his heart. In all the years before, he had never heard it, had ignored it as he had his inhaling and exhaling. But now, too often, it demanded to be heard. There was a heaviness in the right side of his chest, not pain but pressure. He opened the overnight bag, located the bottle of pills that Dr. Ilman had given him, and took two with a half glass of water.

He rang for the room steward, ordered a cheese-and-ham sandwich. Presently, when it came, he gave the steward two envelopes, each with a fifteen-dollar tip in it, and requested that the second envelope be given to the stewardess. Stratman knew that the tips were generous for his budget, but he also knew that the serving people depended on these tips for their livelihood, especially on the run from New York to Göteborg. Too, since the Nobel Prize included a highly advertised sum of money, more would be expected of him, as one of the winners. He allowed the steward to remove his suitcases. After the man had gone, Stratman settled down and nibbled at his sandwich.

Presently, because his mind was on Emily, he returned to her cabin. She was still on the bed, as he had left her, eyes closed, dozing. He sat in the chair beside her, extracted a pocket-sized German edition of a biography of Immanuel Kant from his coat, and resumed reading. When he reached Heine's description of Kant, he reread it: "The life of Immanuel Kant is hard to describe; he has indeed neither life nor history in the proper sense of the words. He lived an abstract, mechanical, old-bachelor existence, in a quiet remote street in Königsberg . . ."

Stratman considered this. There, he thought, but for the grace of Emily, go I. By her sharing of his life, she had infused her guardian's "old-bachelor existence" with an element of normality, yet, ironically, had been unable to retain an element of normality for herself. The terrible incident of the evening underlined for him, in a way he had found impossible to explain to Dr. Ilman, Emily's dependence on him. Without his support, after he was gone, she would have been forced into the turmoil of the working world. Any notion that this necessity would have given her strength had been dissipated by the night's events. As he had long ago guessed, she would not have survived. One cannot expect a person without arms to feed himself. How fortuitous had been the Nobel award. Once he had the check in hand, Emily would have her buffer against the future.

He read more about his beloved Kant, drifted off into numerous speculations, even nodded off several times, hardly aware of the passage of time or of the fact that the ship had ceased pitching and was now rolling less.

The rapping on the door brought him up sharply, and awakened Emily, too.

The steward put his head in. "I'll need the rest of the luggage, sir. We're just outside Göteborg. It'll be less than an hour now."

No sooner had the steward gone with the suitcases, than a young boy in white uniform, wearing the telegraph-office arm band, appeared. There were four long-distance calls from Stockholm. Stratman asked if he might take them here in Emily's room. The boy went to the telephone and made connection with the officer's room. In a few moments, he handed the receiver to Stratman, gratefully accepted his tip, and rushed off.

The first call, and the two after that, were from Swedish newspapers. There was static on the wire, and Stratman had difficulty hearing. He answered the questions that he understood, briefly, precisely, and promised each correspondent that he would give lengthier interviews in Stockholm.

The fourth call was from Dr. Carl Adolf Krantz. Stratman recognized the name and was friendly. He thanked Krantz for his effusive congratulations and welcome. Yes, the voyage had been pleasant and restful. Yes, he and his niece would arrive at eight in the morning. Yes, they looked forward to meeting the reception committee and to participating in the program and ceremonies.

During all these calls, Emily, having washed and applied light makeup, stood at the porthole, half listening, staring out into the rain-crossed night. Spotlights on the water had picked out the pilot boat, and the launch that followed shortly after. The ship was progressing slowly, among what seemed to be dozens of islands, and growing larger in sight was the framework of lights that must be the wharves and the city of Göteborg.

At 10:20, Emily was brought away from the porthole, to join her uncle, by the noise at the door. At once, it seemed, they were surrounded by visitors. The purser was on hand to introduce a First Secretary of the Swedish Foreign Office, who had driven down from Stockholm and would ease their way through customs to the train. Four or five city officials, representing Göteborg, were introduced, and after mumbling their formal greetings, gazed upon Stratman with the awe they had once accorded Wilhelm Roentgen.

For Emily, never leaving her uncle's side, what followed was a continuous flow of movement. Led to the music room, where two Swedish men and two women were stamping passports and checking money declarations, Emily and her uncle were met with silent respect and quickly passed through. From the rail of the open top deck—the downpour had slowed to a drizzle—she watched the ship ease alongside the huge wharf, seeing clusters of Swedes waiting with flowers and from somewhere hearing the strains of "The Star-Spangled Banner."

Following the First Secretary and her uncle downstairs, trailed by the Göteborg officials, she wondered if she would see Mark Claborn again. She hoped not, and she was relieved when they arrived at the head of the gang-plank, and he was nowhere in sight. With the others, she descended the gang-plank, pushing through the customs shed jammed with visitors, porters, officials, and arrived at the counter under a huge "S" that held their five suitcases. The customs examiner was smiling. He had already sealed the bags without opening them. A Nobel winner, his smile seemed to say, could not be suspected of smuggling.

"We had better hurry now," the First Secretary was insisting to Stratman. Two porters carried their bags, and followed them down the stairs to the street. It was raining harder again. The First Secretary's Mercedes, guarded by two policemen, was a few yards away. Emily and Stratman gave their thanks to the city officials, hurried through the increasing rain, and fell into the back seat of the vehicle.

The First Secretary took the wheel, and they were moving. In the rain, Emily could form no impression of Göteborg. The port at the mouth of the Göta River had a population of 400,000. This seemed incredible. The wet, cold streets were deserted. This was the street known as Södra Hamngatan, and that was Milles's Poseidon Fountain in the Götaplatsen, and over there the Röhsska Museum of Applied Arts. While her uncle voiced his appreciation, Emily could make out nothing except two parks that seemed attractive but abandoned in the rain, and the rows of lights about the business district.

They reached the first of the two Stockholm boat trains seven minutes before its departure.

The First Secretary was all efficiency. He guided them to their adjoining compartments. He counted their luggage. He spoke in an undertone—obviously of Max Stratman's importance—to the conductor who wore a black-and-yellow arm band reading *"Sovvagn."* He shook their hands, first Stratman's, then Emily's, and said that he would see them late tomorrow at the Grand Hotel. Then he charged off, and almost instantly the train shook and began to move.

Before Emily and Stratman could leave the aisle, the black-uniformed conductor reappeared.

"Your berths are made," he told them in careful English. "There is no private water closet as in America, I am sorry. The one water closet is at the end of the car. We do not have a porter in each car, but if you ring, I will come swiftly. There is a pull-down basin to wash your hands. I hope you are comfortable."

By the time Emily had entered her compartment, the noisy train was catapulting along at breakneck speed. The compartment was tiny but, she was sure, luxurious by Swedish standards. Everything seemed wooden, except the gleaming steel lever that secured the door.

She was more tired than she had realized. She snapped open the overnight bag on her berth, removed her toilet articles, then opened the washbasin closet. The hot and cold water faucets were both cold. She did not mind. With a Kleenex, she shed her makeup. Then she brushed her teeth, washed and found a towel on the berth to dry. Lifting the basin back into the wall, she searched for a comb, and pulled it through her short bobbed hair twenty times.

She undressed with haste, slipped into her white pleated nightgown, placed the overnight case on the floor, and slid between the tight covers of the sleeping berth. When she laid her head on the pillow, she found no comfort. It was both hard and too high. Poking behind the mattress, she found a second pillow, a hard-packed maroon roll, underneath. The Swedes are Spartans, she thought. She decided against removing the red roll. She would be a Spartan, too.

About to dim the lights, she heard her uncle through the compartment door. "Emily—*wie geht es dir?*"

"Yes? Come in."

He entered, tentatively, glanced about. "Are you comfortable, Emily?"

"Perfectly," she lied.

He balanced himself against the wall. "It is going very fast." He squinted at her. "You are not sorry you came?"

"Of course not, Uncle Max. What ever gave you that idea? I can't wait to get to Stockholm. Can you?"

He tried to reinforce her enthusiasm. "I think it will be an unforgettable week. Not so much this Nobel Ceremony, but the excitement, the new faces. My main wish is that you have a good time."

"I will. Don't you worry. Get some rest."

"Yes." But he was reluctant to leave. He looked down at his niece, so small, so childish, on the large berth. "Emily, I am sorry about what happened tonight." He shrugged. "It happens. It is life. Only it should not happen to you." He hesitated. "I was wondering. Is there—is there anything more you want to tell me?"

"It's out of my mind, Uncle Max."

"Good, Liebchen, very good. You think you will sleep?"

"I took a Butisol."

"Good night. The conductor will wake us in time." At the door, he halted again. "Fix the latch when I go."

"Yes, Uncle Max. Good night."

After he was gone, she did not bother with the latch. She dimmed the lights, and rested on her back, one arm behind her head. The train bounced beneath her, but that was not what made sleep difficult. For the first time in years, she thought of her past, the time before America, her girlhood. Then she thought of the curiously arid, placid period of growing up in the new country. Her mind touched on her resolution, made when she had gone aboard the ship, the determination to become a complete woman, and her consequent failure. The resolution illuminated the events of this night.

That poor young man on the boat, she thought. He was only my guinea pig, and he did not know it. She could hardly remember his name now. But anyway, he deserved more. He would never know how he had been used, and to what extent her experiment had been unsuccessful. She had known psychiatrists, and she had read Freud and Adler, and sometimes she had the objectivity to point their perceptions inward on herself. It was crystal-clear to her now that, unconsciously, she had fully provoked the incident. The drinking had been deliberate. The invitation for six o'clock. The being stark-naked in the shower at six with both doors open. She had invited the ultimate act, not knowing that she had, and expected that he would come as he had, not knowing that she had done so. At the same time—how confusing—her saner conscious ego had not wanted it at all, had feared and despised it. The result had been inevitable. It would forever be inevitable, she knew.

The body, the lie of a body that provoked, the figure stretched below her, detached from her meditations, was her body and she could not disown it, she knew. She did not like it this night, nor any other night in memory. It was crippled inside and soiled outside, and she wished it was not her body, as she had often guessed in Atlanta that some blacks had wished to be white and could not understand a God that had so shown his displeasure. Like them, she resented the curse of Ham, and wanted normality—whatever that was —well, normality, that meant belonging, acceptance, no fears.

It had been 6:18 when the young man had gone from her stateroom. No one would understand, but that had been the exact time that the last of Emily Stratman had died. Did the Nobel people know that their laureate in physics was arriving with a corpse? The celebrated Professor Max Stratman and corpse. Stockholm. She played the word-association game. What does the word Stockholm mean to you, Miss Stratman? Quickly, now, what? And she replied, quickly: trepidation, dread, anxiety, fear, men. All one and the same, all finally—men.

My crazy mind, she thought, wandering. Wonderful, drugful Butisol, work, go on, work. When will I sleep? . . .

On the sunny, late morning of December 2, Carl Adolf Krantz, Count Bertil Jacobsson, and Ingrid Påhl were once more, the second time this morning, the fourth time in two days, seated in the rear of a Foreign Office limousine, en route to the Arlanda Airport. Because two winners and their relatives— Dr. John Garrett and his wife Saralee Garrett, and Mr. Andrew Craig and his sister-in-law Leah Decker—were arriving at 12:35, on the same flight of the Scandinavian Airlines System from Copenhagen, another Foreign Office limousine had been dispatched a half hour earlier to the air terminal.

To make this seventy-minute ride more bearable, Jacobsson had deliberately placed himself between Krantz and Påhl. He wished no more bickering. He wanted unity before the final reception duty was performed.

Carl Adolf Krantz, however, was in no mood for bickering this late morning. His spirits were high, his beady eyes bright, his goatee bristling, as he continued the monologue he had begun after they had finished breakfast with Stratman and his niece and left them in the Grand Hotel.

He had been praising, without restraint, Stratman's findings in the field of solar energy, and now he was extolling the winning physicist's background and character.

"Did you ever meet a more remarkable man?" he asked, and did not wait for an answer. "Wisdom shines in his face. And his true modesty. So rare to find in a famous man. One of the marks of greatness, I would say, a humility that confesses, 'Yes, I have gone so far, but there are more curtains to lift, let us go on, let us go further.' I tell you both, I cannot recollect another laureate who has impressed me more."

"Obviously," said Ingrid Påhl.

"Yes, I liked him," Jacobsson agreed. "I hope he did not mind our staying for breakfast."

"I am sure not," said Krantz.

"I wonder. I had the feeling he was weary—"

"He is not a youngster," said Krantz, "and he has had a long trip. Besides, it was not weariness I detected so much as a sense of a genius whose mind is still on his work. After all, as he told us, he is continuing with his solar investigations. He has only begun. We have just come along and interrupted—"

"He seemed perfectly fine to me," said Ingrid Påhl. "It was his niece— I thought she was a little strange."

"How so?" Jacobsson wanted to know.

"Remote—and—oh, scared." Ingrid Påhl considered the judgment. "To begin with, at the depot. She was separated from him for a moment when the photographers closed in, and she appeared frantic. I saw her face. That was just one thing. For the rest of the time, she was withdrawn. I do not know— as if she were not part of the group, a stranger—"

"She is a stranger," said Krantz.

"At any rate, an interesting young lady. I studied her face. Flawless. She is going to create quite a stir in our little social whirl." Ingrid Påhl leaned across Jacobsson. "And she does not look a bit like Dr. Stratman," she added to Krantz.

"No reason why she should," said Krantz. "She is his brother's child."

"What happened to the brother?" asked Ingrid Påhl.

"How the devil should I know?" said Krantz testily.

Ingrid Påhl opened her voluminous purse and brought out her John Silver cigarettes and holder. "Well, they are settled, thank God. Now, Bertil, what about this noon's visitor? I know all about Andrew Craig. But this Dr. Garrett—"

"You read the typescript I gave you, did you not?" asked Jacobsson.

Ingrid Påhl had the light to her cigarette, shook the flame off the match, and dropped it to the floor. "I read it twice. It was all about his work. What about the man? What are we to expect?"

"There is little I can tell you," said Jacobsson. "He lives in this city near Los Angeles, California, and has three children. He had no reputation in academic circles until he and Dr. Farelli made their heart transplantations. I do not think he is wealthy, but I believe he is well off. I have read excerpts of his speeches in the press. They seem fairly routine. I have the picture of a rather single-minded, dedicated man, with a few outside interests—"

"Dull, you mean," said Ingrid Påhl.

Jacobsson's face looked pained. To him, no winner of the Nobel Prize could possibly be dull. "I would prefer not to characterize him in that way. Rather, I would say that he is a man whose work is his world. Perhaps he is not so colorful in personality as Dr. Farelli, but more the typical, business-like American scientist who has collaborated in producing a marvel for humanity."

Ingrid Påhl's eyebrows shot up. "Collaborated? I did not know he and Farelli worked together—"

"No, no." Jacobsson hastened to amend his statement to Ingrid Påhl. "I used the word only in its broadest definition. They researched separately, and made their discoveries, of an identical nature, quite apart but at the same time. Not unfamiliar in science, as Carl will tell you. You may recall that Dr. Farelli confessed he and Dr. Garrett had neither met nor corresponded."

"Then this meeting in Stockholm will be their first?" Ingrid Påhl savored the drama. "I wonder what they will have to say to each other."

"They will devote hours to discussing immunity mechanism," said Krantz, "as well as organ banks for the heart, pancreas, and liver. Appetizing."

"In any case, you may both have an opportunity to hear what they discuss," said Jacobsson. He bent across Krantz for a view through the window. "We have not far to go. I presume Dr. Garrett and Mr. Craig have had an opportunity to become acquainted in this last hour since Copenhagen. I rather hope so. It'll save us the formal introductions. . . ."

The French-made Caravelle jet, that had taken off from Kastrup Airport in Copenhagen at 11:20 in the morning, had been airborne fifty-five minutes and was twenty minutes out of Stockholm.

It was now precisely 12:14, according to Saralee Garrett's platinum wristwatch, a gift of John's on their recent fifteenth wedding anniversary, and she wished desperately that it were 12:25 and that they had already landed. She wanted them to be swept up in a busy social program, so that her husband would have no more time alone with his ulcerating obsession. Tiny and thin as a hummingbird, Saralee's outward appearance belied her inner resilience. But the last hour with John had proved almost more than she could bear. From the corner of her eye, she espied her husband once more studying the three Copenhagen newspapers, and she knew that he was fuming.

Dr. John Garrett was, indeed, fuming. He would not even allow himself the comfort of sitting back and enjoying the soft leather seat in the airplane. Instead, he leaned forward tensely, in the attitude of a pugilist stalking a formidable foe and awaiting an opening. He jabbed nervously at the three newspapers in his lap, as if they were the embodiment of his opponent, and, indeed, they were, for Dr. Farelli's smiling, cocky Latin countenance mocked him from a photograph on each front page.

Ever since that afternoon seventeen days ago—when he had been lifted to the heights by the announcement that he had been honored by the Caroline Institute of Stockholm for his achievement, and then dropped into the deepest pit of disappointment by the further knowledge that he had to share this achievement with an archenemy he did not know—Dr. John Garrett's mental and pathological state had been one of simmering resentment.

The high regard of his colleagues in Pasadena, Los Angeles, the entire nation, the celebrations that followed, had not been enough to calm him completely. Everywhere, praise had been tempered by acknowledgment that his victory was a joint one. True enough, *Life* Magazine had published separate half-page photographs of Farelli and him, but *Time* and *Newsweek*, while giving him 50 per cent of the text of their stories, had run photographs of Farelli alone. Worse, by far, were the long accounts in *Science News Letter, Scientific American,* and *Science.* They had all assigned special correspondents to interview him at the Rosenthal Medical Center in Pasadena. The correspondents had been courteous and patient. Garrett had been voluble and winning. He had felt positive that his visitors had been dazzled. Yet, when their stories appeared—so important to him in these, his popular trade papers—between 70 and 80 per cent of the stories were concentrated on the specific accomplishments of Dr. Carlo Farelli. In each account—although possibly he had been overly sensitive—he had the definite impression that he had been permitted to tag along as the poor cousin.

Over and over again, he had asked himself—why? Objectivity about his own position was almost impossible, yet he had tried to analyze the results with an investigator's dispassionate appraisal. First of all—an insight of candor injected, perhaps, by his analyst, Dr. L. D. Keller—he was physically less interesting than his rival. He was simply too conventional, too average, too close to the median in his appearance. His brown hair conspired with his rimless spectacles to create the illusion of Undramatic Man. On the other hand, as photographs gave ample evidence, Carlo Farelli appeared the representation of the eccentric genius. His pitch-black, curly, tangled hair hung down over his broad wise forehead. His piercing, fanatical eyes, classical Roman nose, carefree, white-toothed smile, Hapsburg jaw were all made more distinctive by the faintly pitted cheeks and olive complexion of his broad face.

In the second place, Garrett's background had seemed too home-grown and too familiar. Born in Illinois, educated in Massachusetts, he had accomplished his researches in California. On the other hand, Farelli had been born in Milan, educated in Geneva, London, and Heidelberg, and had conducted the majority of his experiments in Rome. This background, Garrett had reasoned, was too cosmopolitan to resist. Finally, all of Garrett's brilliant transplants had been made on unknown, middle-class patients. Almost half of Farelli's twenty-one heart transplants had been successful on patients who were, in the vernacular of the day, "newsworthy"—one a cardinal of the Roman Church, one an Austrian statesman, one a French actress renowned at the turn of the century, one an elderly British playwright. If Garrett saw himself as William Harvey and Joseph Lister, or at least Ambroise Paré, he saw Farelli as only a pale carbon copy of himself made legible, even gaudy, by the methods of Phineas T. Barnum. The fact that the world, or the world's press, at any rate, did not see this so clearly as he, made Garrett a study verging on the paranoiac.

Before his departure for Sweden, he had paid one more visit to his therapy group in Dr. Keller's office on Wilshire Boulevard. What he sought, that day, was not illumination but corroboration of his own current beliefs. On this, his only visit after his Nobel Prize had been announced, his reception had been gratifying, to say the least. For once, Miss Dudzinski had left her mother in peace, and Mrs. Zane had confined her account of her gymnastics with Mr. Zane's employer to ten heated minutes, and Adam Ring had been unnaturally mute and respectful (having decided, no doubt, that his one Academy Award nomination had finally been matched and surpassed by a member of the group).

Unusually agitated, Garrett had accused the Caroline Institute of Stockholm of bias in subtracting half of his honor and giving it to an Italian mountebank. He had railed on against Farelli's self-serving publicity tactics, his unethical standards, his brazen egotism in agreeing to share a citation that was not rightly his to claim. Dr. Keller, so rarely vocal, had been superhuman in his effort to soothe Garrett with calm reason. The analyst had pointed out that if Farelli had drawn upon Garrett's creative genius for his own discovery, he would one day be found out, and in the eyes of the world, Garrett would be properly credited. Meanwhile, he had gone on to say, the best experts of the Nobel Committee had made their studies and had determined Farelli's worth. As a sensible man, it was Garrett's duty to accept the verdict sensibly. This year, he had been honored above all men of medicine on earth. Certainly, at this summit, there was room for another to stand beside him. The accomplishment was no less his, and he should be proud of a contribution to the betterment and longevity of the human race.

And Adam Ring, from deep in the easy chair, had capped it in his own terms: "When you take the Oscar, you don't ask questions, Dr. Garrett. It's the gold medal for life. For the rest of your days, you're the Nobelman, like being knighted. Nobody'll give a damn if there were two winners or ten. All they'll know is you hit the jackpot. Better than an annuity. From now on, no waiting in line, no having your credit checked, no having to pay for it with hookers, no proving anything to anyone. You can't go higher than up, and you're up. Be happy. I'll trade places with you, flat deal, no cash, no questions, right now."

Garrett had departed from the session somewhat mollified.

By the time he and Saralee had entered the Scandinavian Airlines' DC-8 jet at Los Angeles International Airport at 11:30 yesterday morning—despite the well-wishers from Pasadena who had come to see them off—Garrett's temper had again settled into one of controlled resentment. The lulling monotony of the transpolar flight, as Saralee had hoped, had done much to pacify him. The thirteen hours over Canada, Labrador, Iceland, and Norway, broken by only one brief stop for refueling, had been occupied with reading, conversation, lunch, dinner (roast rack of lamb), supper, bourbon, and martinis.

They had slept fitfully, had enjoyed an early breakfast, and had made a roaring landing on the cement strip of the Kastrup Airport at 8:59 Copenhagen time. An undersecretary of the United States Embassy, a beaming, collegiate gentleman not yet middle-aged, had been on hand to welcome them. Since there remained a little over two hours before a Caravelle jet would take them the last lap to Stockholm, the Embassy had arranged an extremely brief tour of the city and environs for them. They had visited the Raadhuspladsen, and then, from the center of the city, had driven through the crowded thoroughfare known as Strøget. They had seen the statue of Christian V in Kongens Nytorv, and later the Nyhavn canal, the Rigsdag, the Rosenborg Castle, and finally, at the end of the Langelinie promenade, rising from the water, the life-sized sculpture of Hans Christian Andersen's "Little Mermaid." The last treat, before returning to the airport, had been *smørrebrød* sandwiches in the festive sidewalk terrace café of the d'Angleterre Hotel.

Garrett, a receptive sightseer, had been considerably soothed by his initial impression of bustling Copenhagen. For almost the first time, he seemed cognizant of the fact that he was on a journey and in a foreign place. When they had returned to the Kastrup Airport, ten minutes before takeoff, he had almost forgotten the existence of Carlo Farelli. But then, just as he was about to go through the door to the runway, passing a newsstand, Garrett's eye was caught by the front page of the Danish morning newspaper, *Politiken*. The photograph, three columns wide, showed Farelli alighting from an airliner, his olive face wreathed in a smile, his right arm raised aloft in greeting.

The United States Embassy escort, over Saralee's weak protests, purchased the newspaper for Garrett, and two others besides, both of which also featured the visage of Carlo Farelli on their front pages. As they strode to the waiting Caravelle, Garrett requested the Embassy man to translate the captions and stories, and, innocently, he did so. Listening to the language of the Danish correspondents in Stockholm—"Italian Savior of Human Hearts," "The Genius Who Has a Heart," "Nobel Laureate in Medicine Arrives in Stockholm in Triumph"—Garrett blanched, and Saralee suffered, seeing the wrath in his twitching features.

Before boarding the jet, Garrett snatched the newspapers from his host, barely remembering to thank him for his kindness, and soon lost himself in his seat. In the hour that they had been aloft since Copenhagen, Saralee observed, he had never once let the newspapers off his lap, and constantly he had returned to them and to Farelli's hateful countenance.

Now Saralee determined to break the spell. "John, you haven't looked around the plane once. Isn't the décor divine? I adore pastel."

Petulantly, Garrett did not lift his head. He had no interest in pastel at the moment.

Saralee would not be put off. "We've still got twenty-five minutes. Why don't you have a drink? I'll have one, if you will. Let's have real French champagne."

"If you insist."

"I'm only thinking what's good for you. Besides, this *is* an occasion. We're almost there. You're going to get the Nobel Prize."

"All right, Saralee, please. In fact, it's a good idea."

She rose from her chair. "You call the stewardess. And no flirting when my back is turned. I've seen them. I'm going to the washroom. I want to look fresh." She crossed into the aisle, bumping his knees, and knocking the newspapers to the floor. "Be right back."

Garrett collected the newspapers, and folded them on his lap once more. He took a cigar from the inside of his coat—cigars were a recent habit, in keeping with his new station—moistened and bit off the tip, and applied his lighter. Puffing discontentedly, he stretched his neck to see what lay outside the window. Nothing met his sight but azure sky. They were at 28,000 feet, he remembered. It only proved that you could be as unhappy close to heaven as on the ground.

He thought that he had heard his name spoken, and rotated his body toward the aisle, past the ball of smoke he had exhaled. He found a serious young lady standing beside his seat, inspecting him. Except for her outlandish hairdo, severe bangs, too girlish, with the remainder of her auburn hair piled vertical in a manner indescribable, she was not unattractive. Her face was young, twenty-five to twenty-eight, he reckoned, and the immediate total impression was that of a hatchet. The bright brown eyes were narrow, the nose an instrument for pecking, the mouth thin and small. Her neck seemed inordinately long, and the effect, created perhaps by the cowl collar of her tweed suit, was that of a woman peeking out of a manhole. The thick suit hid her figure entirely.

"Dr. John Garrett?" she repeated.

"Yes," he replied, shifting, not sure if he was to rise or not.

"I'm Sue Wiley of CN—Consolidated Newspapers, New York."

"How do you do?" he said politely.

"I came into Copenhagen this morning. I was in Berlin on the Spandau Prison story. I'd been assigned to head in your direction—" She indicated Saralee's empty seat. "May I sit down a second?"

"Please do. Wait—" He stood up and moved into Saralee's chair, and allowed Sue Wiley to take his own place.

"I'm doing the big CN Nobel series. I'm sure you've seen the exploitation."

He had no idea what she was speaking about, but he nodded vague assent.

"Fourteen articles, one thousand words apiece," she said. "It'll run for two weeks in fifty-three papers. It's a big one, breaking right after the ceremonies. You're from L.A., aren't you?"

"Pasadena," he said correctly.

"No difference. We'll have outlets in L.A., Frisco, Chicago, New York, anywhere you turn your head. Anyhoo, when I got on this plane, I figured a bunch of nothings and wasted the last hour manicuring my nails. But when the steward was getting me a drink a little while back, he tipped me that there was a Nobel winner on the plane. I could have fallen over. I thought all of you were in Stockholm already."

"No, not really, as you can see," he said cautiously. "As a matter of fact, it is my understanding we're arriving early, as these things go. In past years, most winners came in a few days before the final ceremony. But I'm told, this year, they wanted us earlier. They have a big program."

She blinked her eyes, which he soon learned was with her an unconscious and disconcerting habit, and went on merrily. "My luck, is all I can say, having you cornered here. I wasn't going to get out pencil and pad until tomorrow. But you can save me a lot of time."

"We've only fifteen minutes, Miss Wiley. Wouldn't it be sounder to wait?"

"Mr. Garrett—forgive me, Dr. Garrett—I don't want to boast, but I can make fifteen minutes do like fifteen hours. And it's painless, I assure you."

"What sort of thing do you want to know?"

"From the day one. Not the usual hackneyed platitudes. My byline's going to be on this one, and like I told you, it's a biggie. I want to turn all of you inside out. After all, you've nothing to hide. You know the angle, the Gods as mere mortals. And I'm doing the same with the Nobel crowd. What gives in those smoke-filled rooms? I mean to find out." She unsnapped her purse, preliminary to locating pencil and pad. "Let's plunge."

But, in his own mind, Garrett had made his decision. An unimaginative man outside the laboratory, he was not given to breaking rules. The long letter from the Nobel Foundation, signed by a Count Bertil Jacobsson, had listed precise instructions on handling of the press. While he could speak to the press freely in his native land, it was hoped that once he was on his way to Sweden, and while inside Sweden, he would avoid individual contact with the press as much as possible. If forced to reply to questions while unescorted in Copenhagen or Stockholm, it was hoped that he would make his comments noncommittal and brief. The reason for this advice was that, in past years, statements made carelessly, in unsupervised press interviews, had led to sensationalized stories. With these experiences fresh in mind, the Nobel Foundation had scheduled a series of formal press interviews, for the present winners, in Stockholm on the afternoon of December third. These would be supervised, and the results could be better guaranteed to be favorable.

"I'm terribly sorry, Miss Wiley, but I'm afraid I'm not allowed to talk right now," he said.

Her head swiveled toward him. The eyes blinked furiously. "Are you kidding? Since when are scientists prima donnas?"

"Don't misunderstand me, Miss Wiley," he said quickly. "It's just that I don't want to break the rules."

"What rules?" she challenged.

He tried to explain the strictures placed upon him and his colleagues by the Nobel Foundation.

"Gestapo nonsense," she exploded, when he was through. "They just want to muzzle everyone so the Swede newspapers can get the big breaks. We're Americans—you and I—and we have different principles, don't we? I'll be bending your ear a dozen times. Why not start now? Of course you will—"

Her persistence annoyed him. "No," he said firmly, "I'm afraid not. Tomorrow at the official conference—"

"To hell with that circus." She stared at him. "You really won't co-operate?"

"You make it sound awful."

"It is awful. What happened to freedom of speech? Now, come on, Dr. Garrett, just conversation."

"No."

She snapped her purse shut, too loudly, and sat back, narrow eyes still leveled at him. "You're sure you understand what you're doing? I told you this wasn't the usual handout story. This is a big one, important, personal, behind the scenes." She paused dangerously. "I'd hate to *continue* going to other sources, sources other than yourself, for information about you. I have already, you know. Our bureaus all over the country have pitched in. Quite an eyeful. But I don't like to get it all like that, secondhand. I like to get it straight from the horse's mouth. That's good reporting. That's the way Nellie Bly used to operate." She paused a second time. "You want me to keep getting my material from other sources?"

He shrugged. "I don't know what more to say. I'll cooperate when I can, but not now."

"Okay, Dr. Garrett," she said. She stood up. "But you know, I'll bet Dr. Keller and your group therapy gang wouldn't approve of your behavior."

She smiled a thin smile, wiggled into the aisle, and was gone.

Garrett sat with the disbelieving look of a man who has been handed a grenade two and one-half seconds after the pin has been pulled, and has no place to throw it. His inability to function was total. His brain tried to unscramble the message it had just received. Dr. Keller was a secret. The group therapy sessions were a secret. Garrett had never been sufficiently liberated to discuss his treatment with a soul, except his wife. Who on earth knew of his group therapy? His physician, who had referred him to a psychiatrist, who had referred him to Dr. Keller. And Saralee, of course. But who else? Then he realized that the secret was shared by many: Mr. Lovato, Mrs. Perrin, Mr. Ring, Mrs. Zane, Mr. Armstrong, Miss Dudzinski. Which of them had talked? In what mysterious way had Sue Wiley, or her journalistic network, ferreted out this private information?

He tried to handle the predicament rationally. What did it matter if his group therapy attendance was published? Apparently it had mattered to Sue Wiley and to himself. She had thrown it at him as a threat, a form of blackmail. And he had fielded it as something explosive and destructive. Was it destructive? How would the research staff in Pasadena regard their star, once they knew that he was in group therapy? What would the Nobel Committee think? And the public? Worst of all, what would his archenemy, Carlo Farelli, think? Somehow, it gave Farelli the upper hand by disqualifying Garrett's competence through mental illness—it reduced Garrett's infallibility—it made him less than genius. Would Paré or Harvey or Lister have been in group therapy along with an errant wife, a half-potent actor, and a suffering homosexual? Unthinkable.

He glanced at his watch. Ten minutes remained before Stockholm. He was craven now, and knew it, and did not care, and he was ready for surrender, if that was the price of discretion. He jumped to his feet, just as Saralee came down the aisle from the washroom.

"Where are you going, John?" she asked.

He had no patience for her. "There's a reporter—I promised—I want to talk to her. Sit down and wait."

He brushed past her, trod up the aisle, oblivious of the other passengers, and found Sue Wiley idly staring out the window. She was in the last seat, and, not unexpectedly, as if reserved for him, the chair beside her was vacant. He took it, and she met him with the thin, reptilian smile.

"How sweet of you to come," she said.

"Where did you hear that thing about me?" Garrett wanted to know.

"Group therapy? Oh, we have our sources."

"But where?"

"Now, that's not fair, is it? You know the old adage—newspaper people never reveal the sources of their information. If they couldn't be trusted by informants, they'd never learn half as much as they do. Matter of fact, Mr. Garrett—Dr. Garrett—I was once a cause célèbre in that respect. Right in your fair city. I went to a marijuana party, chock-full of movie stars, and reported it, no names. Your narcotics squad hauled me in and asked for names. I said I'd been invited under the condition no names, and I was sticking to it, and I did. The judge gave me a month, but Consolidated Newspapers and every sheet in the country were up in arms, and I was released after five days. There's your answer."

Garrett substituted self-preservation for pride. "You're not going to publish that—that gossip about my therapy—are you?"

Sue Wiley's reaction was all ingenuous surprise. "I thought most people in psychiatry like to talk about it. That's a signpost of improvement, isn't it? What are you ashamed of, Mr. Garrett?"

"There's nothing I'm ashamed of," he said animatedly. "First of all, it's private, my own business and no one else's on earth. Secondly, it might be misunderstood. The public isn't oriented. They think anyone on the couch—and I'm not on the couch, by the way—anyone like that—is, well, more or less unbalanced, sick."

The wide eyes. "But aren't you?"

"Of course not! I needed some—some advice—that's all. But if you blow this whole thing out of proportion—" He was at a loss for words.

She had the words. "Readers might think you were a screwball? Maybe not to be trusted with that heart transplant routine? Less worthy of sharing a Nobel Prize with Dr. Farelli?"

"All right, something like that, and it's not fair, and you know it. As for Farelli, no one thinks I'm less worthy to share the award than he is. In fact, in many circles, it's believed I should have won the prize myself."

As she listened, Sue Wiley's eyes were more gleaming than before. She smelled something far better, and she wanted to pursue it as quickly as possible. Hastily, she donned a new guise of personality. This one was softer, understanding, all cooperation. "Look, Mr.—Dr. Garrett—what do you think I am, Madame Defarge or something? I'm not out to hurt a great man like you or anyone else. Certainly, I won't mention your private medical history, if you don't wish me to. I only threw it at you to—I guess to show you how thorough we are in our work. If you don't want me to write about your therapy, I won't."

Garrett wanted to kiss this suddenly lovely young lady. "I'd be obliged if you'd forget it."

"Righto. Forgotten. Okay?"

"Thank you."

"I only hoped for a few minutes of your time, to make my stories more accurate."

"I'd be glad to help you in any way, that is, if you don't tattle on me to the Nobel Foundation."

"I told you—we respect our sources."

"Well," said Garrett expansively, relieved, "what kind of stories are you going to write?"

For a fraction of a second, she was tempted to tell him. She was bursting to tell someone. She was proud of the idea, her own, but some inner signal, which she usually ignored, warned her to slow down, take care, and this time she observed it. The success of her series might depend on this crop of Nobel winners. A mistake with one of them, Garrett for instance, might turn them against her, and then her assignment might all be uphill. If she handled the first of them right, it might be her calling card to all the rest.

Her instincts about an assignment, almost infallibly correct, told her that this was the crucial one of her career. But before she could reply to his question about it, she realized that Garrett was on his feet, being introduced by a stewardess to two Swedish gentlemen, fellow physicians, who were eager to have the laureate meet their wives. With an apologetic gesture to Sue Wiley, Garrett asked her leave for a moment, and followed the Swedes down the aisle.

Precious as was their remaining time, Sue Wiley did not resent the interruption. The importance of her new assignment had turned her mind inward, and now she welcomed the interlude to review the circumstances—the triumphal procession through recent years—that had brought her to this turning point.

Sue Wiley, born and raised in that doubtful oasis called Cheyenne, Wyoming, had been the product of loveless parents and their hate-filled marriage. She had grown to adolescence in an atmosphere that was niggardly and penurious. At home she had been unwanted, and at school she had been ignored. Not until her senior year in high school, when she had revealed a gift for composition and journalism, had she known praise and attention. In that period, also, perhaps not by chance, she had read the life of Nellie Bly. Like herself, Nellie Bly had been the product of a small town and had embarked upon a career as a means of self-support. She had exposed the horrible sweatshops of Pittsburgh, had pretended insanity to enter and write about the insane asylum on Blackwell's Island, had found notoriety and $25,000 a year, attired in ghillie cap and plaid ulster, by making a 24,899-mile journey around the world (in the footsteps of Phileas Fogg) in seventy-two days for *The New York World*. For Sue Wiley, encouraged by the success of her high-school compositions, Nellie Bly became her mother, her father, her Deity. For Sue Wiley, the die was cast.

There had been a handful of dim years, hardly remembered any more, as stringer, reporter, rewrite girl, and feature writer, and there had been the opening on Consolidated Newspapers. Here, Sue Wiley had risen almost overnight. She was still only twenty-eight. Her formula had not been unique, but had represented the perfect outgrowth of her character and of the press of her time. Her formula had been juvenile simple: shock by saying nay when all say aye. It would have bewildered her to know that she was less interested in truth than in sensation.

To Sue Wiley, insensitive to all about her, and with her eye on the main chance, the truth was undependable. If you dug for truth, you would uncover no treasure, but instead have dull hard facts, proving nothing, accomplishing nothing. She had been blind to the value of truth, because its rewards were unpredictable. Readers had seemed not to appreciate truth, had even seemed to be discomforted by it. Illumination was not a virtue in itself. It bored and offended. And in the end, who gave a damn? Yourself? Your subject? Yes, perhaps—but the measuring stick for accomplishment was the obscure mass of readers. They wanted variety, gossip, excitement, no matter how superficial. "Make 'em say 'Gee whiz.' " She had once read the command on the bulletin board in a Hearst editorial room, and that was it really, and the devil take the facts. A sound rumor, an apocryphal anecdote, a distorted quotation, a whispered scandal, even if one-half true, or less, was to be preferred to nothing-but-the-truth, if nothing-but-the-truth was an anesthetic. The point was to excite, create talk, sell newspapers.

Sue Wiley was not immoral, but amoral. She was too self-absorbed to anticipate hurt inflicted or wonder about it afterwards. She was not inherently ill-intentioned, even though her technique was often harmful. She was the sum of her culture, and her public, which encouraged and rewarded her and warped her by its own misshapen values.

Sue Wiley perfected her technique by reading biographies. Previously, she had been little addicted to reading, beyond newspapers, but in biographies she tested herself, underlining and copying out what arrested her attention. Her delight was not in learning of Julius Caesar's campaigns but in learning that he wore a crown of laurel to hide his increasing baldness. Napoleon's victories left her cold, but the information that he possessed exceptionally small "reproductive organs" fascinated her. She was not interested in the fact that Francis Scott Key had written "The Star-Spangled Banner," but in the fact that he had no ear for music. And one day was made when she learned that Daniel Webster had been sued for not paying his butcher's bill. In this period, she had also read Dr. William Lyon Phelps's complaint, "Instead of selecting a subject, modern biographers pick a victim. It's getting so that good men are afraid to die." Dr. Phelps's complaint had left her unmoved. She decided that he would have made a poor newspaperman.

Like her idol, Nellie Bly, she had discovered her way—to create news, not wait for it. To electrify the public, and gain its attention. In a thousand editorial rooms, ten thousand reporters, chained to mediocrity and rotting on low salary, bad beer, stale sandwiches, stewed in their daydreams of great beats, and novels, and plays that they would never write. Sue Wiley would not be one of them, and at Consolidated she set out to prove her worth.

The International Red Cross was a sacred cow. Sue Wiley seized upon the 1 per cent of it that was defective, to condemn the entire organization. The Boy Scouts of America were inviolable. Sue Wiley spanked them. Mother's Day was a holy institution. Sue Wiley defiled it. Gradually, she convinced Harold Finnegan, managing editor of Consolidated, to let her expand her target range. On a trip around the world she exposed the lechery aboard luxury cruise vessels, the inadequacy of American embassies, and the graft of numerous customs officials. She also found fault with Tahiti, Israel, Ghana, and Lourdes. On this same trip, she made her best mark. She misused her letters of introduction to Dr. Albert Schweitzer, in Lambaréné, French Equatorial Africa, entirely ignoring the brilliance and selflessness of *le Grand Docteur* during the two hours she spent with him. When she described him later for Consolidated readers, she revealed him solely as an egotistical Teutonic tyrant who inefficiently conducted an unsanitary jungle hospital.

Her salary was larger now, and her reputation with it. What she wanted was one more enormous international killing that would earn her a contract for a syndicate column of her own. "Lowdown on the High-ups," she would call it. And one day after her trip, filing away her Schweitzer notes, she realized that the ex-Olympian had won the Nobel Peace Prize in 1952. This set her mind to thinking of the possible frailty of other Nobel winners and the mysterious aura of sanctity surrounding the prizes in general. Here was humanity's highest reward to its own. The public accepted the judgment of immortality, conferred by a handful of Swedes and Norwegians, without question. The public looked upon the winners themselves as divinities. Yet, had the scalpel of journalism ever been ruthlessly, unsentimentally, applied? Had the judges and the judged ever been thoroughly dissected? Had this hagiolatry ever been defied? What was the truth—Sue Wiley version—behind the Nobel awards?

Bursting with excitement, Sue had bullied the harassed Harold Finnegan into lunching with her in a fashionable bar on Forty-seventh Street. Eyes blinking, words tripping over words, Sue threw out her idea, and Finnegan saw the possibilities at once. He gave her access to Consolidated's bureau heads throughout the nation—within two weeks their copy on the Nobel winners, past and present, filled her New York desk—and he gave her a large expense account and packed her off to Sweden.

Now, after a diversion in Berlin, she was approaching Stockholm in a soundless jet, sitting beside an actual Nobel winner who quaked in her presence, and now Cheyenne was far away, and her future almost secure. This would be the final rung to fame.

With a start, she realized that Garrett was beside her once more, continuing his apologies, but flushed and pleased by his interlude of attention. She tried to remember: what had he asked her before the interruption? What had ignited her inner exploration? Yes, she recalled it. He had inquired about the kind of Nobel stories that she intended to write.

He was chewing his cigar, rather than smoking it, and she was grateful and decided to handle him tenderly.

"As I told you, Dr. Garrett, it's going to be a big series. After all, there is no bigger subject. Everyone wants to know about the machinery of the awards, and the great people who are honored, and I want to tell it all. It'll be highly favorable, of course. Why not? We've researched in depth on all you winners, because we want to transmit complete portraits of human idols, not empty paragraphs about stone gods. I wouldn't write a thing about you that you wouldn't be proud to have your children read."

Garrett did not hide his pleasure. "I'm happy that's your tone. It can be a useful work. It'll inspire a lot of potential scientists. What can I tell you? Do you want to know how I came on the discovery?"

"Another time, perhaps. We can go into it in detail. There was something about a truck driver named—named Henry M.—?"

Garrett leaped at this and, on safe, old ground, began to relate, in sentences smoothed by their frequent repetition, the drama of the historic night. Sue Wiley half listened, poking pencil listlessly at her pad, and surreptitiously following the second hand of her watch. Six minutes and twenty seconds.

The mammalian heart had just been transplanted, and he beamed, and she moved quickly. "Very interesting. I'll want to review all that with you again." Then, almost casually, she laid before him the earlier lead that he had inadvertently given her. "By the way, you and this Italian Farelli, you're cutting up the medical pie, aren't you? How come? Is he a collaborator of yours?"

Garrett was sorely tempted, but this was not Dr. Keller's group. He shook his head. "No. We've never even met."

"Oh, and I thought you worked closely together."

"Absolutely not. I made my discovery alone. In fact, some days ahead of his, if I do say so."

Casually, Sue's hand hooked the shorthand ciphers to her pad, while her blinking, receptive eyes held his own. "Before, you were saying there are people who feel you should have won the prize yourself. Do you think so?"

"It would be improper for me to say." But his prejudice was clear in his face.

"Of course, you will be seeing Dr. Farelli in Stockholm—"

"I would presume so. At least on official occasions."

"Do you intend to—to work out some sort of future research with him? I mean, since you're both—"

"I doubt it," Garrett interrupted. "I have my work and methods, and he

116

has his. However, I do plan to see others in my field, on this trip. One doctor in particular, at the Caroline Institute, in Stockholm. Dr. Erik Öhman. A marvelous young researcher, who is doing transplantation of hearts, and whose ideas are compatible with my own. In a sense, you might say he's a disciple of mine. He was attracted by my papers and corresponded with me, voluminously. He has since successfully accomplished seven cardiac transplants—by the 'Garrett method,' he likes to tell me—and I was recently advised by him that he has three more cases under observation. I'm eager to see what he has done, firsthand, and to make any suggestions I can make. As a matter of fact, if you are hunting for material about me, Dr. Erik Öhman's your man. I think he can speak, with less inhibition, about my work than I can myself. You understand."

Sue Wiley was in no mood to be sidetracked by Dr. Öhman. Perhaps this was evasive action on Garrett's part, although she doubted if he was that clever. Farelli was her boy, and she meant to know more about him, about him *and* Garrett, or him *versus* Garrett. "Very interesting, very interesting," she said. "To get back to Farelli, for a moment. He fascinates me as, apparently, he does the rest of the press. How did he get into your act, anyway? As you said, as I think everyone knows, you were the first to make a successful heart transplant. Isn't it as true in science as in every other field—first come, first served—or, should I put it—first come, first honored?"

"One would think so. But I'm sure, with all your research, you've read Dr. Farelli's statements. He's not given to—to hiding his light."

"You mean, he may have influenced the judges?"

He pretended horror at the thought. "I wouldn't even imply that. It's just that—that his kind of personality—uh—makes itself felt. He's a very colorful man."

She decided to goad him. "You're too modest to defend yourself. I can see that. I can also see that, in these times, the quiet, self-effacing, dedicated scientist, doing his job, doing it magnificently, is often not enough. People are apt to overlook a man like that. They are apt to be swayed by another scientist who is self-seeking, vocal, full of histrionics." She did not ask him if this was so. Brazenly, she assumed that they were in agreement. "It's a shame—isn't it?—how often the public is fooled."

Garrett smiled modestly, warmed by this remarkable young woman's perception. "Yes, it is a shame."

The tin static of the public-address system intruded. They both looked off. One of the stewardesses was speaking. "We will arrive in Stockholm in five minutes. Please put out your cigarettes. Please fasten your safety belts."

There was a rustling among the passengers of the plane. Garrett lifted the palms of his hands helplessly to Sue Wiley. "I guess we ran out of time."

She had what she wanted, and it was enough. In Stockholm, she would learn more, and drive the wedge deeper. "I don't know how to thank you," she said. "Every little bit helps. This gives me a wonderful start. Your first case, that truck driver, will make wonderful telling."

"You're kind," he said.

"And discreet," she added, binding them more closely.

He rose. "I'll see you in Stockholm then."

"I should hope so."

Garrett returned to his seat, and secured his belt. His wife was bewildered at his cheerfulness and good humor.

When the Caravelle touched down on the long runway of Arlanda Airport, braking noisily, a male voice came over the intercom.

"This is your Captain. We have just landed in Stockholm. The local time is exactly twelve thirty-six."

The Garretts were almost the last to leave the jet airplane. They descended the steps, behind the other passengers, and merged into a swarm of people. They shook hands with Count Bertil Jacobsson, with Ingrid Påhl, with Carl Adolf Krantz, and Saralee was effusive over the bouquet of flowers Miss Påhl handed her. They posed for the photographers, while Jacobsson dealt firmly with the Swedish reporters.

They were about to leave for the limousines, when Jacobsson suddenly realized that someone was missing. "Mr. Andrew Craig? Where is he?" Jacobsson tugged Garrett's arm. "The Nobel laureate in literature was on the same plane. Mr. Craig. Did you meet him?"

Garrett shook his head. He had met no one. He did not mention Sue Wiley.

While Krantz and Påhl led the Garretts through the gate to their limousine, Jacobsson rushed among the other passengers, searching for Craig, without any success. At last, he intercepted the ship's Captain, and a stewardess. They produced the passenger list. With Jacobsson, they went carefully down the list of names. There was no Andrew Craig, and there was no Leah Decker.

Utterly baffled, Jacobsson made his way to the waiting cars. He was an old man who lived by plan. Everyone always said that his organizational ability could not be surpassed. This talent was one of his greatest gratifications. The last report, received hours before, had been that Craig was arriving by Scandinavian Airlines, in Copenhagen, at nine this morning. Flight 912, he remembered. The connection for Stockholm was to have been on this plane leaving Copenhagen at 11:20. Could Flight 912 have been delayed? He was certain that he would have been informed. This was a mystery, indeed. It was the first time, in memory, that he could recall a laureate's not arriving as scheduled.

He dismissed the second limousine, and then climbed into the first, taking the jump seat beside Krantz, determined not to worry the renowned Dr. Garrett and wife with his problem.

But all the way back to Stockholm, he wondered what had happened to Andrew Craig.

It was nearly 4:30 in the afternoon when Count Bertil Jacobsson had the answer to his mystery.

Alone of the members of the reception committee, to which a Foreign Office attaché had now been added, he had been impatient during the slow lunch for the Garretts in the Grand Hotel. His anxiety centered on returning to his office at Sturegatan 14, and commanding the telephone, and locating the missing Nobel laureate.

Now, driving his cane nervously into the green carpet of the Foundation reception corridor, he made his way to his telephone. The muffled thud of the cane heralded his arrival, and his secretary, Astrid Steen, materialized in the doorway of the reception office, She held aloft an envelope.

"Telegram for you, sir."

He took it from her, tore it open, and held the mesage before him. The origin, he saw at once, was Copenhagen.

He read the message:

DUE TO CIRCUMSTANCES BEYOND CONTROL HAVE CANCELED FLIGHT TO STOCKHOLM STOP MUST REMAIN IN THIS CITY EN-TIRE DAY STOP AM TAKING NORD EXPRESS TONIGHT AND WILL ARRIVE WITH MY SISTER IN LAW AT EIGHT FORTY FIVE TOMOR-ROW MORNING STOP SORRY IF I HAVE INCONVENIENCED YOU STOP BEST REGARDS ANDREW CRAIG

He heard Mrs. Steen's inquiry. "Anything wrong, sir?"

"No—no—nothing. Mr. Craig has been delayed. He'll be with us in the morning."

He went on into his office, removed his topcoat, and forgot to greet old King Gustaf on the wall.

He settled in the swivel chair behind his deck, flattened the telegram on the ink blotter, and read it again. The mystery had been solved, and yet it was not solved at all. "Circumstances beyond control" had made Andrew Craig cancel his flight. What circumstances? And what kind that were be-yond control?

What in the devil had happened to Andrew Craig, anyway?

Count Bertil Jacobsson had the uneasy, indefinable feeling that things were not going as evenly this year as the last or, for that matter, the year before. The program had not yet begun, and already it was out of line. Jacobsson did not like it. He did not like it at all.

III

The telegram that Count Bertil Jacobsson read in Stockholm at 4:30 had been sent almost five hours earlier, at 11:43 in the morning, from a Danish modern bedroom on the sixth floor of the Tre Falke Hotel in Copenhagen. Although it was signed by Andrew Craig, he had had no part in its creation. It was written and dispatched by Leah Decker, his sister-in-law.

What awakened Andrew Craig from his slumber was Leah's intense, high-pitched voice, in another room, reading the telegram aloud to someone unknown. She read the contents for approval, and the contents were approved. Eventually, Craig would deduce that the person unknown was Mr. Gates, the First Secretary of the United States Embassy in Copenhagen.

Fully aroused from his sleep, Craig tried to familiarize himself with his surroundings. He lay on the black quilt of a daybed, his feet dangling over the edge, in a strange, overwhelmingly citron-colored room, surrounded by severely angled, teakwood furniture, obviously produced in a factory teeming with cubists. The room was efficient, spotlessly clean, lifeless. His suit coat, he realized, had been removed, and his shoes, also. His head throbbed, and his tongue had the leathery consistency of the tongue of a hunting boot. He had been drunk, he supposed, and now he was not quite sober, but sobering badly, and he was thirsty.

He listened to the two voices that came to him through the abbreviated hallway connecting the next room.

A bellboy arrived, and was given the telegram, and instructed to send it off posthaste. Leah worried that, having canceled the flight, they might not obtain a train reservation. Mr. Gates assured her that the train reservation would be forthcoming, and if it was not, there was always another flight. Leah did not want to risk another flight. It was too quick. It would not give her brother-in-law time to rest. He required rest above all else. She implored Mr. Gates to try the Central Railway Station again, and Mr. Gates obliged her. He reminded the reservation desk that he was a representative of the American Embassy, and that two compartments on the Nord Express were sorely needed. There were several pauses, half-uttered phrases, and then it appeared that the compartments had been obtained.

The conversation next door was indistinct, and Craig did not strain to hear it. Suddenly, he heard light footsteps—Leah's, he guessed—and he made an instant decision. He turned his face to the wall, closed his eyes tight, and feigned sleep. As a touch of realism, he simulated labored breathing. Momentarily, he was aware of Leah's unseen presence above him. He heard her sniff twice, clear her throat, and at last, he heard her leave.

When the voices in the next room resumed, this time more distinctly, he opened his eyes once more and listened again.

"He's out cold," Leah was saying. "He'll be out for hours."

"Then we can go?"

"I'm sure it's safe."

"Very well. We'll pick up the tickets at the Central Station. Then we'll lunch at Oskar Davidsen's. If there's time, we can drive out to Elsinore. It's no more than two hours round trip. You're sure Mr. Craig wouldn't want to come along?"

"He's got to sleep this off. Nothing else concerns me. This afternoon, and tonight on the train, will hardly be enough. I just hope the Nobel Foundation won't be put off by the delay."

"They'll be delighted to have you both at any time."

"I hope so."

There was more indistinct talk, and finally movement, and the sound of the door opening and closing.

Andrew Craig lay still. He would give them plenty of time to leave, he decided. Besides, he was too enervated to rise. He wanted the beating in his temples to cease. Given time, it would. Of course, the thirst was distressing. Nevertheless, he would display willpower. He would wait ten minutes. He tried to moisten his tongue against the roof of his mouth, but that was no good, and at last he did so by rubbing his tongue along the inner lining of his cheeks. Ten minutes. He waited.

The couple of weeks in Miller's Dam, before departure, were difficult to recall. The Nobel notification had caught him at the outset of his cycle. After Harriet's death, when he had been recuperating, he had not drunk heavily, no more heavily than when she had lived. It was afterwards—all dressed up and no place to go—wasn't that the old expression?—that whiskey had made each day possible. In the first year, he had drunk blindly, all the time. When the pain had been replaced by conscious emptiness, he had fallen into the cycle. Lucius Mack had told him that it was a cycle. Or had it been Leah? Two weeks drunk and two weeks sober, well, mostly sober. In the last year, it had been three weeks drunk and one week sober, and he had added no more than twenty pages to the meager pile that was entitled *Return to Ithaca*. He had been on his three-week drunk when the notification had come, and he was still on it, he guessed.

It was impossible to recapture more than fragments of the past, no matter how recent, when you had been steadily drinking. The whiskey bottle was the all-inclusive carryall. Into it you could stuff writing, and sex, and hope, and memory, and soak and dissolve them beyond recognition. From the night of the telegram to the morning when he had been driven to Chicago, he could remember almost nothing. Somehow, certain faces were visible, those of Lucius Mack and Jake Binninger, buffers between himself and the outside

122

press; that of Leah, fussing, nursing, complaining; that of Professor Alex Inglis, down from Joliet College, mutely worshipful, mutely imploring.

Yeterday morning—yes, yesterday—Lucius Mack had driven them to Chicago in his station wagon. Leah had been in the best of spirits. She had worn a moss-green knit suit, new, and the black broadcloth coat, new, that Craig had given her as a *bon voyage* gift and her due. (He had not actually bought it himself, but sat in a Milwaukee tavern while Lucius did the shopping and even laid out the money, an advance against the Nobel check.) Not the least of her good cheer was the promise Leah had extracted from Craig the night before, the promise that he would not drink, except socially, until the Nobel Ceremony was ended. These gifts, and the excitement, had served to relax Leah's clenched, Slavic face, and her inflexible body. Her aspect was more feminine, and her pride in him—in the past he had resented it as a subtle pressure—gave him fleeting pride in himself, briefly, briefly, in the way that Harriet had so often given it to him.

The lunch in the Pump Room had been a farewell feast worthy of Lucullus —steadily enlivened by Lucius Mack's moody speculations on the advertising inches he must sell in Miller's Dam to pay for each course—and afterwards they had driven to the airport and entered the Boeing 720 for New York City. What had made the two-and-a-half-hour flight bearable to Craig were the two drinks that he had been permitted in the Pump Room and the two more on the plane. Upon landing, they had been met by Craig's publisher, his agent, and his favorite book-review-page editor, and whisked to a candlelit restaurant, an expensive celebrity haven, and Craig had been miserable. He had been interested neither in the literary talk nor in his future, but only in his desperate need for refreshment. He had been allowed one double Scotch-on-the-rocks, and the mechanics of the occasion made the necessary second and third drinks impossible to obtain. The conspiracy against him was enforced by a publisher who did the ordering and who was determined to see him turn over a new leaf, an agent who had ulcers, an editor who regarded one sherry as daring, and a sister-in-law who hovered over him like an Alcoholics Anonymous convert.

The 7:30 night flight, on the Scandinavian Airlines System jet, the DC-8C, gave more promise of sustenance. Because Leah was satisfied and mellowed, she had joined him in one champagne over Canada and another over Newfoundland, and he had gallantly pressed a third on her (refusing a third himself, and disarming her completely) somewhere early over the Atlantic Ocean. She had taken it and immediately gone off to sleep in her reclining chair, and Craig was saved.

Craig's renown and his mission had preceded him to the airplane, and when he made his way to the lounge to converse and joke with the stewardesses, the *maître de cabine,* and several of the passengers, he was accepted as the party's guest of honor. While the majority of the passengers slept, some fitfully, some soundly like Leah, Craig mounted the cycle. Waving aside the champagne—a come-on for tourists, he announced—he concentrated on

123

Scotch. Through the joyous night, he drank. Into the dawn, come too soon, he drank. Over Scotland and England, he drank.

The fullness of the new day, ashen and remorseful outside the fogged window, found him in his seat, blinds successfully drawn against Harriet and his art, ready for the welcoming oblivion of sleep. The intercom brought the plane, and Leah, awake. Leah hurried to the washroom, and returned with her hair combed back in place, her face stenciled in, and her knit suit unwrinkled.

When she sank down beside him, restored, she asked, "Did you sleep?"

"Won'erfully," he mumbled.

She stretched her neck to the window. "That must be Denmark down there, through the clouds." Without turning from her country-watching, she asked, "Isn't it thrilling?"

"Won'erfully."

When the stewardess announced that there would be no more smoking and that seat belts would be fastened, Craig lighted his pipe and forgot to lock his belt. No one noticed.

They had landed—Leah congratulating herself that they were safe on earth again—and he was shuffling behind her to the plane's exit. As he stepped out on the mobile platform, and tried to find the first step in descent, his jellied knees collapsed. He pitched against the rail, saved from a critical fall by Leah, blocking the way ahead of him, and the strong arms of two passengers.

As she and another assisted him down the stairs, Leah smelled his breath. Her face hardened; the armistice was over.

The rest was sketchy in Craig's memory. Someone, dressed like a butcher on Sunday, had been there to meet them. Black coffee at a counter in the airport. A snatch of Leah's dialogue to their host. "He never drinks. He's not used to it. Everyone's driving him crazy, wanting to treat, celebrating, he doesn't know how to say no. It was too much." And again, at the cash register. "We can't take off in two hours. I can't let them see him in Stockholm this way. He's not like this at all. It would be a disgrace." Then the phone booths, and the host emerging. He had found hotel rooms for them. They had ridden endlessly in someone's automobile. A glossy hotel, with a curved driveway that took them to an entrance that resembled a carport. A busy lobby, reservation counter to the left, elevators to the right. Sixth floor. Right this way, please.

All else, details, were bottled in alcohol. High spirits equal low recall, he told himself. Simple equation.

He sat up on the daybed. More than twenty minutes had elapsed since Leah had left him. He slipped on his shoes and tied them. He found the bathroom and doused his face with cold water, and wet his hair and combed it. He undid his necktie and made it over again. He pulled on his dark gray suit coat and went into Leah's room. It was an identical twin to his own. One suitcase was open and the rest, still strapped, on the floor.

He returned to his room for his trench coat, and then realized that there was a note pinned to the chair beside the daybed. He yanked it free and read it:

ANDREW. In case you should wake up before I return, I have gone out for lunch with a man from the American Embassy. We had to cancel the airplane to Stockholm because you were drunk. We rented rooms in this hotel for you to rest, and are taking a train to Sweden tonight for the same reason. I'll be back by five. Do behave. LEAH.

He studied the letterhead. He was a guest of the Tre Falke Hotel, 9 Falkoner Alle, Copenhagen.

He crumpled the note into a ball, dropped it into the wicker wastebasket, and went out to the elevator. After pressing the button, the wait was interminable. He took out his briar, and by the time it was smoking, the elevator door had opened. It was self-service and carried him downward without a stop.

He inquired of a bellboy for the bar, and the beardless young man led him through the lobby, bearing left, and pointed. The curved horseshoe of a counter, before the dining room, was uninhabited except for the blond, chinless young man, in black suit and white apron, behind it.

As Craig approached, he saw the bartender watching him closely. He lifted himself onto a stool.

"Double Scotch-on-the-rocks."

The bartender hesitated. "Pardon, sir. Are you Mr. Craig, Rooms 607 and 608?"

"Yes."

"I'm terribly sorry, sir. I have strict orders not to serve you."

Craig was more surprised than angry. "How did you know me?"

"Your wife described you, sir."

"She's not my wife."

"The lady, then. She said you were seriously ill—beg your pardon—and the physician's orders were—no drinks."

"Are you out of your mind? This is a public bar. I'm a public customer. I want a drink. Now, please oblige me."

The chinless bartender wavered, but stood fast. "We could be sued, sir, if you fell ill. The hotel rules allow us to serve guests at our discretion. It's posted in your room, sir."

Craig's fury was not with this fool but with Leah. He wanted no argument. He wanted a drink. "Okay, buddy. I'm not sick, and she was kidding you, but we'll let it go." He stood up. "Make it one, then—one shot—for the road. No one'll see."

The bartender hesitated. His only desire, obvious in his expression, was that his customer leave quietly. He nodded, pulled a bottle and a shot glass from under the bar, and filled the glass. "I shouldn't," he said, and pushed the glass at his customer.

Craig downed it in a single swallow. The fluid, moistening his mouth, burning his throat, heating his chest, revived him. "What do I owe you?"

"Nothing, sir." He made his solemn joke. "Remember, you didn't have a drink."

Craig smiled bitterly. "Best drink I never had." He slipped off the stool. "Where's downtown?"

"Twenty minutes away, sir. It's called Raadhusplads. The middle of everything. You can't miss it. You'll find taxis in front here, or you can take the regular buses. Don't forget to change dollars into kroner."

"Thanks, pal."

In the lobby, adjacent to the reception desk, he found the female money-changer with her adding machine. He gave her a twenty-dollar bill, received a handful of kroner, stuffed the Danish money into his wallet as he studied the American, English, German, and French newspapers and magazines at the newsstand, and then went outside.

The day had brightened, but the air was cold. He saw several parked cars in the area ahead, but not a single taxi. He waited, and then approached the doorman, who was busy conversing with a drably clothed porter.

"Where's the bus?" Craig inquired.

"Bus?" echoed the doorman. "Ah yes, yes, the motor coach." He pointed off. "There. It is soon to leave."

Craig thanked him and strode hurriedly to the large blue-and-white bus that stood in the driveway before a cavernous motion picture theater. He climbed into the bus.

The squat, bespectacled driver, polishing the huge wheel with a lint cloth, greeted him with a nod. "Ticket, please."

"I didn't know."

"It is all right to pay—"

Craig extracted his wallet, pulled free a wad of Danish bills, and offered them trustingly. The driver selected several, and handed Craig his change.

Turning to the interior of the bus, Craig saw that it was almost filled, preponderantly with young Scandinavian women. He made his way to the rear, and eased into a tight seat that left little room for his legs.

In a few minutes, the bus engine sputtered and caught. The gears ground. The bus lumbered out of the driveway, wheeled right for two blocks, then wheeled left into a business thoroughfare, and moved forward.

Craig had never seen Copenhagen before. When he and Harriet had taken their six-month honeymoon after the war, they had leisurely made their way to Göteborg by steamer, spent one week in Stockholm, flown to Amsterdam, and taken the train to Paris. They had not wanted to leave Paris, even after six weeks, but had finally rented a Citroën and driven to San Sebastián, down to Madrid, up to Barcelona, then to Nice, stopped at Spezia, defied the mountain paths, and made their way down the road to Rome. Later, they had driven north to Milan and Berne, and then released their Citroën in Paris. Sailing home, they had been full of the wonders of the Grand Tour, and nightly spoke of returning the following summer. But life had closed in on them, and they had never returned, not together, and here he was, in Copenhagen, alone, and he did not look out the window because he did not give a damn.

He heard a crackle overhead, and then the driver's voice on the loudspeaker. "Welcome, everyone, to our daily winter Copenhagen tour," the driver announced professionally. "It is one-thirty P.M. The tour is of three hours' duration. It will end at City Hall Square—what we Danes call Raadhuspladsen—at four-thirty P.M. There will be five stops and visits on the tour, to accommodate camera fans. These will be at Grundtvig's Church, Gefion Fountain, the Little Mermaid in Copenhagen harbor, the Langelinie, and Amalienborg Castle. Among the other highlights of historic interest—"

Comprehending at last, Craig was appalled. He realized that he was not on an ordinary city bus. He had stupidly stumbled into a sight-seeing motor coach. His first impulse was to pull the emergency cord, or accost the driver, explain his mistake, and request that he be dropped off at the next red light. But then he realized that there was no reason to create a disturbance. His destination was merely a bar, any bar anywhere, and this ridiculous conveyance could bring him to one as swiftly as any other.

Despite his discomfort, and his thirst, he was still reasonable enough to be amused. He would soon establish, he decided, the world's freestyle record for being the most briefly seated tourist in the annals of Danish sight-seeing.

The ride seemed endless, but as last they braked to a halt. The loudspeaker announced, "Amalienborg Castle, the eighteenth-century residence of the King and Queen. The passengers may step outside." There was a mass rising and crush to the front doors. The passengers spilled out. Hopefully, Craig followed them.

Outside, the young ladies clustered about their driver-guide. Craig heard the introduction of the spiel—"The royal palaces are among the best representations, in Europe, of the rococo style"—and he drifted away. He searched about him. He was at the boundary of a great square, entirely hemmed in by four towering palaces, each looking exactly like the others. Royal guardsmen, bearskin hats perched atop their heads, stood sentry duty. Nowhere in sight was there a building resembling a bar, a saloon, a tavern.

Craig's good humor crumbled. He felt as frustrated as any character that he had ever met in Kafka. Scanning the arid scene again, he became aware of someone else who had separated from the other tourists and was now crouched a few yards from him, focusing her camera—it resembled Leah's Rolleiflex—on the royal guardsmen. Picture taken, she stood up and gravely concentrated on rolling the film.

Hastily, Craig approached her. He could see, at once, that she was a young girl, looking no more than twenty-one. A white pancake hat was tilted precariously on her head, her silken gold hair tumbling down to her shoulders. A thick, oversized, coral sweater, unbuttoned in front, covered her white blouse and the upper portion of her pleated navy-blue skirt. When Craig reached her, he saw that she was no higher than his chest.

She looked up at him with surprise. Her face was broad and pretty. The eyes were light blue, with laugh wrinkles at the outer corners, the nose was straight and wide, the cheeks shaped high and bony (as Harriet's had been), and the chapped lips full and crimson. The dark dot of a beauty mark, to the right of the upper lip, drew one to the partially open mouth and even white teeth.

Craig was conscious of the girl's appeal, and impatient and annoyed with it, for his mind was on more important matters.

"Pardon, Miss," he said. "I'm one of the passengers on the tour—"

She nodded.

"I just wondered—I wonder if you could tell me—is there a bar anyplace in the vicinity?"

"A bar? You mean, the self-service restaurant?"

"No—no—a place to drink—have drinks—whiskey."

"Oh." She waved at the palaces. "This is Amalienborg."

"I *know*."

"There are no beverage places."

"But somewhere near?"

She shrugged. "I am not familiar with this square. Maybe later." Suddenly, she smiled with a conspirator's enthusiasm. "I will show you when I see one."

"I'd be much obliged."

He stuffed his chilled hands into the pockets of his trench coat, lifted his shoulders into a hunch, and trudged back to the bus. When he entered it, he observed that she was watching him. He hoped that she would keep her word.

For Craig, the motor coach tour proceeded from tedium to monotony to boredom. The driver's soporific phrases flattened against his ears but did not penetrate. He sat cramped in his chair, waiting, as the Ny-Carlsberg Glyptotek ("French and Danish paintings"), the Police Headquarters, Frederiksberg Castle ("officers' training school"), the Zoological Gardens, Nyboder ("built three hundred years ago by King Christian IV") came into his vision, registered dully, and passed away again.

Once more they halted, and left the coach, and stood in a semicircle about the driver, at the edge of the harbor, facing the statue of a mermaid on a boulder. Craig, shifting his weight from one foot to the other, remained at the rear, huddled inside his trench coat, desperate for the one warmth that he desired.

Someone tugged at his sleeve. He turned his head, and she was below him, white pancake hat on golden tresses. Her broad smile was engaging, and her coral sweater was still unbuttoned in defiance of the low temperature. Hearty little mermaid, he told himself. But then he saw that she must feel the chill, for the nipples of her breasts had hardened and were now visibly outlined through her white blouse. For the first time, he noticed the size of her breasts, pressing her blouse outward so that the pearl buttons were strained to the breaking point.

She gestured off. "There."

His sight followed the direction of her finger, and he saw a cluster of shops.

"You will find it cozy in the nearest one," she added.

He started to touch his hat in thanks, but stopped when she winked, to remind him of conspiracy, and then he watched her return and join several girls in the crowd.

Purposefully, he strode away, crossing the street, and entering the first shop. There was a bar, and there were several tables and chairs, and no more. A stout woman appeared from the kitchen, wiping her hands on a towel. He asked for a double Scotch in a hurry. She did not understand English. He surveyed the array of bottles behind her and jabbed his finger at a bottle of Ballantine's. She beamed, brought down the bottle, and started to pour, when he held up his hand, and did a pantomime to indicate that he wished to pour himself and to have the bottle remain on the counter.

He had three shots in a row, as the proprietress watched and counted from a dark recess, before he realized that there was no necessity for haste. He had all day. He filled the midget glass a fourth time, his muscles now eased by the liquor, and this drink he sipped slowly, pleasantly.

He heard the door open, and the jangle of the bell above it, and twisted to greet a fellow member of the club. He knew at once that it was she, white pancake hat still tilted on the golden head.

"The coach is leaving," she called. "They are holding it up, waiting for you!"

He knew, immediately, that he could not desert the foreign legion. It was almost un-American. Bad propaganda. They were *all* waiting for *him*. If he refused to rejoin them, chose to remain in a tavern instead of continuing the tour, it would be a move calculatedly anti-Danish, and set back the work of the White House a decade of years. It distressed him to conform, but the obligations of an American abroad weighed heavily upon him. Also, he was a little drunk.

"Coming," he said.

He downed the fourth drink, splashed a fifth into the glass and took it in a big gulp, and then emptied his wallet. The stout woman separated her due. He pushed an extra bill toward her—for hospitality—scooped up what remained, stuffed it in his coat pocket, and followed the golden blonde to the bus.

This time they sat together, she at the window and he with his lank legs in the aisle, in the last two seats.

The major need of his body had temporarily been fulfilled, and now he was able to study her with detached clarity. The broad face had large spaces of open beauty. Every feature was set apart from the others, without crowding, like well-placed works of art in a superior gallery. Yet the final effect was a blending to achieve a single effect—Nordic perfection, yet curiously un-Nordic in its softness and lack of aloofness and easy smile. Nothing artificial marred the face, except fresh lipstick to hide the chapped lips, and possibly the beauty mark above the corner of the mouth.

"Is that beauty mark real?" he asked.

They had been driving a half hour, and for most of the time, she had gazed out the window to match sights to the loudspeaker's captions, and only occasionally had she smiled at him. Now she turned from the window.

129

"Of course it is real. What do you think?"

"Sometimes women wear them for effect."

"I do not need such effects." There was no arrogance in her speech, only practicality.

"I don't think so either," he hastily agreed. "You're very pretty." Then he added, "And—you're very kind."

She did not acknowledge this, but stared at his eyes until he blinked. "Why did you need to drink?" she asked.

The directness of the question startled him. He had never been asked that before. "I've been ill," he said. There were a hundred answers, and digressions, and involutions, but in the end they came to that anyway.

She nodded, satisfied. "That is what I thought," she said. "Are you happy now?"

"Better."

"I am glad for you."

Craig was enchanted. For the first time in months, he was interested in someone outside himself. "I was going to apologize," he said, "but maybe now you understand. You see, I had nothing against seeing this city—nothing against your country—"

"This is not my country," she said. "I am Swedish."

"I didn't know—"

She smiled. "All Scandinavian girls look the same in the dark. It is a naughty expression I once heard from an English boy. You are not English? American?"

"That's right."

"What place?"

"Wisconsin."

"Is that near California?"

"Far from it. It is between California and New York, a state—a province, you could call it—on the Great Lakes."

"Ah, Chicago."

"Nearby."

"There are not really gangsters there?"

"Not like in the movies, no. But there are some. And cowboys and Indians, too, but only some. Mostly there are people, just like in Sweden. Where are you from in Sweden?"

"Stockholm. It is lovely."

"I know."

"You have been to Sweden?"

Craig nodded. "Yes, long ago." He wanted to change the subject. "What are you doing here?"

"Winter holiday for one week," she said. "Last year, my girl friends and I went to Dalarna for the sports."

"What did you do?"

"Skate, ski, bobsled. This year, they wanted to see Denmark. It is fine, but

I prefer Sweden. I like sports more than cathedrals and palaces and statues. I like to do things more than to see."

He hardly heard her, so intent was he on her face. "I know who you look like," he said suddenly. "I knew I'd seen you before."

"Who?"

"There was an oil painting by Anders Zorn. I saw it in Stockholm the last time. A young girl standing on a rocky ledge—she is nude—her golden hair, reddish actually, is blown from behind so that it is in her face—absolute repose as she stands looking over a blue river—"

"Maybe I posed for it," she said teasingly.

"I think you were only a gleam in your grandmother's eye. Zorn painted it in 1904. Do you like Zorn?"

"I have never heard of him," she said simply.

An earth nymph, he thought, an apparition of the present, no past, no burden of history and knowing, an unaging sprite. His own bondage to his history made him ache in envy of her.

He realized that the motor coach had stopped, and that the passengers ahead were filing out of the doors.

"Strøget," she said. "It is the main street. It is not a regular visit, but fifteen minutes to shop for souvenirs."

She stood up, patting her pleated skirt. He rose above her.

"Do you want souvenirs?" he asked.

"Not specially."

"Have a drink with me."

She considered him, her expression solemn. "You will be drunk."

"Yes, I will."

"Is it important to you?"

"Yes."

"Why do you wish my company?"

There were several answers to this, several dishonest, and several honest and flattering. "I drink more slowly in company," he said.

She laughed. "It is the best reason you could give." She emerged from the seats, and smiled up at him. "Very well." She preceded him into Strøget.

They walked side by side through the busy street, bumping and pushing past shoppers, until they emerged into a vast, vehicle-crowded square, and this was Raadhuspladsen.

She pointed across his chest. "Over there is the Palace Hotel. It is where my friends and I had drinks the first night. It is comfortable."

"The Palace Hotel it is, then."

They made their way slowly, for a block, and then went inside the Palace foyer. Craig had the impression of an old, aristocratic place, quiet and undemanding, and he was pleased with her taste.

"There is the Winter Garden," she was saying, "or a nice friendly room in there to the left."

"What do you prefer?"

"The friendly one."

They passed through an outer room, and into the bar, staid aged wood and grave, a retreat where you think of roaring fireplaces, and they were led to a booth secreted behind a pillar, and there they sat across from each other.

She had what he had, except that she had one single and he had two doubles, and he had not failed his cycle, after all.

A half hour had passed when he glanced at his watch. "We've missed the motor coach, you know."

"Yes, I know."

"Won't your friends be worried?"

"Why? I am not a child."

"How old are you?"

"Twenty-three."

"I don't suppose you're married?"

"No. Are you?"

He saw her glass was empty, and summoned the waiter, ordering a single Scotch for her and a double for himself.

"I was married," he said, finally. It was less difficult when he was becoming drunk. "She died—was killed—three years ago. It was an auto accident. I was driving. I'd been drinking. I suppose you could say it was my fault."

"No one kills anyone like that. It was an accident."

"It was raining. I couldn't control the car."

"It was an accident," she repeated.

He nodded, befuddled by the drinks. "Are you sure you won't miss the sight-seeing tour?"

"I told you I dislike cathedrals. I like to do things."

"This isn't exactly winter sports."

She smiled. "Just as exhilarating."

The drinks were served, and when Craig took his, he ordered another double to follow quickly.

"I'm almost forty," he said.

" 'Almost' means you are thirty-nine. Why do you not say you are thirty-nine?"

"I feel like forty-fifty-sixty. All right, I'm thirty-nine. Why are you with someone who is thirty-nine? That's like sight-seeing, visiting an old historic place."

"You are funny."

"Why did you come with me? Are you playing mother—sorry for me?"

"Why should I be sorry for you?"

"I dunno. Why'd you come?"

"I find it is fun to be with you. I like fun, and so I am here."

This evaluation of himself—fun giver—was beyond Craig's power to grasp or believe.

"You're kidding me."

"Kidding? Oh—like joking? No. Why do you hold yourself so low?"

"Do I? Yes, I do. You're good for me. I should wear you like a charm."

He held up the remnants of his drink, and the new drink arrived. "What do they say in your country—?"

"Skål."

"Skål to you."

He finished the drink, and went immediately to the fresh glass.

"What is the time?" she asked.

"Fourish."

"I must return to my hotel. I have not packed. I go back to Stockholm tonight."

"I will take you." He downed his drink, and paid the waiter, and held on to her arm as they made their way through the hotel and outdoors.

In the taxi, she said, "How do you feel?"

"Drunk. Good. Drunk and good, and good and sleepy."

"I am happy. I will leave you at your hotel first. What is it?"

"No, thass not right. Awright. Tre somethin'—Falke."

The taxi was reckless, and fast, and in less than twenty minutes they drew up before the Tre Falke Hotel.

"Won' you come in?" he asked thickly.

"No. I want you to rest."

"Yes."

He stepped out of the taxi, aided by the doorman, and then freed himself, and came back to the open door.

"What is your name?" he inquired meticulously.

"Lilly Hedqvist."

"What?"

"Lilly."

"I'm Andrewss—Andrews—Andrew Craig—C, R, I, G—Craig."

"Pleased to meet you, Mr. Craig."

"Pleased, too."

Only after she had been driven off did he remember that he had not paid for the taxi, for himself or for her, and he did not know her hotel and could not remember her name, except Lilly.

He walked stiffly to the elevator, and inside punched the sixth-floor button. When the elevator opened, he found the room, the key in his pocket, opened and closed the door. He pulled off his trench coat, and suit coat, felt his way to the daybed, yanked off his shoes, and dropped back on the bed into wondrous oblivion.

How long he slept he did not know—it was more than three and a half hours, he would later learn—but the first consciousness he had was that of being shaken by someone. He opened his eyes, and above him the face was Leah's.

"Are you all right?" she was asking anxiously.

His mouth was dry again, and his eyes were being pinched by something behind them. He felt all right.

"I'm fine," he said, and he sat up.

"You've slept nine hours. Do you know where you are?"

"Of course I know. I got up to go to the bathroom and found your note."

"It's almost eight. The train leaves at seven minutes after nine. Mr. Gates is going to drive us. Do you want a sandwich?"

"No."

She looked at him wearily. "How you abuse yourself. I had to change the reservation, you know."

"Thank you, Leah. I'd better clean up."

They arrived at the hangarlike Central Railway Station with fifteen minutes to spare. Trailing their porter to the Nord Express, Craig halted briefly at a vendor's white wagon to buy some peanuts and an American digest magazine. At their *wagon-lit,* a short, affable conductor, holding a clipboard, checked their names and took their passports.

Once in the car, Craig found their luggage divided between two adjoining rooms, compartments 16 and 17, and saw that the beds were made up, and that there was no place to sit.

Going into the aisle again, he pulled down a window for Leah and one for himself. Gates was below them, on the platform, a Foreign Service smile, like an Embassy pennant, flying from his face. Leah thanked him for lunch and dinner, and Elsinore, and Gates insisted that the pleasure was all his.

He seemed more eager to speak to Craig. "We're all mighty proud of you, Mr. Craig. We'll be looking for every word about the Nobel ceremonies."

"We appreciate all you've done," said Craig. "When I have time, I'll write the Ambassador and recommend a promotion."

Gates depreciated his services with a modest shake of his head. "Don't even think of it," he said. "One thing that would mean a lot, though—my wife, Esther, she's a fan of yours like I am. We'd certainly treasure an autographed copy of your next novel."

Brother, it'll be done in time for your grandchildren, Craig wanted to tell him. But he was almost sober, and fixed on being gracious. "I'll remember that," he said.

"I'll make a note of it, Mr. Gates," added Leah firmly.

Craig had already tired of leaning on the half-open window. "Is there a lounge or diner on this train?" he inquired.

"I'm sorry," Gates called up, "but European trains don't have lounges. One of their major barbarisms. If your room is made up, you can pull down the little folding seat in the aisle and read—"

Craig had almost forgotten. The folding seat was at his knees.

"—and as for a diner," Gates continued, "this train doesn't carry one. They figure everyone has eaten, and you'll be in Stockholm at a quarter to nine in the morning, in time for breakfast. But I'll tell you what, Mr. Craig—if you're hungry—in fifteen minutes, fifteen minutes after you leave here, they'll be loading these cars on the Malmö ferry. It's a seventeen-mile water crossing to Sweden and usually takes about two hours. You can get off this wagon-lit while you're on the ferry, and if you poke around, you'll find two or three places to eat. That should do it."

"Imagine," said Leah, "a train on a ferry. I can hardly wait."

"It's an experience," said Gates. He looked off. "They're buttoning up. I think you're about to go."

"Thanks for everything," said Craig. He closed his window and went into his compartment, leaving Leah to conduct the last farewell. He sat on his bed, taking in the rich, worn brown wooden walls of the small room. He filled and lighted his pipe, and a moment later, the Nord Express was moving. Leah came to his open door. "We're on our way," she said.

"Thank God."

"Aren't you the least bit excited?"

"Only about getting that fifty grand."

"How can you be so—so commercial about it?"

"What do you want me to say, Leah? I'm no schoolboy."

"It's the greatest honor in the world."

"So I'm honored. I also know I haven't written a book in some years. I feel I'm taking the prize under false pretenses."

"Don't say that. I've been reading a biography of Alfred Nobel. It says he thought of the prize in literature to help young or middle-aged writers continue doing idealistic work—"

"Well, I'm afraid your Alfred Nobel made a poor investment this time."

Leah reacted with exasperation. "Why do you always run yourself down, Andrew?"

He looked up sharply. He remembered that the Swedish girl with the golden hair had used almost the same words to him earlier in the day.

"I'm not running myself down," he said defensively. "I simply have a realistic evaluation of my worth—and my future."

"I hope you won't carry on like this in Stockholm. They think a lot of you, and they'll be expecting more than this."

He felt fretful, in no mood for advice from his sister-in-law. "I promise you, Leah dear, I'll be the model of a literary giant in Stockholm."

"Don't joke."

"I'm not. Watch and see."

She was about to leave him. "We should be on the ferryboat soon. Are you going to eat?"

"I don't know."

"If you do, take me along. I'd like to be with you."

Sure, nurse, you'll be with me, in a pig's eye you will, he told himself. "Okay, Leah," he told her, "I'll knock if I go out."

After she had left, and he heard her door and the rattle of clothes hangers in the next compartment, he went into the aisle. He stared out the window at the strings of light in the distance, and his throat and belly twitched in their need for drink. At last, he shoved down the folding seat, and sat on it sideways, stretching his legs and smoking. He wondered why, in the first place, he had not told Leah to go to hell, and packed a suitcase filled with whiskey so that there would not be this problem. Perhaps it was the fear of losing her—although this seemed unlikely—and loneliness appeared more terrifying than sobriety. Perhaps it was something altogether different. People lived by miniature milestones: on this holiday you would begin a diet, on this birthday you would begin economy, on this New Year's Day you would begin a program of work. These were the little rejuvenations, game symbols, artificial hopes, with which people deluded themselves. In an effort to break free of his bondage to the bottle, to leave behind inertia and defeat, he had seized upon the Nobel award as such a turning point. One half-drunk night, after the telegram, he had made himself believe that he would travel to Stockholm sober, accept the award sober, and after, undertake his responsibility as a recently absentee member of the human community sober.

But now he saw, lucidly, the fallacy of the dream. There was no reason on earth not to drink. What mattered it a damn if he went to Stockholm sober and received the award sober? What mattered it if he renewed his subscription to the human race, worked, voted, gave parties, attended them, read, fished, loved? For what, for whom? The argument for permanent euphoria, alcohol-induced, made better sense. It was the medicine man's good medicine for driving away the spirits of Harriet missing and Harriet guilt, of books unwritten, of life promise unused.

The train was no longer moving. Outside the window, there stood a small-town depot, a rail siding, yellow lights, and bundled Danes. The train jolted forward, and then again, and once more. Craig rose, allowing his folding seat to jump against the wall with a bang, and he opened the window. The blast of cold air made him shiver, but he held his place. Not until he saw the railing, and gleam of water behind it, did he realize that they were boarding the Malmö ferryboat.

Again a metallic shudder, and the train was stationary. Quietly, Craig passed Leah's compartment, walked down the aisle to the end of the wagon-lit. The conductor helped him to the tight boat deck. Pressed between the train, suddenly large above him, and wooden cabins to his right, he felt claustrophobic and oppressed. He had forgotten his trench coat, and the night air coming through his suit was like a sheet of ice.

"Where can I get a drink to warm up?" he asked the conductor.

"Stairs to the upper deck," said the conductor. "Restaurant and drinks in the first-class dining room. At the prow."

"Do we have two hours?"

"One hour and fifty minutes. You must return in one hour and fifty minutes."

With the conductor, he backed against the train as a stream of people, all in heavy coats and sweaters, pushed through to the boat stairs. There was a tall woman with a long cigar in her mouth. There were raucous adolescents, most of them smoking cigarettes. There were well-dressed men.

"Who are they?" Craig asked. "Are they on the train?"

"Oh, no. Our express train is from Paris," said the conductor. "The others, they are all down from the waiting room upstairs. The young ones are vacationing, the Swedish returning to Sweden from their holiday, and the Danish leaving for Sweden to begin their fun. The older people go back and forth on business."

Craig fell in behind the crowd, and climbed the metal steps to the top, where a door kept opening and closing. He went through it to find himself on the windy top deck of the ferry, a deck crowded with travelers, Danes and Swedes sitting on benches, standing in groups, walking, all giving off laughter and commotion.

The boat had begun to churn and creak, as he elbowed through the thickly packed deck. An illuminated sign ahead indicated the first-class restaurant, and Craig fought his way toward his goal. One glass door led into a vestibule, comforting as a decompression chamber after the force and stress of the outer cold and the milling passengers, and the second glass door led into an immense, newly decorated dining hall. There were tables and chairs everywhere, but few of them occupied. Immediately to his left, Craig saw a circular counter, with a great array of smorgasbord sandwiches, and sweet cakes behind it. Waiting in attendance were a gray-haired Dane and a thin young woman, both in uniforms.

Craig went to the counter. "I was told I could get a drink here."

"Coffee or tea?" the gray-haired man asked.

"Scotch."

"Whiskey?"

"Yes. Make it a double—two shots—on ice. No soda. Better serve two drinks, both two shots." This needed an explanation. "I'm expecting someone," he added.

The ferry was rolling slightly, and he walked, legs apart for equilibrium, to a table beside a port window. Through it, he was unable to see Sweden, but saw only the prow of the boat beneath, and the reflection of the boat's lights in the water.

Presently, both drinks were served, one before him, and one across from him. His need was terrible, and he emptied the first glass as if he were drinking water. He exchanged it for the glass across from him, and drank that one more slowly. When he was done, he felt in harmony with his surroundings, and he felt relaxed. The glow of the Scotch was high in his head, and, for the first time, Stockholm and what it held for him seemed more probable. Yet he was not sufficiently disarmed to forget the danger that lay ahead. The black night lay ahead, and he had no wish to think.

The gray-haired waiter was nearby, setting a table, and Craig signaled him. "Do you sell bottles on the ferry?"

"Not as a practice, sir."

"I'm on the Nord Express. We're having a little party. I wonder if you could accommodate me?"

"I'd have to take it out of our stock. What do you prefer?"

He tapped his glass. "The same. Any brand."

"I'll see what we can spare."

Waiting, Craig stoked his pipe, and absently scanned the room. He saw her before she recognized him. She was still wearing the white pancake hat on her golden hair, a white blouse strained by her bust, and the open coral sweater. The skirt was different. Navy blue had been replaced by something gray, woolen, and fuller. She stood inside the glass door, tentatively, impermanent, seeking someone.

He leaped to his feet and crossed the dining hall toward her. Only when he was within a few yards of her did she recognize him.

"Hello," he said with real pleasure. For the life of him, he could not recall her name.

"I am surprised, Mr. Craig." She extended her hand formally, and he shook it. "I do not think you remember my name. I am Lilly Hedqvist."

He grinned. "I don't think I was in condition to remember your name. Now I won't forget it."

"I've been looking for my friends. They must be downstairs in the second-class café."

"Won't you have a drink with me first?"

As he spoke, his eyes had gone past her, through the glass door to the outer deck door, to fix on Leah Decker. She was holding the deck door open, standing half in the vestibule, half on the deck, searching behind her for some sign of her quarry.

The sight of her galvanized Craig. He gripped Lilly's arm so firmly that she winced. "We can't stay here. Come with me. I'm trying to get away from someone."

Swiftly, he propelled her around the circular counter, and almost pushed her out the opposite door.

"Where can we hide?" he implored.

"I don't know."

"Follow me."

He went out on the deck, with Lilly behind him. Temporarily, the drinks fortified him against the icy air. He peered down the deck, apparently discovered something, grabbed Lilly's arm, and guided her to the sign over the second-class lounge. They entered. All the chairs and sofas were taken. They stood against a darkened wall.

Lilly's concern was in her eyes. "What is the matter? Are you a criminal?"

"Nothing so romantic. I have a guardian."

"What is that?"

"My sister-in-law. She's on this trip to look after me. She disapproves of drunkards. She's an amateur reformer. When we were standing back there, I saw her on the hunt. I don't want her to find me."

"Why are you afraid of a relative?"

He tried to find an answer for her but could not. "Christ, I don't know why I'm afraid." He glanced about. "This *is* second-class, isn't it?"

"Yes."

"She's too snooty to look here the first time around. But she will the second time. Look, honey, will you do me a favor?"

"What?"

"It's a long night ahead on that train—I'm on the Nord Express—"

"So am I."

"What room?"

"No, it is the second-class compartment in front, for six. We sit up."

"You can use my bed. I'll find somewhere—"

"No. I am with my friends. I can sleep anyplace. What is the favor?"

"Just before you came, I ordered a bottle of Scotch—whiskey—in the restaurant. I need it. I thought—"

"I'll get it for you."

He handed her the last of his kroner. "Go with God."

After she had gone, he leaned against the wall, smoking nervously, waiting, and ever watchful for the appearance of Leah. After five minutes, Lilly returned. She was holding a package that made no pretense of being anything but a bottle.

He accepted it from her, with the change. "I could kiss you," he said. "Do you still want to look for your friends?"

"You offered me a drink," she said.

"Offer still stands. But where?"

Her smooth brow furrowed, and then cleared. She smiled, pleased with herself. "I know where to hide."

"You've been on this boat?"

"No, but my friends have. Follow me. It is a strange place."

He followed her from the lounge to the windy deck. She waited, while he examined the area for Leah. He nodded. She took his hand, and skillfully guided him through the groups of passengers, and then led him down the metal steps to the lower deck. The wagons-lits stood high and immobile. The place was dank and raw and desolate of life. She released his hand and hurried ahead. He strode behind her. They emerged fully into the dark, open prow of the ferry. Parked in front of the train were two rows of four automobiles each.

They stood, shivering, and she waved gaily at the vehicles. "Which will you have?"

"I don't get you."

"The business people drive and take their autos on the ferry. It is too cold to remain in their autos for two hours. The owners go upstairs. The autos are empty. Pick one. It is a perfect place to hide."

"Well, I'll be damned," he said. He joined the fun. "What is my lady's preference?"

"The Volvo."

It was a Swedish runt of a sedan in the middle of the first row, concealed by the darkness and the other vehicles, but nonetheless exposed to the wind. He preceded her, tugged open the front door, and assisted her inside. His teeth chattering, he hugged his package, circled the car, and got in behind the wheel. Only one window was open, on the driver's side, and he rolled it up.

"Sealed tight," he said. "I wonder if it has a heater."

It had none that he could discover. He unwrapped the bottle of Scotch, ripped the seal off with his thumbnail, and removed the cork.

"After you," he said. She took the bottle. His eyes had grown accustomed to the darkness, and he could see her plainly. She had been huddled against the cold, but now she straightened, and lifted the bottle to her lips, her head thrown back. Her coral sweater fell away from her breasts, and he could not help but see what had arrested his attention in the early afternoon—her prominent nipples, stiffened to points by the icy air, protruding through the white blouse.

She had finished her drink, and she saw where his eyes were.

"I do not wear brassières," she said. "Is that wrong?"

He was taken aback by her unembarrassed frankness. "Wrong? It's beautiful." For want of something else to say, he took refuge in intellectualism. "In the Restoration, the great ladies understood this. Sometimes, in the bodices of their gowns, there were holes, for the—the breasts to show through. And in France, under Napoleon, the bosom was exposed for admiration, whenever possible. Marie Antoinette had a drinking cup made from a plaster cast of one of her breasts. It's on display in Sèvres."

She listened, perplexed, then handed him the bottle. "It is not for such display, or to provoke men, that I do not wear the brassière," she said seriously. "It is for reasons of health only." She patted her hip. "I do not wear the girdle either, because of health."

"What's health got to do with it?"

"I belong to a nudist society, like my friends. Health comes from the sun outdoors and not binding the body with artificial garments."

"You mean you actually go around with nothing on?"

"Twice a month, for a full Sunday each time, in the summer. The colony is on a tiny island in Lake Mälaren."

"Well, I must say, it agrees with you." He hesitated. "Aren't you embarrassed?"

"For what? I have a body. Others have bodies. We are interested in our health. Nudism is very popular in Sweden. It is one reason we are strong when we are old."

"Well, I can't say I disapprove."

"You do not?"

"Not at all. I think it's fine."

"I had heard all Americans were prudes. Even the men."

"Some. Not all."

"Your country is obsessed with sex, like the English country, because you are ashamed of it and afraid of it. An American professor of psychology once visited the German and Swedish nudist camps and said if even one little part of the body is covered for concealment—not protection—it makes bad sex thoughts in everyone's head."

"You're a smart young lady."

"I only repeat what I hear at lectures of our society." Suddenly, disconcertingly, she cupped her breasts from underneath and peered down at them behind the blouse. "The nipples are gone. It means I am warm, and the drink is good." She released her breasts and tapped the bottle. "You are not drinking, Mr. Craig."

"I–I guess I forgot."

He could not remember the last time that a conversation had kept him from drinking. He lifted the bottle to his mouth, and poured, and welcomed the burning fluid into his throat and lungs.

"Whew," he said. "That was good."

The heat of it coursed through his veins, and he laid his head back on the seat, then turned sideways to observe that she was staring at him.

"May I ask you a private question, Mr. Craig?"

"Right now, anything."

"Your wife is dead three years, yes?"

He nodded.

"What does a man like you do for love?" she asked.

He pulled himself to an upright posture. He was startled, and going to tease her, but he saw that her face was solemn in the darkness.

What could he tell this serious child in honesty? That he had slept with no woman in desire and love for three years? That once a month, the week that he was sober, he would drive to a boardinghouse thirty miles outside of town, where Mrs. Risten had three girl boarders, and in a businesslike way, and by the clock, release his tensions with one of these girls? That he could hardly remember the faces of any of the girls because he paid twenty dollars a visit to use them as receptacles and nothing more? That he had caressed no woman in passion since Harriet?

"A man like me does without love," he said simply.

"How is that possible for a human being?"

His hand weighed the bottle. "Drink makes anything possible."

"But you sleep with some girls?"

"Yes, but not with love. You cannot pay for love."

"That is dreadful." Her face was soft. "I am sorry for you."

"That makes two of us," he said lightly. "Besides, what do you know about all this, Lilly? Didn't you tell me you were twenty-three? You're still teething."

"I am old enough to have eight children."

"And to know better."

She laughed from deep inside. "Yes, I know better. You drink now, and then I will have one more."

He drank, and drank, and then again. He handed her the bottle, and slid lower in the seat. Slowly, he was being enveloped by the soft blanket of intoxication.

"This sister-in-law," she was saying, "is she pretty?"

"Not like you. But all right."

"Like your dead wife?"

"Not exactly. She has her points, pro and con."

"You have slept with her?"

The question hung above his fogged brain and then penetrated it. "What kind of thing is that to ask?"

"It is a normal question."

"No, Lilly," he said in a humoring way, "I haven't slept with Leah."

"What kind of life do you live? Are you rich?"

"I'm poor, but I live beyond my means."

"What is your occupation? Are you a barrister?"

"I'm a writer, Lilly. I write—used to."

"I knew it!" Her face danced. "I guessed it, but I was not certain."

"How did you guess it?" he asked tiredly.

"Many, many reasons. You are young but look old. You are strange. The pipe. Mainly, the way you drink. Mr. Strindberg also drank."

"You sound like someone who's known writers."

"Some."

He watched the slight shimmy of the auto's ceiling, and listened to the prow of the boat slapping the water. They were silent for a while.

"Lilly."

"Yes?"

"What do you do? Live with your parents?"

"My father is dead. He had a lace shop in Vadstena. My mother is remarried and she lives in Lund. I did not like her husband who has busy hands —so four years ago I moved to Stockholm. I have a nice one-room apartment with a kitchen and a tiny bathroom. I pay a hundred and fifty kronor a month."

"How much is that in America?"

"Thirty dollars."

"Where do you get your money?"

"I sell dresses in Nordiska Kompaniet."

He could not remember. "What's that?"

"One of the biggest department stores."

"Are you happy?"

"Yes. Why not?"

"Why don't you get married?"

"I will when it makes me happier."

"No other reason?"

"Is there one other reason to marry?"

He turned his face toward her. "Lilly, if you are Sweden, I am going to like Sweden."

"You will like Sweden."

"I liked it last time, but I was young—it was my honeymoon. This time, I haven't cared."

"You will like it." They were silent a moment, and then she touched his arm. "Mr. Craig, we must leave the car. We are almost there."

He sat up, rubbed his eyes, and strained them through the windshield. Looming before them were the lights of Malmö.

142

"All right," he said. He started to open the door, when something came to his mind. "Lilly—one more favor."

"Your sister-in-law again?"

"That's right. I'd never get this bottle past her guard without a scene. Can you take it?"

She took it from him.

"I'll show you my car when we go past. I have room seventeen. Will you remember?"

"Seventeen."

"Soon as we leave Malmö, once we're under way, bring it to me. Can you do that?"

"Of course."

"Do I sound terribly drunk?"

"Not very much."

"Good. Thank you for the company."

They left the Volvo, and bucked the knifing wind, which fell away when they reached the haven between the train and the cabins. Passengers were filling their path, and they were slow in reaching Craig's car.

He pointed up. "It's this one. Seventeen."

She bobbed her head. *"Tack för i kväll,"* she said. *"Det var mycket trevligt."*

"What's that?"

"Thank you. I enjoyed myself."

Craig smiled. "How do you say, 'I hope to see you again soon'?"

"Jag hoppas vi ses igen snart."

"Well, *jag hoppas—*"

But she had already disappeared into the crowd.

Craig greeted the conductor, went unsteadily up the steps, and entered the wagon-lit. Leah was awaiting him in his compartment, agitated, as he had expected.

"For God's sake, where have you been?" she cried. "I thought you'd fallen overboard. I looked everywhere, high and low—"

"I was hungry," he said placidly. "I was eating in the second-class café."

"I looked there. You weren't there."

"Sure I was. I was disguised as a Dane. I'm fine, Leah. Never better. All ready for Mr. Nobel."

She eyed him suspiciously, without the nerve to move closer and smell his breath. "You haven't had a drink?"

"On my honor."

"I'm only thinking of Harriet. I keep thinking of her. I want to treat you as she would." Her voice pleaded for understanding. "I'm thinking of you, too, Andrew. I want you to be respected, and proud of yourself."

"You're very kind, Lee." A hollow wooden thud reverberated through the boat, and they struggled for balance.

"What was that?" asked Leah, frightened.

"Malmö. We'll be on shore in a few minutes, hitched up and on our way. I'm going to undress and get some sleep."

She stood at the door. "Don't think I want to nag you, Andrew. When you've needed drink, I've been the first to help you, God forgive me. You know that."

He nodded dutifully.

"But I feel you don't need it now, and if you do, you should conquer your weakness. There's too much at stake." She allowed this to sink in, and then went on. "I know what you are and can be, more than anyone on earth, and that is all that's in my heart."

"I appreciate that, Lee." He wondered what would happen if Lilly should suddenly materialize with the bottle. He prayed that she would not be too soon.

"When you stand on that stage in Stockholm, all straight and dignified," Leah continued, "when you accept the award, it'll make up for everything that happened before."

She buried the shaft deep, and he avoided her prosecutor's eyes. It'll make up for murder, she was telling him without telling him. I, Leah Decker, am my sister's husband's keeper, his probation officer until he has served penance and is again responsible, and I shall release him when his time is served, if ever that be, she was saying.

"It'll be a new day for us," she concluded.

"Good night, Lee."

"Good night, Andrew."

Grimly, he shut the door, removed his coat and tie, and waited for the train to resume its passage and for Lilly Hedqvist to appear. He listened to the train being coupled to a locomotive, and soon they were under way. When the knock came at the door, it was not Lilly but the conductor. He was beaming.

"I told the customs inspectors who you were," he said. "They were impressed. They did not want to disturb you."

"Thanks, my friend."

"I have read all the works of Jack London and Upton Sinclair, but I am sorry to say I have not read your books. Are they translated in Swedish?"

"Yes, they are."

"When I tell my wife, she will buy them."

"I wish I had some copies along, but I didn't have room."

"No—no—my wife will buy them." He was reluctant to leave, but he saw Craig's impatience. "If you need me in the night, you press the bell. I am at the end of the aisle, at my table. Do you wish to leave a morning call?"

"Just wake me an hour before we get in."

"I won't forget, Mr. Craig."

After the conductor had gone, Craig remained at the open door. He bent and peered through the window. In the distance, behind the moat of darkness, a Swedish town, brightened by outdoor fluorescent lights, briefly filled the window and as rapidly disappeared from sight. Shortly, a second Swedish town, also illuminated by fluorescent lights, showed itself, and then withdrew. After the third town came and went, Craig closed his door.

Kneeling, he unsnapped his overnighter, removed his pajamas and the toothbrush and tube of toothpaste, and neatly placed them at the foot of his berth. He took off his shoes, sat on the bed, swaying with the train, and at last he lay down on his back. He was not sleepy, but neither was he wide awake. He was disoriented, not part of this time and place, but contentedly detached. He had consumed more of the bottle than he had realized. He wondered when Lilly would bring what was left of it, and how he would treat her. Was it proper or improper to invite her in to drink with him? . . . *mycket trevligt*—yes, he had enjoyed her, and it would be relaxing to drink with her as they had in the car at the prow of the ferryboat. Still, he did not feel like talking. He wanted her female presence, and most of all he wanted to unbutton her white blouse.

The eroticism of his thoughts surprised him. He felt immature and ashamed and disloyal to Harriet. He tried to explain to her, and went back to find her, as so often he did, and at once he felt more comfortable in the past, which was all solved with its beginnings, middles, ends, than he ever could in the present, which offered him only beginnings and enigmas. It was good to go home again, where everything had happened and was done, and no burdens of proof existed, no demands, no mysteries, because it was done. . . .

It was the winter after the end of World War II, and New York was bedded down in snow. Two days before, he had been honorably discharged from the Signal Corps at Fort Dix, New Jersey, and now he was in an old hotel on Forty-fourth Street, off Sixth Avenue, waiting for the holiday season to end—it was the week between Christmas and New Year's—so that he could see the magazine editors and then leave the city that always made him feel unsure and dissatisfied.

On this day, luxuriating in his civilian status, drawing on his newly acquired Dunhill, he stared into the street below the hotel—even the snow was dirty here—and he could not understand the lyricists and singers of this city. What was there to recommend it? There was no sky, no earth with flowers and all things green, no private air to inhale, no aesthetic beauty, no neighborliness, no place to daydream or meditate leisurely. But its professional spokesmen, with inverted snobbery, treated these lacks as its very virtues. It was a place alive and crackling, a place stimulating, civilization's center. The center of what? He wondered. The plays were mediocre gabble, projected by over-publicized personalities rather than first-rate talents, in shameful, musty old barns. Concerts were no better, their small voices and small orchestral sounds slanted at pseudo specialists and reading aesthetes who would turn off the same sounds if heard in a private room. Businesses were the worst, because here competitors were piled on top of each other like gigantic club sandwiches, yet they were expected to disarm and treat each other civilly at lunch and dinner, which was anti-nature, and there could be no other reason for the statistics on martinis dry, ulcers bleeding, and analysts prospering.

Craig wanted no permanent part of this unnatural club. Before the war, while on the rewrite desk of a St. Louis newspaper, he had tried some short fiction on the side. When he learned the formula, and compromised his fancies sufficiently, the short fiction began to sell. He had determined to free-lance full time, but Pearl Harbor diverted him to a different employment. During his three years of service, especially the months in England and France, he had devoted his leaves to a minimum amount of whoring and a maximum amount of writing. The short stories that he wrote were better, and sold for higher prices, and now that he was free at last, he knew what he would do.

He had arranged to spend the week after New Year's Day going about Manhattan, with his agent, meeting the current crop of editors and telling them some of his ideas. With commitments under his arm, he would return to Cedar Rapids, where he had an ailing father, a robust aunt and uncle, and friends, and he would dig in and write. With the money, he would continue westward. He would live cheaply, but royally, in Taos or Monterey, and he would write the novels that had burned inside him during the war years.

There was one other possibility. He might visit Peru for a year. He had read that it was inexpensive. The purpose of going to Peru would be research. Among several ideas, he had entertained one about Francisco Pizarro. It would be an historical novel about Pizarro and the strange group of 183 men he had recruited in Panama. It would record the changes in the leader and his men, their conflicts and corruption as well as their strengths, from the day of their landing at Tumbez until they sailed for home. It would lay bare in human terms the whole incredible story of how a small, mortal, fanatical gang, armed with only three muskets and twenty crossbows, conquered Atahualpa and ten million Incas and won a vast empire. The idea had been further nourished by the rise and fall of Adolf Hitler and his original small band, but the Nazis were of too recent date to be examined, and a parallel tale about Pizarro might put the whole modern-day tragedy in perspective.

But then the telephone rang, and Craig turned away from the window and his speculations to answer it, and when he was finished, he was also finished with Taos and Monterey and Peru, only he did not know it yet. He did not know, either, that he had just joined the New York club, for most of four years at least.

The telephone had been an invitation to a New Year's Eve party from an army buddy, Wilson by name, with whom he had been discharged at Fort Dix. The cherubic Wilson was not a particularly close friend. He was a lightweight, and wealthy, or at least his mother was, and Craig accepted because he supposed the food would be good, and it was the only New Year's Eve invitation he had.

Fortified by two drinks, he arrived in the plush apartment after ten o'clock. The food was, indeed, good, but what was better was Miss Harriet Decker. When Wilson had introduced him to the nearest drunks at hand, Harriet had been stretched supine on the sofa, in stocking feet, her head in someone's lap, as was the fashion for that age that year. She was one of many guests horizontal, but the only guest completely sober. She had acknowledged Craig by shading her eyes, passing her gaze up his lank figure, and saying, "Hi, up there."

He had come to the party alone, but when he departed at three in the morning, it was with Harriet. At five in the morning of the first day of the brand-new year, he sat in the Automat with Harriet and knew that she had parents and a younger sister in Springfield, Illinois, that she had undergone a mastoid operation at age thirteen, that she had read *Of Human Bondage* three times and Frank Harris's *My Life and Loves* in mimeograph, that she had quit Barnard College in the third year to write copy for a large advertising agency, and that she was in love with him just as much as he was in love with her.

Now he found that New York oppressed him less, and he wrote his stories in the day and saw Harriet every night, and four months after he had met her, they were man and wife. They leased a spacious, unfurnished flat in Long Island, and did it together for comfort, not show, and at the end of the first year, Harriet had a miscarriage, and he had money enough to give her the deferred honeymoon abroad.

The trip was wonderful. They were younger than young, and who on earth had called their new world Old World? They felt wealthy with the black-market money exchanged on street corners, and bought a brown leather-and-teak chair in Stockholm, wooden shoes in Amsterdam, a Picasso pencil sketch and antique bidet in Paris, a Toledo desk set and skin *bota* in Madrid, a crystal chandelier in Venice.

In Rome, the first afternoon, they had a pilgrimage to make. From the starkly modern Mediterraneo Hotel, they took a battered taxi to the Protestant Cemetery, and then dismissed the driver. At the gate they waited, until a little black-eyed boy opened it, and then they went up the gravel walk, climbing, and then turned to the left and continued to the highest rise near the ancient Roman wall, and there they found the white slab pressed in the earth—Percy Bysshe Shelley—or what had been left of Shelley saved from the pyre on the beach at Viareggio—and beside him, so eager to be beside him, the one who had buried him here, the old pirate, Edward John Trelawny.

As Harriet and Andrew Craig stood in mourning, the sun came through the great quiet trees and touched each grave, and the gentle silence that day made death seem lovely and possible, the peaceful resting after the long travail. Later, they had walked hand in hand downward, beyond the Pyramid of Cestius, and arrived below, at the far corner of the cemetery, where stood the majestic shaft without a name—writ on water—and beside it, vigilant, faithful, the resting place of Joseph Severn.

Shelley and Keats. That day, Craig felt an affinity for them, felt a sense of history as had they, felt that he was not one of the faceless of the world, the nonentities of time who come, stay briefly, and are blown away into nothingness, forgotten and unremembered as the flying sands on a windswept beach. He, too, would leave a shaft on earth that would stand as long as men stood or could incline their heads before it. That day, in Rome, he knew strength and purpose, and he was filled with his uniqueness and his mission.

The feeling that had seized him in the Protestant Cemetery expanded and solidified in the next days as he walked beside Harriet through the city. One afternoon, passing the Colosseum and Venus Temple, passing the Constantine Arch, they entered the remains of the Roman Forum, baked hot in the remorseless sun. Ahead of him, beyond the jagged fragments of a powerful and cruel civilization and time, Craig could see the broken colonnades and tossed stones of the once Imperial Palace. Above it was left a pitiful few of the pillars behind which Julius Caesar, writhing like a helpless animal at the base of Pompey's statue, had taken the twenty-three stabs that extinguished his life.

The greatness and smallness of man, and more than that, the continuity and eternity of man, held Craig silent. Minutes later, still looking off, he took Harriet's arm. "I think, at last, I know how, how Edward Gibbon felt—how he could have been inspired to tackle the work of a lifetime—"

Harriet nodded, and quietly, she recited the words of Gibbon. " 'It was at Rome on the 15th of October, 1764, as I sat musing amidst the ruins of the Capitol, while the barefooted friars were singing vespers in the temple of Jupiter, that the idea of writing the decline and fall of the city first started in my mind.' "

Four weeks later, the Craigs arrived in New York City. Five weeks later, Andrew Craig wrote the first page of his first and best novel, *The Perfect State*.

The novel had its roots in history. Somewhere, Craig had read that the philosopher, Plato, having advanced his radical ideas for a Utopia to his students, in the suburban grove known as the Academy, had once been given the opportunity to practice what he had so long preached in his thirty-six Dialogues. In Syracuse, capital of Sicily, the new, twenty-five-year-old dictator, Dionysius II, had been prevailed upon to invite Plato to reform both the dictator and his government. In 367 B.C., Plato traveled to Syracuse to install Utopia. Not only did he attempt to establish a constitutional monarchy, but he tried to introduce the perfect socialized state—the Republic—where men were to be routed into certain occupations by elimination tests. The most brilliant were to continue their study of philosophy until the age of fifty, when they would be made rulers, and would live on together, without personal advantage or gain, in common quarters; children were to be taken from their parents at birth and raised by the state; women to be emancipated and allowed careers, and permitted to marry only under eugenic control; foreign trade was to be eliminated; profits to be curbed so that no single individual might acquire more than four times the wealth of the average man.

This was the perfect state that Plato had intended to experiment with in Syracuse. Dionysius II was horrified by the philosopher's suggestions. He rebelled, sold the hapless Plato into slavery, and returned to his beloved autocracy, his drinking, and his lechery. Meanwhile, Plato was ransomed from his slavery by a pupil, Anniceris, and he returned to Athens and the Academy, considerably disillusioned, and determined to keep his Utopia theoretical thereafter.

Working from these few facts, Craig constructed the plot of his first novel. It was narrated as if the action were seen through the eyes of the young student, Anniceris, as he accompanied his teacher and hero, Plato, to Syracuse to inaugurate a formal Utopia. Taking license with history, Craig had Plato actually put his reforms into practice. Skillfully, he showed that it was not Dionysius II who undermined Utopia, but the people themselves. Plato's philosophic communism fought a losing battle against human nature. Men did not want their life's work enforced and inflexible, and they did not wish limits to their incentive and their income. Women did not want love scientifically controlled, and did not wish their offspring taken from them and raised by the state. In the novel, as Utopia disintegrated all about him, even Anniceris's faith in his master and the perfect state was shaken. In the end, after saving Plato from the fury of the mob, Anniceris returned to Syracuse, thus symbolizing man's preference for individual freedom, despite its attendant ills.

Although his novel was laid in 367 B.C., Craig deliberately aimed his shaft at twentieth-century Communism. While the tale was a drama of ancient times, it was the perfect transmitting agent for Craig's deepest inner feelings about the spreading ideas of Marx and Engels. The novel was published shortly after Craig's second wedding anniversary. The reviewers welcomed it as a minor classic, one told with controlled wit, magnificent irony, and bursts of passion. But its setting, so remote in time, and its subtle allegory had little appeal to the mass of readers. There were two printings, totaling 7,500 copies, and there were no more. Craig had his literary foothold, his cult, and his meager savings account.

It took Craig two years to produce his second book, because he was constantly stopping and starting again, forced to write formula short stories in between, to keep Harriet and himself alive. The second novel was *The Savage*. Again, Craig embellished a factual character and incident. The novel was set in 1782, and the hero was Simon Girty, a fierce and angry American frontiersman, who abandoned his people to become a white Indian and an Indian chief and to lead Shawnee redskins on raids through Ohio, Kentucky, Pennsylvania, and Virginia. History knew Girty for a brutal renegade. Craig saw him as something more, as a nonconformist and a defender of a lost cause. When he wrote of Girty, Craig was writing of all men, in all times, but expecially in his own time, who invite crucifixion by crusading against injustice.

With this book, Craig did not make his point at all. His agent, his publisher, his reviewers, his readers, could not see what he was driving at. They saw only the surface story—an exciting, roughneck hero, an action plot, a slice of Americana, a superior Western—and that was more than enough. The novel sold 22,000 copies in hardback; it sold for a modest sum to a new paperback reprinter; it sold for $50,000 to a major motion picture studio.

The total income from *The Savage* was not a fortune, but even after taxes, it was sufficient to liberate Craig from the tiresome short stories. Creatively, he was bursting with projects. One, especially, appealed to him. If he could carry it off, he knew it would be a tour de force. He called it *The Black Hole*, and lunching at Twenty-One, he told it to his publisher. The framework, he explained, was historically accurate. In 1756, India rose up against the British. The new Indian ruler, nineteen-year-old Siraj-ud-daula, too young to be merciful, captured 146 English fugitives from the garrison and imprisoned them in a Calcutta military cell only 18 by 14 feet in size. In his novel, Craig wanted to dramatize the hell of that one June night in the Black Hole of Calcutta, what the calvary did to men's characters and souls, why 23 survived the night, and how they survived it, and why 123 did not survive it, and how they died. This much Craig related to his publisher, and no more. What he withheld was the theme that lurked behind the mask of history: a polemic against colonialism and white superiority. The publisher's enthusiasm knew no bounds, and the advance he offered was a generous one.

The Girty windfall had freed Craig from magazines; the current advance freed him from New York. Both Harriet and he had grown weary of New York, and both were filled with new life, she with the embryo of their child that she did not wish to raise in the city, and he with the new novel that had grown in his mind. Also, he had become tired of his New York literary set. He had finally agreed with George Bernard Shaw's remark to John Galsworthy that "literary men should never associate with one another, not only because of their cliques and hatreds and envies, but because their minds inbreed and produce abortions."

For months, he and Harriet had spoken wistfully of a town in Wisconsin, once visited while driving to Madison to see Harriet's sister Leah at the university. After four years in New York, Miller's Dam seemed the fairest paradise. When the money from *The Black Hole* came in, the Craigs impulsively pulled up stakes and moved back to their Midwestern beginnings.

Miller's Dam was situated sixty miles northwest of Milwaukee. Riding inland from Lake Michigan, the countryside rose and fell gracefully, like long, lazy ocean swells. This was rich earth, rural earth, and every hillock seemed alive with small living things unseen. The actual landscape that year was bright, clear, and unvaried, except for the occasional billboards and road signs pointing to a gasoline station or hamburger shack that erupted among the endless windmills and red barns, yellow haystacks, fields of bending cornstalks, and herds of speckled cows grazing indolently on the dry green slopes.

Suddenly, homesteads filled the landscape, and they were in Miller's Dam (pop. 1,475), a cluster of shops, a drugstore, a sheriff's station, a hotel, a bank, a pool hall, a theater, all bisected by the little-traveled cement highway. The town was worked in, but not lived in, except for the familiar traveling salesmen in the hotel and the few old couples who dwelt in the rear of their stores. Almost everyone lived on the fringes of the town, where vacant land was plentiful, in two-story flats or frame bungalows with front porches, or farther out, on parcels of worked farmland. Harriet and Andrew Craig conformed, and were glad to do so because they wanted space. They bought the Hartog house, a big stucco-and-frame structure, on two acres, located three miles north of Main Street on Wheaton Road.

From the first day, they felt that they belonged in this isolated, idyllic place, and their feeling of having come home again survived even the pain of Harriet's second miscarriage in her fifth month. Not long after that heartbreak, the routine was once more pleasant and productive. Craig wrote furiously on his typewriter in the mornings, and again after lunch until two o'clock in the afternoon. Then he would read in the backyard, or hit golf balls, or snip at his hedges and plant in his gardens. Often, he would drive into town to pass the time with Lucius Mack, or look in on Randolph's pool hall to learn the baseball scores from Chicago or play a game of snooker, or pick up Dr. Marks and go for a swim at Lawson Lake. Harriet joined the Ladies' Aid Society, and exchanged visits with the faculty wives at Joliet, and sometimes she worked with the summer stock company at Lawson Lake in Marquette County. They belonged to the Lawson Country Club, and faithfully attended the Friday night dances, and when they wanted more excitement, they spent their weekends in Milwaukee or Chicago.

Until Harriet's parents moved to California, they came up frequently from Springfield. Eventually, they were supplanted by Harriet's sister Leah, who had graduated from Wisconsin University and was teaching in a grammar school on Chicago's North Side. In the four years of Leah's comings and goings, Craig was hardly aware of her. He knew that she was in awe of him as a professional writer. He knew that she worshiped her sister. He did not know, until Harriet told him, that she was unhappy. She disliked teaching. She disliked her life in Chicago. She disliked being single, yet could not make up her mind to marry the diffident, shy young man, Harry Beazley, a teacher also, to whom she had been engaged for one year.

Craig was writing well in Miller's Dam. *The Black Hole* was completed in a year, and Craig was proud of it. His publisher had high hopes, and offered a first printing of 10,000 copies. But the public was not interested, and 3,000 copies were remaindered on the bargain counters. There were two play options, but they came to nothing. By then, Craig did not care, for he had researched and was already writing *Armageddon*.

The fourth novel was based on the actual volcanic explosion of the tropical island of Krakatoa, in the Dutch East Indies, in August of 1883. The explosion, which wiped Krakatoa off the map, had sent a tidal wave eighty feet high around the world. It dropped blocks of pumice on Australia. It capsized fishing vessels in the English Channel. It created the sounds of thunder over Texas. It broke barographs in Moscow. It blotted out 163 villages and 36,380 lives. Craig's narrative told the story of the behavior of a seemingly unrelated chain of people, scattered from the Strait of Sunda and Singapore to Washintgon, D.C., under the pressure of a natural catastrophe greater than the lava that covered Pompeii or the earthquake that brought down San Francisco.

The novel was published during Craig's fourth year in Miller's Dam. His parable was missed by no one. Krakatoa was a foreshadowing of the hydrogen bomb and nuclear warfare. What made the terrifying warning and lesson acceptable was that the described event had occurred in the past, and could be digested and understood while there was still hope. *Armageddon* sold 40,000 copies. It received a large advance from a paperback publisher. There were nineteen foreign editions, and it sold to a television network for a two-hour dramatic spectacular.

The money came when it was most needed. Craig invested in stocks and bonds against the unpredictable future of his next novels, painted and repaired his house, allowed Harriet to buy new furniture, and indulged himself in the latest-model low-priced station wagon.

This was their happiest year in Miller's Dam, and the best of their eight years of married life. The month before his birthday, late that year, encouraged by Harriet, Craig accepted the one inner challenge that had so long nettled him. He had been disturbed by his own persistent retreat into the past for settings for his novels. This seemed to be an unconscious avoidance of current hard realities, a continual hiding of today's people and their problems, and himself, too, behind period costumes. The new novel would be a modern one, and tentatively he called it *Return to Ithaca*.

The morning of his birthday, he allowed Harriet to read the first chapter. The afternoon of his birthday, they hiked in the meadows and talked and talked and decided to adopt a child. The night of his birthday it rained, and over his protests Harriet dragged him out to the Lawson Country Club, where he was genuinely overwhelmed by the surprise party that she had arranged. They ate, he cut the cake and opened the presents. They danced. He had four drinks and Harriet had two. He rarely drank, except at parties, and this was twice as many as he usually drank. He felt good and told Harriet that he wanted to get home and make love to her. The midnight of his birthday they slipped out of the party, and he started the station wagon across the slippery highway back to home and bed. Ten minutes later, Harriet Craig was dead and Andrew Craig lay unconscious over the broken steering wheel of the new station wagon.

It was Leah Decker who buried Harriet, and attended Craig in the Joliet hospital, and it was Leah who brought him back to the empty, mocking house. In the months that he was in bed, and then on crutches, he was neither depressed nor moody. His head was vacant, unthinking, and he performed like a post-lobotomy case. Leah was always present, cleaning, sewing, cooking, and listening when he wanted to talk. Once, when his convalescent period was almost over, she said that she would be away overnight. She drafted Lucius Mack to stay with him.

When Leah returned, he remembered to ask where she had been. "Chicago," she said.

"What were you doing there?"

"I gave up my apartment. I packed my things and had them sent here."

"What about your job?"

"Oh, I quit that two weeks after the accident. I didn't like it anyway."

"What about your young man—Beazley—Harry Beazley?"

"He'll manage."

"Aren't you engaged?"

"Not really. Harriet used to call it that. Harry's all right. I'm not sure he's my type. But anyway—he might come up here in the summer, for a week, when school's over."

"It's not right, Lee. I don't want you in bondage."

"It's not bondage. It's what I want. You need me."

"Yes. But there's no reason to turn over your whole life."

"I'm doing what I want to do."

"I don't like it. It's not fair. I can never repay you."

"Just get well and write again. That's all I want."

In the three years that followed, they had never discussed her leaving again. In those years, Craig was not ever sure if he needed Leah, because he needed someone, or if she had made herself indispensable to him, because she needed someone. Certainly, when he had laid aside his crutches, he had not laid them away at all, because figuratively he still had two more. One was Leah. The other was whiskey.

The worst period came when Dr. Marks withdrew the sleep-inducing drugs, and when Craig was well and on his feet. It was then that the full impact of his loss hit him. Harriet's departure from his life had been too unreal to accept, and when he was unwell, and filled with sedatives and sleeping pills, he did not have to accept it. But now he was ready for her again, restored, clearheaded, and she would not come home. No matter where he looked, she was not there. She was in a hole in the ground, as inanimate and wooden as the casket that enclosed her, and there she would be for the rest of his life and for all eternity. The reality was so incredible that he wanted to weep. He could not sleep, and when he slept, he would not wake. He breathed because he did not know how to stop breathing, and he lived only for the passing of the hours and the days. He had no patience for his work or for Leah or for his old friends and old routine.

It was Leah who brought the first bottle of whiskey into the house and who, at least in the early months, drank with him. Later, because she had no taste for alcohol, she gave over her place to Lucius Mack.

In the beginning, the whiskey was of little help, because Craig drank as he used to drink socially, and sobriety came back too swiftly. Gradually, he was able to consume more, and that was better, and gave him something to look forward to when he lifted himself out of bed each morning. The drinking made Harriet's disappearance unreal again, which in some ways was helpful but in other ways cruel.

In the first year alone, after the day's early intoxication, he tried to resume his long walks. Often, he would return to the house, half drunk, half sober, and trudge up to his room, and sit at his desk and stare at the photograph of her face in its leather frame. He would stare at her face and want to share some minute pleasure of the new day, something seen, heard, read, felt, and in his head he would talk to her, and then he would realize with a clutch of inner pain that she understood nothing, heard nothing, that she was only a flat image in black-and-white on glossy paper size 8 by 10.

In the moments after, he would suffer a bottomless despair at life's futility. He would drink again, still at the desk, staring at her, realizing that they had shared nothing since, not gossip and not news, that edicts had been issued from Washington and Moscow and Peiping, that discoveries had been made, that new films and books had been released, that a World Series had come and gone, and of all these things that he knew, she did not know and would never know. The trick of the mirage happened, too, in the mornings. Sometimes when he read the newspaper, he looked up intending to read an item aloud that would amuse her, and she was not across from him to enjoy it with him, because she was not there and never would be again. He had led a whole special life since her death, filled with unshared information and feelings, and he hated every part of it.

Sometimes, when he was drinking more heavily, and there was an infrequent respite, the parched desert of a sober day, he wanted to live too much. It was an odd perversity. On such a day, he would become neurotic about the possibility of dying—move the bristles of his toothbrush across his teeth twelve times, no more, no less, against death, or set the toothpaste tube at a certain angle, against death, or touch the doorknob twice in the same spot, against death. At such times, he wondered about his anxiety for life. Consciously, he would cease his compulsive little acts, and marvel that there still survived within him some fluttering hope that he was valuable to himself and to others. When he sought to approach this hope, to study it, perhaps to use it, he would become frightened and return to the bottle. He did not want to die, but, even more, he was afraid to live.

With fear, and self-hatred because of fear, came his new evaluation of the place where he lived. With Harriet, it had been paradise. Alone, it was limbo. In the sober week of each month, he was critical of Miller's Dam and wondered if he belonged here after all. There was something archaic about these small, sparse, slow Midwestern settlements. They fed the big city markets, true, and there was always talk of the important farm vote and subsidizing the farmer, and learned writings spoke of agrarian economy, but underlying was the feeling that all the fuss was about a museum, really. Craig wondered what would happen when the produce of the earth was inevitably supplanted by produce of the chemical laboratory. Would Miller's Dam cease to exist? How would the people who lived in Miller's Dam—"hid" was the better word—justify hovering outside the mainstream of the country?

He tried not to deceive himself. He tried to be blunt with himself. The thousands or the millions who populated the Miller's Dams of the nation did so because they were afraid of life. That was it. They were anti-life. Perhaps Thoreau would have disagreed with him. Perhaps Thoreau, whom he admired, would say here was the essence of life, with the sky and earth so near and the meadow smells and the brooks and the freedom to contemplate. But in all honesty, what in the devil did these people have to contemplate with? No, he was positive that he was right, and that his poor, misguided friend from Walden's Pond was wrong. In the twentieth century, Miller's Dam was anti-life, a perfect hideout from competition, judgment, action, the gauntlets of urban existence. Miller's Dam was a refuge for cowards. Men stayed here because they were scared of leaving, scared of what they might learn about themselves, and this rural womb was a better preparation for dying without disillusion. Over and over he asked himself: why am I still here? And he answered: because here no questions are offered and no demands are made. Because here was Sydney Smith's "healthy grave," the elephant's burial ground, where the beast could die alone, out of sight and far from pity. . . .

What aroused him, transported him in a flash from Miller's Dam to the Malmö train bound for Stockholm, was the series of sharp rappings on his door.

Lilly.

He leaped from the berth, and shook himself alive. She had come in time, and he blessed her. There had been too much memory, too much introspection, and there would be more in the night, unless he was diverted. Lilly and the bottle were the saving smorgasbord.

He stepped to the door and pulled it open. There was no one in sight. He looked up the train corridor. It was empty. He turned his head, and saw only the conductor at the far end, capless now, dozing over his folding table. Then, at his feet, he saw the bottle.

He took it up and retired, shutting the door, and lifting the bottle, saw that a piece of paper was fasened to it by a rubber band. He removed the paper and opened it. It read: "Welcome to Sweden. Lilly Hedqvist. Polhemsgatan 172C, Stockholm."

He had looked forward to seeing her, but it did not matter, because he was tired, and the bottle was enough. It was still half filled. He propped it on the berth, stuffed her note in his pocket, and then changed into his pajamas and brushed his teeth.

The drinking cups were paper, and when he poured his whiskey, he watched with fascination as the cup blotted up the liquid. Discarding the foolish cup, he sat down on the middle of the berth, legs crossed, and swallowed straight from the bottle. The fluid was welcomed by every taut nerve in his system, and he continued to gratify his body by drinking steadily.

In an hour the bottle was empty, and he was satisfied. Thank you for me, he told the bottle without speaking, and thank you for my body. He pushed the bottle under the berth, turned down the lights, and crawled under the cover.

Stretched flat and inert, he was momentarily nauseated. Behind his eyelids the scene loomed. Their speed was moderate, because the highway was wet. The curve, which was sharp, he had met and traversed hundreds of times. Unthinking, he had flicked the wheel, and the station wagon had left him, gone out from beneath him, as a child's legs the first day on roller skates. Harriet, head thrown back on the seat, had been saying lazily, "I had a lovely day, didn't you?" But he could not reply, because there was this unruly, shocking thing happening to him. They had skidded completely around, smashed into the fence along the embankment, rolled over once into the ravine, and pancaked in a geyser of metal and wood and glass against an oak tree. That was it, and that was all, and later he remembered that he had taken four drinks and that he had meant to reply to Harriet, "Yes, yes, my darling, the loveliest day of my life with you."

The nausea passed, and the scene, and he curled on his side to sleep. It did not come immediately. Instead, a memory he had missed floated to the surface. The last time he had slept with Harriet had been three days before his birthday, in the morning, when he had kissed her awake, and she had pulled him down.

His mind weakly groped to recall the details of their last loving. He threw aside the blanket, and she lifted her nightgown above her breasts. The room was night-chilled, and he hurried for their flesh to warm them, and poised above her he saw that the nipples had hardened to points in the cold, and the cold had come across the prow of the ferry and into the car. He searched the face and was not surprised it was Lilly's.

He pressed his head into the golden-haired pillow and remembered no more, except—

Welcome to Sweden.

IV

The seven-story Grand Hotel of Stockholm, located on the quay at S. Blasieholmsh 8, faced the majestic Royal Palace, directly across the Strommen canal, as an equal.

Few hostels in Europe, and none in Scandinavia, surpassed the Grand Hotel of Stockholm. It had been erected in 1874, when Ulysses S. Grant was President of the United States and Benjamin Disraeli the Prime Minister of England, and except for certain renovations of the rooms and suites in a recent decade, it remained unchanged, proud of its years and high esteem.

Unlike most hotels, in dark December the Grand was more crowded and more festive than in the summer months. While the two veranda grills were closed, because of their exposure to the cold weather, the ornate inner Breakfast Room, off the lobby, and the enormous three-story Winter Garden, with its dome of glass, and balconies, and pillared arches, abounded with visitors and their hosts.

There were precisely 297 rooms in the Grand Hotel, smartly serviced by a trained staff of 550 men and women, and on this early morning of the third of December, every room was accounted for if not occupied. There were six choice suites, each with its pair of entry halls, sitting room, one bedroom with twin beds or two bedrooms with single beds, and large bathroom furnished with two wash basins, toilet, and bidet, and annually, at this time of the year, these suites were held in reserve for the Nobel Prize winners summoned to Stockholm. The use of these rooms for seven days, and the Continental breakfasts, were entirely paid for by the Nobel Foundation.

This year, five of the six choice suites had been reserved, and this early morning of the third of December, four of the five were already filled by Nobel guests from Paris, Rome, Georgia, California, and the fifth was being held in immaculate readiness for the delayed arrival of the literature laureate from Wisconsin. . . .

The sleek Foreign Office limousine made a graceful U turn, bending around the row of taxis parked on the quay, and drew up before the impressive, gaping entrance to the Grand Hotel.

Andrew Craig, crowded into a corner of the rear seat by Ingrid Påhl's ample person, puffed his pipe, perhaps faster than he knew, and waited. During the entire drive from the station, he had been relatively uncommunicative. He had replied to the questions directed at him briefly, and in as friendly a manner as possible, then lapsed into silence, while Leah nervously carried on, making fanciful excuses for their change of plans in Copenhagen and bubbling over the sights outside the car window. Craig hardly glanced outside the window at all. His disinterest and silence came, not from the Scotch—nearly a fifth—that he had consumed in the night or any resultant hangover, but from a growing apprehension, a reluctance to revisit the hotel where Harriet and he had spent their first honeymoon night abroad a decade ago.

Now they had arrived, and the emotionally charged meeting was at hand. The doorman, wearing a long military coat that made him resemble a refugee White Russian officer, had opened the car, and stood rigidly at attention, fingers to the brim of his cap. Krantz scrambled out first, and then Count Bertil Jacobsson closed Krantz's jump seat, and his own, and worked his way out of the car. Leah followed him, and Ingrid Pähl followed her, and then it was Craig's turn.

While porters struggled with the bags, Craig stood on the wooden board walk and surveyed the magnificent vista that he had remembered so well. The Strommen canal was placid and unfrozen beneath the pale sun. Off to one side, two white excursion boats lay at anchor before the National Gallery. Across the way, like an ancient lion at rest with paws extended, sat the familiar eighteenth-century Royal Palace, and behind it was the spire of the hallowed Riddarholm Church. Over the canal, linking the new city with the Old Town, stretched the bridge known as Strömbron, dotted with pedestrians and pygmy automobiles and a bright blue tram. At a distance rose the massive Royal Opera House, and hidden behind it, he recalled, was the busy square called Gustav Adolfs Torg.

Jacobsson was beside him, blowing condensed air into the palms of his reindeer leather gloves. "I am truly regretful we could not order warmer weather for you, Mr. Craig. The sun is deceptive. Actually, it is below fifty degrees Fahrenheit. But at least, it has not snowed. I am told it will not for another month."

"I'm used to this weather, to worse weather, where I come from," said Craig.

"You mentioned that you were here before?"

"Yes. Some years after the war." He turned and recognized the huge revolving doors. "Nothing has changed."

"Well, we might as well go inside, get the chill out of our bones."

Craig saw that Leah, flanked by the other two members of the reception committee, had preceded them, and he followed the old Count through the revolving doors and inside. Slowly, he ascended the eight stone stairs, the rubber matting muffling his shoes, and now he was in the lobby.

While Jacobsson continued after the others to the reception desk, Craig remained motionless at the top of the stairs.

Nothing had changed, nothing at all. The main lobby was as vast as ever, and between the two pillars, the sitting room and on either side of the pillars, the elevators marked *Hiss*. Walking slowly to his right, he circled the main lobby. There was the smaller reading room, with its fat chairs, and glittering glass showcases featuring Guerlain perfumes, Silvanders' neckties, Kosta goblets, Sjögren jewelry. Next came the towering door with the sign, "Grands Veranda," and this was the Breakfast Room. Alongside were more showcases with Orrefors vases and Jensen silver, and then a candy booth, and suddenly he came upon the narrow newsstand with its assortment of foreign newspapers and magazines. Here it was that Harriet went daily, every afternoon before cocktails, for her day-old Paris edition of *The New York Herald Tribune.*

He was not moved. There was no nostalgia at all. No bittersweet memory ached inside. Yet nothing had changed, except himself.

When he reached the others at the *portier's* desk, Leah was before him. "There's no mail, except a funny cable from Lucius and something about the new omnibus edition from your publisher. Do you want to read them?"

"Later."

Her forehead creased. "You were looking around. Is it different?"

"Oh, yes. I'd almost forgotten everything. After all, we were here only a week."

"I'm terribly excited, Andrew. I've never been in a place like this before."

Jacobsson approached them from the reservation counter. "I am sorry holding you up," he said courteously, "but there was a blunder about your rooms. They gave you suite 225. That is one of the most desirable suites, looking down on the canal, but it has only one bedroom with twin beds. They thought you were married."

Leah's color rose in her cheeks. "What are you going to do?"

"I explained. You will have the same suite, of course, but they are arranging to free an adjoining single bedroom. It will be ready in an hour. It can be made to connect with the drawing room. Meanwhile, the original suite is ready."

"I can't wait to unpack," said Leah. With Jacobsson and Krantz, she started for the elevator, then turned. "Aren't you coming, Andrew?"

"In a moment. I just want to pick up some reading."

"I'm afraid you won't have much time for that," said Jacobsson with a chuckle.

They continued to the elevator. Ingrid Påhl, steadying her floral hat, hastened from the information counter to join them, but Craig intercepted her.

"Oh," she said, "I thought you had already gone upstairs."

"Miss Påhl, I—where can I get a drink here?"

"Do you mean coffee?"

"I mean a highball."

She did not disguise her confusion, and Craig understood this, knowing that it was only 9:40 in the morning.

"Why, of course, Mr. Craig—"

"It's been a grueling trip, and I'm still on Wisconsin time. I can't think of anything more distasteful than Scotch before breakfast, but I'm afraid I need a bracer."

The explanation was satisfactory. "Here, let me show you," said Ingrid

Påhl, taking his arm. "Do you mind if I join you? I could stand a hot cocoa."

They found a table next to the dance floor at one side of the Winter Garden. Except for a few other couples, the mammoth room—Craig had always thought that it looked like a college field house decorated for a prom—was devoid of life. At this hour, most guests were having breakfast in their rooms or off the lobby.

Ingrid Påhl fiddled inside her embroidered purse, until the waiter materialized. Craig ordered a cocoa and buttered toast for her, and a double Scotch-and-water for himself.

"It was more awkward getting a drink when I was here last time," he said for conversation.

"When was that?"

"Ten years ago."

"Yes, we had liquor control in those days and that horrible Bratt System. Well, there is no use lying about it, we are a nation of drunkards—well, heavy drinkers, anyway. It is the long winter nights, I think—the dampness, the gloom this time of the year—that makes men turn to strong brännvin. But Dr. Ivan Bratt—you know, his national law to control sales of alcohol went into effect way back in 1919—solved nothing, made matters even worse. To obtain a ration book for beverages, you had to tell the district system company your whole life story. It was a terrible, prying thing. And then you had to stand in line at the *systemet*, like sheep, to get three liters—less than a quart a month. Can you imagine that? And there were inequities. Married women were not permitted to have ration books at all. It created all sorts of evils. A black market in ration books. Bootlegging from Finland. Home distilleries. Evils Sweden had never known before. Having a drink in a restaurant was even worse. I am sure you remember, Mr. Craig."

"Vaguely. You couldn't have a cocktail without ordering food, something like that."

"In the restaurants, wine and beer were unlimited, but did you ever try the beer in those days? Distilled water, I assure you. No drinks were served before noon. A woman could not really have a full drink of hard liquor until three o'clock. And then, as you point out, when you were served, you had to buy food with it, if you were hungry or not. No food, no spirits. Most restaurants became quite clever. They would serve you the drink with an old, old egg they used over and over again. And no matter what your needs, you were limited to what you might call four shots a day. It did not help a particle. In the ten years before the end of the war, there were a quarter of a million people here found guilty of misdemeanors induced by alcohol. Even the prohibitionists were against Bratt, though for different reasons. There was one temperance society, the Blue Band, that objected because the law made people waste valuable food to obtain drink, and this while half of Europe was starving. Well, we're a rational country, and the people would not stand for it. It was our one national deformity. Bratt had been so personally abused that he had gone into exile in France. So, in 1955, the Riksdag abolished liquor control, overwhelmingly. And I am proud. You do not fetter an entire people's thirst. I do not drink—oh, a medicinal sip or two at nights before bedtime, to keep me tuned—but I am proud. If you wish a bottle, you can now walk two or three blocks from here, to the first package shop, and order whatever you like. No ration books, and no questions, although they will not sell to a customer who is obviously drunk. Of course, a new inequity has already arisen. The price of a bottle of alcohol, and the tax on it, makes it very dear. I do not believe that is fair, either. Pricing hard drink out of reach may be a means of creating a false temperance, but it only indulges the rich who can afford to drink as much as they please, and it deprives the laborer and the poor. Everyone who reads me thinks I am an eccentric old lady who lives in the country and thinks only of nature's beauty and bird-watching, but I am more than that, Mr. Craig. I am concerned about all injustice. I abhor it on any level."

"I'm on your side," said Craig. He had read about Ingrid Påhl, but had never read her books, and had not known what to expect. Now, he liked her enormously.

"Here is your drink," she said. "I am sure I have made you ravishingly thirsty."

The waiter served them, and after a short argument, Craig won the right to sign the bill.

Ingrid Påhl lifted her cup of cocoa. "Down with Bratt and up with skål," she said.

"Skål and down with Bratt," said Craig, and he drank.

"I have your program," she said, and touched the folded paper that she had found while fumbling around in her purse, and had placed beside her saucer. "Do you want to see it now?"

"I'll read it later. What are the highlights?"

"The first highlight is today, two o'clock, at the Swedish Press Club. You and the other winners will be formally interviewed by the world press. Tonight, at seven, cocktails and dinner in the Royal Palace with the King. It is full evening dress only for the nobility. Tomorrow, a grand tour of the city. Count Jacobsson and an attaché will be your guides. The day after, a formal dinner in the country tendered by Ragnar Hammarlund, our billionaire industrialist. It is optional, but as an author, I would not miss it. After that, all sorts of small events, until the final Nobel Ceremony at Konserthuset—Concert Hall—at five o'clock in the afternoon. Does your head spin?"

Craig smiled. "A little." He consulted his watch. "Do you mean in only four hours from now I have to meet all those reporters?"

"I am afraid so."

He shook the ice in his glass. "I'd better stick to one drink." He looked at his companion. "How are these press conferences? Are they rough?"

"Very."

He brought the glass to his lips. "I've changed my mind. I'd better make that two drinks."

161

It was 2:10 in the afternoon, and the four press conferences of the Nobel laureates were already under way.

With a sigh of relief, Count Bertil Jacobsson sat in the straight-backed chair behind the reception table in the seclusion of the second-floor cloakroom of the Swedish Press Club. Under his direction and that of his secretary, Astrid Steen, the Club had been prepared earlier for these interviews. The immense hall, beyond the closed door of the cloakroom, had been partitioned by a half-dozen screens into two separate and private rooms. The Drs. Marceau had been installed in one half, and Professor Stratman in the other half. Off the hall, the confined rear reading room had been assigned to Dr. Farelli and Dr. Garrett. The nearest, larger lounge had been turned over to Mr. Craig.

It had been planned that the different winners would meet one another formally this evening, during the cocktail period, at the Royal Palace. But since they were all assembling here in the afternoon, Jacobsson felt that their simultaneous presence, without introduction, might be awkward. At the last moment, he had requested the participants to arrive at a quarter to two, instead of two, so that they might become acquainted informally.

The fifteen minutes before the press conference, when the laureates had been herded together in the hall, introduced to one another, and served sherry and whiskey with ice, had been curiously uncomfortable minutes for Jacobsson, and apparently for all concerned. Individually, each of them seemed sociable, even amicable, but together, as a group, they did not jell. It was odd, reflected Jacobsson. Perhaps it would have been wiser to invite their wives and relatives, who were at this moment elsewhere, being treated to luncheon by the wives of the various members of the Nobel academies.

Except for Dr. Farelli, an overpowering and gregarious personality, none of the others had mixed or conversed easily. They had met as strangers, and they were strangers still, despite their common victory. Professor Stratman had taken several pills with his sherry and had appeared preoccupied. Drs. Denise and Claude Marceau had not exchanged a single word with each other—there was definitely some disagreement between them—and had been too strained to mingle with the others. Dr. Garrett, whom Jacobsson had introduced first and properly to his co-winner Dr. Farelli, had seemed to be struck dumb. He had stammered several inarticulate words to the Italian, and then left him as he might a leper, and he had thereafter been mute and unaccountably agitated. Mr. Craig, who had arrived last, had been disinterested in the others and had devoted most of his attentions to the waiter, consuming three Scotches with ice in the fifteen minutes. It had been with sincere gratefulness that Jacobsson had greeted the first press arrivals, and had ordered Mrs. Steen to take the laureates to their separate stations.

Drumming his fingers nervously on the cloakroom table, Jacobsson wondered if the mistake had been his own. Perhaps he should have avoided their meeting until evening when the different winners, without the stress of a press conference ahead, mellowed by the spirits and food of the Royal Palace and the presence of His Majesty, would have been more receptive to one another. The idea of a simultaneous press conference, never before attempted, had been his own touch of showmanship. Several local newspaper executives had protested, for it meant assigning four reporters instead of one to manage full coverage. But Jacobsson had been adamant. He had felt that requiring more reporters in attendance this year would make the newspapers even more conscious of the importance of Nobel Week. Furthermore, he had assumed that the concurrent release of interviews with all six winners in the four categories would make a greater impression on international readers. Now he hoped that he had not been wrong.

The turnout had been promising. The racks of the cloakroom were thick with coats, male and female, of every description and color. The open guest book, at his fingertips, gave further evidence of a success. He scanned the four pages and estimated that over one hundred reporters were present. Representatives of all the Swedish newspapers and periodicals had signed in, and so had, he could see, foreign representatives of the great weeklies of the world, *Der Spiegel* of Hamburg, *Świat* of Warsaw, *L'Express* of Paris, *Il Mondo* of Rome, the *Spectator* of London, *Life* magazine of New York, and *O Cruzeiro* of Rio de Janeiro. Above all, there were present the foreign reporters of the important wire services, Associated Press and United Press International and Consolidated Newspapers of America, Tass of Russia, Reuters of Great Britain, Agence France-Presse of France, and so on and on.

He was alerted to the hall door of the cloakroom softly opening. Mrs. Steen wriggled in and closed the door behind her.

"How is it going?" Jacobsson inquired anxiously.

"Smoothly, as far as I can tell, sir."

"No trouble from the press members?" asked Jacobsson. He did not object to good-natured raillery. (Along with the reporters, he had enjoyed the fun at the press conference in 1960 for young Dr. Donald Glaser, the American laureate in physics. Dr. Glaser's trip to Stockholm had doubled for a honeymoon, and jesting reporters had inquired of Mrs. Glaser, "Did you know he was going to get the Nobel Prize—is that why you married him?") What Jacobsson did object to was celebrity baiting. Every year, there proved to be several reporters who invited irritation by asking rude or personal questions, in order to create front-page copy.

"The press seems tame enough," said Mrs. Steen, "but then, it is still the early stages. A few more drinks, and—" She shrugged her shoulders.

"And our laureates—are they controlled?" By this, Jacobsson really meant, had any one of them made any intemperate remarks. Only this noon, in an hour of divine privacy in his apartment, he had added a painful jotting to his Notes: "In September, 1930, in Paris, Eugene O'Neill, who would become a literary laureate six years later, told Nathan, the American critic: 'I think the Nobel Prize, until you become very old and childlike, costs more than it's worth. It's an anchor around one's neck that one would never be able to shake off.' Distressing."

"They are all being most moderate," Mrs. Steen was saying. "But the questions are still moderate, also. They are being asked their feelings when informed of winning the prize, and about their trips to Sweden, and about their first reactions to Stockholm. That sort of thing. I do not know what they will say, when the interviews become bolder."

Jacobsson lifted himself erect. "Perhaps I had better look in myself to see if the interviews are becoming bolder. Our guests may feel less uneasy, if they see a familiar face and an ally."

As quietly as possible, Count Bertil Jacobsson took his place on a vacant folding chair to the rear, and peered past a portion of the fifteen or twenty press members to see how Dr. Denise Marceau and Dr. Claude Marceau were performing.

Claude Marceau was speaking to a reporter in the first row, measuring and doling out each phrase, brandishing his burning cigarette as he spoke. His full graying hair, serious Gallic countenance almost handsome, neat pin-striped dark-gray suit, offered the appeal of assurance and authority. In the opposite corner of the divan, at least four feet apart from him, sat Denise Marceau. She did not watch her husband as he spoke. In fact, she hardly seemed to be listening to him. She sat tensely, with her back straight and knees together, her hands working a white handkerchief in her lap. Occasionally, she jerked her shoulders, as if even the gently shaped green tweed suit she wore were too binding. She stared impassively ahead.

Jacobsson wondered if anyone else noticed that she was unhappy. Perhaps, he hoped, he was wrong, and she was shy of public appearances and merely nervous. Chemists often were a peculiar lot. It was probably the result of too many hours among their glass stills, and heaters, and vacuum pumps. Perhaps their compounds and camphor, unbeknownst to themselves, depressed them. Jacobsson prayed that *Madame le docteur* would eventually say something amusing.

On the divan, so composed and detached to the unprobing and insensitive eye, Denise Marceau was not entirely unaware of her husband's monologue. He is hypnotizing them, she thought. He is impressing them favorably, the great genius offering the chiseled phrases and opinions from Olympus, she thought. And then she thought: I wonder what those reporters would say if I told them the old lecher's condition when I informed him that we had won this damn prize. And I wonder how they would react if I suddenly stood up, and shouted at Claude, "Oh, *merde!*" and walked off.

The impulsive thought pleased Denise, and forced a smile to her lips, and she realized that her smile had been noticed by the ancient Swedish Count in the back row, and that he was smiling back. For a moment, her ordeal became less tormenting. She told herself that after all, if she divorced Claude (and, much as she detested the necessity, she could see no other course this afternoon), she would be a widow, no, not a widow but a divorcée, a single unit, and she would have to stand on her own feet. Her future would then be based on her fame as one Curie, not two. She must not allow Claude to leave her behind, floundering, helpless, dependent upon him. She must rise alone, and show the world that she never needed that skirt-chasing fool. In short, she must be practical. And the time was now. The Nobel Prize was their steppingstone to immortality. If she permitted him to dominate it, the world would think that the honor was his alone. Her duty was to make it her prize, too, as a safeguard against the near future.

She pushed the fantasy of Claude and Gisèle on their future wedding night —how could he enjoy that bag of bones? but he had, damn him!—out of her mind, and became attentive to the opportunity at hand.

"—and so we stopped our researches on coenzyme A," Claude was saying, "and we concentrated our full attention on this new possibility, which we had conceived, that of preserving and banking male hereditary semen."

"Did you tell them, dear, exactly how we came on this new project?" Denise asked with a tight tiny smile.

"Well, as you heard, I indicated that we had both become interested—"

"Of course. But I mean the *whole* story, dear."

The Stockholm *Expressen* reporter in the front row was immediately interested. "What is the whole story, Dr. Marceau?" he asked her.

Denise abandoned Claude to his perplexity and firmly took over the reins. "I think it is rather amusing, an ironic sidelight, that this discovery of ours, for which we are being honored, deals with the male spermatozoa, yet the project was initiated by a female. As my husband will generously corroborate, it was *I*, quite by chance—but who knows? perhaps nothing like this is pure chance—who first brought up the possibility."

The *Expressen* man sniffed his lead. "Pardon, Dr. Marceau, but are you saying that you, alone, hit upon the discovery?"

Denise could feel the divan move beneath Claude's angry quiver, and she was pleased. Still, it would win her no sympathy to let this get out of hand. "Oh, nothing like that, *exactly*. My husband and I worked closely, *after* I had brought up the possibility. Make no mistake about it, we are a team. We are *ensemble*. Our accomplishment, for whatever it be worth, cannot be divided in two, now or ever. All I have tried to say is—and I thought it would amuse you gentlemen—someone had to conceive the hypothesis, and, in this case, it happened to be I."

"Yes, in that sense it is true," Claude said, too quickly, too uneasily, suspecting danger and trying to avert it and keep the peace. "Six years ago— we were having lunch, with colleagues—a new paper on the female ovum was being bandied about. The talk turned to heredity—heredity control—"

"—and I looked at Claude," interrupted Denise, determined to have the attention of the press, and concentrating on the *Le Monde* reporter, "and I said—I remember the very words this day—I said, 'Suppose it were possible to preserve the living spermatozoa of a Charlemagne or an Erasmus, or the unfertilized egg of a Cleopatra, and implant them today, by modern means, centuries after their donors were dead?' Those were my words, and that was our beginning." She turned sweetly to her husband. "Remember, dear?"

"Yes," he said dully, "it was a fortuitous remark. It was then that *I* suggested—" Ah, thought Denise, he is irritated. Good, good. "—that we look into the matter further." He turned to the reporters. "And we did, for six years, together."

Denise beamed at the rows of faces. "I could never have done it *alone*. My husband was wonderful. It was a work of devoted collaboration. There is a telepathy between us, you might even call it a mystique bond. I know what he thinks, he knows what I think, and we save precious time by these perceptions."

Claude shifted uncomfortably on the divan, and reached for his sherry on the end table, as the reporters bent their heads and scribbled on their pads.

The Agence France-Presse man lifted his hand, and then posed the next inquiry. "Dr. Marceau," he asked Denise, "I wonder if you could clarify for all of us—not in scientific detail, necessarily—we are laymen—but clarify what your discovery is all about. Were you the first in this field or had others worked on the same problem?"

"Now, that is two questions, but I will do my best with both of them," Denise replied with a charming smile. "Let us take the last one first. What made our discovery possible was the successful application of artificial insemination to humans. This was first attempted in London a century and a half ago. The greatest advance in artificial impregnation was made in 1939, by Dr. Gregory Pincus of America, Clark University, if I recall correctly. He transplanted the egg from the ovum of one female rabbit into another female rabbit, and an offspring was successfully produced. Now, despite religious opposition, and sometimes legal barriers, artificial insemination is widely practiced. In America alone, I am told, there have been fifty thousand so-called test-tube children, that is, children conceived without intercourse. Once this artificial means of procreation was possible, and acceptable, the next step was —well, the step my husband and I took—controlled heredity." She turned to her husband. "Before I inveigled you into this field, Claude, how many others, would you say, were researching along the same lines?"

Claude did not deign to look at her or reply directly to her. He addressed the Agence France-Presse man. "In France, our own Dr. Jean Rostand, back in 1946, kept a frog's seminal cells alive. In London, a bull's semen, treated with glycerine and carbonic snow, was kept alive. You must understand, sir, that the problem was to keep the male sperm from perishing, so that it could be transferred. In artificial insemination, the donor's sperm was rarely more than two hours old. The problem was—how to keep this same human sperm alive not for two hours but two months or two years or two centuries, and still preserve its power to fertilize the female egg. The Dr. Pincus of whom my wife spoke, with Dr. Hudson Hoagland, both Americans, made remarkable experiments in this field. They thought it possible that a genius could sire a family of several hundred and do it a century after he was in his grave —by leaving behind him vitrified sperms. The hopes this opened for humanity were staggering. Our own Dr. Rostand remarked, 'Under a system of artificial selection, the proportion of human beings of high quality would be bound to become greater—and, indeed, much greater—than it is in our time.' It was our problem to make this dream a reality, and I am proud that we have succeeded."

"And the means?" repeated the Agence France-Presse man.

"I promised to answer that," said Denise Marceau, deliberately taking over again. "After I convinced Claude it was more than a fancy—he is at heart a skeptic, like all fine investigators—he joined me wholeheartedly in tackling the problem of vitrification. We followed the leads of other geneticists —that is, apply glycerol to protect the sperm before freezing and later thawing. We found glycerol little more than sixty per cent effective. Only six out of ten human sperm cells survived this freezing at one hundred degrees below zero Fahrenheit. The problem that haunted us was to get a higher percentage of sperms to survive freezing, and to have them survive not a few months of cold storage but many years. After ceaseless trial and error—I suspect Claude wanted to throw up his hands many times, but I had a woman's persistence, abetted by intuition, about the project—we finally discovered the compound that we call P-437—our private joke is that the P stands for patience—and our experiments have proved that we can keep a male sperm in storage, and alive in suspended animation, for more than five years, probably ten."

"Magnificent," said the Agence France-Presse man, writing furiously.

"Doctor," the *Svenska Dagbladet* reporter called to her from the third row, "you originally suggested that the living spermatozoa of a Charlemagne or Erasmus could be implanted in a modern-day woman. Dr. Marceau, your husband, spoke of dead geniuses giving the world today newborn children, families of hundreds, from their frozen sperms. Do you honestly believe this will become a reality?"

"I believe so," said Denise, flatly. "Now it is possible, at last. There is a practical obstacle, of course. It requires fifty million sperms for a single human artificial insemination. Most geniuses, unfortunately, are recognized when they are old, less fertile than in their youth, sometimes sterile or impotent in their last years."

"Mozart was a genius at six," said the *Svenska Dagbladet* reporter.

"*Voilà*," agreed Denise. "And he lived until thirty-five. The perfect subject. Had our discovery been made in the eighteenth century, what a heritage the world might now have from its Mozarts."

"Did you entertain such notions during your six years of research?" inquired the Reuters man who sat in front of Jacobsson.

"Constantly," said Denise. "I am a scientist first, but also a woman and a romantic." She glanced playfully at Claude's stern face. "My husband, perhaps to our advantage, is less tolerant of romantic fairy tales. His life is the test tube." She turned toward the Reuters man. "When we had almost succeeded, I was beside myself with my imaginings. And now that our work is a reality, I am as thrilled as before by the human possibilities. Consider. If our P-437 had existed in the sixteenth century, Anne Hathaway might have loaned your Shakespeare to the cause. Today Shakespeare's actual sperms might be taken out of storage, thawed, and a dozen of your English ladies impregnated with them and in nine months these ladies would bear his children. Consider further. If our P-437 had existed in the last five hundred years, we would today have a storage bank containing the living reproductive sperms of Galileo, Pasteur, Newton, Darwin—Voltaire, Milton, Goethe, Balzac, Guy de Maupassant—Garrick, Casanova, Napoleon Bonaparte, Nietzsche, Benjamin Franklin—and tomorrow morning, I could go to this storage bank, remove and thaw the sperms of any of these geniuses, impregnate selected women in Sweden, England, America, or in my native France, and by next autumn, there would be delivered squealing sons and daughters spawned decades or centuries ago by Galileo or Goethe or Benjamin Franklin. Had we made our discovery earlier in our own lifetime, we might have in the storage bank the living sperms of Luther Burbank or Professor Einstein or Paderewski or, for that matter, Rudolph Valentino."

"Or Judas Iscariot," muttered the *Die Weltwoche* reporter from Zürich.

"Oh, we need never take him out of the storage bank," said Denise. "Or we could thaw his sperms and throw them away."

"When do you start collecting the sperms from our present-day geniuses?" asked the Associated Press man.

"Not yet, not so soon," said Denise. "But perhaps soon enough. More work must be done, more experiments by others. Claude and I have finished our work. Others must carry on, find the limits. And then we will be ready."

"What new field are you going to enter into next?" asked the Associated Press man.

Denise demurely gestured toward Claude. "I prefer that my husband give that reply."

Claude was caught off guard. "I—I do not know what we will try next. We have some ideas, but it is too early—we shall see."

"Madame—that is, Docteur—Marceau," called the Reuters representative, "to return, for a moment, to your rather optimistic hopes about the value of storing the sperms of the genius—do you mind?"

"Go ahead, please."

"I could not help but remember a well-known anecdote about George Bernard Shaw. One day, the wild, uninhibited Isadora Duncan suggested to him that they cohabit in order to produce a perfect child. 'Think of it,' I believe she told him, 'our child would have my beauty and your brains.' Shaw replied, 'But suppose, my dear, it turned out to have my beauty and your brains?' " Everyone in the room laughed, including Denise, and then the Reuters man added, "Well, Dr. Marceau, in the case of your sperms, what if the result were the other way around?"

When the laughter subsided, Denise assumed a solemn demeanor. "Yes, I understand. It is really a serious matter. Of course, genius does not always, or even frequently, produce genius. Lincoln's son, Robert Todd, did not automatically inherit the abilities of his illustrious father. And Lord Byron's surviving daughter, Ada, what did she produce in maturity? A system for betting on horse races that was a failure, and she died at thirty-six, shattered and deranged. On the other hand, John Adams, the second American president, gave the world John Quincy Adams, the sixth American president. And consider, also, Dumas *père* and Dumas *fils*. Here, genius was passed on. No doubt, it is a gamble. Yet controlled breeding, as applied to bulls and cows, has shown gratifying results in England. From the standpoint of modern eugenics, we can improve the human race by skillful mating of pedigreed human beings, men and women physically fit and of measured high mentality. Genius may not always be the result. Borrowing the heredity of Erasmus may not give us another Erasmus centuries later. But the odds would favor the possibility. Certainly, by using the sperms of brilliant men or physically healthy men, and implanting them in young women with the same characteristics, we will improve our chances of populating the world, one day, someday, with a superior people. There is no guarantee, but this is the hope, and for myself, I believe it is a promising one."

An aged waiter, in a white jacket, appeared with a tray crowded with glasses, some filled with sherry, the rest with whiskey. He glanced at Denise, and she nodded, welcoming the respite.

She accepted a whiskey from the waiter, and settled back on the divan, pleased with herself. She watched him pass before the members of the press, and saw them taking drinks and whispering among themselves.

Suddenly, she was aware that Claude had moved closer to her, and that his features revealed cold anger.

"I see you have taken over completely," he said in a low, harsh, shaking voice. "What in the hell are you trying to do to me?"

It was a moment that she had fancied for weeks, and now she savored it. She smiled at him with her lips. An American vulgarism came to mind, and she cherished it. She had first heard the vulgarism as the ending of an off-color story told at a reception—months ago—by the intoxicated and raucous wife of a visiting chemist from Pennsylvania. Were she to abandon refinement, Denise told herself, how perfect could be her retort. At once, Claude's brutal persecution of her filled her mind, and, at once, she thought, *"Au diable!"* and abandoned refinement.

Her lips still smiled. "What am I trying to do to you? Why, dearest, I am simply trying to do to you what your darling Balenciaga mannequin has already done." Her smile broadened. "I, too, am trying to screw you."

Delighted with Dr. Denise Marceau's reversal of form, her sudden display of verbal pyrotechnics, Count Bertil Jacobsson used the interlude of the serving of refreshments to transfer his presence to the Stratman press conference progressing in the rear half of the hall, behind the series of screens.

Finding an empty chair at the periphery of the gathering, Jacobsson was not surprised that the attendance here exceeded, by one-third, the conference that he had just left. Physics and literature, he had observed in past years, almost inevitably outdrew chemistry and medicine. He had always assumed that this was because physics and literature were more publicized and controversial, and therefore more comprehensible to the layman.

What did surprise him, when he revolved slowly in his chair the better to observe the circle of journalists, was to find that he was sitting beside Carl Adolf Krantz.

"Well, this is unexpected," he said in an undertone. "What brings you here? Are you writing for the newspapers? I thought you and Ingrid were happy to have the afternoon off."

Krantz, absently manipulating a crooked metal puzzle in his hands as he sat absorbed in the questions and answers, acknowledged his older colleague. He brought a finger to his lips to indicate that silence must be observed in this holy place. "I could not miss the opportunity to hear the great Stratman," he whispered.

"How does he handle himself?" Jacobsson wanted to know.

"With understandable assurance," said Krantz. "But they plague him with nonsensical questions. Our Swedish reporters are becoming as foolish as the Americans." He returned his gaze to the front of the room. "Soon we will arrive at the essentials."

Looking from Krantz beside him to Professor Stratman almost out of sight in the recesses of a deep leather chair, Jacobsson was fascinated by the general similarity between his colleague and the Nobel laureate. Both were stunted men, almost dwarfish, like Charles Steinmetz, the electrical engineer, whom he had once met. Both, when seated, gave the impression of the human embryo curled within the amnion in the female womb. Both resembled round and wrinkled infants, incredibly advanced in age. This was the first and general impression—perhaps the one that unconsciously drew Krantz to his more celebrated counterpart—but, Jacobsson could see, the similarity dissolved when specific differences were considered at a second glance. Krantz, in his pinched suit, seemed the disapproving pedagogue; Stratman, in his baggy coat and trousers, seemed above criticizing or criticism. Krantz's hair, dyed black, the porker features of his face, his sour mouth caught between mustache and goatee, gave one the feeling that here was disputer and complainant, analyzer and annotator, all but creator. Stratman's outsized cranium, shiny red and almost hairless, his amused eyes all-seeing behind steel-rimmed bifocals, his nose as prominent as a Christmas tree decoration, the ready smile, gave one the feeling that here was genius so simple and assured and secure that it dwelt high above all mundane carpings and concerns and criticisms. Here was the originator. Here was the Maker. No wonder at Krantz's reverence.

Jacobsson tried to concentrate on the laureate as mere man, not Maker, and momentarily regretted that he had to subject such a one to the low curiosity of the press.

How, he speculated, could a Stratman bring his lofty brain processes down from the rarefied summit to consider earthly matters of a telegram from Stockholm, a sea passage on a Swedish ship, a reaction to a Baltic community? Could Jacobsson have known the reality of the brain processes of the laureate, he would have had his answer and have been astonished.

For Professor Max Stratman, folded into the leather chair, one hand rubbing the meerschaum pipe, legs comfortably crossed, had his mind on matters of less than cosmic interest. Earlier, replying to questions about his trip from Atlanta to New York to Göteborg, he had been reminded that for the first time since the end of the war he was in a foreign country, no more than two or three hours from his native land, the land of his birth, and upbringing, and learning, and sorrow. Proximity evoked ancient memories: taking turns with Walther at the keyhole of the library for glimpses of the peasants his physician father treated in their country home; he and Walther running and skipping, beside his father, through the pungent grass, to the stable; Walther and Rebecca and the infant Emily—no, not infant, she had been older and hitting a rattle against the high chair—gathered about the table, to partake of the roast chicken, on Christmas Day when dinner was not lunch but dinner at noon, and he was there, glowing with pride in his family and with pleasure in the woolen muffler that Rebecca had knitted for him.

His thoughts had turned to his Emily—could he have imagined then that she would be *his* Emily?—and now he fixed on her, once more, as he had with compulsive regularity since the arrival in Stockholm. It was for Emily that he had made this long, risky journey, or perhaps less for Emily than for Walther and Rebecca and the remembrance of that Christmas noon.

Only after his arrival in Stockholm had Stratman authoritatively learned that the trip had not been necessary. The Nobel Foundation made occasional exceptions to the rule that their winners appear in person. He was told that when Ernest Hemingway won the literature prize, he had been recovering from a skull fractured and a spine broken in an African airplane crash, and he had been permitted to accept the $35,000 reward by mail in Cuba. Had the Nobel givers known his own heart condition, they would, Stratman was sure, have granted him the same consideration as Mr. Hemingway. He decided for the tenth time, despite Dr. Ilman, that the trip had been worth the chance, rather than make public—to his colleagues and to Emily—his impairment.

The episode on the ship had proved him right. That last night at sea, even Emily's slight security had been proved wanting. What on earth had possessed her to encourage that young man to violate her privacy, knowing full well that she was incapable of accepting his attentions? *Ach,* the distortions of the human head, forever substituting wish for reality. No doubt, it had been an irrational effort by Emily to stand on her own two feet, mature and independent of her Uncle Max, to cut the final umbilical cord. The not unexpected disaster had been a setback. Now, in Stockholm, she was edgier than at home, more withdrawn, and the evening before had even turned down the invitation of a gallant Swedish attaché to escort her to the opera. Yes, the episode on the ship had been the setback. It had reminded Emily that she was helpless, and certainly, Stratman told himself, it had reminded him of her need and his responsibility.

Dimly, he heard his name, and then realized that he had another responsibility, and that to perform attentively for his generous Nobel hosts.

"Professor Stratman," the Stockholm *Aftonbladet* journalist was repeating, "would you not say that the Nobel Prize was given you more for an invention than for a discovery?"

"I would put it this way, more precisely—I made a discovery, and then I made an invention."

"But it was the invention that won the prize, nevertheless."

"It is possible."

"Do you believe that this is in strict observance of Alfred Nobel's wishes? While it is a fact that, according to his 1895 will, he offered one part of his money 'to the person who shall have made the most important discovery or invention within the field of physics,' the Swedish Academy of Science has traditionally ignored inventions. After all, your American, Thomas Edison, who died only in 1931, did not win the Nobel Prize for that reason. How do you feel about this?"

Stratman studied his meerschaum a moment, then looked up. "It would be presumptuous of me, a guest as well as a beneficiary of Mr. Nobel's will, to comment on how the Academy of Science chooses to interpret that will." He paused, reconsidered, then resumed. "I think it would be fair to say this much. To the best of my knowledge, the prize in physics *has* frequently been given to inventions in physics. The Academy of Science has in no way ignored Mr. Nobel's desires. Several examples come to mind. I think of Herr Guglielmo Marconi. In 1895, he invented the wireless telegraph. In England, using a kite as an aerial, he demonstrated that this invention worked. Soon he was building a radio station for the Pope and amassing a fortune of twenty-five million dollars for himself. In 1909, I believe, he was awarded half of the Nobel Prize for 'services in the development of wireless telegraphy.' That is one case. I give you another, in another field. In 1903, my friend Willem Einthoven began constructing an instrument to detect heart ailments. In 1924, he won the Nobel Prize 'for his discovery of the mechanism of the electro-cardiogram.' That was an invention, pure and simple. A more recent case comes to my mind. In 1956, three Americans, William Shockley, John Bardeen, Walter Brattain, all of the Bell Telephone Laboratories, shared the Nobel physics prize for 'their discovery of transistor effects.' This, too, was an invention, the invention of the transistor to replace vacuum tubes. It turned upside down the world of electronics. In those terms, is the photochemical system I have discovered to convert and store solar energy an invention? The answer is yes—it is an invention. Does this kind of invention fall within the boundaries of the Nobel awards? Again, evaluating against historical precedent, the answer is yes."

Someone in the middle row raised his hand and began to ask another question, but Stratman held up his pipe for further attention. He was not through, and again he addressed himself to the busily writing *Aftonbladet* journalist.

"I might add—in honesty, I might add one more point," said Stratman. "You made mention of the neglect of Thomas Alva Edison by the Nobel Committee. Strictly speaking, Herr Edison was not a physicist, not a chemist, not a physician. He was entirely the inventor. I do not know, but possibly this made him ineligible for a Nobel Prize. I want to say, I think he was one of the most remarkable scientists that the world ever produced. He took out over one thousand patents—he invented the phonograph, the electric lamp, the mimeograph, the alkaline storage battery, the kinetograph—but he conceived only one scientific discovery as such, the Edison effect, so vital to radio and television. Perhaps I am, as my colleagues call it, sticking my neck out to speak further, but at my age, such things do not matter. It is my opinion that between 1901 and 1931 Herr Edison should have received a Nobel Prize in physics. This is not an adverse commentary on the judges of those days. Their task was not an easy one. Indeed, they had to give themselves limitations. Omissions are understandable to me. I only make an opinion, with the comfort of hindsight. Herr Edison should have won the prize.

"Also, while we speak of these matters, I believe Herr Wilbur Wright, who lived until 1912, and Herr Orville Wright, who lived until—I think, yes, 1948—both alive during the time of the Nobel Prizes—should have been honored in physics for developing the first practicable aircraft. Now, my neck is far out, but you see I favor the inventions in physics as much as the discoveries. I think the Swedish Academy of Science does, too—or why would I be here?—and that their sins of omission have been admirably few. The only overall omission I would criticize is the pitifully few prizes given to pure theorists—let us say like Herr Einstein and Herr Bohr and Herr Schrödinger. Experimentalists—discoverers, inventors—are too frequently honored. They are important, very important, but most discoveries utilize and verify either Einstein's theory of relativity or the old conversion of momentum theories. At the same time, the abstract theorists, the elite of physics, are too frequently overlooked. To my mind, that is the major defect in Soviet science today. The Russians devote so much effort and money to satellites, nuclear weapons, rockets, that they neglect basic research and abstract theory, and one day, they will suffer for it."

Stratman raised his head, seeking the *Aftonbladet* journalist, and said, "I hope that answers your questions." His eyes swept the hall. "You see what happens when you ask me provocative questions? You will be here all the day and tonight. Now, I am ready for more, if you are."

The reporter from the Stockholm *Dagens Nyheter* was standing, and Stratman acknowledged him by adjusting his bifocals and nodding.

"Herr Professor," the reporter began, "so far we have been discussing discoveries and inventions in general, and of the past, and I should like to bring the interview to a specific point and to the present—"

"*Jawohl,*" Stratman agreed.

"You have been awarded the Nobel Prize in physics for the 'discovery and invention of a photochemical conversion and storage system for solar energy' and for the 'practical application of solar energy to produce synthesized solid rocket propellants.' Except for reading, everywhere, that you have harnessed the rays of the sun, found a way to stock it and transport it, and proved that this kind of energy can help turn out rocket fuels, making obsolete the energy derived from coal and other fossil sources, I nowhere have read or been able to learn precisely what you have done."

There was appreciative laughter in the room, and even Stratman responded with an understanding smile.

The *Dagens Nyheter* reporter earnestly continued. "I am not alone in wanting to know your process, your instrument or container, the means exactly for which you are being honored. I have asked the Royal Swedish Academy of Science, and they cannot—or will not—tell me. Will you?"

Stratman peered impishly over his bifocals. "They cannot tell you, because they do not know—*exactly*."

"Herr Professor, I have no intention of being disrespectful—but how could they honor you for an invention about which they know so little?"

"Because, I am told, your Swedish investigators came to the United States and learned from my government and my colleagues what I had done. They were shown proof of what I have done. They were shown results at our fuel plant in the Mojave Desert. But, for reasons of national security, they could not be shown the means, the process, the storage system."

A woman from United Press International called out, "Professor Stratman, can you give us any detail of your actual discovery?"

He shook his head. "No. I am sorry, no."

"Not so much as a hint? Something to write about?"

"Not even so much. I apologize deeply. It is highly classified military information."

The *Neues Deutschland* man, who was from East Berlin, spoke up. "I am surprised they let you out of the country."

Stratman smiled. "Because they saw I was an old man who needed a vacation. Besides, they agreed that I was an absent-minded professor who would never remember the formula, anyway." Suddenly, he was serious. "It is an unhappy state of the world, to have this censorship, I agree. It is not an exclusive symptom of my adopted homeland. Secrecy, in certain circles, is a way of life, an attitude toward survival, in your Sweden, your England, your Russia, too, I assure you. No longer can the scientist think of himself as a citizen of the world. The frontiers of his mind, once boundless, are now constricted by nationalist barriers. The fraternity of the past, exchanging ideas and findings, cooperating, is no more, to the detriment of humanity. But that is the fact of the situation. When there is a common effort to halt competition and erase fear from all minds, the international fraternity of science will meet and come to order again. Then, all men and all nations will profit. It is the day I hope to see, still, in my lifetime."

There was a spattering of applause among the reporters, and someone shouted, "Hear, hear," and Stratman seemed surprised and pleased.

"Herr Professor," said the reporter from *Svenska Dagbladet*, "if you cannot give away the secrets of your invention, maybe you can tell us something useful in a general way. Why did you interest yourself in solar energy? What is the value in harnessing the sun's rays?"

The press waited, as Stratman weighed his reply. At last, his dome of a head bobbed in the affirmative. "*Ja*, the questions are fair. It would be wrong to send you back to your editors empty-handed. So—the questions. I will try to avoid the lecture room, but speak in such a way that you will understand, at least, what the motive behind my work was, and what it has accomplished."

He pointed his meerschaum toward the windows. "Out there is the sun. It is ninety-three million miles away, yet sun's outer atmosphere engulfs our earth, and its rays of atomic energy—hydrogen atoms converted into helium atoms—dominate our daily lives. What kind of potential energy, in earth terms, does this sun offer our tiny planet? If our entire earth were covered with an ice layer four hundred twenty-five feet thick, and if it could be melted—which it could not—the sun's rays would melt all of it, every inch of it, in twelve months. It would take twenty-one billion tons of coal to match the solar energy that covers the earth every sixty minutes. In the Sahara Desert alone, the solar energy imparted in one day—one single day—is three times as much as all the coal used in the world in three hundred sixty-six days. In any two days of the year, sunshine offers more energy than may be found in all the coals and other fossil fuels yet untouched beneath the earth's crust. Potential power fantastic—*ja*—but how to enslave it?"

Stratman paused, allowing the interviewers time to absorb and record his remarks. When the heads began to look up, he went on.

"Many men tried to enslave the sun power, and to small degrees, some succeeded. In 1864, a French physicist, Professor Augustin Mouchot, constructed a power boiler that was heated to run by sunrays instead of coal. The sun was funneled through a truncated cone to the boiler, and it developed steam for use in irrigation. In 1870, a Swedish-American, John Ericsson, who had built the *Monitor* to fight the *Merrimac,* constructed a solar plant of mirrors, but the expense became prohibitive for the horsepower generated, and Ericsson quit. Persistent men, some dreamers, some practical, took up the work. The list is too long to recite—Eneas in 1901, Shuman in 1907, and since the First World War, Dr. C. G. Abbot, and a hundred more, with their parabolic mirrors and flat-plate collectors.

"The major problem was always the same—it was intermittence of supply. By that I mean, the sun shone only in the day, and then not every day at that. How could one depend on such erratic power? The solution, of course, was not to depend directly on each new day of sunlight, but to collect the light, convert it into energy, returning more than thirty per cent efficiency, and then store the energy away for use whenever needed. But how to store solar energy? It would take me many hours to relate all the methods that have been tried. Men worked with thermocouples, and with photoelectric cells, and chemical cells. All of these were successful, but efficiency was far too low. Of one hundred per cent sunlight, only ten per cent could be saved and used. The pioneer work was dramatic, challenging, and I could not resist it. I entered the field. I concentrated on the means by which green leaves—plant organisms—flora—store carbohydrates. I wondered if the same process of nature could be simulated mechanically and in closed vessels. By chance, I was fortunate. I was able to improve the known methods of collecting and converting solar energy, both nature's and man's methods. More difficult and more important, I was able to find the means to store successfully and cheaply this energy for use when needed. My government colleagues assisted me in applying my findings to manufacturing solid fuels for heavy rocket propulsion."

A hand shot up. It belonged to the representative of *Berliner Morgenpost*. "Professor Stratman, do you intend to continue to work in the field?"

"Definitely. We have not even scratched the surface."

"What more can be done?" asked the journalist from *Jerusalem Post*.

"Infinite possibilities. We want to learn how to run factories with solar energy, and give inexpensive power and heat to homes through cheap roof collectors and individual power suppliers. We want to irrigate deserts with it, and illuminate entire cities by night. There is no end, and it all lies ahead. We are at the primitive beginning."

The reporter from the Oslo *Aftenposten* made himself heard. "Does Soviet Russia have a similar invention?"

Stratman shook his head. "No comment." Then he added quickly, "Of course, they have been in the solar energy field since 1933. It is known that they built a power plant in the Uzbek Soviet Republic. Today, they have a Russian Solar Power Institute. They have made great advances all along the line. As to their possessing what is now in our possession—of this I cannot speak further." He scanned the room. "I prefer not to discuss national policies. I will be cooperative in answering all general questions about science— or myself."

"Herr Professor." It was the Stockholm *Expressen* journalist. "You were at the Kaiser Wilhelm Institute in Berlin throughout the Second World War, were you not?"

"That is true."

"Why did you not leave Germany?"

"I could not. I am a Jew."

"We all met Dr. Fritz Lipmann, the biochemist, when he came here to receive the Nobel Prize in medicine during 1953. He was at the Kaiser Wilhelm Institute, and he also was a Jew. He got out to Copenhagen, and later to Boston. He did not work for Hitler. It is a matter of curiosity to many of us why so many of you Jewish scientists stayed behind."

Stratman sat very quietly. He was tempted to say to the Swedish journalist: So many of my American colleagues fought Hitler, why not you? But it was foolish. The man was a journalist. He wanted a story. You provoked, and this way, you obtained a story. "I do not know Dr. Lipmann's circumstances at the time," said Stratman slowly. "I know my own. Those dearest to me were in concentration camps. As long as I cooperated, they were kept alive. That is all I wish to say on that subject."

A new voice, rather loud from the rear row, was heard. It was the Tass Agency man speaking. "Is it not true, Professor, that you were kidnaped by the Americans in Berlin, and taken to the United States at gunpoint?"

"It is *not* true," said Stratman forcefully. "What is true is that I had been coerced into working for one totalitarian state, and I did not wish to be coerced into working for another. I went with the Americans voluntarily, and I have never been sorry."

He wondered if they would publish that statement in *Pravda* or *Izvestia*. His heart hammered with old resentments. Control, he told himself, control. He must remember Dr. Ilman. He must think of Emily. He thought of Emily, and waited for the next question.

With an air both curious and troubled, Count Bertil Jacobsson stood inside the door of the confined reading room and watched and listened to the third press conference taking place, now half over.

After eight minutes in the room, what bothered Jacobsson was this: if an innocent bystander had stood in his place, and seen what he had seen, he would surely have believed that only one person had won the Nobel Prize in physiology and medicine, and not two, and he would have been convinced that one laureate was being interviewed, instead of a pair.

The group of journalists in the room, a smaller group than those in the previous two sections of the hall because both winners had already been so widely publicized for their dramatic discovery, had been aiming almost all of their questions at Dr. Carlo Farelli, of Rome, while Dr. John Garrett, of Pasadena, California, sat beside him like an inanimate piece of sculpture that needed the dustcloth.

Jacobsson asked himself why this was so, but the question was purely rhetorical. Dr. Farelli's presence, as he leaned forward from the sofa, intimately addressing his audience, made the answer obvious. He was an attractive, dynamic human being. Dr. Farelli was a large man, not in height, but in width of face, and neck, and shoulders, and chest, and in the breadth of his gestures. Dr. Farelli conveyed the confidence of raw power. From some depth of academic memory, Jacobsson resurrected an image of the twenty-seventh Emperor of Rome, Maximinus I (235–238 A.D.), a giant of eight feet who was half Goth, half Alan, a giant who wore his wife's bracelet on his thumb as a ring and consumed forty pounds of meat and ten gallons of wine daily. The comparison was inaccurate, even absurd, but it came to mind, nevertheless.

Spoken in a resounding basso, Dr. Farelli's phrases seemed to be slung at his cowed listeners as if thrown by a catapult. His damp, black locks hung over his forehead, shaking as his head moved. His dark eyes sparked, his hooknose quivered, his white teeth gleamed, and his protruding jaw dared all disbelief. Beside him, as unremarkable as a slight blemish, sliding lower and lower into the sofa as if sinking into a quicksand patch of inadequacy, was Dr. John Garrett, brown hair and rimless spectacles and lackluster countenance slowly fading into the wan beige of the sofa, until both were one, and Farelli seemed quite alone.

Yet Jacobsson tried to judge the phenomenon fairly. This dominance was not of Farelli's doing. It was invited, nay, desired, by the dozen journalists. In the Italian they sensed excitement, and they wanted to draw upon it and inject it into their routine accounts, so that their stories would be as alive as their subject.

Jacobsson pondered the possible results of this group interview. Did Dr.

Garrett realize that he was being made as extinct as the dodo bird? Did he realize what was happening to him?

On the sofa, melted into the fabric, nearly vanished, Dr. John Garrett felt no pain. From the second that he had been introduced to Farelli, his immediate surface anger and antagonism had been blotted up and absorbed by the Italian's overpowering charm. Thus drained of righteous indignation, he was less man than automaton.

When the interviewing had begun, Garrett had been offered his fair share of questions, and had answered them simply, but then there had been fewer questions, and finally none, as if the audience had made a choice as to the player they preferred. Now all questions were being directed at Farelli, and all replies were being given by him. Oddly, Garrett experienced apathy, not rebellion. To join Farelli, to participate, would seem to be intruding on an enchanting Pirandello play. Gradually, Garrett had become so mesmerized by the Italian's words and histrionics that he felt he no longer shared the laureate sofa with him, but rather belonged apart, to the press audience, logically listening with them.

Even now he listened, still bound helplessly in the same hypnotic trance of inferiority, as if his contribution to their great work had been a minor accident, and now he wished to make amends through apologetic silence.

"One asks oneself, after all, what is this organ, the heart, that it is so difficult to replace?" Farelli was saying. "It is a simplified pump, a hollow muscular bag somewhat larger than a tennis ball or my fist, weighing no more than ten ounces. Seventy-two times a minute it beats, perpetually beats, and through it, each minute, pass six quarts of blood. One sees that in its design the heart is simple to duplicate, yes? Though, do not be fooled by its simplicity. For sixty or seventy or eighty years, it pumps with no rest. Where can one buy a machine guaranteed to pump for sixty—seventy—eighty years without failing once?

"Both Dr. Garrett and I fell into the error of trying to find such a man-made machine to use as a model, a machine that would equal or surpass the living heart. There were many models, of course. For several decades, scientists have been constructing artificial hearts to perform outside the body. One remembers the year 1935, when Dr. Alexis Carrel admitted that he and Colonel Charles Lindbergh had kept alive an animal organ with the first artificial heart made of a pump and coiled glass tube. One remembers Dr. John H. Gibbon, of Jefferson Medical College in Philadelphia, who was among the first, possibly the first, to employ an artificial heart-and-lung machine on a living patient, to keep the patient alive forty-five minutes, while surgery was being done. One remembers Dr. Leland C. Clarke, in Yellow Springs, Ohio, who kept a fireman alive seventy-five minutes with a heart-and-lung machine, while chest surgery was completed.

"In the world, there have been thirty or forty such artificial heart devices. And other remarkable cardiac devices, too, such as the recent electronic pacemaker. One saw the brilliance of these efforts, and the progress made, but still one—who was a perfectionist—despaired. For all of these machines were temporary devices outside the human body. They could not, in any form, be trusted inside the body—and will not be trusted, until we have discovered perpetual motion. Dr. Garrett and I saw that the practical heart, the one that might prolong or even double longevity, must be alive and mammalian and in the image of the human heart. Here was a goal for a Dr. Frankenstein—but where, my friends, where in the medical profession, was there a Mary Shelley?"

Farelli had spread his broad palms in a gesture of helplessness, and the audience, almost collectively, sighed in distressed understanding of his problem, as a theater audience might sigh at the dilemma of the beset hero. Farelli cast a friendly glance at Garrett, who sat agape, like a boy child waiting for Father to turn the page.

Farelli met the attention of his audience again. He would not let slack the communicative bond between them. "The goal was clear, but so, also, were the steep hurdles. What kept us from grafting lower mammalian hearts into human bodies? Preliminary attempts had been made on dogs, in England, in America, and the animals had survived three weeks. Why not men and women? The hurdles were these—to find an animal heart of similar structural design to the human heart, to find a means of storing this organ, to find a workable operative technique, to find a way of preventing irreversible ischemic damage to the transplanted heart—yes, I could go on and on. These were hurdles, but they were not the largest. The largest was the one I speak of last—to find means of preventing the rejection mechanism of the cells from marching out to attack and crush all invading material trying to enter the body.

"Those of us who dreamed of an eternal body spent our long nights of lonely strategy devising means to overcome these hurdles. In the Istituto Superiore di Sanita, in Rome, I did my research and experiments. In the Rosenthal Medical Center, in Pasadena, my admirable colleague, Dr. Garrett, did his research and experiments. We met our difficulties, one by one through the years, and we overcame them. Blood for the brain during surgery? We used a plastic booster heart, a pump oxygenator, outside the body. Clotting? Anticoagulants, of course. The replacement heart? One grafted from a mammal near the weight of the patient. Storage of the replacement heart? Perfusion and cooling, now useful for several hours, but already progress is being made on a special drug which will arrest metabolism. Suturing of blood vessels? Prosthetic materials like Teflon or dacron, or sometimes spare blood vessels from human cadavers. Technique of suturing? Our adaptation of a vessel-suturing instrument, resembling a miniature sewing machine, first used by the Russians at the Sklifosovskii Institute. And the rejecting mechanism? Ah, here the fight was the longest. We employed massive radiation, various radiomimetic drugs, steroids—and discarded them—and went on—and in the end we found the combination, Dr. Garrett in Pasadena, and I in Rome, to neutralize the enemies of our transplanted hearts. We found what my colleague has so aptly named Antireactive Substance S." He paused. "I have been too verbose for your purposes—and too brief for mine—but that is the answer to what was asked, that was our long road to Stockholm."

Farelli settled back and enjoyed the intermission of journalists recording his story.

Garrett, bewildered and muted by the Italian's glib locution, watched Farelli find a lozenge and place it on his tongue. Spread before him, Garrett observed the reporters writing. What were they writing? Farelli said, Farelli said, Farelli said, the renowned Farelli, the incredible Farelli, the genius Farelli. In the center row, a lady's hand waved, her bracelet jangling.

Garrett stirred himself from the long sleep. "Yes?" he called out weakly.

"Dr. Farelli—" replied the lady's masculine voice. Her demand buried Garrett deeper into the obscure corner of the sofa.

"Dr. Farelli, I am *Stockholms-Tidningen*," she said. "I would like from your own lips the story of your first successful case."

"You have all read about it," said Farelli with a self-deprecating gesture. "It has been made romantic enough."

"Yes, but in your words, no matter how briefly—"

"Very well. I was at the Istituto, early one afternoon, preparing to transplant a mammalian heart into a St. Bernard dog, for the benefit of foreign physicians en route to Milan for a medical convention. In the midst of my preparations, I was informed of an important emergency case. The patient, in his seventies, was a great international figure. He was an English expatriate, a playwright, who had known James McNeill Whistler and Oscar Wilde and Lily Langtry, and for some years had been living in Ravenna. He was on a business visit to Rome, and he had suffered a coronary thrombosis only a few blocks from the Istituto. I rushed to save him, but there seemed little hope. His common-law wife, an Italian lady from a titled family, a lady I had met socially and who had attended my lectures, knew of my dreams and begged me to replace her playwright's dying heart with the mammalian one I had ready for my exhibition experiment. Even as she signed the release, and my equipment was being set up in surgery, the playwright expired on the table. I had no more than five minutes to open his chest and begin a cardiac massage, while my anesthesiologist established an airway. When the patient had first been wheeled in, expiring, I had been frightened. But now that he was dead, all hesitancy left me. I worked like ten demons. Massage immediately reactivated his heart, his breathing, so no brain damage was incurred. Next, I put into use the cardiopulmonary bypass machine. After ninety minutes, I was able to effect the transplantation of the new mammalian heart into his chest. I then connected his circulatory system to the new heart, closed his chest, and resumed treatment with my antireactive drug. In three months, he was on his feet—and just before coming to your gracious city I received, by air post, an advance copy of his latest play—his best yet!"

The *Stockholms-Tidningen* lady clapped her hands, and several other reporters joined in applause.

Farelli cast his eyes downward, modestly, and then he looked up. "That was my first case. Since then, I have made twenty additional human heart transplantations, on qualified patients, and I am proud to say that there has not been one failure. So much for my work. Now, I am certain, you would like to hear my fellow Nobel laureate tell you about his." He opened his hand toward his companion on the sofa. "Please, Dr. Garrett—"

The sudden invitation to share honors and newspaper space had caught Garrett completely off guard. He had been dazzled by Farelli's account, and felt shrunken and wizened after the applause. Now, to follow Farelli was as impossible as to conclude a story that had been half told by Scheherazade.

"I—I don't know if—" He found himself speaking to Farelli, and he realized that this was all wrong. He faced the reporters, and imagined that he saw impatience, even hostility, in their faces. Desperately, he sought a thread of coherent narrative. "I was in the hospital in Pasadena—it's in California—I had my calf's heart and had been working on a canine specimen—it was late, after dinner—this truck driver—sixty-seven—Henry M., I called him in my paper—I made the heterograft of the organ—and he's alive today. It was— there were obstacles, still—"

Garrett became aware that one reporter, not listening to him, had completely turned his back to consult with another reporter behind him. He heard the rustling of paper. There was an excessive amount of coughing. A chair scraped the floor. They wanted Scheherazade, Garrett knew. The inattention flustered him. He was in full rout.

"—anyway, it was a gratifying experience, and the reception was gratifying, and I was gratified." The record needle was stuck and Garrett wanted to quit. He quit. "That was my first case," he concluded lamely.

The waiter appeared with his tray of drinks, to which cigarettes had been added. Farelli accepted a sherry, and, dazed, Garrett took one, too, though he detested the drink. The waiter circulated among the press, and Farelli sipped his sherry, and Garrett did the same.

Garrett tried to think. Had Farelli deferred to him, offered him the chance to state his own case, out of genuine respect? Or had the Italian been sensitive to the fact that he had been putting on a one-man show and felt a pang of guilt? Or had the Italian elected to display his superiority by deigning, on his terms, at his command, to allow a lesser royalty to speak?

Considering Farelli's motive, Garrett emerged from his hypnotic trance, reminding himself that beside him sat the usurper, the rival, the enemy, a crafty Machiavelli of medicine who must be battled word for word, to the death. He had been given an opportunity, moments before, and he had fumbled it badly, out of surprise, out of self-imposed inferiority. This must not happen again, and it would not. Farelli was a blowhard, a highwayman, an alchemist. He, Garrett, had been first in the field, first acknowledged and first recognized, and now, because he was humble and kind, he had allowed the Italian to take the lead through dubious forensics. He must sharpen his wits, become a recognized member of the press meeting, and hold his own. He gulped the distasteful sherry, pushed himself to the very tip of the sofa, like an anchor man on a relay team awaiting the baton, and poised himself for the next questions.

A distant hand went up. It belonged to the *Il Messaggero* man from Rome. "Dr. Farelli, did you and Dr. Garrett work together, and if so, to what extent?"

"I will answer that!" Garrett shouted, and then, horrified at the loudness of his voice and at the suddenness with which he had attracted the attention of the whole room, he modulated his next utterance to a whisper. "We did not work together at all."

Farelli waited until he was sure that Garrett had nothing more to say, and when he was sure, he added his own comment, addressing the reporters. "Dr. Garrett and I, unfortunately, never set eyes upon each other until one hour ago. We never corresponded. We knew nothing of the progress or details of each other's work—except, of course, what we read in the scientific journals."

"Is that not unusual?" asked the *Il Messaggero* man.

"Not at all, not at all," said Farelli. "There are many examples, in science, of similar parallel researches. I will submit two examples. Years ago, in Rochester, Minnesota, a biochemist, Dr. Edward Kendall, worked on secretions of the adrenal glands. At the same time, in Basel, Switzerland, another biochemist, Dr. Tadeus Reichstein, also worked on adrenal glands. By 1936, both biochemists, independent of one another, had discovered a new hormone, the same one, which later led to cortisone injections for arthritis. In 1950, these two men, and a third, Dr. Philip Hench, made a three-way share of the Nobel Prize in medicine for 'discoveries relating to the hormones of the adrenal cortex.' Similarly, in 1956, Dr. Nikolai Semenov, of Soviet Russia, and Sir Cyril Hinshelwood, of Great Britain, won your chemistry prize, shared it, for work in the field of reaction rates—the mechanism of chemical reactions—although they experimented separately, far apart, but going along on the same researches." He paused. "You see, it happens. Dr. Garrett and I are not so unusual."

"Gentlemen, we are all wondering about the future," said the Associated Press man. "What will your heart transplant eventually mean to all of us and our children?"

Garrett was not certain if Farelli had deferred to him once more, and politely held back, or if he, himself, had merely leaped to the reply more rapidly. In either event, he had not given himself time to consider the question before answering it. His only objective now was to have the floor on his own. "That—that is a difficult question," Garrett began, "because it requires a prediction." He would make a joke. That would even him up with the Italian. He made the joke. "After all, Nostradamus never won the Nobel Prize."

He waited for the loving burst of laughter that would greet his sally. There was none. He felt humiliated and undignified, and he tried to recover. "It is too early to guess at the future of our discovery. At present, the transplant can only succeed in limited blood types. The two of us have attempted the heterograft thirty-eight times, each time successfully, but still, in science, thirty-eight times is a conservative number. We are too deeply engaged in the present to give our thoughts to the future."

He liked the roll of his last sentence, and examined the audience covertly to see if it was being preserved. It was not. The pencils of the press remained stilled. Disheartened, he withdrew, and was not surprised to hear the Italian speak.

"I should like to extend my American friend's remarks a little further, if I may," said Farelli. "Dr. Garrett is a scientist, as am I, and naturally reticent. Everything he has said is correct, of course. Our work is in its pioneer phase. Yet I think this much can be added—both of us have our private, and similar, visions of the future. We are working toward the same end—and the end, with the Lord's approval, is really the beginning—it is the immortality of man. A dream? *Sì, sì*, a dream, but now more, now a scientific possibility. As our work is improved, spread, the longevity of human beings will be doubled and trebled, and—who can say?—one day man, bolstered by artificial organs, may live forever."

Farelli paused, and the pencils moved steadily, and Garrett was dismayed. Garrett was not dismayed at his personal failure alone—his reply had been dry and colorless, and the Italian's had been a fairy tale that made copy—but also at his rival's instinctive perception of what laymen wanted to hear. Farelli's tactics, Garrett told himself, were not worthy of the medical profession. Was it right to feed them pap, optimistic tabloid pap that could not be supported, in order to make headlines? What would Dr. Keller and the therapy group in Los Angeles think of all this? Perhaps the psychiatrist might disagree with him, and state that great scientists must have great dreams to justify the minute drudgery of the laboratory and thus give themselves lofty goals far beyond the immediate scalpel and surgery room. He prepared to argue with his psychiatrist, but was interrupted by Farelli's basso, as it boomed again.

"If we cannot be satisfied with our way of life and our society," Farelli was continuing, "we cannot afford to be satisfied with ourselves, with man himself. It is not cynical or irreligious—the Lord forgive me, if it is—to observe that man is an imperfect mammal. In the age of the machine, compared to the machine, man is poorly and frivolously designed and built. Think of a heavy machine standing precariously upright on two thin legs. Think of a machine, that must have vision, limited to two small eyes on one half of its head, instead of three, four or five all around. Think of a machine with wasted, useless parts, parts of the brain, an appendix, extra toes. Worst of all, think of a machine whose manufacturer gives no guarantee on moving parts, and who sells his apparatus at enormous cost without the promise of replacement parts. We want to improve on this machine. Man is a marvel, but he must be made more durable. Too much of years, and love, and money, is expended on each man to have him degenerate, part by part, and waste away so quickly. Schopenhauer once said, 'It is clear that as our walking is admittedly nothing but a constantly prevented falling, so the life of our bodies is nothing but a constantly prevented dying, an ever-postponed death.' It is true, but it is wrong, and we—those of us in physiology and medicine—defy it. Our goal is immortal man, and it will never be less!"

Once again, applause rang through the small room, and even Garrett was moved beyond his resentment. As the clapping of hands ceased, and the pencils moved once more, Garrett castigated himself for his lack of imagination. Why could he not speak up in this way? Why was he handicapped with so narrow a funnel vision? Why was he not poet as well as scientist? Yet, answering the last, and applauding himself slightly, he reminded himself that the scientist's business was science, not poetry, and that this was his strength and his rival's weakness.

A feature writer, a woman, from *Svenska Dagbladet,* had the floor. "Do other medical researchers entertain your same goal of the future? Are there others attempting to improve your findings in heart transplants?"

Garrett, grasping for another chance, replied immediately. "Many others have learned our techniques. The work goes ahead in six nations, other than the United States and Italy."

"As a matter of fact," added Farelli, "one of the most important extensions of our work is right here in your native Sweden, in Stockholm itself."

There was a murmur of interest in the room, largely from the Swedish press members, and someone called out, "Can you be specific?"

"I am proud to give credit where credit is due," said Farelli. "Among the first to take up heart grafting, after our discoveries, was Dr. Erik Öhman, a member of your magnificent Royal Caroline Medico-Chirurgical Institute. He has already accomplished three transplantations, and will be doing more."

Garrett bounced on the sofa, steaming with rage. He felt cheated and robbed by an unscrupulous business partner. Dr. Öhman was Garrett's personal property, his protégé even, and here was Farelli stealing this possession and making it his own. It was unfair, blatant larceny, an obvious trick to butter up the Swedish press, and ingratiate himself with the general public by making them proud of their own native-born surgeon. Garrett had no objections to that aspect of it, only that he, himself, should have been the spokesman on Sweden's behalf, linking Dr. Öhman with his own name, as Öhman would have preferred. Why had he not done it? Why had he not been clever enough?

"Are you acquainted with our Dr. Öhman?" the woman from *Svenska Dagbladet* was inquiring of Farelli.

"Not personally, I regret to say. I have read about him in the medical journals and have been pleased to see a Swedish doctor carrying on our work."

Garrett could contain himself no longer. "I know him!" he cried out.

"You have collaborated with Dr. Öhman?" the *Svenska Dagbladet* woman wanted to know.

"Not exactly collaborated, but—"

"Have you met him?"

"Not yet, but—"

"How do you know him, then?" the woman asked piercingly.

"Through correspondence," said Garrett weakening. "I—I have tried to help him." He realized that this might sound condescending to Swedish listeners. He tried to improve upon it. "I've made available to him all my findings—to add to his own—which have been most creative—his own, I mean. I admire him very much. I intend to meet with him this week."

"Uh—Dr. Garrett—" It was the *Expressen* reporter.

"Yes, sir?" Garrett was alert, pleased to be recognized before Farelli, at last.

"I am sure that you are familiar with the research of many renowned men of medicine, today and in the past. Can you think of any great names that have been overlooked by our Nobel Committee, any doctors who justly deserved the award and did not receive it?"

Garrett could think of several such names, but his natural timidity prevented him from putting them forward. The Nobel Foundation had been generous to him. He did not want to insult its judges. "No," he said, at last, "I can't think of one great name your committee has ever overlooked. I concur with their decisions completely. Since 1901, they have honored all who deserved to be honored."

He relaxed, satisfied with himself. He had accomplished what Farelli had tried to accomplish—he had given the Swedes pride in their judgment—and he had done a better job of it.

"Dr. Farelli." It was the *Expressen* reporter again. "Are you in agreement with your fellow laureate?"

The Italian smiled at Garrett, and then at the press. "I believe Dr. Garrett and I are in accord on most matters, but I am afraid we are not so on this one. You wish to know if your Nobel Committee has overlooked any great doctors, deserving of the prize in the past? Yes, indeed they have. Two unfortunate omissions come to mind. One was an American. I think Dr. Harvey Cushing, of Boston, deserved a Nobel Prize for techniques he introduced in brain surgery. The Caroline Institute had thirty-eight opportunities to reward him, and failed to do so. The other omission, that of an Austrian, was even more serious. I refer to Dr. Sigmund Freud, founder of psychoanalysis. I find his neglect by the Nobel Committee, between 1901 and 1939, incomprehensible. I cannot imagine why he was not honored. Because he had once dabbled in hypnotism? Because organized medicine in Austria fought him? Because psychoanalysis was not an exact science? All mere quibbling. He remains the colossus of our century. His original discoveries in the field of psychology and mental disturbance have enriched our medicine. Those are the only black marks against the Caroline Institute in an otherwise brilliant record of judgment. I am proud to belong to their honor roll."

Garrett had listened to all of this with an increasing sense of shame at his own dishonesty and lack of candor. With envy, he watched the scribbling pencils among the press corps. He glanced at Farelli's profile, and hated its Latin smugness more than ever before. He hated Farelli for his own weakness and the other's unerring showmanship. He hated Farelli, an Italian, for extolling the virtues of an American, Dr. Cushing, and thus marking Garrett's own lack of patriotism. He hated Farelli, an extrovert, for robbing him of Dr. Freud, an introvert's property, a property that was justly his own every time he paid ten dollars to Dr. Keller for another group therapy session.

He hated Farelli, but it seemed useless, like abominating an overwhelming force of nature.

Garrett closed his eyes and sank back into the sofa. His mind sought not justice, but survival. He must crush the Italian soon, or himself be liquidated from existence, as he was being liquidated this afternoon. The necessity to act was clear. Only the act itself was cloudy. Yet here he was, the discoverer of the means to transplant an animal heart, the winner of the Nobel Prize, an acclaimed and approved genuine champion pitted against a windy Cagliostro. Quality would win. The odds always favored the champion.

He opened his eyes, now burning with confidence. He would find a way. He saw Farelli's profile, and its inevitable defeat, and at last, he felt sorry for the man. . . .

In all the Nobel press conferences that Count Bertil Jacobsson had attended in the past, and they were many, he had invariably enjoyed most the interviews with the literary laureates. The others, those starring the physicists, chemists, doctors, had always possessed merit, offering stimulation and high purpose, but somehow their language and content had little to do with the world of ordinary men. You admired, but you did not identify yourself with them. Who could identify with a neutron or the exclusion principle or colloid solutions or enzymes or aortic mechanisms or the citric acid cycle? Literature, on the other hand, was another matter. Almost everyone could read, and if you did not read, you could appreciate the offering of a book through secondary media like the stage and films and wireless and television. Too, you could identify with authors, poets, historians, for even if you did not write books, you wrote diaries and letters and scraps of messages and telegrams, and if you could not write, you told fictions to your wife or tall tales to the children at bedtime. And, if you were Count Bertil Jacobsson, why, you wrote your precious Notes.

These were the thoughts in Jacobsson's mind, that spurred his anticipation, as he crossed from the medical press conference to the larger private lounge, where the literary press conference was being staged. Another thing, Jacobsson told himself: the literary interviews were better sport because the authors were often used to the limelight, whereas few of the scientists had known attention outside of their academic circles, and so authors were more clever about public appearances. Furthermore, except for the literary minority of cultists and precious dilettantes who rarely reached Stockholm anyway, most authors were articulate, uninhibited, contentious, and unafraid of controversy. Scientists, too often, were the opposite. They behaved as prophets of the Lord's Word, and chilled the respectful press into reticence. This was not always so, of course. Sometimes, it was the author who performed as if his current work in progress were the Sermon on the Mount, and the scientist was earthy and argumentative. But more often, you could wager on the author as being the better copy.

Opening the door to the lounge, Jacobsson wondered to which camp the new literary laureate, Andrew Craig, belonged.

He had hardly seen Craig since the novelist's arrival in the morning. The sister-in-law had been attractive enough, although inclined to resemble somewhat Shakespeare's shrewish Katharina of Padua. As to Craig, Jacobsson had not been in his presence long enough to form an opinion. Later, after they had left the Grand Hotel, Krantz had been quick to assert his minor disapproval. He had defined Craig's withdrawn silences as snobbery. But then, Krantz did not like Americans in general. On the other hand, Ingrid Påhl, who had breakfasted with the visiting novelist, had been enthusiastic without reservation. Ingrid's enthusiasms for fellow members of her craft were frequently misplaced, and grew from a loyalty to their common vocation, but this time (Jacobsson believed) her judgment was more profound.

Jacobsson entered the lounge at the moment of interlude. Craig's press conference had been going on for one hour and ten minutes, and now he and the journalists were accepting drinks before the last curtain. Unlike the other rooms, this one was a scramble of chairs and occupants irregularly placed. The gathering, even larger than that attending Professor Stratman, was the most informal now meeting in the Swedish Press Club.

In the far corner of the room, below the wide window, Craig sat alone on a spacious cream-colored couch. Fresh whiskey in one hand, briar pipe in the other, stilt legs crossed, he resembled a giant blue heron, species American. The elongated countenance, beneath the unkempt black hair, Jacobsson observed, seemed more gaunt than this morning, so that the ridges of facial muscle between cheeks and jaw were more apparent. He is tired, Jacobsson decided, but relaxed; he will get through the rest of it.

All about Craig, in unsymmetrical semicircles, were the press people in their folding chairs, smoking, drinking, conversing with one another. Jacobsson guessed that the efficient Mrs. Steen had undoubtedly organized the chairs in even rows, but during the excitement of the interview their owners had pulled them out of line, to hear and view their subject better.

Only a few of the chairs were unoccupied, and Jacobsson selected one near the exit, where his presence would go unremarked. Quietly seating himself next to a chain-smoking and youthful female, who wore a Robin Hood hat and blinked her eyes unceasingly, he waited for the interview to resume.

"Pardon me, sir, but are you Count Jacobsson?"

The question came from the youthful female, and Jacobsson slid around in his chair to meet her full face. It was a humorless visage that he now encountered, one given the appearance of severity by the sharp auburn bangs on her forehead and by two penciled lines of lipstick, rimming the mouth and serving carelessly for flesh lips that were nonexistent.

"Yes, I am Count Jacobsson," he said.

She transferred her loose-leaf pad to her left hand and extended her right. "I'm Sue Wiley," she said. "I've been sent here by Consolidated Newspapers of New York. You were pointed out to me, when I got off the plane with the Garretts."

Jacobsson inclined his head courteously. "It is a pleasure to meet you. We have your credentials at the Foundation."

"I'm not here for a one-shot, Count Jacobsson. It's a tremendous assignment." Her visage was alive with dedication. "I'm going to do fourteen—fourteen articles—on the Nobel Prizes, past and present. They'll break in fifty-three papers. Isn't that something?"

"I could not be more pleased," said Jacobsson. He tried to place Consolidated Newspapers, tried to sort them out of the classification of memory, and then suddenly, he remembered. Consolidated Newspapers was a features syndicate, servicing America and Great Britain, much devoted to exclamation points and inside stories and rude sensationalism. Once they had issued an account—unfortunately published throughout Sweden, also—implying that Dr. Albert Schweitzer, of Lambaréné, was arrogant and vain, basically disinterested in individual human beings, and that his hospital in Africa was unclean. Jacobsson had been offended by the appalling account. His own memory of Schweitzer, with whom he had dined in Stockholm before 1924, when the universal man had been doing organ recitals and lectures to raise money for his hospital, had been highly favorable. He had affected Jacobsson in a way that clergymen often affected him: uneasiness in the presence of someone in touch with metaphysical secrets beyond our grasp, someone deceptively in our image yet known to be a favored son of God. Now Jacobsson tried to remember who had maligned this genius, this St. Francis with his reverence for life, but could remember only that the account had been credited to Consolidated Newspapers of America. If Miss Wiley was from this same syndicate, his guard had better be up.

"—would be impossible without your full cooperation," she was saying, and Jacobsson realized that he had not been listening. "This isn't the usual ephemeral newspaper nonsense," she went on. "I want it to be so thorough, so correct, that students reading it will feel they are learning all there is to learn of Alfred Nobel, your Foundation, the history of the prize giving, the stories of the many winners, the ceremonies, and so forth. I want to do full profiles on this year's winners. Make the series topical, you know. I'll want to see each of them personally. Do you think you could arrange it?"

"I'm afraid, Miss Wiley, that would be somewhat outside my province. I would suggest you contact the parties personally."

"I'll want to talk to you, too, and loads of the Nobel judges and officials and so forth. Certainly, that kind of cooperation is in your province?"

"Yes, it is. The only difficulty will be the matter of time. I am certain you understand. This is Nobel Week. All year, we aim toward this one week. We are hosts, and we have duties and functions. The demands on our time are great."

"I can't think of anything more important than what I'm trying to do for you."

Jacobsson smiled bleakly. "We appreciate it, Miss Wiley. Do not misunderstand. We are here to serve you. I would suggest you telephone me at the Foundation tomorrow morning. After ten. I shall do my best to arrange what

I can for you." Jacobsson heard his own voice, and realized that the room was beginning to quiet. He looked off. "I believe the interview is commencing again."

Straightening in his chair, Jacobsson remembered one point and was curious about it. He leaned toward Sue Wiley. "How has it gone so far?" he inquired. "How has Mr. Craig been?"

Sue Wiley blinked, sniffed, and looked off. "I don't like him," she said. "He's too disdainful."

Across the room, setting down his empty glass on the end table beside the couch, Andrew Craig, preparing to endure the last portion of the press conference, felt no emotion akin to disdain. If some few, like Sue Wiley, had misinterpreted his too quick, too curt replies or his overly casual attitude, as scorn for them, the rabble journalists, and their stupid questions, it was an unfortunate accident of behavior. As a matter of fact, Andrew Craig, when he was able to pin his mind to the activity at hand, had been favorably impressed by the intelligence of his inquisitors and the quality of their inquiries.

What had affected Craig, shortly after his arrival in the Swedish Press Club, was not scorn for Grub Street, but rather self-despair. If he hoped, as Leah and Lucius hoped, that the change of scene and the high honor accorded him would revitalize his interest in life, in creativity, he was wrong, and they were wrong. The laureate Craig was a mockery of the other man he had once been. The reception and adulation, also, seemed intended for someone else, someone who had written *The Perfect State* and *Armageddon*, and not for him, this day, an impostor, an impersonator of the real Andrew Craig. His attendance at the Press Club seemed even more futile. The questions asked were being asked of another man, and his replies were by proxy. The other man might have cared. He did not. It all seemed wasted, like giving information for a story that would never be printed.

The fresh drink had helped, and he uncrossed his legs, and put the unfilled pipe in his mouth, and leaned forward, elbows on his knees, trying to appear interested, determined to do better by that other man who had written those books.

The room was attentive, and the interrogation resumed.

"Mr. Craig," said the man from the Stockholm *Dagens Nyheter*, "is it true that you are only thirty-nine years of age?"

"Only?" echoed Craig with surprise. "Since when is anyone *only* thirty-nine?"

"In terms of the Nobel literary award, sir, that is extreme youth. I believe you are the youngest winner to date. Previously, Rudyard Kipling was the youngest. He was forty-two when he came here in 1907, and Albert Camus was the second-youngest, forty-four when he came here in 1957."

"Well, I assure you, I've established no record," said Craig. "I would allow Mr. Kipling to remain your juvenile lead. He was always younger than forty-two, and I've always been older than thirty-nine."

"Thank you on behalf of the British Empire," called the man from Reuters.

Everyone laughed, and Craig smiled boyishly, and good cheer was restored to the room.

"I wonder," said the man from *Dagens Nyheter,* "why our committees honor so many *young* scientists and *old* writers? Would you have any comment on that?"

"I didn't know you favored young scientists," said Craig. "It's hard for me to imagine. When I see news pictures of them, they always seem wrinkled and stooped, as though they invented seniority to give you confidence in their magic."

"Quite the contrary," the man from *Dagens Nyheter* persisted. "The Nobel Prize-winning physicist in 1960, Donald Glaser, was thirty-four years old. Chen Ning Yang and Tsung Dao Lee, of your country, who divided the physics prize in 1957, were thirty-five and thirty-one, respectively. Dr. Frederick Banting, of Canada, who won the medical prize in 1923, was just thirty-two years of age. William L. Bragg, of England, who won the physics prize in 1915, was only twenty-five. I believe that is the record. But you are the first winner of the Nobel Prize in literature under forty. Can you explain that?"

"I should imagine the reason for this may be found in the nature of the awards," said Craig. "You give all your science prizes for a single discovery. A man may make this discovery in his twenties or thirties as easily as in his fifties or sixties. But you give the literary award not for one work, but for a body of work. It takes a long time to build up a list of books. It's taken me thirty-nine years to write four novels, and you say I'm the youngest. Most writers are elderly gentlemen by the time they have produced sufficient quantity to be judged. Also, I believe, writers ripen more slowly than scientists. A brilliant physicist can often display his genius all at once, at an early age. Experience is less important to him than flash perception and inspiration. Writers, no matter how brilliant, are immature and callow when they are young. Words are not enough. Life provides their materials, and usually they are not good enough until they have lived enough." He half smiled. "Living enough takes time."

"Despite the necessity of the aging process, do you not think too many old authors are given the prize?" asked the *Dagens Nyheter* man. "Many of us believe Alfred Nobel meant his prize money to help the struggling and promising young, and did not want it wasted on the advanced in years who are usually secure and perhaps no longer productive. Nobel once said, 'As a rule, I'd rather take care of the stomachs of the living than the glory of the departed.' Another time, he said that he wanted 'to help dreamers, for they find it hard to get on in life.' Do not these statements imply an interest in aiding younger artists who lack means?"

"I hope so," said Craig with amusement, "I hope that is what Nobel wanted —for, by your standards, I am young—and, by my standards, I lack means."

The *Dagens Nyheter* man would not be put off. "Then why do our committees pour all their funds into the laps of old men who do not need it? The first seven literary winners averaged seventy years of age! Anatole France was seventy-seven when he doddered in here for the Ceremony and check, and his countryman, André Gide, was seventy-eight. Sir Winston Churchill was seventy-nine. Why does our Swedish Academy do this? I do not think it is fair. We wish your opinion, Mr. Craig."

"It comes down to the purpose of the award," said Craig carefully, "and that was not defined by Nobel and has never been clear since. I'm not sure I agree that the handling of the literary award is as unfair as you imply. I don't think age should be the issue at all—only merit—and older writers, proved writers, generally have more merit and deserve more honors. This may be playing it safe, true enough. But honoring younger men, simply because they are younger and promising, may be equally unfair. They may not improve, may not endure—indeed, may retrogress. I have heard that your Academy considers Sinclair Lewis a case in point. I'm no Pollyanna, and I'm not given to toadying, but all things considered, I think your Swedish Academy is doing the right thing. I'm sorry I can't agree with you, but that's how I feel. Call the Nobel Prize in literature an old-age pension, if you will, but I think that is better than turning it into a young man's subsidy." He might not receive the most sympathetic write-up from the *Dagens Nyheter,* he told himself, but it did not matter. His attention was diverted to someone else's upraised hand. "Yes?"

The young male correspondent, with the short-cropped beard, was standing. He introduced himself as representing Sweden's *Bookseller Magazine.*

"Mr. Craig, past winners of the literary award, in recent years, have often stated—whether out of honesty or modesty—that they were less deserving than some of their contemporaries. Sinclair Lewis, in his public speech here— that was back in 1930—felt that James Branch Cabell, Willa Cather, Theodore Dreiser, Upton Sinclair, all were Americans more deserving of the Nobel Prize than he. Six years later, when Pearl Buck was notified of our award, she called it incredible and ridiculous, and stated that the honor really belonged to Dreiser. In 1954, Ernest Hemingway said that Carl Sandburg, Bernard Berenson, or Isak Dinesen should have had the award before him. Three years later, Albert Camus said, 'Had I been on the Swedish jury, I would have voted for Malraux.' This brings us to Andrew Craig. What other author alive would you consider as deserving as, or more deserving than, yourself of the honor you are receiving here?"

Craig struggled with his conscience briefly. Leah had begged him not to derogate himself. But honesty forbade evasion or silence. Yet he hated to name names. There were so many. Well, without fully exposing his inferiority, why not complete candor?

"I cannot name one author more deserving than I—because there are half a hundred who should have this prize before me. There are at least ten in the United States, perhaps fifteen in England and France, several in Japan, and many more elsewhere. I can think of several in Scandinavia, certainly one right here in Sweden."

"Would you name Sweden's candidate?" asked the young man from *Bookseller Magazine.*

"I'm reluctant to name names—second-guess your Academy—but I will say that I've read two novels by your Gunnar Gottling, and for all his irreverence, explicit sexuality, crudity, he is a major talent."

"He does not qualify in certain areas."

"Well, I don't know the facts," said Craig, "and I have no wish to argue in favor of authors who should be here in my place. You asked if there were others that I thought should be here in my stead, and I said yes. I'm sure no author can ever be certain that he alone, above all others, deserves the world's highest literary compliment. Nor, I am sure, can any annual award satisfy the entire public."

The *Svenska Dagbladet* reporter had risen. "Mr. Craig, I suppose you are acquainted with our Nobel machinery? Former Nobel winners are allowed to nominate. French and Spanish and other recognized Academies are allowed to nominate. Professors of literature in universities are allowed to nominate. And, of course, our own Swedish Academy has given itself eligibility to nominate. These nominations are submitted in person or by cable or by letter. I am sure you know all of this—"

"No," said Craig truthfully, "I had no idea of all these formal preliminaries."

"Of course, I am leading up to a question," said the *Svenska Dagbladet* reporter. "Please bear with me a moment longer. Early in 1950, I am informed, there were over one hundred nominations for the literary prize from abroad. Many were from America, and not one included the name of William Faulkner, of Oxford, Mississippi. Consequently, our own Swedish Academy nominated Mr. Faulkner, and then voted him the prize for 1949, which had been held open. I am also informed, from an excellent source, that you won your prize in the very same fashion. Did you know that?"

"I had not heard it, no."

"You were not nominated by your fellow countrymen in America or any other nation abroad. You were nominated right here in Stockholm, by our Swedish Academy, who then later voted you the prize."

"Again, I can only say I am grateful—now doubly so."

"The point I am leading up to is—why was it left for a Swedish jury, so far from your homeland, to introduce your name? In short, why are you so neglected—unappreciated, I should say—in your native America?"

Craig shook his head. "You've posed a tough question. Well, I'll do my best. For years, Faulkner was relatively obscure because his admirable Yoknapatawpha County was obscure—in the eyes of critics and public alike. Happily, your Swedish jury, with the insight of distance, found him less so. My output has been relatively neglected, in my own country, for similar reasons."

"Obscurity?"

"Yes, I think so. I write about the present, but I write about the present in terms of the past. Most Americans have been conditioned to believe that historical fiction should be romantic and escapist. To them I am an odd duck, out of joint with time. My historical fiction does not fit the popular mold. It is neither romantic nor escapist, but puzzlingly realistic, and touches their contemporary lives. It worries them. It confuses them. They find my method obscure, and they turn their backs on it. For some reason, which is a mystery to me, your Swedish jurors understood what I was doing and admired it. I was fortunate to find understanding an ocean and half a land away from where I live."

The London *Spectator* man was on his feet. "Mr. Craig, you were especially cited for *The Perfect State* and *Armageddon*. The Academy called them 'writings in support of humanitarian ideals.' Can you elucidate, in your own words, the humanitarian ideals these two novels represent?"

"Certainly. In *The Perfect State*, I was saying that communal government cannot work unless the nature of man is changed. I doubted if the nature of man would change, or even that it should. I was saying that the socialized state—now exemplified by Communism—was basically anti-man, and could not dominate man, and that man would fight it and survive it. I was saying this was true in Plato's day, and it is true in our day. As to *Armageddon*, I was simply adding my voice to many, to remind readers of the magnitude of catastrophe conceivable on this planet, and of their own microbe-insignificance and helplessness in the face of it. It was as if ants had finally invented their own insecticide. I was pointing out that, at best, man is a frail, wispy creation, with an uneasy and precarious foothold on earth, and that he had better think twice about outdoing the Maker in competing for destruction. Perhaps the Maker challenged man with Pompeii and Herculaneum and the Lisbon quake and Krakatoa, but He did not obliterate him. By imitating God, without God's wisdom and mercy, man can destroy his kind forever with nuclear weapons, his homemade Krakatoas."

The *La Prensa* man from Buenos Aires looked up from his pad with a question. "Sir, do you have another work in progress?"

"Too long in progress, I'm afraid."

"Is that the novel entitled *Return to Ithaca* that I've heard about recently?"

"Yes."

"Is this also a novel set in an historical frame?"

"No, it's modern, it's contemporary."

"Isn't this the first time you've gone modern? What made you change?"

Craig hesitated. He had always wanted to be a part of his time, and had been afraid, and it had been Harriet who had encouraged the project. But Harriet was the dead past, and they were wanting to know about the present. "I don't know," he replied, "except that's the way this new idea came to me. Possibly, too, like most writers, I felt I'd been in a rut and wanted a change of scenery. I guess I got tired of my costume parties—decided that the Mardi Gras was over—wanted to remove the mask and show the world my own face. I'm not sure. I'm just repeating the first thoughts that come to mind."

"Sir, can you tell us what the new novel is about?" It was the Japanese gentleman from *Yomiuri Shimbun*.

"This much—a twentieth-century Odysseus, his wanderings through the labyrinth of life, fending off its monster perils, fighting attacks—from within and without—on his liberty to speak and think, on his right to worship alien gods or none at all, on his ethics and moralities in averting poverty. It's an oft-told tale, but each generation must tell it in its own way. I hope I live long enough to write it."

A lady from *Aftonbladet* spoke up. "What authors, now regarded as classical, influenced you?"

"I won't vouch for any direct influences, but I know who has interested me and moved me. Will that do? Very well. The writings of Tolstoi, Stendhal, Flaubert and Sir Richard Burton meant a good deal to me. The life Shelley lived, that rather than his poetry, was valuable to me."

"Are you aware, sir, that Shelley was also one of Alfred Nobel's favorites?"

"No, I wasn't."

"Oh, yes, he adored Shelley's philosophy and rebellion. Nobel's only published book, a tragic play, *Nemesis,* was based on the same theme Shelley used in *'The Cenci.'* "

"I'd certainly like to read Nobel's play," said Craig.

"I'm afraid that would be almost impossible," said the *Aftonbladet* lady. "After his death, Nobel's relatives burned every copy of that play they could find. Since it was a horror story, they felt that it was not worthy of a legendary prize-giver. I believe only three copies survived."

Craig nodded his thanks for the information, and then acknowledged the *Expressen* representative.

"Mr. Craig, I understand you have visited Sweden before?"

"Yes, after the war."

"We always welcome opinions on our country, good or bad. Do you have any?"

"Well, I don't think I'm qualified—"

"What have you liked about Sweden?"

Craig was amused by the journalist's persistence. "All right. I've liked—let me see—most of all I've liked the island of the Old Town, Carl Milles's fountain in Haymarket Square, your lobster in cream sauce, the store called Svenskt Tenn, your actresses Greta Garbo, Ingrid Bergman, Märta Norberg —especially Miss Norberg—why won't she do more plays?—and what else do I like? Yes, the trip to Uppsala by boat, Orrefors glass, your cooperative movement, your abolition of poverty, and, yes, Ivar Kreuger—I don't want to outrage you, but the grandeur of the man fascinates me. That's a partial list."

"And the other side, Mr. Craig—what have you *not* liked about Sweden?"

"That's not quite fair."

"You are not the type to like everything."

"Of course, no one does. All right. I'll be brief, and not elaborate. I think you put too much store in conformity, you make too great a virtue of politeness and manners, you have sex but too little romance, you reap the benefits but suffer the consequences of the middle way—no highs and lows, overblandness, overneutrality. I love Sweden, but these are the things I love least of all. I would not speak of these things, but we are here to question and answer, and that is my answer."

Craig had a half minute's respite, as the reporters wrote. He made a gesture toward taking up his glass, but saw that it was empty. He filled his briar and lit it.

Across the room, a young woman in a Robin Hood hat was standing. Even at the distance, Craig could see that she was blinking nervously.

"I am Sue Wiley of Consolidated Newspapers, New York," she said loudly. "Do you have any objections to personal questions, Mr. Craig?"

"Many objections, I assure you—"

Several reporters tittered.

"—but I acknowledge your right to ask them," Craig continued. "By being here, I'm fair game, I suppose. And I do confess, I'm more interested in Charles Dickens's relationship with Ellen Ternan than in his paper heroines. I must assume your readers are, too. So, though I'm a reticent person, Miss Wiley, do go ahead."

Sue Wiley remained standing. "Speaking of relationships, who is the lady you have traveled to Sweden with?"

He did not like her tone, or its edge, and he sat up. "She's my sister-in-law, Miss Decker, and she's quite inoffensive and having a marvelous time, thank you."

"Your wife was killed in an auto accident three years ago."

Since it was an announcement and not a question, Craig did not reply to it. But he did not like Miss Wiley's prosecutor mannerism, either.

"Do you have any immediate plans to marry again?" she demanded.

This was impertinent, and Craig tried to contain himself. "I have none. If I had, it would remain my own business."

Sue Wiley stood unabashed and blinking. "I want to ask you about your work habits."

That was better, and Craig's arm muscles eased slightly. "Okay," he said.

"Do you find that drinking hard liquor stimulates the imagination?"

Craig tightened, and he pulled himself completely upright on the couch. The clever, insensitive bitch, he thought. He was in for a dogfight, and smelled it at once. "You were inquiring about my work habits," he countered coldly.

"Yes, Mr. Craig, that's what I'm talking about. I have my research. It's no secret, is it? I've met and heard of writers who use dope because it helps their work. Look at De Quincey. I have it that you drink when you work."

He would not concede a public display of bad temper. All eyes were upon him, and he forced a smile to his lips. "Miss Wiley, if I drank when I worked, I wouldn't write at all."

"But that's the point, you haven't written at all, not for three or four years," Sue Wiley shot back triumphantly.

This brazen public exposure, by a sensation-mongering bitch, brought the heat of color to Craig's face. He found it hard to contain his fury. "Now, wait a minute, young lady—" he began.

Before he could go on, to what regrettable end he knew not, he was interrupted.

"Mr. Craig, may I have the floor for a moment?" The request, clear and confident, had come from Count Bertil Jacobsson, who had raised himself to his feet and now stood beside Sue Wiley.

Craig bit his lower lip, and held his tongue.

Jacobsson had moved apart from Sue Wiley, so that he could address not only her but the rest of the press.

"When unfounded accusations, such as those just made by the lady press member, are directed against an honored guest from abroad, I feel that it is my duty—and not his—my duty as a host of the Nobel Foundation and a representative of His Majesty, to intervene and make the reply." Jacobsson studied the hushed audience with awesome patriarchal gravity. "Let me make clear our position. We of the Nobel Foundation do not judge our nominees and laureates by their personalities or characters or eccentricities. We are not interested in whether our winners are drunkards, heroin addicts, or polygamists. Our judgment is not based upon human behavior. That is a task for Sunday schools. Our decision, in literature, is based solely on whether or not we think we are satisfying Mr. Nobel's desire to reward 'the most outstanding work of an idealistic tendency.' "

"What about freedom of the press and what readers want to know?" demanded Sue Wiley. "We're servants of the public. Why did you invite us to this press conference anyway?"

"We invited you, and everyone," said Jacobsson calmly, "to meet a laureate but not so that you could malign him with inference, gossip, and unseemly questions. I do not know Mr. Craig's personal habits, and what is more, I am not interested in them. I am interested in his genius, and I want you to be, also, and that is why I invited you here this afternoon." He studied the members of the Swedish press corps, and suddenly a smile broke across his wrinkled features. "And suppose Miss Wiley could prove that Mr. Craig is, indeed, a most obnoxious drunkard—which you can see he is not—but suppose she could prove it? What would be proved, after all? The majority of us in this room are Swedes. I should wager there is not a teetotaler in the group. What true Swede would claim that he does not, on occasion, have his love affair with snaps or beer? Are we children? Or do we possess the mature tolerance of an Abraham Lincoln? Do you recollect the well-known Lincoln anecdote? Gossips had warned him that his most successful general, Ulysses S. Grant, was a poor drunken imbecile. 'If I knew what brand of whiskey he drinks,' said Lincoln, 'I would send a barrel or so to some other generals.' "

Laughter rattled through the room, and Sue Wiley blinked furiously.

With aristocratic ease, Jacobsson went on. "I can speak to you with some authority of previous Nobel laureates in literature, whom I have met and known personally and respected highly. Needless to say, I would not wager that all of them were abstainers and prohibitionists. I remember when we notified one Scandinavian author that he had won the Nobel Prize, he went on a two-week drunk. It is a fact. It is also a fact that when Knut Hamsun came from Norway to get his literary award in 1920, he was thoroughly inebriated the night of the dignified Ceremony. He pulled the whiskers of an elderly male member of the Swedish Academy, and he snapped old Selma Lagerlöf's girdle!"

There was laughter once more, and much note taking, and before Sue Wiley could speak again, Jacobsson hastily added, "We have taken enough of Mr. Craig's time, and surely, we have made him thirsty. While I join him in toasting Mr. Hamsun, I suggest you write your stories. *Det är allt.* The press conference stands adjourned!"

Afterwards, after the Press Club had been cleared of reporters, and the Marceaus, Stratman, Farelli, and Garrett had gone off with Krantz and the attachés, Andrew Craig lingered behind. The drinks had disappeared, so he leaned against a wall of the cloakroom and smoked, watching Mrs. Steen and Count Jacobsson gather up their papers.

When Mrs. Steen said her good-bye, Craig joined the old Count.

"Thank you," he said.

"For what? Everything I told them, I will tell you. It is true."

"You may have put yourself out on a limb. What if I am a drunkard? It would make a fool of you."

"I am sure you are not. And if you are, I could not care less. Every few years, we have a witch like Miss Wiley, and she must be put down. It is dangerous, that sensationalism. It obscures all that is important here."

"Well, at any rate, you were right about one thing—you did make me thirsty. Do you know where I can buy some liquor to take to the hotel?"

"I will direct you. We will walk together."

They went down the stairs and into the street. It was late afternoon, and already the darkness of winter had fallen on the city. A chill wind whipped up from the canal, and both men buttoned their topcoats. They walked across the square, Craig chewing his empty pipe, Jacobsson swinging his cane in a wide arc and thumping it on the brick pavement, and then they entered Fredsgatan, passing Fritze's, who advertised themselves as booksellers to the court, and turned the corner into Malmskillnadsgatan, where they found the package shop.

Craig fell in line, behind several Swedes, at the long counter of the package shop, and waited patiently, studying the half-filled shelves behind. When it was his turn, he requested three bottles of Ballantine's.

Later, returning to the Grand Hotel along the canal, Craig wondered if the anecdote about Knut Hamsun were true, and Jacobsson said that he had witnessed it. For a moment, Jacobsson considered revealing to Craig a more recent incident: that of the elderly literary laureate who had arrived in Stockholm with two bountiful young ladies who, while introduced as his secretary and his interpreter, were rumored to be his two current mistresses. It had been a situation fraught with the possibilities of scandal, but Jacobsson had artfully managed to hide it from the press.

Now, Jacobsson decided against alluding to the lechery. Instead, he said that the details of the Hamsun anecdote were carefully recorded in his Notes, and then he told Craig of his Notes, and did not conceal his envy for writers who actually wrote books. He spoke fondly of his quarters, above the Nobel Foundation, and of his private museum, which was really his study, filled with autographed photographs and memorabilia of previous Nobel laureates. He hoped that Craig would find time to pay a visit to his museum, and Craig, with growing affection for the old gentleman, said that he would.

"Do you think your press conferences were successful today?" Craig asked.

"Among the best in a decade," said Jacobsson. "I looked in on each one, you know. I believe you met Dr. Farelli?"

"The medicine man?"

"Yes. He made an interesting remark in his interview. Someone asked him what he thought was the most serious omission in the history of the medical awards. He said Sigmund Freud. Of course, he could not know the truth. I think it might amuse you."

"What is it?"

"Sigmund Freud was never formally nominated for the medical award, true—but once, he was nominated for the Nobel Prize in literature. Did you know that?"

"Are you serious?"

"Absolutely. It is a fact. And, for that matter, why not? I should guess he was as qualified for that award as Winston Churchill. In our literary awards, we respect gifted amateurs."

"When was Freud nominated for the literary prize?"

"In 1936, in his eightieth year. It had been predicted, you know, but rather as a sarcastic joke. In 1927, the psychiatrist and physician, Julius Wagner von Jauregg, won our medical award for malaria inoculation used in paralysis. Well, the Freudians, of whom he disapproved, crowded about to congratulate him, and von Jauregg told them, 'Gentlemen, someday you will all get the Nobel Prize—for literature.' And it almost came to pass. In 1936, Romain Rolland and Thomas Mann nominated Freud for the Nobel literary award. Freud was a serious candidate that year, but in the end, the Swedish Academy voted him down. Sigmund Freud lost out to Eugene O'Neill. There is hidden history for you."

They had arrived at the entrance to the Grand Hotel, and Jacobsson took his leave. He indicated the bulging package of three bottles nested in the crook of Craig's arm.

"Do not let Sue Wiley see you," he said with a smile. And then he added, almost too gently, "And do not forget tonight you are a guest of the King."

Watching Jacobsson depart, Craig wondered about the old gentleman's last remark. Did he suspect what that bitch, Sue Wiley, already knew? Had he, in his indirect and courtly way, tried to put Craig on his guard and warn him of the consequences of a scandal?

Hell, Craig thought, nothing happened to Knut Hamsun, did it? He hugged the package more tightly in his arm. Momentarily, he felt secure, three bottles secure. But he would go easy right now. He regretted that he had not reassured Jacobsson. He could have told him that tonight he would be fit for a King.

V

In a corner of his restfully quiet, lamp-lighted library, Count Bertil Jacobsson, attired in starched shirt, white braces, cummerbund, and formal trousers, sat at his antiquated walnut desk—a reproof to the new generation's intense modernism—and thoughtfully tapped the capped end of his pen against the open green ledger before him.

He contemplated the shadows cast on the high ceiling, and across a wall of books, and on the nearby glass case that held his Nobel award souvenirs, and at last, knowing the hour was late and the limousine would soon arrive, he resumed his Notes. In his pinched chirography, he wrote:

—was one of the rare occasions in which I had to intercede between a laureate and the press. It may be true that Craig drinks—I do not know yet— but if it is true, his resultant behavior could damage us and ruin him. The Knut Hamsun incident still haunts me. We shall see how matters develop tonight.

He read over what he had written, and was about to put the pen back in its holder when he decided to add a paragraph less speculative and more factual.

The Royal Banquet has been moved up to tonight, which is December 3, and will formally inaugurate Nobel Week. Except for the afternoon of the climactic Ceremony, and the Town Hall dinner that follows it, the Royal Banquet, highly exclusive and dominated by the presence of the King, is often the most memorable social event of our winter season. I remember that after he had received the prize for literature in 1923, William Butler Yeats, the Irish poet, wrote of the Banquet, "I, who have never seen a court, find myself before the evening is ended moved as if by some religious ceremony." I trust that this year's winners will be similarly impressed.

Carefully, Jacobsson blotted the page, closed the green ledger, and placed it in the middle drawer of his desk.

With an indistinct complaint, he stood up, pulled on his formal jacket, and then started for the bedroom to find the decorations that he must wear. The decorations, he knew, would soothe him. They would remind him of long experience and exemplary performance, in the service of the throne, in handling all manners and nationalities of men. He hoped that he would not need the confidence of these decorations this night.

It was almost seven o'clock when Andrew Craig finished changing from his single-breasted tuxedo into his freshly pressed dark blue suit, and it was the second time he had dressed for the evening.

The half bottle of Scotch that he had consumed through the late afternoon, sparingly and in the privacy of the bathroom, out of sight of Leah's disapproving gaze, had made him forgetful of the mimeographed instructions about attire for the Royal Banquet. It was only after he had answered the door earlier, and admitted Mr. Manker, the prim and punctilious young attaché with the high pompadour who had been assigned to him by the Swedish Minister of Foreign Affairs, that he had been tactfully reminded of protocol.

Mr. Manker had removed his felt fedora and topcoat, and placed both neatly on a maroon chair, and had sat stiffly on the sofa, while Craig, his mouth cottony from the drinking, had tried to think of conversation. The awkward pause had been filled by Leah's zestful entrance from her bedroom.

"Hello, Mr. Manker! Have you come for inspection? How do I look?" She pirouetted once, gaily, rather clumsily, Craig thought. Her brown hair was swept back and bunned more tightly than usual, her face unlined and flawless and unsoftened by the pancake makeup, and the evening gown of red satin that hung straight downward along her rigid figure.

Mr. Manker had leaped to his feet, clucking approval, then gallantly clicked his heels and bent over her hand. "Exquisite," he had murmured, and Craig, watching hazily, detected false professionalism and disliked it. "It is a terrible bother, this protocol," Mr. Manker went on, "but it is the way of monarchies, no matter how democratic. I, for one, approve. It gives us islands of dignity in the drab land mass."

"I approve, too," said Leah with pleasure.

Mr. Manker took brief stock of Craig, and his lower lip worked in and out. "For the annual Royal Banquet," he said, "His Majesty the King wears formal evening dress—"

"And a crown?" asked Leah.

"Heavens, no. The crown is there, but as a symbol," said Mr. Manker. "You shall see for yourself at the dinner. The King's family and relatives, and the few higher-ranking members of royalty who have been invited, also are in formal evening garments. Perhaps some will wear the uniforms of their station. The Ambassadors whose nations are represented in the Nobel awards, and our Cabinet members, wear dark but informal suits. The ladies of the court, and commoners, all wear similar dresses—black taffeta or velvet with puffed sleeves. This is to prevent one from outdoing the other. The wives or relatives of the laureates may wear evening gowns of any design or color. Miss Decker is handsomely attired. The male laureates, like our Cabinet members, are expected to wear informal dark suits. Full dress is only expected at the Nobel Ceremony on the tenth."

Craig realized that Mr. Manker had been addressing him, and suddenly he realized what was wrong. "I'm not supposed to have a tux on for this brawl, is that it?"

"You will not be barred," Mr. Manker said with his trained smile, "but you may be mistaken for a member of the royal family. Yes, as you understand it, a plain dark suit is preferred."

"I'll change," said Craig.

"As you wish," said Mr. Manker, his face reflecting relief. "But before you go, while we have the time—I came early for this—a few words about further protocol. I hope you do not think me insufferable, but it is my duty. I extend this briefing to laureates every year."

"Go on," said Craig.

"Cocktails will be served in one of the salons off the dining hall. This will take place for a half hour to perhaps one hour before the dinner. The purpose is really for our laureates to meet distinguished members of our government, and to meet each other."

"I already met the other winners at the Press Club this afternoon," said Craig.

"Ah, yes, but this will be, it is hoped, a more social and relaxed meeting. After the cocktails, and immediately before dinner, the King and princesses and princes will appear. For Mr. Craig, it is only necessary to take the King's hand when it is offered, to speak after being spoken to, and to address him as Your Majesty or Your Royal Highness—either one will do. Our King is not withdrawn, and his informal cordiality will please you. At dinner, there will be place cards. You will remain standing until His Majesty is seated, and then, of course, you may sit, too. As for you, Miss Decker, when the introduction to the King is made, you will curtsy deeply—"

"I've never done that, I wouldn't know what to do!" Leah cried out. Her concern was genuine.

"That is why I am here," said Mr. Manker calmly. "I will demonstrate the curtsy, and then we will rehearse it together while Mr. Craig is changing."

Craig regarded the cue as a form of insolence, but his alcoholic intake allowed him to accept it with equanimity. He left the sitting room, pulled the sliding drapes across his bedroom entrance, and began to undress.

Now he stood before the full-length mirror in his dark suit and knew that only one thing was missing. One leg, he told himself, was still hollow. He went into the large bathroom, located the half-filled bottle of Scotch on the tile behind the bidet, unscrewed the cap, and swallowed once, twice, three times. This meant three ounces, and this meant he was fortified and informal.

He hid the bottle again, and returned to the bedroom. Momentarily, he eased himself into the chair across from the double bed. He wanted the good feeling to invade and occupy every limb. He thought that he could hear the creaks and compliments that accompanied the art of the curtsy from the sitting room. Above his bed, he noticed for the first time, hung a copy of a painting in a mahogany frame appropriately royal. Napoleon Bonaparte was playing with his ill-fated son, L'Aiglon, as set on canvas by Jules Girardet. It struck Craig not as a work of art but as a sigh for a past glory, and, somehow, it was as much an anachronism as the night that lay ahead.

Craig reached over and took the mimeographed sheet from the bedstand. Once more, he read it:

His Majesty the King has been graciously pleased to invite the Nobel Prize laureates with their husbands, wives, or relatives to a banquet at 7:30 P.M., December 3, in the Royal Palace of Stockholm.

Auto will be in waiting at the hotel at 7:10 P.M., and the persons invited will be accompanied to the Palace by the attachés attending.

Dress for the evening will be . . .

The words had begun to cloud. Craig crunched the sheet into a ball, and in pleasant emulation of a basketball idol of his youth—was it Hyatt at Pittsburgh? Murphy of Purdue? McCracken of Indiana?—he pegged the wad of paper at the distant wastebasket, and missed.

His watch read 7:07. Unsteadily, he rose to attention before the mirror, and was satisfied that nothing was missing now.

Throwing aside the drape, he entered the sitting room. "Okay, Mr. Marker —Manker," he said thickly, "take me to your leader."

Their noiseless limousine sped across the Strömbron bridge in the bitter-cold blackness of early evening, and swiftly approached the festively illuminated, massive Royal Palace on Skeppsbron that guarded the medieval island of the Old Town.

"Kungliga Slottet," announced Mr. Manker, unnecessarily giving the Royal Palace its Swedish name, as they drove into the vast main courtyard bathed white in the blaze of lights. The towering guards were wearing gleaming spiked steel helmets, and black leather boots, and traditional dark uniforms adorned with white epaulets. They seemed forbiddingly Prussian, until you discerned that the faces were bland Swedish, like the faces of a million boy children who required no gun permits for their toy weapons. The guards snapped to attention as Craig emerged from the limousine, followed by Leah and Mr. Manker, and for a moment, Craig enjoyed this unreal play-acting, enjoyed his impending coronation, and regretted the French Revolution, and wished the drabber parts of democracy dead.

Hastily, a resplendent officer helped Mr. Manker lead them across the uneven stone paving, up three steps, and out of the relentless cold into the small reception room of the Royal Palace. A servant took Craig's hat and topcoat, and Leah's coat, and disappeared. Mr. Manker, retaining and carrying his topcoat, escorted them to a business office where an equerry, in regimental garb, greeted them effusively.

There was a singsong exchange between Mr. Manker and the equerry in Swedish, and when it was done, the attaché turned to Craig. "You are the first of the laureates to arrive. Would you like to go immediately to the salon, or perhaps spend ten or fifteen minutes seeing a portion of the palace?"

Still chilled by the ride, Craig desired the salon and the comfort of the drinks, but he did not wish the strain of being the first of the guests, either.

Before he could make his decision, Leah had his arm. "Oh, let's see some of the palace while we can!"

"So long as it's not drafty," added Craig glumly.

Mr. Manker led them to a curving marble staircase, made all the more magnificent by the two stiff guards flanking the bottom steps, their silver breastplates glistening over their Charles XII uniforms.

They climbed between walls decorated with ancient, yellowed tapestries, and when they reached the top, and moved through the gaping corridors and ornate museum rooms, Craig's impression was of enormousness, mediocrity, and expensive shabbiness. As they walked and walked—here King Oscar II's bed, there Charles IV's dishware, here *objets d'art* belonging to Gustavus III —Craig felt smothered by prosaism and commonplaceness. Sweden was a small and remote land, yes, but it had spawned better names than these palace puppets—it had spawned Tycho Brahe and Emanuel Swedenborg, Jenny Lind and Carolus Linnaeus, and yes, even his patron, Alfred Nobel.

As they progressed from room to room, inundated by medieval furniture and French rococo and more tapestries and porcelain and classical sculpture that Gustavus III had permanently borrowed from Italy, Mr. Manker attempted to enliven the tour with a running commentary. It was made without hesitation, almost without inflection, and Craig knew that the attaché had dutifully led many other Nobel laureates across this path before.

"This Royal Palace is the largest still-inhabited palace in the world," Mr. Manker was saying. "There are six hundred eighty rooms here. Our present King uses thirty of them for his private quarters. In the thirteenth century, there was a castle here. The royal family moved in about 1754, and their descendants have lived here ever since."

"Why all those paintings of Napoleon and Josephine?" inquired Craig, interested for the first time. And then, he remembered his history. "Because of the Bernadotte family?"

"Exactly," said Mr. Manker.

Leah, whose reading of history had ceased on the day of her graduation from college, spoke up. "I'm afraid I don't know what you two are talking about."

"Our present royal line," said Mr. Manker, "derives from France, and has since 1818. It is a curious story. By 1809, we had suffered reverses inflicted by Napoleon and Russia, lost our empire, and our Gustaf IV was overthrown and sent into exile in Switzerland, where he died in poverty. Some of our insurgent noblemen were dissatisfied with the heir of our ruling family and wanted to import a new one. One of these noblemen, Count Carl Otto Mörner —a distant relative on my father's side, I am pleased to say—went to France on a mission. There, he met one of Napoleon's favorite military aides, Jean Baptiste Jules Bernadotte, a sergeant who had risen to the rank of field marshal. Count Mörner was impressed, and took it upon himself to sound out Bernadotte on the possibility of his occupying the Swedish throne. I do not believe Bernadotte took him seriously. But Count Mörner was very serious. He returned to Stockholm and began to make propaganda for Bernadotte.

At first, the idea was resented. The ruling class had another outsider in mind for the throne—a Dane—Prince Christian August. But before the Dane could be elected, he pitched off his horse one day, dead from a stroke, although there was a suspicion that he had been poisoned. That left the door open for Bernadotte, and gradually his name grew in popularity. Eventually, Bernadotte was offered the throne, elected crown prince, and adopted by old King Charles XIII. Bernadotte changed his name to Charles John, and in 1818, he became King Charles XIV John of Sweden. He turned against his former commander, Napoleon, sided with England and neutrality, and regained Norway for us.

"Incidentally, Bernadotte's wife was Désirée Clary, the daughter of a Marseilles merchant. She had been Napoleon's first love. When Bernadotte became heir to our throne, and later our ruler, Désirée refused to follow him from Paris to Stockholm. She adored Paris and had the idea that Stockholm was a primitive outpost of civilization. After ten years alone, she thought that she would see for herself, and, reunited with her husband, she found that she preferred Stockholm to Paris, at least for a while. She demanded, and received, a separate coronation as Queen of Sweden. She was extremely irregular—used to wander the streets incognito—outlived her husband, most of her contemporaries—and in her old age was found dead, of natural causes, in someone's doorway. Such were the first Bernadottes, Mr. Craig, and we have had them ever since. Our present King is of French origin."

"It's a most unusual story," said Leah. She turned to Craig. "It would make a wonderful book."

Craig shook his head. "No, thanks." Drunkenly, he apologized to Mr. Manker. "No offense intended. I like your rulers, but their virtues destroy them for the novelist. They're all too do-good, too amiable, too pacifistic. There's not a hell raiser or a son of a bitch in the lot."

"Please, Andrew, your language," Leah protested, and worried over whether he had been drinking.

Mr. Manker ignored her and went directly at Craig. "You are wrong—forgive me, Mr. Craig. You do not know our history. It was not always so. We have had many—very many—uh—colorful rulers. I can think of three immediately."

"Name one immediately," Craig challenged with mock belligerence.

Mr. Manker pointed to a wall that they were nearing. "There you see a painting of Gustavus Adolphus. Our Sweden had only two million inhabitants when he made it the greatest power in all of Europe. After that, there was his daughter, Queen Christina—"

Craig snapped his fingers. "I forgot about her."

"—and certainly, she was by no means colorless. At eighteen, she refused to take the oath as Queen of Sweden, but took it as King of Sweden. She refused to marry. 'I would rather die than be married,' she used to say. 'I could never permit anyone to use me as a peasant uses his field.' She worshiped scholarship. It was she who brought Descartes to Stockholm, where he died. Because her health was poor, she traveled through the warm countries of Europe. She fell in love with Italy, became converted to Catholicism, and abdicated the throne of Sweden. She was received in splendor by the Pope of Rome and by King Louis XIV of France. Her eccentricity got worse. She dressed like a man, planned to become Queen of Naples, and allowed two members of her royal household, Santinelli, her Grand Chamberlain, and Monaldeschi, her Grand Equerry, to compete for her favors. When Monaldeschi incurred her wrath, she encouraged Santinelli to murder him. She is the only one of our rulers not buried in the Riddarholm Church—you have seen it—located about a kilometer from the palace. Her father, Gustavus Adolphus, rests there. So, also, does Charles XII—another colorful figure— who, at the age of eighteen, with a cavalry of four hundred, routed eight thousand Russians led by Peter the Great—they are all there, except Christina. She died in Rome, impoverished, and in Rome she is buried."

The liquor was mellowing Craig, and he had grown sorry for the attaché, who was trying so hard, and he relented. "Maybe I was hasty in my judgment. Too many of us know too little about Sweden. Yes, Christina was quite a character. From the writer's point of view, certainly the best of the lot. Of course, in a sense she wasn't really a Swede—"

"She was as Swedish as I am," Mr. Manker insisted. "She was merely seduced by the passion of Latinism."

"But that's interesting," said Craig. "That means all of you up here are not simple little igloos. Inside each igloo burns a fire. Properly fed, it becomes a bonfire."

Leah frowned. "I don't think that's nice, Andrew, saying those things to Mr. Manker."

"No, it's all right, Miss Decker," said the attaché. "I appreciate Mr. Craig's frankness. It is stimulating, like his writings." He addressed himself to Craig again. "No, we are not simply igloos, as you so curiously put it. We are as warm as citizens of any country, perhaps more so. And we are enlightened about our passions, also. Swedish children are given sex education their first year in elementary school. High-school students—what you call teenagers—are taught in the use of contraceptives. We are healthy and open and normal about sex. From what I have read, you Americans are quite the opposite, you are quite furtive about sex."

"We're furtive as all hell," Craig agreed cheerfully. "No nation on earth talks and thinks as much about sex, and does so little about it, as Americans —per capita, that is."

"What kind of conversation is this, anyway?" interrupted Leah, blushing.

"My sister-in-law is right," said Craig to Mr. Manker. He waved his hand at another assembly of paintings, tapestries, and historic furniture. "It ill befits us to bicker about carnality amid the grandeur of Kings." He halted. "Mr. Manker, my thirst for knowledge is quenched. Thank you. Now, let us satisfy a lesser thirst. Where in the devil is the Banquet?"

"I apologize for detaining you so long, Mr. Craig. Right this way."

He led them to a marble staircase, and then started down. Craig was about to follow when he felt Leah's restraining hand on his arm.

"Andrew, please," she whispered, "you're behaving rudely, baiting the nice man. Have you been drinking? You have, haven't you?"

"Lee, dear, I'm a wasteland—in need of irrigation still."

"You're drunk. I can tell, when you talk like that, so loose and crazy." Her features bore the suffering of all Motherhood. "Please, Andrew," she implored, "don't make a spectacle of yourself before the King."

The word *spectacle* conjured up for him the marvelous picture of his predecessor, Knut Hamsun, gaily snapping Miss Lagerlöf's girdle, one Nobel laureate to another. He smiled inwardly at the tableau.

"I'll behave, Lee," he promised. "Miller's Dam will be proud of its hero son." He started down the steps. "I'll remember to nurse my drink, and you remember to curtsy."

"Don't joke. If not for my sake, then for Harriet's. Your whole future depends on how you act this week, and this week starts tonight, right now."

"You take care of the curtsy, and I'll take care of the drink," Craig called over his shoulder, "and neither of us'll fall on our face."

Mr. Manker had led them to the doorway of the large salon, adjacent to the royal dining room, and then he had summoned Count Jacobsson and had excused himself. Mr. Manker's rank, that of third secretary, was not sufficiently high to warrant invitation to the Banquet.

Count Jacobsson had brought Craig and Leah into the spacious salon. "This is *Vita Havet*—the White Sea room," explained Jacobsson. "It was once used for court balls, and Oscar II liked to distribute his Christmas presents here. Beyond is Charles XI's Gallery—the dining hall. And over there, through the small chamber or cabinet room—if you follow the narrow corridor—you will come upon Sofia Magdalena's state bedchamber. You might have a look later."

At the moment, Craig took in the large salon called the White Sea. The room appeared to be designed in Empire style, blue and white, made loftier by gold-and-white pillars, softly illuminated by burning candles in the sparkling chandeliers, and heated by roaring fires in two huge open fireplaces. Despite the density of guests, Craig could make out enormous unfamiliar oils, marble-topped commodes, faded divans, tables and chairs. Jacobsson pointed to the three rugs covering the floor—"Gustavus III received them as gifts in France almost two centuries ago." Craig became aware of a small balcony, filled with onlookers, above the entrance. He inquired about these spectators. Jacobsson explained that they were the more distinguished members of the press corps. Craig tried to locate Sue Wiley among them, and could not, and felt easier.

Now, with Old World correctness, Jacobsson maneuvered Craig and Leah about the room, smoothly introducing them to knots of the select. As they made headway, from someone in formal dress to someone in business black to someone in yellow court knickerbockers, steadily hand-shaking, the names

206

fell back from Craig's ears, but the titles remained: a Prince, a Bishop, a Baron, a Professor of the Nobel Committee of the Royal Caroline Institute, the French Ambassador, the Prime Minister's wife, the Swedish Minister of Foreign Affairs, the Permanent Secretary of the Swedish Academy, and a dozen others.

Along the way, Leah had accepted the invitation of a prodigious lady in waiting to the court, who had relatives in Minnesota, to join in a discussion that was then going on, about child welfare in Sweden. Craig and Jacobsson had reached, at last, the liveried servant with his tray of effervescent French champagne, and now, at this oasis, both held their goblets, sipping the wine as they surveyed the scene about them.

There were forty to fifty people in the salon, and conversational groups everywhere—Craig could see Professor Stratman almost hidden from view by his admirers—and yet there was no raucous babel of talk. There was the hum of voices, stray sentences that floated high and indistinctly and evaporated, an occasional careful chuckle, a muffled exclamation, but in total resonance the salon was as reserved and hushed as any library reading room.

"Now, over there is a pair you should meet," said Jacobsson, nodding off in a direction past Craig.

Craig tried to follow his direction, but could distinguish no pair in particular. "Which ones?"

"The toothpick man with greased reddish hair—he is in full dress—is Konrad Evang. He is a Norwegian millionaire, the owner of many department stores in Scandinavia. Several years ago, he was in the United Nations. He is an important member of the Stortings Nobel-komite in Oslo—the Nobel Peace Prize Committee. Since there is no peace award this year, he has the time to represent his country at this affair. The one he is speaking to, the bald-headed one in the pin-striped suit, he is Sweden's wealthiest man today, no doubt a billionaire. Perhaps you have heard of him. He is quite world-famous. He is the industrialist, Ragnar Hammarlund. Do you see them?"

Now Craig saw them, and was surprised that he had not identified them before. They were a bizarre pair in a room of figures so alike and monotonous. Suddenly, he remembered Hammarlund's name from news stories and magazine articles, although he could not recall his face.

"Yes, I know Hammarlund's name," he told Jacobsson, "but I never knew what he looked like."

"He does not permit photographs," said Jacobsson. "He is a fabulous figure, most mysterious. I suppose everyone who has made his first billion inevitably becomes mysterious. He is ageless, but possibly sixty. He was at the Hotel de Paris, in Monte Carlo, negotiating his first international deal with Sir Basil Zaharoff, when the munitions king died there in 1936. Hammarlund became interested in high finance when, in his youth, he was briefly employed by our Ivar Kreuger, whom you admire. In 1928, I think, four years before Kreuger shot himself through the heart in Paris, he hired Hammarlund to set up a holding company, the Union Industrie A.G., in the tiny principality of Liechtenstein, next to Switzerland. This was at a time when

Kreuger had loaned seventy-five million dollars to France, had big factories in thirty-four countries, and was making sixty-five per cent of the world's matches. But I think Hammarlund smelled the rat. He considered Kreuger the world's first money wizard, but he also guessed that he might be a super-swindler. So he got out in time and went off on his own. He enjoys to speak of Kreuger, and the old days, but I have heard him say many times, with pride, it is not necessary to emulate Kreuger to become wealthy. Shrewdness is better, even easier, than thievery, he likes to say. And I do believe he is honest, ruthless perhaps, but honest, anyway as honest as a man can be who has made so many millions."

"Does he manufacture matches?"

"Nothing so fragile. He is in everything, I am told, in Scandinavia, in America, everywhere in the world. He once owned a part of Bofors with Axel Wenner-Gren and Krupp. He has hydroelectric power plants, a merchant shipping fleet, forests, iron mountains, several airlines, newspapers, oil wells, banks—endless banks. I could not begin to enumerate his holdings. You will learn more of him, when you visit his villa in Djurgården—the Animal Park not far from here—on the sixth. It is Hammarlund's dinner for the Nobel laureates. Surely you will attend?"

"I wouldn't miss it."

"I think maybe it would be proper to meet him now. However, I must warn you, he is not an easy talker when he is away from the villa. At home, he is engaging and outspoken. Elsewhere, he is reticent and on guard. No, Hammarlund will not offer much tonight. But I do think you will enormously enjoy Konrad Evang. He is a delightful man, but serious. He is a virtual encyclopedia of information on his Oslo Peace Prizes—perhaps I value this trait in him too highly, since information on the prizes is my own field, too. Would you like to meet them?"

"Yes, I would," said Craig, "but first, I'd like another drink."

A flicker of apprehension showed on Jacobsson's face, but then he signaled the liveried servant, who came with the tray. Craig placed his empty goblet on the tray, and taking one filled with champagne, began to drink it at once.

"All right," he said finally, "let's find out about peace—and money."

The four of them had been talking—or rather the three of them talking, with Hammarlund, for the most part, listening—for five minutes. Evang had governed the conversation, graciously discussing and praising Craig's novels, with occasional interjections of assent from Jacobsson and Hammarlund. Craig, his reactions dulled by a morning and afternoon of whiskey and two recent champagnes, pretended attention but remained indifferent.

Concealing his impatience, he found his eyes seeking the servant with the tray, but the man was nowhere in the immediate vicinity. With effort, Craig tried to concentrate on Evang, who was extolling the merits of Oslo. He observed that Evang's rust hair was touched with bleach, and the pince-nez on his thin nose had a golden chain, and a network of veins showed through his cheeks, and the cords of his throat stood out as he spoke.

Almost stealthily, Craig transferred his scrutiny to Ragnar Hammarlund. He could not help but stare. The abnormally albescent skull and face were entirely devoid of a single bristle. Hammarlund's head was glabrous and his face hairless. Peering hard, Craig thought that he detected white eyebrows of almost invisible down above the eyes, but he could not be sure. No wrinkle added character to the face, no wart, no scar, and almost, or so it seemed, no human feature. The eyes lay evenly pressed into the head, neither concave nor convex, miniature flat mirrors of watery gray. The broad nose was shapeless, melting into the center of the face, so that only the nostrils showed. The mouth was a delicate roseate. No more than an inch beneath the lower lip, the pretension of a chin receded, giving the disconcerting effect of no chin at all. In summary, a soft, smooth larva countenance, the consistency of a white slug. The frame beneath the remarkable head was medium in height and width, and garbed impeccably in an old-fashioned, expensive custom-tailored suit.

Craig tried to detect something human about this legendary figure. The feminine hands held a silk handkerchief, and several times, quickly, almost unobtrusively, the handkerchief was touched to the place where Hammarlund's forehead must be. The forehead perspired, Craig was pleased to note, and then he remembered that on their introduction, he had shaken Hammarlund's limp hand, and it had been clammy and repellent.

Raised on the traditions of Commodore Vanderbilt and Gould and Fisk, the blustering and savage robber royalty, Craig could not conceive of how this pulpy being had made his first billion. Fleetingly, he wondered what Hammarlund was doing at this affair. What was his connection with Nobel? Or the King? And what was his interest in the laureates, anyway?

He realized that Hammarlund's head had turned to meet his stare, and quickly he returned his attention to Konrad Evang, apostle of peace.

"Yes, my friend," Evang was saying to Jacobsson, "you get all the attention in Stockholm. I suspect most of the world hardly knows that we in Oslo are responsible for possibly the most important of the five prizes."

"If you wanted attention, you should have given a prize this year," Jacobsson chided him.

"It is not so easy, not so easy, my friend," said Evang. "Ours is a perilous task, and infinitely more controversial—political—than any of the four under your guardianship."

"Well, why did you skip this year?" Craig inquired.

"We were hopelessly deadlocked over three candidates," said Evang. "Not one could win a majority of the votes. It is just as well, I believe. How could we honestly give a prize for peace in a time like this?"

"I should think there would be no better time," said Craig. "There are plenty of men and organizations working to keep the world from being blown apart. Why not recognize and encourage them?"

"Because," said Hammarlund, speaking at last, in a tone so satiny and faint that it automatically forced everyone to lean closer to him, "our Norwegian neighbor prefers to keep peace rather than honor peace. An award to any party, no matter how neutral, might be interpreted as an affront to the Soviet Union or the United States."

"Come now, Ragnar, that is not so," said Evang without anger. "We are judicious men, not frightened men, and you know it."

"I am not so sure." Hammarlund's handkerchief flicked his forehead. "I know your awards very well. You gave your first one to a seventy-three-year-old Swiss, Henri Dunant, because he founded the International Red Cross. I have heard it said that he deserved not the Nobel Peace Prize, but the Nobel Prize in medicine. You could have done better, but you were playing it safe. In 1946, after World War II, you honored the American Quaker, Emily Greene Balch, who had done her best work in World War I, and John Raleigh Mott, the Protestant, who was in retirement. You would not honor an active worker, because you feared controversy. You reached into the forgotten past. As for you and your colleagues being judicious men—"

"Now, now, Ragnar," protested Evang, "do not start in on us again."

"I am speaking for the benefit of our guest, Mr. Craig," said Hammarlund softly. His glance included Craig, but he continued to address the Norwegian. "In 1906, you gave thirty-six thousand dollars and a Peace Prize to Theodore Roosevelt—to the Rough Rider—an obvious warmonger like all the others. Did not this Roosevelt once say, 'No triumph of peace is quite so great as the supreme triumph of war'?"

"He mediated the Russo-Japanese War," said Evang.

"Mediators are not good enough for me," said Hammarlund. "Then go and honor all referees and umpires on earth. They are mediators, too. I know your list of Rough Riders—you honored Elihu Root, Aristide Briand, Gustav Stresemann, General George Marshall—you call them all genuine pacifists?"

"You must be fair, Ragnar," interrupted Jacobsson. "Our Norwegian friends have also honored Woodrow Wilson, Fridtjof Nansen, Albert Schweitzer, Ralph Bunche, Cordell Hull—"

"I know about Hull," said Hammarlund placidly. "Franklin D. Roosevelt wrote Oslo every year between 1938 and 1945, nominating Hull, before Mr. Evang's committee saw fit to elect him." He turned to Craig. "This may interest you, Mr. Craig. In 1937, Cuba nominated Franklin D. Roosevelt for the Peace Prize, and Hull seconded it. That was one election your Roosevelt lost. The Peace Prize went to Viscount Cecil of Chelwood instead, a League of Nations man."

Evang appealed to Craig. "My friend Hammarlund is teasing. He knows of our courage. Take the year 1961. Did we not defy the white supremacy people of South Africa to give our honor to Albert Luthuli, a dark-skinned former Zulu chief who fought apartheid?"

"Too easy," said Hammarlund. "You were not afraid of South Africa. You were picking on someone your own size."

"All right, then," persisted Evang, "let us speak of someone bigger. In 1946, the Finns nominated Aleksandra Kollontai, Russia's first female Ambassador, an advocate of free love, for helping to shorten the war between

Finland and Russia. It was outrageous, a Russian propaganda move. We voted her down, despite the threats of *Pravda*. And long before that, we had suffered when the Czar of Russia and Kaiser Wilhelm of Germany were nominated for the Peace Prize, and we had voted them down, too."

"How did you ever get saddled with that award?" asked Craig. "Why was that single one taken away from Sweden?"

"Nobel had intended that Sweden give the Peace Prize, too, with the other four awards," said Evang, "but at the last moment, he had a change of heart. At the time, Sweden and Norway were under a single ruler, King Oscar II, and Nobel wanted to bind the countries more closely together. Also, he felt that we in Norway could be more impartial about a political hot potato than his fellow Swedes. There were other reasons, but those were the principal ones."

Abruptly, Evang turned away from Craig to face the bland Hammarlund once more. "I will tell you this, Ragnar—we have made our blunders, yes, but we have had our moments of truth, too, truth and courage. I will mention one name, and then you judge us as you wish." He paused, and then he said slowly, "Carl von Ossietzky."

There was a silence. Hammarlund remained imperturbable. His handkerchief flicked. His hairless head moved ever so slightly up and down.

"Yes, Konrad," he said, "Ossietzky was your finest hour. For giving the prize to him, I forgive you all else."

Craig tried to identify Ossietzky in memory, and failed, and was about to inquire who he was, when the liveried servant materialized with a tray, freshly filled with goblets of champagne. Gratefully, Craig traded his empty glass for a full one. By the time the servant moved on, the thread of conversation had been lost.

He prepared to speak to Hammarlund, when he saw that Hammarlund was gazing intently off toward a far corner of the room.

"Bertil," Hammarlund murmured, and Jacobsson was immediately alert. "Bertil, that couple over there before the fireplace—the handsome gentleman and his Gallic lady in light blue décolletage—would they be the Drs. Claude and Denise Marceau, your chemistry winners?"

Jacobsson squinted off. "Yes, the Marceaus."

"Introduce me," said Hammarlund. It was not a request, but a command. "Introduce me," he repeated. "I am keenly interested in them. I must know them tonight." He nodded at Craig. "Forgive me, Mr. Craig. It has been a pleasure." He glanced off at the Marceaus again, and then added enigmatically, "It is ever thus—business before pleasure."

The moment that the Ambassador had left them, and they were alone for the first time this evening since leaving the Grand Hotel suite, Denise Marceau flung her accusation at Claude.

That same moment, as he stammered in his bewilderment at her charge, she saw two men approaching them. One she recognized as the Swedish Count who had been on the Nobel reception committee and who had welcomed them at the afternoon press conference. The other, a fantastic, so bald, so white, so singular, she had never seen before. Suddenly, nearing, the Count had whispered to the other, and they had veered off in another direction and attached themselves to a group nearby.

Immediately, Denise perceived what had kept the two men from joining Claude and her. They had seen her face, distorted with rage, when she had spat her accusation at her husband. They had deduced that a family quarrel was in the making. Tactfully, they had steered clear of the battle. Thank God, Denise thought. She wanted to settle this with Claude alone, uninterrupted, and right now, here and now.

"You have not answered me," she challenged Claude. "Did you or did you not arrange an assignation with that girl, in Copenhagen?" Then, without waiting for his reply, she went on angrily. "It is not enough to insult me in Paris. Now, you throw discretion to the winds. Now, you must have your favorite courtesan follow you through Europe, always near, always at your beck and call. I do not know what has got into you. I swear, you must be insane."

Claude listened to the tirade in befuddled silence. What he had feared the most was happening before his eyes. Denise had been too distraught to reveal, in continuity, what new fantasy was troubling her. She was making charges that were not only riddles but utterly senseless.

"Denise," he pleaded, again fearful of a scene, "what are you going on about this time?"

"Do not lie to me. I am sick of lies."

"Denise, I swear, I simply do not know what you are talking about. *Qu'est-ce que c'est?*"

"Oh, yes, I can imagine you do not know." She had unsnapped her sequin evening bag, and pulled out a crumpled envelope. She thrust it at him. "*Voilà.* Now tell me you do not know."

He flattened the envelope in his palm. The envelope was addressed to him, typewritten. It bore a French stamp, and a Paris postmark, and the imprint *Par Avion.* He turned the envelope over, unable to guess its contents, and saw that the back flap had already been torn open. He fingered inside for the letter, and found only a short newspaper cutting. Across the top, in block lettering had been printed in pencil, *Figaro.*

With anxiety over an unknown threat, heightened by Denise's accusing eyes, he read the cutting. It told him that the French government, in a gesture of good will toward Denmark, had arranged to transport ten of its foremost Parisian mannequins, and the latest Paris fashions, to a Copenhagen winter fair. The mannequins would be guests of the Danish government, at the Hotel d'Angleterre, for three days, commencing December 6. The names of the ten mannequins from Balmain, Dior, Balenciaga, Ricci, and La Roche were listed. The fourth name in the list of ten read, "Mlle Gisèle Jordan, Balenciaga."

The news of Gisèle's impending nearness stunned Claude. He kept his eyes fixed on the cutting, to give himself time to regain his composure before the inquisition continued.

"Well," Denise was saying, "how long ago did you arrange that little rendezvous?"

"I arranged nothing. Can you not read? This was arranged by the French government."

"Est-ce que tu veux me faire prendre des vessies pour des lanternes?"

"No, I am not trying to prove to you that black is white. I am simply saying I knew nothing." He held off the cutting as if it were contagious. "This is the first I know of it."

"Parbleu!"

"I am sorry. It is the truth."

"That skinny *putain* sent it to you—you will not deny that." And then Denise added, "Or do you have some concierge for a go-between?"

Claude examined the envelope. There was no doubt that Gisèle had mailed it. Such indiscretion was unlike her. Yet, no doubt, she had assumed, as a single person who knew privacy, that in all marriages this privacy was maintained. She had believed Claude opened his own mail, and Denise her own. She could not know that, in the long years of their work, with most of their correspondence scientific and technical and meant for their collaborative eyes, they had always opened each other's mail. His bad luck, he told himself. It was done, and he would have to make the best of it.

"I will not deny it is from Mlle Jordan," he said at last. "There is no one else who could have sent it. But I assure you, Denise, I had no idea of her visit to Copenhagen. I suppose it just came up—"

"—and now she lets you know she is waiting, flat on her bed, ready, your divine *sous-maîtresse.*"

"I can endure anything from you, Denise, except crudeness."

"And I can endure anything from you except humiliation." Denise's lips trembled. "When have you agreed to see her?"

"Please. We have agreed to nothing. She will be in Copenhagen, at work with her friends. I am in Stockholm with you."

"Copenhagen is an hour or two from here. Like taking the *métro.*" She paused. "You intend to see her, do you not?"

"I am not seeing her," Claude said firmly.

"If you humiliate me once more while we are in Stockholm, you can go on that stage yourself and take the whole damn prize for yourself."

"You are suddenly generous," said Claude, weary of his defensive position. "You were less so this afternoon."

"What does that mean?"

"At the press conference," said Claude, bitterly. "You certainly did your best to castrate me—"

"I would not do it with words—I would do it with a dull spoon, if I had one," Denise interrupted.

"—to make a fool of me in public," Claude went on. "I would like to see a transcript of that interview. One would think you had won the Nobel Prize alone, and I had come along to help you carry the medallions."

"I told them nothing but the truth," said Denise.

"We did the work together, and you know it. Since when do we say, 'I have done this' and 'You have done that'? What have we come to, Denise, even to have to discuss this? We are a team of two—"

"I thought it was three. My roll call shows three."

"*Mon Dieu,* stop it!"

"I married you to collaborate not only in work but in pleasure. When you take your pleasure elsewhere, and leave only the work part for us, then there is not enough for me. I am left alone. I have to think of myself alone, now and in the future, and so I spoke for myself."

"Denise, I told you we would work things out."

"How?"

"I do not know yet," he said miserably, "but we will, I guarantee it." His hand took in the salon. "Surely this is not the time and place to make decisions."

"I am telling you this—I am not waiting for your decisions. Henceforth, I shall make my own."

"Then make your own," he said.

Her eyes blazed at him, and she wanted to say many cruel and important things, but she suppressed further combat. "Get me a drink," she said.

He searched the room until he located a servant, and then summoned him. When the tray appeared, and they took fresh champagne, Denise became aware that the pair of men who had originally approached them, and then detoured, had now decided that the family quarrel had ended.

Count Bertil Jacobsson joined the Marceaus with a slight bow. "How do you do? One of our most celebrated citizens is eager to make your acquaintance." He brought Hammarlund forward, as if from the wings. "Dr. Denise Marceau—Dr. Claude Marceau—our eminent industrialist, Mr. Ragnar Hammarlund."

Hammarlund took Denise's hand, prepared to kiss it, but since this was a gesture of greeting which she habitually resisted in France (as being archaic and insincere), she brought the industrialist's smaller hand down sharply and converted the gesture into a masculine handshake. Having gripped his hand hard, she found that it squashed in her palm like a broken snail, and she withdrew quickly. Next, Hammarlund offered his clammy grasp to Claude, who took it without attention.

Hammarlund addressed Denise. "Count Jacobsson tells me you were brilliant at the press conference this afternoon."

"He is unnecessarily flattering," said Denise, with a smile for Jacobsson and a triumphant sidelong glance at her husband.

"It is so," said Jacobsson enthusiastically. "I have heard many chemistry laureates, but few more articulate than *Madame le docteur.*" He turned to Claude. "I hope you are having a pleasant time this evening."

"It would be more pleasant," said Claude lightly, "if I could have a Swedish drink instead of champagne. For a Frenchman—champagne is like milk for an American."

"But of course, you may have anything," said Jacobsson, fussing nervously.

"Also where is the lavabo?" Claude asked. He nodded to his wife. "Darling," he said, and then to Hammarlund, "Mr. Hammarlund, do excuse me for only a minute. I shall be right back."

He backed away, and then went hastily off with Jacobsson.

Denise watched him leave, more annoyed than ever with him for having stranded her with a perfect stranger, and wondering if he could no longer endure her company and merely wanted a respite from her.

"I have followed your work in the journals for years," she heard Hammarlund saying. "No chemists on earth more deserved this recognition."

"And I have read about you for years," said Denise with effort. "Is it true you were once with Ivar Kreuger?"

"An early and instructive phase of my life. It convinced me that honesty is, indeed, the best policy."

"I was a little girl in Paris when the scandal unraveled," said Denise. "I remember my father pointing out the apartment in the Avenue Victor-Emmanuel where he shot himself. What happened to you after that? And to all Kreuger's holdings?"

"I had got out months before," said Hammarlund. "I left Kreuger with his matchstick empire and made a connection in munitions. Much less breakable, and much more in demand. As to Kreuger's holdings, only his home firm, the Swedish Match Company, survived the scandal. It still owns, I believe, over one hundred factories in three dozen countries. However, I have little interest in matches—though several of my researchers have labored several years trying to produce a permanent match, one that will last its owner's lifetime."

"I did not know you were interested in research," said Denise, and because she was too impatient to be polite, she added, "I thought men like yourself were only interested in money."

"But we are," agreed Hammarlund, without humor. "Men such as I also have foresight. In the end, research means money. I own nine industrial laboratories in Sweden alone. I even have two in your native France. They do not carry my name, but they are supported by my endowments."

"This is not altruistic, I presume?"

"Not one bit. We work toward a practical end. Most of the alchemy is hopeless and wasted, but one day, one of my laboratories will produce a perfume that stays on the skin indefinitely or a textile that never wears out or an automobile tire that lasts forever—and my enormous investment in improbability will pay off. Right now, I am interested in synthetic foods. I still have an old paper, in my files, that you and your husband published. It concerns experiments you made with a certain strain of algae, as a possible food substitute."

"Yes, that was shortly after our marriage."

"Why did you abandon the work?"

"We saw no future in it, and we were young and filled with a thousand hopes. We worked at a dozen projects until we found the one we could fully embrace."

"I cannot say you were wrong. After all, here you are for the Nobel Prize."

"Yes."

"But from a selfish point of view, I wish you had gone on in synthetics. I believe it is the most promising field of the immediate tomorrow, and there are too few geniuses in the field. Although, I must say, I do have one excellent analytical chemist working directly under me, in my private laboratory behind my villa. His name is Dr. Oscar Lindblom, an unknown young man who will one day have a reputation. This very morning, we were preparing a homogenate together. Food synthetics are rather a hobby of mine. Would you care to know why I became so interested in the problem?"

Denise did not care to know. She searched off for Claude, seething at him, and then remembered her companion's question. "Why you became interested? Money, I suppose."

"This time, in all honesty, no, at least, not at first. You see, Dr. Marceau, I am anticreophagous—anti-flesh eating—a lifelong practicing vegetarian."

Somehow, aware of his bizarre appearance again, she was not at all surprised. "Is that sensible?" she asked.

"Oh, I enjoy good company. Plutarch was a vegetarian, and so were Voltaire and Schopenhauer and Tolstoi and our own Swedenborg. I have never gone as far as Shelley, who would not eat crumpets because they were likely to be buttered—but I simply will not eat anything that I can pet. Curiously, this attitude made me speculate on synthetic foods—including algae, which I classify with the synthetics, and then, gradually, I saw that the commercial importance of such products was more important than the aesthetic benefits. One day, soon, no one on earth will go hungry or be ill-nourished, thanks to cheap synthetic foods."

"Which you will manufacture?"

"It is my dream. At any rate, I hold almost a hero worship for superior chemists, and since it was announced that you were coming to Stockholm, I have looked forward to meeting you."

"You are kind, Mr. Hammarlund."

"Not kind, never kind." He dabbed his face with his silk handkerchief. "If you have read your program, you know, perhaps, that I am having a dinner this week for the visiting laureates—"

"Of course. I had forgotten."

"We would be honored—"

"You say 'we.' You are married?"

"I am quite alone, by choice. I hold with our Ibsen, 'A strong man is strongest alone.'"

"And a strong woman?"

He stared at her, the flat mirror eyes catching a vision of her dissatisfaction and bitterness. "I am not so certain about a woman—a woman is different."

He waited for her comment, but she was contained again. "By 'we,'" he went on, "I mean my friends and I will be honored to receive you. Dr. Lindblom will be at the dinner, of course—I think he will interest you—and Miss Märta Norberg will graciously act as my hostess."

"Märta Norberg—the actress?"

"None other."

"I am not a *dévote* of the stage or cinema, but when I have attended, it has most often been to see her. I have not seen her for several years. Is she in retirement?"

"An actress is never in retirement. She is always awaiting the proper role. It is like asking an actress about her comeback. Inevitably, she will say, 'Comeback? But I have never been away.' You and your husband will be my guests?"

"I never speak for my husband," said Denise. "You must invite him yourself. As for me, yes, I will be delighted—on two conditions—that you do not insist that I visit your laboratory, and that you do not serve me a meal either synthetic or vegetarian."

Hammarlund patted his glistening albino face with the handkerchief, almost merrily, and then replied, "I promise you—no laboratory—that would be rather a busman's holiday, would it not?—and the meal, strictly food you can pet." He studied her a moment. "If your husband is otherwise occupied, and you come alone, I assure you, you will not be sorry. Our Swedish young men are most gallant and attentive—and appreciative of the best France has to offer."

Her face grew suddenly grim. "Mr. Hammarlund, I may have my problems, but a need for gigolos is certainly not one of them."

Hammarlund opened his hands toward her, at once self-reproachful and penitent. "Forgive me, Dr. Marceau—at times, I am so clumsy with the language—but I meant to imply no such thing. I apologize, believe me, if I exceeded good taste in a mere desire to be hospitable."

Convinced of his sincerity, Denise softened. "No, the fault is mine. I am afraid I am overwrought. Blame it on the trip, the excitement, this whole royal formality—" Beyond him, she saw Claude and Jacobsson walking toward her. "Here they come now. You will enjoy my husband. He is better-behaved at these social affairs."

When Claude, holding a new drink almost colorless, arrived, with Jacobsson a step behind, Denise immediately spoke to him. "Mr. Hammarlund has been most engaging, but I have given him a difficult time."

"Quite the contrary," Hammarlund protested.

Denise continued to address her husband. "You will find Mr. Hammarlund a patron of chemistry, and you will be flattered to know that he is acquainted with our earliest work." She turned abruptly to Jacobsson. "I have exchanged hardly a word with the other winners. I think I should do so." She took Jacobsson's arm. "Will you escort me, Count?"

The gathering, the largest in the White Sea Room, had been kneaded into a tight circle by the comings and goings at its periphery and by a common desire to keep the discussion informal. Included in the gathering, from the point where Denise Marceau had been admitted to it five minutes before, were—left to right—Saralee Garrett, John Garrett, an earnest and acne-riddled young Swedish Prince in uniform, Margherita Farelli, Carlo Farelli, Konrad Evang, Emily Stratman, Max Stratman, Carl Adolf Krantz, and Count Bertil Jacobsson.

The young Prince, in a learned falsetto, was giving a biographical discourse on Alfred Nobel, in response to Margherita's thickly accented question about the donor. John Garrett listened with impatient courtesy, shifting his weight from one leg to the other. Garrett was interested in neither information nor entertainment, but in assassination. Like a hunter in hiding, he had no time for the appearance of the minor animals. He wanted only the king of beasts.

Since his fiasco at the press conference, Garrett had revaluated his own worth and decided that he was deserving of a defense to the death. Never again, he had vowed, would he let the Italian treat him as a satellite ally. Now, as the talk flowed, he waited for Farelli to speak up, so that he might interrupt or contradict him and thus reveal him as unworthy of invitation to this select circle. The wait was irritatingly protracted. Eager as Garrett was to pounce, there was no prey. The Farelli of the afternoon, vocal and vulnerable, was no longer in evidence. Tonight, he was subdued. Tonight, handsome in a black wool suit, English-tailored in Rome, he listened. It was as if he scented a lurking danger and preferred to hide beyond anonymity. Garrett ground his teeth and marked time.

The young Prince was going on shrilly about Alfred Nobel. "—is another reason we so fervently admire him. He overcame all odds. His father was twice a bankrupt. Nobel, himself, had no formal education, never once graduated from a school. This will interest you especially, Professor Stratman. You were speaking of John Ericsson—the builder of the *Monitor* for Lincoln —and his early experiments in trying to accomplish what you accomplished, harness the sun's rays. Did you know that Nobel met Ericsson in America?"

"That is really true?" asked Stratman.

"It is in our histories," said the young Prince. "Nobel was only seventeen. Ericsson showed him the engine he hoped to run with solar energy, and this inspired the inventive streak in Nobel."

"And then Nobel invented nitroglycerine," said Garrett importantly.

"I do not believe that is quite correct, Dr. Garrett." It was Farelli who had entered the conversation. "Nitroglycerine—blasting oil—was discovered by one of my countrymen, some time before Nobel—Professor Ascanio Sobrero, of Turin."

"True," the young Prince confirmed.

Garrett's confidence sank beneath the new setback. He had been overeager. The prey had stalked the hunter. Farelli was again ahead. Garrett determined not to make the same mistake twice.

"What Nobel accomplished was to invent the blasting cap," the young

Prince was saying, "and later safety powder, made of nitro combined with German clay, which was what started the great dynamite business and made him a millionaire. But as I was remarking, for him it was always a battle against odds. In the pioneer stages, the explosive blew up his factory and killed his younger brother. He had to move his laboratory to a pontoon raft in the middle of a Swedish lake. By accident, this liquid exploded ships off Germany and Panama, a whole city block in San Francisco, a warehouse in Australia. Once, I am told, your American Senate"—he spoke to Garrett now—"seriously debated a bill to make the shipping of Nobel's liquid a crime to be punished by hanging."

"Yes," said Garrett, "my fellow Americans are often very suspicious of science. When I was doing my work in heart transplants, I received many threatening crank letters warning me not to try to compete with God."

Farelli said nothing, and Garrett felt the warmth of a small victory.

"Fortunately, Nobel learned to tame and control his dynamite," said the young Prince, "and in ten years, he had fifteen factories and was one of the richest men in the world—almost as rich for his day as our celebrated Mr. Hammarlund is in this day."

Farelli moved to speak, and immediately Garrett was ready. "Most interesting," Farelli said. "But I am curious about another thing. Here we all are, the laureates from the ends of the earth, the benefactors of Nobel's generosity. Yet I know next to nothing about my benefactor himself, his personal character, life. What was he really like?"

Garrett pounced. "Surely, Dr. Farelli, you have read at least one of the countless articles or books on Nobel? They are there for all to see. I have read many, and I feel I know him as well as I know any of my relatives."

"You must read between the lines then, Dr. Garrett," the Italian replied. "I was not saying that I had not read about Nobel. I was saying that, despite all I have read, I still know nothing about him. What kind of man is it who can put forth dynamite, so destructive, and also put forth prizes for peace on earth and idealism in literature and discoveries that benefit mankind?"

"Guilts, all guilts," said Garrett in a fading tone, desperately drawing on the patois of Dr. Keller and the therapy group. "He was compensating for his guilts. It is obvious to see."

Count Bertil Jacobsson cleared his throat. "If I may comment—"

"Count Jacobsson knew Nobel personally," the young Prince interjected.

All eyes were on Jacobsson, as he went on. "—I would be inclined to agree with Dr. Farelli that Nobel remains, to this day, an enigma. No book has captured his contradictory nature. Yes, I knew him briefly, but in a sense, I have lived with him all of my life, yet I doubt that I know him at all."

Listening, Garrett hunched his shoulders, to bury his head, as had been his habit when teachers had rebuked him in grammar school. He felt Saralee's sympathetic arm link inside his, but it was not enough.

"Nobel was an atheist, but he read the Bible," Jacobsson was saying. "He was a bachelor who regarded women as repulsive, yet he admired the shapeliness of American young ladies. He would have been much impressed by Miss Stratman here."

Farelli, Krantz, Evang, and the young Prince obeyed Jacobsson's implied directive, and as one, appraised Emily Stratman's endowments. Momentarily, she lost her poise, blushing, and then, automatically, she brought a hand up to hide the deep cleft between her breasts revealed by the low-cut gown that she had hesitated to wear and then defiantly worn.

Cognizant of her acute embarrassment, and sorry he had caused it—having wished only to crown her quiet beauty—Count Jacobsson quickly resumed his recital. "Nobel was a Socialist, but on the other hand, he believed in an elected dictator and in suffrage limited to the educated minority. As to prizes, Nobel ridiculed them. He liked to say that he owed his award of the Swedish Order of the North Star to his cook, because his cook's dishes had seduced those who gave the medal. He insisted that he received the Brazilian Order of the Rose only because he knew Dom Pedro, ruler of Brazil. He detested publicity, and would not give interviews or allow himself to be photographed. 'That is for actors and murderers,' I once heard him say. Yet he created his world-famous Nobel Prize. I wonder what he would have thought of our press conferences this afternoon."

Stratman spoke. "And I have wondered, Count Jacobsson, why he settled on merely five awards. One would think he would have thought to honor also the best in botany, biology, zoology, psychology?"

"His omissions were even more numerous," admitted Jacobsson. "He also neglected to will money in such categories as architecture, economics, music, and art. This was not accidental. He wanted to reward only the fields that intensely interested him. Caruso would never win a Nobel Prize in music, because Nobel himself had no interest in singing. Paul Cézanne would never be honored, because Nobel had no interest in painting. Luther Burbank would not receive a prize, because Nobel had no interest in botany. To be perfectly honest, an earlier will even omitted literature—but Nobel corrected that omission when he began to read and write in his last years, and his interest in literature revived."

"His will, it caused trouble, I understand," said Stratman.

"Yes, I am afraid so." Jacobsson wanted to be discreet, but the pedagogue inside him elbowed aside all prudence. "He had a distrust of legal minds, so he wrote an amateur's will by himself. He left a fortune, but named no one to—to dole it out. Fortunately, the King took over this responsibility. Nobel had relatives in Russia and Sweden, and the Swedish branch objected to the will and for five years fought it. At last, the matter was settled, and the prizes were given for the first time in 1901, in the Academy of Music, six years after Nobel's cremation."

"I, for one—Margherita and I—are grateful," said Farelli cheerfully. "Not only the honor—Nobel was wiser than that—but the lire, I should say kronor, will be useful in a time when money seems the only honor."

"What are you going to do with your share?" asked Garrett, aggressively, across the group, of Farelli.

"I am giving it all to my favorite charity," said Farelli, "the Carlo Farelli Fund to keep Carlo Farelli and all little Farellis alive."

"You're going to keep it?" demanded Garrett accusingly.

"Certainly."

Saralee Garrett tugged at her husband. "John, I think how people spend their money is a private affair."

Garrett ignored her, still intent on the prey. "Every man to his own taste. I'm giving my share to the Rosenthal Medical Center in Pasadena—for basic research. Basic research needs every dime it can get."

"Good for you," said Farelli, "I am in envy that you can afford to do this."

"A scientist has no choice," said Garrett pompously.

Carl Adolf Krantz made a gesture toward Stratman. "And you, Herr Professor, do you wish to speak of this?"

"I must side with my friend from Rome," said Stratman. "I will keep the cash prize. The world has had sufficient contribution from me. The world can keep solar energy, but I will keep its money."

"Bravo, I approve," said Krantz with worshipful enthusiasm.

Garrett flushed. "All right, the vote is two to one, but I still think—"

Count Bertil Jacobsson saw that the moment for diplomatic intervention had come, and he broke into the American's protest smoothly. "There is no right and wrong on what is done with the prize money," he said. "There is no morality about such income. Each laureate has his own needs and requirements. Many, like you, Dr. Garrett, have turned their winnings over to admirable causes. Albert Einstein kept none of his Nobel check. With the approval of Elsa, his second wife, who was also his cousin, he gave half the money to his first wife, Mileva, for her devotion in his struggling early years. The remainder he presented to charities in Berlin. Romain Rolland gave his check to pacifist organizations. Fridtjof Nansen gave his money to build two agricultural schools in Russia. Sir Rabindranath Tagore turned over his Nobel money to his international school in India—"

"Jane Addams," interrupted Konrad Evang, "gave her half share of $15,755 to the Women's International League for Peace and Freedom."

Jacobsson nodded. "Yes. But on the other hand, an equal number have preferred to keep the money. Selma Lagerlöf bought back her three-century-old ancestral home. Björnson paid off the mortgage on his farm in Norway. Marie Curie installed a new bathroom in her place, and her husband kept the money so that he could give up teaching. Yeats wanted the security, and the physicist, Dr. Clinton Davisson, paid off his debts. Knut Hamsun was impoverished, and the award saved him. So you see, gentlemen, there is no rule, no precedent."

"The important thing to remember," said the young Prince, "is that Nobel's nine million dollars, except for a quarter of a million in American blue-chip stocks, has been soundly invested in Swedish securities, railroads, real estate, and that there is always a large amount of interest to divide and give to prize winners. I cannot recall any year when an individual prize was less than thirty thousand in American dollars, and this year it is over fifty thousand. I believe that is a tribute to our sound economy—and our years of neutrality."

Jacobsson squirmed at the mention of neutrality—a touchy subject with him, for he had been so passionately on the side of England, America, and France, in two wars—and he was sorry that the rash young man had brought it up with such vanity. Without offending the Prince, Jacobsson felt that he must correct the impression that was being made.

"I do not know how much our economy has been aided by our so-called neutrality," Jacobsson found himself saying, "and I am less sure that our highly publicized neutrality was quite so neutral. The majority of Swedes favored the Allied cause in the Second World War, and—"

"Nonsense," said Carl Adolf Krantz in a harsh undertone.

"—and, despite the objection of my colleague, the majority of Swedes aided the Allied cause whenever they could. We sent a hundred million dollars and nine thousand volunteers to Finland to fight Russia in 1939. When we found a Nazi V-1 rocket, we rushed the parts to England. We had a center for Jewish refugees in Malmö, and we refused to give asylum to Nazi or Fascist war criminals. We saved almost twenty thousand Danes and Norwegians from concentration camps."

"Sweden was pro-German, and you know it," Krantz, bristling, shot at Jacobsson. "King Gustaf V was married to a German. All our scientists, like myself, went to German universities. German was our second language in Stockholm. As for the war, we had refused to let England send troops across our country to Finland, but in 1940 we allowed Hitler—and rightly so, at the time—to send troops on our railroads, armament, too, to Narvik and Trondheim. In 1941 we let an entire German division march across our land to Finland for the attack on Russia. We delivered ball bearings to Germany, and a hundred other necessities. I regret Nazi excesses, of which even the *Führer* was unaware, but one cannot blot out all of the good that was in Germany, just because of popular prejudice. Germany was and remains the land that nurtured Beethoven, Goethe, Kepler, Hertz, Hegel—"

"Also, Joseph Goebbels, Heinrich Himmler, Julius Streicher, Reinhard Heydrich, Ilse Koch," said Stratman mildly.

Disconcerted, Krantz stared at Stratman. "Yes, of course, I agree with you, Herr Professor—but surely—wherever there is good, there is also evil. When the evil passes, the good remains. All Swedes understand this. As perpetual onlookers, we retain our objectivity. I am proud I was active for Germany during the war. Why not? In peace, it has offered us more than England or America."

When Krantz finished, a heavy silence hung in the air surrounding members of the group. There was embarrassment, and it was shared by all. For a moment, Stratman considered disputing Krantz further, but the awareness of Emily at his elbow restrained him from speaking.

It was the young Prince who broke the stillness. "I believe it is understood that Sweden was not pro-German or pro-Allied. Sweden was pro-Sweden and pro-humanity, as witness our beloved Dag Hammarskjöld's martyrdom in the cause of peace. Our instinct, like Switzerland's, is for survival, our own and everyone else's. Is that wrong? On the contrary, I think it is civilized and godly not to want to kill and to want to live. Perhaps if we were big and strong, we would have been forced to take sides. As it was, we remained history's bystander. It is not a happy role, but there is much right in it."

"I was in the medical corps, attached to the Marines, in World War II," said Garrett. It was a complete *non sequitur,* at least to those who heard it, and several of the others appeared confused. But Garrett was, for himself, purposeful. "I saw combat at Iwo Jima," he went on. He was staring at Farelli. "Where were you in World War II, Dr. Farelli?"

There was a hush.

Farelli remained unperturbed. He regarded Garrett coolly. "I was not at Iwo Jima, but I was at Regina Coeli in Rome," he said. "I was an inmate of the prison. Not all Italians were Mussolini's blackshirts, you see."

Garrett felt the slap, and stood defeated, his mouth slack.

Farelli turned to Stratman. "However, I am sure Professor Stratman knows more of such misery than do I. As a Jew, he must have suffered more."

Stratman felt Emily shiver beside him, and he replied in a low, serious tone. "I did not suffer, at least not physically. I spent the entire war in a laboratory, as a hostage. It was my sister-in-law who was in Ravensbruck and then Auschwitz."

In his personal shame, Garrett wanted to say something, anything, to regain respect. He would show compassion. Without further thought, he blurted to Stratman, "Was she put to death in the crematorium?"

Stratman winced, and looked quickly at Emily. Her eyes had filled with tears, and she was frantic at her own emotional display. "I—I want a drink," she gasped, and then pivoted and hastened away.

Stratman watched her briefly, as she headed for the waiter, and then he faced the others and Garrett. "Yes, she was put to death in the gas plant. She was Emily's mother. Emily spent the war in Ravensbruck. She is now my charge."

The conversation had reached its dead end. Saralee pulled John Garrett out of the group, and they drifted off, and then the group disintegrated, and individuals of it attached themselves to other guests throughout the salon.

With a fixed fascination, made more intense by his inebriety, Andrew Craig had been staring for several minutes at the slender brunette with the provocative features, in the nearest gathering. Of all the young women in the large salon, she was the only one who captured his interest. While pretending to attend to the conversation of Ingrid Påhl, and a scholarly member of the Swedish Academy, and the Italian Minister, he was heedful only of the girl who stood so close beside Professor Stratman. He had known her before, he was positive, but where or when he could not remember. Yet, he told himself, had he known her before, he would not have forgotten. Suddenly, he was less positive that they had met.

Now he was startled to see her face writhe in agitation, and he watched her wheel away from the group, and remove herself from it. His eyes followed her as she went aimlessly about the room, and then he realized that she was heading for the liveried servant at a point midway between the girl and himself.

Acting on an impulse of the instant, moved by an unconscious necessity that he had no time to fathom, Craig unceremoniously excused himself from his gathering. Although his legs were not entirely obedient to his desire, and he weaved a little as he walked, he tried to reach the liveried servant at the same time that the girl reached him.

Emily Stratman had already confronted the tray, and taken the last champagne goblet from it, when Craig arrived.

"Oh," he said, "well—I guess you beat me to it."

"I'm sorry," she said, hardly noticing him. "I'm sure there is more where this came from."

Craig looked at the servant inquiringly. The man held up a finger, to tell him to wait a moment, and then hurried off.

Craig considered the girl, whose head was bent over her drink. "I'm sure I've met you somewhere," he said.

For the first time, she lifted her head to scrutinize him. "No, you haven't," she said. Suddenly she wrinkled her nose, as if it bothered her. "It tickles," she said, and indicated her champagne. "Bubbles."

"You have to be French—or a skin diver—to avoid that."

"Mmm." She sipped the drink, avoiding his eyes.

"Well, if we haven't met—we might as well. I'm Andrew Craig. I'm—"

"I know," she said. "You were pointed out to me when you came in. Congratulations."

"Thank you. Are you Professor Stratman's daughter?"

"I'm his niece."

"I see. He's a bachelor, isn't he?"

"Very."

"And you take care of him?"

"Probably the other way around." She hesitated, and then added, "My uncle is self-sufficient. I'm not."

He regarded her closely. She was taller than he had expected. The short black hair shone as it caught the lights. The curls along her cheeks enclosed her maiden's face and gave it piquancy. The words "vestal virgin" crossed his mind, yet the slanting eyes, Oriental emerald in color, made "vestal virgin" impossible. Her serenity enchanted him. Here was the picture of self-possession, yet she had just remarked that she was not self-sufficient.

"I was watching you, a few minutes ago, in that group with your uncle," he said. "I was impressed by your poise—the gift of *sangfroid,* which the French so admire—until you suddenly seemed upset and broke away. Are you still upset?"

She considered him, for the first time, with wonder. "Yes, quite upset. Don't let the façade deceive you. It took years to build, to have a place to hide." She paused, as if astonished with herself. "I don't know why I'm telling you this. I must be drunk. This is my fourth champagne."

"I'm the one who must be drunk, to have even brought it up." He was compelled to go further. "I only asked about your being upset because I didn't want to say the wrong thing to you. I can't explain. It suddenly seemed important, that's all."

"I don't mind. It's all right."

"You know my name. I don't know yours."

"Emily Stratman. Birthplace Germany. Naturalized American citizen. Raised in New York City since fifteen—or was it sixteen? Now resident of Atlanta, Georgia. Have I left anything out?"

"Yes. Marital status."

"Aggressively single."

"The result of a broken marriage?"

"Is this how writers get their material? No marriage. Not past, present, or future."

"How can you know about the future?"

"Because I know about the present. What did you do before you won the Nobel Prize—write advice to the lovelorn?" Quickly, she repaired this. "I was just joking. I didn't mean to be fresh."

"Please don't apologize for being 'fresh' to me. That word freezes me. One is fresh to elders. I'm not an elder. I remember the first time a pretty girl, introduced to me at the country club, said 'sir' to me. That was the day I realized I was middle-aged."

"I don't mind middle-aged men," she said. "In fact, I prefer them. They're more comfortable to be with."

"Another barb. Are 'nonromantic' and 'nonthreatening' synonyms for comfortable?"

"I hadn't thought, and I won't try. No deep thinking for me tonight. No self-analysis. Only champagne and the King."

"In other words, you're still upset?"

"And you're too damn perceptive. Don't undress my poor psyche here." She spoke without anger or objection, in a flat, low, matter-of-fact voice. She held herself in reserve a few seconds, peering at her drink but not drinking, and then she met his eyes. "Yes, I'm still a little unstrung. I suppose you want to know why?"

He nodded. "I want to know."

"Here's material for your next book, Mr. Craig. We were talking back there, and Dr. Garrett was baiting Dr. Farelli—with little success, I might add —and Dr. Garrett told what he did in the war, and then Dr. Farelli mentioned that he had been interned in an Italian jail, and he questioned my uncle, and my uncle spoke of being held as a hostage for my mother and me. We were in Ravensbruck through the entire war. Then my mother was separated from me and shipped, in a cattle train, to Poland, to Auschwitz. Anyway—anyway— Dr. Garrett asked if she had been—what was the fashionable word?—liqui- dated in a crematorium? And I don't know—that just made me ache—as if it had just happened—as if I was just looking into a—someone's coffin, someone close—and I guess I—lost my poise. It's silly, because I hadn't thought of my mother, in that way, for years. And then out of the blue, among strangers, in this formal place, it all welled up. Now, there you have your material, Mr. Craig."

He was deeply moved. "I don't want material from you, Miss Stratman."

"What is it you want?"

"Someone to talk to like this."

The liveried servant had returned with his plentiful tray, and Craig took a glass of champagne, and waited for the man to go. When he was gone, Craig at once resumed with Emily, as if fearing that he might lose her.

"I'll revise what I just said. What I want is not someone to talk to—but specifically you to talk to. No explanation. You see a girl, a young lady, and because her eyes are green, or her smile crooked, or she brushes her hair back from her eyes—"

"Or she's upset."

"—yes, most anything like that, you want to know her. Sometimes you know her, and it's a mistake, and you know once again you were duped by an illusion, and sometimes—" His voice drifted off, and he shrugged and drank.

"Is the woman you came in with a member of your family?" she asked.

"My sister-in-law, yes. How did you know she wasn't my wife?"

"I read the newspapers, Mr. Craig. I read books, by the bushel, and I read about their authors. I knew you were a widower."

"Yes, I am. My sister-in-law has been wet-nursing me for three years, ever since." He considered evoking Harriet, but felt that he owed her nothing tonight, not in this reality, and so he did not speak of her.

"Your sister-in-law is handsome."

"I guess so. I really don't know."

"Did your wife look like that?"

"My wife was more feminine, in a way." He was not exactly sure, right now, how feminine Harriet had been. It was a relative matter, anyway. In relation to Leah, Harriet had been more feminine. In relation to the girl before him, Emily Stratman, Harriet—the vagueness of her Slavic features and brisk efficiency—seemed less feminine. "Leah, my sister-in-law, planted a proprietary flag on me early, and that's the way it's been."

"How do you live?" asked Emily. "I know you live somewhere in Wisconsin—but how?"

The unlovely film of the last years unreeled in memory, and he weighed the masochistic and repulsive truth, and then instinctively vetoed this truth. Like an adolescent, he wanted to impress a beautiful girl. "I own a sprawling farmhouse in southern Wisconsin, at the outskirts of a charming small town," he heard himself saying. "I walk or garden in the mornings, ride sometimes, see friends. After lunch, I lock myself in my study upstairs and write until evening. My nights are quiet, a few companions, or cards, or reading. Some-

226

times I take a few weeks in Chicago or New York, to get the hay out of my hair. I'm afraid it sounds a little dull."

"It sounds divine."

Craig smiled wryly. If only Lucius Mack could have heard him. He would have said: well, old man, glad you're turning out fiction again, and about time.

"What do you do with yourself?" he inquired.

"I—I tend my uncle's house, and work in a veterans' hospital outside Atlanta, and, as I told you, I read a good deal." The statement was so devoid of life that she was ashamed, and made up her mind to embellish it. "And then, of course, all sorts of famous people are always down to see Uncle Max, and I'm his hostess. We have too many dinners, too many late nights. I—I go out the usual amount, like all unattached women—I don't care for nightclubs, but you know, the theater, drives, private homes. It's enough to keep one busy." She was more ashamed than ever, and wanted desperately to change the subject. "I'm reading one of your books now. I bought it for the boat."

He was pleased, and showed it. "Which one?"

"I'd read them all, I thought, and then I found I'd missed *The Perfect State*. I'm almost through. I believe it's my favorite. I liked *The Savage* the least, because it's brutal—"

"Like our time."

"—yes, like our time, and that frightens me. *Armageddon* was exciting and moving, but it scared me, too. *The Black Hole* was almost a classic, I think, though I assure you it didn't sell well in Georgia. I remember the bookdealer trying to talk me out of it. 'That's a No'thern book, ma'm,' he kept mumbling. But this one on Plato peddling his Utopia—I think it'll live. Uncle Max was saying it came out not long ago in Scandinavia, and that's what got you the prize. You deserve it."

His instinctive affection for her had become adoration. "I'd like to bring you to my publisher's next sales meeting."

"It's not necessary. You don't need puffs any longer." She stared at him. "It's odd, meeting the author," she said, finally. "I couldn't imagine what to expect. Two of the books, three actually, were so violent—no, I mean indignant—furious. You're not like that at all."

"My gift for outrage is well hidden, and only brought out for special occasions, like when I write a book."

"Why? It's a virtue, not a fault."

"Outrage is a red flag—it invites conflict—it invites grappling with life—and the obvious part of me is withdrawn and scared and wants no trouble. Do you understand?"

"Completely."

"Maybe that's why I retreat into history, where my real self won't be spotted and forced to fight. It's cozier. It's a weakness, a kind of flight, but there you are."

"I understand that, too. I'd wondered."

He looked about the salon, and realized that either he was myopic or a haze had fallen over the occupants. Too much to drink, he thought, far too much, and now he regretted the escape. He wanted to belong here, faculties intact, but it was too late. "Enough of this talk," he said to her, "the wrong note for the eve of the Royal Banquet." He drained his glass of champagne in a final flagellation. "Now," he said, setting the goblet on a marble-topped commode, "I want to show you something."

He took her arm, but she held back. "Show me what?"

He pointed off. "See that chamber door down there? Count Jacobsson was telling me it leads to one of the historic state apartments—Sofia Magdalena's state bedchamber—he said it's worth seeing if I have a chance. Let's look."

She hesitated. "I don't know—"

"Be adventuresome." He divested her of her drink, and placed it on the commode, and then swiftly led her across the French rugs to the chamber entrance.

"Follow me," he said, and she went after him through a dim passage into a tiny, bright drawing room. He opened a door, peered inside, and announced, "Sofia Magdalena awaits within." She crossed into the state bedchamber, and then he stepped inside, shutting the door behind him.

The majestic bedchamber, dimly lighted by a single lamp, was white and gold with a baroque ceiling. The pilasters bore the feminine touch of rose laurels. The ceiling represented an overwhelming allegory of the four continents. The rest was lost in the shadows.

Craig remained weak-kneed inside the door, his reddened eyes following Emily as she went directly to an alcove to examine two Gérard portraits of Eugène Beauharnais, Napoleon's stepson, and Eugène's wife, Princess Amalia Augusta of Bavaria. In the salon, Craig had been aware only of Emily's face, but in these private quarters, he saw, as if for the first time, her slim body, accentuated by the black evening sheath slit up to the knee. Then, when she turned in profile, and next, three-quarters, he realized that she was not slim at all. The flesh of her shoulders, above the protruding breasts, appeared warm and soft, and the hips and thighs spread generously outward from the tiny waist.

Rocking uncertainly, he realized with a pang that he had not been absorbed by a female body, as he was now, since the time of Harriet. Discounting, that is, his dream of Lilly last night. But that was different, fleeting. Now it was as if he had been revived from a long sleep of death. He wanted a claim on Emily's physical comeliness, and the need, which was desire, and so long foreign to him, now was the strongest unreasoning part of him.

Drunkenly, he traversed the bedchamber, and planted himself in front of her. She looked up, with surprise, at his face. His head was a turmoil, and his heart pounded, and he felt wild and extravagant.

"I wanted to be alone with you," he said.

Her eyes showed alarm, but she did not move. "We are alone."

"You're so beautiful—it makes me shake inside—you're beautiful—I have to say it—"

228

"Thank you," she said, stiffening. "Now, I think we'd better—"

"Emily, I want to kiss you. I haven't touched a woman I cared for—someone beautiful—since—"

He placed his hands on her arms, felt their softness beneath his palms. He tried to draw her into him, but she was suddenly all resisting sinew and bone.

She tore free, and backed away. "Don't you touch me!"

"Emily, listen, I'm trying to tell you—"

"Get away! Go away!" She started past him, almost running, but he caught her shoulder and spun her to a halt.

He saw her then, as he had not seen her before, breathless, quivering, cornered and at bay, and then he perceived a secret damage in her that he had only known in himself. The enormity of the new hurt that he had inflicted overwhelmed him, and his shame was suicidal.

He released her. "I'm sorry, Emily. I apologize, believe me. I'm—I'm not like this at all—not at all—I had too much to drink. I lost my head. Can you forgive me—forget it? Please forget it. It was all the drinking—all day long—and now—and more than just that—"

A sudden, loud creak broke his plea, and a shaft of brighter light from the drawing room laid them bare. As one, they whirled toward the doorway. It had been flung wide open, and in its frame stood Leah Decker, stern as conscience.

She advanced slowly, mouth compressed, looking from one to the other, until she was a few feet from them.

It was Craig whom she addressed coldly. "I saw you go in here. I thought I should tell you—you'll be missed. The King is making his appearance."

Craig inhaled, straining for composure. "This is Miss Emily Stratman—Professor Stratman's niece—my sister-in-law, Miss Leah Decker."

"How do you do," said Emily, in a voice flat and dulled. She took several steps away. "If you'll both excuse me—my uncle—"

She exited quickly, head high, not looking back.

Leah watched her speculatively, and then turned to Craig. "Well," she said.

"Well what?"

"Never mind . . . Good Lord, you're a mess. Your eyes all bloodshot. Your tie. And you need a comb. Here's mine."

"Don't waste your time." He felt funereal, and wanted to chant a dirge. "'All the King's horses and all the King's men—couldn't put Humpty Dumpty together again.' Remember? Come on, let's curtsy."

As Count Bertil Jacobsson's cane rapped three times on the floor, the occupants of the salon fell back against its walls, forming a long, irregular semicircle, waiting. No sooner had the echo of Jacobsson's cane ceased than the King of Sweden entered through the arch. Behind him came the elegant royal princesses and princes. While the retinue remained stationary, the King, in severe evening dress without ornament, moved ahead and surveyed the room with the briefest smile.

Jacobsson jumped forward, crossing the carpet toward his ruler. When he reached the King, he stamped to a halt, stood rigidly at attention. The King proffered his hand, and Jacobsson, inclining his head, took it—touched it, really, and no more.

Now the King moved toward the semicircle of guests, with Jacobsson a half step behind, whispering introductions as His Royal Highness welcomed each guest, male and female, with a handshake, a nod, a muted word.

Andrew Craig, situated beside Leah in the first third of the semicircle, had observed all of this through bleary eyes, steadying himself by leaning against the commode behind him. Just as the King had done, moments before, now Craig too surveyed the guests. The majority were counting the progress of His Royal Highness. The rest, mostly Scandinavians, stared straight ahead, as if soldiers at an inspection. Craig explored the visible faces of the women rising and falling from focus, seeking the one from which he wanted understanding and forgiveness. But Emily was nowhere in the range of his vision.

He was conscious of an extraordinary movement beside him. He investigated, and was amused to see his sister-in-law dipping and lowering herself, in what seemed jerky and convulsive motions made more awkward by the straight lines of her gown, and then he realized that this was her interpretation, recently acquired, of the curtsy. He saw her rise again, slowly, laboriously, like something reaching upward from a launching pad, and then she was once more perpendicular.

That moment, he heard his name distinctly spoken, and the words "literature" and "laureate," and like a Pavlov dog, without thought and by reflex, he pushed himself from the commode and straightened and faced the King of Sweden.

The King extended his hand. "Welcome to our country, Mr. Craig."

Woodenly, Craig took the King's hand and released it. "Thank you"—he was about to add the word "King," banished it, sought frantically for the lesson of protocol, and found it—"Your Majesty."

The monarch lingered. "I enjoyed your novel, *The Perfect State*. Its sentiments coincide with my own."

"I appreciate that, Your Majesty."

"I look forward to the completion of your next work."

Supported by the battalion of bottles consumed, Craig felt as reckless as a young Socialist. "Is that a command, Your Majesty?"

The King was amused. "If you wish so to regard it, Mr. Craig."

"I am sincerely flattered and inspired. You shall have the first copy, Your Majesty."

The monarch moved on, to the continuous hand shaking and curtsying, and Craig realized that he had, indeed, been flattered by the ruler's interest, but not inspired, not inspired at all, for the King's sovereignty was temporal and earth-bound to this land, and Craig paid obeisance only to the Muse—once Clio, now Calliope. With regret, he resigned from his promise to the King of Sweden.

He heard Leah's troubled whisper. "How could you joke with His Royal Highness like that?"

"He didn't seem to mind."

"How do you know? Oh, Andrew, I'm so mortified—"

"He enjoyed it," said Craig between his teeth.

"Even if he did, you're so irresponsible when you drink—what'll you do next?"

"For Chrissakes, Lee, we're the hit of the evening. I won't criticize your curtsy, and don't you knock my dialogue. Now, please behave."

"Everyone saw you go in that corridor to the bedroom—"

"What of it? It's not a whorehouse."

Leah gasped, blushing and pulling back. Her eyes darted around the room, seeking to learn if Craig had been overheard. She saw that he had not been, and she started to speak again, and then held her tongue, and settled into sullen taciturnity.

Across the salon, the King had finished his social duty, and now, at the entry to the Charles XI's Gallery, he waited for his royal entourage. Followed by the royal princesses and princes, he went into the dining room. At once, the semicircle of guests broke forward, unevenly, falling into a column at the entry, and marching in to the Royal Banquet.

Presently, Craig found himself seated, by place card, between Leah and Ingrid Påhl, and perhaps thirty feet from the King, who was at the head table, quite isolated except for two princesses to one side of him, a prince and another princess at his other side, and a private uniformed waiter hovering nearby.

Befuddled by drink, Craig squeezed his eyes to make out his surroundings. He owed this careful inspection not to his writer's memory file, but to Lucius Mack, his favorite pallbearer, as a conversation piece. Craig's eyes studied the Gallery hall, and sorted out busts of a King and Queen of long ago on a shelflike cornice, and several cabinets containing silverwork and amber and porcelain. The painted ceiling above—as he would later learn—recorded events in the reign of Charles XI and Ulrika Eleonora. From the ceiling hung a glittering chandelier, and immediately beneath it, on the table, a magnificent elevated vase, and before him, lustrous silver service.

He peered to see if the King had the same silver service, but something else beside the King's plate caught his eye. It was a proletarian egg, curiously majestic, in a brilliant golden egg cup.

He shook Ingrid Påhl's flabby arm, and pointed. "What's that?

"Where?"

"Next to the King's plate. Looks like a plain ol' egg."

"But it is, Mr. Craig," said Ingrid Påhl gaily. "It is a tradition. A long time ago one of the earliest Swedish Christian rulers—possibly Olof Skötkonung or Erik Jedvardsson—sat down to dinner with a bellyache, and rejected his rich meal, and demanded one ordinary boiled egg. This was unheard of—the egg was fare of the peasantry—and for one hour, the kitchens of the palace were ransacked for the simple egg, while the King sat fuming with impatience. At last the egg was found and served, but by then the King was beside himself. He made a royal proclamation. From that day forward, there must always be one plain boiled egg beside the King's plate, ready and waiting, should he ever desire it. For ten centuries the tradition has persisted. So now you see the royal egg."

"Charming," said Craig. "And over there, on the table behind him—?"

"Yes, yes, his jeweled crown, his scepter, his sphere and cross—power and justice—his horn holding the anointing oil. All symbols of his authority and prerogative. Again tradition, Mr. Craig. He does not wear the crown, and he does not brandish the scepter. But they are there, you see, and he knows it, and the democratic government knows it, and the Swedish people know it—and for all, it is something to trust and hold onto in perilous times. I think, Mr. Craig, there can be worse virtues than the secure knowledge of continuity existing from the distant past and offering reassurance for the future. It is something that atheists and republicans miss, I imagine."

"It is a knowledge many Americans miss," said Craig sadly. "I envy you what you have—something to believe in."

By then the caviar had been served, and Craig picked at it without appetite. Glancing across the table, to see who was opposite, he recognized Stratman adjusting his bifocals, and next to Stratman, there was Emily, also picking at her caviar, eyes downcast.

Craig had no interest in the splendid dinner. All of his effort was concentrated on catching Emily's eye, and somehow letting her know that he had been foolish and must have her pardon. From time to time, steadily, in the next hour and a half, he stared at her. Ingrid Påhl spoke to him, and Leah spoke to him, but he did not hear them. The hot dishes came and went—the consommé, the *marinerad sill* (which tasted like sweet smelts), the large cut of venison with currant jelly, the tender reindeer steak, the concoction of lettuce, fruit, peas, shrimps and sliced mushrooms identified as *västkustsallad*, the traditional bombe with its regal crown of sugar—but Craig left most untouched, and when he ate, he ate sparingly. He had requested more champagne, and this he drank through the entire feast. In all this time, as he stared at Emily, she refused to lift her head and acknowledge his existence. Since the table was wide, and the vase was a barrier, and Leah another, he could not address her.

Morosely, he drank, once responding to a formal toast to His Royal Highness, and another time toasting the memory of Alfred Nobel. His inner emotional barometer rose to self-righteousness and dropped to self-pity. For a short period, he resented the injustice of Emily. After all, he asked himself what had he done that was so sinful and wrong? He had lured a pretty girl into a private room and had told her that she was beautiful and that he wanted to kiss her. Was that a crime? Hell, no, it was a compliment, and any other girl would have been proud of it—from a Nobel laureate, at that. The failure was her own, not his. Chrissakes, he hadn't violated or hurt her, had he?

Then, for another period, he decided that he had, indeed, violated and hurt her. Every woman, he told himself, is vulnerable in different ways, and hurt has its many varieties. One woman you would injure and spoil by physical defilement—by forcible entry into her body. Another woman you would wound by mental defilement—by insult and disrespect through words or actions. Obviously, Emily Stratman was the second woman. Undoubtedly, she was shy of men, probably a virgin, who regarded even the small acts of coercion—words of seduction, a kiss, an embrace, a stray hand—as an attack on her private and individual womanhood and an act of ravishment. When he came to this understanding of her, Craig was once more depressed and mortified.

But then again, after yet another goblet of champagne, the barometer rose in his favor. What did he give a damn about her for anyway? There had been no real women since Harriet, and he had been spared emotional turmoil about other women because he had been so devoted to his personal turmoil and guilt. Under these conditions, this Emily person was an intruder. For a moment, finding her, he had been bold enough to cross the forbidden frontier back into reality, and it had been as unpleasant as he had always feared it might be, and now he was glad to go back to where he had come from. Women died with Harriet. To hell with them all. Good-bye, Emily.

He was surprised to see that everyone at the table was rising. With a start, he realized that the Royal Banquet was ended and that the King had departed. With difficulty, he pushed himself to his feet.

"There'll be coffee in the salon," Ingrid Påhl was saying.

"Good," he said.

He noticed that Leah was engaged in conversation with a diplomat, and had preceded him. He fell in beside Ingrid Påhl and returned to the salon, where a long buffet held the coffee.

His meditations at the table had disturbed him, and now he wanted to avoid formal company and idle talk and to think himself straight in privacy. He was in no mood for Emily now and less in a mood for Leah. He wanted to flee from the rejecters, the embodiments of disapproval.

Nearby, Count Bertil Jacobsson stood momentarily alone, fixing one of his decorations. Craig went to him.

"Count," he said, "when you see my sister-in-law, Miss Decker, tell her I left early, I wanted to walk back to the hotel, get some air."

"Certainly, Mr. Craig." Jacobsson did not hide his concern. "Are you all right?"

"Never better. Memorable evening. Excellent dinner."

"You'll be pleased to know His Majesty was positively delighted with you."

"Tell that to my sister-in-law, will you?" He wanted to add: and tell it to Emily Stratman, too. But he refrained. He said, instead, "And by the way, thanks, Count."

With that, Craig went for his hat and topcoat, and then left the Royal Palace.

He waited on the windswept curb, in front of the lonely small hotel, for the taxi that he had summoned from the cheap bar inside. A waiter had directed him to dial 22.00.00, and he had, and then given the girl his address and name, and she had said, *"Bil kommer,"* which the waiter had told him was good, and now in the cold, he waited for the taxi.

The last time that he had looked, it had been near midnight, and now it must be much later. After leaving the palace, he had walked and walked, not covering much ground in his old man's walk, staggering sometimes, and leaning against frozen walls of darkened buildings. In the late winter hour, the city had been desolate of life, and without sound except for the heavy clop of his shoes on the pavement and stones and the occasional whirring passage of a motor vehicle. When his nose, mouth, and chin felt numb, almost frost-bitten, he had found the gloomily lit hotel in the side street and the empty bar, and for a half hour had defrosted himself with whiskey.

For the most part, his brain had been too soggy to entertain logical thought. But an immediate matter had frequently drifted in and out of his head, until, in the bar, he had captured it and made a decision. This night, it seemed, he had reached the nadir of his existence. A glamorous occasion, of which he had been a part as a highly honored guest, had proved one more of life's Waterloos. For a moment, in that occasion, he had come alive, felt old stirrings, and because he was no longer armed to be alive, he had failed and sunk back into easier demise. Yet, strangely, in all his walking, some persistent fragment of an emotion—infinitesimal but pulsating—survived. The emotion, long dormant, was identifiable: the desire to be loved, not pity-loved, not respect-loved, but simply loved.

When the emotion came clear, he knew what must be done. In sobriety, it would have been madness. Insobriety had a logic all its own. Craig had made his telephone call for the taxi, and now on the curb, worn and quivering, he waited.

At last, the black sedan with the meter arrived. Craig ducked into its rear seat. For seconds, he searched for his wallet, then located it, and removed the slip of paper that he had found attached to his bottle on the train from Malmö.

"Drive me to Polhemsgatan 172C," he said.

The ride was fast and skidding and of brief duration. He gave the cabbie a large bill, so that he would not have to figure out the kronor, accepted the change, handed over a three-kronor tip, and found himself before a seven-story apartment building. On the glass door hung a wreath of Christmas lights, disconnected. Craig punched the buzzer, and the door sprang open. He entered.

Above each mailbox, in the hallway wall, was a name, an apartment letter, and a floor number. The fifth from the right read "Fröken Lilly Hedqvist, Apt. C., Fl. 6."

Dizzily groping his way in the faint light, Craig reached the elevator. It was an unusual triangular cage, meant to accommodate two thin Lilliputians, and Craig stuffed himself into its confines as into a foxhole. He squinted at the buttons, hit No. 6, and ground upward to the topmost floor.

234

When the elevator shuddered to a halt, Craig squirmed out of it. The short, dim corridor swam before his eyes. He wondered if he would make it, or should—the search for love seemed less reasonable now—but suddenly, he knew, this was a better folly than returning to the Grand Hotel and Leah.

With one hand on the wall to support himself, he traversed the corridor. The last apartment door, near the window and fire escape, bore the letter "C." He rapped gently, and when there was no immediate response, he rapped harder.

Her voice came from behind the partition. *"Ja?"*

"It's I," he said.

He heard the lock turn, the door opened partially, and then, at once, it opened fully.

He recognized only the cascade of golden hair. "Mr. Craig," she whispered with concern, drawing her lavender robe about her.

She swung back and forth before his eyes, like a metronome, and he made one desperate effort at courtliness. He removed his hat, he thought, and said, "Miss Lilly—" and could not remember her last name.

"Come in, please."

Her tone was so beseeching that he obeyed at once. His impaired vision could only furnish part of the single room: a mosaic on the wall over a pine-wood divan with striped cushions; a glass coffee table on a black tubular frame; two wicker spoon chairs; a small television set; a double bed pulled down from a recess in the wall. Somehow, he reached the bed, and came down on the fat comforter.

She was before him, he knew.

He tried to explain. "Lilly, I—I'm very drunk—and very old—and don't care—except—tonight—I wanted to be with someone who would know and not mind—and I thought of you, Lilly. Do you mind?"

She knelt before him. "Oh, Mr. Craig, I am happy for me that you came."

"I'll just rest a little and go back to the hotel."

She took his chilled hands and rubbed them, transmitting her warmth into him. "You will stay. I will take care of you. Lie down, lie down and sleep."

He felt satisfied and welcomed, and then realized that she had taken off his topcoat and suit coat and that his head was deep in the feather pillow and that his legs had been lifted on the bed. She was undoing his collar and shirt, he thought, and she was above him, tending him, and perhaps what had brushed his cheek was her breast. It was wonderful to imagine this before sleep, and then, at once, he slept.

He became conscious behind his eyelids, and he waited, motionless, while gradual awakening crept downward through his outstretched body.

When he opened his eyes, he saw the thin drapes, and he saw that the city was still dark behind them. The room in which he lay was partially illuminated by some night lamp out of sight, and from a far corner came the hushed purr of radiator heat. He had expected to find himself in his upstairs bedroom at Miller's Dam, and then remembered that he was in the Grand Hotel in Stockholm, and then, with increasing bewilderment, he understood that he was in a room unknown to him.

Against the gravity of sleep weight, he sat up with effort, pushing off the blanket. Except for his shorts, he was naked. He had no memory of undressing for bed, when suddenly the last memories of the night flooded into his brain. The image came clear—the cascade of golden hair, the lavender robe—and he swiveled from his sitting position to fill in the rest.

Lilly Hedqvist, curled beneath the blanket, slept a few feet from him on the double bed. She slept with the easy innocence of a child girl, strands of her tangled hair across her cheeks, hiding all but the beauty mark above her mouth. The blanket was drawn to her shoulders, so that only the flimsy white straps of her nightgown were visible.

Studying her in this unguarded moment of inanimateness, Craig was touched. He had invaded her privacy, a stranger, a foreigner, a drunk, and she had taken him in with unreserved kindness and open trust, and offered him her care and her bed. Craig owed her much, he knew, and what he owed her first was to leave her undisturbed and to remove himself from her presence.

Reluctantly, he eased himself off the bed, wishing he had been given this meeting before the time of his disintegration. But then, he told himself, this meeting would not have occurred, for it had been born of pity—hers for him, and his for himself.

He padded after the bathroom, opening a closet by mistake, and then finding the bathroom. With the fluorescent light on, and the inevitable mirror before him, he tried to see in the reflection what Emily Stratman had seen before midnight and Lilly Hedqvist had seen since midnight. He saw a gaunt and angular face ravaged by weakness, and it sickened him. Turning on the tap, he doused his face in cold water and then washed. He rinsed his mouth. Briefly, he felt revived. He was sober and, incredibly, without hangover. He took a silent vow: a new leaf, no more drink, no more self-destruction, no more anti-life.

Tiptoeing into the living room, he picked his shirt and trousers off the chair beside the bed, and then, suddenly, as he stood there, he was too fatigued to dress. He wanted only the bed again, that and an infinity of warmth and peace, and a later awakening to a world where something mattered. Weary and dispirited, he lowered himself to the edge of the bed. He sat hunched, inert, knowing it was almost nine of a dark winter's morning, knowing Leah waited and the Nobel committees waited and the program waited, and he was not ready for celebrations.

"Where are you going, Mr. Craig?"

Lilly's voice startled him, and he spun around. She was on her back, beneath the cover, head turned toward him, one hand brushing the hair from her eyes and the other holding the blanket to her throat.

"To the hotel," he said. "I wanted to get away without awakening you."

"Why?"

"I didn't want to compromise you." He considered this. "No, that's not it at all. I was ashamed to face you."

"There is no reason for shame."

"The way you saw me—"

"I saw a man who drank too much and was tired. I did not care. I had thought of you—the funny time we had on the Malmö ferry—and I was glad you thought of me and came to me."

"Yes, I did think of you."

She pushed herself upright, against the pillow, still holding the blanket before her. With her free hand, she patted the bed. "Come here, Mr. Craig."

He dropped his clothes, and went around the bed, and sat beside her.

"Why did you think of me last night?" she asked.

"I don't know exactly, Lilly."

"You do know."

"I wanted to be alone at first, and I was beaten, and then I didn't want to be alone—I wanted companionship—and you came to mind—I had enjoyed you—and somehow I came here."

"But you have not had companionship, as you say. You have slept, and now you go, but you are still alone."

"Yes."

"Is this the way you want it—to still be alone?"

"Lilly, for God's sake—"

"No, you must be truthful with me and yourself. You must learn that. Why did you really come to me?"

"All right, you asked—because I wanted you, dammit—"

"You wanted me," she repeated, flatly, levelly, without the inflection of a question. "Yes, that is true. Then why are you afraid of it? Why do you make such complexity of loving and being loved? Why do you come alone and go alone?"

"It takes two—"

"We are two." She threw the blanket off her body and held out her arms. Immediately, he was beside her, in her arms, embracing her, kissing the hollow of her throat and neck and cheek.

"Wait," she said softly, "we are still apart." She settled his head on the pillow, and bent and disrobed him completely. Then she took the hem of her white nightgown, and, gathering the nylon folds, she lifted it and pulled it over her head and dropped it to the floor. "There, now we are the same, both nudists."

She was on her knees, posing for him, smiling. He studied her sensuous young body with pleasure. From the pink expanse of her chest her bust developed gradually, in a classical protruding curve, to the great circles of red nipples with their hardening points, and then the breasts rounded back into the full flesh of the body. The breasts were young and bursting, suspended straight outward, yet were not appendages but part of a symmetry of the whole, all faultlessly circular, like her rounding belly, the navel almost hidden, and the hips and thighs.

She came off her knees and stretched out full length, pulling his head down between her breasts. "You are tired, I can see, but now you will not rest alone."

For a long time, he lay against her bosom, luxuriating in the pervading heat and knowing peace within himself, until slowly, slowly, tranquillity was kindled into desire. He began to kiss her, and could hear her heart as he heard his own. And now she had his head in her hands, and kissed his forehead and eyes, and at last, his lips.

"Lie back," she whispered. "Yes—"

He felt his shoulder blades on the bed, but still held her waist, as she came over above him, encompassing him, burning her flesh into his until her flesh was fused to his trunk, and their corporeality was consummated.

All reason left him, and as he gave himself to sensation, he gasped, "Thank you, Lilly—"

Her voice was far away, and reached him from a distance, riding the surge and swell of a comber. "Never—thank me—never," she whispered. "Lovers do not thank—"

And the rest was her sigh lost and suffocated by the onrushing whitecap of passion.

"Lilly—Lilly—"

Her breath was on his cheeks, and her oscillating murmurs were in Swedish, and he opened his heavy eyes and saw her, almost unreal with her tumbling flaxen hair and swaying breasts and creased belly, like some transported Norse goddess.

He wanted to tell her that she had come from heaven, but then she curled forward, closer and closer, her presence flowing over him, so that it was not a breaker that engulfed him but lava, and he could not speak. Her open mouth touched his, and he thought her to whisper, "Freya."

And he remembered Freya, Swedish goddess of carnal love, and he was shorn of control, and all gentleness was out of reach. He took her arms, and pulled her down, rolling her over to her side, so that they were side by side. The waves again buffeted him, and consciousness flickered low, but she managed to hold him to her. And suddenly he was released from the eddy, freed of the vortex, and lay spent in her arms.

"Do not move," she said, and seconds later, she gave a convulsive shudder, and fell back, hands covering her eyes.

After a while, she removed her hands, and opened her eyes.

"*Du är inte ensam*," she said. "You are not alone."

But he had not heard her. He slept.

VI

It was early afternoon when Andrew Craig returned to the Grand Hotel.

His mood had improved over the previous day. Physically, he felt cleansed of old poisons, and consequently rested and at ease. For the first time in several years, he had slept without drink or drug, and the sleep had been dreamless and relaxed.

When he had awakened, in a natural way, he had found the place beside him in bed empty. Of Lilly there had been left only a note pinned to the pillow:

DEAR MR. CRAIG, the coffee is on the stove, and you can heat it. I am off to work. I hope we will meet again. LILLY HEDQVIST.

After dressing and coffee, he had added a line in reply to her note. "I'll see you soon," he had written—and then he had gone down into the street. Outside the entrance, the elderly *portvakt*, the Swedish doorkeeper of the apartment, had been kneeling, adjusting the Christmas lights. Craig had almost bowled him over. But the old man had not been annoyed, had even been friendly, as if Craig were one of his tenants, and Craig guessed that Lilly had spoken to the portvakt of him.

Daylight had come to the city, and the air was windless and surprisingly mild, almost balmy. The sun hung high and bright in the cobalt sky, and Swedish pedestrians appeared gay and appreciative of the spring interlude.

Carrying his topcoat on his arm, Craig had made his way leisurely to the nearest square, noticing that the colors everywhere, and of everything—the women's clothes, the pottery on a sill, the yellow furniture in a store window, the red-ribboned holiday packaging in a Tobak shop—were more vivid than before, either because of the sun or because of his own sobriety.

At the square, he had hailed a taxi and been driven back to the hotel that he had not seen in seventeen hours. Only when he was in the elevator, ascending, did he suddenly remember Leah and the new day's official program. He could not recall what the Nobel people had scheduled for this day, but he hoped, for their sake, it was not important, yet, for his sake, sufficiently interesting to have removed Leah from the premises. If Leah was in, he would have to have an excuse, and a plausible one—the more difficult to conceive, he told himself wryly, because he had not written fiction for so long —or suffer her chastisement. What he needed was a respite, time to think of a likely story, and he prayed fervently that Leah was out.

When he entered the suite, his agnosticism was confirmed. His prayer had not been answered. Leah's purse stood unyielding and stern, like a motorist's warning sign, on the hall table.

Leah sat stiffly on the maroon chair in the living room, holding the telephone in her lap, her bunched features as reproachful as those of a young widow.

"Well," she snapped, "I see that you're alive anyway. I've called everywhere but the morgue."

Craig had crossed the room and dropped his coat on the sofa. "I'm sorry, Lee. I suppose I should have phoned."

"Should have phoned?" she echoed shrilly. "How inconsiderate can any human being be of another? Here I am, a foreigner, an absolute stranger a million miles from nowhere, without a friend, with no one except you—what am I to think? It was bad enough leaving me flat at the palace last night—absolutely humiliating—but knowing you had gone out drunk as a lord, I stayed up half the night, until I fell asleep right in this chair, and since then, worrying—Did a car run you over? Did you fall in a canal?—God knows what I imagined."

"I couldn't find you after the dinner," he said lamely. "I needed some air. Didn't the Count give you my message?"

"He didn't say you'd disappear until the next afternoon."

"I didn't mean to—"

"You're impossible," she scolded. "It'll be so embarrassing now. What will they think? I called Count Jacobsson at the Foundation—Mr. Manker at the Foreign Office—I even talked to Professor Stratman."

Craig flushed. "Stratman? What's he got to do with me?"

Leah was less certain now, and immediately less aggressive. "I don't know. I was frantic. I—after all—you had been with his niece last night. And then after I got the message that you'd gone, I saw Professor Stratman leave early with the girl, and I thought—well, maybe that you were meeting them—"

"Or meeting her? Isn't that what you mean?" Craig was suddenly infuriated. "What if I had met them or her? Wouldn't it be my business? Don't I have any private life?"

"Andrew, it's not right to talk like that. I was worried about you, in your condition. Besides—besides, you'd brought me and—I don't want to be an albatross, but—it's etiquette, decent, to at least escort me back first."

"I just don't like your notifying the whole place of every movement I make. You were worried about how I'd behave—a scandal. Well, if there is one, you'll be the one who's inviting it, with your hysterical calls."

He was headed for the bedroom, when the telephone in Leah's lap emitted a muffled ring. Leah started, almost dropping it, and Craig halted.

She was on the phone. "Oh, you're very kind, Count Jacobsson. He walked in this minute. . . . He's fine, yes. He'd gone to visit some old friends, people he'd known when he was here before. . . . What? Oh yes, yes, certainly, we'll be ready. We'll be in the lobby."

She hung up, and looked at Craig unhappily. He wanted no victory such as this, and his anger evaporated. This was Sweden. When in Sweden, do as the Swedes do, invoke the Middle Way. Pacifism at any price.

"Look, Lee, let's not fight—"

"I don't want to fight. I just want you to be safe and well. I keep thinking of poor Harriet—I can't help it."

Inwardly, he winced. He had defenses for all but this: his debts. Leah had again sent him the remainder of payment overdue and ever-mounting interest.

"Lee, we were both wrong. You were wrong to churn up such a storm. I was wrong to have let you worry. I was terribly drunk, last night, and I did want to walk it off, so I went out and walked. It was cold and I wound up in a hotel bar for coffee, and then felt ill, and the bartender saw that, and saw I was an American, and he packed me off on a cot in his back room to sleep it off. I suppose I needed that, because I slept through the night and morning."

She wanted to believe it, and she wanted peace, but she could not help but be herself. "Your clothes aren't rumpled," she said.

"I didn't wear them to sleep," he said patiently. "The bartender got me out of them and hung them up."

"What if someone had discovered who you were—a Nobel laureate without his clothes—passed out on a cot in the back room of a bar? It would be terrible."

He agreed with a penitent nod, and thought of the sharp young lady at yesterday's press conference, Sue Wiley of Consolidated Newspapers, and how she would savor such a story. But he reminded himself that the story was not true, and so Miss Wiley was no threat. Then he remembered what was true, and revived the fresh memory of Lilly Hedqvist, Nordic girl goddess, and her uncomplicated and lusty abandon, and he wondered what Miss Wiley would think of that, and, indeed, what Leah would think, also.

The full import of his position—he was in the international limelight this week and the big microscope of journalism waited to magnify and enlarge every move he made—meant that he would have to be cautious of his every action, if he cared about his future. Until this morning he had not cared at all, but now there was some self-concern, mysteriously motivated, and he determined to be discreet about public drinking and private fornication.

"You're right, Lee," he said. "We don't want any headlines until the Ceremony is over, and we have the fifty thousand."

"It's not just that."

"I'm kidding. I said you're right, Lee. Now I'm sober and properly regretful, and I have vowed reform. Add to that a meteorological fact: the sun is shining—an exceptional thing for winter in Sweden, I'm told—and the day lies ahead. Let's go out for lunch."

"I've had lunch, and we have a date. Don't you know the program, Andrew?"

"I haven't the faintest idea. We've been to the palace. What else is there?"

"We're doing Stockholm today. I haven't seen a bit of the city yet. Mr. Manker and Count Jacobsson are taking us and one other couple, one of the other laureates. And, oh yes, your Swedish publisher is going to be along."

"What's his name?"

"Mr. Flink. Don't you remember? He had a funny first name. Let me see —margin—setback—Indent! I was associating. That's how I remember. Mr. Indent Flink. I think that's another reason Count Jacobsson phoned back. He wanted to be sure you'd be here for the tour—because he wanted you to meet your publisher."

"Lee, I've already seen Stockholm with Harriet—"

"That was so long ago. Besides, you should meet your publisher. In a way, his editions helped you win the prize."

"I can meet him, and make some apologies, and just skip out. You go on the tour. I'd rather kind of browse through the city on my own—"

"No, Andrew, it would be rude."

"You're getting to sound more like Harriet every day."

"I hope so."

It was a lie, he knew, and he did not know why he had said it. Harriet would have conspired with him to avoid a formal tour. Or at least he thought so, as best as he could remember her. Suddenly, he was unsure.

"Okay, Lee, you win." He started for the bedroom to change. "HSB, here we come."

"What does that mean?"

"You'll see," he said enigmatically, "you'll see."

"Our first stop on this informal tour," said Mr. Manker, as he swung the Foreign Office limousine away from the curb before the Grand Hotel, "will be the HSB cooperative housing units on Reimersholme island, in the south section of the city. HSB, I am sorry to say, stands for Hyresgästernas Sparkasse- och Byggnads-förening, which means Tenants' Savings and Building Society, a title I shall not further burden you with. Henceforth, I shall refer to this cooperative company as HSB."

Craig squirmed in the jump seat, and glanced at Leah in the rear, and she acknowledged the clarification of enigma with a satisfied smile.

Mr. Manker fingered the brim of his fedora with his free hand. "If the ladies do not mind, I shall remove my hat and enjoy the full benefit of the sun, which Herr Professor Stratman has so recently tamed."

"No objections from Miss Stratman or Miss Decker, I am sure," said Stratman pleasantly.

Mr. Manker deposited his hat on the front seat, between Count Jacobsson and himself, exposing with relish his high pompadour, meticulously waved, to the solar rays.

Craig wished that Emily had not been seated behind him. His long legs were cramped in the jump seat, and it would take the limbs of a contortionist to wind around and speak to her.

The knowledge, received when he had entered the limousine with Leah, that Stratman and Emily were the other guests on the tour, disconcerted Craig completely. Without meeting Leah's eyes, he sensed, from her greeting to the Stratmans, her immediate wariness. His own accosting of Emily had been cordial but brisk, as if to prove to her that he was a new man, the soul of sobriety, and that this was a new day. Her acknowledgment of him, in turn, had been distinct but detached, with no intimation of forgiveness or approval.

Now they rode in silence between the canal and the buildings, Leah, Stratman, and Emily in the rear seat, and Indent Flink, the publisher, in one jump seat and Craig in the other. Flink proved to be more probable than his name, a prosperous, corpulent man in his late forties, conservatively tailored in dark gray, a business man who smelled of Danish beer and Baltic herring and was proud of his colloquial command of the American language.

"I guess you've seen today's papers," Flink said to Craig. "You got considerable space in all of them, and so did Professor Stratman. Rave notices. Count Jacobsson has clippings for Professor Stratman, and I have five for you." He pulled the newspaper accounts from his pocket and handed them to Craig. "See for yourself."

Courteously, Craig leafed through the clippings, and found them as baffling as the inscriptions on the Kensington stone. "I'm sorry I can't read Swedish," he said.

As he handed them back to Flink, Leah leaned forward and protested. "Andrew, keep them for souvenirs."

"Okay," said Craig, "but I'd like to know what's in them. Don't read them, for heaven's sake—I don't want to bore the Professor or Miss Stratman."

"I'm interested." It was Emily. Craig twisted to thank her, and was again fascinated, as he had been the evening before. Her brunette hair glistened in the dusty sun, and the loveliness of her green eyes and tilted nose was heightened by carmine lipstick, still moist and fresh, and the only makeup she wore.

Disinclined as he was, for he felt Leah's scrutiny, he faced the publisher once more. "Just give me the gist of the stories," he said.

"The gist," said Flink, "is this." He reviewed the leads of the stories in a monotone. Two newspapers played up the fact that, although Mr. Craig was the youngest literary laureate ever to win the prize, he approved of the award's going to established authors, no matter how elderly. One newspaper featured Mr. Craig's remark that Gunnar Gottling, the controversial Swedish novelist, was a "major talent" who had been overlooked by the Swedish Academy. Another newspaper devoted its first paragraphs to the things Mr. Craig admired about Sweden and the things he did not like.

"What's in that last clipping, Mr. Flink?" Craig asked.

The publisher shrugged. "Nonsense. It speaks of an altercation between you and an American correspondent, Miss Wiley, which broke up the press conference."

Craig scowled. "Does it say more?"

"Well—"

Immediately, Craig realized that the article had sensationalized and gone into the argument about his alleged drinking habits. It was the last thing on earth he wanted brought up before Emily and Leah.

"Never mind," he said curtly to Flink.

But Leah had pushed forward. "What's this all about? What are they writing? What happened at the press conference, Andrew?"

Suavely, from the front seat, Jacobsson interceded on Craig's behalf. "It was nothing at all, Miss Decker. We suffer at least one such incident annually."

"What incident?" demanded Leah shrilly.

"Miss Wiley writes for an American syndicate that lives by scandal," said Jacobsson, "and when there is no scandal, she must make it up for her bread and butter. She asked Mr. Craig some personal questions, and he felt—and correctly so—that his private life, his habits, his marriage, had no place in an interview. That was all. To prevent the woman from tormenting us, I called the interviews to a halt."

"The nerve of those reporters," said Leah, still confused.

"And now, Professor Stratman, would you like to know about your clippings?" asked Jacobsson.

"A summary will do," said Stratman.

"The emphasis," said Jacobsson, "was on the fact that the details of your discovery are being kept top-secret by the American government. Everyone quoted your predictions as to the future of solar energy. Two periodicals discussed your life in Germany and—"

Stratman, ever sensitive to Emily's hatred of their homeland, held up his hand. "That is enough, Count Jacobsson. Who wants to relive the past when this day is so brilliant and Stockholm is before us?" He called to Mr. Manker, "Where is your cooperative housing?"

"Right ahead," said Mr. Manker.

The HSB cooperative housing village on Reimersholme consisted of nearly one thousand apartments that were occupied by three thousand middle-class Swedish citizens. The buildings were difficult to tell apart. All were clean and modern and seemed new, although they had been constructed in the latter years of World War II. All were set back from the canal, all were wood, concrete, and stucco, painted either white or beige, and all carried proud little balconies, most now filled with sun seekers.

Mr. Manker parked the limousine before one of the apartment buildings. For several minutes, he explained the nonprofit evolution of the communal housing unit beside them. When he finished, he inquired, "Would you like to visit inside?"

They all left the vehicle, and gathered on the sidewalk in the gentle sun. Craig said to Mr. Manker, "If you don't mind, I'll stay out here and have a smoke. I've seen your co-ops before."

"As you wish," said Mr. Manker.

"I think I'll keep Mr. Craig company," said Indent Flink.

Mr. Manker herded the others toward the apartment building entrance. Craig watched Emily Stratman as she proceeded on beside her uncle. She was taller than her uncle, and she wore a gray suede jacket and tight blue skirt, cut short, revealing her long legs and the perfect curves of her calves filmed over by sheer nylon. As she walked, her ample buttocks and generous hips moved freely, and Craig realized that she wore no girdle. He had earlier been so absorbed in her virgin face that it now surprised him that her figure could be more feminine and provocative than Lilly's figure.

Briefly, he made his mental apologies to Lilly, remembering her uninhibited giving, yet the difference was clear. You associated Lilly with health and nature and spontaneous animal sex. You put her against the background of a forest, with the forest sounds and the sky patch above, and you took her at once, without sparring, for carnal pleasure alone, on the earth and grass. But Emily Stratman—you imagined her, and you thought of unblemished maidenhood, reserved and withheld, tensely waiting on one desired, and you thought of love and romance and the long hungry building. You put her in the softly lighted boudoir, with the caressing breeze coming through the open French windows, and the wan moon and the faraway music, and you carried her from the chaise to the canopied bed, and you embraced her and kissed her and touched her unviolated flesh, until at last a low fire burned, and then you took her slowly, ever so slowly, with art and soothing, until the low fire grew to blaze.

Craig shook himself. The incongruity of his fancy, here on a Stockholm sidewalk, before a cooperative housing structure, struck him fully, and as being ridiculous, and he banished the daydream. Emily and the rest had disappeared into the building. Craig found his briar pipe, packed it, and Indent Flink was waiting with the match.

"What do you think of our cooperatives?" asked Flink.

"I admire them," said Craig, drawing on his pipe, "as I admire a nation with no slums. I think it's advanced and a great gift for the majority. But I'm a writer, an individualist, and I suppose I'd rather live in a tent, simply to be alone and not belong and be leveled off, because I prefer ups and downs."

"It will interest you that our cooperatives have even got into the writing game," said Flink.

"In what way?"

"The co-ops publish a magazine, and they publish books at lower cost. They even sponsor a yearly lottery to raise money for maybe three dozen deserving writers."

"You mean there's that much interest in authors here?"

"Enormous interest," said Flink. "There are seven million people in Sweden. Sixty-five per cent of all adults are regular book readers."

"Remarkable," said Craig.

"Our problem here is the critics. Everything succeeds or fails on the reviews. If they are good, a book becomes a best seller. If they are bad, we can dump our stock in the canals. *The Perfect State* got unanimous raves. What irked me was that the raves were not only for its literary merit, but, I suspect, because a story of Plato gave the critics a chance, in their articles, to display their own erudition."

Craig laughed. "I suppose that does happen."

"I am sure," said Flink seriously. "It happened with each of your books.

The critics used them all to show off themselves. I believe this sometimes influences even the Nobel Committee. Jacobsson was telling me about the contest for the second Nobel literary award in 1902. There were many nominees considered behind closed doors—Anton Chekhov, Thomas Hardy, Henrik Ibsen—but who were the final contenders in the last ballot? Theodor Mommsen, eighty-five years old, with his five-volume *History of Rome*, and Herbert Spencer, eighty-two, with his ten-volume *A System of Synthetic Philosophy*. So there they were for the Nobel literary prize, a German historian and an English philosopher—and not Chekhov or Ibsen. Mommsen was elected and given the prize. Why? The Nobel Committee said for his artistry. Compared to Ibsen? For myself, I suspect a prize for Mommsen was an advertising for the Nobel judges, of their own erudition and scholarship. Possibly, this same egotism worked in your favor, too. I don't know."

Craig and Flink paced before the cooperative building, discussing publishing and books and public taste, discussing the cynical and morose outlook of Swedish writers (a rebellion against the idyllic welfare state), and the taste of Swedish writers for Faulkner and Kafka and Gottling and their distaste for the valentines of Ingrid Påhl, until, presently, Mr. Manker emerged with his conducted tour.

Leah burst forth toward Craig, taking his arm and attention possessively, and bubbling on about soundproof rooms and stainless steel and garbage-disposal equipment. Feigning a show of interest, Craig covertly sought out Emily Stratman. A quarter of an hour before, he had wished she would turn around so that he might enjoy her fully. Now she was turned around, in his direction, across the lawn. She wore a high-necked pale blue sweater beneath the suede jacket and over the tight skirt. Her bosom, rising and falling slightly —had they climbed stairs or was it the day?—was spectacularly abundant, and Craig was unaccountably pleased as he enjoyed it, and her, in the sun.

They drove on now, with Mr. Manker at his voluble best, fluently reciting capsule histories of this museum and that gallery and endless chapels of worship. On lovely Helgeandsholmen—Holy Ghost Island—he idled the car, and they considered the unlovely, Germanic Riksdagshuset or Parliament Building, and learned that it had been established in 1865, and that the aristocracy had been oppressive (did Count Jacobsson squirm ever so little?) and allowed only 10 per cent of the population to vote until after the fall of the Hohenzollerns and Romanovs, so recently, when universal suffrage and true democracy finally came to backward Sweden.

They drove farther through Stockholm—"a community of twelve islands connected by forty-two bridges," recited Mr. Manker—until they reached an immense underground garage, known as Katarinaberget, and they were told that this had been specifically constructed as a shelter to protect 20,000 persons against nuclear explosions. Now, for the first time, Craig was fascinated by a projection of the future.

"We hope that people will take the lesson of your book, *Armageddon*," said Indent Flink to Craig, "but if they don't, you can see, we are ready to survive."

"How many of these have you got?" asked Craig.

Mr. Manker replied. "We now have four of these huge atomic bombproof shelters in Stockholm, to save fifty thousand people, and, in all, nineteen such large ones throughout Sweden, and also thirty thousand small ones, to hold all together over two million people. The rest of the people we could evacuate in minutes from the cities to rural areas. The subterranean shelter you observe here has electricity, heat, water, and food, even preparations for schools. Much of our heavy industry—Bofors and Saab—make their antiaircraft and jet airplanes in subterranean factories carved into granite hills. Other nations only speak of civil defense; we in Sweden have already acted on it."

"Perhaps you shall inherit the earth," said Stratman glumly, "and by then, you can have it."

Emily stared at the cavernous underground garage. "It's awful," she murmured.

"But why?" asked Mr. Manker. "We are so proud of this—"

"I don't mean what you think," said Emily quickly. "Of course, you've done the sensible thing. I mean"—she waved her hand toward the shelter— "the completed cycle, the irony of going back to where we came from, Neanderthal man scooping out his prehistoric caves, except now, the caves are air-conditioned."

Solemnity had settled on all of them, and Count Jacobsson was anxious not to have the afternoon spoiled. "Now you must see the lighter side of Stockholm," he announced. "Mr. Manker, will you kindly drive us to Djurgården and Skansen?"

Concentrating on his new goal, the attaché maneuvered the large car through the busy mid-afternoon traffic, conforming to the left-lane drive that unnerved all but the Swedes. He continued eastward through the city, until gradually he began to shed the traffic, and they drew closer to the vast pastoral island known as Djurgården.

Easing up the pressure of his foot on the accelerator, Mr. Manker slowly circled the vehicle around a clustering of odd and elaborate buildings. "We call this Diplomat's City," said Jacobsson. "Here you will find most of the foreign embassies and legations. There, you see the Italian Embassy—"

As each was identified, it amused Craig to reflect on how each Embassy took on the character of its nationals abroad. The British Embassy was staid and sturdy brick, aloof, dignified, conservative and no-nonsense, like the majority of its nation's travelers. The United States Embassy, across the way, squatted high on a small cliff. It was a modernistic horror, awkwardly trying to belong to the country it was visiting by imitating that country, and failing miserably, so that it was finally no more than a caricature of an American abroad trying desperately to be a part of Sweden.

With relief, Craig observed that they had crossed a bridge over a small canal and arrived at the winding road of the great island. To the left stretched acres of wood-fringed meadow, similar to the fields of Wisconsin and Minnesota, and to the right rose the stately villas of Sweden's elite. "Djurgården means Animal Park," explained Jacobsson. "In its early days, this was the King's hunting preserve. Now the forests and clearings are a public pleasure park. As to the rest, the estates of our aristocrats and millionaires and artists, I think Mr. Manker is better qualified to point out things of interest."

Enthusiastically, Mr. Manker resumed his recital. There was a series of villas, many hidden from view by foliage or sunk below road level, belonging to princes of the blood, but of the names of their owners, Craig recognized only that of Prince Bernadotte. And finally, on that portion of the Djurgårdsbrunns Canal that resembled a lake tinted blue and green, stood Åskslottet—Thunder Palace—a miniature but ominous version of the Taj Mahal and the home of Ragnar Hammarlund.

"Pull up there before the manor gate," Jacobsson directed Mr. Manker. "Our guests have all met Mr. Hammarlund—in two days they will be enjoying his hospitality at dinner—and they may have special interest in his residence."

"You mean, someone actually lives in that place?" asked Leah incredulously, as they drew up before the metal gate.

"Indeed, yes," said Jacobsson, "and a bachelor, at that."

A pure-white gravel walk led dramatically to the statue of a white sea nymph by Carl Milles. The nymph guarded a magnificent rectangular artificial lily pond. On either side were walks and gnarled oak trees, and at the far end, almost in replica of the marble Mogul tomb, was Åskslottet. The mansion was two stories in height, square and light gray, with a steep reddish roof. Four slim pillars, like minarets, towered before the entrance.

"Of course, Hammarlund is not quite alone in there," Jacobsson was saying. "He has his staff of mysterious retainers. At any rate, it is all impressive to look at. . . . Well, Mr. Manker, shall we go on?"

As the limousine started forward, everyone but Leah settled back for more of Djurgården. Leah craned her neck for a last sight of Hammarlund's castle.

"It's hard to believe that he's a millionaire and owns that big place," she said. "I mean, when I met him, he seemed so ineffectual and ordinary."

"On the contrary," said Emily, "he was exactly what I had expected—type-cast for his role—right out of a hundred suspense novels about tycoons, munitions makers, merchants of death."

Since Craig was interested, Leah could not allow herself to be contradicted by this young woman. "You're being romantic," she said to Emily. "What's so different about him?"

"For one thing, he's bizarre," said Emily. "For another, when I think of Hammarlund, I suffer astigmatism—I see him in plural—the limp personality we meet by day, and the other personality he keeps locked up until night."

" 'I want to write about a fellow who was two fellows,' " quoted Craig. "That's what Robert Louis Stevenson once told Andrew Lang, and that's how Jekyll's Hyde was born."

"We're all two fellows," said Stratman with a grunt.

Leah grasped for any ally. "I agree with Professor Stratman," she said vaguely.

"So do I, Lee," said Craig. "However, I suspect Hammarlund's two fellows are more interesting than mine or yours. And that's where I side with Miss Stratman. I, too, think he's bizarre, a cache of secrets, and that he only permits his second self out at night when there's empire work to be done, and no one's looking. That's the self we never meet, the one who assembles cartels and makes millions. The self we see is simply too soft, too bland, too hairless and chinless, to be believed. There most be more."

"Oh, there is more, indeed there is," Jacobsson said from the front seat, "but perhaps not so exciting as you imagine. Hammarlund has his intrigues constantly, of course—is that not so of all big businessmen today, in a business world?—but he has no double life or private band of assassins, as far as I can ascertain. The Zaharoffs of private enterprise are dead in a world of expanding socialism."

"I can't wait for his dinner party," said Leah.

"It will be correct and lavish," Jacobsson promised, "but do not expect hidden doorways and secret passages and bodies that fall out of closets." He smiled indulgently, and one almost heard the facial parchment crackle. "Of course, for your sake, Miss Decker, I hope that I am wrong." Jacobsson peered through the windshield, and then said, "And now we approach an institution no less glamorous but far more innocent, one in which we Swedes take great pride. I refer to our celebrated Skansen park. Once more, Mr. Manker is the authority."

Mr. Manker shifted into low gear, sending the limousine grinding up the rising highway, and then he spoke in his rehearsed Cook's Tour monotone, the words floating forth too easily, as if lacking the ballast of thought. "Skansen is unique," said Mr. Manker. "It is not an amusement park like Disneyland or Tivoli. It is a museum in the open air, a condensation of Sweden's past, presented visually in the present. It was opened in 1891, and in the decades since, it has become one of our foremost attractions. You will see our manor houses, centuries old, reconstructed . . ."

By the time Mr. Manker had finished his description, they had arrived at the foot of the final ascent, and entered the parking place reserved for them. Emerging from the car, after Emily had stepped down, Craig studied the main entrance gate of Skansen and remembered the humid summer's day when Harriet and he, carrying cameras and ice cream cones, had first walked through it. He remembered it as fun, that time, like discovering an old *National Geographic* in the dentist's office. But he was in no mood for visual history today. The lack of a single drink, since the night before, had left him parched and restless. He required something to comfort him, either Emily to talk to or a whiskey, preferably both and at the same time. If he went on this visit, he decided, it would only be to seek a moment with Emily.

Stratman had been conversing in an undertone with Emily, and now the physicist waddled over to Jacobsson and Mr. Manker.

"If you will forgive me," said Stratman, "I think I will sit this one out. The spirit is willing, but the bones are weak." He looked off. "Your Skansen appears too formidable."

"There is a modern escalator," said Mr. Manker.

"Thank you. I believe I will just sit in the car and doze. I am sure there is much more to see after this. I must conserve my strength."

Emily had come up alongside her uncle, and her face showed concern. "I'll stay with you, Uncle Max—"

"*Ach,* no—no fuss, now—please go with the young ones."

Some unconscious purpose, in Craig, made him speak. "I'll be here, Miss Stratman, so you needn't worry." He turned to Jacobsson and Mr. Manker. "I don't want to be a spoilsport, but I've already been through Skansen, top to bottom. It's worth another visit, but like Professor Stratman, I'd like to conserve my strength. I still haven't got over the plane trip."

Emily was not appeased. "Uncle Max, I prefer—"

"No," said Stratman firmly, "I want you to go and tell me all about it. Mr. Craig and I have had no time together. I will teach him physics, and he will give me a course in literature appreciation. Please, *mein Liebchen*—"

Emily glanced worriedly from her uncle to Craig, and at last capitulated. She permitted Mr. Manker and Jacobsson to lead her to Leah and Indent Flink, and together the party started for the Skansen gate. Once, Emily looked back, and Stratman reassured her with an uplifted hand.

After they had gone, Stratman shook his head. "The child troubles too much about an old man. It is my fault."

With a sigh, Stratman went into the limousine, loosened his collar, and laid his head back comfortably on the rear seat. Craig took out his pipe, and after lighting it, he sat down on the front seat.

"I have my meerschaum, but I forgot my tobacco," said Stratman.

"Have some of mine," said Craig, quickly passing his pouch.

When Stratman was puffing contentedly at last, he spoke again. "As you add years, your pleasures subtract. Once, my years were few, but my pleasures were many, many. Long ago, I would fish, play billiards, hold a Fräulein's hand, stay up the entire night with my brother in card games, go to the opera, read for pleasure, stuff myself with schnitzel, smoke my pipe, and work—work was always pleasure." He held up the brown meerschaum. "Now only the pipe remains, this and work. I do not complain. It is enough."

"I envy you," said Craig. "I have only the pipe."

"And not the work?"

"No."

Stratman was silent a moment. "Emily told me you lost your wife recently. Is that the reason?"

Separate emotions struggled inside Craig. One was of elation, that Emily had actually spoken to her uncle of him. The other was of shame, that he had indulged himself in prolonged self-commiseration. "When I lost my wife, there seemed no point any longer."

"Is not work itself, creation, solitary accomplishment, the real point?"

"One would suppose so. I remember one of Mr. Maugham's characters once saying that an artist should let his mother starve, if necessary, rather than turn out potboilers to save her. In short, the artist's work, his devotion to it, was all that mattered. You know, Professor, that takes terrible strength."

"For strength, I would substitute something else—an unrealistic sense of divinity—that the Lord gave you, only you, the Golden Plates."

"I used to feel that."

Stratman nodded. "I am sure you did. If you had not, you would not be in Stockholm today. Then, what has happened to you? I am no psychologist, but I can guess. The unrealistic sense of divinity was violated by a horrible accident of reality—your wife's sudden death—and you have been brought down, and your faith shaken, and you are still in shock. It happens, young man, it happens."

Craig tried to think about this, sort it out and spread it before him, but he was not ready to understand it, and finally he decided to defer analysis for another day. "Perhaps you're right," he said, and said no more.

Both men had lapsed into silence, puffing their pipes and listening to the remote sounds of Skansen and welcoming the winter sun as it filtered through the openings of the automobile.

"Why did you remain behind?" Stratman asked suddenly. "To keep an old man company?"

"No, not at all."

"Then what? To speak of yourself?"

"Not that either. Instinctively, I wanted to be near you, because you are close to Emily."

"Emily, eh?" But there was no astonishment in the red face. Stratman emptied the bowl of his meerschaum, lifted his bifocals higher on the bridge of his nose, and peered at Craig uncritically, seeming to regard him for the first time not as a fellow laureate but as a human being. "So," he said, "what does Emily have to do with us?"

"She told you that we met last night?"

"She mentioned it. We reviewed the affair together, afterwards—we have often done that after social gatherings—and she told me a little about you—and, as a matter of fact, about some of the other guests, too, ones she had met."

"I see." Craig felt disappointed. He had hoped for more, some affirmation, some special interest. "Did she tell you what happened between us?"

"What happened between you?"

"I was drunk, and I offended her."

"Umm." Stratman digested this, perhaps tried to define it. "I am sorry to hear that. I could have told you—she is extremely sensitive and withdrawn about men. So—you made her angry?"

"Yes, I did. I've been waiting for the moment to apologize. She won't permit it."

"That is right. It is her way since childhood." He paused. "Why is this so important to you, Mr. Craig?"

"I'm attracted to her. I want her good opinion."

"Then, you have an unenviable task—"

"A hopeless one?"

Stratman shrugged. "I cannot think for her. I know her better than I know any person on earth. I have a father's love for her. I raised her. I know her quirks and fancies and most of her reactions. But each day is a new creation of life, and to some minute degree, each person enters that day as a newborn. The brain, the nervous system, the muscles, the glands, the conditioned reflexes, all go through the life of the day responding in set and familiar ways —but then, there occurs one new accident or adventure or confrontation, one exceptional stimulus, and suddenly past performance means nothing— and the person's brain or nervous system reacts differently, in a way previously unknown. So—how can anyone judge anyone else or speak for them? How can I know what Emily feels about you today?"

"But you have an idea?"

"Of course, I have an idea. I have past performance. After I brought my niece out of Germany, to England and then America, I saw her adhere to one pattern of behavior, and this has remained remarkably unchanged. She does not trust men. She does without men. If by some voodooism you managed to make her lower her guard last night, and then took advantage of it, I would predict that her distrust would be stronger than ever—of men in general, of you in particular. So—you ask if it is hopeless to win her good opinion once more? As her relative, and a scientist, I would say the odds are against you, Mr. Craig. Certainly, I would not wager on your chances. But still, the imponderables—we have them in physics—a new day with a life cycle of its own, and possibly, somewhere between dawn and dusk, a new Emily. I am sorry, Mr. Craig, but this is the best I can offer. I am sorry to be so ponderous and long-winded. I am German born and raised. You are a product of optimism, a society of optimism, so your own decisions, for yourself, will be fairer than my own. And this, too—you are a spinner of tales, greatly honored, so no doubt you have perceptions about people much keener than mine. Apply your optimism and your genius."

Craig smiled. The old man was teasing him now, he was sure. He replied in kind. "My stories are of the past. I am a stranger to the present, and unarmed."

"There is no present," said Stratman. "One minute ago is the past." His eyes twinkled behind the thick lenses. "You are armed." He settled lower in the seat, and crossed his chunky legs. "I will have my beauty nap."

Craig pushed himself off the front seat, stood up, and stretched. "And I'll take a walk."

Stratman's eyelids had already drooped, but now they winked open. "Mr. Craig—"

Craig moved to the open rear door and leaned in. "Yes, Professor?"

"I think you will try to win her good opinion."

Craig said nothing.

Stratman sighed tiredly. "Should you succeed where others have failed, and make her lower her guard once more, do not disappoint her—or me."

He yawned and closed his eyes, and Craig remained standing, moved but unmoving, reflecting on how Victorian the scene had been and how Herr Professor Stratman, guardian of the sun, and of his brother's daughter, had momentarily sounded like Edward Barrett, of 50 Wimpole Street, London, guardian of the invalided Elizabeth against the young Browning. Yet the comparison was odious and unfair. Stratman was no jealous tyrant of Wimpole Street, suppressing latent feelings of incest. Stratman was a rutted bachelor, who had come into unexpected fatherhood late, and who was burdened with a responsibility that exceeded normal parental obligation. His first thought was for Emily, and not for himself. All things considered, Craig knew, Stratman had been kind.

Craig ambled off, without destination, without curiosity, about the perimeter of Skansen, sometimes halting to watch children play, once stopping for a lemonade. He meandered on and on, letting fantasies slip in and out of mind, occasionally letting himself become absorbed in the new characters who peopled his life, and then Miller's Dam and the frame house on Wheaton Road and Lucius Mack, and even Harriet—yes, Harriet in the ground—seemed far away and of another time.

A half hour had elapsed before Craig returned to the limousine. He saw that the others were already in the car, and Mr. Manker was wandering nearby searching for him, and he quickened his step. Once inside, squeezed into the jump seat, he apologized, and could not, for the life of him, explain, in retort to Leah's question, where he had been and what he had done.

Mr. Manker was behind the wheel, and they were on the road again.

Craig listened, as Emily behind him reported to her uncle, briefly but brightly, on some of the highlights of the Skansen visit. When she had concluded, she asked her uncle how he had occupied himself.

"Mr. Craig and I had a long, long talk," said Stratman.

"About what?" Emily wanted to know.

"Shop talk, *mein Liebchen*. He advised me how to put plot in my papers, and I advised him how to employ solar energy in his typewriter. After that I napped."

"How do you feel now?"

"Refreshed and a tourist again. . . . Count Jacobsson, what is your next propaganda to convert us all?"

"The best we have to offer," said Jacobsson. "Mr. Manker is driving us to the Old Town—specifically, Stortorget—the Great Square—the original site of Stockholm seven centuries ago."

Presently, going the long way around, they crossed the Norrbro bridge, swung past the Royal Palace, slowed before the Storkyrkan Cathedral, which had been built in 1260, proceeded up a narrow, ancient street that opened into the spacious square, and parked before the Börssalen, which Mr. Manker identified as the Bourse or Stock Exchange Building.

After they had left the car, Mr. Manker guided them around the Stortorget. The square, paved with aged, uneven bricks, was dominated in its center by a huge round ancient well. Surrounding the landmark, there were public benches, and because the day was mild, the benches were filled with old men reading newspapers and middle-aged lady shoppers resting and gossiping.

They strolled along the sides of the square, which were lined with severe stone buildings, four to five stories high, housing commercial shops on the ground floor level and apartments in the floors above. Following Mr. Manker, they visited the hoary alleys and side streets leading into Stortorget. These shadowed streets were twisting and dark, as in medieval times, walled in by antiquated gabled houses that seemed to have been designed by the brothers Grimm.

"Today, almost everyone wishes to live here in the Old Town," Mr. Manker was saying. "To live here is what you call in America a status symbol—is that right? The exteriors of the apartments are the originals. They cannot be renovated. They are left as they were in the beginning, and are now beaten by weather and chipped and peeling, and that is their charm. However, inside the apartments, I assure you, most of the quarters are spotlessly modern, with all the latest appliances, including oil burners for these winter months."

Slowly, Mr. Manker led them back to the ancient well in Stortorget's center. "This is a hallowed place," he announced, as the party gathered more closely about him, and several Swedes on the benches looked up curiously. "This is the very spot of the infamous Stockholm Massacre or Blood Bath. In 1520, a Danish king, who controlled all of Scandinavia, offered amnesty to eighty rebellious Swedish aristocrats, invited them to this square for a celebration, then betrayed them by beheading all eighty." Mr. Manker pointed off. "Now, there is a more pleasant object for sightseeing."

The members of the party turned to examine, once more, the rococo Stock Exchange Building before which the limousine was parked. "That palace was built in 1773," said Mr. Manker. "On the ground floor is the Exchange, but upstairs are the offices and library of the Swedish Academy, where André Gide and T. S. Eliot and Andrew Craig were voted the Nobel Prize in literature."

Leah took Craig's arm. "Isn't it exciting, Andrew?" Craig grimaced at his sister-in-law's display, and then, worried that his hosts would be offended, he summoned forth a slight smile of pleasure.

"Alfred Nobel is not your only benefactor," Mr. Manker told Craig. "There is another, and he is King Gustavus III, who came to our throne in 1771 and fifteen years later founded the Swedish Academy. For all of his faults, and they were many, ranging from a disinterest in the poor to a lavish spending on himself, Gustavus III has our high regard because he gave us much of our culture before he was assassinated at the masquerade ball in 1792. He gave us our opera. He gave us works of art from every corner of the world. And finally, to promote literature, he imitated the French by establishing the Swedish Academy. Because he superstitiously favored the number eighteen, he founded the Academy with eighteen members, taken from Sweden's most respected authors and scholars. Gustavus III's number has survived to this day. Eighteen members, Mr. Craig, voted you the Nobel Prize."

254

Jacobsson came forward and touched Craig's shoulder. "Perhaps it would interest you to see the place where you were elected?"

"I'd enjoy it," said Craig sincerely, "but I'm afraid the others might be bored. Maybe one day I can come alone—"

"Nonsense," interrupted Stratman. "All of us would like to see the inside of the Academy."

The members of the party fell in behind Count Jacobsson, and with him crossed the square, and turned the corner into the side street. They followed Jacobsson up the street, until he came to a halt before two giant, timeworn doors at Källargränd 2. To the right of the entrance, fastened to a granite block, was a plate bearing the legend: SVENSKA AKADEMIENS NOBEL-BIBLIOTEK.

They all went inside. Mr. Manker and Jacobsson led them through a gloomy hallway, up wide stone steps to the first floor above the one at ground level, and then through a beige door into a long corridor, which was cheerfully lighted and awesomely scholastic. To their immediate right was a librarian's desk, now unattended, and next to it the portal to the Nobel Library, whose stacks bulged with the literary produce, in almost every language, of the Nobel winners, contenders, as well as associated material.

With a possessiveness that came from familiarity, Jacobsson took them along the corridor, lined with shelves of books on either side, to another door that opened into a colossal auditorium. As they passed through the auditorium, Jacobsson said, "We are approaching our Kaaba, the holy place where the Academy members convene annually to elect a Nobel winner. The secret chamber is called the sessions room. And here we are."

They entered one more door and found themselves in a bright, broad room, high-ceilinged, with tall windows looking down on the historic square below. Beneath a sparkling crystal chandelier rested a rectangular table, which seemed to fill the room, and drawn up neatly around the table were twelve ornate chairs, their seats, backs, and armrests covered with blue plush. The glossy table was bare, except for a wooden tray holding a pen set that had belonged to King Gustavus III almost two centuries before, and a pewter pitcher and a glass vase. Against the walls were a blue-covered sofa and additional pull-up chairs, and on one wall hung a gleaming gold medallion engraved with Gustavus III's royal symbol, bound wheat stalks. At the head of the table, behind the Permanent Secretary's chair, stood the Academy's ever-present conscience—a marble bust of the founder, Gustavus III, perched on a circular stone pedestal.

"Yes," Jacobsson was saying, as he patted the marble bust, "ever since 1914, when the Academy took over this room, His Majesty has sat here listening to secrets the entire world would like to know. Before that, the voting was held in the Permanent Secretary's home on Skeppsbron, then in a rented apartment at Engelbrektsgatan, and then in the old Nobel Library at Norra Bantorget. But since Romain Rolland was selected in 1915, every literary laureate has been voted the prize right here."

"How often do the Academy members meet in this room?" Emily inquired.

"I will explain the modus operandi," said Jacobsson. "Let us take the case of our current winner—Mr. Andrew Craig. Nominations for the Nobel Prize in literature this year, as always, were closed this last February first. Nominations, usually in writing, were submitted to the Swedish Academy. There were forty-nine this year. Thirty came from properly accredited sources—previous winners in any category or recognized academies throughout the world—and nineteen came from unaccredited sources, such as authors' publishers or wives or the authors themselves, and were thrown out. Mr. Craig's name was formally submitted, not from a foreign source, but by eligible admirers in our own Swedish Academy, led by Miss Ingrid Påhl, a voting member. I think Mr. Flink can better tell you how that came about."

Indent Flink addressed himself to Craig and Leah. "I claim no credit," he insisted with false modesty. "I am in the business of publishing, and I have a part-time book scout in New York, just as I have scouts in Paris and London. Mr. Craig's last novel, which had been overlooked in Scandinavia, was sent to me with a bushel of other books. I was impressed—it's a rattling good story—and I bought the Swedish rights on *Armageddon* for five hundred dollars. I believe that was the price?"

"That was the price," said Leah.

"I had the translation made, and brought the novel out in September of—let me see—four years ago. The reviews were so overwhelming that, I believe, many of the eighteen members of the Academy read it and became acquainted with Mr. Craig."

"Quite so," said Jacobsson.

"Well, to make a long story short," Flink continued, "I bought up two more of Mr. Craig's novels, the sales were gratifying, but the enthusiasm in literary circles was even greater. Then I acquired a copy of *The Perfect State*, and it was the best of the lot. I translated it myself, and published it early last year. This time, I had my cake and ate it, too. It was a runaway best seller, and it was a critical rave. Well, I think that did it. An Andrew Craig cult had sprung up in the Academy—not only Miss Påhl, but others—and he was nominated for the prize in February."

Craig had listened attentively, detached, as if hearing another author being discussed. Then he realized that the others in the room were looking at him, and among them Emily, and almost for the first time he became aware that it was he himself who was the subject of Flink's little reminiscence. He knew that something was expected of him. "My American publisher thanks you, my agent thanks you, the Miller's Dam Security Bank thanks you, and I thank you, Mr. Flink."

"In turn, the world thanks you," Flink said grandly.

Embarrassed, Craig sought to change the subject. "Count Jacobsson, exactly what happened after the nominations last February—or is that secret?"

"Not at all," said Jacobsson. "Four members of the Academy's eighteen serve as a weeding-out board. The leading books, by the thirty official nominees, were turned over to them. Many of the works, like your own, were already in Swedish and easy to read. Others had never been translated, and so the four board members had to read them in their original languages. Besides Swedish, the board members read well in English, French, German and Spanish. Where a nominated work might be in an exotic language like Chinese or Hindu, it would be turned over to special consultants who are linguists. Language is a barrier, but I doubt if it has ever barred consideration of a work of real merit. I am thinking, at the moment, of 1913, when Rabindranath Tagore, of India, was nominated for his poetry. He had only one volume in English, when he was nominated. There were none in Swedish. The cream of his creativity was in his native Bengali. The four-man sifting board located a Swedish professor, an avid Orientalist, who could read Bengali. So charmed was he by Tagore that he tried to teach our Academy members Bengali that they might appreciate the poet in his own tongue. But the Academy members found Bengali too formidable, and awaited the professor's translation. It was accurate enough, and beautiful enough, to convince all that Tagore must have the prize."

"Then the literary award is actually in the hands of four men," said Stratman.

"By no means," replied Jacobsson. "The four-man board merely does the preliminary job. This year, they read the primary works of the thirty nominees, and eliminated twenty-four, and settled on six names as the final contenders. The best books of these six—Mr. Craig, another American author, two Germans, one Englishman, and a Japanese—were sent to all the other Academy members, along with excerpts, translated into Swedish, of other writings of the nominees. All through this past summer, the eighteen members of the Academy read and read.

"And now to reply to your earlier question, Miss Stratman—in the middle of September they all met formally, for the first time, in this room, to discuss what they had read, to sound out one other, to speak for their favorite works. One morning last month, in November, they met in this room a second time—gathered about the table here, the door locked, visitors not admitted —and they prepared to select the year's winner. The chairman of the four-person sifting board rose to his feet, right over there, and he said, 'We have reduced the thirty nominations to six, and of these six, we wish to recommend two names in particular.' He then offered Mr. Craig's name as a first choice, and an English author's name—I am not at liberty to identify him—as a second choice. He then read biographies of Mr. Craig and the five other nominees. After that, he read both favorable and unfavorable critiques of each man's literary work. Then the debate began. It lasted six hours. If you think Swedes are calm and pacific, I wish that you could attend one such wrangle. There was much passion, for and against—not only you, Mr. Craig, but every nominee. At last, ballots were passed down the table. Sixteen voted and two abstained. I am happy to say, Mr. Craig, you won by a creditable majority. Immediately, I was informed. I prepared the notification cable that same evening, and it went out to you directly. Shortly after that, the press was given the news by the Foreign Ministry."

Stratman advanced to a chair, and held it for support. "This wrangling, Count Jacobsson, this passionate debate you speak of—can you give any other specific instances?"

"To discuss this year's or last year's closed meetings might be improper," said Jacobsson, "but I suppose there is nothing wrong with relating a few historic disagreements. I relish them, and do not mind sharing them." He noticed the physicist's weariness, and said suddenly, "Please, Herr Professor —in fact, everyone—sit down for a few minutes while we talk. Take the chairs. This is not a museum—the chairs are for use."

Quickly, he helped Stratman off his feet, while Craig held a seat for Emily, and Mr. Manker and Flink vied to assist Leah. Soon, everyone was at rest around the long table. Jacobsson settled himself at the head, before the bust of Gustavus III.

"You know," said Jacobsson, "on many days every November and December, people all over the world pick up their newspapers and read of Nobel Prize winners. They come to believe, without thinking, that the laureates are demigods, and that the award is divinely ordained, but I am the first to admit that the winners, often geniuses and saints, are not demigods but human beings. At the same time, I am also the first to admit that the awards are neither divinely ordained nor decided by judges endowed with superior wisdom, but rather they are voted upon by ordinary men, of fine intellect, but of human frailty. I make these preliminary remarks because you wish to know what has gone on in this room, in secret sessions behind locked doors— and to appreciate what I will tell you, you must understand that our eighteen, like members of the other prize-giving committees, are merely mortals, after all. Most are experienced and knowledgeable men and women of scholarship and objectivity and great integrity. But, I repeat, they are mortals—they have personal prejudices, likes and dislikes, neuroses, vanities. They can be influenced by others, and influence one another. They can be bold, and they can be frightened. They can be cosmopolitan, and they can be provincial. They can be overspecialized in one area, and completely ignorant in another. But all of this considered, they are the best eighteen minds in this field that we have to offer. Once appointed, they serve for life, and to a man, they are the dedicated servants of Alfred Nobel's will. They are the judges of an Academy which has honored Rudyard Kipling, Gerhart Hauptmann, Romain Rolland, Anatole France, George Bernard Shaw, Sigrid Undset, Thomas Mann, Bertrand Russell, and Boris Pasternak. They are also the judges of an Academy which has ignored or rejected Émile Zola, Leo Tolstoi, Henrik Ibsen, Marcel Proust, Mark Twain, Joseph Conrad, Maxim Gorki, Theodore Dreiser, and August Strindberg. You see, they are wise, and they are foolish, but no wiser and no more foolish than other men."

Craig caught Jacobsson's attention. "Your selections I understand," said Craig, "and for the most, I heartily approve—my own included."

Leah, Flink, and Stratman laughed appreciatively, and Jacobsson permitted a flitting smile to cross his wrinkled features.

"But I still don't understand your omissions," Craig went on. "Some of them were brought up at the press conference yesterday. They seem to be brought up everywhere, and often, and never answered. Why didn't Zola and Tolstoi win one of the early prizes? Why weren't Ibsen and Strindberg, two of your own, ever honored? Was it that the judges, at the time, were dunderheads? Or were actual pride and prejudice involved?"

"Ah, I was coming to that," said Jacobsson, "I was leading up to that. Yes, generally it was prejudice—sometimes pride—often politics and weakness. Let us consider the specific names you have mentioned. Émile Zola was alive until 1902, and therefore twice eligible for the Nobel Prize. It is a fact that he was officially nominated for the first award by Pierre Berthelot, the celebrated French chemist. But, you see, Alfred Nobel had died only five years before, and his powerful ghost cast a long and influential shadow over the Academy members. In his lifetime, Nobel had detested Zola's *Nana* and the rest of his naturalist novels. Nobel considered them too—how shall I put it?—too earthy, coarse, realistic. Do not forget, in his will Nobel offered the literary prize for 'the most outstanding work of an idealistic tendency.' In Nobel's opinion, Zola had been anything but an idealist, and the Nobel judges knew this, and they had to consider the benefactor's tastes in disposing of his money."

"That I can understand," agreed Craig. "For the first time, the omission makes sense."

"You spoke of Tolstoi, Ibsen, Strindberg," continued Jacobsson. "Here, it was largely the strong prejudices of one man—one judge—who kept all of them out."

Craig did not hide his surprise. "Actually?"

"Yes, yes," said Jacobsson. "Certainly, there were other factors. Not only were the Academy members handicapped by the idealism edict, but they were conservative and poorly read. That was long ago, and I think we can admit it today. The majority of the judges were limited in their literary outlook. They were historians, religionists, philologists. Only three of them, I believe, knew anything of literature. One of these, a remarkable man, a poet and a critic, was Dr. Carl David af Wirsen. When the Academy took over the Nobel awards, Wirsen was its chairman, its most powerful figure. He was about fifty-eight at the time, wise and learned, but a person of strong personal prejudices. As an example of his control of the Academy, I need only cite what occurred in 1907. When the Academy loses one of its eighteen, and elects a replacement for life, the King must give his routine approval. In 1907, a new member, an eminent literary historian, was elected over Wirsen's objection that the new member had once committed *lèse-majesté* by publishing a volume critical of Gustavus III, the Academy's founder. When Wirsen found that he had been overruled, he went to King Oscar II and persuaded him to veto the new member—and the new member did not get in until Gustaf

V was on the throne. That was the power of Wirsen. And it was he who kept out Tolstoi."

"How could he do it?" asked Emily.

"It is not easy to explain, Miss Stratman, but let me see if I can," said Jacobsson. "The French Academy had nominated a relatively unknown poet, Sully Prudhomme, for the first award. The Swedish Academy was impressed by its French counterpart. Furthermore, our judges wanted a safe, uncontroversial choice. So they gave Prudhomme the first prize. The literary world was shocked. Even here in Sweden. Forty or fifty Swedish writers and artists castigated the Academy and offered a petition favoring Tolstoi. As a matter of fact, Tolstoi could not have been elected that first year, because no one had officially nominated him. This oversight was repaired the second year. Tolstoi was, indeed, nominated in 1902. But now Wirsen, the chairman of the Academy, came into the picture. I have seen the minutes of the stormy meeting when the judges had to select a laureate from among Mommsen, Spencer, and Tolstoi. It was Wirsen, almost single-handed, who struck down Tolstoi. Wirsen admitted that *War and Peace* was an immortal work. But he charged that Tolstoi's later writings were sensational and stupid, that Tolstoi condemned civilization, that he advocated anarchism, that he had the effrontery to rewrite the New Testament, and, greatest crime of all, that he had denounced all money prizes as harmful to artists. Wirsen's fiery diatribe carried the day, and the great Russian was defeated, and although he lived through eight more awards, he was never again a serious candidate."

"And Ibsen and Strindberg?" asked Craig.

"Again, as I have said, Dr. Wirsen's was the decisive veto. Ibsen's name was offered in 1903. Wirsen argued that to honor Ibsen then was, in effect, to honor a dead monument. Wirsen seemed to be saying that Ibsen's best plays had been done between *Peer Gynt* in 1867 and *The Master Builder* in 1892, and that in the eleven years after, his talent had declined. On the other hand, one of Ibsen's fellow Norwegians, Björnstjerne Björnson, a writer Nobel himself had admired, was still at the height of his powers. The argument carried the day. Ibsen was voted down and Björnson elected." Jacobsson paused, lost in thought a moment, and then resumed. "The opposition to August Strindberg was unfortunate, but even more bitter. Wirsen judged Strindberg's plays as 'old-fashioned.' That may have decided the matter. On the other hand, I sometimes think Strindberg was his own worst enemy. Wirsen and the majority of the Academy, and the King of Sweden, too, were appalled by the dramatist's private life. Strindberg had been thrown out of school for low grades. He had been fired from every job he had undertaken. He had been married and divorced three times. He had been sentenced to jail for blasphemy. He was a drunkard, an anti-Semite, and an advocate of black magic. And if there was ever any hope for him, he destroyed it by ridiculing the Swedish Academy in print. I believe it was in *Aftontidningen* that he wrote, 'The anti-Nobel Prize is the only one I would accept!' No men enjoy honoring someone who persistently insults them, and so Wirsen and the Academy had little difficulty in keeping the prize from Strindberg. Of course, for accuracy, I must add that Wirsen did not always have his way. There was an awful fight in 1908. Wirsen and the board were behind Algernon Swinburne, and half the Academy was behind Selma Lagerlöf. A deadlock resulted, and a poor compromise candidate, Rudolf Eucken, a German, was elected laureate. After a year of politicking, however, the Lagerlöf adherents managed to acquire a majority vote, and in 1909, over Wirsen's opposition, they gave her the prize. With that defeat, I believe, Wirsen lost his power over his colleagues."

"The Strindberg veto still fascinates me," said Craig. "Have many authors been deprived of the prize because of their personal lives?" Shortly before, Craig's mind had gone back over his last three years, his alcoholic bouts, and he had wondered if the Academy would have elected him had they known the truth. Now, he was curious.

"Unfortunately, a writer's behavior is often an issue," confessed Jacobsson, "but, aside from Strindberg and D'Annunzio, I cannot think of a single case where it has been the determining factor. Although, now that you bring it up, I do recall one laureate who was almost passed over because of his private life. If the ladies will forgive me, I must mention the example of André Gide. Year after year, he was a contender, and year after year, he was voted down because of his homosexuality, which he had admitted and defended in public. In 1947, Gide's name came up again. By this time, many members of the Academy had become more tolerant of him. His perversion was still an issue, but there was an odd switch in the balloting. One of Gide's most ardent supporters suddenly became prudish and turned against him, while at the same time, several members of the conservative bloc suddenly favored him. As you know, he was finally elected and, because he was ailing, had the French Ambassador to Sweden pick up his prize."

"You've been speaking of personal behavior," said Emily. "What about personal beliefs? Do the ideas an author stands for ever affect the voting?"

"Definitely," said Jacobsson. "In 1916, the Academy board recommended Zenito Pérez Galdós, a Spaniard. But a majority of the actual Academy was impressed by Romain Rolland's pacifism, his unpopular stand against World War I, which caused his self-imposed exile, and his leaving belligerent France for neutral Sweden. As a result, Rolland won the prize. In 1928, Archbishop Nathan Söderblom, although not exactly a literary figure, was a member of the Swedish Academy. He was an ecclesiastic of considerable prestige—a few years later, he would win the Peace Prize—and when he backed Henri Bergson for the literary award, because he venerated the Frenchman's philosophic beliefs, all opposition to Bergson fell aside. However, Miss Stratman, sometimes an author's beliefs will act against him. In 1934, Benedetto Croce, of Italy, was the favorite to win. It was a time, in Italy, when Benito Mussolini and his Fascist blackshirts were on the rise. Croce was anti-Fascist and outspoken in his hatred of Mussolini. A Nobel award to Croce would have been a slap in the face to Mussolini, and the Italian dictator knew it. I cannot substantiate what happened next—some say that Mussolini got in touch with his Ambassador in Sweden, and the Ambassador got in touch with the

Swedish Academy—but, at any rate, Croce was voted down for his beliefs, and his relatively harmless countryman, Luigi Pirandello, was given the prize. I know that this sounds weak-kneed, but you must remember it in the context of the time, a time when Fascism was a fearful threat. Anyway, I believe our Academy members made up for it in 1958, when they courageously gave Boris Pasternak the prize for *his* beliefs, despite the Communists holding a gun to our heads."

"But you can be pressured and bullied?" said Stratman.

Jacobsson lifted his palms upward and shrugged. "I have told you, Herr Professor, we are only men. More often than not, the pressures are lesser ones, and they come not from without but from within this room. There is always what you Americans call lobbying."

Jacobsson paused. He had something on the tip of his tongue, and hesitated, as if to reconsider it, but then spoke again. "There is one notorious case—an American author—I do not think I should mention the name. This author had produced several novels that, for reasons of personal taste, had impressed two senior members of the Academy, Dr. Sven Hedin, the explorer, and Selma Lagerlöf. These two tried to convince their colleagues that the American must have the prize. The majority of the Academy considered the works of this American potboilers and, as the chairman put it, 'mediocre.' Nevertheless, Hedin and Lagerlöf persisted, dramatizing the polemic value of the American's books, and finally invoking their seniority as judges until the Academy capitulated. The American won the prize, although originally opposed by the majority of members."

"I wonder who it was," said Leah.

Jacobsson waved his finger. "Not important. The American was certainly as deserving as many laureates before or since." Jacobsson looked across the table at Stratman. "Have you had enough of our little bouts in this sacred room, or do you have an appetite for more?"

"The entree was excellent," said Stratman with a smile. "I still have room for a dessert."

"Very well." Jacobsson thought a moment, reliving his precious Notes in his mind, reviewing this story and then that, censoring some and considering others, and when he was ready, he leaned his elbows on the table, and resumed. "In 1921, the two leading candidates were John Galsworthy and Anatole France. The board recommended Galsworthy, considering France's output as 'a dainty hothouse,' but the majority of the Academy favored France for injecting a new romanticism into literature. Anatole France was elected. It was eleven years before Galsworthy was offered as a serious candidate again. This time, his opponents were Paul Ernst, the German poet, and H. G. Wells. The argument for Ernst was that he was not only gifted and uncommercial in his creativity, but that he needed the money more than Galsworthy. Nevertheless, the final vote was in Galsworthy's favor.

"As to the argument that a candidate's financial straits be considered, that may have been an influential factor when William Butler Yeats defeated

Thomas Hardy in 1923. That, and also the fact that Yeats's advocates inveighed against Hardy's pessimism, which they felt did not meet the specifications of Nobel's will."

"Were there ever such intense debates over an American laureate?" Craig wanted to know.

"Several times," admitted Jacobsson. "Perhaps the meeting in this room in 1930 was the strongest. For three decades, the Academy had passed over American candidates, men such as Mark Twain, Edwin Markham, Stephen Crane. But in 1930, both Sinclair Lewis and Theodore Dreiser were leading rivals for the prize. To be perfectly honest, not much enthusiasm was generated over either candidate. Lewis was considered too prolific and popular, and only one of his novels, *Babbitt*, was held in high esteem. Dreiser was criticized for being too ponderous. In the end, Sinclair Lewis was chosen. I remember him well, all arms and legs, studying Swedish on Linguaphone records. He was most gracious. He was proud of his honor, but he told us all that many others deserved the prize before him." Jacobsson looked down the table. "I see Mr. Manker is signaling me. I am afraid I have talked too much, when there is more of the city you must see before the sun sets." He pushed his chair from the table and rose to his feet. "We have had enough of the sessions room."

Fascinated by the Count's recollections, Craig felt for the first time since his arrival in Stockholm a glimmer of gratification in his own triumph. He felt undeserving, yet reassured. He had courted extinction for many months, and feared it, and now there was relief in knowing that, despite himself, he would never die as long as the Nobel pantheon of accomplishment meant something to the civilized world. In many ways, the conversation in this room had been his best moment in Sweden, this and Lilly's love and the hibernating emotions that had awakened in Emily Stratman's presence. It was as if his dark soul was admitting its first shafts of light since mourning and guilt had drawn the shutters against life.

Rising, he murmured his thanks to the old Count.

"For what?" asked Jacobsson.

"For pride," he said, and knew that Jacobsson had not heard him, and that if he had, neither he nor anyone on earth would understand what he really meant.

The sun was lower, but still warming, when they arrived at the Town Hall, and clustered together on the open terrace, beneath the arches of colonnades, to listen to Mr. Manker.

The Town Hall, their guide had promised, would be the most inspiring building that they would visit in Stockholm. They were not disappointed. They had driven northwest of the Old Town to Kungsholmen island, and here, set sturdily on a small peninsula that crept into Lake Mälaren, between the Lake and the Klarasjö inlet, they found Stockholm's rare municipal structure.

They saw first the stark square tower of Town Hall, climbing 350 feet into the sky. They saw that it was russet red, as indeed was the entire building, with three crowns adorning its summit. They saw, also, that the red was brick, each and every brick lovingly set by hand. The roof of Town Hall was burnished copper, the gates of oak, and, below the arches and thick columns of the terrace, the balustrade that stretched over the water was of marble.

As Mr. Manker explained the history of the Town Hall, Craig noticed that Emily Stratman had drifted away from the gathering, and was now seated on a marble bench in the garden nearby, half listening and smoking a cigarette. Craig tried to concentrate on Mr. Manker's history, but his attention continued to be diverted by Emily, so trim and still with her legs crossed, so withdrawn and preoccupied.

"Now as to the magnificent interior of Town Hall," Mr. Manker was saying, "I will let you go inside and see for yourselves. We shall visit first the gold banquet hall, and I will direct your attention to the gold mosaic mural, made of one million pieces of colored stone, which depicts the story of Stockholm. Please, if you will follow me—?"

They had started off then, following the Foreign Office attaché into the courtyard, with Craig alone in the rear. As they filed past Emily, she quickly dropped her cigarette, ground it out, took her purse, and prepared to rise. Craig reached her at that moment, with the others continuing ahead, and he halted between her and the others, and smiled nervously down at her.

"Miss Stratman, if you don't mind, I'd like a word with you." He had not meant it to come out so formally, but it had because his instinct told him that too familiar or abrupt an approach might frighten her away.

She remained sitting, but uncertain. "They're expecting us."

"There's plenty of time for that," he said. He sat down on the marble bench, a few feet from her. "I think people absolutely ruin their travel by compulsively trying to see everything, grinding through city after city, trying to store up more see-manship than the next fellow. I'm for unplanned travel, with an occasional art gallery or historic site thrown in. If I ever give up writing, I'll start Aimless Tours, Incorporated—and I'll advertise, 'We Take You Nowhere, but You'll Find Yourself or Money Back.'"

She smiled. "Where do I make a reservation?"

He pointed off. "Look at that. Don't tell me what's inside can be better for the soul than that."

Staring out at the lazy blue waters of Lake Mälaren, they both watched the graceful gliding sea gulls, and the hazy fairyland outlines of Riddarholmen island beyond.

"Peace, it's wonderful," she said softly. She opened her purse, found the package of cigarettes, and took one, and he lit it. He filled his pipe and lit that, too. They smoked in silence for a while.

"What are you thinking?" he asked.

"As a matter of fact, I was thinking of you. That visit to the Swedish Academy—all that insider talk by Count Jacobsson about such legendary names—it made a deep impression on me. And I was thinking now—imagine,

Emily, you are sitting here on a stone bench in Stockholm with a man—with one whose name, in later years, will be discussed exactly as you heard Anatole France and John Galsworthy discussed today."

"Well, hardly—it's flattering, but not the same."

"Oh, yes."

"I may be the Eucken or Bunin of the Nobel roll call. Just as all our Presidents were not Lincoln. Some were Polk and Pierce."

"I think not."

"You don't know a thing about me, Miss Stratman."

She swerved toward him on the bench. "How is one transformed from Emily to Miss Stratman overnight?"

"By the wondrous sorcery of sobriety."

"I see. Well, wet or dry, I'm still Emily."

"In that case—I'm Andrew."

Her brow furrowed. "That's hard for me. It would have to be Mr. Craig for quite a while. After that, the next step would be—well, dropping Mr. Craig and not using your name at all—the transition—and then long after, maybe your first name. But we have only a week."

"Andrew's so easy. Try it."

"I couldn't."

"Simply say it after me. Andrew."

"Andrew."

"There, you see. Was that so difficult?"

"No—because I didn't believe it, it didn't connect with you."

"Well, when you're by yourself, practice it, rehearse constantly. Andrew—Andrew—where is Andrew?"

She smiled. "All right, I'll skip the Mr. Craig, I'll use no name for the time and see what happens."

"The weekly news magazines refer to us as Nobelmen. I wouldn't mind that."

"I'll oblige you in my next incarnation—when I'm a weekly news magazine."

She drew on her cigarette, and dropped her shoulders slightly, as if more at ease. "Back at Skansen," she said casually, "did you and my uncle really discuss physics and literature?"

"Not a bit."

"I thought not. What did you talk about?"

"You."

She showed no surprise, and pretended no immediate curiosity. "That must have lasted a quick ten seconds."

"Why do you say that?"

"Some people are conversation pieces, and some aren't. I'm 'aren't.' I hate to admit this, Mr.—sorry, I promised transition—I hate to admit this, but I'm enormously unexciting."

"How would you know?"

"Who else would know better? I'm cerebral and unadventurous. Not dull, mind you. I'm extremely clever in my head, and original, but there's nothing for a biographer or novelist. Shouldn't a good character provide conflict and excitement—action, eccentricity, passion—something?"

"Not necessarily, but it helps. Most people are good characters, not from the skin out, but beneath the skin."

"Perhaps," said Emily. "Anyway, I can't see two great Nobel brains discussing me at any length."

"I brought you up," said Craig, "because somehow it seemed to matter to me. I told your uncle how I'd behaved the night before, and that I owed you an apology, not only owed you but myself, because I wanted your good opinion."

"What did he say?"

"I think he advised me to go find another girl and start from scratch." Emily laughed. "Oh, he couldn't have—;"

"No, not in those words. But he made it clear that if I had offended you, I shouldn't hold too much hope about unoffending you."

"Well—I've got to admit I have thought about last night—"

"I was drunk, Emily, absolutely plastered. The way I behaved then has nothing to do with the way I am now or usually. I don't ordinarily take pretty girls, whom I've just met, into private rooms and try to kiss them. I'm much too reticent. But my inhibitions had dissolved, and I was impelled to perform, in short minutes, as I normally might perform after long weeks. So, forgive me—and pretend I've found another girl, and I want to start from scratch."

"If you'd waited a moment, you wouldn't have had to apologize at all," said Emily. "I was trying to say—I thought about last night, and there is simply nothing to forgive on your part. If there is to be an apology, it should come from me."

Craig knitted his brow in bewilderment.

"Yes," continued Emily, "from me. I'm not a child, but sometimes I behave like one. I knew you were—well, that you'd had some drinks—and so had I, and I was amused by you, and more awed than I let on. I went to that room with you because I wanted to. And as to your—your advances—I could have handled all that in good humor, or seriously but nicely, instead of playing the swooning nineteenth-century maiden. My behavior was involuntary—that's the best I can say for it—as I'm sure yours was, too. So, as you put it, let's start from scratch, Andrew."

"There, you said it—Andrew."

"I did? I guess I did. Isn't that strange?"

"Now, then, I know the way to start from scratch," said Craig. "First, we must enlist you in Aimless Tours, Incorporated. The first tour is downtown—Kungsgatan. I haven't had lunch—let's get me a sandwich, and you something, a soft drink, and just walk and look or not look and do absolutely nothing."

She hesitated, then nodded toward the rear. "What about all of them?"

"I'll run in and tell them we have to do some shopping."

"I actually do. I haven't bought a thing."

266

Craig jumped to his feet. "I'll tell your uncle you'll see him at the hotel a little later."

"You're sure no one will mind?"

"They may. But I'll mind more if we don't do this. Now, just sit and wait for me."

He strode hurriedly across the court toward the building, just as Mr. Manker emerged and waved, and started toward them.

"Miss Decker became worried," said Mr. Manker, "so I said I'd find you."

"Thanks, Mr. Manker. I was going in to find you. Will you tender our thanks and regrets to one and all, and explain to Professor Stratman and Miss Decker that Emily and I have to go into the city—some shopping, some errands—"

"But our sightseeing, Mr. Craig, it is not done."

"Wonderful as you've been, Mr. Manker, I've decided to join another group for the rest of the day. Aimless Tours, Incorporated. I recommend them highly. They're good for what ails you—myopia, bunions, buzzing in the head, and cathedralitis. See you later, Mr. Manker."

After leaving the taxi, they had walked only a short distance on Stockholm's main street before they had come upon the Triumf restaurant at Kungsgatan 40 and peered inside and decided that it might be a lunchroom.

They sat on high green stools behind one of the three horseshoe-shaped counters and consulted a menu relentlessly Swedish. Timidly, Emily suggested a translator, but Craig thought that would spoil the game. After considerable speculation, Craig settled upon *Kyckling med grönsallad och brynt potatis* at 5.25 kronor. Emily was amiable to his suggestion. Confidently, Craig put in the order, reassuring Emily that there would be little surprise since two of the Swedish words related to English words. The element of surprise and fun lay in "Kyckling." Each of them had wild interpretations. Emily was sure that it meant pregnant herring. Craig voted for boiled Lapp.

When their dishes came, they were both dismayed. "Kyckling" proved to be fried chicken.

"One world," said Craig grimly, but they both enjoyed the chicken, and the potatoes and green salad, because this was their first adventure shared in common.

Later, after Craig had his black coffee and Emily had her cigarette, and the tipping problem had been simply solved by leaving a handful of öre (because the coins were small, and as apologetic as centimes), they strolled leisurely, side by side and self-consciously, on broad Kungsgatan.

Sometimes, in the crush of the heavy foot traffic, especially at intersections, they were thrown against each other, their shoulders bumping, their arms rubbing, but this was their only physical contact. Craig was careful not to take either Emily's elbow or her hand when they crossed a street. The walk on Kungsgatan was as unceremonious as any walk on a similar street in New York, Atlanta, Chicago, or Kansas City. There was a lack of foreignness about Kungsgatan. The business buildings and commercial stores, the women with packages and the men with briefcases, had all been seen before. Of course, the Swedes looked at you and somehow knew you were American, and you looked at them and knew they were Swedish, but the differences were small and subtle. Except for the street and store signs, which were foreign, and the persistent *tack, tack, tack* of passers-by (which Craig knew to mean thank you-thank you-thank you), Craig and Emily felt that they could not be far from home.

"The time I was here before," Craig said, "there was a record being played up and down this street. It was called, 'There's a Cowboy Rolling Down Kungsgatan.' I asked someone about it. Why a cowboy on Kungsgatan? Well, it turned out that some American flyers had come down over Sweden, during the war, and had to be interned. However, they were given the freedom of the city, and some of those big Texans loved to walk, in their rolling gaits, up and down Kungsgatan. So, after the war, it became a romantic song, very popular, to celebrate a moment of light excitement in a time of drab neutrality."

"Why did you come to Sweden at that time?" Emily inquired.

"I'm not sure. I think we kept hearing about the bad plumbing in Paris, and how the Italians rob you, and we wanted to start our honeymoon in a faultless and antiseptic place. It was fun, because it was our first country abroad, but frankly, Paris and Rome were better."

"Was the plumbing bad? Did they rob you?"

"Of course. Two tenderfeet full of compassion for France and Italy after the war. But who needs plumbing, when you have the Tuileries? And who cares about overpaying when you get, in return, the Borghese Gardens?" He pointed off. "Over there, you must see that. Let's cross the street."

They waited for the light to change, and then made their way, in the crowd, to Hörtorget square.

"That building to the left is Concert Hall," explained Craig. "In there is where your uncle and I will receive our Nobel Prizes on the afternoon of the tenth."

Emily studied Concert Hall. It was an immense square building, seven stories high, fronted by ten pillars and nine latticed entries. On the expanse of stone steps, a dozen or more Swedes, mostly young people, sat basking in the last of the day's sun. Emily followed Craig to the dark-green statue, so modern and fluid, of a godlike youth, airborne, playing a lyre, while four mortal youths and maidens gathered below.

"Is that Carl Milles's 'Orpheus'?" asked Emily.

"Yes. What do you think?"

"Incredible—to find that right off the business street. I'm not sure I like the representation, but I like the idea—this sort of thing here—instead of some granite general or obelisk to the war dead."

Craig had been impressed with the "Orpheus" work when he had first come upon it with Harriet, so long ago. It was still impressive, he found, but less so. What disconcerted him was not the art but the unreality of the art.

The maidens were too much like the boys, their hips too narrow, their buttocks too flat, and now that he had known Lilly, he believed Milles less.

"Let's sit on the steps a minute," he said to Emily, "if it isn't too cold."

They climbed ten steps to the top and sat apart from the Swedish students and facing the square.

"The square is quite a sight in the summer," said Craig. "It's an open-air market jammed with flower stalls—marigolds, sweet peas, lilies—overwhelming in color and fragrance. And across the way, the department store, that's P.U.B. Do you know why it's famous?"

"I haven't the faintest idea."

"A girl named Greta Gustafsson was a saleslady there. She sold hats. That was before she became Greta Garbo."

"Is that really so?"

"Absolutely. When I was here the other time, P.U.B. used to advertise the fact. Remember how everyone talked about Greta Garbo's big feet? Well, I went in there and asked someone in the shoe department her size. It was nine. Is that big?"

"It's not small."

"What's your foot size?"

She held out a leg and wiggled her sandal. "Six. Why?"

"Women's sizes fascinate me."

"Well, don't ask any of my other sizes. I'd be embarrassed. It's like undressing in public."

He moved back and eyed her with exaggerated lechery: "I'd say thirty-eight, twenty-four, thirty-six. Am I right?"

"Never mind, Mr. Craig."

"I've been demoted."

"Banished."

"I'll earn back my Andrew."

"You were doing as nicely as Mr. Manker. How do you remember all those things?"

"You know, Emily, I haven't thought of Sweden in all these years. When we sat down here, it all came flooding back. Lucius Mack always said my mind's a repository of useless and footnote facts. I think that's true of certain writers. When it comes to knowledge, there are three kinds of writers. First, the one who knows only one field—himself. Remember Flaubert's admission? 'I am Madame Bovary.' Second, the writer who knows two or three fields in depth—the Civil War, Zen, and Palestrina—and nothing else. Third, there is the one who knows a little about very many things—from European rivers called Aa to the biological name for ovum which is zygote—and Lucius Mack puts me in that category."

"Who is Lucius Mack?"

"Didn't I introduce you? I'm sorry. He edits our weekly newspaper in Miller's Dam. Our answer to William Allen White. My best friend. A wonderful old-young codger. You'd adore him."

"I like journalists."

"The trouble with newspapermen is that they think they want to be something else. That's what corrodes television people, and dentists, and accountants. But not Lucius. He made his peace. Are you cold?"

"A little. I guess the sun's gone."

"Let's walk."

They descended the stairs, and continued slowly along Kungsgatan, and then turned off on Birger Jarlsgatan, which had the expensive look of the smaller Fifth Avenue. Several times, shop windows caught Emily's attention, and then they would go inside and poke about, and by the time they had reached Berzelii Park, she had purchased an Orrefors ashtray, a Jensen serving spoon and fork of silver, a miniature Viking made of wood, and a box of Vadstena lace handkerchiefs.

In Berzelii Park, they stood in the darkness, among the denuded trees.

"I'd like to buy a Swedish language book," said Emily. "Do you think all the book stores are closed?"

"It's not that late," Craig said. "It just gets dark early in winter. I know the bookstore for you. Fritze's. A wonderful old shop founded in the 1830s. I think J. Pierpont Morgan used to buy there. It's a medium-long walk. Are you up to it?"

"I wouldn't miss it."

They crossed Gustaf Adolfs Torg under the street lamps and arrived at Fredsgatan 2, which was Fritze's. Inside, they browsed for a half an hour. Emily found a Svensk-Engelsk phrase book, and then also purchased a Stockholm edition of *Alice in Wonderland* and three copies of an enchanting and sophisticated juvenile cartoon book, *Mumintrollen* by Tove Jansson, to be given as gifts. In turn, Craig purchased a copy of Indent Flink's Swedish version of *The Perfect State* and gave it to Emily as a supplement to her language booklet.

After they had left Fritze's and gone several blocks along the canal, Craig suddenly stopped. "Why are we going all the way back to the hotel to join that mob for dinner? Why don't we eat out alone, together? I know exactly the place. It'll charm you."

"How can we after walking out on them this afternoon? The Nobel committee might consider it rude—"

"But nothing formal's been planned. There's nothing special on the program."

"And my uncle—"

"I'll phone him. I'll tell him I'm taking you to dinner, and I'll have you back safe and sound in a few hours. How's that?"

"I'm not sure—"

"I am. Let me call him."

"All right."

They walked another block, until they found an outdoor public telephone booth. Emily gave Craig two ten-öre pieces, and he closed himself inside the booth while she waited beyond the glass pane, smoking.

Craig got the operator, and she put him through to the Grand Hotel, and the Grand Hotel connected him with Professor Stratman's suite.

Craig identified himself, and Stratman asked immediately, "How is Emily?"

"Never better. I'm looking at her right now through a window of the booth. She was worried that you might be concerned, so I offered to call."

"You are thoughtful. So—you gave us the slip today."

"I'd seen it all, and Emily wanted to shop. She just bought a copy of *Alice in Wonderland* in Swedish."

"For me, you do not have to make up stories, my laureate friend." Stratman's chuckle came over the wire. "I see I would have lost my bet. Your case was not hopeless. She accepted your apology."

"Yes, Professor."

"And now you are—how do they say?—on the wagon."

"Definitely."

"I wish you luck."

"I'll need it. I was really calling because I want to take Emily to dinner, and she wondered—"

"You tell her Uncle Max is all right. The Count is coming over to take me, with the Farellis and Garretts—and also your sister-in-law—to eat in the Winter Garden. You go and have your good time."

"How was my sister-in-law?"

"Like the Queen of Hearts," said Stratman.

It was not until Craig had hung up, and was leaving the booth, that he understood Stratman's allusion. Stratman had meant Lewis Carroll's Queen of Hearts, who had been furious, and who had ordered that Alice's head be cut off.

They had gone down the steep stone staircase, through the winding narrow passageway, until they emerged into the long cellar grotto, hewn out of rock. This was the Old Town's most renowned and beloved ancient restaurant, known to Swedish bohemians as Den Gyldene Freden and to visitors as The Golden Peace.

Now they sat at a tiny table against the rock, across from each other, while an attractive waitress in a white-and-coral apron took their order for dry martinis. After the waitress left, Emily looked about, filled with wonder. At this early evening hour, the quaint restaurant was only half filled with customers, informally dressed, but already gay and noisy. The room quieted somewhat when a respectable-looking troubadour, wearing horn-rimmed glasses and dark suit, appeared at the cellar entrance and began to play the lute and sing the old songs of Carl Mikael Bellman.

"Well," said Craig, "what do you think?"

"I've never seen anything like it," said Emily. "I'm glad you brought me here. Is it as old as it looks?"

"Older. Remember when we were driving through what used to be the King's hunting grounds today, and Mr. Manker pointed out the place where Carl Mikael Bellman lived? Well, Bellman made Den Gyldene Freden. He was its leading customer. He came here every night and wrote his lyrics, and sang them, and got drunk and wild. They say he used to dance on the tables. That was back in the 1770s, so it's old enough. In modern times, Anders Zorn, the painter, bought the restaurant and restored it as a sort of artists' hangout, which it is now. Notice how wide these chairs are? Zorn's doing. He was fat, and used to get caught in the old chairs, so he had these made to his specifications and installed. Eventually, Zorn turned the restaurant over to the Swedish Academy, and I think they still get part or all of the profits. The first time I came here, after the lute player and orchestra were through, some customer pulled his guitar out from under the table and began to strum, and everyone in the place joined in a community sing."

The waitress set the martinis before them, and Craig said, "Skål," and sipped the drink slowly, determined to have no more than one.

"Did your wife come here with you?" Emily asked.

"Oh, yes. She loved it, naturally. But one visit was enough. She wasn't an on-the-town type. Are you?"

"Heavens, no."

"I didn't think so. I'm not, either. But Harriet liked to collect quaint restaurants. She liked to go once, and that was it. When she was a student at Columbia, she lived in Greenwich Village a while. I don't believe she ever got over it. Whenever we went into a city, she would try to find its Greenwich Village."

"How did she like living in a small town?"

"Very much. But had she lived, I don't think we would have stayed there. She was a homebody, but always at civil war with her arty side. She was satisfied to stay inside, if she knew Greenwich Village was available somewhere outside."

"And you?" asked Emily.

"I'm not Greenwich Village at all. I was headed in that direction once—Taos, I thought, or Monterey—but I was saved in the nick of time. In those days, I wanted to write, not talk about it. No, I'm not Bohemia. I'm grass roots. What are you, Emily?"

She revolved her drink slowly in her hand. "I'm wherever I am. I merge with the landscape. What is outside doesn't matter, because I live inside myself."

"Are you satisfied?"

"Who is ever satisfied? I'm content. I manage."

"That's a big thing," said Craig. "That's a kind of peace."

"So is dying, I suppose. Don't envy me. I'm a vegetable. Can you envy a vegetable?"

He smiled. "Yes, I can." Suddenly, he could not allow last night's lie about his way of life remain a deceit. "You see, I don't even have a vegetable's peace. At least, not recently. Last night, before the banquet, you wanted to know how I lived, and I wanted to impress you. I gave you the country squire routine. Not true, I'm afraid."

"What is true, Andrew?"

"Well, no laments, no dirges, on a night like this, in a happy place with a pretty girl. But—"

He hesitated and then was silent.

"I want to know," she said.

"For three years, I haven't worked and haven't lived. Until this trip, I haven't been fifty miles out of Miller's Dam. I haven't gone back to recreations, haven't had a date, haven't written so much as a letter." As he spoke, he automatically expurgated the drinking and the suicidal guilts. "I wake up and don't know the day or the weather or if there is a bird or flower left alive. I go through each day eating Leah's cooking, and holding books I don't read, and playing cards with Lucius Mack, and falling asleep. At least, a vegetable grows. I'm a fossil."

"Is it all your wife?"

"It used to be. I'm not so sure of that any more. I haven't thought of her too much in the last year. But the inertia remains. Well, at least until today. I felt alive, today, and growing again. I think I mean that as a compliment to you."

Emily was shy, but not coy, and she said simply, "Thank you, Andrew."

"I know I chattered on a good deal about her and us and our honeymoon today. But it wasn't longing that inspired my monologue. It was being alive, in the streets, with a woman again, someone before whom I wanted to perform as a man, and I found I could discuss the past quite naturally. What started all this outpouring?"

"You envied a vegetable." She paused and examined her drink. "Don't. Because I lied to you, too, last night, with my usual surface fairy tale. All the big people coming and going, myself the ravishing hostess, the glamorous dates in Atlanta. None of that is true. All that exists to be had, but I don't have it. I exile myself to my bedroom. I drug myself with my books. Except for Uncle Max, I'm alone."

"How can that be? A girl like you—I would imagine a hundred suitors beating a path to your door."

"Not a hundred, but some. I won't deny that. I've let them know I'm not available. I do not choose to run."

"Don't you want a husband, children, a home of your own?"

"I want children and a home of my own."

"I see." He finished his drink and regarded her thoughtfully. "You let me speak of my loss. What about yours?"

"You mean my mother and father? That's so long ago—"

"Is it?"

She stared at him. "No, it isn't. My mother was wearing a faded green cotton dress that day. It had been mended a hundred times. And she always kept it clean. I was asleep in the barracks—it was dawn—and she leaned over and kissed me, and I saw she was wearing the green dress. 'Emmy,' she said, 'the Commandant wants to see me. Maybe it will be good news. I will wake you when I come back.' She never came back. They put her on the cattle car for Auschwitz. My father was in Berlin with Uncle Max. I'd forgotten his face by then—except his funny nose—he and Uncle Max had twin noses, like two tulip bulbs—but aside from that, I could remember nothing but the smell of the lotion he wore after shaving and an expression of endearment he had always used when we played together—and so, after my mother went, I was alone. It was like being a child and waking up suddenly to find the house empty and dark."

Craig was silent, for there was nothing to say.

She glanced about the room absently and then looked at Craig. "When Uncle Max brought me to America," she said, "I made up my mind that I was just born and had come from nowhere. I never spoke German again, or read it, or even thought in German. I extinguished it through sheer willpower from my life. To this day, I won't read a book by a German author or buy a product made in Germany. If this award had not been so important to Uncle Max, I would not have made this trip with him—because Sweden is so near to Germany. Being here, a few hours away, I can't tell you how it makes me feel. It makes me vengeful—and it makes me afraid—both, at the same time. Why am I vengeful? Who is there any longer to punish? Why am I afraid? Don't I have a United States passport? But anyway, there it is. And now, I have talked too much. Let us put away the past and speak of the present." She tried to smile. "I had a happy day today, Andrew. I'm grateful. I don't think I'll ever forget Stockholm."

"I don't think I will, either," he said. "Let's wait and see."

It was almost eleven o'clock in the evening when Craig returned to his Grand Hotel suite.

The spell of the evening, of Emily's allurement, was still upon him. Their dinner at Den Gyldene Freden had stretched lazily over three hours. There had been comfortable talk and comfortable silences. They had discussed the better parts of their pasts, and dreams and desires half forgotten, and, several times, they had timorously made mention of their separate futures. All through dinner, the cellar had filled with customers, and when dinner was over, encouraged by the lute player, they had blended their voices with a hundred others, humming melodies that were international.

Afterwards, they had promenaded through the Old Town, and when it became too cold, they had made their way more quickly over the bridge that led them to the Grand Hotel. Although they had been close all the evening, Craig deliberately took no advantage of it when they reached the door of the Stratman suite. He was not sure what Emily expected, but the first experience with her and a sure instinct told him that she would be apprehensive. As she put the key in the door and opened it, his demeanor changed to one of friendly formality. He had said that he hoped he could see her tomorrow, and she had replied that she hoped so, too, although she did not know what her uncle's schedule would be. She had extended her hand, thanking him for their sightseeing and the dinner, and he had taken her cool fingers and palm, thanking her for her company. And then, swiftly, he had departed.

Now, entering his suite—their suite, he remembered, and this brought Leah back into his life—he saw that the entry hall was lit, but the sitting room darkened except for a single lamp. Leah was nowhere to be seen, and he guessed that she had retired. He went to her bedroom door, to observe if the crack below showed light, but he could not tell. He was tempted to knock, to reassure her that he was home safe and proudly sober. But he resisted the temptation. He was no little boy who must parade virtue and observance of curfew before Mother. He owed Leah none of this. Moreover, his appearance at this hour—had not Stratman warned him that Leah had been irritated by his flight with Emily?—might only bring on a scene. He wanted no scene. He wanted no defect in an almost perfect day.

Stealthily, he tiptoed across the carpeted sitting room, held aside the drawn drapes, and entered his bedroom alcove. The soothing yellow light on the bedstand showed the bed neatly turned down, and his pajamas folded and lying across the blanket. He wondered, briefly, if the floor maid or Leah had prepared this.

He was as peacefully tired as he had been in the long-ago morning, after he had left Lilly's apartment. The bed would be welcome. He would lie in it, and review the day, not his past but the day, and eventually, he would rest without a drop of Scotch. He considered writing a short victory note to Lucius, but realized that he would be home almost as soon as the note, and he decided that he would relax in a warm bath instead.

After undressing, he took up his pajamas, turned off the bedroom lamp, and went into the bathroom. He closed the door softly, and then drew the water, adjusting the faucets until the water was exactly right. At last, he immersed himself in the water, not washing, merely soaking, sometimes splashing and rubbing the water over his face, shoulders, and chest.

His writer's mind fastened on the day, and outlined its wonders in specific categories. The major elements of the day had been Lilly Hedqvist, the Swedish Academy, Emily Stratman. Each had served him with the stuff of life. His writer's mind went on—the anatomical categories—Lilly had served his torso below the waist, the Academy had served his head, Emily had served his heart—but that wasn't quite it, and he continued to refine the categories. Lilly had given him sexual release and comfort, and knowledge that he was worthy of love and was not alone. Jacobsson had restored his pride in his work and past, and had given him a solid sense of achievement. Emily had offered him a romantic hope for the future, a vision of normality, a goal for living. And together, unwittingly, all had combined to prove to him that he might survive a day unaided by drink or drug.

After he had dried himself, and pulled on the bottom half of his pajamas, he was ready for sleep.

He opened the bathroom door, flipping off the bathroom light, padded into the bedroom, sat on the bed, and stretched his bare arms, yawning.

In the dark, he lifted the blanket, and eased himself under it, and then squirmed to the center of the bed. Suddenly, as he moved, his leg and hand touched a solid object. At once, he knew that it was heated flesh and bone—a human body.

His heart leaped to his throat, throbbing uncontrollably at the surprise and shock of this presence.

"Who is it?" he gasped in a strangled voice.

There was no reply, and then there was a reply, almost inaudible. "It's me." The voice was Leah Decker's voice.

He lifted himself to an elbow, waiting for the thump of his heart to lessen and his incredulity to recede.

"Lee?" he whispered.

"It's me," she repeated.

"What in the devil are you doing here?" He had recovered his wits. "Let me put on the light."

He sat up in the bed to grope for the lamp, but quickly she rose in the darkness beside him and fell across his chest, fumbling for his outstretched arm. "No, Andrew!" she cried. "Don't, please don't—"

He was pressed back against the headboard by her body, and felt the weight of her loose pendulous breasts, flaccid and milky, against his eyes and mouth. Their enormousness and sag confounded him, for they had always been bound tight and flat, in the Japanese manner, inside her dresses, and he had never imagined them released. Her hair was undone, he knew, for he felt its mass brushing his forehead as she tried to recover balance. For a moment, she tottered over him, and he smelled the whiskey on her breath. Before she could fall on top of him, he reached up in the darkness to help her, gripping her ribs so that his hands were enfolded beneath the swinging breasts. He pushed her across to her side of the bed, and felt her convulsive movement as she slid beneath the blanket.

"Lee, for Chrissakes, are you drunk or what?"

"I am not drunk," she replied in a shaking voice. "I—I had some drinks, because I needed courage, but I am not drunk." She paused. "Andrew, I have nothing on. I'm naked."

"I know you're naked," he said with distress.

"Andrew, don't talk, please don't talk, don't say a word. Let's not spoil it. Listen to me. Are you listening?" She went on breathlessly. "You know how hard this is for me. It's taken me three years to get up the nerve. I know it was wrong of me to be so prim. I couldn't change my nature, much as I knew you needed me. But since we got here—seeing what's happening to you, knowing the crisis you face—I made up my mind—I made up my mind tonight—I must think of you—it's the right thing—"

"Lee—"

"Don't worry about me, Andrew. It's the right thing, I'm positive now. It's what Harriet would have wanted. You're the important one. I've found my role in life—*it's to make you happy.*"

"Lee, I'm—I don't know what to say—"

She was not listening, so intent was she. "I'm throwing off the blanket, Andrew. I'm naked. You can come here. You can do it. You can show me what to do. I've never done it in my life, Andrew. You won't believe it, but

276

you're the first. No man's ever touched me that way. But you can. Now I'm ready."

He lay back against the headboard, dazed. The darkness had dissipated, now that he was used to it, and the lone sitting-room lamp behind the drapes lightened the room enough, so that he could distinguish the lines of her, the silhouette of her body, on the bed.

He sat up again to speak to her, but she mistook his rise for the complementing passion, and immediately, she extended her legs so that one touched his own.

"Lee, wait," he said. And then he said, "Tell me why you're doing this. In bed, there's no dishonesty. Be truthful. Do you need it? Is that what you want?"

He heard the intake of her breath, and the horrified tone of her reply. "What a thing to say, Andrew! What do you think I am—a nymphomaniac? Of course, I don't need it. You know better. Women don't need it. But I know about men, and you're a man. I came here to make you happy the best way a woman can."

"Lee, you've got it all mixed up. I am happy. You don't have to be a sacrificial lamb. You don't have to offer your body to make me happy. I wouldn't do that to you."

"Let's not talk, Andrew. I know you're embarrassed. You don't want to feel you're taking advantage of our relationship. I promise you, I won't think so. But I've seen you drinking yourself to death. I've seen your misery. No one has seen it as I have seen it. And, here, you seem to be worse than ever— doing strange things—going off by yourself—and starting to look at women— I can see the way you look at them—and then it all came to me—that I'd been a fool—that you were too sensitive to tell me your need. And I thought —I kept thinking—what would Harriet want of me—and I knew that she would approve, she would be the first to call down and say help him, Leah, save him, make him happy and normal. And that's all I want to do, Andrew. It's no sacrifice for me. You know how I feel about you. It would be good. And I'm glad, I'm really glad I saved it for you. And tonight won't be the only night, so don't worry about that. This is not an impulse. I've thought it out. We'll be gone from here soon, and you'll have me always there, and you don't have to worry and have tensions. I'll be there, and you don't have to drink any more or be a celibate. You can have pleasure again and be your old self again. Don't make me talk any more, Andrew, please—"

"Oh, Christ, Lee, listen."

"—because that's not the way I planned it. I only had the drinks to get up my nerve, and because I was worried I wouldn't please you, because I'm not Harriet, and I've never slept with a man. But I'll be good, you'll see. Just have patience, and show me, and don't hurt me—but even if you do—I don't care." Her voice became smaller, and now it caught. "You can take me now, Andrew."

"Goddamit, Lee, no. Goddamit, I won't take you, I can't." He was furious with the predicament in which she had placed him. "I don't want intercourse with you—or maybe I do, I don't know—but even if I did, I wouldn't."

Agitated, he swung off the bed, felt under the lamp, and turned on the light. He stood beside the bed, in his rumpled pajama drawers, hitching them up, ashamed to have to see her here. Her head, her free hair matted, was on the pillow, and now averted from the light. Her hands knotted tightly on the blanket top, pulling it to her neck.

"What are you doing?" she groaned. "Turn off the light."

"I won't. I don't trust myself in the dark. I am a human being."

She kept her face averted. "Then why are you scared?"

He knew that this rejection was terrible, and so he softened toward her, made the fault his own. "I don't want your pity, Lee. This—it's not good for us. Can't you understand, Lee? It's nothing for a man. It's easy for a man. It would have been pleasurable for me. You're an attractive woman. I mean that. I think you may even be a passionate woman. But what would be the point? You're not on earth to accommodate me—to be my bondmaid. I'm not that selfish. That's all it would be. I could never promise you more or offer you more. So it would be wrong for me to be the first, unless you needed it. That would be another matter. But you don't. You say you don't. And if you haven't up to now, I think you should wait until it means something more, until you have someone. There's that nice fellow in Chicago—Beazley—Harry Beazley—it would mean something with him. It would mean a whole life for you. But you know me. I can promise you nothing—not love—not even affection. And marriage—I can't think of marriage. I just won't have it with you this way. Now, let's not think of it or speak of it again. Let's just go on as we have."

For the first time, she turned her face to him. Her thin lips quivered. "Go into the other room," she said in a cold, expressionless voice, "until I'm decent."

He retreated awkwardly through the drapes, and then pulled them chastely across so that they covered every inch of the bedroom entrance. Moving to the coffee table, he found a pack of Leah's cigarettes and took one and lit it. His hand shook, as he held the cigarette, and he could not remember when, since Harriet's death, he had been more dismayed.

He listened to the creaking of the bed, as she got up to dress, and he paced back and forth across the sitting room.

Presently, the drape was flung aside, and Leah appeared. She wore a flannel bathrobe over her nightgown, and slippers. Her hair was long, but combed. Her face was composed, but glacial.

She advanced toward him without shame or timidity. He read her attitude at once. Her every movement spoke her thought. She was saying: I am blameless, the fault is your fault. She was saying: I offered, in all charity and kindness, to save you from yourself, and you rebuffed me. She was saying: the Lord will punish you, not me, for I am the handmaid whose name is Hagar.

Against fanatic righteousness, Craig knew that he was helpless.

"I've listened to your pack of lies," Leah began stridently, "and I just want you to know you're not pulling the wool over my eyes."

"Now, what does that mean?"

"It means I see through you, better than anyone on earth. All that holy talk about thinking of me, about saving me for someone else, about not wanting to hurt me. I know the truth. I suspected it, but now I know it."

"Maybe you'll let me in on your secret."

"You didn't need my love, which is clean and decent, because you've been getting too much these last couple of days from that little Nazi whore-bitch from Atlanta!"

"Leah!"

"I could see it from the first minute she set eyes on you. She put her hooks in you fast. She gave you what you needed fast. She's got one Nobel winner in the family, but that's not enough. Now, she wants two. She saw you were weak—any experienced woman could tell that—and she played on your weakness, and now she's got you, and that's what is wrong. Andrew, Andrew, you're such a guileless fool!"

He tried to repress his anger, for he knew her hurt, but it was impossible. "You're the fool, Lee, if that's what you believe," he said quietly. "Emily Stratman is as much a virgin as you are."

"I see, you know that. You found out?"

"Dammit, Lee, shut up. She's attractive, of course, and I'm not a eunuch. You bet your life I tried to make time with her. I didn't get to first base. I haven't touched her. I haven't even kissed her."

"You were with her all day."

"So I was with her. So what? I was sick of the tour, and I wanted to be on my own—I told you that this noon—and she had some shopping to do, and I wanted companionship, and we went walking. That's all. Is that wrong?"

Leah had listened, and her outrage was spent and her jealousy relieved and she saw a new hope. "If it's true, it's not wrong, and I'm sorry."

"It's true, and I swear it. And everything I told you in the bedroom is true, also."

"You said we wouldn't discuss that."

"All right."

There was nothing more to argue about, but Leah was not ready to go. "I—I suppose you have to know other women besides me. Especially now that you're famous. But what you see in a German foreigner—"

"She's an American, Lee."

"Whatever she is, I don't care. What you can find in common with a perfect stranger—"

"Harriet was a stranger before I met her. And so were you. And so is everyone to everyone, until they communicate. Miss Stratman and I simply walked and talked about nothing important—I showed her some of the places in downtown Stockholm where Harriet and I had been—"

"You did that?" It was as if he had been an infidel who had violated

Mecca. Again, Leah's displeasure was evident. "You mentioned Harriet to her?"

"Of course. Why not? I told her about Harriet and our life, certainly."

"How could you? It's improper. You never talk to me about Harriet and you. How can you do that with someone you've only known for two days?"

"Maybe because I only knew her two days. You're Harriet's sister. That makes it difficult."

Leah pursed her lips tightly. "I don't know what's going to become of you, I really don't. You're simply acting without restraint in every way. You're getting worse all the time. I can see what's ahead for us. Drinking and more drinking, and now, added to that, strange women, with all your pitiful confessions, embarrassing both of us by pouring all your troubles into everyone's ears. You can't do that, Andrew, not now—now that the entire world knows you—now that you're a Nobel winner. What would people think if they knew you killed your wife? What if it got out? I suppose you got drunk and told that to the Stratman girl? Did you?"

It was almost as if Craig had known from the beginning, from the moment of his rejection of Leah, that the blow would fall again, as it always had when he displeased her. It was the one blow that could bring him to his knees. Against it he had no shield. And now, inevitable as death, it had fallen, and he was once more defeated. He hated the past, that had provided her with the ultimate weapon and had left him disarmed.

"You don't have to worry," he said, suddenly tired. "I didn't tell her about the accident."

"Thank God for that much restraint," she said. "The accident—as you call it—is in the family. That's what worries me about your drinking. And seeing strange women. If you need the company of women, and you—you have too much respect for me—I wouldn't care if you went to a prostitute once in a while. At least, you wouldn't talk too much to them. It's the ordinary girls that I worry about, the ambitious ones who worm their way into your confidence. Keep that in mind the next time you see the Stratman girl. In the end, I trust your common sense, Andrew. You have a new position to maintain now, and a new future, and if you think of Harriet once in a while, and remember that I'm your best friend in the world, you won't ruin it or yourself. I think we understand each other, don't we?"

"Yes, Lee."

"I was upset by your behavior in the bedroom," she said briskly, again self-assured and in full control. "I was going to move out of this suite, even go home, and just leave you. Now I see that would be wrong of me. You need me for a rudder. So you needn't worry. I'll stay. You can depend on me. Good night, Andrew."

"Good night, Lee."

She went into her bedroom, and he shuffled slowly into his. With distaste, he viewed the mauled bed, the heavy impressions on both pillows. He knelt beside the overnight bag, unlocked it, and removed a bottle of Scotch. In the bathroom, he took one of the two empty glasses, then came back into the bedroom, filling the glass as he walked.

He settled into the easy chair, and he drank deeply, and when the glass was empty, he immediately filled it a second time, and drank again.

The almost perfect day had become one more day of disaster, and Leah, in her misguided, stupid desire to help him, had been the instigator of the calamity. Yet he was uncertain of one point. He asked himself a question: had Leah, with her rigid naked body, sincerely set out to help him? He asked another question: or had Leah, consciously or unconsciously, set out to help herself, herself alone? Now, Hamlet, Horatio, whoever, that was the question—or, rather, the questions.

Craig gulped down the liquid, which no longer stung, and relaxed in the chair as the savior fluid coursed through his veins and numbed his tormented brain.

The questions and now the answers. His writer's mind wrote the story, the deductive story, on paperless air. The words floated . . .

Under the influence of whiskey, an author accidentally kills his wife. Unofficial manslaughter. The wife's sister comes into the house to care for the widower. The sister has a fiancé, but her obligation to her adored relative's memory makes her sacrifice her own life plan. Then, overnight, the author is catapulted into renown and invited to make a trip, and the sister accompanies him. To her dismay, her ward, the author, is exposed to the outer world and the charms of a beautiful, chaste girl of German descent. The sister sees her selfless good works threatened by another. She must protect her ailing author for the one he had sent to the grave. It is her sacred duty. She must accomplish this at any cost, in a single stroke, a stroke that will bind his guilts to her forgiveness forever. She offers her body—so naïvely, so rooted in the old belief that sexual intercourse must lead to marriage (for Harriet, for Harriet)—and she is sure this will carry the day, and she will possess him and hold him in thralldom (for Harriet, for Harriet). But he has come alive, and is alert, and retreats from the tendrils and palpi of the Madagascar man-eating plant and is saved from the past. The end.

Was it the end? Or was it To Be Continued?

Craig finished the drink, and as he poured one more, his writer's mind knew that his story was incomplete. Too many loose ends and no denouement. There would have to be another installment, and perhaps even a rewrite of the first installment. After all, was his story accurate? Had that been Leah's hope and her plan? Suppose his perception was correct, and it was her plan. What then? The loose ends: the author was not yet saved, for if he had repulsed the sister once, he was still the slave of their secret and the ugly guilt. The loose ends, add: the sister was still an unpredictable threat, for she was a woman scorned. Didn't women scorned always do something? They surely did, for if they didn't, half the libraries of the earth would be devoid of novels. And the denouement? Craig could not imagine it. His writer's mind had fogged. The future was impenetrable.

A sense of uneasiness pervaded Craig, overcoming even the settling effects of the alcohol.

Perhaps he had Leah all wrong, and he was at fault. Maybe he did owe Harriet's memory, and his debt to her, a final payment through her younger sister. She had wanted that payment in bed, in bed without end, and if he made it, he might be free inside. His thick logic dissolved into fantasy. What would the payment be like? He had felt the contact of those ample breasts, and observed the mound under the blanket, and he wondered. And then he knew, he was positive that he knew, and that he could write it as D. H. Lawrence might write it or Henry Miller or John Cleland. His writer's mind tried and tried but couldn't rise above the layer of intoxication. But Craig knew, nevertheless. If he came out of his chair now, and crossed the sitting room, and rapped on her door, and went inside her bedroom, she would be waiting and as ready as before. He would kiss her lips, and she would respond, and she would yield to him fully. It would be onerous, and she would be lifeless as a marble statue, with no resilience, with no rhythm, with no giving, and yet it would be physically pleasurable for him and mentally pleasurable for her. And that would create the mold into which they would both be locked for life. Later, she would be more mechanically giving, and with security, more doughy in her flesh offering, and she would perform as dutifully on the mattress as over the stove, in return for his name on their mail and her name in the dedications of his books. They could live forever, thus, the three of them—he, and Leah, and Harriet. His body would be fettered, but his conscience would be clear. That was the dismal payment.

Should he make it?

He finished his drink, and this was the moment. He had but to rise and go to her, and the battles were done. With wavering aim, he poured whiskey into the glass until it came to the top.

Unexpectedly, his almost perfect day floated before him. Lilly. The Swedish Academy. Emily.

Suddenly, he thought, to hell with conscience, and the consequences of a woman scorned. He could always cross the sitting room to that other bed. He would have another day, another day or two, without commitment. He would take his chances. He would see what the second installment brought.

He was drunk, and the room was a ferris wheel. He lowered the glass to the floor, and slumped back into the chair.

Jesus, what confusion.

He let his drowning brain have a life of its own. Go ahead, brain. His brain offered him an Irish gravestone epitaph, somewhere read, somewhere seen. He accepted it with cynical joy. It would be Andrew Craig's epitaph this night of reburial:

> Here lies the body of John Mound
> Lost at sea and never found.

VII

"You say you are in trouble, Mr. Craig?" repeated Count Bertil Jacobsson into the telephone. "I do not understand. What kind of trouble?"

From behind his desk, beside the second-story window of the Nobel Foundation at Sturegatan 14, Jacobsson's expression of regret reached out to his two early morning guests, Dr. Denise Marceau and Dr. Claude Marceau, and begged for their indulgence over the interruption.

Claude's understanding shrug told Jacobsson that they did not mind, and, to reassure the old aristocrat, Claude opened his silver cigarette case and offered it to his wife. The Marceaus settled back on the blue sofa, smoking. Absently, Claude gazed at the portrait of King Gustaf on the wall, while Denise half listened to the Assistant Director's pacifying of the unseen Nobel literary laureate.

"Now, let me see if I understand you," Jacobsson was saying into the mouthpiece. "You tell me you were awakened ten minutes ago by a group of college students, out in the corridor, serenading you? Is that correct? . . . Yes, I see. And this young man, their spokesman, Mr. Wibeck, says they are the delegates from Uppsala University who have been assigned to escort you to a lecture? . . . Umm, true, true, it could be a mistake, Mr. Craig, but the printed program of your appointments, the one I gave you upon your arrival, that will tell you if it is actually on your schedule or not. What is that? . . . Oh, well, if Miss Decker has your copy, and she is out for the morning, then I will be glad to assist you. I believe I have a copy readily at hand. If you will—what was that? You cannot hear me because . . . I see, yes. Well, please, Mr. Craig, simply request Mr. Wibeck to have the Uppsala students halt their serenading until you are off the phone. He will not be offended. I am sure he is in perfect awe of you. While you speak to him, I will search for the program."

Count Jacobsson placed the receiver on the desk blotter, next to the telephone, cast one more apologetic glance at the Marceaus, and searched the middle drawer of his desk. At last, he had what he wanted, the mimeographed program, and picked up the receiver again.

"Mr. Craig? . . . Good, good, I understand. I have no ear for music in the morning either. Now I have the program before me. Today is December fifth. Ah, here it is. Are you listening? . . . Very well, I will read it to you. 'Mr. Craig's schedule for December fifth. Nine-thirty, morning. Address the creative writing class of Uppsala University on the subject, 'Hemingway and the Style of the Icelandic Sagas.' Three-thirty, afternoon. Address the literature and poetics classes of Stockholm University and Lund University combined on the subject 'Literary Criticism in the America of the Fifties and Sixties.' Eight o'clock, evening. Optional. Free time, or attend performance of *La Bohème* at the Swedish Royal Opera.' " Jacobsson paused. "There you have it, Mr. Craig. I am afraid you have promised the two lectures. You recall—your letter from Wisconsin? What? . . . I appreciate your problem. But even if you have not prepared, I am sure the students would be glad to hear you on any subjects about which you choose to improvise. They are not there to learn of Hemingway and the Icelandic sagas or American literary criticism. They are there to see you and hear you. They will be forever grateful. . . . I am sorry about that, too, Mr. Craig. I would suggest two or three aspirin, or our Magnecyl which are less expensive. . . . No, I wish it were possible, but we are all tied up this morning. Miss Påhl is taking Dr. Garrett to the Caroline Institute. Dr. Krantz must meet a colleague who is flying in from Berlin. I am this moment occupied in giving the Doctors Marceau a little tour of our institution, such as I gave you yesterday. I am positive that you will find young Mr. Wibeck most cordial and cooperative . . ."

As she listened to the predicament of a fellow laureate, and to the Count's soothing but firm replies, Denise once more examined the latest development in her own predicament. Without hesitation, she would have traded predicaments with Craig. His were minor, and of easy solution. He need only fortify himself with aspirins, or something stronger, and mumble a few words before two meetings of students, throw the lecture open to questions, answer them briefly, and he was done with it. Her own dilemma was far more pressing, and there was no easy solution.

Before yesterday's sightseeing tour, and after, in the fleeting moments that they had alone, Denise had finally made it clear to Claude that if he dared to see Gisèle Jordan for so much as an hour, tomorrow, or the day after, or the day after that, in Copenhagen, it would mean an immediate separating and divorce. And more than that, Denise had warned her husband, knowing his main vulnerability, his bourgeois fear of disgrace, she would make the separation a public matter through the press before the final Nobel Award Ceremony.

Her threat had been delivered so passionately that Claude did not doubt her or attempt to conciliate her, as he had been doing, with vague promises of working out their problem in the future. He had vowed, invoked the name of the Lord, that there would be no assignation with his mannequin in Copenhagen.

Yet, sitting here now—they had not had time on yesterday's tour to visit the place where they had been voted their chemistry prize, and Jacobsson had informally invited them over for this morning—Denise felt no relief from or security in her husband's fervent promise. She wanted a guarantee. She could conceive of none. He had proved before she had discovered the affair, and again following it, that the flesh was weak. The arrival of his young mistress tomorrow, in a location only an hour or two away, would be a temptation.

Denise remembered the visit to Balenciaga, remembered the lithe ash-blonde with the high cheekbones and pouting lips and sensuous walk, and remembering this, she knew that Copenhagen might just as well be a room adjacent to their suite in the Grand Hotel of Stockholm. What bothered her was a hypothesis, with no scientific evidence to support it, that if her husband copulated with his mistress on this trip, in glamorous surroundings, their relationship would become permanent and unbreakable, and all of Denise's hopes would be in vain. Claude had given his word that this would not occur. Denise wanted not his word but a bond.

She became aware that Jacobsson's conversation with Craig was almost at an end. Apparently, Craig had come around and was ready to conform to his schedule. Jacobsson was reminding him of the place of his lectures.

"Do you recall the situation of the Swedish Academy, Mr. Craig?" Jacobsson was asking. "There was a large auditorium—the Stock Exchange Hall—right before we went into the voting room. Well, that is where you will be taken for both addresses. I am positive you will not regret it. Many of those students are promising writers, and all are tremendously appreciative of advice from a great author. As to your remaining schedule, I shall send you another copy of the program for yourself. There are other events you will have to remember to attend. We do not wish to overwhelm our honored guests, but you can understand the demand for their presence. . . . Yes, any time, Mr. Craig. I am here to serve you. And thank you very much."

For want of anything better to do, Denise Marceau had listened attentively to the last of Count Jacobsson's telephone conversation. During the last of it, something creative had begun to arouse itself inside her head, something useful, something hopeful. The exact moment that Jacobsson's receiver had clicked into place, Denise had been struck by an idea. Quite by accident, Craig's call to Jacobsson had given Denise Marceau what she had sought since yesterday—the guarantee that would keep her husband apart from Gisèle Jordan, at least for the critical present.

Jacobsson had set the telephone to one side of his desk, and now he swiveled his chair toward the Marceaus.

"I am sorry," he said, "and I am grateful for your patience. I can sympathize with Mr. Craig. There are days when our program does seem heavy."

"I do not find it so," said Denise quickly. "I feel that when one is abroad little more than a week, one owes it to oneself and one's hosts to put every moment to use."

"I wish everyone was as—" Jacobsson began to say.

"As a matter of fact, Count Jacobsson," Denise hurried on, "I do not think my husband and I have enough to do here. I am sure Claude agrees with me—"

Taken unawares, Claude was too perplexed with her opinion to make any comment.

"—and that was why I wanted to request a favor of you this morning," continued Denise to Jacobsson. "I should have brought it up the first day. Perhaps you will think it presumptuous."

"Anything, anything," said Jacobsson.

"I notice by the program, we have two unoccupied evenings in the next three days. There is the Hammarlund dinner tomorrow, and then the two free evenings. Also, there is one open afternoon. Claude and I would like something scheduled for those times. Nothing frivolous. Rather, appointments that would bring closer ties between us and your scientists in Scandinavia."

Jacobsson clucked his approval. "Most admirable of you, Dr. Marceau. I had turned aside many invitations tendered you for fear that you might be exhausted."

"Not at all," said Denise firmly. "We are eager to meet as many Swedish chemists and Nobel personnel as possible. You cannot keep us too busy."

Dimly at first, and now clearly at last, Claude perceived his wife's strategy. Since he had had no intention of seeing Gisèle in Copenhagen—it had seemed unnecessarily risky when he had considered it in bed last night—there was no reason for Denise to build this cage of activity around him. It was wearisome and foolish. "Denise," he said quietly, "are you not being overly ambitious? I want to participate as much as you do. But I will not have you tax yourself to the limit."

Denise flashed her husband a hypocritical smile, and returned to Jacobsson. "Is he not considerate, Count? He has always been thus. It has made our collaboration possible."

Jacobsson had tried to understand the nuances of the exchange between the couple, but without further information, he could not have full understanding, and so he gave the lady the benefit of the doubt. "I shall contact the Royal Institute of Technology," he said, "and the Institute of Inorganic and Physical Chemistry at the University of Stockholm. They had been pressing for you to conduct a seminar. However"—he glanced at Claude Marceau's weary face, and offered him a palliative—"if you should have a change of heart, find the strain too much, I can always cancel the meetings I intend to arrange."

"We will not have a change of heart," said Denise firmly. "Inform us of our new schedule, and we will *both* comply." She opened her purse for a cigarette. "Enough of that. Before the telephone rang, you were speaking of the first chemistry award."

"Ah, yes, yes," said Jacobsson, relieved to be returned to a subject less controversial. "I was trying to brief you on the background of the chemistry award, before showing you the conference room where the Nobel Committee for Chemistry debated your candidacy this past year." He tilted back in his chair, his fingertips touching and hands making a pyramid on his chest. "As I was saying earlier, Alfred Nobel left one-fifth of the interest on his prize fund to the person or persons 'who shall have made the most important chemical discovery or improvement.' That was all the guidance that he gave us. In 1900, the Academy of Science sent letters to ten institutions and to three hundred well-known scientists in every corner of the world, inviting them to make nominations for the first Nobel Prize in chemistry. Out of this, only twenty nominations were made and of these, eleven suggested the name of one man—Jacobus Hendricus van't Hoff, of the Netherlands, who had founded stereochemistry, as you know. He became the first chemistry laureate. Our choice was universally praised."

Jacobsson was lost in thought a moment. "In those early years, we committed only one serious blunder in chemistry. We neglected the American, Professor Willard Gibbs, of Yale University."

"Gibbs was an absolute genius," agreed Claude. "I read his monograph, 'On the Equilibrium of Heterogeneous Substances,' with complete absorption. However, you can have no shame in overlooking him. I am told that his fellow countrymen did not appreciate him either. One American scientist who visited our laboratory in Paris told me that when Gibbs died—in 1903, I think—his American colleagues and students hardly noticed it. They considered him an eccentric old man. The majority of condolences came from scientists around the world, who had read him and understood his worth."

Denise addressed Jacobsson. "Why did the Royal Academy of Science neglect him?"

"He was too far ahead of his time, and no one here understood his abstractions," Jacobsson said simply. "As I told Mr. Craig yesterday, our judges are only too human. They make mistakes. Usually, though, they are right."

"Yes, usually they are right," said Denise. "Have any of your chemistry judges won the Nobel Prize?"

"Professor The Svedberg was elected in 1926, most deservedly, and he has balloted on many awards. A remarkable man, Svedberg, a one-man faculty, library, student body, all condensed in a single brain. He spoke seven languages, read poetry in Latin, learned Spanish in two months before taking a trip to South America. We have had our share of geniuses. The annual balloting is in good hands."

"How do your judges determine if a certain candidate should be honored in chemistry or physics?" inquired Claude. "To my mind, there is often considerable overlapping."

"You have touched upon one of our major problems," agreed Jacobsson. "When such a decision has to be made, the chemistry and physics committees of the Academy of Science exchange their views and make an arbitrary judgment. I would guess that such a decision might have been made in 1944, when Dr. Otto Hahn was a candidate for discovering nuclear fission, which affected physicists everywhere and led to the atom bomb. But Hahn's experiments were actually in chemistry, and so he received the chemistry award. I suspect that our chemistry judges are happiest when there is no overlapping, and they can vote for candidates whose findings are unquestionably in the chemical realm. Many such clear-cut decisions come to mind at once—Sir William Ramsay's discovery of helium, Henri Moissan's isolation of fluorine and adoption of the electric furnace and his production of artificial diamonds. Actually, in the case of Moissan, a majority of the Academy had favored the Russian, Dmitri Mendeleev, for inventing the periodic system—but one minority judge impressed the others with Moissan's versatility, and those artificial diamonds carried the day. Other clear-cut decisions? Richard Willstätter's work, and later Hans Fischer's, on chlorophyll, and, in 1960, Willard F. Libby's atom time clock, which could tell the age of fossils fifty thousand years old, dating even the hair of an Egyptian mummy. Those are the chemistry awards our judges like the most."

"And you, Count Jacobsson," said Denise, "what do you like the most?"

Jacobsson was startled, and then he smiled. "I concur with the majority. I am only an innocent bystander." He considered this a moment, and recollected his Notes, and then he added, "As a matter of fact, the 1957 medical award—which was a case of overlapping and might very well have been the chemistry award, instead—that one gave me a good deal of satisfaction, because it was deserving, and, as one advanced in years, I had profited by it. I am sure you know of Dr. Daniel Bovet's discoveries. He was a Swiss who became an Italian citizen. For a while, I believe, he worked at your Institute in Paris."

Denise nodded. "Yes, shortly before our time."

"Bovet made three thousand experiments in four years. As a result, he produced the sulfas, and the great antiallergy drugs—antihistamines, and synthetic curare to be used as a muscle relaxant in surgery, and so on. In your Paris, Bovet fell in love with the daughter of a former Premier of Italy—her name was Filomena Nitti—and he told the press, 'I proposed immediately. It was a lightning chemical reaction.' After that, they worked together like the Curies, and Joliot-Curies, and yourselves. I think it is wonderful, a man and wife, to have so major a common interest."

Claude squirmed, and Denise glared at him, and the last was not lost on Count Jacobsson. Claude fished for his silver cigarette case, and Jacobsson, while mystified, sensed the ferment in the room.

Instinctively, Jacobsson wanted this couple to be happier, to be drawn closer together. He wanted to inform them of how happy Marie Curie, the first woman to win the prize, had been to share it with her husband, and how sad she had been, when she arrived in Stockholm for her second prize, to come without him, for Pierre Curie had been killed in an accident in 1906. Jacobsson wanted to tell them how well another husband-wife team, Drs. Gerty and Carl Cori, who had won the medical prize for isolating enzymes, had got on together and were a family. But somehow, Jacobsson felt that this might not be the time for such examples. Yet there was his job and the dignity of the awards, and he must think of something to give the Marceaus subtle warning. Then he thought of Irène and Frédéric Joliot-Curie, who had shared the $41,000 prize in 1935, and with them he thought that he might make his point.

"Indeed, you are in a select circle," Jacobsson told the Marceaus. "You are only the fourth husband-and-wife pair in our history to win the prize. We are sentimental about such awards, and the winners, with one exception, have made us proud."

"One exception?" said Denise carefully.

288

"I am thinking of your countrymen, Irène and Frédéric Joliot-Curie, who won the chemistry award for their discoveries in radioactive elements."

"What of them?" asked Denise.

"They earned the award for artificial radium, and they received it here in Stockholm, and we would give it to them again. But their subsequent history, after the prize, was—in some respects—unfortunate."

"They were a devoted couple," said Denise sharply, with an eye on her husband.

"Oh, yes, yes, nothing like that," said Jacobsson hastily. "Indeed, they were heroes of the Second World War. Frédéric Joliot-Curie stole the world's greatest supply of heavy water—then important in atomic research—from under the noses of the Nazis in Norway. He got it safely to England. And in France, despite the Gestapo, he organized eighteen underground laboratories to make incendiary bottles for the maquis. I have no doubt you know all of that."

"Yes, we do," said Denise.

"It was their activity after the war that most Swedes deplored," said Jacobsson. "They joined the French Communist Party. And Madame Irène Joliot-Curie told an American visitor that the United States was uncivilized, and that the workingmen should overthrow the government. I remember more that she said, for I have recorded all in my Notes. She told the American, 'You are deliberately fomenting war. You are imperialists, and you want war. You will attack the U.S.S.R., but it will conquer you through the power of its idea.' I tell you, this caused much headshaking in the Swedish Academy of Science."

"Unfortunate," said Claude. "However, surely you judge by the scientific achievement of your laureates, not by their personal activities."

"True," said Jacobsson. And then, he added slowly, "Still, our laureates are so much looked up to, so widely respected, that when they commit scandals, we are unhappy—extremely unhappy."

The shaft, motivated by instinct and not information, hit its targets, Jacobsson was certain. For Denise regarded her husband coldly, and Claude avoided her gaze and lifted his heavy-set frame from the sofa.

"I am eager to see the room where the chemistry awards are voted," announced Claude.

Jacobsson rose. "I had better explain that the room you will see is not exactly where the balloting takes place. In this room, the Committee for Chemistry often holds the preliminary meetings that lead to the recommendation of the ultimate winner. The actual final balloting, ever since 1913, takes place in the session hall of the Royal Swedish Academy of Science building, located at Frescati just beyond central Stockholm."

Now the three of them walked through the Executive Director's office into the corridor, and then into what Jacobsson called the conference room of the Nobel Foundation.

"Here," said Jacobsson, as they stood inside the door, "is where the Nobel committeemen determined upon the two of you as the favorites for the prize in chemistry, and where the physics branch weeded Professor Stratman and several others out as the foremost candidates for the prize in physics."

The Marceaus surveyed the green room. It had none of the shine of a tourist showcase and none of the petrified appearance of archives. It conveyed the impression of a room in which living men did living work and did it frequently. Most of the conference room was filled by the table, its surface overlaid with leather, worn and beaten, and surrounded by ten chairs covered with oxhide. Directly across, overseeing the table, hung a large oil painting of Alfred Nobel, seated, the work executed posthumously in 1915.

Jacobsson led the Marceaus around the room counterclockwise. To the right, a long marble ledge ran along the wall, and atop it were boxed redbound albums. Jacobsson removed one album. "In each album, we keep photographs of our laureates, autographed whenever possible. The day after the final Ceremony, you will be asked to come here to receive your check and to sign your photographs." He opened the album. "Here you see signed photographs of two fellow chemistry winners. This is Professor Richard Kuhn, of the University of Heidelberg, who was voted the 1938 prize for his work in vitamins. And on this page is Professor Adolph Butenandt, of the University of Berlin, who shared the 1939 prize for his work on sex hormones. As you know, Hitler would not allow his subjects to accept the Nobel Prize. Both Kuhn and Butenandt were forced to refuse it. However, in 1948, after the war and Hitler's death, these two wrote to thank us for the honor which they had wanted but not been permitted to accept. We gave them their gold medals and diplomas, but could no longer give them the prize money. By regulation, it had been held one year, and then returned to the main fund. Too bad, too bad."

Jacobsson restored the album to its slipcase, then indicated a lively portrait of a woman, hanging above the ledge.

"Alfred Nobel's mother painted by Anders Zorn," he said. "Nobel had tremendous affection for her. Even when he was traveling, he tried to come back to Stockholm annually for her birthday. She died six years before he did."

They moved on to the far wall of the room. Jacobsson identified the paintings on either side of the oil of Nobel himself. "This is Bertha von Suttner, the most important woman in Nobel's life besides his mother. She had been a titled governess in Austria, and fired, when she read an advertisement in a Vienna newspaper—'Elderly, cultured gentleman, very wealthy, resident of Paris, seeks equally mature lady, linguist, as secretary and supervisor of household.' She answered the advertisement, and Nobel was the elderly, cultured gentleman, very wealthy. She became his secretary, and often his adviser. Later, she left him to marry a young baron and become one of the world's foremost pacifists. It is possible that she influenced Nobel to create the Peace Prize. At any rate, we feel that she belongs beside him on this wall. The painting on the other side is of Ragnar Sohlman, an executive director of this Foundation, who died in 1948. He had been a personal friend of Nobel's and one of the executors of the famous will."

Jacobsson pointed out the three bronze busts in the room. "This one is of Nobel. We move it to Concert Hall on the tenth for the Ceremony, and then bring it back here. That one is Nobel's father, and the other, one of his brothers. Now, perhaps, you are curious about what took place in the session hall the afternoon your names were presented?"

"I am most curious," Denise admitted.

"The four leading chemistry candidates were decided upon earlier in this room," said Jacobsson. "You yourselves were one. Two Americans, as another team. A Dane. And a candidate from Israel. Of the other candidates, one was considered for his pioneer work in the creation of life, of a living cell. But it was felt that his findings were not yet conclusive. Another had accomplished much in the dissolving of blood clots. Again, the work was considered in its primitive stage. The third, our American candidates, had made progress in new drugs for mental unbalance. In one case, I will admit, a certain prejudice was held against the candidate. He was wealthy and his work commercial, and certain judges were against him for no other reasons. You will understand the sensitivity of the judges when I explain that, although Nobel had once stated that he wanted to reward dreamers who found it hard to get on in life, in contradiction to this, the chemistry committee had given the 1931 award to Karl Bosch, head of the I. G. Farben cartel, and to Friedrich Bergius, also of Farben, for making coal into oil. The committee was soundly criticized for its choice. At any rate, the current judges decided that both of you were dreamers, qualified in every way, and your discovery of sperm vitrification thoroughly proved. The debate lasted less than two hours. You were elected laureates by a vote of better than two to one."

"We are very humble," said Claude sincerely. "I thank you for the information."

They had gone back into the hall as Jacobsson was talking, and now Jacobsson saw them to the exit at the end of the corridor. After shaking hands, Denise reminded him, "Count Jacobsson, you will not forget to fill our schedule. We want to be busy every minute."

"I shall be delighted to oblige," said Jacobsson.

As they went through the door, Jacobsson closed it and turned to find Mrs. Steen waiting directly behind him with some papers. Because he halted beside the door to consult with Mrs. Steen, he was able to hear what went on beyond the door.

He heard first Claude Marceau's muffled voice and then Denise Marceau's reply.

Claude had said, "Very clever with that schedule, but idiotic. Do you think that could keep me from Copenhagen if I wanted to go?"

Denise Marceau had said, "Go to hell."

Embarrassed, Jacobsson stared down at the green carpeting, until the footsteps of the laureates had receded and were gone.

Jacobsson made no pretense of not having overheard the exchange. Lifting his head to meet Mrs. Steen's phlegmatic gaze, he said, "What do you think, Mrs. Steen?"

Like her adding machine, Mrs. Steen was without deviousness. She replied, "If they should ever win a second prize, like the Curies, I am sure only one of them would return to Stockholm—the one who had murdered the other."

"Mmm. That is my thought, too, Mrs. Steen. And my prayer is—should homicide happen, let it not happen before the Ceremony."

In the gloom of the cold winter morning, the three-cylinder Saab-93 sped over Solnavägen toward that area where the many buildings of the Caroline Medico-Chirurgical Institute were located.

At the wheel of the Saab was a young driver for the Institute. In the confined back seat, normally loose and removable because it covered the car trunk, the displacement was three-quarters Ingrid Påhl and one-quarter Dr. John Garrett. Wearing her enormous new hat banded with artificial roses and her heaviest woolen coat—she was sure the temperature was close to Celsius O°, which would be Fahrenheit 32° and freezing—Ingrid Påhl had lost her earlier look of misgiving, and her puffy features were once more unburdened and even buoyant. When Krantz had pleaded emergency the night before, and backed out of taking Dr. Garrett to the Caroline Institute, and Jacobsson had telephoned her to replace Krantz, she had protested. She knew nothing of medicine. What would she have to say to Garrett? Nevertheless, as a duty, she had agreed to perform as hostess. But Garrett had proved to be a simple, friendly man, much engrossed in his own thoughts, and that had made her task easier.

For Garrett, pressed into the corner of the Saab, this was a crucial morning, and he was living inside himself. At his own request, the visit to Drottningholm Palace had been replaced by this appointment at the Caroline Institute. His protégé, Dr. Erik Öhman, was expecting him and waiting. Although Öhman could not know it, he was a vital weapon in the offensive Garrett was mounting against Carlo Farelli. This day, Garrett had determined, the counterattack must begin.

There was nothing complex about Garrett's battle plan. By his aggressiveness at the press conference, Farelli had claimed most of the space in the newspapers the following day. Garrett had been treated as an unwanted relative who had had to be introduced. He had been relegated to an occasional interjection or the spare room of last paragraphs or the graveyard of publicity that read, "also present was—." When Garrett, in his desperation, had attempted an impromptu guerrilla campaign against Farelli in the salon of the Royal Palace, he had been repulsed, and the defeat still rankled. Now he knew that his tactics must include, first, a carefully organized frontal assault on the battleground of the world's front pages.

The meeting with Öhman would be Garrett's first foray. He would learn of Öhman's progress and future, all an extension of his own heart discovery. He would study Öhman's three successful transplantations, and the three additional patients he now had under observation. This done, Garrett would then telephone Sue Wiley. He would offer himself, this very afternoon, for an interview more spectacular than the one he had given her on the airliner.

He would reveal colorful details of his meeting with Öhman, human interest facts about Öhman's patients, and in praising Öhman's accomplishments, he would be praising himself. He would give Miss Wiley some concrete predictions about the future of his work. Farelli would be out of it entirely. It would be as if he, alone, were in Stockholm, as indeed he should have been. The story for Consolidated Newspapers would be carried throughout the world. That would be the beginning. He would hurl the monarch of darkness from the dais and have his rightful seat of honor at last.

It was all so satisfying. Garrett sighed with pleasure at the justice of his plan. Outside the window, the bleak morning appeared less forbidding. Beside him, Ingrid Påhl, screwing a cigarette into an ebony holder, appeared more attractive.

Garrett decided that he owed her the courtesy of conversation. "Are we almost there?" was all that he could muster up to ask.

"Any minute," said Ingrid Påhl. She had a lighter to her cigarette, and now exhaled a stream of smoke. "I have only seen the hospital twice myself. And my knowledge of medicine is limited to patented treatments of heartburn, upset stomach, and constipation. Lest you think it is odd that I—scientifically, the least qualified member of the reception committee—was assigned to escort you this morning, I had better explain."

"As a Nobel Prize winner yourself, I can think of no one more qualified," said Garrett with heavy gallantry.

"You are a gentleman, Dr. Garrett, but it is no use flattering me." Her obese presence exuded cheer. "I am not a fit companion for you. I do not even know where the human kidney is located. And as to the heart, I never remember—is it on the right or the left?"

"Left."

"There you are. The truth is, Dr. Krantz was to have been your escort this morning. You could have talked to him. I daresay he is a grouch, but a brilliant one. Unfortunately, for you, Dr. Krantz had to rush off to the Bromma Airport to receive an old friend and distinguished visitor from East Berlin."

"East Berlin? Are they allowed out?"

"Of course, Dr. Garrett. Do not believe everything you read. Most Germans—while I do not have excessive affection for them—do not live and work there by choice. I have no idea about Dr. Krantz's friend, but, at any rate, it was someone who had to be met personally. So the honor of taking you to the Caroline Institute fell upon me. I hope you are not too disappointed."

"Miss Påhl, I've told you—"

"Actually, I suppose I do know a little about the Caroline Institute. Some years ago, an English periodical inquired if I would write a series of articles about Sweden. Journalism is not my cup of tea, but I needed the money, and I considered the offer. The first article was to be on the Caroline Institute, since it has some reputation as the source of the Nobel medical award. I did a week or two of preliminary research—took a tour of the hospitals, renewed acquaintance with their Nobel committeemen, asked questions, made notes—but when it came down to it, I could not write the article. Some writers are simply no good with facts, and I am one of them. Facts are like figures with me; they baffle me entirely. I never wrote the article, but I did not starve, either. A Swedish film company bought one of my old novels, and I was saved to write again, to the dismay of a majority of my critics. Anyway, all I have left of the experience are some unorganized facts about the Institute. You may have them as a gift, if you are interested."

"I certainly am interested," said Garrett, trying to hide his restlessness, for he wanted to be where he was going and get on with Öhman and begin the march against the enemy.

"Fact one," said Ingrid Påhl. "The Caroline Institute was started in 1810, to supply military surgeons for the Swedish army, which was having one of its periodic wars with Denmark and Russia. Fact two. Alfred Nobel was fascinated by medicine. On different occasions, he had friends make blood transfusion and urine experiments under his guidance. It was natural that he would give a prize in medicine, and select the respected Caroline Institute to confer it. Fact three. The Caroline committee had to determine what Nobel had in mind when he wrote in his will that he wished 'the most important discovery' in medicine or physiology honored. Did he want to reward practical advances only? Or theoretical progress as well? The Caroline committee decided to reward both types of discovery. And they did not limit their prizes to doctors. Through the years, they also honored biologists, chemists, zoologists, and once a biophysicist. Fact four. Nominations for the award that you won come from professors within the Caroline Institute, from members of the Swedish Academy of Science, from former Nobel medical winners, from faculties of all major universities in Scandinavia, and from faculties of outstanding universities in twenty foreign countries. There are about one thousand persons eligible to make nominations. Should I go on?"

"Please," said Garrett, who involuntarily found himself absorbed.

Ingrid Påhl ejected her cigarette butt into the car tray. "Fact five. There are three permanent members on the Nobel medical committee who advise and recommend. Usually, temporary members, experts in this or that, are added to the committee from the Caroline teaching body. The medical winners are elected each year in the session room on the ground floor of the Caroline Institute. It is a light airy room, with the longest modern table you have ever seen, and modern Swedish chairs for the judges. As I recall, there are sixteen or eighteen oil portraits of eminent Swedish physicians and Nobel personnel on the walls, and two white marble statues between the windows. The final vote is made by forty-five physicians and instructors on the Caroline staff."

The car slowed, and Ingrid Påhl gestured with her head. "And lo, there it is now—the Caroline Institute."

The Saab turned off the main thoroughfare, and drove through a gate and across a private road that wound through a landscape of icy trim lawns, clipped hedges, and many clusters of aged trees. Again, the Saab slowed, and wheeled left through an opening between two rows of frozen foliage.

The car drew to a stop on a paved lot. The young driver tumbled quickly out of the front, trotted around, and opened the rear door. With some difficulty, fighting gravity and density, he freed Ingrid Påhl from her place and helped her out of the sedan. Then he gave Garrett a hand.

Before them stretched a squat three-story oblong building of red brick. Its rows of windows peered down at them like a montage of square eyes. Three cement stairs led to two heavy doors, and above the entrance were projected letters that read, MEDICINSKA NOBELINSTITUTET. Garrett glanced off to his right. A bench rested in the open, on the pavement, before a miniature park of withered plants and barren trees. Behind the bench, on a high stone pedestal, stood a weather-beaten black bronze bust of Alfred Nobel. There were touches of frost around Nobel's eyes and his set mouth.

Garrett brought his topcoat collar around his neck.

"You would not believe how lovely this is in the summer," said Ingrid Påhl. "Now it is impossible. Either we build a fire, or we go inside."

The two of them hurried inside.

Dr. Erik Öhman, sitting with one knee propped up against his desk, a cigar between his teeth, was scanning a newspaper held wide open. The moment that Öhman saw them, he leaped to his feet, almost upending the chair, and pounded around the desk. Ignoring Ingrid Påhl's formal introduction, he grabbed Garrett's hand and pumped it with unrestrained enthusiasm.

"Dr. Garrett," he said, "Dr. Garrett—what a pleasure this is for me. How I have looked forward to it—"

Somewhat taken aback, for he was not a demonstrative man, and (despite the prize) he had never valued himself highly in his secret heart, Dr. Garrett tried to return his host's ardent and worshipful greeting. "Believe me, it's good to meet you at last, Dr. Öhman."

"Sit down, both of you—please sit down," said Öhman, herding them to the chairs. "There will be hot coffee in a moment." He looked at Garrett with bright eyes of disbelief, as lowly subject to his sovereign. He tried to speak, but no sound came forth except a drawn-out rumble, which Garrett would learn was a speech impediment. "Uhhh," was the embryonic sound seeking the birth of vocabulary, "uhhh—Dr. Garrett, I am so privileged." He ran behind his desk, and brought forth the chair, so that he could sit directly opposite Garrett and Ingrid Påhl.

Garrett was surprised by the appearance of the man with whom he had so long corresponded. He was unable to define to himself what kind of person he had actually expected to find. Possibly someone more Swedish, more genteel, more dignified. Instead, Öhman, his reddish hair cropped short, resembled, for all his agility, a European middleweight prizefighter who had fought several years too many. The face, the cauliflower ears, and gross features above a thick neck were not Garrett's conception of a doctor's head. And the hands, like blunt instruments, stubby fingers round as sausages, were not a heart surgeon's hands. Yet Garrett saw at once the face's kindness, the admiration it now reflected, and from Öhman's letters he knew the man's scientific soundness and learning.

"Uhhh, Dr. Garrett—uhhh, tell me, you must tell me what you think of our Sweden. How thrilled I was when your prize was announced. You had my cable? Uhhh—you must tell me what you have seen here, and wish to see, and what I can do for you. Your wife is with you? You must dine with my wife and me. Uhhh—my patients, they are as much your patients as mine, and you must see them and tell me what you think. And questions, I have a hundred questions."

He went on and on, punctuating his excitement with his stammer and asking questions that he did not wait to have answered, but when his boyish exhilaration had finally run down, he was ready to listen. He begged Garrett to speak of this and that, and Garrett spoke. Ingrid Påhl was interested and receptive, and Öhman worshipful and memorizing every word for the long winter ahead, and Garrett reveled in the attention. Before Dr. Keller and the therapy group, he had always felt inadequate to hold center stage. What was the old psychiatrist joke—who listens? But group therapy had given Garrett experience in monologue, and this experience, combined with an attentive audience, now gave Garrett license to discourse freely and at length.

Garrett had been relating, in some detail, his adventures in California after having been notified of the Nobel award. Now, encouraged by Öhman, he reminisced about the years during his transplantation research, and, rather effectively, he thought, he recreated the dramatic case history of Henry M. He was pleased to note that Ingrid Påhl was enthralled by the last, and Öhman as intrigued by this as he had been by all that had gone before.

At this point, Garrett had the feeling that he had monopolized the meeting long enough. Three-quarters of an hour of autobiography was more than sufficient. The time had arrived for self-effacement. If his battle plan was to work, it was necessary that Öhman be encouraged to reveal more of himself and his career.

"At any rate, to sum it up, here I am, an actual laureate," he said. "It's hard to believe." During his monologue, he had taken notice of Öhman's office, which, except for the padded chairs, seemed furnished entirely in efficient gray metal. But now he realized that two walls of the room were entirely covered by framed photographs and snapshots, some autographed, and Garrett recognized several as former Nobel laureates.

"You've never told me, in your letters, Dr. Öhman, if you have any connection with the Nobel medical awards. Have you?"

"In a way," said Öhman.

Before he could continue, there was a knocking at the door. A trim girl, wearing tortoise-shell-rimmed spectacles on a scrubbed face, backed in pulling a serving cart, carrying hot coffee and sweet rolls, after her. Öhman introduced her as his secretary, and she apologized for being late.

After she had poured coffee and gone, and they were all sipping, and nibbling rolls, Öhman cleared his throat. "Uhhh—Dr. Garrett—you had inquired about my position in the Nobel picture. Uhhh—a minor one, minor, I assure you, at the same time—uhhh—interesting. Do you know anything of the medical awards?"

"Miss Påhl was kind enough to give me some background on the drive here."

"Very little, Dr. Öhman," said Ingrid Påhl. "For all I know, Dr. Arrowsmith got the prize."

Öhman laughed. "Well, as a matter of fact he did, did he not? Martin Arrowsmith, Gottlieb, Sondelius—how alive they were to me. What was it Arrowsmith fought? Uhhh—yes—the bubonic plague in the West Indies, yes. Our committee has great respect for plague fighters, but it has always distressed me that some of the best have not been honored."

"Are you referring to anyone in particular?" asked Garrett.

"I am," said Öhman. "Uhhh—it has always been my belief that Walter Reed and General Gorgas, as well as Noguchi, should have shared an award for their work against yellow fever. Gorgas was nominated many times, I am told, but since he had made no new discovery, he could not be elected. Reed died too early, I think. At any rate, that is neither here nor there—more coffee, Miss Påhl?"

He filled Ingrid Påhl's cup again, and then Garrett's and his own, and settled back in the chair.

"Did Miss Påhl tell you of our nominating procedure?" Öhman inquired of Garrett.

"Yes," said Garrett.

"Then you know of our special investigators?"

"No, not that."

"I must tell you, then. For it is in that capacity that I have several times served the Nobel Committee. In fact, because of my knowledge of your discovery, I was one of the two so-called experts assigned to investigate your candidacy, Dr. Garrett."

"I didn't know that," said Garrett. "I really owe you a debt of thanks."

"Not a bit," replied Öhman. "Any fool would have understood the—uhhh —magnitude of your discovery and verified its worth. The Caroline Nobel Committee uses its investigators—detectives, you might call them in America —more than the other prize-giving committees, because of the intricate nature of medical research. There are so many varied specialties. There is so much complexity. Consequently, when the candidates are narrowed down by the committee, one last step is necessary. Each candidate is turned over to a member of our faculty, who is an expert in the candidate's field. The expert or investigator makes a thorough study of the candidate's discovery. Is it complete? Is it proved? Is it new? Is it worth while? The investigator will read everything on the discovery, and seek opinions, and sometimes even travel to the homeland of the—of the—uhhh—candidate, to see for himself without giving away the—uhhh—reasons for his visit.

"When Ivan Pavlov was nominated for the first award in 1901, for his experiments in the physiology of digestion, two of our investigators, the great Professor Johansson and Professor Tigerstedt, traveled to St. Petersburg, in Russia, to meet Pavlov and his dogs and verify, firsthand, his accomplishments. Pavlov was given special attention, too, because it was known that—

uhhh—Alfred Nobel himself had been interested in the Russian's work and had once contributed a large donation to Pavlov. So our investigators went to Pavlov's laboratory and observed the results of his experiments in conditioned reflexes. Apparently the final report of the investigators was not fully satisfactory, for, as you know, Pavlov did not win the first Nobel Prize that year. He had to wait three more years to win it."

"Who did win the first medical prize?" asked Ingrid Påhl. "It is shameful of me, and do not repeat it to Dr. Krantz, but I simply cannot remember."

"It was a close contest that first year," said Öhman. "A small number of judges supported Pavlov. The committee's recommendation was that the award be divided between Niels Finsen of Denmark and Ronald Ross of Great Britain. But there was also substantial backing for—uhhh—Emil von Behring of Germany. Eventually, the debate raged around von Behring. Some considered his discovery of the serum against diphtheria an old discovery and therefore disqualified. Others felt that it should be honored, because it was long accepted by the public, and would be familiar and noncontroversial. Uhhh—well, von Behring won, he won because his serum was popular—serums always are with our medical judges—and the three losers, Ross, Finsen, Pavlov, won their prizes later, in the next three years."

Garrett's attention had strayed, again, to the framed photographs on the walls. "Those pictures, Dr. Öhman, are they all medical winners?"

Öhman surveyed the photographs with pride. "My little hobby," he said. "I was a mere lad—long ago—in the thirties—when my father invited me to attend with him a Nobel ceremony. My father was a journalist and had a press invitation, and then a colleague became ill, and there was an extra invitation at the last moment, and so my father took me. It was a memorable occasion for a young boy. I watched Sir Charles Scott Sherrington receive the diploma for medicine, and my father told me all about Sherrington—how he had been nominated regularly for thirty years, and, for one reason or another, the investigators always recommended against him—and now, in his old age, they had relented. I was moved. That night, my destiny was set. I, too, would become a physician. Sherrington's was the first photograph I hung on this wall, so long after. It's there, behind my desk."

Öhman leaped to his feet, and went around his desk, squinting at his photographs. "Eventually, I acquired photographs of all the winners, and the autographs of at least half of them. An inspiring hobby." He pointed to a fuzzy photograph. "Uhhh—the celebrated Dr. Paul Ehrlich. In the first eight years, he was nominated seventy times by professors in thirteen different nations. His work in immunology was recognized, at last, in 1908. There is a story—the Kaiser of Germany was like a peacock over Ehrlich's conquest of the spirochete causing syphilis, and at a public banquet told him—ordered him—as if it were the easiest thing, 'Now, Ehrlich, get on with it, get rid of cancer.' "

Rapidly, Öhman bounced from picture to picture, tapping some and adding vocal captions. "Here—uhhh—Sir Alexander Fleming. University of London. He was looking into influenza when a blue-green mold spoiled on one of his culture plates. It was the shape of a pencil. He named it penicillin. That was 1928, yet he received no Nobel Prize for it until 1945, seventeen years later, because initially, he had no practical use for the discovery. Then, Sir Howard Florey and Dr. Ernst Boris Chain, of Oxford, began to wonder if it had a use. They injected mice with fatal doses of streptococci, and half of the mice with this penicillin, and the half with penicillin lived and the others died, and they had found a use, at last, for Dr. Fleming's accidental find. They *all* got the prize."

He had reached a larger frame bearing two portraits. "Uhhh, the first joint prize—this will interest you especially, Dr. Garrett. For five years the Swedish Academy resisted splitting a single prize. Finally, in 1906, they broke down and divided an award between Camillo Golgi, of Italy, and Ramón y Cajal, of Spain. Since then, the prize has been divided many times, as witness—Dr. Farelli and you."

The blood seethed to Garrett's cheeks, and he wanted to speak against the outrage of Farelli, but some restraint kept him from bringing up the matter before Ingrid Påhl. Instead, he said, "Do you think those joint prizes are fair?"

"So many candidates are often in the same field, it is impossible to credit only one." Öhman had arrived at an elderly face on the wall. "My favorite since 1949. Dr. Antonio Egas Moniz, of Lisbon, Portugal."

"Who is he?" asked Ingrid Påhl.

"In 1936, he introduced the prefrontal lobotomy," said Öhman. "There was no cure for certain cases of severe mental distress, apprehension, depression. Drugs would not help. Psychiatric treatment would not help. Dr. Moniz found that these acute fears, verging on insanity, came from the frontal lobes of the brain, certain gray matter in the skull above the eyebrows. By incisions in the side of the head, the size of a dime, and severing the nerve fibers of the front lobes with a long thin knife, Dr. Moniz learned that a patient's anxiety could be dramatically reduced."

"It sounds horrible," said Ingrid Påhl.

"It is to be preferred to suicide or insanity," said Öhman flatly. "It cuts away all apprehension and worry. It makes these patients happier. The only unfortunate aspect is that it frequently makes them into irresponsible dullards."

"But that's like cutting away a man's conscience, the soul that God gave him," said Ingrid Påhl.

"In medicine, we are less concerned with a man's soul than with his life," said Öhman objectively. "Uhhh—I am sure that Dr. Garrett will not disagree with me. The brain is the unexplored Mato Grosso of the human body. For that reason, I have always respected Dr. Moniz's find above all others—until lately. Now, I have a new favorite."

Öhman hurried back to his desk, opened a drawer, and took out a photograph. He offered it to Garrett with a pen.

"Will you sign your photograph, Dr. Garrett? It shall henceforth have the main place—above Dr. Moniz."

Garrett accepted the picture and pen. "I hardly know what to say."

"You need say nothing. Your accomplishment speaks for you."

Garrett signed the photograph: "To my favorite co-worker and friend. Dr. Erik Öhman, with best wishes, John Garrett." He returned the photograph and pen, and Öhman fondled the photograph with the reverence often given an early church relic.

"Now," said Garrett, pointedly, "I'd like to talk a little shop."

Ingrid Påhl could not miss the meaning of Garrett's remark, and she did not. She pushed herself from her chair. "If it is going to be shoptalk, this is no place for me. I have some friends here I want to see. When do you want me to pick you up, Dr. Garrett?"

"Well—"

"Not for an hour anyway," said Öhman. "Uhhh—there is much I want to show Dr. Garrett. I want to take him through my ward and discuss various problems."

"An hour, then," said Ingrid Påhl, and she waddled out of the room.

The moment that they were alone, Garrett began to adhere to his battle plan. "When do you perform your next transplantation?" he asked Öhman.

"We go into surgery at seven in the morning of the tenth. I am still making tests on the patient, and still trying to find the correct-sized young bovines or sheep, in order to acquire the best fresh hearts available. The case is an interesting one. Uhhh—I should say, in some respects, the most challenging and important one I have yet undertaken. The patient is a Count in his early seventies, a distant relative of His Royal Highness. Much public attention will be given to the result."

Garrett's heart leaped. This was what he had hoped for, this was the main chance.

"Will there be any difficulties?" Garrett inquired.

"Uhhh—frankly, some aspects of the case worried me, but now, I am confident again—since yesterday, when Dr. Farelli was in to examine the patient."

Garrett felt the blood siphon from his face, and he thought that he would faint. "Farelli?" he gasped.

Öhman's brow wrinkled with surprise at his guest's emotional reaction. "Why, yes—Dr. Carlo Farelli. He appeared yesterday with a newspaperwoman who had been interviewing him—a Miss Wiley from America—and without protocol, he introduced himself and said that he wanted to see my ward, my patients—all most flattering—"

"And you—you took them through—both of them?"

"Why, certainly. And he was kind enough to study the patient's history and charts and offer some advice. As I said, it was flattering and generous of him—"

"You fool!" shouted Garrett.

Öhman stood stunned. "I beg your pardon?"

"You heard me. Generous of him? What a laugh. He's an arrogant, vain publicity monger and a thief."

Öhman looked as if he had been slapped. He swayed, speechless, the pupils of his eyes dilating. "Dr. Garrett, I—uhhh—uhhh—uhhh—are you referring to Dr. Farelli—?"

"None other," said Garrett, rising, all restraint cast aside. "I suppose the reporter, Miss Wiley, I suppose she took notes? She did, didn't she?"

"Why, of course." He lifted the newspaper from his desk. "She filed the story last night. The Swedish papers picked it up today."

"And it's all about that bastard Farelli?"

"I—I—uhhh—yes, I mean—naturally, the new Nobel laureate comes to our hospital to pay his respects—offers to advise us on an important patient, a royal patient in critical condition—it is a story, naturally—uhhh, Dr. Garrett, I cannot understand—you are so upset—what is it? Is there something I should know?"

"You're damn right there's something you should know." Garrett's lips worked, and steadily he pounded a fist of one hand into the palm of the other. "You sit down," he commanded. "I'm going to give you an earful about that charlatan Farelli—trying to use you—making fools of both of us—and the Nobel Committee besides—now, sit down."

Dazed, Dr. Öhman sat down, staring up at his deity, who had so suddenly been transformed into a vengeful Mars, and slowly, with relentless hatred, Mars began the case for the prosecution.

Carl Adolf Krantz, who, among other human frailties, was a hypochondriac, had fortified himself against the freezing weather with earmuffs beneath his hat, a swath of knitted muffler, a bearish topcoat, and it was with difficulty that he was able to maneuver the Mercedes-Benz sedan into the parking slot outside the vast glass-and-metal Bromma Air Terminal.

He knew that he was late, and the moment that he left the car, this disgraceful fact was confirmed by the Arrival and Departure Board. The Czechoslovakian Airlines four-engine plane—an early morning telegram had informed him that it was leaving two hours earlier than scheduled, and so would arrive two hours earlier—had taken off from the Schönfeld Airport in East Berlin at 9:55 in the morning and was expected in Stockholm, en route to Helsinki, at 12:55. It was now 1:06. An immediate inquiry calmed Krantz's nerves. The passengers from East Berlin were still going through customs.

Outside, near the rows of windowpanes and the Royal Waiting Hall, Krantz removed his earmuffs, fearing their absurdity, and tucked them inside his coat pocket. He wondered if Dr. Hans Eckart had looked for him, before going into customs. Had Krantz been able to hire a chauffeur for the morning, as he had wished, there would have been no tardiness. But he knew, understanding his visitor, that Eckart would have severely disapproved. He and Eckart had private matters to discuss, and Eckart was, above all things, cautious, and a third party in the car would have been inhibiting. It was too bad, because a chauffeur would have readily fixed the flat tire of the Mercedes that Krantz had so lavishly rented on Klarabergsgatan at twenty kronor for the day (minus 10 per cent discount for the winter season) plus twenty-five öre for every kilometer to be driven. Without the chauffeur, Krantz had wasted precious time hunting a garage and, beyond that, he had probably driven the rim through the deflated tire, which would force a costly penalty upon him. Still, these expenses were minor, and the irritations minor too, when he considered the importance of his meeting with Eckart.

As he thought of their reunion, Krantz's spirits lifted. The assignment that Eckart had so mildly suggested in East Berlin, more than a year ago, one that had seemed so impossible at the time, had now culminated in complete success. Krantz had done his job magnificently, and Eckart must deliver what he had promised. In that sense, the German physicist's arrival in Stockholm was today not only a congratulation but a guarantee of payment. Severe as the day was, Krantz shivered with warm anticipation at the guttural assurances that would soon give him the prestige and security that had become his full-time obsession, ever since the vacant chair of physics at the University of Uppsala, rightfully his by accomplishment and seniority, had gone to another.

Waiting in the icy air of early afternoon, Krantz felt like any child on Christmas Eve. He knew, at once, that the simile was incorrect. He had never been "any child" on Christmas Eve. This he could not forget. His gruff father had always been off to Frankfurt on holidays, and his mother had consequently been fretful and angry, so there had never once been a celebration. It irked him to remember the pointless past in this his maturity, when he had made his own cause for celebration.

As he smoothed his mustache and goatee with his gloved fingers, his earlier and happier mood revived. But that he was nervous there was no doubt. Automatically, his gloved fingers scratched for the metal puzzle in his coat pocket. He took the puzzle out, clumsily but absently twisting and turning it, and suddenly he heard his name.

Dr. Hans Eckart, a single light bag in hand, was goose-stepping toward him. At least, his exact military stride gave the impression of a modified goose step, and while it often made many heads turn, it no longer seemed surprising to Krantz, to whom it had been familiar since the war.

Depositing the puzzle in his pocket, tearing off the glove of his right hand, Krantz bolted forward to welcome Eckart with a hospitable handshake and relieve him of his bag.

"*Guten Tag,* Hans!" exclaimed Krantz exuberantly. "*Wie geht es Ihnen?*"

"*Es geht mir sehr gut, danke—und Ihnen?*" Eckart stepped back and surveyed Krantz. "You need not answer. I see you are fit. No older, you appear no older than the last time."

"How long has it been, Hans? A year—"

"One year and twelve days," said Eckart exactly. "It is considerate of you to meet me, with all the duties you must perform in the Nobel Week."

"Receiving you is my happiest duty of the Nobel Week," said Krantz with sincerity.

"Not quite, not quite," said Eckart with Wagnerian humor. "There was another I am sure you welcomed more."

Krantz understood the dig, which was not meant unkindly but was their mutual pleasure, and he smiled. "Yes, Hans, it is true the other gave me pleasure, also. . . . I am sorry for the weather. Come, I have a Mercedes waiting."

"A Mercedes, eh? We will have you for an honorary citizen yet."

They walked in step, stride for stride, Krantz's short legs pumping to match Eckart's long ones, toward the parking area. Glancing sidelong at his liberator, and superior, Krantz was proud as ever to be seen with him. Dr. Hans Eckart was a gentleman of admirable bearing. Although in his late fifties, he carried himself like a young Prussian officer. When Krantz had first met Eckart, after the war, he had regarded his appearance as an affectation. Eckart wore a monocle, but the glass was not convex but flat, and one suspected that he did not need the eyepiece. On the side of his chin, like a battle ribbon, lay a jagged scar, to conjure up memories of Heidelberg, and Ludendorff and all the best of another Germany, but Krantz had heard—from jealous detractors—that Eckart had earned the scar in a pedestrian ice-skating fall. There was no Junker tradition in Eckart's past, yet he had imposed such an inheritance upon himself, acquired from museum figures he had met in his youth and from history and from the cinemas of UFA. Eventually, a new generation had come to believe that Eckart was what he pretended to be, and to respect him, and eventually Krantz had come around, too, for this was the private vision that he held for himself.

During the war, Eckart, a minor researcher in physics who knew considerable about heavy water, had been ostentatiously arrested by the Gestapo, briefly confined, and at last placed for the duration in that section of the Kaiser Wilhelm Institute where non-Aryans were kept under protective custody to toil for the Fatherland. It was announced at the time that Eckart was one-fourth Jewish. But in the years after, various German scientists in Berlin whom Krantz had come to know had winked at him and hinted the truth. Eckart had not been Jewish at all, not one-fourth, not one-millionth. He had been as pure, as Nordic, as Krantz himself. It had all been a sham, a playlet, his arrest, his custody, to plant someone among the Jew scientists, who were untrustworthy and had to be watched. There was no proof behind this rumor, but Krantz liked to believe it and did believe it. And what corroborated Krantz's belief was the rapid promotion of Eckart since the war. At first, Eckart, after choosing to remain in East Berlin, had returned to his old teaching post at the Friedrich Wilhelm University, now renamed the Humboldt University. Almost overnight, Eckart had risen in station. To teacher, he had added the title Chairman of the Physics Department. Now more administrator than teacher, he was soon on the university board. But his position went far beyond control of faculty and 9,000 students. He had been sent on several key government missions, and had become the unpublicized spokesman for East German science. Because one of the earth's two powers—and the greater of the two powers, in Krantz's opinion—backed him, his political influence was inestimable.

Now, observing Eckart clean the fog from his monocle with a handkerchief, Krantz felt the snug security of having such an omnipotent patron.

"Here we are," said Krantz.

He hastened to open the front door for Eckart, and when his visitor was inside and comfortable, Krantz unlocked the trunk of the Mercedes, lifted the bag inside, closed it, and then got behind the wheel.

They had driven a minute or two, but it was not until they had left the Bromma Air Terminal out of sight that Professor Hans Eckart spoke at last.

He was a man with no small talk, and he had no small talk now.

"You are waiting for me to congratulate you, Carl—"

"Well—" said Krantz, unsure if he should be perplexed or modest.

"—and I do congratulate you, on my own behalf, and on behalf of my colleagues."

"Thank you, Hans," said Krantz earnestly, with deep relief.

"To be frank, we had expected this to be Max Stratman's year all along. But we could take no chance. You Nobel people are too easily misled or diverted. It was because we could take no chance that we had you in Berlin, Carl."

Deferential as he was, Krantz could not let this go by so easily. His own services had to be put in true perspective. "It is never anyone's year for the Nobel award," he said mildly. "As a matter of fact, before last February, there was even some doubt that he would be nominated. His old accomplishments were dated and had long been superseded. And as to this new discovery, there was some question about his work in solar energy, not only in the Royal Swedish Academy, but in those eminent faculties throughout the world who nominate. There was a widespread feeling that it had not yet been proved, that it was too early. What reinforced that resistance was the cloak of secrecy the Americans threw about his find. Because of lack of information, there were many judges who said, 'Perhaps it is overrated. Perhaps it is a hoax.' "

"It is no hoax, I promise you."

Krantz looked at his German friend thoughtfully. "You are sure of that?"

"We are sure," said Eckart.

"That was my feeling, all along, of course," said Krantz. "In any event, no nomination of Stratman had come through by early January, and the whole possibility became more precarious. It meant that if no one had nominated him, I would have had to do so at the last minute. Had that happened, I freely admit I do not think I could have put him over. Fortunately, at the eleventh hour, three strong nominations came in, one each from America, England, France—"

"Naturally," said Eckart with a tinge of acidity. "They all share his find. They *know*."

"And so, then, to add weight, I submitted my own nomination of Stratman, too. That made four. That made him a more promising candidate, but by no means a favorite, by no means. At least three other candidates had an inside track, with cliques behind them. I never faced a more arduous task."

Dr. Hans Eckart was as much a diplomat as a scientist, and he knew when to crowd and when to coddle. This was a moment for graciousness. "Do not misunderstand me, Carl. I was merely feeling you out, to learn what your position was when the contest began. Your letters were guarded, but I suspected your difficulties. We are all overjoyed by your incredible achievement. My congratulation was not an empty formality. It was given in sincerity."

"I hoped you would understand, Hans."

"We do. We appreciate your abilities. More than that, your comradeship, also. Would we have given you this assignment—where there could be no failure—unless we wholeheartedly believed in you?"

"I thank you for your trust, Hans."

"Now my inquisitiveness has got the better of me," he said. He stared out of the moving car window, at the frost-nipped, barren Swedish countryside, and then he returned to his host. "I know a little about your precious prizes, of course, but I am curious about how you put Stratman over. You said there was resistance from the start. How could one man possibly overcome it? In short, how does one man win, singlehandedly, a Nobel award for another?"

Krantz was pleased. With one hand free of the wheel, he tugged at his goatee. Now he understood. At the outset, Eckart had minimized his part in the physics award, because he did not wish Krantz to get out of control or demand too much. It was their clever technique. Krantz knew them well. He was one of them. But underneath it all, they knew that he, Carl Adolf Krantz, a voting member of the Royal Swedish Academy of Science, had indeed swung the award to Stratman, the man they wanted to have the award this year. And now the jockeying was done, and Krantz's achievement had been recognized, and he could speak with self-complacent honesty.

"I will not make more of myself than I am," he told Eckart disarmingly. "Three or four times, in past years, in different categories, a single member, one judge, has been able to take a minority candidate and convert him into the first choice. It takes careful handling, believe me. Usually, especially in physics, there is a heavily favored candidate, and he sweeps all before him, and nothing can be done about it. Such was the case when Wilhelm Roentgen won the first award for his discovery of the X ray. It was the same when Enrico Fermi won, and again when Ernest Lawrence received the prize for the cyclotron. On the other hand, there was Albert Einstein, and he proved vulnerable. Outside influences kept us from honoring his general theory of relativity. You remember Philipp Lenard, your fine Nobel winner? It was said that Lenard became an anti-Semite after Germany lost World War I. Possibly because Einstein was a Jew, Lenard was opposed to him. Lenard made a great campaign against Einstein, telling our judges that the theory of relativity was not actually a discovery, had not been proved, and was valueless. This gave our judges pause. They avoided Einstein for seven years, and when they elected him physics laureate in 1921, it was for the lesser law of the photo-electric effect and not for relativity. I relate this only as evidence that our judges can be moved in one direction or another. Not usually, but on rare occasions. To have one man influence the judges, for or against a candidate, especially a minor candidate, this one man must know where the competition is vulnerable and have unlimited enthusiasm for the candidate he is promoting. Had you suggested any physicist other than Stratman, I might not have been able to summon up the necessary enthusiasm. But we talked about this at Humboldt—Stratman is a candidate I believed in from the start. His harnessing of solar energy will, I am convinced, change the face of the world—"

"Yes, yes, we agree," interrupted Eckart.

"—and so you gave me a name worthy of my devotion. Very well. That is first. You had asked me how one man, by himself, could win a Nobel Prize for another. And I have said that it has happened on several occasions. I will cite one, for your edification. It occurred during 1945, in the Swedish Academy, when they were preparing for the year's literature award."

"Literature," said Eckart, removing his monocle. "Hogwash."

"You will have to take that up with Alfred Nobel," said Krantz flippantly, and then regretted his levity and retreated. "I am inclined to agree with you, of course. But there is an award, and eighteen judges, and how does one put over a minority candidate? Well—1945. The favorite candidates, that year, were a number who later won, André Gide, William Faulkner, Hermann Hesse, and others like Jules Romains, Carl Sandburg, Benedetto Croce. There was even talk of giving Thomas Mann a second award. During all of this discussion and byplay, one of the judges in the Academy, Hjalmar Gullberg, a poet, fell in love with the verse of an obscure teacher from Chile named Gabriela Mistral. Have you ever heard of her?"

"No."

"But of the others?"

"Of course, Carl. What do you take me for?"

Quickly, Krantz went on with his story. "Gabriela Mistral had been published in Mexico and Latin America, and almost nowhere else. As far as Sweden was concerned, she was unknown. Her chances for a Nobel award were less even than Max Stratman's. Gullberg tried to sell Gabriela Mistral to his colleagues, but they curtly rebuffed him. Undeterred, Gullberg made up his mind to win singlehandedly for his candidate the prize. An ambitious undertaking, I assure you."

"I can see that."

"Gullberg set himself to work translating her best poems into Swedish, a formidable task, and then he had the translations published. He promoted the published works. He sent copies to all members of the Swedish Academy. His translations were magnificent, and this, along with other politicking, I imagine, turned the tide. Gabriela Mistral, an unknown, an underdog, really an impossibility, Hans, won the Nobel Prize in literature for 1945. Now, there you see how it can be done."

Eckart allowed this to sink in, and then he inquired, "Now tell me how you did it, Carl."

"Stratman?"

"Yes, Stratman."

"We must go back to our meeting in Berlin," said Krantz. "You had summoned me to inquire if I would consider taking the chair of physics at Humboldt University, and I said it was the dream of my life. And you said that my application would be entered, there might be an opening soon, but you did not wish me to resign yet from my membership on the Nobel Physics Committee of the Academy of Sciences. You said that it was important to you, the university, to the East German government, that Max Stratman be awarded the physics prize and be brought to Stockholm. Since you knew my respect for Stratman, his work, you preferred to have me in Stockholm, doing my part, until Stratman won the prize. The understanding was—when I had delivered Stratman, you would favorably act on my application."

Eckart flinched slightly. "I do not think we put it as bluntly as that, Carl."

Krantz would not be turned aside. This was vital. "That was your implication, Hans."

"Implication, yes. No question. We respect and reward our friends."

"I did not ask you why you wanted Stratman in Stockholm. I felt that was not part of our—the implication of our deal."

"I think I have told you—we wanted him here, nearby, in a free and neutral climate, away from his captors and bodyguards, where we could talk to him —I could see him as an old friend, merely that, nothing more."

"The point I make is that I did not bother you with my ambitions," said Krantz. "You spoke to me of a position to which I have aspired all my life. Quite reasonably, you asked if, first, I could remain where I was, to throw my influence as a voting judge behind a candidate you desired to be elected. Your wish was my wish, as if a command. I tell you that in sincerity, Hans."

"We are proud of your friendship, Carl."

Krantz nodded. "I promised you that I would do what I could do, but even then, I did not foresee the difficulties. Stratman was duly nominated, as I have told you, and that was a beginning. All through the spring and summer, I acquired Stratman's published papers, and, like Gullberg, translated them with care, and sent them to my voting colleagues with personal notes. I tried, through faculty friends abroad, to learn what details I could of Stratman's actual discovery, the specific solar conversion and storage method, but I ran into a stone wall. American security deprived me of precious details. What I did obtain were zealous endorsements of the discovery, from those who had been eyewitnesses to its results and values. All of this correspondence I translated, and passed around to the other judges. During the summer, I was instrumental in bringing two physicists, one English, the other Russian—"

"Yes, we helped clear the way for the Russian to come here."

"Did you? Well, I thought it had been too easy. It was wise of you, Hans. He came, and the Englishman, and since they were specialists in solar work, they gave valuable lectures—I saw to it that my colleagues attended—and I saw to it that the speakers gave praise to Stratman, and in both cases, my encouragement was not necessary, for their praise would have been lavish anyway. By then, I think, my fellow judges were properly oriented, Stratman-conscious, and for the first time, he was a serious candidate."

"You are a wonder, Carl."

"You have only heard half of it, Hans. The most decisive half lay ahead of me in the fall. My original work had been constructive. To build up Stratman. Now, I shifted my gears. My next work became, necessarily, destructive, to destroy the competition. Believe me, the competition was serious this year. We are in the age of physics, and there is an overabundance of eligible candidates. A series of informal lunches with my fellow judges produced the names of three favorites running ahead of Stratman. I will not bother you with full-length biographies. Suffice it to say, one was that damn Norwegian with his latest findings in the low gravitational field. Another was the Spaniard, the meterologist, the one with the new cloud chamber, who claims to have made the first inroads in weather control. The third was an Australian team that had made advances in high-frequency transport—I must confess, fascinating—an elaborate theory, and some evidence, of building underground cables beneath concrete highways and rails to propel vehicles electrically. There was competition, you can see, and demonstrated, whereas Stratman's findings, though doubtless more important, were made to seem impractical by loathsome secrecy."

"What was your next step, Carl? How did you sabotage the competition?"

Krantz felt uncomfortable. He pretended to devote himself to his driving, eyes on the three-pointed silver star above the grille. "I do not think the exact details are pertinent."

"They are to me," said Eckart. "We know your resourcefulness in theory. We want to see it proved."

"The Norwegian was easiest to dispose of. I wrote a learned paper—I must show it to you—proving that antigravity, if controlled by Norway, could be harmful to Sweden. It would give our neighbor terrible ascendency in rocket propulsion and whatnot. I knew that this would strike at our judges' nationalistic pride. Moreover, to give them a graceful backing off, I indicated that many of the Norwegian's experiments had dealt with the value of antigravity fields in medicine as well as physics—you know, relief of heart sufferers—and I indicated that his candidacy should be considered, next year, by the Nobel Medical Committee. I circulated my paper, and I am happy to say that the Norwegian received only two votes. As to the Spaniard, with his weather control, I was able to learn that he was a Falangist, and so I located several exiled Spanish scientists, of unimpeachable repute, and invited them to be my devil's advocates. Their letters were 'volunteered' to the leaders of our committee. Their disparagement of the Falangist's discovery was most effective, I must say. The Australians were another matter. Their high-frequency invention was well regarded everywhere. Moreover, it was a safe prize, noncontroversial. There was no chance of my getting at them through their work."

"What could you do?"

"I could get at them through themselves," said Krantz placidly. "I have a man here in Stockholm, a refugee of long standing, who is useful in these matters. He is a Hungarian. He had served one of the Axis powers, in World War II, as a minor espionage agent. He likes to think of himself as a free-lance spy, still, but he is actually a pathetic buffoon. Yet, on several occasions, I have employed him for research and found him valuable. He is literate and bookish. He has good connections among the international press. They feed him tidbits in exchange for news trifles. He thinks of himself as another Wilhelm Stieber or Fräulein Doktor Schragmüller, but he is actually a librarian, a researcher. I hired him to investigate the Australians."

"How could you take such a risk with an irresponsible Hungarian buffoon?" asked Eckart bitingly.

"Because he depends on me, Hans," said Krantz. "He is stateless, and I, and several like me, have intervened on his behalf with lesser government officials, to keep him here. Also, he needs the few kronor we dole out to him now and then. I used him to discover that the Spanish candidate was a Falangist. When it came to the Australians, I used him once more."

Krantz's lips curled in self-satisfaction as he negotiated the Mercedes around a curve. When the car was straight again, he continued to speak.

"The two Australians were homosexuals. We gathered the proof, and when the final voting conference was held last month, I deferred to one of my conservative colleagues—I had shown him the facts and said I thought he might be interested, although I thought it was no issue—and at the critical moment, he burst forth and made it an issue. Professor Max Stratman was elected our Nobel laureate in forty-five minutes."

Eckart shook his head. "Carl, Carl, what is there for me to say? You are a master. I would hate to be a candidate before you."

"You would have no problem, Hans. I would favor you."

"So that is how it was done?" mused Eckart.

"In this case, yes. I would not guarantee it again. The circumstances were exceptional. At any rate, you see the work that went into it."

"You will make a scintillating addition to our staff at Humboldt, Carl."

Krantz took his eyes from the road and looked at his guest. "When?" he asked.

"Soon, soon," said Eckart. "Have no doubts. I will see Stratman. You will finish with your Nobel circus. I will return to East Berlin, consult with the board, and you will be confirmed."

"Must it wait that long?"

"How long? It is nothing. Two weeks or three. The formalities and no more. I will phone you, and you will be on your way. Incidentally, you have seen Stratman?"

"Certainly. I am on the official reception committee. I welcomed him at the train. I attended his press conference. I spent considerable time with him at the Royal Banquet."

"How does he look?"

"What do you mean? When did you last see him?"

"The week our Führer died."

"He is not a young man any longer—that you know, Hans. Sometimes he appears quite sprightly, other times feeble."

Eckart fiddled with his monocle. "Has he spoken of the past, of Germany?"

Krantz squirmed in his place behind the wheel. "Several times. The Americans have brainwashed him with their propaganda and money."

"They have? How so?"

"At the press conference, he defended the secrecy of his discovery as necessary. He said that he was forced to work at the Kaiser Wilhelm to keep his relatives alive. He denied that the Americans kidnaped him. He said that he left Germany voluntarily, because he had worked for one totalitarian state, and he did not wish to remain and work for another."

"He said that?"

"It was in many newspapers the following day."

"And in your other conversations, anything else?"

"At the Royal Banquet, before dinner, there was a trifling exchange. There was conversation about money—what to do with the Nobel money—and Stratman made it clear that he was keeping his prize."

"Because he needed the money?"

"That is my guess. Later, I had a disagreement with Count Jacobsson—you have met him—"

"Yes."

"An officious ass," said Krantz. "We were arguing Sweden's neutrality. Jacobsson, as usual, said we were pro-Allies, and I had no stomach for that lie. I told the truth about public sentiment."

"How did Stratman react?"

"He made no comment on that, but when I praised German genius, he disparaged it. Then, right after, the two medical laureates told what they did in the war, and one of them asked Stratman what had happened to him, and he said that he had been held a hostage—that was his word, hostage. Then, there was an incident. Stratman had said he was a hostage, he and his brother—"

"Yes, Walther Stratman."

"—to keep his brother's wife and daughter alive in a camp. Well, the brother's daughter, Stratman's niece, was right there in the room with him, and when someone asked what had happened to her mother, she broke up and ran off. It was needless and embarrassing. Stratman, I must say, remained unruffled."

Eckart folded his hands in his lap and stared out the windshield. "Stockholm," he said.

"We will be in the city in a few minutes."

Eckart was silent a moment. "Then Stratman is here with his niece?"

"They are always together."

"What is she like?"

"A cold fish. But one never knows. If I were twenty years younger, I would be sorely tempted, even if she is a Jew."

310

Eckart smiled. The picture of the crusty gnome beside him being tempted by fleshly desire was too improbable to formulate. "Keep your mind on your work, Carl."

"My work is done," said Krantz.

"One never knows. I want you to keep in close touch with me."

"I expect to, Hans. I must remind you, I made your reservation at the Grand for only two days. It was not easy. The city is crowded. Do you intend to remain longer?"

"I cannot say for certain, Carl. I might stay through the tenth."

"Well, tell me the second you know. If you stay on, I will have to tackle the manager of the Grand again. Oh, he will extend your accommodation, but I must know so that I can arrange it."

"I will let you know tomorrow, Carl."

"When are you seeing Stratman?"

"In the next hour. As soon as I have checked in, I will call his room. I cabled. He is expecting me."

"And you know he will see you?"

Eckart rubbed his scar meditatively. "Why should he not see me, Carl? You forget. Max Stratman and his brother and I worked side by side at the Kaiser Wilhelm all through the war. We are friends, old friends. Today, we will have lunch. We will speak of many things. *Gemütlichkeit* will be the note. You make a reservation for us, the moment I register. The Riche, I think. That would be the best restaurant. . . . Yes, Carl, have no fear, Max Stratman will be waiting for this reunion."

Andrew Craig and Leah Decker occupied the desirable corner suite 225 in the Grand Hotel. Directly above it, having the same dimensions and identical in furnishings, was suite 325 which, for the duration of Nobel week, was tenanted by Emily Stratman and Professor Max Stratman.

At 1:20 in the afternoon, Craig arrived at suite 325 and rapped on the door.

After a moment, the door opened, and although Emily was not visible, he heard her voice. "You can roll it right in the living—" And then her head appeared around the door, and she saw Craig. "Oh, it's you—forgive me—I'd ordered lunch from room service and—please come in."

He followed her through the entry into the sitting room. His eyes were on her semishingled dark hair, and when she turned to take his topcoat, he enjoyed again the black curls that curved forward on her cheeks, framing her face in piquant loveliness. She wore a loose forest-green tunic of jersey, that draped outward and straight down from her breasts, and the tight cotton-knit green slacks beneath, smooth and chic, adhered to her hips and thighs. He had never seen her dressed this informally, and there was an ease about her that pleased him.

"Are you hungry?" she asked.

"Famished."

"I can still catch them downstairs. Will you join me?"

"Why do you think I'm here?"

She picked up the white room-service telephone, and was instantly connected. "This is Miss Stratman in 325. If you've still got my order, I'd like to add another to it." She listened, said, "Please hold on," cupped the mouthpiece and told Craig, "In the nick of time. They'll keep mine warm while they get yours ready. What are you having?"

"Whatever you're having."

"That's Swedish roulette," she said. "I don't know what I'm having. They brought the *middagen* menu—that's what it said—and I pointed to *Kalvschnitzel med spaghetti.*"

"That sank the Titanic. Okay by me. And any kind of Danish beer."

She put through Craig's order and sat several feet from him on the sofa. "I want to thank you again for last night, Andrew. It was lovely."

"For me, too."

"I can always tell when it's good. I went to bed early, because I wanted to think about it and nothing else, and before I knew it, I was asleep. What did you do after?"

How could he tell her of his similar good intention, and how quickly it had paved the road to hell? How could he tell her of finding Leah naked in his bed—so fantastic now, in the daylight—and of their bitter quarrel? Even to hint at it would frighten Emily.

"I read a Gideon Bible," he said.

"Did you really?"

"I wanted to see what those boys had. It needs a polish job. They're on to a good idea, but the characters aren't believable, and the sex is too explicit and there's no book that can't be helped with a little cutting. I think one rewrite would do it."

"Silly."

"I had a good night's sleep, too, Emily, until the Uppsala boys' chorus woke me at some ungodly hour."

"They serenaded you? I heard they did that."

"Warn your uncle. Tell him to wear earplugs every night. No, I'm kidding. It was very nice. It turned out I was supposed to lecture them this morning on Hemingway and the Icelandic sagas."

"Did you?"

"I lectured, all right. I just came from there. They got an Icelandic saga, I'll say—Miller's Dam, Wisconsin, on a winter morning. The snow sometimes piles up five or six feet."

"Did you discuss writing?"

"I said authors want to write, have to write, and all the rest don't want to write, they only want to be authors. I said that was the essential difference, the one that separates the men from the boys. They got the message. Most of them will wind up manufacturing matches, but they were a nice bunch. I have to do a repeat performance for a group from two other universities at three-thirty." He paused. "What have you been up to this morning?"

"Uncle Max wanted to rest. He has an old friend coming in from Berlin, and he has to see him for lunch. He's dressing right now. We just stayed in and lazied. It's too cold out, anyway. I studied all morning—"

She picked up a book, one she had purchased the day before at Fritze's, from the coffee table.

"—Swedish into English, English into Swedish. I'm determined."

"Anything I should know?"

"Indispensable," said Emily. She opened the language book and leafed through it. "Here is the Swedish phrase, and here it is in English. 'Who will pull me across the lake?' Now, how could you get along without that? Here is another. 'Please get me a clean knife.' That one haunts me, like the ending of Dickens's *The Mystery of Edwin Drood*. And here we have 'The wine is too warm, fetch some ice.' And the pessimism. Here is a little exchange one is expected to learn in Swedish. Question: '*Hur går affärerna? How is business?*' Answer: '*Stilla. Dull.*' Question: '*Hur mår Eder man? How is your husband?*' Answer: '*Han är mycket sjuk. He is very ill.*' Cheerful, isn't it?"

Craig laughed, and took the book from her. "Have you learned anything yet?"

"Several words."

"Let's find out." He read aloud. "*Spottning förbjuden.*"

"Heaven help me. What does that mean?"

"No spitting . . . what every young lady should know . . . *Glogg*. What's glogg?"

"I know that! Brandy—burnt brandy."

"Very good, Miss Emily." Craig consulted the book again. "*Helge-flundra.*"

"Halibut," said Emily promptly.

"My God, you're right. And *mässling?*"

"*Mässling—mässling*—sounds like something you chew or an Oriental form of wrestling."

"You are quarantined. It means measles. Here is one you can't do without —*ormskinn.*"

"I surrender."

"Snakeskin. Had enough?"

"Well, one more."

"All right," said Craig. "What does *renstek* do to you?"

"It gives me indigestion."

"Right. It's reindeer steak. Oh, wait, just one more. What if a stranger said to you—*avkläda?*"

"I'd say you're welcome."

"It means undress."

"Mr. Craig!" But she smiled when she said that, and Craig knew everything was fine between them.

He threw the book down. "My only advice to you, young lady, is don't go out with a Swede."

"If I do, I'll stick to 'Please get me a clean knife.' "

"I see you don't need me."

"But I do," said Emily.

There was a knock on the hall door, and Emily called out, "It's open!"

The waiter, in a white jacket, towel over one arm, came in pulling a portable table filled with covered plates, the coffeepot, and a bottle of beer.

As the waiter reached the sitting room, Professor Max Stratman, wearing a hat and short overcoat, emerged from his bedroom.

He did not seem surprised to see Craig. "Good afternoon, Mr. Craig. Are you going to keep Emily company?"

"Until three, I hope."

"Very good." Stratman kissed Emily's cheek. "Do not let him charge any more to our bill. Let him spend his prize, and we will spend ours."

"I'll watch him, Uncle Max. Where will you be? Downstairs?"

"No. We are having lunch at an elegant restaurant around the corner. At least, that was the way Eckart put it. He was always the one for fancy places. I remember during the war. He was the only one of us who could talk his way into Horcher's." And then to Craig, "That was where Göring ate, so it was good. Take care of my girl."

He went slowly, thoughtfully, out the door.

The waiter had almost finished arranging the luncheon, when Emily suddenly rose. "Excuse me a second." She hurried into her uncle's room.

Craig had signed the bill, and the waiter had left, before she returned. She was reading a telegram, and her face was troubled.

"What's the matter, Emily?"

She looked up absently. "What? Oh, I always check his room after he goes. He's so forgetful. Sometimes he leaves his pipe lighted on the table, and the hot ashes fall out. We had two small fires last year." She sat down next to Craig. "The pipe was all right—but I found this wire."

"Anything wrong with it?"

"Not exactly, but—" She folded the telegram. "It's from this friend he used to work with in Berlin, the one he's lunching with now. This man, Hans Eckart, says he has read my uncle is in Stockholm for the Nobel Prize and congratulates him. He says he, too, will be in Stockholm, and would like to have lunch with him today and will phone him. He says they have much to talk about, and he brings news of Walther."

"Walther?"

"My father. Strange, after all these years."

"Not so strange," said Craig. "This man stayed on in Berlin, and may have heard more of what happened to your father, and it's a natural thing to pass it on to his old friend."

"Yes, I suppose," said Emily slowly.

Craig studied her face. "You're still not convinced. What's bothering you?"

"The origin of the telegram," she said. "It was sent yesterday from *East* Berlin. I tell myself—what good can come from East Berlin?"

Riche's restaurant, located at Birger Jarlsgatan 4, several long blocks behind the Grand Hotel, was one of Stockholm's most expensive and superior restaurants. Every international capital has its elegant dining place where the elite—the wealthy, the titled, the powerful businessmen, the renowned artists —are recognized at once, and, as the ruling class of celebrity, they are seated promptly and kept apart from the ordinary customers. Riche was one of these.

The glassed-in veranda facing the street—where the music was soft and the voices hushed, and one could look out and take pleasure in the tall, well-dressed Swedish men and tall, well-dressed Swedish women passing by in the prosperous thoroughfare—was the choice site for dining. And here, through Krantz's intervention, Dr. Hans Eckart, of East Berlin, Germany, and Professor Max Stratman, of Atlanta, United States, had been seated a half hour before.

Now Eckart had ceased speaking. He waited as the empty consommé dishes were removed, and their waiter served rare beef cuts off a wagon, and the sommelier brought fresh beers and poured them.

From beneath his half-closed eyelids, arms folded on his vest, Stratman pretended to watch the elaborate service, but actually observed the man across the table from him. Their meeting in the lobby, their walk to the restaurant, their beginning at the table, had come off easily and without incident. To Stratman's eyes, Eckart, except for the thinning and graying of his hair, and wrinkles at his neck, and an air more authoritative than before, had not changed since the war years. The monocle was still caught in place, and it reflected light whenever he moved his head. The scar was as livid and dramatic as before. The corded Prussian rigidity of the face was inhuman as it had ever been. All that had really changed, Stratman decided, was that Eckart had not been given to wasted words, but in the past half hour he had been relatively garrulous, and pointless, in his conversation. Stratman made up his mind that Eckart was nervous. Since he, himself, was not, he felt comfortable, and remained calm.

In the half hour, after profusely congratulating Stratman on becoming a Nobel laureate, Eckart had devoted himself to reminiscing about the lighter side of the past that they had shared in common. He had recalled anecdotes of their long days in the Kaiser Wilhelm Institute, and joked about their colleagues, and provided information on those who had survived and what had become of them. Eckart had a clever way of making that gruesome period of enforced confinement, of toil for the devil, seem congenial and sport, as if they had all had membership in a jolly men's club, and as if this was now their best memory of the past.

As the waiters tactfully disappeared, Stratman realized that he did not like this spurious talk, that his dinner companion had never really been his friend (but only someone who had come and gone from the laboratory for two years), and that he was too old to fritter away his time on inconsequential prattle.

Eckart lifted his beer stein. *"Bitte*—your health, Max."

"To yours," said Stratman, and he drank, and then set his thick glass down decisively. "You seem to have tremendous affection for the past, Hans. I have less. My only affection for the time we shared is a memory of my brother

315

Walther. Your cable spoke of him. I cannot imagine why. Maybe you are ready to tell me."

Eckart, who was no longer used to brusqueness, frowned, but tried to convert displeasure into nostalgic pain. He had wanted the conversation to go his way, to be its sole pilot, but now he remembered that Max Stratman had often been called headstrong and impatient. He pretended to give consideration to his reply, to measure it, as he efficiently sliced his roast beef.

"What do you know of Walther's death?" asked Eckart.

"What do I know? I know that when I was in England, before emigrating to America, the British advised me that he had been arrested by the OGPU immediately after my escape, for his role in it, and deported to a Siberian labor camp. There, a month or two later, he died or was put to death—I do not know which—even while I was still in the custody of the Americans in Germany. That is all I know."

"You have been misinformed," said Eckart.

"Have I?"

"Absolutely, my old friend. The British were propagandizing you. They wished an alliance with your hatred. Siberia? Labor camp? What a crazy story that is. No, believe me, I have the facts. Walther was not sent to Siberia but to a nuclear laboratory seventy miles from Moscow. When he was being screened, it was discovered—from a paper he had published—that he was an expert on the bubonic plague. At once, he was offered a better post. He was asked to join a team of other researchers, led by the renowned Dr. Viktor Glinko, engaged in experiments concerned with biological warfare—bacteria bombs—a magnificent attempt to simulate, for purposes of peace, the bubonic plague that killed five million people in France and England in 1348. In the initial experiments, there was an accident, many were killed, and Walther was among those declared missing, presumed dead. I give you my word, Max, and I believe it will relieve you to know this. Walther was never arrested or pressed into slave labor. He was intrigued by this new field. He volunteered to enter into it, and undertook a crash course that converted him from physicist to bacteriologist. He was given every consideration and comfort, until the end. And why not? You know how the Soviets respect scientists."

"So he volunteered to develop germ bombs?"

"Yes."

"I am sorry, Hans. I do not believe you. I think I knew my older brother better than you. He would have been incapable of such a thing."

"Come now, Max, I understand your love for him, but that is all long ago, and you must be sensible. What was so wrong about that? He was an investigator, above petty politics. It was a challenge, and he was interested. Had he not always been interested? I have read a reprint of his scientific paper on the bubonic plague—"

"Child's play," interrupted Stratman. "He wrote that silly paper when he was in his twenties. Disasters of history were a hobby with him, and to have some fun, a small sensation—oh, possibly because he wanted attention, his vocation was so routine and dull—he applied the scientific attitude to the bubonic plague of 1348. Such child's play is one thing. But to bottle black death for the Russians is quite another, and I will not accept it."

"His so-called child's play was a bit more lethal," said Eckart insistently. "The Russians saw that, and so did I, when I read Walther's paper. I do not refer to the history—all the detail about the bubonic plague killing off one-third of the population of France and England. I refer to Walther's prophetic speculations on the possibilities of one day compounding biological agents to produce artificially the same epidemics as those once produced by the buboes-type plague and the pulmonary-type plague."

"I repeat—juvenile strutting. It was his only weakness. Walther was far too kind and good—"

"Be that as it may. It is useless to labor the fact further. But you will not deny this, my friend—Walther did work on nuclear fission with us throughout the war."

"Of course, he worked on nuclear fission, as I did. We did it because we knew that the program was so depleted of funds, so hamstrung by Hitler's politics, that Germany could never have an atom bomb before the Reich was defeated. If there had been any other possible outcome, Walther and I would have died in Hitler's ovens before cooperating. And Walther would have let his wife and daughter die, too." Stratman snorted with anger. "As it was, Walther's wife died in Auschwitz anyway, and for nothing."

Eckart quickly wore his mask of mourning. "That was a pity, a cruel mistake. I agree it was for nothing. I deplore that tiny Nazi gang as much as—"

"What do you mean—tiny Nazi gang? The guilt was national, all Germany's guilt, not the mere madness of a small political party."

"Come now, Max, you cannot believe that, no matter how bitter you may be. People are sheep. They go along. They have no idea what is happening around them. Each lives at his hearth, in his block, and no farther."

"It took thousands to shovel the bones out of those incinerators and millions to make up the *Wehrmacht*. To me, that is people. And the Russians are no better. So—now we have a lovely fairy tale to soothe the survivors. Walther was treated in a courtly way, and he died happily in the line of duty. Is that the news you have for me?"

"I am sorry you will not believe it."

"I wish I could," said Stratman. He drank his beer, no longer having taste for the meal. "What is your source for the fairy tale?"

"As you know, I hold many positions of—of importance in East Berlin today. I have access to every record, all data. I made it a project to find out what happened to our old Kaiser Wilhelm Institute alumni. I thought I might bring them all together for peaceful nuclear researches."

"And you found Walther's obituary?"

"His entire history. And yes, his obituary, as you put it. You see, Max, for a long time, after we heard of the accident, the explosion at Dubna, near Moscow, and saw the list of dead and missing—many of our old colleagues were lost there—a few of us had unrealistic hopes that the missing had not been killed but had disappeared somewhere, possibly escaped, and we might one day see them alive. Unfortunately, it was not to be. As I say, it was un-realistic of us, this faint hope. For now I must tell you, among the papers I found were some recent untranslated ones—and one of these, several years old, declared Walther officially dead. So that is it."

"So that is your great find," said Stratman bitterly.

Eckart nodded solemnly, as if in reverence for one departed. "Yes, that and something more." He reached down beside his chair for his briefcase. Stratman had forgotten it. Briefcases were so much a part of German costume that one hardly ever paid attention. As he opened the briefcase, Eckart went on. "I understand Walther's daughter is alive and with you in America."

"How do you know?" asked Stratman quickly.

Eckart was all innocence. "I read the newspapers, Max. You are a celebrity, you forget. Well, now, I was able to locate—it was not easy—some of Walther's personal effects. I had them returned to Berlin, because I am a sentimentalist like you. I had love for your brother."

Stratman poked at the beef and was silent.

"And when I learned his daughter had survived, the first thing I thought was that she might like these souvenirs."

From the briefcase he had extracted a silver wristwatch, dented but recently polished, a worn Talmud, a yellow-brown portrait on stiff cardboard of Walther, Rebecca, and Emily at the age of two, and a chipped enameled cigarette case initialed W.S., which Walther had received as a gift from his prewar employers on the anniversary of his tenth year with them as an engineer.

Accepting the objects one by one—passing through his hands a dear and precious human being's entire life—Stratman's eyes brimmed with tears, and his heart felt near bursting. Slowly, he stuffed the wristwatch, small Talmud, cigarette case into his pockets, and the five-by-seven portrait he turned face down beside his plate.

"I am sorry," said Eckart. "I was only trying to help."

"Thank you," said Stratman sincerely. "Let us eat."

They ate without another word for five minutes, until Eckart saw that Stratman had recovered his composure.

"As you have said, Max, you have no affection for the past. So let us forget the past. We are alive in the present, and we have too much to do."

Stratman nodded, and chewed his meat, and made no comment.

"I am now the senior member of the board of Humboldt University," said Eckart. "Did you know that, Max?"

"No."

"The future is in the hands of science, and I am a scientist. I am seeing that the university has the broadest basic research program in the world. We are making a home for the leading minds of every land. Would you like to hear of some of our plans?"

"Not especially," said Stratman. "For me, this is a vacation, not a business trip."

Eckart, fork poised in mid-air, sat nonplused. Again, he was not used to such offhand treatment. It was with difficulty that he remembered that Stratman, as a Nobel Prize winner, might consider himself his equal.

Uncomfortably, Eckart tried a chuckle. "Well, now, you are right. But I still have my curiosity. My only interest is science. That is my business and my pleasure. What are your plans, Max?"

"About what?"

"The field you are in. You have perfected conversion and storage of solar energy. That is what I read. What next?"

"I will remain a servant of the sun."

"For peaceful purposes, I hope?" inquired Eckart.

"Who says the energy we now use to make rocket fuel is not for peaceful purposes?" Stratman shoved his bifocals higher on his nose and squinted at Eckart. "I think my discovery will keep the peace. And work I plan for the future will doubly assure it."

"I cannot tell you how happy that makes me, Max—to know we are both working to the same end. This makes it easier for me to reveal a thought that has come to my mind."

"Yes?"

"Max, I want you to keep an open mind about this. Hear me out." He paused, and then he asked, "Have you ever considered returning to the Fatherland?"

Stratman looked up. "What does that mean? Hans, your circumlocutions make direct conversation impossible. What are you talking about?"

"A high position—the highest—in Germany—for you. You would be the most brilliant scientist at Humboldt University, among your own kind. We would furnish you a home, any home, of your choosing. A private laboratory building. And three times the salary you now make. All this, to bring you back to the land of your birth. For the first time, you would work for yourself, for us, and the devil take both our enemies."

Stratman laid down his fork and knife. "You mean I should defect from the West and join the Communists?"

"Childish nonsense—communism, communism. They fill you up too much with that poppycock in America. Who cares about communism? Am I a Communist? I am not. I am a German citizen and a German scientist, and that is the best religion, and you belong to it, too."

"Do I? Recently, it was not thought so. Recently, my religion was Jew, not German."

"Max, we have washed our hands of those gangsters."

"There will be new gangsters. I know my Germany. On the outside, the beautiful peak—the peaceful Ku'damm, and cafés, and Fräuleins with braided hair and miniature cameras, and toy fairs—and underneath, down inside, the lava cooks and steams and waits to explode. I have no love for Germany, Hans. I have love for my youth. But not for Germany. That was an accident. My seed might have grown anywhere."

Honest astonishment showed on Eckart's face. "I cannot believe you."

"It is so. But suppose this is only grief at what has happened. Suppose I did wish to return to the old place. It would not be Germany but Soviet Germany."

"That is not so. That is propaganda."

"Who pays you your salary, Hans? Who would pay mine at Humboldt?"

"The German government, of course."

"The *East* German government, you mean. East of the Brandenburg Gate is Russia and Marxism. That is your supreme authority. You have come to me at the wrong time, Hans. You see, I have been spoiled. Yes, little golden America with its milk and honey has spoiled me—because it is golden, and there is milk and honey. I think and speak as I wish, and read what I wish, and, within the law, do as I wish, and when you have known the beauty of freedom, you cannot go to a pimp and his whore."

Eckart's lips had compressed until they were blue. "This freedom of yours —do you take me for a provincial dolt, Max? I have seen pictures of your slums, and unemployment offices, and black people beaten on the streets. And despotism over science—Oppenheimer—the rest—this is your freedom? I swear to you, you will find no such savagery and primeval living in East Germany."

Stratman pushed his plate aside. He was still calm, but he missed his meerschaum. "Freedom breeds its own canker sores," he said. "The colored man was once slave, now he is only half slave, soon he will be free. Under Communism, Germans will never in our lifetime, or after, be free. We, in America, have hope. You have none."

"Max, I do not want to argue with an old friend. I want nothing of politics and neither do you. Max, I want you with us. It is simple as that. Not in Russia. Not in America. In Germany. And if, for personal reasons, it cannot be in Germany, I will compromise. I will let you do your work in a neutral climate—Sweden, Switzerland, as you wish—as long as the work you do is for us. Why? Because to work for America or Russia is not to work for peace. But to work for your Fatherland, which with strength will enforce peace, that is the only sense for all of us."

Stratman sighed, and tried to maintain a pleasant demeanor. "Do not waste your energies on me any longer, Hans. I see you did not arrange this lunch to speak of Walther, but to proposition me. It is no use. If I took your money, I could not face myself or my niece Emily, or the ghosts of Walther and Rebecca. I am an American now, Hans, and so I shall remain to the last of my days."

There had been many shifts of emotion on Eckart's countenance, and the one that deliberately remained was of friendly resignation.

"Well, Max, I respect your feelings. You cannot blame me for trying to hire the world's foremost physicist, can you? It would have been a fine feather in my cap. But your work is so important, I pray you point it toward peace."

"Let me care for my own child, Hans."

"How long are you remaining in Stockholm?"

"Until the day after the Ceremony—the eleventh, I think it is—just time enough to pick up my check. I may take Emily to Paris for a week. Every girl should see Paris once. After that, I sail for home. There is much I have to do. And you, Hans?"

"I have some other business. I may stay a few days longer." He hesitated, then resumed. "Max, if ever you should need money, and wish to reconsider—"

"At my age, I will not need more money. I have my salary. It is generous. And now, I have Nobel's legacy."

That moment, Eckart hated the Nobel Prize, which, ironically, had given Stratman the independence to reject his offer. But, at the same time, the prize had been necessary to bring Stratman here so that he might be tempted. Eckart's own design, and Krantz's execution of it, had been intelligent, correct. It had quite simply backfired.

"People are known to change their minds," said Eckart hopefully. "Possibly, one day, I can make the inducement higher."

"Never high enough."

"I can hope. We shall see. . . . Will you have a dessert, Max?"

Stratman shook his head. "No. I think I have had just about all I can stomach for one day."

Except for the inadequate circles of artificial light thrown by the street lamps, the city of Stockholm was pitch-black at 5:40 in the afternoon, the time when Andrew Craig returned from the Stock Exchange Hall to his suite in the Grand Hotel.

The last lecture had been successful, but enervating. Despite his physical weariness, he felt at peace within himself. The reception accorded him by the university students, and their faculty, had shored up his writer's pride, and it reinforced the tenuous structure Jacobsson had built for him at the Swedish Academy on the ruins of his old self. The frivolous lunch with Emily, in the Stratman suite, had also played a positive part in his well-being. Gradually, Emily was beginning to accept and trust him, and for the first time in three years, he was enjoying companionship with a young woman of his own choosing.

The terrible guilts of the night before, revived by Leah's hysterical offering, he had managed to put aside. What remained in mind was the vivid sensation of Emily's living presence, and the growing knowledge of his own rights and his own worth. This precarious resurrection of himself, as author and man, had made him vow, in the late afternoon, that he would not again drown himself in drink.

The fact that now, sprawled on the sofa of his sitting room, he held a double Scotch with water in his hand was in no way a breaking of the vow. Craig knew his history as a drinking animal. There was the normal Craig, in the indistinct Harriet days, who, like most men, would have a relaxing double before dinner, and no more. And there was the suicidal Craig, of recent years, who would have a compulsive fifth or more, after the double, in the daily descent to oblivion.

Tonight—it was already 6:14—he was the normal Craig, with the relaxing double before dinner, and there would be no more.

He was appreciative of his solitary confinement in the suite. He would like to have had dinner with Emily, of course, but she had promised to accompany her uncle, and members of the Royal Swedish Academy of Science, to the opera. On the other hand, if the opera took away pleasures, it gave them, too. For, upon arriving in the entry hall, he had found a brief note from Leah that she was off to dinner with Mr. Manker, and then, like Emily, to the opera, also. He wanted none of Leah this night, and so he blessed the opera, and he drank his drink.

He enjoyed being alone to reflect. And he enjoyed his drink, because it would be his only one, and he could taste and savor it and not use it as a lethal potion. What would he do this evening? He would buy some American magazines at the newsstand in the lobby, dine by himself at an isolated table in the Winter Garden, and then come back to the suite. He would change into his pajamas, crawl into bed, make some notes on *Return to Ithaca*—several ideas for scenes had occurred to him in the last day or two—and then read a new English biography of Kierkegaard that the students of Uppsala had given him. He would fall asleep early, and awaken early, refreshed, and take Emily out for breakfast and a long walk.

He finished his drink, went into the bathroom, rinsed the glass and left it beside his toothpaste, found his knit tie and knotted it for dinner. He had pulled on his dark gray suit jacket, when he thought that he heard someone at the door. He went to the curtain and listened. The knocking was repeated.

He hurried to the door and opened it.

A young lady stood beyond the doorframe, in the corridor. "Hello, Mr. Craig," she said.

He did not recognize her. A Robin Hood hat was tilted above her auburn bangs. She had a nose like the beak of the common tern. Her lips, closed, seemed to give her no more than one lip. She was garmented in a thick coat of military cut, and under an arm, like a diplomatic pouch chained to a wrist, she carried an oversized black leather purse.

As she prepared to introduce herself again, her eyes began to blink disconcertingly, and Craig immediately established her identity. "Don't you remember?" she asked. "I'm Sue Wiley of Consolidated Newspapers."

He remembered, and he wanted to slam the door in her face, but he was too sober for rudeness. "What can I do for you?" he said coldly. "Or are you here to see if I can walk a straight line?"

"I'm sorry that upset you so, Mr. Craig. I was only doing my job. How am I supposed to get stories, if I can't ask questions?"

"There are jobs and jobs," said Craig. "Lizzie Borden had a job, too."

"She was acquitted," said Sue Wiley. "Look, Mr. Craig, I told you I'm sorry if—"

"I'm not going to invite you in," said Craig, "and I'm not just going to stand here. Tell me what you want."

322

"I have someone downstairs who'd like to meet you—someone I think you'd want to know—"

"Who?"

"At your press conference you praised Gunnar Gottling as the most talented writer in Sweden. He's in the lobby. I promised to introduce you."

Immediately, Craig was interested. Still, he hesitated. "What's Gottling got to do with you?"

"I happened to meet him in the line of duty. I've been interviewing all prominent Swedes about the Nobel Prizes. I arranged to see Gottling this afternoon. We had some drinks. He's a great talker and bursting with information. Anyway, your name came up, naturally, and he had a lot of things to say about you and the literary awards. I told him you were at the Grand and asked if he'd like to meet you, and he said he would. I suggested maybe the three of us could have dinner. So he drove me over—"

"Miss Wiley, I'd like nothing better than to meet Gunnar Gottling. But not with you, no thanks."

Sue Wiley's Univac brain digested, calculated, and computed rapidly, from long training. She fed the machine Gottling. She fed the machine Craig. She fed the machine herself. Apparently, the combination did not add up. One click, and she subtracted herself. Gottling and Craig added up. Another click. When flint struck flint, there would be a fire. If she could not have the story firsthand, she could have it secondhand. Reinforced by alcoholic fuel, Gottling would give her the result tomorrow. Click.

"All right, Mr. Craig, no hard feelings," she said. "If you don't want me around, it's your privilege. I've got my story from Gottling already, so it doesn't matter. I'll limit myself to good Samaritan, and maybe you'll give me one mark on the credit side of your judgment ledger. I'll introduce the two of you and make myself scarce. How's that?"

Craig remained suspicious. This was a young lady who did not wear altruism well. He watched her blinking eyes. "You'll make yourself scarce? How scarce?"

"Totally, completely. I'll introduce you and vanish into thin air. I'll even drop dead, if that's your wish."

Craig still did not like Sue Wiley, but he could no longer be suspicious. A meeting with Gottling, on an unplanned evening, was irresistible. He admired Gottling's uninhibited, earthy, iconoclastic prose. Craig as author had breathed life again, and now he wanted to sustain this existence. Dinner with another writer, a foreign writer, one whom he admired, would be stimulating. "Okay," he said to Sue Wiley. "Let me get my overcoat."

They went through the corridor together, and then down in the elevator, without exchanging a word.

As they emerged into the bustling lobby, Sue Wiley pointed across the way toward the newsstand.

"There he is," she said.

Gunnar Gottling was stamping around a table at the far end, hands clasped behind him, ignoring the stares of whispering guests. What Craig saw first was a barrel figure of medium height, made to appear shorter by his bulk. He wore an eccentric fur cap and a mangy fur coat, open and billowing, as he paced. As they drew closer, Craig could make out the fierce Cossack face. The brow was narrow Cro-Magnon. The eyebrows were shaggy and unkempt, like strips of rug samplings. The sunken eyes were more red than brown, because they were bloodshot. The mustache was not a mere lip adornment but two wild bushes of hair that covered the mouth and portions of the cheeks. The chest was that of a bartender at the turn of the century, and the suit coat over it was pocked with drink stains and cigarette holes.

"Mr. Gottling," said Sue Wiley, "this is Mr. Craig."

Gottling gargled and coughed, and enveloped Craig's hand in his own, crunching it. "So—so—so," he growled.

"I know you were both looking forward to this meeting," said Sue Wiley, trying to watch both men at the same time.

"Yes, I've enjoyed two of your books, Mr. Gottling," said Craig.

"You are a good reader," said Gottling. "About your writing—we will talk soon. First, we must drink." He looked about the lobby, sniffing with distaste. "This stinks. It's for the fat ones. Are you a fat one, Craig?"

"I'm not sure what you mean."

"Flesh and gut flabby with security and gadgets and showing the Joneses?"

"Hardly," said Craig.

"Don't let that Nobel bribe get you that way. That's Judas money. It sells you out to conformity, to pleasing, to commercialism. Never a damn honest word written by any prize winner, after he got the boodle. Christ, this place stinks. Where should we drink and eat?"

Sue Wiley caught Craig's glance, and quickly said, "Count me out, Mr. Gottling. Work, work, you know—"

Gottling glowered at Sue Wiley. "What do you mean—work? For a female, that atrophies the ass. The best thing you can do, young lady, is go out and get yourself laid."

Gottling's voice acted like a sonic boom, and there were many in the lobby who turned, wide-eyed and horrified. Craig wanted to crawl under the table. But Sue Wiley was the product of countless city rooms and pressrooms, and she did not flinch. "Mr. Gottling, thank you for your advice, but I like my work. And thank you for the interview. It was swell. I hope you'll see me again. And good night, Mr. Craig."

She took her leave with dignity.

"Cerebral and sexless," grunted Gottling after her. "Your typical American dame."

"If she were typical, I'd give up my citizenship," said Craig. "I promise you, she's not."

"Not? The hell she's not. How many American women you slept with, Craig?"

"I don't know. A dozen. Two dozen. I've never counted."

"I, Gunnar Gottling, have counted. I did not count after the first one hundred. All of them the same, the same, except the Polacks. All the same.

Ouija boards have got more movement." He snorted. "I know where we'll tank up. Ever been to Djurgårdsbrunns Wärdshus?"

"I'm not sure."

"If you been there, you'd be sure. Best tavern in Sweden. Fifteen minutes from here, out in the park. Come on."

Gottling stalked out, with Craig towering over him, a stride behind. The frozen night air hit them with a blast, and they both staggered, then bolted for Gottling's compact Volvo station wagon.

A few minutes later, they were speeding to the outskirts of the city. Craig suspected that his host was myopic, but too vain to wear spectacles, for Gottling hung over the wheel, his eyes squinting through the close windshield, as he concentrated on the road ahead.

"You like my English?" boomed Gottling, as he wrenched the car around a turning.

"It's colloquial enough. One would think you'd lived in the United States."

"Where do you think I lived? Six years in your lousy country when I was a kid full of piss and vinegar. Got me off a Norwegian freighter and thumbed my way to Chicago. Worked in the stockyards and as a bouncer and then mixed drinks in a joint on the South Side. Used to spend my day off in Comiskey Park so I could get drunk with company and yell, and spend every night humping those colored girls. Ever tried that for luck, Craig?"

"Never. Only for lack of opportunity."

"You missed nothing. They smell good, and they got big tits, and they go through the motions, but they're overrated. The white boys imagine too much. Expect all kinds of African animal pleasures. Not so. Those colored broads in Chicago are too neurotic and bound up and angry. How can you give out to someone you resent? So it comes out just like with the white broads—except the Polacks, they're special. They got the tiger in them."

"Why did you go to the United States, Gottling?"

"Like I said, I was a kid, piss and vinegar. And I'd done my share of reading. In those days, Sweden wasn't for poor kids. That was before all this fancy welfare state crap. In those days, there was the muck-a-muck on top, and the serf on the ground. I wanted a place where I could flex my muscles and be what I wanted to be. It was either Russia or the United States. Well, I didn't go for that Bolshevik crap, never did, and still don't. No lousy commissar's ever going to tell Gunnar Gottling what to do. So I took a flyer at the United States. That was crap, too. Blue laws and puritans and bloomers. Except for some cases used for advertising in your history books, the real story was—the poor stayed poor, and the rich got richer. Democracy. Ha!"

In the darkness of the bumping car, Craig looked at this outspoken, angry man. "I know what you're against, Gottling. What are you for?"

"Anarchy, pure and simple. I talked to those boys down in Barcelona once, several years back. They got it right, if they ever come out in the open. Anarchy, that's right. Back to the tribes and freedom absolute. That's my allegiance, to that and the Republic of Gottling. Three bona fide citizens in the Republic of Gottling—me, myself, and I. Title of my autobiography, if I ever get down to writing it."

He drove in silence, and then took his eyes off the road a moment. "You said you read my books, Craig. Which?"

"The two published in English. The one about the Lapland girl who comes to Stockholm, and what civilization does to her. And the other one, about the farmer who gets a job in—in Malmö, I think—and brings his family to the cooperative housing place."

"Did you like them?" he asked brusquely.

"I told you, they were damn good. A little long, a little rough, but first-rate."

"You're damn right. I wish I could say the same for your books."

Craig stiffened. "Say whatever you want. This isn't the Boy Scouts of America on an outing."

"You're a featherweight, Craig. You write scared. That's what makes you a featherweight."

There was a squeeze of resentment in Craig's chest. Who the devil was Gottling anyway? The bully boy of unread literature. Craig was not letting him get away with anything tonight. "Who writes scared?" he said. "I've tackled important themes, problems. That's more than you've done."

"Don't go thin-skinned on me," mocked Gottling. "I know your goddam important themes. But why sneak off and do your hollering a century or two ago? Now's the place, in this world, among the bastards of this world, to do your sounding off. Belt them head on. The day you do that, you'll be great, the champ. Right now, you're only cute, a fancy Dan who gets it on points, but nobody knows if he's got a punch. Know what I mean?"

Craig knew too well what he meant, and he knew what Harriet had once meant, but tonight he did not like it at all. He had come out with Gottling, he realized, to have his ego further inflated. And now, this. His ego had been too recently revitalized to stand up under punishment.

He sat sullen and wordless.

"Here we are," said Gottling. He yanked the wheel, and they spun off the road, parking at the foot of a flight of stone stairs. These climbed to the entrance of a building that resembled an eighteenth-century English inn.

It was too cold to linger outside in the Volvo station wagon. They hurried up the steps and into the warm reception room of Djurgårdsbrunns Wärds-hus. As a waitress helped him off with his topcoat, Craig observed, to his left, the main dining room, immaculate white tablecloths and several early couples, and to his right, the barroom, which was more densely populated.

"What'll it be, Craig?" Gottling wanted to know. "Food or spirits?"

"I could stand a drink."

Gottling grinned grotesquely from beneath the ferocious mustache. "I can see we'll get along."

They made their way into the noisy barroom. There were about a dozen men in the room. Some were on stools at the bar, several watched a Swedish play on the television set, and the rest hunched about the wooden tables. Al-

326

most everyone, it seemed, knew Gottling, and they greeted him with affection, and he cussed at them with affection. He led Craig to a corner table, somewhat apart from the others, and they settled on chairs covered with a plaid material as thick as horse blankets. Gottling ordered a double gin on ice, and Craig ordered a double Scotch on ice, and they both waited, pretending to be absorbed in the activity of a young man throwing darts at a worn board beneath the television set.

When the drinks came, Craig downed half of his in a single gulp, enjoyed the familiar spread of heat through his veins, and then drank again. He became aware of Gottling's gaze and half turned to meet it.

Gottling nodded in approval. "I'd heard you were a drinking man, Craig. I think that's why I bothered to come out and meet you."

"Who said I'm a drinking man?"

"That dame with ground glass in her genital canal—your Miss Wiley."

"That bitch."

"If she didn't tell me, I'd know anyway. I can spot a pro when he bends his elbow. Amateurs sip and suck and nurse, and they make it a secondary occupation. But the pros, you and me, we pour it down like we know there's a lot more where that came from and like it's the most important thing, which it is, except for an occasional lay and sometimes writing."

"I don't like drinking, Gottling. I take it the way Socrates took the hemlock cup—a necessity better than living."

"You're a mighty complicated guy."

"Sure I am. Did Sue Wiley tell you that, too? Let's have another drink."

Gottling shouted across the room at the bartender, and in seconds, fresh drinks appeared.

"Why'd you see her?" Craig asked.

"Who? The dame with the ground glass down under?"

"That's right. Did you want publicity?"

"You baiting me, Craig? I get enough publicity. This dame called up and said she heard I'd been nominated six times for the Nobel Prize and never got it, and she was writing a series about the whole machinery, and did I have anything to say. Well, my friend, that Nobel Prize is one of my favorite table topics. When I can let off steam on it, it gives me as much pleasure as an orgasm. So I told her to come right over. She filled two notebooks."

"Why didn't you ever get the prize, Gottling?"

"Why didn't Strindberg get it? Same difference. Consider my track record. I've been divorced twice, the first time for beating my wife's head against the wall and the second time for laying my stepdaughter. I've had a Danish mistress for five years—she wears glasses to bed, and that's what gets me—and I let her give interviews for me. I've had four illegitimate children. I've been arrested and in jail six times, for drunken behavior in public. And my literature isn't exactly idealistic. And that book where the Lapp girl comes to Stockholm, and the city corrupts her and turns her into a whore, well, my fellow Swedes are touchy as hell. They didn't like it a bit. Still, I didn't put the blast on them, and I kind of waited, because I figured I'd get the prize sooner or later, like old Gide and old Hamsun. I mean, I'm the only Swede writer around who can write his name. And that Swedish Academy, those academic boys, they love to masturbate—honor themselves, their own—and sooner or later, I figured, they'd want to honor a Swede, and it would have to be me. I don't give a damn about the honor. I wanted the dough. I can always use the dough. But I have my pipelines, and about two years ago, I found out it was no soap. So I said what the hell, you can't have everything in life, and now I'll have some fun with those bastards. So in six weeks of boozing and scribbling, I got me a novel about the eighteen immortals in our Academy—thinly disguised, thinly—what they're really like after hours—and, man, what a yelp there was. I made the kronor, and they made the threats about hauling me into court, but they were afraid. The book's never been published in your country. Too special. But I settled our Nobel Committee good, and that's why you're never going to see my name beside yours and old Thomas Mann and old Rudyard Kipling."

Craig downed his second double, and ordered a third, and so did Gunnar Gottling.

"What did you mean about the judges liking to honor themselves, their own?" Craig asked.

"Nepotism, my young buck, good old-fashioned nepotism," said Gottling. "Four small Scandinavian countries—Sweden, Norway, Denmark, Finland—with about as much talent, per capita, as you could put in a thimble, but one big mutual admiration society. Take the first sixty years of the Nobel Prize. Those Scandinavian countries got thirty-one of the prizes. Can you believe it? Thirty prizes in the first fifty years. Sweden and Norway kept patting themselves on the back, and each other, and their Nordic neighbors. What crap."

"It's not what Nobel wanted, is it?"

"Who knows? I don't suppose so. He said the prizes should be given without regard to nationality. But his heirs didn't believe him. They put the screws on right from the beginning. You've heard of Bertha von Suttner? Nobel's secretary? Well, when she didn't get one of the first Peace Prizes, the Nobel family went to Oslo and said, in effect, look, Nobel set up the Peace Prize for old Bertha, so let's get on the ball. Sure enough, in 1905, old Bertha got the prize. After that, the doors were wide open. Who in the devil ever heard of Nathan Söderblom outside Scandinavia? But look up 1930. He won the Nobel Prize for peace. Why? Why not? He read the services at Nobel's funeral. And he was the Archbishop of Uppsala. And so it's gone. How many people outside Scandinavia read von Heidenstam, Gjellerup, Jensen, Sillanpää, Pontoppidan? All Nordics. All laureates. Hell, in 1931, the Swedish Academy broke its most inflexible rule to give their prize to a dead man. They sure did. They loved their Secretary—nice guy—poet by the name of Erik Axel Karlfeldt, and his widow and daughters needed the dough, so they gave him the prize. Very touching. But what has all that got to do with honoring great writing, and what does that make of the prize itself?"

"It's still the most respected prize on earth," said Craig.

"Of course it is. You know why? Because most of the democratic world has abolished titles and all that crap. But men are human. They yearn for titles, for an elite, for an upper class. The peasants have their equality, but there is the old nostalgia for royalty. So along comes the Nobel Prize, at the right time, at the turn of the century when everything is drab and dull. The masses were waiting for it. They made it the new knighthood. That's why it's respected and popular. Because people are masochistic, inferior fools." Gottling swallowed his third double gin. "If they only knew what crap goes on behind the scenes of the awards, not only nepotism, but all the narrow prejudices and politics."

"I don't think that's a secret," said Craig. "Jacobsson took me up to the Academy yesterday, and he was damn honest about the literary voting. He said there was good and bad."

"Jacobsson," Gottling muttered, rolling his glass on the table. "Count Bertil Jacobsson? That old stuffed parrot, he should have been put in a time capsule years ago. He lives in the past. He has nothing to do with breathing people. Why do you think the Foundation supports him? Because he's a front—he's got blue blood, he knew Nobel, he makes with the erudition and history—and part of his gambit is to anticipate criticism. I wager you ten to one, he gave you the old routine—why Tolstoi and Ibsen and Hardy didn't get it—but reminding you of all the big names that did. It's all technique to disarm visitors and send them off beaming. Studied frankness to strip you of your objectivity. And another wager. I'll bet you he wasn't frank enough to confess how the Nobel committees have always sucked around the Germans—like that turd, Krantz—and looked down their noses at the Americans, at least until the Second World War, and how they got a permanent boycott going on the Russians."

The whiskey had gone to Craig's head, and the room reeled. "I like Jacobsson," he said.

"You Americans love everybody," growled Gottling, "just to be sure somebody loves you. What crap. So you like Jacobsson. But did he tell you how his Nobel crew ass-licked the Germans and put the knife in the Russians?"

"No, he didn't. I better have another drink."

"Me, too. . . . Hey, Lars, refills!" He turned his bloodshot eyes back to Craig. "You like this old Wärdshus?"

"Greatest place on earth," said Craig thickly.

"You're damn right."

"What about the Hun?" asked Craig.

"Germans? Forty-nine prizes in sixty years. Russians? Seven prizes in sixty years, and lucky at that."

"I'd say that shows courage," said Craig, "thumbing your nose at Russia, when they're looking down your throat."

"Courage, ha!" exploded Gottling. "Every Swede is scared stiff of Russia, and when it counts, Sweden crawls. Why do you think we didn't join NATO? Because we're afraid of Russia, that's why. I wish we had half the guts that Norway has. They defied the Nazis, when we didn't, and now they defy the

Communists, when we won't. Like giving that 1961 award to old Dag Hammarskjöld, knowing the Bolshies hated him dead or alive. But us next door? We're yellow, a yard wide, and we know it, and we don't like it. So how do we salve our national conscience? We make believe we're men by childish crap—by sticking our tongues out and keeping the Nobel Prize from Russia. So where does that put the holy Nobel Prize? It puts it in local politics. It makes the prize a political instrument that you dumbheads in America —except the Polacks—consider an honest honor. Christ, what crap."

The new drinks came, and Craig spilled part of his before he brought it to his mouth. "You said something about the prize being anti-American and pro-German—"

"That's what I said. Cold figures. I may be looped, but I got it all in my head. Take chemistry. Only one American, Richards of Harvard, won it in thirty-one years. Take physics. Only one American, Michelson of good old Chicago, took it in twenty-two years. Take literature. Only one American, Red Lewis, in thirty-five years. Take medicine. Only two Americans, Carrel and Landsteiner, in thirty-two years. But the Germans—oh, our Nobel boys worshiped them. Fifteen winners in the first ten years, not counting the peace prize, which isn't worth spitting on. In Sweden, if you could show a degree from Frankfort on the Main or Heidelberg, you were practically nominated. For forty-some years, those krauts were the superior race over here, Nordics just like us. But when you kicked the hell out of them in the Second War, and when you came up with the atom bomb, there was a fast shuffle in all the Nobel committees—and now they pour prizes at you and Great Britain like it was confetti. Don't ever talk to me about impartiality, when you talk to me about that lousy prize you won."

"What's wrong with the prize I won?" Craig peered at Gottling with owl eyes and spilled his drink again.

"What's wrong? Haven't you been listening to me? You plastered or something? I told you about Russia—"

"I forgot."

"Seven Russians in sixty years in five categories, and not one of them a clean-cut award. It's not just anti-Communism. It's plain anti-Russianism. We been shaking in our boots since the time of the Czar. What happened in physiology and medicine in the first sixty awards? Old Pavlov should have carted off that first award hands down. But no, the Committee kept snubbing him for four years, until there was so much pressure they gave in. And they had to give half of Ehrlich's prize to a Russian in 1908, because it was on the record he deserved half the credit for advances in immunity. Two stinking medicine awards to Russia in sixty years and none in a half century of that sixty years. Take a look at chemistry. One-half of the 1956 prize, and that's it, brother, that's all in sixty years. What about physics? One prize, divided among three Russians, in sixty years. There's your science awards. I'm not a Russky lover. I told you before, they stink. But what's that got to do with accomplishment? That's a country where they've done the best work in longevity and genetics and stuck a Sputnik and a guy named Gagarin in the sky. That's a country where they invented artificial penises for soldiers wounded in the war. That's a country where Popov demonstrated radio transmission before Marconi, and where Tsiolkovsky had multistage rockets in 1911. But not according to our Swedish Academy of Science—no. According to our Nobel idiots, Russia is the land without scientists. And those idiots in Oslo are just as bad. Russia didn't get a single Peace Prize in sixty years, but Germany—Germany!—got three and France eight and you Americans twelve. And now, my son, we're home again—literature."

"Bunin and Pasternak," mumbled Craig.

"Ivan Bunin and Boris Pasternak—two Russians in sixty years. Ever think who lived and wrote in Russia in those sixty years? We all know about Tolstoi being turned down nine times. But what about Chekhov and Andreyev and Artsybashev and Maxim Gorky—Gorky was around until 1936. Nothing."

"Bunin and Pasternak," repeated Craig.

"Phony!" bellowed Gottling, but no one in the Wärdshus bar so much as looked up. "Bunin was a White Russian refugee, an anti-Communist, who lived in Paris and translated Longfellow's 'Hiawatha.' He hadn't been in Russia in fifteen years, when you Americans pitched for him and put him across in 1933. And old Boris Pasternak, the matinée idol with good guts, out there in his *dacha*—who gave a damn about him when he was writing solid poetry? Who honored him then? Not the spineless Nobel judges, I guarantee you. But the minute he put out that novel that criticized communism, the minute he had the nerve to say what every Swede was afraid to say, they crowned him with the prize he couldn't accept. Someday, I got to write advice to writers all over the world. I got to tell them, 'Writers, arise! If you're Russian, if you're American, no matter what, grind out an anti-Russian potboiler and get it translated into Swedish, and you're in. You get the Nobel Prize and the big boodle. Just like Andrew Craig.'"

Craig squinted at Gottling through bleary eyes. "What in the hell does that mean?"

"The facts of life, kid," said Gottling, belching, and swallowing his gin, "the facts of life. Why do you think you got the Nobel Prize? Because you're a hotshot author? Because you're the best this year? Because you're the leading idealistic literary creator on earth? That what you think? That what Jacobsson and that bag, Ingrid Påhl, told you? Because you're somebody, in the league with Kipling and Undset and Galsworthy and O'Neill? Crap! You're nothing, and the Nobel boys know it, and everyone in Scandinavia on the inside knows it. You're here on a phony pass, because they wanted to use you, and that's all. And, brother, that's the truth. Have another drink?"

"What are you talking about?" said Craig. His brain and mouth were fuzzy, but a distant alarm registered. "Is this some more of your sour grapes?"

"I'm the only guy in Sweden with guts enough to level with you, Craig. I got enough pity for that. I don't want to see you making a horse's ass of yourself. The Nobel Prize for literature to Andrew Craig? Ha! Crap. The Nobel Prize for anti-Russian propaganda, that's what it should be. You won because the Swedes have been having a diplomatic squabble with the Russians over two islands in the Baltic Sea—you never read about that, did you?—and the Swedes are going to lose, and crawl, and eat crow. But they got to keep face—that's our one Orientalism, keeping face—and so, knowing they got to lose, they unloaded a rabbit punch at the Commies by honoring your little anti-Communist fiction, *The Perfect State*. That's to show we're big boys, not afraid of anybody, even when we crawl."

"You're making it up, Gottling. You're bitter, and you've got to get your jollies some way. If the Swedish Academy wanted to blast Russia through an award, they could find novelists in a dozen countries who'd written stronger anti-Soviet books."

"Oh, no. You're blind, man, you don't see at all. An award to a writer of a work overtly anti-Russian would be too dangerous—they don't want Pasternak all over again. That was too much of a sweat—they don't want to stand up and body-punch. Like I said, they just wanted to sneak in a quick rabbit punch, for face, for conscience. Your novel is anti-Russian, all right, but you got to cut away the sugar coating to know it. If Moscow gets sore, and they have—I read *Ny Dag*, that's our Commie sheet here—the Swedish Academy can just look surprised—and they have, too—and shrug and say they were honoring a pure historical novel about Plato and ancient Syracuse. You see? But everybody knows different. Only the way it is, nobody can prove it. It's a scared gesture, like whistling in the dark, just like yours is a scared book."

"To quote Gunnar Gottling—you're full of crap."

"Am I? The hell I am. Listen, if I wasn't loaded to the gills, I wouldn't be telling you this. But I got two good friends in the Swedish Academy. They're the ones who nominate me every year. And after every voting, I get a play-by-play. When your name came up, there were only three of the twelve, the Påhl witch and two other innocents, who thought you had more on the ball than A. A. Milne or Edgar Guest. You were dead, until somebody brought up Russia and those two Baltic islands. Then there was heated talk about Russia, and then someone said the only good thing about your book was that it showed the Russians up—that is, if you read between the lines—and in about an hour, the majority agreed that if you got the award, it would show those Russians, it would really show them. And so you got it. And we've shown them. Sorry, kid. You'll write some real books one day, but that wasn't the one, and we all know it—so go home with your money and your title and don't knock luck."

Craig sat very still. The film of alcohol that covered him, like a placenta in the prenatal chamber, was not enough to protect his frail rebirth as a man. Until now, he had only listened to Gottling, only taken him half seriously. The ravaged Swede was a carper and a dissenter, who made himself larger by making other men smaller, and once you understood that, you understood him, and relaxed and enjoyed it. But this last had the sound of truth, and if it was truth, it was devastating. Craig wanted his rebirth here in Stockholm, one last rebirth of his ego and soul, whole and healthy. If this one miscarried, if this one was stillborn, only the death of sterility as an author lay ahead. He would not accept Gottling's rotten exposé.

"You're trying to get me sore, Gottling. You can't. I've got your number, you see. You're a defeated, bitter wreck. You can't get up with the rest of us, so you do the next-best thing. You try to drag us down into your gutter. You get away with each ambush by flying the flags of candor and honesty, but your real banner is a deep sickness of the soul. If you weren't paying for these drinks, I'd bash your nose in."

Gottling grunted, and he twisted to face Craig fully, his eyes twinkling. "Don't try it. I eat laureates. I break them in small pieces and eat them."

"Not this one. I doubt if you could take this one. You *are* paying for the drinks?"

Gottling was silent a moment. "Yeah. I'm paying."

"Okay, then."

"Craig, you can't get me to fight you. Because I like you, I like you too much."

Craig's eyes mirrored his surprise.

"Sure," said Gottling. "I know you're a zero, and I know you know it. Maybe someday, you won't be. Someday, you'll be a figure—if you live that long—but now you're a zero. Still, I like you—you know why? I'm not ashamed. I'll tell you why. Because you put it in the papers that I'm talented and should've won the prize. You put it in the papers that I'm talented. Nobody's said that in a long, long time, and nobody with a title ever said it at all. I can live off that until I die."

"But if I'm a zero, and say you're talented, what does that make you?"

"Maybe you're not a zero, and maybe even I'm not. I never was good at figures. Have another drink, Craig. It's on me. I'm paying all the way."

How Craig had arrived outside this large gymnasium, on Valhallavägen near the old Olympic Stadium, some time before 10:30 at night, was not clear to him.

He did not remember Gunnar Gottling's dropping him off at the Grand Hotel, and driving away. Craig had stood swaying for some time before the entrance, wondering what he should do. The weather was freezing, and the area before the entrance was deserted—even the saluting doorman had taken cover inside—and the only signs of life were the two taxi drivers locked snugly in their vehicles and asleep.

At first, Craig had not minded the cold. Alcohol seemed to preserve him against it. He had stood there, rocking from leg to leg, and weighed his one problem and his three possible solutions.

His problem had been—emptiness. The brainchild, the child of hope, attended and nursed to life by Jacobsson at the Swedish Academy, by Emily, by the students in the morning and afternoon, had been delivered stillborn, after all. Gottling's self-serving attack had shattered him. He was no more alive than he had been that late afternoon, in Miller's Dam, that hour before the telegram, when Lucius Mack had put him to bed, and he had passed out. Yes—emptiness.

As he had stood there in the biting wind, the solutions were three. If the opera were over, there would be Emily, restorer of life, life giver. But to come to her this way, shorn of strength, weak of will, muddled and sottish, might repel her forever. And another thing, another thing, and this you felt at once in your head and your heart and between your thighs. You wanted the reviving clamp of woman love.

Craig desired this desperately, the potion of anti-emptiness, to prove his worth to himself and the earth's worth to him. He wanted to put a needle in a doll, deeply, and incant the magic that would dissolve the big, bad Gottling. He wanted Emily, but she would be unprepared, unbriefed, without the knowledge necessary for understanding, and the force of his passion would start her running, and after that, he would never find her. No, it could not be Emily.

He had considered the second solution, which had a sanity and logic of its own this wintry night. Leah, the rigid Leah. His loss and drunken need would be familiar, understood, readily accepted. He thought of Leah, hair loosened to her shoulders, known Slavic features, sagging teats, and muscular thighs. There he would find easy admittance and comfort, and later he would sleep well, released of ambition and guilt, and the battle would be over, at last. For long moments, in the cold, the temptation of it, the simplicity of it, had almost drawn him inside. But then, in the clarity of the icy wind, the hotel became the house at Appomattox, and if he entered now, he would be Lee, when he really wanted to be Grant. No, this was not surrender day.

For, by then, he had pictured the third solution. Freya, Swedish goddess of carnal love. The solution was a night's miracle, inviting no danger, demanding no surrender.

Immediately, Craig had gone to the nearest taxi, awakened the startled driver by rapping on the window, and asked to be taken to Polhemsgatan 172C.

When they had arrived at the apartment, the elderly portvakt had been in the entry hall, performing some repair. He had come to the door out of curiosity, and then recognized Craig from the other time. At once, he had hobbled outside, waving his hands, and making a long and negative speech to the taxi driver.

"He is saying," the driver had told Craig, "your lady friend is not home tonight. Once a month, she goes to her club, and that is tonight." Craig had wanted to know when Lilly would be back. The portvakt could not say, although he thought it might be late, it was usually late. "Find out where she is," Craig had ordered the driver, "and then take me there." He had not thought it out. He had only considered his need, and her unselfish readiness to serve him. He had only known that he must rescue her from the banality of clubhood so that, in turn, she might save him.

And that was how, at this late hour, on this freezing night, he came to be standing unsteadily before the entrance of the square gymnasium on Valhallavägen.

He made his way, stumbling, across the walk to the green door, pulled it open with effort, and staggered inside. Despite the cement floor of the entry hall, the room was well heated by a pounding radiator. The room was barren of all furnishings, except for a table and a chair behind it, now filled by a masculine, middle-aged woman in a brown suit. She had a metal card file open before her, and was sorting cards and stacking them, and she looked up with a puzzled smile when Craig approached her.

"I'm looking for Miss Lilly Hedqvist," said Craig, enunciating each word clearly. "I'm told she is a member here. I'm an American friend. I wonder if I could see her?"

"Well—" said the receptionist.

"It's very important that I see her."

The woman rose. "If you will excuse me." She strode off vigorously, quickly opening and closing an inner door.

For Craig, the delay was tedious. There was no place to sit, so he tried to pace, but his gait was unsteady, and at last he resigned himself to immobility by leaning against the wall.

Suddenly, the inner door swung open, and the receptionist held it, while two people passed into the entry hall. One was a tall though stooped elderly gentleman with the face of a fox, wearing incongruous attire. He was clothed in a polka-dotted blue bathrobe and beach sandals. The other was Lilly Hedqvist, and she wore a white terry-cloth robe and was barefooted.

While the elderly gentleman hung behind at the table, with the receptionist, Lilly, her golden hair gathered up with a ribbon, her brow pinched with concern, padded quickly across the cement to Craig.

"What is it, Mr. Craig?" she asked in an undertone. "Are you well?"

He was fascinated by her terry-cloth robe and bare feet. "What kind of club is this, anyway?"

"Our nudist society. I told you once, remember? In the winter, we meet once a month in this gymnasium, for sunbathing under lamps and for lectures. Tonight is a special meeting for the new membership. How did you know I was here?"

He told her, but he was still fascinated by the terry-cloth robe. "Is that what everyone wears—robes and swimsuits?"

"No. You do not understand. This is my nudist society. I have nothing on underneath the robe. We are all free and open, for good health. New members sometimes wear these transition robes for a few minutes, until shyness is gone, and then they take them off. I borrowed this from the closet to come out. I could not dream who was here."

"Lilly, can you get away now? I've got to see you."

"It is impossible, Mr. Craig. I am secretary this year. I must make notes on the meeting. Then, I want to hear the lecture for the new members."

"How long will it be?"

"One more hour."

"An hour? I can't wait alone that long. What'll I do?"

She was troubled by his mood, and she wanted to help, and at once her face brightened. "I know what. You can come inside and sit with me. It will be a good lesson for you, anyway. Maybe you will learn health."

"Sure, if I can be with you."

"Let me see. I will ask our director."

Craig remained leaning against the wall, and watched and listened, as Lilly went to the elderly gentleman, with the polka-dotted robe, and began addressing him in rapid-fire Swedish. The gentleman replied, and then Lilly spoke some more, and the gentleman kept glancing across at Craig, as if evaluating him. At last the gentleman nodded, and left the room.

Lilly returned triumphantly to Craig. "It is all right," she said. "He was worried at first, because they have not interviewed you, but I said you were an old friend of my relatives in Minnesota—"

"You have relatives in Minnesota?"

"Of course not. I convinced him when I told him you belonged to the American Sunbathing Association in New Jersey—I have read about it in our pamphlets—and I told him I had seen your card, and you were interested in our Swedish nudism and wanted to attend a meeting."

"Then it's all right for me to be with you?"

"It is all right."

They started for the inner door. The receptionist, still standing, bowed her head in welcome, and then they went through the door. Craig followed Lilly, and wanted her more than ever, but restrained himself from touching her. They reached two more green doors.

Lilly pointed to the right-hand door. "That is to the gymnasium. When you are ready, come in. I will be waiting for you. Try to hurry. The lecture begins soon." She indicated the door to the left. "You go in there. That is the locker room for men and women. You will find an empty locker for your clothes."

She started to leave, but Craig grabbed her shoulder.

"What do you mean—locker for my clothes? What am I supposed to do?"

She seemed surprised. "Undress," she said simply. "This is the nudist society. I am nude. Everyone is."

"Lilly—for God's sake—I've never done anything like that."

"I have seen you naked. You were not ashamed."

"Of course not. But this is in public—men and women—"

"Mr. Craig, you will find it is easier than you think, and normal. There is nothing indecent about human anatomy. Clothes, even a little clothes, that is what makes people curious and lascivious. When everyone is unclad, there is nothing to it. It is so natural, you will see. You will not be curious and think evil thoughts, and you will feel different. Now, quickly undress, and come so we do not miss the lecture."

Craig knew, as Lilly spoke to him, that some of her phrases had the quality of pamphlet phrases being recited. But her face was earnest, with a kind of religious fervor, and Craig did not dispute what she had to say.

Having finished her sermon, Lilly hastily opened the gymnasium door and was gone. Craig stood drunkenly by himself, trying to make sense of this comedy. Then he remembered that Lilly, in all solemnity, was waiting, and that he could not disappoint her. My God, he thought, do all drunks have

336

these strange adventures, all drunks and rudderless people? And then he thought, what the hell, they're here for kicks, so give them some and have a few yourself, and get it over with. With that resolve, he went into the locker room.

Inside the narrow locker room, that resembled all the locker rooms he had known in boyhood and in the army years, and that smelled of wet shower floors and slippery soap, he removed his topcoat and jacket. Seeking an empty gray locker, he opened three that held garments, two that were filled with men's suits and one that held a woman's skirt, blouse, and underthings, and for another moment he hesitated, wondering if he dared give in to Lilly's caprice.

The fourth locker was vacant, and in it he hung his topcoat and suit coat. As he sat on the bench to remove shoes and socks, he tried to articulate to himself what bothered him. Despite Gottling, he was a man of importance, in a time of importance. What if Sue Wiley or some other member of the press, or even Jacobsson, should learn he had been here? It would prove the suspicion, held by some, that he was a hopeless alcoholic. He could see the headlines in the American tabloids: DRUNKEN NOBEL WINNER GOES NUDIST. No honor would counteract this damage. Decidedly, Alex Inglish and Joliet College would not have him on their staff.

Once he was barefooted and shirtless, he knew that his fear was not of scandal but of something else, and that, as ever, he had been rationalizing his hesitation. He unbuckled, and unbuttoned, and unzipped his trousers and stepped out of them. What remained was his blue shorts, and what remained was his real fear. Mentally, the evening had depressed him, but physically, drink and despair had stimulated him. He had wanted Lilly's body, in nudity, and he had wanted it savagely, and he wanted it still. Now he would face her disrobed, and see her stark naked, and the emotional charge would be uncontrollable. And there would be other girls, perhaps as beautiful as Lilly, and he would see their private parts, and be a slave to wild imaginings, and would react sexually. Would it happen to him? Did this happen to men at nudist gatherings? If it did, God help him. What a spectacle he would present.

He took off his shorts, threw them into a locker, and now he was a nudist, the nudist laureate.

He strode into the corridor, looked off to see if the receptionist was watching for him, but no one was there. At the gymnasium door, he wavered a last time. He stood straight and unclad and wondered what you did with your hands. Where were modesty's pockets? He would keep his arms dangling straight down at his sides. Well, the hell with it. He yanked at the door and went into the gymnasium.

The lights—not the overhead lights, but the banked sunlamps across the floor—blinded him, and he shaded his eyes. Before he could adjust himself to the vast hall, or to who or what was in it, he saw Lilly. She was advancing toward him, carrying a pad and pencil in one hand, and she was smiling. He had not seen her completely naked in the light before, and now there was nothing to conjure up in passion's mind. It was all there before him, revealed, obvious, matter-of-fact, and natural. The two young-blown fleshy breasts bobbed as she walked, and the nipples were not points, as he had remembered them, but circular crimson stains, flat and soft and the texture of velvet. Below the navel fold, the body rose and fell and swelled in perfect lines of classical Hellenic female maturity.

Craig was moved that this was his, and yet, to his relief, he was not moved with desire. It was as if, with many others, he was sharing enjoyment of a wonder of nature. There was detached, objective pleasure, but there was no sexual involvement.

"Now, do you not feel better?" Lilly was asking.

"I'm still a little drunk."

"I know. But it is good to have your clothes off and be like God made you and be healthy, is it not?"

"I suppose so. . . . You're incredibly lovely, Lilly."

"We do not speak or think of such things here," she said, but enjoyed the compliment. "All nudists are lovely in one way or another."

"What's going on here?" he asked, looking off. His eyes had become accustomed to the glare, and now, for the first time, he could make out the nudists in the gymnasium.

There were bodies everywhere, and of every description, at least two hundred men and women, young and old, some lying on mats beneath the sun lamps, some sitting on the rows of wooden benches communing with one another, some standing about in conversational groups, and a dozen or more playing volleyball. There were lanky men and chunky men and skinny men and fat men. There were middle-aged women and young women, and small immature breasts and mountainous breasts and some as perfect as Lilly's own. There was no self-consciousness, no inquisitiveness, no atmosphere of sexuality. Almost no one looked at Craig, as he moved toward the front of the row of benches with Lilly, and soon he found that there was no need to study or stare at anyone else.

Lilly indicated the third bench, and they seated themselves, and she crossed her bare legs to support her pad.

"Well, what do you think, Mr. Craig?"

"I'd never have believed it possible," he said.

"What do you mean?"

"To see so many females in a state of undress and not be a bit aroused."

"I told you it would be so," she said. "It is clothing that arouses. If a woman wears a dress, there is always a man who thinks of what is beneath it. And little pieces of clothes are the worst, like the low-cut gown or bathing suit or bikini, because they put your eyes and attention on certain places of the body. But if you are nude and see those places of the body revealed on everyone else, there is no mystery or stimulation, and you take it for granted, and you are healthy. Mr. Tapper—he is our director you saw in the entrance —he has said it is suggestion that makes all the trouble. He has said millions of dollars are made through suggestion of sex, because people are curious about the mystery. The burlesque in the nightclub, the fadeout in the cinema,

338

the asterisks in the book—they are to tease you about the anatomy. But if you are a nudist, you are not teased, and it is open and better."

"I never knew you were a student of morals, Lilly," said Craig with a smile. "But yes, Mr. Tapper is right, and you are right. All I've got against public nudism is that it would do away with sex."

"Oh, Mr. Craig, you are joking."

"Yes, I am joking," he said.

Mr. Tapper, divested of his polka-dotted bathrobe, proved to be all ribs and knob knees, and looked oddly incongruous behind a public address microphone. He was calling the meeting to order in Swedish. Men and women lifted their bodies from the mats, and the conversational groups broke up, and the volleyball game ceased. Everyone was being seated, row upon row of shoulder blades, spines, and buttocks against wood.

"He will speak in Swedish," Lilly told Craig. "I will translate for you."

In a dry monotone, Mr. Tapper began his address. While she was making her jottings, Lilly interpreted the address for Craig. Mr. Tapper was tracing the history of the nudist movement. It had begun, in theory, in Germany during 1903, with the publication of a book entitled *Die Nacktheit* by Richard Ungewitter, the son of a watchmaker. The author had advocated a nude society, to relieve men and women of constricting attire, to give them freedom of movement and enjoyment of air and sun, and to make all parts of their anatomies commonplace so that seduction and adultery and perversion would be reduced. Shortly afterwards, perhaps inspired by Ungewitter's proposal, another young German, Paul Zimmerman—a schoolteacher turned farmer, who had raised his four daughters to disdain clothes—opened the world's first nudist camp, called Freilichtpark, in Klingberg am See. To enter the park, one had to give up alcohol, tobacco, meat-eating—and all garments. The nudist park was a success, and within twenty years, there were 50,000 nudists in Germany alone. The idea spread quickly, to Switzerland, to Scandinavia, to England, and finally, by 1929, to the United States. The same year that nudism reached America, it had its mightiest triumph in Germany. For, that year, in Berlin's Volksbühne Theater, a nudist troupe staged a vaudeville show. This show, composed of dances and acrobatics, was open to the public, although every performer was naked. Today, said Mr. Tapper, nudism had spread to nearly every nation on earth, and was universally accepted.

"Now, before anticipating the questions that new members have in mind, I should like to say a few words about nudity in general," said Mr. Tapper. "Modesty is unnatural, and it takes on various forms throughout the world. If you came upon a naked Swedish or French or American woman by accident, she would first cover, with her hands, her pubic area. But, as one Langdon-Davies has remarked, if you came upon a naked Arab woman, she would first cover her face before all else, and a Laos woman would first cover her breasts, and a Celebes woman would try to hide her knees, and a Chinese woman her feet, and a Samoan woman would try to conceal her navel. As you see, this reduces modesty to the ridiculous, and shows you how unhealthy it can be. Under international nudism, the naked woman's face, breasts, navel, pubic area, knees, feet, could all be revealed, and she would have to cover nothing, for there would be nothing to fear."

Mr. Tapper droned on in Swedish, and for a while Lilly was too busy recording in her notebook to interpret his remarks. Once Mr. Tapper paused to accept a drink of water, and then Lilly whispered to Craig, "Now he will give questions and answers to the new members."

Mr. Tapper scratched his abdomen, cleared his throat, and resumed, and Lilly interpreted his words as best she could.

"Our new members may wish answers to certain questions. I will give them. What is our goal? To provide, through nudism, better health, more relaxation, cleaner minds and higher morals. Do we permit cohabitation and sexual activity in our outdoor park? No. Such misconduct means immediate dismissal. Can members wear shorts? No. Concealing garments of any kind only provoke and excite. The only exception made is that women may wear shorts during their periods of menstruation. Will members, primarily the male members, ever have to worry about becoming sexually aroused and embarrassed at our meetings? No. This has never once occurred in our history. The mind, from which sexual passion originates, is apparently not stimulated by large groups of nude people. I am reminded of the experience of Jan Gay, who wrote a book about her first visit to Zimmerman's nudist park. The new members among you may find Miss Gay's first reactions similar to your own. 'To be sure,' wrote Miss Gay, 'the first time one enters such a class, one is aware of other people's bodies to a considerable degree; but when one mingles all day, day after day, with naked men and women, a penis comes to be not much more unique than an elbow or a knee and little more remarked; and the contours of one woman seem very much like those of another, save that some are more shapely.' New members will soon understand this reaction.

"But let us resume our answers to questions. Will membership in a nudist society ever cause you trouble if it is publicized in the less tolerant outside world? No. In America, nudists know each other by their first names only, and membership lists are never made public. In Sweden, we do not have such a problem. As you know, our Stockholm newspapers, as well as the newspapers in Copenhagen and Oslo, annually publish photographs of our summer festival King and Queen, and these photographs are entirely nude, and the winners are much admired and respected."

Listening, and somewhat sobered, Craig realized how absorbed and diverted he had been. And the interesting part of it was that his absorption had not been in the shapes of the nude young girls all around, but in the director's talk.

Although he was a writer, in these last years his roots had not spread, had not found new areas of interest and experience, had almost withered and died. Tonight, he had been entertained by an absolutely new adventure on earth. The subject of nudism, as such, was nothing that personally attracted him. But the fact that there was here a whole new level of living and devotion, nonconformist and even bizarre, yet attracting so many fellow humans, and he had known nothing about it, was what interested him. His thirst for knowledge, for hearing facts, for observing people and incidents, was once more alive and a part of his being. In his absorption, he had been able to forget, for a time, the bitter encounter with Gottling and the hollowness of his Nobel victory. He had almost been able to forget his earlier sexual desire for Lilly, now unclothed beside him. He had not even given thought to Leah or Emily. He was once more, as he had not been for three long years, a writer-sponge, soaking in fresh sensation. It was strength to know the writer-sponge was not completely atrophied.

Presently, Mr. Tapper was finished, and the formal part of the meeting was ended. Most of the members rose, some to return to their mats beneath the bank of sunlamps, some to resume their volleyball game, and the rest to enter the locker room and dress for the outer world.

"It is over now," said Lilly. "We can put on our clothes and leave."

She stood up, while he still sat, and her naked body—from the full pink breasts thrust forward as she straightened, to the dipping lines of flesh curving down to her groin—loomed above him in female beauty. This was what he had imagined, in the earlier evening when he had hunted her. Yet now it moved him not at all. It was one more naked body, out of so many, without mystery or provocation. He sighed, and came to his feet. Perhaps this was not their night. Perhaps it would be best to drop her off at her apartment and go back to the hotel and sleep.

They followed the others to the crowded locker room, a mass of men and women dressing amid a babble of Swedish talk. Her locker was across from his, and they separated briefly. Hurriedly, he pulled on his shorts and trousers, and got into his shirt, stuffing the tails carelessly inside the trousers, and then he took his socks and shoes and sat down on the bench to put them on. As he sat, he could see Lilly directly across the way. She was still naked, and had just finished talking to a plump young woman who was securing her dress.

Tying his shoes, he watched Lilly arrange her clothes on the bench and automatically begin to dress. It fascinated him. It was like a filmed striptease run backwards. She held her brief nylon panties before her, and stepped into one leg opening and then the other, and pulled them up tightly so that the elastic band came to her navel. Then she sat on the bench, rolled her sheer nylons, inserting one foot, then the other, and unwinding the nylons up her slender calves and up her thighs, and fastening the stockings at her thighs with garter bands.

Now, when she stood, her nudity partially clothed, her bare breasts seemed to expand and grow. A trick of the imagination, Craig knew, because the panties and stockings had focused attention on what was still revealed. She slipped into a white cotton blouse, and began to button it, and Craig remembered that she had disdain for brassières. The indigo jersey skirt was on, a single tug of her hands circled it into place, and she was pulling the zipper. Her sandals were on her feet, and her thick woolen sweater was over her arm.

Craig was ready, and he met her between the benches, and they went into the corridor. Briefly, they were alone. She halted to put on her sweater. She poked one arm into the sweater, and tossed her golden ponytail, as he assisted her with the other arm. Coming around her, face to face once more, he could see that the upper button of her blouse was open, and he could see the cleavage between the breasts.

He tried to picture the breasts and nipples now pressed behind the blouse, and he tried to picture the thighs beneath the skirt, and at once, all at once, in that instant, he was moved by a consuming passion for what could not be seen, and by a hungry desire to see it and possess it. For the first time since entering the gymnasium, he was physically aroused.

It amused him, and he smiled.

She saw his face, and took his hand. "What is it, Mr. Craig?"

"Just a private thought," he said. "I was thinking of the most incredible thing on earth."

"What?"

"Man," he said.

And then he squeezed her hand, and started with her down the corridor, wondering how long it would take her to undress.

VIII

What awakened Andrew Craig was the sound of voices from another room.

When he opened his eyes, he instantly realized that he was lying on the folding bed of Lilly Hedqvist's living room. Hazily, the events of the night before were recalled—Gottling, in the Wärdshus, drunkenly revealing how the Nobel Prize in literature had been inspired by politics, not art; the nudists in the gymnasium, unclad and bizarre, listening to a speech by their director; Lilly and himself, on this bed, performing their protracted lovemaking.

Only the last memory made sense, and Craig tried to revive the details of it, but at last he gave up. He had been more inebriated than he believed. A few fuzzy amatory pictures remained. The rest was a void. The surviving evidence of pleasure, aside from the rumpled bed, was his languid body frame. His mind contained neither hangover nor remorse; his limbs were loose.

He would have chosen to remain in bed all morning, but then he remembered the voices that had roused him. Undoubtedly, one voice was Lilly's. He glanced at the clock. It was already after nine o'clock. Why was Lilly here? Why wasn't she at work? And the other voice. Who had come into the apartment—friend? enemy?—and seen him this way, and was now in the kitchenette?

The voices, indistinct, resumed their give-and-take, and Craig realized that one of the voices was male. Alarmed, Craig immediately sat up, and then lifted himself off the bed, gathered up his clothes and shoes, and hurried into the bathroom.

The shower and drying, the dressing and grooming, took him twenty minutes. When he emerged, somewhat combative over the compromising position Lilly had put him in (alleviated quickly by the realization of the compromising position he had put her in, and by the further realization that she had no idea at all, or at least had not expressed an idea, of his importance and news value), he noted that the pull-down bed had apparently been made and raised back into the wall, and that the living room was all neatness and chastity again.

He went into the kitchenette, prepared for anything.

At first he thought that Lilly, at the two-burner stove in the foreground, was now alone. The morning was dark, and there was but a single window and a weak lone electric bulb overhead. She was a delight to the eye, as usual, golden hair combed free and long, throat exposed and young, wearing a crisp cocoa dacron blouse and dark tan swing skirt. She had just finished pouring coffee, as he entered, and her spontaneous friendly smile showed him even white teeth and no regrets.

"Good morning, Mr. Craig. Did you rest?"

"I'm wonderful, Lilly. I thought I heard—"

He stopped short, in mid-sentence. His gaze had gone past Lilly, to the shadowed end of the kitchenette, where, leaning casually against the service porch door, holding a saucer in one pudgy hand and a steaming cup in the other, stood a man.

"I want you to meet my best and oldest friend in Stockholm, Mr. Craig," said Lilly. "This is Nicholas Daranyi. He does not like to be reminded of the Nicholas. Everyone must call him Daranyi."

"Like Garbo or Duse," said Daranyi. "Or, for that matter, Kitchener. It would be less to call him Horatio Kitchener. Immodest of me, perhaps. But we all have our little vanities." He had set down cup and saucer, and now he came forward to accept Craig's hand. "I am pleased to know you, Mr. Craig."

Under the electric bulb, Craig was able to appraise the intruder. Daranyi was in his fifties and below middle height. His head was large and fleshy, and was sparsely covered with hair that had been oiled, then parted well to one side and combed to cover a balding spot. His face was sleek, too closely shaved, and the jovial cheek fat made the eyes into slits. But the eyes were merry, and the long nose and mouth amused, and you thought of yuletide and were sure he wore a costume to surprise all children at Christmas. Preceding him was a considerable potbelly, and you wondered how the legs, so thin, held him upright. His gray suit, faintly checkered, was short at the sleeves and short at the trouser cuffs, but pressed and clean and fastidious, with signs of rubbed usage. His total appearance was unmistakably Middle European, and even in this foreign place, he looked foreign. He smelled of exotic soap and strong cologne.

"I confess a certain embarrassment," said Craig frankly.

"By why?" asked Daranyi ingenuously. "Because you overslept?"

Lilly turned from the tray she was preparing and clapped her hands with delight. "Oh, Daranyi, do you not understand? Mr. Craig is a nice American with Pilgrim morals. He is ashamed to be found in the bed of an unmarried woman."

"Yes, I see," said Daranyi gravely. "But, Mr. Craig, you are in Sweden, not in your native Minnesota—"

"Wisconsin," interjected Lilly.

"—native Wisconsin. Moreover, I am like a father to Lilly." Then, he added quickly, slit eyes bright, "A tolerant and sophisticated father, that is."

"I don't know how I would have lived without Daranyi," said Lilly, finishing the tray. "When I left Lund four years ago, I knew no one here except for three letters of introduction. One was from an aunt to Daranyi. He found me the job with Nordiska Kompaniet. He helped find me this apartment.

He bought me my television. And on my two mornings off, and on Sundays, he drives me wherever I must go. Without him, I would be lost."

"Pay no attention to Lilly, Mr. Craig," said Daranyi. "She overvalues me constantly, to my secret delight."

"And Daranyi knows," Lilly went on gaily to Craig, "that the Swedish girl has a trial, with more women than men in Sweden—"

"Six women to every five men in Stockholm," said Daranyi precisely.

"—and a girl so old as twenty-three, like myself, will be an old maid, and mean and nervous, if she does not have a man she admires in her bed at least every fortnight. So do not be embarrassed, Mr. Craig. I am sure Daranyi will tell you that when he came this morning, he was pleased to find you in my bed."

"It is true," said Daranyi with equanimity.

"Now, into the living room, gentlemen," said Lilly. "We will have breakfast."

Somewhat bewildered, but enjoying himself, Craig followed Daranyi into the living room. Daranyi cleared the glass coffee table and drew up the two wicker chairs, and Lilly served fruit juice, ladled out the scrambled eggs from an earthenware dish, and put cups of coffee before them. Then they all sat and ate.

"Lilly tells me you are a writer," said Daranyi to Craig.

Craig, his mouth full, nodded.

"Fiction or nonfiction?" inquired Daranyi.

"Fiction," said Craig.

"Then it is unlikely I have read you. In my work, one has little time for novels. I must spend my book time with politics and biography, current and past, and most of my time for reading I give to newspapers and periodicals."

"What is your work, Mr. Daranyi?" asked Craig.

Daranyi had brought the fruit juice to his lips, but now he held it poised. "I am a spy, Mr. Craig," he said, and then, he slowly drank down the juice.

Craig knew that his face was foolish with astonishment. He had made his inquiry casually in passing, not expecting anything of interest, expecting perhaps that Daranyi might be an insurance salesman or shoe clerk or civil servant. Instead, he had named the most improbable profession on earth. Craig decided that his ears had deceived him. "Did you say—spy?"

"That is correct," said Daranyi, wolfing down his eggs. As he chewed them, he went on. "It is not the happiest profession any longer. Once, it was. But no more. If I had a son, I would not let him follow in my footsteps. I would rather let him be a dentist."

Craig remained nonplused. Was the potbellied man having sport with him? He appeared serious enough, and Lilly, committed to her breakfast, was hardly listening and certainly no part of a joke. "But if you're a spy," said Craig, "whom do you work for? And how can you even mention it?"

"Among friends I can mention it," said Daranyi. "If I do not mention it, how will I find clients? Besides, most people do not take me seriously. It is an unlikely profession, is it not? Most people think I am having fun with them. There is no need for secrecy, except when I am actually at work. When I am at work, I am undercover and discreet. As to whom I will work for, the answer is—anyone who will pay well. I am the last of a breed almost extinct—the free-lance spy."

"Exactly what does that mean?"

"It means, Mr. Craig, that ideological amateurs have almost put the professional spy out of business. The operation of the Soviet Union is typical. Their intelligence need not shop for expensive agents abroad. They know there are enough idealistic Communist fanatics or fellow travelers who will do the job with dedication at cut-rate fees. The Dr. Allan Nunn Mays, and Dr. Fuchses, and Rosenbergs have made my lot a hard one. There were always national agents, of course, but there were free-lance spies, also. For example, Gertrud Zelle—you know her as Mata Hari or H. 21. Hundreds of men and women who had no allegiance but to themselves and the nobility of their profession, worked for any nation, at any task, on a flat-fee basis. As a young man, in Budapest, I aspired to this profession, as one does to law or medicine. From my reading, it appeared that while there were risks, the inducements were worth while—constant travel, interesting people, excellent food, considerable income, and possible immortality in histories. In the Second World War, I worked for the Germans in Istanbul. I had cultivated some peculiar talents —one of them lip reading—and I would sit in the cafés and restaurants and read the moving lips, across the room, of American and French and English diplomats and pass on their conversations. After the war, I did some valuable work for the English in Jordan and Palestine. You see, I play no favorites. Emotionalism is synonymous with starvation for one like me. The German mark and the English pound buy the same food and clothing."

"How did you come to Sweden?" Craig wanted to know.

"I could not go back to Budapest, nor did I wish to," said Daranyi. "I was stateless. I had no genuine passport, although I had several faked ones that I had used. I cold-bloodedly selected Sweden as a perfect base of operations. It is near Moscow, near the two worlds of Berlin, and yet with powerful American and English influences. And Sweden itself, in its anxiety to remain neutral, is an excellent espionage customer. It was not difficult to obtain an assignment here as a minor foreign correspondent. Once here, I made myself useful to several persons in high places, and they have seen that I am permitted to remain. Stockholm has its faults. It goes to sleep too early. It is not Paris or Rome or Vienna or Istanbul. But there are worse places. My income is limited, but my needs are modest. I have a pleasant routine. I have good friends like Lilly."

"Tell Mr. Craig about Enbom," said Lilly from her coffee.

"Enbom, yes," said Daranyi. "Lilly is proud of my part. So am I. You see, Mr. Craig, I make no pretenses with you. I am no great one like Alfred Redl or Jules Silber or Fräulein Doktor Elsbeth Schragmüller. First, I came too late to my profession. My kind of espionage is now outmoded, as I have said. Second, I am a coward. I am not ashamed to confess it. I am a spy who is scared. With such limitations, I do not receive many important assignments. In some ways, I have been reduced to a researcher. My last assignment, a month ago, was for a Danish industrialist, who desired certain private knowledge of a new Swedish competitor. Before that, I made an investigation for a member of the Royal Swedish Academy of Science—"

Craig was surprised. "A Nobel judge?"

"As matter of fact, yes," said Daranyi. "Dr. Carl Adolf Krantz, an old client of mine. You have probably never heard of him. At any rate, I had better not speak of that."

Craig said nothing, although he was curious. He found his pipe and filled it, and remained attentive.

"But occasionally, rarely, but sometimes, an important case comes to me. Such was the one Lilly refers to—the Enbom case, in 1952. You have heard of it?"

"I'm sure I read about it," said Craig, trying to remember.

"It was the most important spy trial in our history," said Lilly. "And Daranyi played a role."

"Fritiof Enbom was a reporter for a Swedish Communist newspaper in Boden," Daranyi said to Craig. "That is our vital fortress in Lapp country, near Finland. He was a Swede, and one of those ideological spies I was telling you about. He was an agent for Soviet Russia. He started during the Second World War for Russia. He had secreted a radio transmitter. He came often to Stockholm. When he did, bringing with him reports of our fortifications, he would leave a twisted hairpin in the crevice of a house near the Russian Embassy, and then the Russians would call on him. All went well, until 1951. Then he had a falling out with the Communists, quit his newspaper in Boden, and moved down here to Stockholm. Since Enbom needed a job, he asked help of some of his old Swedish Communist comrades in the government. They refused him. Enbom was extremely put out. One night, complaining to a friend, he told what he had done for the Communists as a spy. The friend, a loyal Swede, went to the Ministry of Defense. Enbom was promptly arrested. So were his brother and mistress—here is where I came into the story, but I cannot yet reveal what I was hired to do or who hired me—and also arrested were four others. Enbom was charged with selling military secrets to Russia for ten thousand kronor. The others were charged the same. Enbom was convicted and given Sweden's harshest penalty—life in prison at hard labor. Of the others, one was acquitted, and five also sent to prison, although for lighter sentences. But, you see, sometimes my life is not so drab. Perhaps someday you will want to write my story, Mr. Craig?"

Craig smiled. "Perhaps, someday."

"The real point," said Daranyi, "is that Stockholm deceives tourists. It is orderly, immaculate, prosperous, so much so that it seems hopelessly dull. But it is not as it looks. Neutralism makes this a free playground for conspiracy. The Enbom case was one that happened to be made public. You take my word, there are a hundred other intrigues, as varied as the smorgasbord, in this city."

"It's hard to believe—like being told the Brontë sisters were really a spy ring," said Craig. He looked at Lilly, who was patting her mouth with a napkin. "I suppose Lilly is one of your agents?"

"No, she is quite hopeless," said Daranyi. "She has no talent for the devious."

"I think," said Lilly, "my frankness upsets Mr. Craig. I tricked him into joining our nudist society last night."

Daranyi shook his head. "Not for me. You have more courage than I have, Mr. Craig. Never in a million years would I expose my belly to that pack of health fiends."

"I don't remember much about the experience," said Craig. "I'm afraid I was drunk."

Lilly lifted her arms behind her head and stretched. Her breasts expanded outward against the cocoa blouse, but nothing was revealed, and Craig realized that, for the first time, she was wearing a brassière. Craig wondered why.

"Well, whatever it was, the drinking or our nudist meeting, it agreed with you," said Lilly to Craig. "You were wonderful in bed last night."

Craig felt his face redden. "So were you, Lilly."

Daranyi coughed and spoke. "We used to have a Prime Minister in Sweden —Per Albin Hansson—who was a prohibitionist, and his favorite quotation was from Aristotle. It was, 'Those who go to bed drunk beget only daughters.' A word to the wise."

Lilly waved her hand at Daranyi. "Do not be an old father goat. Am I a child? When I was in school in Vadstena, and I was seven, I was taught about the fertilization of the ovum, and by the time I was twelve, I had learned in the classroom about contraceptives. You tell your Aristotle I will beget no daughters." She turned. "Are you relieved, Mr. Craig?"

"Not if they'd look like you."

"American men make prettier speeches than Swedish men." She glanced at her wristwatch, and suddenly leaped to her feet. "We will be late. Hurry, Daranyi." She looked at Craig. "Are you busy at the hotel?"

"Not especially."

"Then you must come along with us. There is someone I wish you to meet. It will delay you only an hour. After that, Daranyi will drop me off at NK and return you to the hotel. Is that all right?"

"I'm with you," said Craig.

Lilly did not bother with the dishes, but hurriedly brought her coat, and the men's coats, from the closet. She was all rush now, as they made their way into the hall, down the elevator, and outside.

"Some of the canals are frozen over from last night," said Daranyi, as they walked to his car. "But today is not so cold. Gloomy, though. Yes, look at the clouds."

"Do not waste time," said Lilly. "You know it is bad if I am late."

The car proved to be a black Citroën. Despite its age—it was at least ten years old—it gleamed with care and polish. There was not a nick, not a dent, and the chrome was shining. Craig helped Lilly into the front seat, and, himself, got into the rear, as Daranyi squeezed behind the wheel with an exhalation.

They started with a forward jerk, and then smoothed out. Daranyi drove stiffly, like all fat men, and correctly, like those on a temporary visa, and he drove not at excessive speeds but steadily.

"Where are we headed?" Craig once asked.

"Near Vällingby section," said Lilly. "You will see. No more questions."

Craig settled back, and smoked contentedly, as Daranyi related anecdotes of the life of a Hungarian in Sweden, and Lilly was quiet, lost in her own thoughts.

In a short time, on a wide street of apartment buildings and modern shops, Daranyi slowed the vehicle, and edged into a parking space against the curbing. They left the Citroën and made their way, with Lilly several strides ahead, to a two-story stone building. Craig could not make out the Swedish lettering above the door, as he dutifully followed the other two inside.

They were in a hall, and then in a reception room. The room was neatly furnished with an oak sofa that had a wickerwork back and four chairs featuring cowhide seats and a large center table holding two rows of Swedish magazines.

"You sit and be comfortable," said Lilly. "I will be right out."

She disappeared through a glazed door. Daranyi sat and picked at a magazine. Craig hunted about.

"What is it?" inquired Daranyi.

"I'm trying to find an ashtray."

"They always forget. Mostly women come here, and rarely do they smoke in public." He pointed off. "There is one, on the window ledge."

Craig crossed, mystified by their locale, emptied his pipe of ashes into the ceramic tray, filled the bowl again, lit up, and found a chair.

"Why all the mystery?" Craig demanded to know.

"Sometimes Lilly likes her fun," said Daranyi.

They waited five minutes, neither speaking, when suddenly the glazed door opened, and Lilly appeared. She was carrying a straw-haired boy in blue jeans, a little over a year old, and she was cooing at him and rubbing his nose with her own, and he was giggling.

She turned him around in her arms, handling him as she would a puppet, and she bowed him toward Craig.

"Arne, I want you to meet a friend of ours from far away—Mr. Craig." She smiled across the room at Craig, who half rose, blinking in stupefaction. "Mr. Craig," continued Lilly, "I want you to meet my son."

Then, without waiting for Craig's reaction, she pointed the boy toward Daranyi and lowered him to the floor. "There is Uncle Daranyi. You may kiss him."

The little boy waddled, unsteadily, but with secure familiarity, to Daranyi's outstretched arms. Daranyi engulfed him in a hug, and then worked through his coat pocket and produced a grape lollipop, and handed it to the boy, who took it and kissed him. The little boy turned, saw Craig's strange and amazed countenance so high above, backed off in fright, and trying to run, fell down. Lilly was on her knees at once. She scooped him up, cuddling him. "Did Arne hurt himself?" she whispered. "Mommy loves Arne."

Standing with the boy in her arms, Lilly faced Craig. "What do you think of him? Does he look like me? He is so smart for fourteen months, but he is shy."

"He's beautiful," said Craig, and he meant it. "I didn't know you'd ever been married, Lilly."

"But I have not ever been married," Lilly answered cheerfully. "I am still an old maid. . . . Excuse us now. Arne and I must meet the guardian. See you later."

Craig considered himself sophisticated in many respects, and Stockholm had made him more so, but his amazement had turned to undisguised shock. Dazed, he watched Lilly leave the room with her son.

He felt Daranyi beside him and looked down. "You are startled, yes?" the Hungarian asked.

"I'm stunned."

"But not appalled?"

"Nooo. Not appalled."

"I am pleased with you," said Daranyi. "Lilly would not want your disapproval. She did not tell you before, because she feared that you would not understand with words. She is a woman who lives by instinct. Her instinct was to let you see her son first. When you saw him with her, you would understand better."

"I'm not sure I understand anything," said Craig, "but I'm not appalled."

"Exactly," said Daranyi. "Perhaps I can make you understand. Come with me. There is a Norma chain restaurant on the corner. Lilly will meet us there soon. We can have coffee, and I can make you understand."

They walked outside, and the short distance to the corner, and in the Norma restaurant they took the counter seats at the far end, apart from the other morning customers.

After Daranyi had ordered coffee for Craig, and coffee and a sweet roll for himself, he spun on his counter stool toward Craig.

"To make you understand," he said seriously, "I must request a trick of magic. Presto, you are no longer in your Wisconsin or on America's Main Street or anywhere in your United States. You are in Scandinavia, in a different moral climate, a more unusual and progressive moral climate. Is that something you can do?"

"I can try. She called him her son. You can't have a son by yourself. Was it an accident?"

"Not at all an accident, Mr. Craig. Arne's conception and birth were planned."

"You're kidding?"

"Mr. Craig, divest yourself of the old shibboleths. One out of every ten children born in Sweden is illegitimate."

"I'm not a puritan, whatever Lilly says. Far from it. But somehow, you don't expect this of someone you know—know intimately—or thought you knew."

"But it always has to be *someone*. Why not someone you know? People become millionaires, and sometimes it has to be someone you know. People murder and are victims, and sometimes it is someone you know. People divorce, and they commit suicide, and sometimes it is someone you know. Little Arne is the one out of ten in Sweden."

"How did it happen? You said it was planned."

"Two years ago, a well-known Swedish architect, rather handsome and impressive, came into Nordiska Kompaniet to buy a dress for his wife's birthday. Lilly was his salesclerk. They fell in love with each other. Young women like Lilly do not believe in promiscuity, but they do believe in love, not sublimating it but expressing it and enjoying it. They had an affair. As I said, this architect loved Lilly, but he also loved his wife and three children. Lilly is sensible, you can see. She knew that she could never possess him legally. But if marriage was denied her, she wanted the fruit of marriage. She wanted a child in her lover's image. So they talked it over, exactly like married couples, and they went ahead. Soon enough, Lilly was pregnant."

Craig tried to keep an open mind. Daranyi was making it too reasonable. "But the consequences—didn't she think of that?" Craig asked.

"There are no consequences in Sweden," said Daranyi. The coffee had arrived, and he dropped two cubes of sugar in his cup and stirred them. "The word bastard is unknown here, and that is as it should be. After all, Mr. Craig, the newborn child has committed no sin."

"Right," said Craig, "but still—"

"Sweden does not encourage illegitimacy. Women like Lilly do not prefer it. Marriage is still the ideal. But life goes on, and love happens, and Sweden faces these facts. Because every child's birth, by either a married or unwed mother, is recorded here, and accepted, Sweden has the highest illegitimacy rate in the world. Sometimes, I wonder. I think that is only because they admit to what other countries hide and make ugly."

"You mean Arne actually won't suffer?"

"He won't suffer at all. When Lilly was ready to give birth, I drove her to a state hospital, and the father, the architect, was already there. After Arne was born, Lilly was put in a room with two married mothers, and treated exactly as they were. The cost of the hospital and doctor was only one krona a day—maybe twenty cents American—a virtue of socialized medicine so detested by your American doctors. The government gave Lilly four hundred kronor as a gift, for her immediate needs. While she was still in the hospital, the appointed guardian appeared. You see, the Swedish welfare state thinks of everything. In 1917, around that time, they established what they call the Svenska Barnavårdsnämnden or Child Welfare Committee, to supervise unwed mothers. This organization has female guardians, trained for two years in sociology, psychology, child care, and it assigns a guardian to each unwed mother. The guardian gives advice, sees that there is money, and so forth. Lilly's guardian has been visiting her and the boy every month—today they are meeting in the government nursery building, where we were—and soon, the guardian will look in maybe only twice a year, until Arne is eighteen."

"How does Lilly manage?"

"I was coming to that, Mr. Craig. The Swedes, as I have said, are sensible. Every child must have a father. Very well. If the father does not volunteer his responsibility, as Arne's father did, the state finds the father with help of the mother. If he admits paternity, all is well. If he refuses to admit it, he is given a blood test. If the blood test is positive, he is automatically the father."

"But blood tests aren't always accurate," said Craig.

"No, they are not, but they are better than nothing. There are a few inequities, I am sure, but very few. If the blood test is negative, and the father cannot be found, or if the father is found but too poor to help, the state takes over financial support of the so-called illegitimate youngster. Lilly's architect, of course, admitted paternity at once. He now gives Lilly ten per cent of his monthly income to take care of Arne."

"What does the architect's wife say to this?"

"He has never told her. If she outlives him, one day she will know, for Arne will receive part of the inheritance. More often, the men tell their wives. There are scenes, but I have never heard of a divorce over this."

Craig stared at his coffee, but had no interest in it yet. "Mr. Daranyi, I don't want to pry, but—does Lilly still see her son's father?"

"No. That was over with a half year ago. The decision, you must believe me, was Lilly's own. She finally fell out of love with him. She saw that he was not really her type. She is happy now that he was not free to marry her, or there would be either an unhappy marriage held together by the child, or there would be a divorce. In case you wonder, she is still pleased to have the little boy. For the time, Arne is her life. She keeps him in the state nursery all the time now. But later, she will let him be there only in the day, while she works, and at night and Sundays she will have him in the apartment."

"And there is no disgrace whatsoever?"

"Mr. Craig, when Arne was born, Lilly put a birth announcement in the newspapers, and she sent blue cards of happiness to all her friends. She has several friends in similar circumstances. One girl, in the nudist society, and with a good job—she was thirty-four and dying to have a baby, but because of the man shortage she was afraid she would never find a husband. At her job, she discussed this problem with her employer, whom she admired, and he cooperated, and now she has a daughter. Is that not better for a normal woman than living barren and sterile and withered? And is it not better for the child, at least when he comes by accident, to recognize him and make him like everyone else, not to do what is done in other countries, make him sinful or dead by abortion, or make the mother a fallen woman or a suicide or forced into a shotgun marriage? I think so."

Craig nodded slowly. Understanding had come, and in an hour he had grown again. "Yes," he said, "I think so, too."

"You heard Lilly speak of her sex education in school. That is universal here. No girl, no boy, graduates without complete knowledge about intercourse, birth, abortion, contraceptives. That would be impossible in your country, because the churches would not allow it. But here the Lutheran Church is the state church, and the state dominates it. Here the church is weak. Hardly anyone attends it. Education and realistic government supplant it. Is that so bad? Let us be honest. Swedish young people are no different in their sexual needs from American young people. At seventeen, eighteen, nineteen, the urges are the same everywhere. But in America, the love is illicit, all behind the barn and in a lovers' lane and in motels, and spoiled by shame and guilts and secrecy. Here the love is not illicit. It is natural. If a girl loves a boy, she has intercourse with him because it is the normal thing to do. If the love continues, they marry. If it is not good, they do not marry. I have read the findings of your Dr. Chapman, who took the sex survey of your married women in America. What were his statistics? Four out of ten married women had premarital sex relations. Well, there was a similar survey in Sweden. Here, eight out of ten married women had intercourse before they were married, and the majority by the age of eighteen. You see, Mr. Craig, they are freer here, and no worse for it. In fact, better for it. Marriages here are more solid. A man does not marry a woman so that he can sleep with her. He sleeps with her, and then marries her because he does not want to be without her."

Craig sipped his coffee absently. Lilly was on his mind. There was a question, and by now, it should not have troubled him, but he was a product of his past. "What will happen to Lilly?" he asked.

Daranyi shrugged. "Who knows? She is still young. Swedish women marry relatively late. I believe the average marries at twenty-six or so. Lilly has found men she loves. Maybe one day, she will find one she loves enough to marry."

"Why did she—why did she submit to me?"

Daranyi smiled. "She did not submit to you, Mr. Craig. You submitted to her."

"I'm not so sure."

"I am. Lilly has love on her own terms."

Craig set down his empty cup. "It all seems different now," he said. "Up to last night, it was just a—a side adventure—a tumble with a lovely girl. But now—"

"Now what, Mr. Craig?"

"I can't say exactly. It seems she deserves more. And her son, despite what you've said—he deserves more."

"Mr. Craig, I detect in you the incurable disease you hold in common with all your countrymen."

"What is that?"

"Guilt, Mr. Craig, guilt—from cradle to the grave."

"But the boy—"

"Do not worry about the boy. He is Arne Hedqvist, secure and accepted. He does not have horns. Lilly knows—I have told her—that some of the greatest names of history were illegitimate children—Leonardo da Vinci, Erasmus,

Pope Clement VII, the younger Dumas, your Alexander Hamilton, our Strindberg. They managed. Arne will manage better. And Lilly will manage, too. She has no guilts. Perhaps this is a good day for you. Perhaps after today you will have no guilts, either."

Daranyi looked past Craig and waved.

"Here she comes now," he said, turning his seat and rising. "We must go."

Craig came to his feet slowly. He wished he could discuss all this with someone, someone close. He tried to think of Miller's Dam and Harriet, but neither came alive. What came alive was the vision of Emily Stratman. If only he could speak to her, but he could not, because between them was an invisible barrier. Both had reached to surmount it, but they had not touched. Emily was, as yet, unreal. Only the girl with the golden hair, before him, was real, but here again was guilt, the smooth-rubbed Leah guilt.

What, he wondered, does one owe all others?

When does one belong to oneself alone, oneself alone?

Dr. Hans Eckart had left the taxi, and, in his unbending, goose-stepping stride, approached the goateed, diminutive figure who had answered his summons, and now waited on the street corner.

"Carl," said Eckart.

Carl Adolf Krantz whirled around, and without bothering to take Eckart's formal gloved hand, he grabbed his arm and pushed him toward a doorway.

"In there," said Krantz with urgency.

Annoyed, Eckart made the concession to the Swede's foolish melodrama, and permitted himself to be pushed into the open recess of a *konditori* entrance.

"What has got into you, Carl?"

But Krantz was peeking at three receding figures, a stout man, a tall man, and a young woman, across the street. *"Gott sei dank,"* he muttered at last, "he did not see us together."

"Who?" asked Eckart with exasperation. *"Um Himmels willen*—what is this idiocy?"

Krantz had recovered, and was immediately humble and apologetic. "Forgive me the bad moment, Hans. I did not wish to inconvenience you. But just as you came toward me, I saw across the street, coming out of the Norma restaurant, the Hungarian."

"Zum Teufel! What Hungarian?"

"Remember when I spoke to you of"—he paused discreetly, looked behind him, but the door of the tea shop was closed—"the secret Stratman vote, how I maneuvered it?"

"Yes, yes—"

"I told you of a Hungarian clown who passes for a spy—he is an investigator, actually, with good press connections—and how I hired him to inform me of Stratman's rival candidates in physics. Do you recall? He was the one who learned the Spaniard was a Falangist and the two Australians homosexuals."

354

"Vaguely, I remember."

"He was across the street just now. There would have been nothing wrong in his seeing us, but he is curious—by nature of his calling—sometimes gossipy, and I thought it wiser—"

"You did the correct thing," said Eckart, mollified.

Krantz poked his head out of the recess and looked up the street. He could see a tall gentleman helping a blonde into an automobile. He could see Daranyi, identifiable by his shape, waiting, and then getting in behind the wheel. Daranyi's companions, the blonde and the tall gentleman, had been too distant and indistinct to be recognizable. Briefly, Krantz wondered who they were and what Daranyi was up to these days.

When the Citroën drove off, Krantz returned to Eckart. "They are gone," he said. "We are free to go wherever you like. You said on the phone you wished a brief conference?"

"I do."

"Well, where we go depends on what you want to discuss." In his heart of hearts, Krantz hoped that Eckart had arranged this meeting to report good news of his appointment to the staff of Humboldt University. More realistically, he realized that it might be too soon for that, and more likely Eckart had immediate problems on his mind. Probably he had seen Stratman, and wished advice. "If it is nothing important," continued Krantz, "we can go to the Norma restaurant across the street. However, if it is privacy you prefer—"

"It is privacy I prefer," said Eckart sternly.

"I have a Volkswagen at my disposal. It is around the corner. We can sit in it and talk or drive about—"

"We will sit in it and talk," said Eckart.

From Eckart's tone, Krantz sensed something disagreeable in the air. He fretted about the appointment, as he led the way around the corner to the Volkswagen sedan. Krantz opened the door for his German visitor, and Eckart stiffly stepped inside and sat on the leatherette seat, blue-veined hands folded on his lap. Krantz slammed the door, becoming more nervous, then bounced quickly around the car and settled straight behind the wheel.

"Do you want me to leave the windows rolled up or do you want some air?"

"Leave them up."

Krantz tugged off a glove, and located the metal puzzle in his pocket, and worried it with the fingers of his bare hand.

Eckart, who had been collecting his thoughts, was suddenly diverted by the metal puzzle, and regarded it with distaste. "Carl, *höre doch auf* with that puzzle—put that infernal game away. I must concentrate, and I wish you to concentrate. This is serious."

"Yes. Sorry." Krantz shoved the puzzle back into his coat pocket and waited penitently.

"As you know, I saw Max Stratman at lunch yesterday."

"Ah, good."

"Not good," snapped Eckart. "It was a wasted meeting."

355

Krantz was anxious that his own valuable contribution to the meeting, the production of Stratman in Stockholm, not be diminished. "I warned you of the possibility, Hans. Remember? Do you remember? He told the press he did not wish to work for a totalitarian state. He said he had left Germany voluntarily." Worriedly, he glanced at Eckart. "Is that what he repeated to you?"

Echart ignored Krantz's question. "I offered him a place at Humboldt University at three times his present salary. I offered him a house. I offered him freedom. No one but an addled and sentimental fool would have turned down that offer. He turned it down."

Almost physically, Krantz felt the pain of Eckart's words. From the first, he had understood, without being openly told, that Eckart and his East German comrades wanted Stratman in Stockholm so that they might woo him back to the Fatherland. But, somehow, it had never occurred to Krantz that they wanted Stratman for a post at the university. That was a surprise, and it disturbed Krantz deeply, for it was also a threat to his own future. After all, how many positions were there in the physics department of the university? If the great Stratman had one, would there be another for the less important Krantz? This was all that mattered to Krantz, now. He did not give a damn about Stratman's refusal. Except, of course, if it helped his own application. But he knew that Stratman's post, still open, did not automatically make room for him. Rather, as he suspected from the first, the refusal detracted from his own accomplishment. About Stratman's turning Eckart down, he had no emotional feeling. Krantz was a Swede, pro-German but a Swede, and officially neutral in these affairs. All that mattered was himself, his future. Which way did his best advantage lie?

Eckart's feelings had been made clear, and Krantz's shrewd judgment advised him to agree with his patron. "I am surprised as yourself," he said. "How could any scientist refuse so magnificent an inducement?"

"We dug our own grave," Eckart mused, almost to himself. "I always knew they went too far with their liquidation of undesirables. They should have screened more carefully, looked ahead. It was madness, and we are the heirs to it." He met Krantz's eyes. "Stratman will not forgive Germany for killing his sister-in-law, and Russia for killing his brother. This niece who survived—he spoke of her as Emily—it is she, I suspect, who keeps the unreasoning hatred burning within him. He is subservient to his military masters, I am certain, and prattles on about the wonders of America and the virtues of capitalist democracy, but that is all camouflage. He is a German still. Our fault is we made him a Jew, also."

"Was his refusal absolute?"

Eckart was silent a moment, staring through the windshield. "So he says, so he says."

"Then it is impossible," said Krantz. "There are other talents. You must turn your mind elsewhere."

"No," said Eckart angrily. "There is one Stratman. There is not another."

"But hundreds of physicists have worked in solar energy. Perhaps if you hired—"

Eckart turned on Krantz with a fierceness bred of frustration. "Are you a fool? Do you not see what we are after? Stratman alone has the key. The door he has opened for our enemies he has closed to us. Someday we will find that key. But it is the many other doors he can now open that worry us. We want him in East Berlin not for what he can give us of his discovery. No. Not even for what he can give us in new discoveries. We want him with us so that he will no longer work for them, help them, arm them. We want him not as an addition to us, but as a subtraction from them. That is what we want, and that is what we will have. Why do you think I am telling you all this? Because we have hope, still, and we know we have you, as a friend, a future colleague, to depend upon."

Krantz received the last with mingled pleasure and misgivings. "What more can I do for you? I have done my part."

"Only a share of your part," said Eckart roughly. "Your work is done when we are satisfied. We are not yet satisfied."

Krantz felt himself pulling at his goatee, and he knew his hand was trembling. "That is not so, Hans, that is not so, and you know it. It was an exchange of favors. I had a simple demand, and you made a difficult one. You asked me to make certain that Stratman won the Nobel Prize in physics and came to Stockholm to collect it. That is what you asked me, and no more. In return, you promised me a full professorship in the physics department of Humboldt. I have done my whole part, and now you should do yours."

"Really, Carl, I respect your meticulous and matter-of-fact mind, I respect it highly," said Eckart, his tone softening and sucking, "but there are limits of exactness in the human relationship. We are not measuring molecules. We are concluding a—a happy trade. Yes, it is true, you have brought Stratman here. To your eternal credit. But as long as he is still here, and not compliant to our wishes, he is still a matter of contention. In a broad sense, he is not delivered."

"He *is* delivered. He is here."

"Fleetingly. Why this resistance, Carl? You do not even know what I want of you."

"My position is precarious, that is all I know," said Krantz. "I have gone as far, in my position as a Nobel judge, as is humanly possible. What more can you want of me?"

"A minor request, a routine performance, and nothing else. Were I in a position to carry it out, I would do so. I am an outsider here. You are still an insider. A task that is formidable for me becomes easy for you. And this I can promise you, Carl—acknowledge your responsibility to finish the work you have begun—finish it—and before I part company from you and your capital city, I shall offer you the contract for your chair at Humboldt and a residence visa to East Berlin. Now, what do you say to that?"

Krantz knew that there was no bargaining. He must go on, or forfeit his dream of the future. Well, he told himself, it would all depend on what was demanded of him. "Exactly what is it you want me to do?"

"All yesterday afternoon and evening, I have given the problem my full mind," said Eckart. "The problem is one of providing greater inducement for Stratman. What can we offer him that he cannot reject? This is the scientific and civilized approach to the problem. But to make the proper offer, I have told myself, I must know more of the man and his requirements. What are his needs? What does he want? For what would he trade his allegiance? What are the necessities and luxuries that would bring him to our side? These questions are the ones I wish you to find answers for, Carl. When I have them, I will arrange a second meeting with Stratman. This time, I will have the bait. I guarantee you, it will hook him."

"How can I find out about Stratman's wants? I am not a detective."

"You were once, not long ago. You can learn his wants by learning about his life, and the lives of those around him, like the niece, anyone else. After all, you told me yourself that when you had to find out about the Spanish physicist and the two Australians, you found a way, and the information was useful. Now, that is all I require of you again. Is it so much?"

"I see," said Krantz, thinking. "If that is all—"

"That is all."

"It might be possible. I suppose I could employ the Hungarian again—Daranyi. He is experienced, a workhorse, and he has sources."

"Is he reliable?"

"Perfectly. I have said, his residence here is dependent upon several like myself. And he is always desperate for money. You would supply cash for the services, of course?"

"Money is not an issue. Within reason, that is."

"How soon do you need this dossier on Stratman?" Krantz asked.

"How soon? Yesterday, if that were possible." Eckart's Prussian face sniffed slightly in heavy humor, and then it relapsed into severity. "Let me see. What is today? The sixth of December? By the night of the ninth, no later."

"Three days for such a job? Impossible."

"Nothing like this is impossible, and you know it. I must have the information by the ninth, so that I can engage Stratman that evening, or the morning of the tenth. By the afternoon of the tenth, he will have the prize, and the next day be gone. He told me so himself. You can try, Carl. You can do your best."

Krantz sighed. "I will try," he said.

"When you brief the Hungarian—or anyone else you hire, for that matter—you must be clever, clever and cautious. Your agent must not know precisely what you are after. You understand? The slightest slip could be an embarrassment for me—for *both* of us. But do not fret. What is this, after all? An innocent little sport. A harmless research to give us some psychological understanding of Stratman. It will not be difficult for one of your stature and mentality. Already, I look forward to the day when you are in Berlin with us.

You and Stratman, our proudest advertisements. How your Swedes will envy you then, eh, Carl? . . . Now, drive me back to the hotel. You can drop me off a block or two before. Remember to telephone me tomorrow, after you have made the arrangement. I will be waiting. . . . Now, Carl, let us relax and speak of other things. Are there any worthwhile revues in Stockholm this season? And the girls—how is the current crop of Nordic beauties, my good friend?"

The embossed invitation, engraved on the most expensive linen paper, had gone out to twenty guests.

The invitation was for a formal dinner party, given by Ragnar Hammarlund, host, and Märta Norberg, hostess, honoring the visiting Nobel Prize laureates. The time was seven o'clock of the evening of December sixth. The dress was, in Swedish, *smoking*, which meant black tie and evening dress. To this was added *O.S.A.—om svar anhålles*—meaning R.S.V.P., and below that was listed Hammarlund's private telephone number.

While all twenty guests had responded to the invitations affirmatively, several hours before the dinner it appeared that the list might be reduced to nineteen. Emily Stratman had telephoned Hammarlund's secretary to explain that her uncle was not well—nothing serious, simply fatigue—and that he wished to rest and begged to be excused. When informed of this, Hammarlund had personally telephoned Count Bertil Jacobsson at the Foundation and requested him to substitute for Professor Stratman as Emily's escort. Jacobsson had been agreeable, and Hammarlund was satisfied that the guest list would once again number twenty.

Now, it was 7:15 in the evening.

On the Djurgårdsbrunns Canal, beyond the ornate metal gate and artificial lily pond, the first-story windows of Hammarlund's pillared Taj Mahal—Åskslottet—were ablaze with festive light. Since the Scandinavian guests had been bred on Swedish punctuality, and since the foreign guests had been forewarned about it, all twenty visitors were inside the huge and splendid main living room.

The last callers to arrive had just come through the living room archway. This party consisted of Jacobsson, Emily Stratman, Andrew Craig, and Leah Decker. Their host and hostess waited inside the entrance to welcome them with handshakes.

Ragnar Hammarlund, attired in faultless evening wear by Bond Street, seemed more featureless than ever. His white, hairless visage could hardly be discerned, so that his person resembled some eugenic cross between headless horseman and invisible man. Beside him, as fill-in hostess for the evening, a role she so often performed, was the legendary Märta Norberg.

As they awaited their turn to be greeted, Leah whispered to Craig in the tremulous voice of fan worship, "My, doesn't she look just like she did in pictures?"

Indeed, Märta Norberg looked just as she had looked on thousands of billboards and magazine covers and in legitimate theater and motion picture advertisements. She also looked at forty-two as she had looked at thirty-two and twenty-two, the perfectly preserved product of the most costly international beauticians. Despite the trademark slouch of her broad shoulders—that had long reminded awed audiences in London, New York, Cairo, and Bombay of disenchanted world-weariness and that had offered overtones of a sexuality both mystical and unique—Märta Norberg was tall, considerably taller than Hammarlund beside her. The other trademarks were also in evidence, the trademarks so endlessly celebrated in the fan magazines: "her mouse-colored hair, to the shoulders, abandoned and recklessly uncombed . . . her sunken pool of gray eyes, bearing the unconquered enigma of all womanhood . . . her patrician nose that launched a thousand theaters . . . her maddeningly superior smile, the smile of a Valkyrian Mona Lisa . . . her insinuating voice, a husky throb caught in a swan throat."

Awaiting his introduction, Craig found himself almost as captivated as Leah. If he had passed her on the street, and she an unknown, he wondered if he would have bothered to turn. Technically, her features and physique were imperfect, the face too long and sunken, the bosom—breasts like matched oversized buttons—too flattened beneath the clinging silk crepe gown, with high front, bare back, and the body too straight. What made it all desirable was the worldwide reputation that she wore like a royal cape.

But then, when he was the last to take her firm, slender hand, he felt the electric current of her magnetism and understood the allure of her personality.

"Craig," he said, introducing himself in the formal Swedish fashion.

"I know," she said deeply. "I have been entranced by all your books. I am Märta Norberg."

"I know," he said. "I have been entranced by all your faces—Camille, Nora Helmer, Beatrice, Sadie Thompson, Lady Windermere."

Her lips curled ever so slightly. "You speak as well as you write, I see. Come, Ragnar will lead you to the guests."

Again, Swedish formality prevailed. The protocol of introduction had been given Leah by Mr. Manker, and Leah had passed it on to Craig. Apparently Emily, so delicate in her sleeveless silk jersey evening dress, had been well briefed by Jacobsson, for she was performing as Craig knew that he must perform.

The fourteen guests who had arrived before stood waiting, some with cocktails, some with highballs, in an uneven semicircle, a formation almost identical to the one Craig had witnessed at the Royal Banquet. He moved awkwardly inside the circle, behind Leah and Emily. As he came face to face with each new guest, he introduced himself by surname, and the guest murmured back his or her surname. The ones he had met before—the Drs. Marceau, Dr. Farelli and his wife, Dr. Garrett and his wife, Konrad Evang, the Norwegian—these, Craig met again with spontaneous informality. But with the new ones, he conformed to strict etiquette. There were Baron Johan Stiernfeldt, a representative of the King, and the Baroness Stiernfeldt. There was Miss Svensson, the opera contralto. There were General Alexei Vasilkov, military attaché of the Russian Embassy, and his wife Nadazhda Vasilkov. There was Mrs. Lagersen, with the countenance of a monkey, whose claim to fame was that she had known the friendship of Mette Sophie Gad, Paul Gauguin's bewildered Danish wife, in Copenhagen during 1905, and had recently published *A Memoir of Mette and Paul*. There was Dr. Oscar Lindblom, Hammarlund's research chemist, who was thin and uncomfortable.

The moment that the formal introductions were concluded, since it was known that these were the last of the guests to arrive, the semicircle of formality splintered off into conversational foursomes and pairs.

Leah, who pretended to have forgiven Craig for their bad night and now had resumed her old relationship of domineering nurse and ever-present conscience to him, began to rave about the expensive living room, decorated in late Georgian style, and for the first time, Craig became attentive to his surroundings.

The great room, wainscoted from floor to ceiling, every panel featuring eighteenth-century engravings, was broken on one wall by an enormous fireplace faced in Carrara marble. At the far end, atop a small platform, beside the French doors that led onto a terrace overlooking the botanical gardens, was a five-piece orchestra, definitely Parisian, that was playing muted standbys and operetta classics. A wispy, tiny French *chanteuse*, attractively anemic, all gesticulation, joined them to sing unobtrusively, nostalgically.

Against the opposite wall stood two Chippendale sideboards of mahogany with ornately carved legs, one magnificently laden with a peacock sculptured of ice and surrounded by cut hothouse orchids and a rainbow of smorgasbord —pickled salt herring, salmon cutlets, marinated mussels, veal meatballs, Gotland asparagus, braised beef rolls, boiled potatoes, rye rusks and saffron bread, smoked goose breast, endless cheeses—which was served by two wholesome Swedish girls in Dutch aprons. The second table held glasses and bottles of drink, and was officered by two bartenders in red-and-black uniforms. Circulating through the room was Hammarlund's liveried butler, Motta, an elderly Swiss with the face of an inebriated St. Bernard. Motta carried, and tendered, a large tray of hot American-style hors-d'oeuvres. Behind him, with dishes and napkins, dainty in her starched dress, was the Finnish vestibule maid.

Leah had become separated from Craig by Saralee Garrett, who felt safe with Leah, and now they were intently discussing Swedish shopping bargains. With relief, Craig turned away and sought Emily. He had not seen her all day. After Daranyi had left him at the hotel, Craig had tried to call Emily but learned that she was out with her uncle. During the drive to the Hammarlund dinner, Jacobsson and Leah had dominated the conversation, and Craig had been unable to do more than smile at Emily. Now he was impatient to speak to her.

He beheld her at last. Jacobsson had her arm, and had brought her into a group that contained Baron Stiernfeldt and his wife, Mrs. Lagersen, and the Farellis. Craig knew that he could not extricate her, not yet. That left one immediate alternative.

He made his way to the temporary bar and ordered a double Scotch on ice.

Waiting, he observed on the end of the table a placard propped against an easel. It bore the legend *Placering*. Beneath the legend was the seating plan for dinner. Craig studied the table arrangement etched in pencil. He would be seated between Margherita Farelli and Leah Decker. He frowned, and studied the chart further. Emily would be seated between Jacobsson and General Vasilkov.

Craig accepted his drink, and pursed his lips, as he glanced at the seating plan once more. It was unromantic. It would require one rewrite. He promised himself that he would take care of that later.

Briefly, flanked by Lindblom and Märta Norberg, the evening's host stood apart from his guests and surveyed the room.

Every important Swede—that is, a Swede with social position—was expected to sponsor three formal dinner parties a year, usually in the dark winter season when life was monotonous and unbearably dull, but Hammarlund always preferred to exceed this requirement. Essentially, he was a lonely man. This, however, was not the motivation behind his formal party-giving. He hosted his expensive dinners because, from an Olympian height, he looked down upon smaller men, regarding them as being helpless as insects, and the antics of the species *Homo sapiens* amused him and later filled his reveries. This was Hammarlund's ninth formal dinner of the year, but only the third time in his life that he had invited Nobel laureates as guests.

The first two Nobel dinners had been, for him, disasters, because he had found the scientists dreadful and dogmatic bores. He had vowed to avoid another Nobel party, and limit his guest lists to the people that he enjoyed the most—fellow industrialists who spoke the common language of legalized piracy, and the foolish, crazy children of the entertainment world. What had changed his mind this year, and prodded him into one more Nobel feast, was the award of the prize to the Marceaus of Paris. He had seen, at once, how they could be valuable to him, in a way beyond their understanding or beyond the conception of ordinary beings. Knowing that it would have been unseemly to honor only the Marceaus in Åskslottet, he had taken on the responsibility of his third Nobel dress dinner. So far, he decided, all had gone well. Soon, he must instigate the business at hand.

Märta Norberg was speaking. "That author person, Craig, has a certain charm. I daresay he could be fun."

"Forget Craig," said Hammarlund curtly. "I have told you to devote time to Claude Marceau." He addressed Lindblom. "And as for you, Oscar, you know your duties." Hammarlund took Lindblom and Märta Norberg by their arms. "Come. Let us begin before they are involved."

The three advanced across the room to where the Marceaus stood together, moodily drinking, speaking neither to each other nor to anyone else. Irritation between the Marceaus had mounted in the past twenty-four hours. Claude chafed under the relentless new speaking schedule Denise had imposed upon him, through the Foundation. And Denise was tense because she had read of the arrival of the French mannequins in Copenhagen early that morning. Under these circumstances, the appearance of Hammarlund, with glamorous Märta Norberg and young Lindblom, was not entirely unwelcome.

When he put his mind to it, Hammarlund was a master of social tactical diversion. With practiced ease, he paired Märta Norberg and Claude Marceau, and pointed them toward the sideboard-bar to obtain a cocktail for Märta. Relieved to be free of his wife's abuse, and, indeed, impressed by the attentions of the renowned actress, Claude had gone off too willingly to please Denise.

Alone with Hammarlund, and his skinny, youthful employee whose name she could not remember, Denise decided to make the best of a bad thing. She imbibed her dry martini and left the burden of sociability to be borne by her repulsive host.

"You met Dr. Oscar Lindblom, I believe," Hammarlund was saying.

"Yes, of course I remember," said Denise. "He was the one who blushed when we were introduced tonight."

Now that Lindblom had once more been identified, Denise considered him objectively, as he stood beside his employer. Lindblom and Hammarlund were physical opposites—one an ectomorph and the other an endomorph—yet they seemed to blend because of one characteristic held in common. Both were supremely colorless. If Hammarlund resembled a mound of mash, Lindblom's aspect was that of a blank human figure outlined in a juvenile coloring book, not yet filled in with crayon. Except for a mop of dark brown hair, and insomnia traces under his gray eyes, Lindblom's regular Nordic features, thin but handsome, were bleached out by a personality that was tentative and introverted.

At once, Denise realized that Lindblom's blanched face was tinged with pink, and she remembered that she had accused him of blushing, and here he was blushing again. He had started to say something gallant, stuttered, and then said to Denise, "It is not every day, Dr. Marceau, one can meet a genius in one's own field whom one idolizes."

Denise inclined her head. "I thank you, Dr. Lindblom." She gave regard to Hammarlund's pleased reaction. "You must be lax with him, M. Hammarlund. When a chemist has time to learn pretty compliments, he cannot be giving enough time to his test tubes and mice."

"Good," said Hammarlund. "Then you recall my telling you that Dr. Lindblom is head of my private laboratory?"

"Certainly I remember."

"But you do not recall my telling you that he is one of the most promising chemists in Scandinavia? Mark my word, he will one day have the Nobel Prize like your husband and your—"

Lindblom blushed once more, and his bow tie danced nervously on his prominent Adam's apple. "Mr. Hammarlund, really—"

Hammarlund brushed aside his protest with a gesture, even as he would brush aside a gnat. He continued addressing Denise intently. "You are quite wrong about the time he gives his test tubes and mice. He gives all of his time to his experiments. He is on the verge of an important breakthrough in synthetic foods. Only now, just recently, he has become bogged down."

"I am sorry, but it happens," said Denise to Lindblom with fervent disinterest.

"I do hope he will tell you all about his work," said Hammarlund energetically. "I know he wants to. And as for gallantry, you will find him charming." He looked off, as he had planned. "I see I am wanted by General Vasilkov. Excuse me for a moment, please. You will enjoy each other."

Quickly, Hammarlund left Denise and Lindblom. He had grafted them. He hoped the graft would take.

Denise watched her host depart with a relief that she made no effort to disguise. But what she was left with was equally boring. She considered the straw man before her, a Swedish oaf, a science amateur, and she wondered how long it would be before she could gracefully escape from him.

"I must apologize for Mr. Hammarlund," Lindblom was saying with some mortification, his bow tie jigging. "Everything he possesses must be the best, and he permits these enthusiasms to include his employees."

"I have no idea what you are talking about," said Denise tartly.

"I mean—I mean—his prediction that someday I may earn the Nobel Prize like your husband and you. I would not allow myself to imagine this, or let you think that I believed I was on the uppermost plane of science with two great laureates. I am relatively a beginner, a student almost, in comparison to your genius. It embarrasses me to have—to have my name brought up in the same conversation with yours. That is why I apologize for Mr. Hammarlund's extravagance."

Denise's eyes narrowed, and she considered her companion more keenly. His lean face, the gray eyes, not entirely unattractive, were sincerely abject, but the one thing that Denise could not bear in a male was weakness. "Never mind that," she said. "We each have our work, our place."

She knew that she would have to give an ear to his work, before she could be free of him. She might as well get it out of him and over with as speedily as possible. She could see her husband, at the bar, speaking too animatedly to Märta Norberg, and standing too close to her. Now that Claude's moral balance was gone, and he had sunk to the depths of philandering, there was no telling how far he would let himself slide. If he could not have Gisèle Jordan in Copenhagen, the old fool might try to have that overpublicized iceberg, Märta Norberg, right here in Stockholm. It would be just like that old roué, that pitiful Casanova, to feed his vanity with another affair.

Denise bit her lip in resentment, and then knew that she was marring the lip rouge, and quickly opened her evening bag to repair her face. She was not yet alarmed by Claude and the actress, but it would be foolhardy to let the flirtation go on at length. She would do her face, and finish her drink, and hear this oaf out, and then take herself to the bar and break that new thing up.

As she worked with her lipstick, and then her powder puff, Denise said, "Mr. Hammarlund told me something of your work. Do you wish to tell me more? Of course, this is no place for laboratory talk—but a little might be interesting. Just what are you up to, Dr. Lindblom?"

Denise's peevish tone inhibited Lindblom and, at the same time, made him venerate her the more. This female genius, so otherworldly, her head doubtless teeming with a hundred projects requiring talents beyond his mundane limitations, had actually encouraged him to speak of himself. He wanted to, desperately, and yet feared her impatience. What forced him to speak, at last, was a remembrance of Hammarlund's command earlier in the day: "Oscar, when you are alone with her, interest her in your work—that is one of the main purposes of the party."

For an introvert, the assignment was as impossible to envision as daring to monopolize the time of a Marie Curie, but the necessity of reporting back to Hammarlund enforced a superhuman effort. "I am sure Mr. Hammarlund told you the motivation behind our research into synthetics?"

"Yes. Personal aggrandizement."

"*His* motive, for the most, but not *my* motive. He is a vegetarian, as you know, and he did not want to consume foods—meats especially—that came from the corpses of once-living animals. Yet he knew also that the proteins of meats were necessary to his survival. He posed the problem of synthetic proteins to me, some meat substitute with the same values that would be morally and aesthetically acceptable. I pointed out that with time and money, anything was conceivable in the area of synthetics. When soldiers suffered from malaria in the last war, the cure was quinine. But not enough quinine, from tree bark, was available. This vital necessity mothered the invention of synthetic quinine, known as Atabrine. I pointed out to him that when there is an important need, there is always a possible solution."

"And you felt your employer's vegetarianism was an important need?" remarked Denise acidly.

"By no means. While his need was for a solution to squeamishness, and later, a chance to make added millions, my motives were entirely different. For one thing, as I worked in the laboratory, I saw that natural foods were not at all as efficient and wholesome as people imagined. Synthetic foods could be made free of nature's defects, and promise more health to humanity. For another thing, once food came out of the laboratory and then could come off the assembly line, there would be food, always, for the entire world—no more undernourishment, no more famines. I saw the goal was worthy. I have devoted myself to it ever since."

"I admire your humanitarianism," said Denise, who had long since tired of the subject, "but in the end, you may be manufacturing only fool's gold."

"No, no, Dr. Marceau, you must take my word that anything can be done in this field. Consider what Bergius has accomplished in converting sawdust and wood shavings into carbohydrates of the sugar type, and Fischer, synthesizing proteins that provide full nourishment. Most of us tend to forget that synthetic elements already exist in natural food. What is ice cream? Is it natural? Is it picked in the field? Does it grow? It is the result of combining natural products with chemicals. Or baking powder. Is that grown from trees?

Synthetics are employed, chemicals like monocalcium phosphate. Or, for that matter, what shall we say of baked bread—?"

He was going on and on, warming to his subject, but Denise was no longer listening. With her concentrated glare she tried to hold her husband, across the room, in check. He had ordered, and was now accepting, fresh drinks for Märta Norberg and himself. He was standing even closer to the bitch in heat, addressing her more confidentially, beguiling her with his heavy-handed wit, now touching her bare arm and laughing, obviously working at seducing her (had he not had recent practice in the technique?).

Denise only half heard Lindblom's hymn to synthetics, and the word caught in her mind, and she wished that chemistry could produce synthetic men, with synthetic faithfulness and a love that did not revolt against becoming middle-aged, and synthetic sex as well, that was geared to one mate and one mate only.

"—and so I am trying to reproduce, in the laboratory, the taste of meat, the nutritional content of meat, the resemblance of meat," Lindblom was saying. "At the same time, I am exploring new areas, algae strains—"

"Fascinating," said Denise with firmness and finality.

Lindblom knew that Her Majesty had dismissed him, but he was not dismayed. He was flattered to have held her attention at all. He was relieved that he could report some success to Hammarlund after the dinner.

"Someday," Denise went on, "under more propitious circumstances, in a more appropriate place, you must explain your concrete accomplishments and the problems that have prevented your going further. Right now—"

"I would be honored," Lindblom hastily interrupted, "to have you visit my laboratory on the grounds, show you about, let you see my work."

"Thank you, thank you very much. Our time, as you know, is not our own. We are in the hands of the Nobel Foundation. Count Jacobsson appears to have filled every hour of our stay. But as I said, some day in the future—"

"You and your husband will be always welcome."

"Yes, my husband," said Denise, glancing toward the bar. "I fear I have neglected him. A tribute to your elocutionary powers, Dr. Lindblom, and the drama of your work. Now I had better see my husband. Thank you so much."

Abruptly, she left Lindblom and strode across the living room. Claude and Märta Norberg both had their glasses to their lips when she came between them.

"I wondered where you were," she said to Claude viciously.

Claude's social smile froze. "Miss Norberg was interested in spermatozoa—"

"Quelle surprise!" said Denise.

Märta Norberg appeared not to have overheard her. She was searching off for someone in the room. "Well, I'll leave you two together," she said formally. "Your charming husband, Dr. Marceau, made me entirely forget I was the hostess. I must circulate." And then to Claude she added, "It was divine. Now, remember, my dear, keep one frozen sperm for Norberg. I may need it one day, if I don't find a man soon."

Gracefully, she inclined her head, and slouching, long-striding, she was gone.

"'Keep one frozen sperm for Norberg,'" Denise mimicked. "The shameless bitch. I will wager this is the only time she has been vertical all year."

Claude showed pain. "Denise, is this continuous vulgarity necessary? Miss Norberg is a decent, utterly captivating lady."

"Like someone else we know?"

He affected not to have heard her. "How was your Dr. Lindblom?"

"A hotheaded Don Juan," she said savagely. "I had to fight to keep from being raped. . . . Now get *me* a natural drink, you synthetic husband."

"What does that mean? Are you going to be difficult tonight?"

"You may be sure of that, *mon brave*," said Denise Marceau.

All through the cocktail hour, Andrew Craig had been trying to catch Emily's eye. Now, with his second double Scotch in hand, he succeeded. She turned her head in his direction, knowing that he was staring at her, and he made a movement of his head to invite her to join him, but she replied with a quick, helpless shrug.

He understood. Her circle had enlarged. Baron Stiernfeldt and his wife, Mrs. Lagersen, and Margherita Farelli were still there, although Dr. Carlo Farelli had disappeared. And to this group had been added, since the last time Craig had looked, the persons of Ragnar Hammarlund, Konrad Evang, and General Vasilkov and his wife. It was the largest circle in the room, and it irritated Craig that the men were being attentive to Emily. Inevitably, he thought. She was irresistible to the male. Wherever she shone, the moths would bat about the flame.

At last, he conceded to himself that she could not escape from the others. He was on his own. He wheeled slowly to take in the remaining occupants in the room. Leah was still involved with Saralee Garrett and another woman, Miss Svensson, the opera singer. Craig saw that Leah kept glancing at him worriedly, and this posed a minor threat, for she might make up her mind that he was lonely. A second threat, too, was gradually drawing nearer. The actress, Märta Norberg, appeared to be approaching him. For a time, she had been with Claude Marceau, but twice he had caught her studying him. She had left both Marceaus at the other end of the bar, and by a circuitous route, first briefly engaged with Dr. Lindblom in conversation, then exchanging a few words with the butler, Motta, and now, after looking in on Leah and her ladies, she would undoubtedly be headed for him. He was next. There could be worse fates, he knew.

As a younger man, watching Norberg's unapproachable enlarged image on countless motion picture screens, enchanted by her gifts behind the footlights, Craig had shared in common with millions of other males certain wish fantasies. The years had been kind to Norberg, he told himself now. She was ageless, and still a lithe symbol of all desired and unattainable. Yet through some perversity, now that he had an opportunity to converse with her on intimate terms, as an equal almost, he was reluctant to do so. He was in no mood for banter about the entertainment world. He was in no mood to listen to her glories. His mind was on Emily Stratman, only Emily, with an occasional bewilderment about Lilly.

He gulped down the last of the second drink, and suddenly felt stifled in the overheated room. He wondered where he might cool off, in isolation, free to sort out his thoughts. His gaze passed along the exits from the living room, and held, finally, on the French doors near the indefatigable orchestra. One of the French doors was ajar. It was all the encouragement that Craig needed.

Giving his empty glass to Motta, and rejecting a refill, he walked to one French door, and, hoping that he was not being observed, edged through it and closed it behind him.

The cold night air, not so bitter as other evenings, braced him. For the eternity of a minute, he stood motionless on the flagstones, inhaling the night and peering up at the clear navy-blue sky with its infinity of miniature stars like erratic strands of gay Christmas-tree lights. After a while, he drew back into himself, and strolled around the veranda, romantically and dimly lighted by antique English coach lamps. He considered Emily, and then Leah, and then Lilly, in that order, and tried to relate them each separately to Miller's Dam and Lucius Mack and Joliet College and *Return to Ithaca*.

He had reached the low stone balustrade that partitioned the veranda from the gardens, and absently he looked below, at the bush clumps and intersecting paths, and the hothouses in the distance. That moment, he realized with surprise he was not alone. Two male figures, directly beneath him, were moving across the lawn from the veranda stairs to the nearest garden path.

By straining his eyes, he made them out at last. The bulkier one, progressing with fluid ease, was Carlo Farelli. The other, progressing in fits and starts, nervously, jumpily, was John Garrett.

Briefly, Craig speculated on what the two winners in physiology and medicine, who were comparative strangers, would have to say to one another. His writer's mind wrote. Would they exchange shoptalk, medical talk? But why out here in the cold night? Why not inside the warm house? Or was it something else? Something private?

"Because it's something private, that's what," said John Garrett belligerently, in reply to Farelli's question, as they reached the gravel garden path.

Farelli good-naturedly protested once more. "But in this frozen weather? I am a Latin, do not forget. My blood is thin."

"I know, I know about your blood," said Garrett with a rasp. Whenever he drank excessively, and tonight he had, his voice grew hoarse. Now it was not only hoarse but strained with hatred long repressed.

"If what you must tell me is so private, we can ask Hammarlund for his library. We can enjoy the civilized amenities as we converse. Shall we?"

Farelli halted and looked hopefully at Garrett's unremarkable face, now flushed. Garrett halted, too, and swayed.

"No," he said. "What I have to say—there should be no one around."

368

"You are certainly enigmatical, Dr. Garrett."

Garrett pulled himself together, trying to attain his full height, trying to match his enemy in strength and power of physique. It had been after the meeting with Dr. Erik Öhman, on his return from the failure at the Royal Caroline Medico-Chirurgical Institute, that he had come to this decision, the decision to have a showdown with Farelli. He could no longer postpone the inevitable. Farelli's promoter tactics were steam-rolling him. Farelli's trick at the Caroline Institute, taking advantage of Öhman and him, using Sue Wiley, crowing to all the world that he alone was the medical savant, that Garrett did not exist. Well, at least in one intrigue, Farelli had tripped. Now Dr. Öhman knew that Farelli was a charlatan, and a disgrace to the profession and the Nobel honor roll. Now Dr. Öhman knew that Farelli had used him badly.

Garrett's intensity, overlaid on Öhman's debt to Garrett and worship of Garrett, had converted the Swede into a dependable ally, if one were needed. But now, Garrett did not need an ally. He had looked forward to this night's truth session with Farelli. Once Farelli realized that Garrett had his number, once Farelli understood that Garrett was on to his manipulations, the Italian would cease and desist. He would not dare to continue as he had. Then, and only then, would Garrett be free, at last, to receive the full credit for discovery that was rightfully his own.

He realized that he had been lost in thought, and that Farelli was staring at him strangely. "Is anything wrong with you, Dr. Garrett?"

"What makes you say that?"

"You seem—somewhere else. I had been asking you what mysterious matter brought us out here in the night to get pneumonia."

"I'll tell you what—I'll tell you what—" Garrett's reserve had burst, and he was shivering. "I brought you here to say what I think of your getting half of my money!"

At first Farelli's leonine head shook with lack of comprehension. His tone of voice was incredulous. "Do I understand your English, Dr. Garrett? Do you say I am receiving half of *your* money?"

"For the Nobel Prize, yes, yes, that's what I'm saying. I should have gotten $50,300 instead of $25,150. You don't deserve the other half. You never have, and you know it. I made the discovery first, by myself, but you took the credit, you took most of it, like Cook and Peary—you're Cook—you're a pretender."

Farelli's jaw was agape. "Dr. Garrett, I do not believe my ears. You are joking with me, of course. It is a joke."

"It's not a joke. Don't give me any of that clever pretense. You can hoodwink the Nobel Committee, and the press, and Sue Wiley, and Öhman, and half the world. But some of us know the truth. We're on to you."

"On to what? What are you on to? Your crazy words make my head swim."

"You know what I mean. You want me to spell it out? I know a good deal about psychology, not just pathology but psychology, and I know what makes a pretender like you tick. History's full of impostors and frauds. I've read about them all, and on every page I see you—I see you in Psalmanazar, and Tichborne, and the so-called Dr. Graham with his Temple of Health and celestial bed, and Colonel Ghadiali, and all the medical quacks. You used my findings, my years of labor, you used my papers, and you had spies in my laboratories—"

Farelli's dark face had hardened. "*Che faccia tosta!*" he growled. "Dr. Garrett, if I did not believe you were either drunk or paranoiac, I would slap your face."

"Go ahead, try it, try it, try it," Garrett chanted, like an inciting boy roughneck who wanted to be struck so that he might have a cause. "I've watched you here, Farelli. Öhman and I have watched you, the greatest operator of all time. You've got the wool over their eyes, all right, you sure have. Taking over our press conference, trying to blot me out. And the Royal Banquet, trying to make me ridiculous in front of the others. And now—now—pretending you want to help Öhman—using him so you can get a lousy, cheap story from that Wiley girl."

Garrett reeled with the excitement of his temper and the alcohol high in his throat.

"You couldn't steal the whole prize, the whole credit," he went on in a shriek, "so you're trying to do it now. But I know you're a phony, and others are beginning to know, and you keep it up, and you're asking for trouble. Yes, *trouble!* You're a phony, goddamn you—"

Farelli's big face was livid. "Shut up, you stupid man. *Si calmi.* Make yourself sober, and maybe I will let you apologize someday."

He turned to leave, but Garrett was not letting him have the last word, not tonight, not this exulting night that was Garrett's night and his hour of truth.

Garrett reached out, almost falling, clutching Farelli's arm, and pulling him around.

"You're a phony, a rotten Dago phony!" he shouted.

Farelli slammed at Garrett's hand, knocking it free of his arm. "Do not touch me, you sick, crazy man! Go away—*imbecille—pazzo!*"

It was this, nothing else but this, that goaded and incensed Garrett beyond all final restraint. Dr. Keller would have understood. The group therapy patients would have understood. Garrett departed from himself and his senses. With all frustration and fury unleashed, he swung his fist at Farelli. The blow landed high on the Italian's shoulder and skated off. It was less the impact of the blow than the surprise of it that staggered Farelli, and sent him reeling backwards a few steps.

"I'll show you!" Garrett was shouting, choking.

Blindly, he charged at the Italian, swinging both arms clumsily, like all middle-aged, sedentary men who become violent. But Farelli had his balance now and control of his temper. Quick of foot, he stepped aside, and as one of Garrett's fists missed him entirely and the other glanced off his ribs, Farelli rammed his beefy right hand wrist-deep into his attacker's stomach. Aggression and oxygen went out of Garrett. He doubled in two, and then as he slowly folded like a jackknife, Farelli catapulted a hooking left to the exposed jaw. The sound of knuckles on flesh was short and sharp, like a handclap, and Garrett, head jerking, fingers holding his belly, went over backward as if axed.

He sat on the gravel path, whimpering, spitting blood and alcohol and, like a sand sucker, chewed for air.

He looked up, eyes crossed and maniacal, and suddenly, from some reservoir of strength, he lifted himself, groaning, to one knee, and then, throwing himself at Farelli's legs, tried to pull the other down. Farelli kicked loose, with a curse in Italian, but when he attempted to retreat, Garrett was upright on his feet again, wobbling. Garrett threw himself upon the larger man, bear-hugging him, attempting to wrestle him to the turf, attempting to destroy all that stood between himself and self-respect. Farelli fought to tear Garrett's clawing hands from his shoulders, and in this way, into the frosted loam of the garden, they grappled and cursed.

It was then that Andrew Craig came on the run, having watched the altercation from the terrace. Craig pushed between them, and because he had will and no anger, his authority was felt, and Garrett released Farelli, and staggered backward, panting, lips working, but speechless.

"Are you insane? Are both of you insane?" Craig demanded.

"He insulted me," said Farelli with bedraggled dignity. "He struck first."

Garrett found his voice, which was broken. "He's a liar—a hoax—he provoked—"

"I don't give a damn what happened, or who's right, or who's wrong," said Craig furiously. "For Chrissakes, you're two adults—holies—the great Nobel winners—behaving down here like two saloon brawlers. Now, cut it out and forget it. What if this got out? What if someone found out?"

He turned to Farelli. "You go first. Better comb your hair and straighten your jacket. The lapel's ripped. I think you can disguise it before you get inside."

Craig turned back to Garrett. "I'll try to put you in shape. Here's my handkerchief. Wipe the blood. It's only a lip cut. I'll clean you up and sneak you into the bathroom."

"*Benissimo,*" Farelli said to Craig. Then he studied Garrett with contempt. "*Arrivederci, fratello mio.*" He started to go.

Garrett glared past Craig, making a ball of his fist and shaking it at the Italian. "I'm not through with you, you quack. I'll fix you yet—I'll fix you— you wait and see."

And then Garrett turned back into the dark of the garden, crying and vomiting at once, not out of physical pain, but out of humiliation and loss and gross injustice and inadequacy, all in one, and all in his bursting heart.

There were six in this group now, near the improvised bar, Denise Marceau between Hammarlund and Evang, and then Leah Decker and Jacobsson and Mrs. Lagersen.

Hammarlund, to impress the Marceaus, had given the familiar cue to Mrs. Lagersen. He had mentioned, proudly, the latest original Monet and Sisley oils that he had acquired, through his agents, at a Paris auction, oils now on their way to Stockholm, and soon to enrich his living room walls and gallery beside the other Impressionists. What he missed the most was a Gauguin. He had always desired a Gauguin. This was the cue, and Mrs. Lagersen was on.

She remembered Paul's death in distant Dominica, and how she had been with Mette in Copenhagen the week the news came, and Mette's resentment of a life so irresponsibly wasted. She remembered how Paul's personal effects —furniture, paintings—had been auctioned off in Papeete to pay a court fine. There had been great fun, that day, over the effects of the demented and deceased French painter, and when Paul's last oil came up for bidding, the auctioneer had turned it upside down. "What will you give for Niagara Falls?" he had called out, and someone gave seven francs, and that was the end of Paul Gauguin, they thought, even Mette in Copenhagen thought, but now Ragnar Hammarlund, with all his fortune, could not find an available Gauguin.

Listening, Denise had become absorbed in Mrs. Lagersen, museum piece, living link to an immortal. The firsthand stories, along with the drink, and the music, had drawn off the poison of Denise's anger somewhat. How much fun all this might have been, she thought, studying Claude's profile. Another anecdote had begun, and Denise gave it her attention. It was near the end of this that Motta, the butler, materialized, and hovered behind Claude. He seemed anxious, but kept his distance with phlegmatic respect.

Then the anecdote was finished, and they all laughed. With this intermission, before a new story could begin, Motta quickly sidled up to Claude, and touched his arm. Claude leaned sideways, toward the butler, and Motta whispered in his ear. Evang was speaking, and no one took notice of Motta and Claude, no one except Denise. She saw her husband's brow furrow, and his nod, heard him murmur an indistinct apology to no one in particular, and then watched him hastily leave, following the butler out of the room.

Denise lost her interest in Evang and Mrs. Lagersen and their anecdotes at once. Her mind was on Claude. What was the message? She pondered the mystery of where he had gone and what was happening.

Evang had been telling a long story, and this was followed by an interlude of broken chatter. Hammarlund bent toward Denise.

"Do you like the music?" he inquired politely.

"Most enjoyable, both orchestra and vocalist," she said absently.

"I flew them in from Paris for you. I thought they would make you feel at home."

Denise cocked her head at Hammarlund with surprise. It would dismay him to learn that while she lived in Paris, she was not of Paris, not these last laborious years, no part of the city's night life, its song, and that she could not tell a French orchestra from a Swedish one. But why had he done this? "You did it for me?"

"To accommodate a great lady I admire."

"Well, I thank you, sir."

"Dr. Lindblom informs me that he had a most inspiring conversation with you."

She found it difficult to recall Lindblom or the conversation. "Yes," she said, "yes, a promising young man." Her mind was gnawed by Claude's sudden disappearance. What had taken him away? And then she was aware that Motta had reappeared, and was preparing to resume his duties.

She clutched her handbag. "Excuse me a moment," she said to Hammarlund.

She headed toward the butler, intercepting him before he could begin his inquiries of the guests about the next round of drinks.

"I am Dr. Marceau's wife. Is anything the matter?"

"Nothing at all, Madame. It was merely the Grand Hotel. They had an urgent business call, long distance, for Dr. Marceau, and they wanted to speak with him, to know if he would take it. He is waiting for the call to be transferred."

"Long distance?" said Denise mildly.

"Copenhagen, Madame."

Denise felt an immediate hot flash in her temples, and for a moment she was faint. "Where is Dr. Marceau taking the call? It may be of concern to me."

"In the rear library, Madame. If you will kindly follow—"

She followed the butler out of the living room, along a corridor with several doors, and a turning, until they reached a rich oak door.

Motta put his hand to the brass knob. "Right in here, Madame."

"Never mind. I will let myself in. You can go back to the other guests. Thank you very much."

Motta had already turned the knob, partially opening the door, but now he released his grip, bowed, and silently disappeared around the corridor corner.

Denise waited, frozen, for the servant to be gone, already hearing Claude's voice. The second that she was safely alone, she turned back to the oak door. She wondered if it would squeak if she pushed it, and then she did not care. It opened a few inches and then a few inches more. Claude's voice was low but distinct. She could not see him from this angle, but a trick of the subdued lamplight threw his shadow, elongated like a thief in the night, against the trophy-covered wall that was visible.

She stood hypnotized by his black silhouette on the wall, and clenching her dry hands together, she listened without shame. She felt dull and hollow, helpless and dreading, like an agent parachuted among the enemy for the first time, overhearing at some headquarters of a surprise attack, and girding herself with the advantage this knowledge gave her homeland, which was herself.

Her ear was sensitive, alive to every inflection, pause, remark.

"I cannot hear you. *Répétez, s'il vous plaît*," Claude was saying. "Yes, yes, I am on the line. The connection is poor."

Pause.

"Yes, fine, Gisèle, fine. I am busy, but there is excitement. It is a great honor. And you, how are you, my dear? How was the flight?"

Pause.

"I am happy. You sound wonderful. It is rather difficult in this place. I will be missed."

Pause.

"Oh, it is a dinner party, formal. One of Sweden's millionaires is giving it. But someone may come in. I am glad you called. But why the risk to call me here? *Qu'est-ce que c'est?*"

Pause.

"You what? Here in Stockholm? When?"

Pause.

"I know, I know, Gisèle. I miss you, too. But you do not understand. I am obligated—the schedule—everything, every moment, planned—it would be most awkward—what?"

Pause.

"Well, you know how I feel. Of course, I want to see you. When would it be? For how long?"

Pause.

"The ninth, you say?"

Pause.

"Only the afternoon? I understand. But you will get back for the evening show in time?"

Pause.

"Of course I want to, Gisèle, you know that. It will work out. I shall see you somehow. Of course, I will not be able to take you to the airport, but—oh, another thing. Remember this. You are not to stay at the Grand. . . . What? What did you say?"

Pause.

"You have? Excellent. Then wait there for my phone call after you arrive. It will be before one o'clock. I may be a few minutes late phoning, but I will, and I will see you, be sure—"

Pause.

"What gives you such ideas, my darling? *Je te trouve toujours ravissante!* Nothing has changed."

Denise pulled back from the door as if it were a guillotine, and from within, Dr. Guillotin's dooming voice. *Nothing has changed.* Nothing, nothing. Denise's eyes brimmed with tears, and she could hardly keep from audibly sobbing.

Spinning away, she ran to the turning, and then up the corridor. Approaching the bright lights from the living room entrance, she slowed, then halted, shaken, trying to collect her poise. She found a handkerchief in her purse, and carefully picked at her eyes, drying them without disturbing the makeup. Next, she found her compact, snapped it open and studied her reflection—so worn, so defeated, too old—in the circular mirror. Stalling for time, she touched powder to her pale cheeks and then added the slightest edge of rouge.

She had lost, she knew. The final debacle was in the making. Three days from this night, less than three days, Gisèle Jordan would land from Copenhagen for an afternoon's assignation in a hotel room, hidden and secure. And with some lie, carefully invented, Claude would leave her to carry out alone the hateful schedule she had wished upon them. He would leave her, the used, tiresome person known too long, leave her, the forty-two-year-old dowdy who smelled not of perfume but of chemical compounds, leave her with her unforgiving, curdled hostility; and he would go to the other one, so fresh, so unencumbered, so blond and tall and perfect, so exciting with the fragrance of youth, flesh and high fashion and murmuring approval and secret skills; and after this exchange, Denise would suffer total obliteration.

Despite the headache, her mind ranged for some hope of survival. How could she contest this superior opponent, survive this uneven match? Continuing anger would only drive Claude away, for as it was, she had become for him the embodiment of guilty conscience. What if she thwarted his rendezvous on the ninth, followed him, exposed him, or, less crudely, revealed to him what she had just learned? Impossible, her intuition warned her. It would enforce upon him the ultimate decision, and she dreaded an ultimate decision now. Inevitably, she believed, proceedings for divorce would follow. If it must be black or white, she was lost. Yet she could not go on in this directionless fog of gray. More important now was the impact of one decision made, or made for her by some second self: Claude must not be lost to her; she must not be deserted, condemned to embittered and solitary confinement. The question mark remained, but what preceded it now was different. No longer how to punish him—now how to hold him?

At once, Denise remembered where she was. She could not remain rooted in the corridor another instant, brooding, for Claude would appear and find her. Not only her location, but her face, might give her away. That could drive him to the choice too fast. Or worse, might induce pity in him. She shuddered, dropped her compact into the bag, and then returned to the masquerade in her guise of imperturbability.

Scanning the room, seeking for someone, anyone, to attach herself to, and to be busy and vivacious with when Claude came back, her eyes came to rest on Lindblom, that ridiculous, sallow chemist—whatever was his first name?—standing off to one side, nearby, shyly isolated and sipping a drink.

While she studied him, unseen by him, something clicked in Denise's head. No hypothesis, and experiments, and trying and discarding, and formulating, and deducing. Simply—click—a find—idea—discovery. But she was scientist still. She never leaped. Always the magnifying microscope first. She put her mind's eye to the invisible microscope and enlarged the image of Dr. Lindblom—Oscar Lindblom—Dr. Oscar Lindblom, boy chemist. She enlarged and enlarged and studied the validity of the idea.

As specimen for use, he was not her ideal. Quite the opposite. Too weak, yet there was strength in this, for he would bend with her strength, he would comply. Also, another fault, too lacking in distinction. He had definitely taken on Hammarlund's absence of coloration, the pallor of the face chalky, and all else, features and frame and personality tentative, inconclusive. For such an experiment, one wanted strength, daring, dash, masculinity. Still, the microscope was unerring, the virtues were evident, also. His face, for all its monotony, was well made, even pleasing, the features regular. Despite his thinness, there must be six feet of him, with the limbs finely proportioned if not muscular. He was single, she remembered, and unattached. And most favorable quality of all—potentially troublesome, but now favorable, none the less—he worshiped her.

With an incisiveness that she had not known since her laboratory period, she made her decision. It was this or nothing. In less than three days, Claude would be beyond retrieving. She must stake all on this, trusting her suspicions of Claude's vulnerability and knowledge of the power of her own sudden ingenuity.

Boldly, she advanced on Lindblom. "Well, hello," she said cheerfully. "A handsome young bachelor like you all alone?"

Lindblom came around startled, recognized her and beamed, heard her and blushed. "I—I get this way sometimes at parties. Not exactly unsocial, but—"

"I understand," said Denise softly, searching his eyes, which he quickly cast downward. "May I stay with you?" she inquired.

"May you? Why, Dr. Marceau—I cannot tell you—this I esteem. It is a glory for me."

She decided not to waste time. Elaborations and seductive dances were not necessary to win over this callow youth. "Dr. Lindblom, do I remember correctly—did you invite me to inspect your laboratory?"

"Yes, I did. It is what I wish more than anything. You said that you and your husband might someday—"

"I am a woman. Do I possess a woman's privilege—?"

"Privilege?"

"—to change my mind?"

Lindblom's gray eyes were wide with revival of a lost hope. "Would you? Is it possible?"

"My husband and I have another Nobel function in the morning. But it is unimportant. He can manage it himself. I have had enough of those formal duties. I plan to have a migraine headache tomorrow morning. Once I have got out of the engagement, my headache will vanish. And I will be quite free to do as I please. And you? Will you be free, Dr. Lindblom?"

"I will see that I am free," said Lindblom with rising enthusiasm. "I have nothing but my work. Besides, Hammarlund will be so pleased."

"Forget Hammarlund," she said curtly. "I find him tiresome and opportunistic. No, not Hammarlund or anyone, for that matter. If I am to have a busman's holiday, I wish to have it on my terms. It is you I want to see, quite alone, undisturbed by others. You will show me your experiments, charts. We will go over them together in peaceful quiet—"

"Oh, Dr. Marceau, I cannot express to you my joy!"

"Perhaps we shall find ways to be useful to one another."

"For me, it will be memorable—"

"Yes," said Denise with a faint smile, "I expect so." Then she added in a crisper tone, "Let us say eleven o'clock tomorrow morning. Where will I find you?"

"The private laboratory is a half kilometer from the house, back in the small forest. I will tell you what I can do. I shall send a car for you, with instructions, and I will wait for you at the forest path."

"At eleven?"

"I could not forget in a million years."

From the corner of an eye, Denise observed Claude re-enter the living room with studied casualness. She pretended not to see him. With an elaborate show of gaiety, she slipped an arm inside Lindblom's arm.

"Now we must celebrate," she said. "Take me to the bar. We shall toast our—scientific assignation."

Waiting for one more drink before dinner, Andrew Craig greeted Denise Marceau and Lindblom with a noncommittal smile, and gave his attention once more to the troublesome seating-plan placard on the easel at the end of the table. He had promised to look in, once more, on John Garrett in the bathroom, but he was sure that the ammonia and cold water had been sufficient to repair the medical researcher and revive his sense of propriety.

Since he had been separated from Emily for more than an hour, the prominent seating plan took on even greater importance for Craig.

Nonchalantly, he drifted to the end of the table, pretending to have just noticed the placard bearing the legend *Placering*, scrutinized it closely, and then picked it off the easel and took it to the carved mahogany armchair against the wall.

Sitting, Craig held the placard before him as a shield. His pose was of absorption, but looking past it, he could see that no one in the room was paying attention to him. Quickly, he pulled the gold pencil from inside his jacket, uncapped the top with his thumb, and made two erasures and revisions. Now, no longer did Jacobsson and Vasilkov enjoy Emily Stratman between them. Instead, they had the pleasure of Leah Decker's companionship. And Craig, now deprived of Leah, was soothed by the presence of Emily on one side and Margherita Farelli at the other. Craig was pleased with his handiwork. Signora Farelli was not meddlesome, not demanding, and Craig would have Emily at his elbow the entire dinner.

Getting to his feet, he brought the improved seating plan back to the easel.

As he left it, Craig saw Märta Norberg step away from Leah, excusing herself, stare across the room, and then start directly for him. With Emily taken care of, Craig did not mind. He braced himself, and swallowed Scotch, and waited.

Märta Norberg, with a toss of her unruly hair and a disconcerting smile, was before him.

"Have you been trying to avoid me?" she said teasingly.

"What ever gave you that idea?"

"I don't know. You've been monumentally disinterested in your hostess."

"Quite the contrary. My hostess seemed well occupied."

The superior feline smile came and went. "Occupied, yes. Well occupied, no. However, your sister-in-law was quite interesting."

"Was she?"

"Her delivery may leave much to be desired, but her material is interesting," said Märta Norberg. "She talked a good deal about you."

"I see."

"At any rate, when I observed this paragon of hers all alone in the armchair, so forlorn, reduced to reading the seating plan, I thought I might provide more amusing company."

He wondered if she had seen him change the seating plan. He decided that she had not. "To confess the truth, Miss Norberg, I am an avid and indiscriminate reader—anything I can find—railroad timetables, old telephone books, seed catalogues—dinner seating arrangements—and when there is nothing else available, I even read palms."

She held out her slender hand, slowly revolving it until the palm was upward. "Read mine."

He shaded his brow, set his face in a feigned trance, and touched Norberg's palm with his forefinger. "I see one woman, majestically alone, and thousands at her feet."

"I hate crowds, Mr. Craig," she said quietly. "If you look closer, you might see more. Not the career line, the personal life line. You mean you don't see a man coming into my life?"

Craig knew that she was frankly staring at him, but he did not lift his eyes. Was an invitation couched in the child's play? It was possible, anything was possible, and the likelihood of it amused him. He remembered, at once, Gottling's little speech: democracy had virtually swept away titled royalty, and then, to fill the gap, created a royalty of its own—the elite aristocracy of celebrity, wealth, and prize winners. In this rare circle, background did not matter. A boy might come from New York's lower East Side or Coney Island, be born of semiliterate parents with unfashionable ghetto accents, uneducated beyond grammar school or high school, or he might emerge from a farm in Iowa or a ranch in Idaho, be born of narrow peasant stock, unread and unlearned and unsophisticated, but if he could floor any man on earth with a punch, or crudely and savagely outwit all competition and amass vast wealth, or, yes, write a book that moved millions—if he could have his image before the world on magazine covers, or his name in print, if he could become a Success—he was of the elite. A single unique talent or sometimes luck alone, either one was enough. He was of the earth's anointed. Overnight, he was in that higher place. Overnight, the ones who would previously not have deigned to look at him or speak to him, the ones who considered him of the herd, would now recognize his aristocracy and accept him as their equal. Overnight, what had so recently been impossible was all-possible. Overnight, he could banter with a King, share food with a millionaire, and know flirtation from an unapproachable sex symbol. So incredible. For he was no different than before the ascension. He had not changed in his eyes. He had changed in *their* eyes.

And tonight, Märta Norberg could say to him, "You mean you don't see a man coming into my life?"

A month ago, he would have been timorous of asking for her autograph. Now she was asking for his.

He bent over her hand. "I see many men," he said.

"Unlikely," she said, and instantly withdrew her hand. "You are a faker, Mr. Craig. Confine your reading to timetables and telephone books." Then her mouth smiled, as if to remove any hint of annoyance. "I read in the newspaper the other day that the things you like most about Sweden include Carl Milles, Ivar Kreuger, and Märta Norberg."

"And Orrefors glass," said Craig mildly.

"Yes, of course." She considered him. "Am I to feel complimented in that company?"

"You all have this in common—divine artistry. Except that you and Orrefors have also beauty."

"Orrefors is transparent and hard. Whatever you think, I am neither." She ran her fingers through her hair. "But I have artistry and beauty, yes. I can see it is a compliment."

"I always looked forward to your plays and pictures," said Craig honestly. "Going to either, when you starred, was forever an event. I've missed you, and I know I'm not alone. Why did you quit?"

"I didn't quit," said Märta Norberg testily. "It is the creative writer who has quit. I have waited for one to invent a role worthy of my time. In the last four years, I have read nothing but trash. Why don't men write about women any more—women as large as life, as tragic, as important? Why are men afraid? Where is Anna Karenina? Where is Emma Bovary? Where is Marguerite Gautier? Why have women diminished in size?"

"Women are not smaller today," said Craig. "The problem is that men have shrunk—withered by complexity—and men are so busy growing up to women, they no longer have time to sing of them."

"You may be right," said Märta Norberg thoughtfully. "Perhaps it is up to us. . . . At any rate, I've been made so desperate that I am involving myself in rehashing Rachel's old repertory. I'm considering Eugène Scribe's *Adrienne Lecouvreur*. Do you know the play?"

"Not the play but the subject. Lecouvreur was the eighteenth-century actress Voltaire loved, wasn't she?"

"Yes. And Marshal de Saxe. It's an old play, perhaps dated. But it has a woman. It has grand passion. At least the heroine is worthy of Märta Norberg." She measured Craig briefly. "Would you like to see me rehearse the role?"

"I would like nothing better."

"Very well. I'm at the Royal Dramatic Theater every afternoon. Cronsten is directing me. Why don't you drop in tomorrow? As a matter of fact, there is a business matter I'd like to discuss with you. This is no place for it. But if you came by late afternoon tomorrow—five or six—when rehearsal is almost over, we can have a cocktail and talk in peace. May I expect you?"

"I'll be there, Miss Norberg."

She glanced off. "Ragnar has his handkerchief out. That is his distress flag. It means he wants to be rescued. Very well. Tomorrow afternoon, Mr. Craig."

"Thank you, Miss Norberg."

His eyes followed her to Hammarlund's group. Her stride was a man's stride, and her carriage slouched and poor, and yet there was utter femininity and provocation in her lanky figure. Around her, like the circles around Saturn, there was an atmospheric film of inscrutability. Or had that been manufactured in a hundred press agents' typewriters? No, he told himself, you did not create such things. It was there. You wanted to know what she was really like, deep inside, and if she possessed, to a degree more than mortal, the mystic power to make a man feel he was superman. Thus spake Zarathustra. Thus spake Märta Norberg.

As he watched Norberg link her arm in Hammarlund's arm, and join Hammarlund's company, Craig saw Emily Stratman detach herself from that group. He fancied that she had tried to catch his eye, but he was not certain. She had placed her empty glass on a table, and was moving toward the French doors. Craig's gaze followed her passage, and Norberg was forgotten. If femininity was desired, femininity and provocation and mystery, Emily carried all these more naturally. The silk jersey gown clung to the contours of her body as she walked, to the wavelike vacillation of her breasts, to the sinuous, rippling thighs. She had lifted the latch on the French door, and then she was gone.

Craig looked over his shoulder. Leah was elsewhere absorbed. Immediately, he started for the terrace.

Outside, the air was colder now, and the English lamps seemed shrouded. At first, he could not find her, and then he made her out at last, her back to him, arms folded against the weather, in a shadowed corner of the veranda.

He went to her. "Emily—"

She revolved toward him, slowly, without surprise, her green eyes and innocent face serious and trusting.

"—it's too cold out here, but"—he faltered, because her eyes were intent on his mouth, and she was not listening—"I had to see you alone."

She said nothing, but her bare arms crossed, she seemed to lean toward him, and he placed one arm around her shoulders, spontaneously, unthinking, to draw her close and give her garment warmth and body warmth.

In his half embrace, she lifted her face, eyes closed, soft lips parted, and momentarily he was mindless of discretion and consequences. He brought her up to him, her back arched against his hand, until his mouth met her moist lips. The kiss held for a small infinity, until both his arms had gone around her, and the kiss deepened, and rising passion gripped them both.

Suddenly, with a gasp, she withdrew her lips from his mouth, eyes still tight, but averting her face, yet remaining in his hold.

"Emily," he whispered, "my darling—"

She buried her face low in his chest, saying not a word, and as he stroked her shining hair, the sounds of a brass gong from within, once, twice, three times, brought them back to themselves, their separateness, and the stone terrace, and the night's chill.

The butler's voice in the living room followed the echoes of the gong. "Dinner is served . . . dinner is served."

Emily pushed free of Craig. "They'll be looking for us," she said.

He caught her arm. "No, Emily, wait—"

"We must," she said, and she went inside.

For a few seconds, Craig remained stationary, unconscious of the weather, still savoring her lips and the compliance of her body and their intimacy. At last, eager to lead her in to dinner beside him, he went through the French door.

He saw at once that most of the guests had disappeared. Four couples were still in line, in the regulation Swedish manner, ladies to the right and their gentlemen partners to the left.

He was surprised that Emily had not waited for him. Perhaps, he told himself, she had not seen the revised seating plan.

Since he was tardy, he decided to take a short Scotch in to dinner. Ordering it, his gaze fell on the placard marked *Placering,* and then what held him—unless it was a trick of vision—were two blotches. Perhaps his erasures were clumsy, he thought.

He made his way to the chart to enjoy again his arrangement: Emily Stratman, Andrew Craig, Margherita Farelli.

The blotches he had observed were real, but they were not from his erasures. Firm new erasures were on either side of his name.

Emily Stratman was no more. In her place was written the name of Leah Decker. The return of Leah Decker, neatly written in a hand he recognized as the familiar hand of Leah Decker. Craig's own name remained untouched, unchanged. But like Emily, his other partner had disappeared also. Margherita Farelli was gone, and in her place, in an unfamiliar hand, but in a hand distinctively feminine, was penciled the name of Märta Norberg.

"Here you are, Mr. Craig."

He turned to find Märta Norberg smiling at him. "You see what we think of you? You are the partner of the hostess. You are to be at my left. Ragnar is about to make his speech of welcome. Will you take me in?"

IX

In the center of the Old Town of Stockholm there exists one of the architectural curiosities of the city and among the foremost of its tourist attractions. This is Mårten Trotzig's Lane, an official street no more than three feet wide. The lane is not level, but consists of worn stone stairs that descend steeply, between the caked walls of old buildings, beneath two wrought-iron public lamps, into Västerlånggatan.

Mårten Trotzig's Lane was both Nicholas Daranyi's cross and vanity. His ground-floor, three-room apartment was located flush with the thoroughfare of Västerlånggatan, and only a few buildings down from the lane. The disadvantage of this was that being on the street, so close to traffic, so near a guidebook site, made quiet and peace almost impossible for Daranyi to achieve. In summer and winter alike, the bands of tourists were chattering magpies beneath his window, running to and from the lane, constantly vocal —in English, in German, in Danish—in praise of its oddity. Daranyi liked to read and contemplate what he read, and meditate on things he had seen and things he had done in his wandering life, but the location of his apartment made such monastic retreat impossible.

Yet, for almost no money on earth would Daranyi have surrendered his apartment and lived in a more modern and tranquil one in the new city. Even though his apartment's situation had its shortcomings, and even though the rent was slightly beyond his means (which meant skimping on other necessities, here and there), Daranyi treasured it for its address. This was snobbery, and he knew it, and did not mind, for such superficialities were of importance to him. His apartment was in one of the most respected and desirable sections of the city, and one of the most ancient, and for a stateless man who had lived from hand to mouth so long, it was worth anything to have the dignity and rooted tradition of such an address.

The best times in all the year were the dark early mornings of winter and the dark long nights of winter. Then the tourists did not come, and few trod the steps of Mårten Trotzig's Lane, and Daranyi had his address and peace as well.

Now it was Daranyi's favorite time, the dark early morning of December seventh—8:15 in the morning—with the air in the streets like the wall of an iceberg. Occasionally, snowflakes flurried and swirled and briefly hung suspended in the frozen air, before slowly parachuting to the pavement. It was a morning to be off the streets, to be snug and comfortable in a heated apartment, and Daranyi was, indeed, snug and comfortable in his heated apartment, and convinced that he was one of God's favored souls. However, what made his bliss complete was not warmth and roof alone, but an added security that was man-made—the immediate prospect of considerable income.

Daranyi was proud to have so distinguished a figure as Dr. Carl Adolf Krantz call upon him at this address, seek him out with restrained urgency, partake of his hospitality—the brown leather chair, antique table from Bukowski, steaming coffee, buttered rolls—as Krantz was now doing, and offer, by his very presence, the promise of money in a period of financial drought. Krantz's visits to this address were infrequent, but always welcome, for they were never merely social or frivolous. When Krantz appeared, cash was not far behind. True, during his cryptic call to Daranyi shortly after his return home late last night, and during the first ten minutes since his arriving this morning, Krantz had not spoken one word of an assignment, but Daranyi *knew*, felt it beneath the layers of flesh, perceived it in his bones.

Determined to show his occasional employer that he had no anxiety, anticipated nothing but a friendly call, Daranyi squatted on his chair across from Krantz, and blew on his coffee, and listened to banal comments on world events, and waited. Presently, Krantz ceased the irrelevant conversation, and devoted himself to the rolls and coffee, and they both had their breakfasts in silence. With this, from previous observation of Krantz's behavior pattern, Daranyi understood that the waiting game would soon be over. Shortly, there would be a few indirect questions, the tentative posing of an idea that wanted looking into, direct questions, then orders.

Krantz's empty cup clattered to his saucer, and Daranyi started to rise to bring the bamboo-handled pot, but Krantz's lifted hand stayed him in his place.

"Never mind, I have had enough," said Krantz. Genteelly he patted his mustache and goatee with his napkin, then took a metal puzzle out of his pocket, swinging it, and finally letting his short fingers twist and untwist it. "Tell me, Daranyi, what have you been up to these days? Have you been behaving yourself?"

"At my age, Dr. Krantz? I practice celibacy, and good eating three times a day. Food and first editions, those are my excesses."

"Are you busy?"

Daranyi swiftly weighed his answer: very-busy implied unavailability and might scare the customer off; not-at-all-busy implied undesirability and might make the customer a stiff bargainer. "Moderately, moderately busy," said Daranyi. "There is always something going on, you know."

Daranyi weighed elaboration: if he was not specific, the customer would think he was lying; if he was too specific, the customer would know he could not be trusted. "I am concluding two industrial accounts—of course, Dr. Krantz, I am not at liberty to divulge—"

"Yes, yes," said Krantz impatiently. "I will tell you why I am here—I have an idea. A minor matter has come up—something of concern to me—and I would need some—some intelligent, discriminating research. I could think of only you, Daranyi. The question is—your immediate availability."

Would you be able to put your other work aside, at once, to undertake short, intensive investigation? Be truthful, Daranyi. We know each other. We are old friends. I would have to have your complete dedication, your full cooperation. I could not have you being diverted by any other project. You know my requirements—thoroughness, promptness, prudence. What do you say to that, Daranyi?"

"As I have told you, my other assignments are about done. Fortunately, the deadlines are still a while off. But even if they were not, I would put them aside for you." Fleetingly, to Daranyi's mind came *The Faerie Queene:* this the temple of Venus, and here inseparable friends, here Damon and Pythias, Jonathan and David, Hercules and Hylas. Daranyi's smooth, plump countenance assumed the hood of Damon, earnest, sincere, faithful to whatever end. "You have always been generous with me, Dr. Krantz," continued Daranyi, "and I cannot help but stand ready to serve you, with all devotion, at any time. Your word is my command."

Krantz's uneasiness gave way to comfort. "Good, good."

"You need only speak of the problem, and I will address myself to it immediately."

Krantz, who had been deep in the leather chair so that his stumpy legs dangled and his shoes barely touched the carpet, pushed himself forward in what was to be a gesture of confidence. Now he perched on the front of the chair, his shoes solidly planted before him. He stuffed the puzzle in his pocket —it was as if Eckart was over his shoulder, judging him—and proceeded to the business of the morning.

"As you know, Daranyi, this is Nobel Week, one of my busiest weeks of the year—"

"So it is. How time flies. I had almost forgotten."

"Have you read of this year's crop of laureates who have come to us from America, France, Italy?"

"I am ashamed to confess this, Dr. Krantz, but I have been so busy, I have hardly had time to glance at my newspapers this week."

Krantz brushed at the air with his hand. "No matter. The assignment I have for you concerns these Nobel winners. Because of their importance, and the nature of what you must learn, your research—the assignment itself —must be strictly confidential."

"Dr. Krantz, I have never failed you." Then Daranyi added with pride, "I am professional."

"Take no offense. I merely emphasize the—the stature of the persons being investigated—and remind you they are in the international limelight. Now then, a rumor has come to the attention of several of us on the prize-giving committees. One of our laureates, I know not which, may have an unsavory —no, let me put it this way—may have a questionable past and be of questionable character. There could be a scandal, before or after the Ceremony. If this is true, we must know about it in advance, we must be informed, prepared to take preventive action. The good name of the entire Nobel Foundation is at stake."

Daranyi nodded gravely, and did not believe one word of what Krantz had told him. Daranyi's professional assets were distrust and suspicion, and long experience had taught him that the motives men pretended to have in hiring him were always to be doubted. But Daranyi never fussed about this. Morality had nothing to do with free-lance espionage. An ethical spy was an impoverished spy, or worse, a dead one. You took a job. You rendered efficient services for a fee. You did not think. You survived.

Daranyi did not think now. He wore the Damon hood. "I can see the importance of this, and your concern," he said.

Krantz appeared pleased with himself. For him, so dryly factual, so lacking in the art of fable, the worst of it was over. The rest would be relatively simple. "In quite a natural way, several of us on the committees banded together on the matter—unofficially, of course—and determined to take action, *sub rosa*. I mentioned to my colleagues that I knew someone who could help—and here I am."

"I am grateful," said Daranyi. "You wish me to proceed as I did in the investigation of the Australian physicists?"

Krantz recoiled slightly at the bald mention of an old intrigue, best forgotten. "Not quite," he said. "That was a leisurely research done at long distance. In this research, there is a time element, and the subject—subjects —of the research are close at hand, and therefore your inquiries will be more dangerous. Now, I have spoken of rumor of a scandal, but I do not want you out blatantly snooping for one—not at all. As a matter of fact, you may find no evidence of scandal at all. But we on the committee have our information, our half of the jigsaw, and by supplying us more information, you may supply us with the missing half of the puzzle. Do you understand?"

"I fully understand."

"I will leave with you pocket-sized photographs of the laureates, a record of their recent activities in Stockholm—public activities, that is—and the remainder of their schedules. I will also leave you condensed public biographies of each laureate, containing their backgrounds, statements, habits, as taken from our official records and gleaned from the press. This we have and is of no importance. I will give it to you merely so that you may familiarize yourself with the subjects, know who they are, know the quarry."

"Everything will be useful."

Krantz's beady eyes glittered. "What we require, and do not possess, is *personal* data—as much as can be obtained in a hurry—on each laureate, and his or her relatives and associates. I repeat, do not look for overt scandal. What we want is that which has been kept secluded from public view—the small weaknesses of the present, indiscretions of the past, the personal histories unknown, the expurgated sections of experience or conduct. I am certain I need elaborate no further. You are practiced in these matters."

"Thank you," said Daranyi modestly. "How many subjects will I research?"

Krantz dug inside his suit-coat pocket and brought out two envelopes. One he placed on the end table. "The photographs," he said. He opened the second, longer envelope and took out and unfolded what appeared to be a half-dozen closely typed pages. He leafed through the pages. "Six laureates," he said finally, "and two wives, one sister-in-law, one niece. Perhaps, because of time limitations, all should not be given equal emphasis."

For half a minute, Krantz was lost in thought. Eckart had suggested the red herring: because you can trust no one in these affairs, do not give the impression you want only one laureate, Max Stratman, investigated, but make it appear you wish all six laureates investigated, Stratman being only one more among them. This was safe, Krantz realized, but the fallacy was that it spread Daranyi's investigation too thin. They would obtain a little about everyone, and possibly too little about Stratman. Krantz weighed the risk of emphasizing several names, instead of all, and then he took the risk.

"I will tell you what," Krantz resumed. "I want to make your inquiry easier. Here, we have ten persons to be looked into, but because of what we already know, perhaps more attention should be given four of them. In your place, I would expend maximum effort on—let us say—Dr. John Garrett and Dr. Carlo Farelli, the laureates in medicine—their wives are of lesser moment, although one never knows—on those two gentlemen, and—let us say—Professor Max Stratman, also—Professor Stratman and his niece, whose name is Emily Stratman. You will keep this in mind, Daranyi?"

"My memory is unfailing."

"Yes, Garrett, Farelli, the Stratmans." He examined the papers in his hand. "As for the others—the Marceaus—Andrew Craig—"

Daranyi's bland face almost gave away its first surprise. "Andrew Craig?" he echoed.

Krantz looked up. "The literary laureate," he said. "You know him?"

Daranyi's mind had gone back to the tall, gaunt American in Lilly Hedqvist's bed, to their breakfast, to his monologue on sex life in Sweden with Craig in the Norma restaurant. There could not be two Andrew Craigs, both writers, in Stockholm in one winter. The heavy-drinking man—my God, he had even been to the nudist society with Lilly, the puritanical, troubled, attractive man who was Lilly's lover—was no more a wanderer, tourist on the run, but he was one of the world's great authors, a Nobel laureate, no less. And Daranyi remembered that he had lectured this giant as he might a farm lad. Suddenly, he felt foolish and weak, and tried to pin his mind to Krantz's question, and with effort succeeded.

"Know him? No, no, of course not. I had been reading some books by an American named Craig—"

"Undoubtedly the same, but we have no time for literary digressions, Daranyi."

Daranyi's mind leaped to Lilly: did she know the august position of her paramour? Probably not, or she would have mentioned it. Certainly not, he decided. Lilly, for all her alertness and native wisdom, was widely unread. She was a delightful little animal of the senses, whose frankness sometimes passed for knowledge and erudition. Daranyi, as her fatherly mentor, knew her better. Except for occasional periodicals devoted to health and nature and popular psychology for mothers, she read next to nothing, certainly not books, in fact, not even newspapers. She would know neither Craig's creative work nor his new reputation. Was there an advantage for her, in knowing? Craig enjoyed her, it was evident, and had interest in her and sympathy for her. What a catch he might make for Lilly.

Daranyi realized that he would have to give the problem further thought when he was alone. Now his duty was to Krantz, and the physicist's obvious red herring. The interior titillation was—which of the four emphasized was the one that Krantz was trying to hide from him, and yet learn the most about? Dr. Garrett? Dr. Farelli? Professor Stratman? Miss Stratman? Well, that was the fun of it, above and beyond the kronor involved.

"—can give them less time," Krantz was saying. "Mind you, I want something on the Marceaus and Craig, indeed I do, and the wives and the Decker lady—one never knows—but I want you to use your time where it counts the most. I will trust your judgment."

"You have made everything clear, as ever, Dr. Krantz. Now as to the time—"

"The time limitation is immutable," said Krantz firmly. "I must have your data by the early evening of December ninth, and if you can bring us the research earlier, I might arrange a bonus. But the ninth—"

Daranyi whistled. "Impossible."

Krantz recited Eckart's words to him. "Nothing is impossible, Daranyi. I do not ask you to move mountains. A few facts from here, from there—"

Daranyi had been calculating. "You are giving me forty-eight hours—sixty at most."

"I am fully cognizant of the difficulties, and I come prepared." He took out his wallet, removed a wad of bills held together with a paper clip. "Two thousand five hundred kronor for expenses alone," he said.

Daranyi picked up the bills and weighed them with satisfaction. "This will help."

"I presume you are going to do as you have always done—?"

"How is that?"

"Buy information from foreign correspondents, among other sources?"

"That is likely."

"The timing is fortunate. Reporters are here from all over the world—the Grand, Hotel Stockholm, Eden Terrace, Foresta, Carlton are teeming with them. Many need extra money. The sum I have given you should go far."

"Except with the Americans."

"True," said Krantz. "But you will find other means with them. For one lead, I might mention a young woman named Miss Sue Wiley, who represents Consolidated Newspapers of New York—you will remember her name?"

"Sue Wiley."

"I happen to know that she is preparing an exposé, on the sensational side, of the Nobel history and its many winners, past, present. I suspect she would do anything for new information."

388

"Are you suggesting, Dr. Krantz, that she might give me specific information I need, in return for such gossip as I can supply for her stories?"

"No question about it. But I would not pretend for her that I was a journalist. She might worry about the competition—Americans are so conscious of exclusivity—whatever the word is they use."

"Scoop."

"Yes, yes, idiotic word. But give yourself another identity."

"You can leave that to me, Dr. Krantz."

The physicist combed his goatee with his fingertips. "You might pay heed to the program that the laureates have been following. You will find they have been drunk at the Royal Palace and at Hammarlund's villa—"

"Do not worry," Daranyi reassured his visitor, "I have my sources everywhere—and with two thousand five hundred kronor—" He hesitated. "All that bothers me is the time limitation."

"You will do your best. I ask no more."

"Very well. You can depend on me." There was the final matter. Daranyi coughed and cleared his throat. "Now, as to my services—"

Krantz came to his feet and pulled his jacket straight. "Your fee is not yet settled, Daranyi. I am having another meeting with my colleagues. You will have to trust my judgment. Have I ever failed you in this respect? I have not. It will be good pay for forty-eight hours' work. It will be more than adequate recompense, more than you received on your last assignment, that I pledge. And I repeat, if you can deliver material earlier, there will be a bonus."

"In financial affairs, I trust your generosity, your knowledge of my usefulness, entirely."

Krantz had taken his overcoat, and now Daranyi was on his feet and helping his employer into it.

At the door, Krantz paused. "Utmost discretion, Daranyi, I warn you."

A smile enlivened Daranyi's face. He made his joke. "I have a neck, too. I like it."

Krantz grunted. "Then it is settled. At any hour of the ninth, when you are ready, telephone my private number. I will be waiting in the apartment until you call. Then I will expect you right over."

"I hope I have something," said Daranyi.

"I expect you will," said Krantz.

He left. The meeting was over. Daranyi stared absently at the closed door. He wondered what was behind all this. Soon enough, he might know. That was the sport of it, that and the money.

He returned to the end table and took up the biographies that Krantz had left behind. Slowly, he read. His forty-eight hours of voyeurism had begun.

At exactly 11:05 on the same morning—the air still as frozen as it had been in the earlier hours, but with the landscape of Djurgården now painted zinc-gray rather than black—Denise Marceau had been driven through a rear gate behind Åkslottet, and had seen Dr. Oscar Lindblom through the wind-shield, slapping his arms and waiting at the forest path ahead.

As he assisted her from Hammerlund's Bentley, a luxury that she enjoyed, so fitting for her mood, she was pleased to observe that Lindblom appeared more handsome, more definite, more manly than she had remembered. His hair had been caught by the wind, and rumpled, and the weather had made his cheeks ruddy and alive. The woolen muffler he had bound about his neck and shoulders—the muffler with no topcoat—gave him an indefinable dash. He looked less like a cavity, praise the Lord, she decided, and she went cheer-fully on his arm through the rows of stripped trees. Lindblom said that there were some tame deer in the forest, but Denise saw none.

The private laboratory, a one-story cement building, thirty by sixty feet, stood in a clearing, isolated from all other construction and habitation. Al-though the inside of the laboratory—two rooms and a bath—had the familiar appearance of a dozen laboratories Denise had known in France, this one proved infinitely more up-to-date.

Lindblom, attentive as a military school junior, had helped her off with her heavy gray strolling coat. She had been pleased, certain that she had not imagined it, that he had furtively admired her new silk shantung dress, low-cut and stylishly short for daytime wear.

After lighting her cigarette, he had guided her proudly through the larger room, the work section of the laboratory, meticulously pointing out and dis-cussing each glass still and its contents, each high vacuum pump, the tem-perature gauges and heaters and flasks and beakers, the spectrophotometer, the high-speed centrifuge, the experimental rodents in stainless steel cages. Despite her lack of interest in science at the moment, Denise was impressed at the cash outlay the private laboratory represented.

As they marched up and down, past the counters, Lindblom discoursed with nervous enthusiasm about the work in progress. His love for algae stains and soybean nodules and Rhodophyceae and Chlorella dinned on her ear-drums. His hatred for the chemicals of natural food, his devotion to synthetics, were passionate. What interested Denise was not the knowledge that Lind-blom imported, but rather that he possessed any range of emotion at all. She wondered if only the chemistry of food stimulated him. She wondered if he would react, similarly, to the chemistry of woman.

She listened occasionally, but for the most part she did not listen at all. It was one of her gifts: the ability to shut off almost all human sound, yet to know intuitively when to nod and when to give assent and when to interject a comment of praise or displeasure. She had employed this ability through the laboratory tour and lecture. She had more momentous things in her head.

From the moment of her decision at the Hammarlund party last night, until the moment Claude had left her this morning, she had been of cheerful dis-position, secure with her secret inner hope. This sudden change in her tem-perament had confused and dismayed Claude, and she had seen it in him. She had even guessed that he might be suspicious of her. At the end of break-fast, in the hotel suite, he had interrogated her carefully about her activity and enjoyment of the Hammarlund meeting. He had probed, and for the first time since her humiliation, she had felt real superiority.

The odds, she had known, despite her secret inner hope, were against her still. Gisèle's imminent coming from Copenhagen might obliterate her entire effort. Still, she had made up her mind to do something, to make a fight of it, and that was heartening.

But her effort, she had known, was yet to be launched. Last night, she had made the crucial initial decision. In this laboratory, this morning, she would have to make the ultimate decision. And, once it was made, she would have to see it through.

Trailing Lindblom, she peered at her watch. She had arrived at 11:05. It was now 11:55. The zero hour that she had set herself loomed close. The ultimate decision. Question One: Should she do it? There were two courses open: (a) mild flirtation, a holding of hands, an embrace, a kiss, romantic whispering, to be followed by similar meetings devoted to the same and no more; or (b) sexual intercourse.

Instinct advised her that moderation would not work. Claude's infatuation —hypnotized as he was by Gisèle's sexuality—would not be shattered by mere retaliatory flirtation. She could not play-act the pretense that it was more, and she knew that Lindblom was even less capable than she. Claude would view the flirtation as a juvenile's revenge, rather ridiculous, rather foolish, a pathetic joke. On the other hand, illicit love had a sweeping power that could bring real response. Here, no play-acting would be demanded of Lindblom. He would be her lover and know it and show it. And real possession of her body, unviolated by another since her marriage, would be a shattering blow to Claude's ego. If it was not, her marriage was done anyway, and nothing would be lost. But if his ego was injured, and what remained was jealousy, there was hope.

She followed Lindblom about the laboratory and continued to reason with herself. She was satisfied that Question One had been resolved. Should she do it? Yes, she should. Now Question Two: Could she do it? This was a difficulty. She had been raised a French Catholic. Her parents had been stern overseers. Yet, in young maturity, free of them and adrift from the Church, she had enjoyed three brief but earnest affairs with male students of the Sorbonne. But after she had met Claude, and made her vows, she had not once cheated, not once flirted, despite the legendary nonsense about the loose morals of French women. She had not even thought of such a thing.

She walked and deliberated: but now, it was all different, and Claude had made it so. What vow policed her? The vow had been mutual, in partnership, and he had broken it. What chastity need she preserve and for whom? And what fears need she have? She was a woman, and that made it easier. She was a woman scientist, and that made it far easier. She was a woman scientist of forty-two years, matter-of-fact, unromantic, not widely experienced but fully experienced, and that made it far, far easier.

Two factors made it possible and a necessity. Lindblom had halted to point out a beaker of liquid. Standing there, staring at it, by some curious metamorphosis, the beaker became a vessel, and the association was Gisèle Jordan's young vagina given to Claude, to her husband, and his taking it, and she hated the image and drove it off, but her fury with the offenders in her life remained. Then, to forget the image, to please Lindblom, she had stepped beside him to lean closer to the beaker, and inadvertently, she had leaned forward across his outstretched arm so that her generous breasts, loosely bound in a thin lace bra, had pressed deeply against his arm. She had felt, with excitement at her power, the sudden rigidity of his arm, of his entire frame beside her, in fact, and she knew at once that he could be had with ease and that it would be painless. And so Question Two was answered. Could she do it? She could, indeed.

And now, hardly able to contain herself, she was ready for her plot to spin to its climax.

She had backed off, and she considered Lindblom with friendly pleasure. My collaborator, she thought, but said instead, "This has been absolutely fascinating, Oscar—if I may call you that?"

"Please, please—to be sure—"

"Now where can I get off my poor feet and have a cigarette and—"

"Forgive me, Mme Marceau. I am afraid I was carried away by all of this. How thoughtless of me. Come, we will go in the next room—what Hammarlund calls my 'think' room."

Quickly, he led her into the doorless adjacent room, a small carpeted study, a modern desk to one side bearing a portable typewriter, a pile of charts, and an electric coffeepot. Against the wall was a sturdy sofa covered with heavy fabric and a bookcase packed with scientific journals. Two light chairs stood nearby.

"Would you like to use the bathroom?" He pointed it out.

She shook her head.

"Coffee?" he inquired.

She shook her head again. "No, I merely wish to sit and smoke—and find out all about you."

She sat in a corner of the sofa, crossing her legs so that the short silk dress pulled provocatively above her knee. Lindblom tried not to see this, as he bent forward to light her cigarette.

She stretched backward against the sofa, inhaling deeply, so that her breasts bulged outward. Lindblom remained standing awkwardly before her.

"Do you mind telling me about yourself?" she asked.

"Not at all. But I am afraid you will not find me very interesting, outside of my work, Mme Marceau."

"Let me be the judge. How old are you, Oscar?"

"Thirty-two."

Not too bad, she told herself. A respectable age, at least, she told herself. "And still a bachelor?" she inquired. "How do you manage to keep free—with your good looks?"

Lindblom blushed at the compliment.

Before he could reply, she said, "You need not blush. In France, we are used to being frank in all matters. I understood it was the same in Sweden?"

"Not precisely, Mme Marceau. We Swedes are quite a formal and inhibited people."

"What of all the wild reportage I have read about your open sex lives?"

"Some is true, some is not."

"I see. But still, you have managed to escape the girls, Oscar?"

"I am not exactly a cinema star. Besides, I am devoted to my work."

"That I can understand," said Denise in a kindly way, to relax him. "But your social life—do you keep a girl friend?"

He seemed startled. "I am not sure what you mean."

"A mistress? Do not be annoyed with my candor or curiosity. It is simply, having come to know you a little more, I am intrigued. You are quite attractive, you know. So I wonder who the lucky young lady is."

"There is none," he blurted.

"You mean no single one? Surely, you see women?"

He wriggled uncomfortably before her. "I go on dates now and then, but not too often."

"How are these Swedish girls of yours? Do they readily let you make love to them?"

His cheeks were crimson. "Oh, Mme Marceau—"

She smiled. "I *am* giving you a hard time. But I mean to know. Do you make love to your little friends? Or do you not? You can be perfectly honest with me . . . you are not undersexed, are you?"

"Certainly not!" he said indignantly. And then added, "I do not go out with women much because of this long research of ours. Ragnar Hammarlund pays me well, but he is exceedingly demanding. I work day and night—"

"You have not answered me fully."

"Of course, I make love to certain women, when I must, when it is necessary."

"How often?"

"I do not know. I do not think about it. Really, I admit it, I am embarrassed, Mme Marceau—"

"Nevertheless, how often?"

"Once a month maybe, sometimes more, when I can get away. These algae strains—"

"Never mind that. I am truly sorry I have embarrassed you. I did not mean to."

"And I did not mean to be impolite to you, either," he said hastily.

"You are a dear young man. You are not impolite at all." She smoothed the sofa cushion beside her. "Come, sit beside me. I have only been asking these questions because"—she waited while he lowered himself to the sofa, a foot or two from her—"because," she resumed, "I am quite enchanted by your person, your intelligence, and—I warned you we French are candid—your physique. I cannot know too much about you. It is unfair to you, but I confess, I cannot control myself in your presence." She found another cigarette. "Here, light me." She offered him her lighter.

He snapped the lighter, and as he offered the long flame, his hand shook. She reached up and took his hand in her cool hand and steadied it. She moved her hand caressingly over his, closed the lighter for him, but did not release his hand, instead kept it in her own on the sofa between them.

She stared at him. "I must frighten you, Oscar. Do I?"

"Not at all," he said tremulously.

"My failing is that I do not know restraint. I am what I am. I confess what I feel."

"That is admirable," he said, his Adam's apple as busy as a Geiger counter in the Congo.

"It is my weakness, and my weakness is affected by you." She pulled his hand. "Come closer to me."

Stiffly, he moved closer, until their hips and thighs touched. She did not take her eyes off his face. "You are the most handsome man I have known in years, and sweet—do all the girls tell you that?—so sweet, with your devotion to synthetics, with your gorgeous wavy hair and beautiful mouth. I cannot take my eyes off your mouth."

She leaned against him, cupping his intimidated face in her hands, and bringing her lips to his. His lips were unyielding and withdrawn, but she worked her mouth until his lips parted and softened and began to respond. He did not touch her. His arms were limp at his sides, but now he responded with his mouth. She felt his thin body shuddering with excitement, and she feared what might happen, and withdrew from the kiss.

"Now, was that so bad?" she asked.

"No—no—"

"Is that the best you can say?"

"It was wonderful. I am honored—"

"Do you like me a little, Oscar? You can be truthful."

"Mme Marceau, what can I say? You must know how I feel inside. You—you and your husband—you have been my idols. The thought of even meeting you, of daring to be alone with you—"

"Do not be so foolish, Oscar. Make such speeches when you speak of historical figures like the Curies. I am not the Curies. I am not entombed in history books. The Nobel Prize has not mummified me—not my heart or flesh or emotions. I am a human being and young, and I am fortunate enough to be with a human being who is also young, a male who electrifies me. I do not want your admiration for my achievements. I want your admiration for my person. Am I attractive to you?"

"I have dreamt of one like you—"

"But am I attractive?"

"Of course you are, Madame—"

"Of course—who?"

"Madame—"

"Is that the best you can find to call me?"

"But anything else—I could not—"

She considered the tense sallow face and the tic that had come to the corner of his right eye. He was as foolish, as incredible and introverted, as every Stendhal hero, but his fear and inhibition whetted her appetite to bring the experiment to a successful conclusion.

"Oscar," she said softly, "loosen your tongue and let your heart escape. Do you not see what I am trying to learn from you—what I want to hear—what every woman in the prime of life must know from a man who affects her? Do you care for me as a woman? Just as a woman—a female denuded of records and accomplishments and prizes—a female who is not above you, but your equal or less—who wants your admiration—"

Lindblom's face was contorted, and the words choked before they came out. "I worship you," he cried. "I worship you above all women!"

Denise felt victory near. "If you could, Oscar, if it were possible—would you love me?"

"I cannot allow myself to think of such a—"

"Then you would!" she said triumphantly. She turned, half faced him on the sofa, her manner at once businesslike. "Now, we will be sensible about this, while we can be. We are both, the two of us, adult persons of science. At the same time, we admit, we are both human beings. We are people with emotional needs, which require gratification, and that is often as important to us as our work, is it not? Do you grant that to be true?"

"Oh, yes, yes—"

"I have tried desperately to tell you—do not be misled by my public reputation, for I have a private life. I am as much a female woman as any. I have passionate needs, and one of them, the most enslaving, is love, physical love of a man who attracts me. I can no longer endure austerity, pretense. I must humble myself before you." Impulsively, as she had planned, she reached for his hands and gripped them tightly. "Oscar, I need you. Can you understand that? It is a terrifying hunger for a woman, because she must passively wait for fulfillment. For a man, it is so simple. When he has a need, he goes into the street, anywhere, finds someone, and is sated. For a woman, it is unendurable, especially for one in my public position. But today, I can contain myself no longer—because of you. Through these hands of yours, I feel the surge of passion. I am putty. Mold me as you wish."

She closed her eyes, and wondered if she was going on too theatrically, like someone in *Poetry of the English—Blake to Byron*. Perhaps she was talking too much. But then, she decided that she must, for she was playing both roles, both woman and man.

She heard Lindblom's small distant voice. "I would like to—but are you sure—I mean—your husband—"

Denise opened her eyes, about to speak rudely of Claude and to chastise Lindblom for his reticence, but she instinctively knew that either derogation might reduce her partner to impotence. The last word in her thought—impotence—gave her the clue to her reply. She must dissolve Lindblom's fear and guilt potential, by explaining away Claude and her own behavior.

She dropped her gaze and turned her head and furrowed her features in secret suffering. "My husband—my husband"—she was finding it an affliction that curbed speech—"he is impotent. I must not speak of this—"

At once, Lindblom sought to comfort her. "Do not then, please do not torture yourself."

She went on, nevertheless. "Five years ago—after many excesses—ill-using himself—abandoning me—he was stricken by a grave disease. In recovery, he lost his powers of manhood. I had planned to leave him, but now there was his pitiful need for companionship, and I could not. I knew my fate. I must forego all normal womanhood, become his cloistered nun. I did, and have done, my duty. I sublimated my natural wants in our work—*pas facile,* believe me—but his bestiality made obedience a cross too heavy—ah, dear Oscar— my life has been cruel, my body starved and withering for love, for love—"

Carried away by her improvised scene, Denise managed to squeeze tears to her eyes.

She saw that Lindblom's face was all tenderness and empathy, and that his eyes, too, were wet. He stroked her arm. "Poor, poor dearest—" he was saying.

Denise had had enough of verbal foreplay. She sniffled and tried to compose herself. "Oscar, are we alone here?"

"What do you mean?"

"Does anyone come here?"

"Only Hammarlund, and he is gone for the day."

She bent forward and brushed his pale cheek with her lips. "Lock the door, my darling," she whispered, "and draw the blinds. I must go into the bathroom. Be here—wait for me."

She rose with her purse and quickly went into the bathroom, shutting the door behind her.

A few minutes later, she emerged, eyes bright. The room was considerably darkened, more intimate, she saw that the blinds were drawn. Lindblom stood unsteadily beside the sofa, worriedly clasping and unclasping his hands.

She went directly to him, putting her hand on his chest, hearing his wild heart beat, and slid her arms around his waist. "Take me, Oscar," she whispered. "I am in your hands."

He embraced her hard, almost suffocating her, and kissed the top of her head.

She groaned, and whimpered, "Oscar, be kind to me," and pulled him down on the sofa. She kissed his eyes, and then his mouth, all the while unbuttoning his shirt, and then she had her hand on his jumping chest, on his ribs, on his bony back.

Her mouth was at his ear, kissing it, filling it with endearments. "I am ready, Oscar. I have removed my girdle, and taken precautions. There is nothing beneath my slip but love—"

She felt him shiver.

"Poor darling," she whispered, "do you want me to help you off with your clothes—?"

"No—no—"

He tore himself away, almost falling, and then stood upright. Hastily, he shed his trousers and shorts, and stood overwrought before her in shirt and shoes and nothing else.

"Ah, how magnificent you are," she said in a voice muffled and pride-giving. "I am so fortunate. I will cherish this love forever."

She closed her eyes, and wished Claude could see, and awaited the coupling. Seconds passed, and when he had not come to her, she opened her eyes once more and realized that he was not above her, but kneeling beside the sofa, staring at her.

He tried to speak, and strangled, and his Adam's apple was everywhere. "Mme Marceau, are you sure—?"

Her patience was gone and in its place came indignation. "Oscar—it is not fair—you have me hanging here, excited beyond belief. Now—are you or are you not going to—?"

With that, she lifted her slip, and bunched it about her waist, half twisting toward him, showing him her white belly and thighs.

Her voice—she was certain not even the Divine Sarah could have improved upon it—was weak with passion. "Oscar, do not deprive me—I will die without you—"

"Ah, *älskling*—my darling—my darling—"

At once, he was beside her, suffocating her with kisses, caressing her throat and chest. She squirmed sensuously—the last months had been so barren—and made believe that this was the Claude of long ago, and she held her lover tightly.

"I am ready," she murmured. And then, "Are you?"

"I—I think so—"

Her uncertainty alarmed her, and she forgot fantasy and brought herself back to the living task at hand. She understood that, like it or not, she must participate, or there would be no consummation, and the long seduction would be wasted. What to do? She quickened her breath, mouth at his ear and against his face. She gasped and gasped and brought her fingers fluttering, like broken wings, across his lank thighs. His arousal was almost instantaneous, and at once—and during this she recollected the Bible euphemism for sexual intercourse—he had "gone in unto" her.

She had thought that consummation would end her role, and that she could wait out the rest with no part in it, but after several seconds she saw, with objective detachment, that still more was demanded of her. If he would have value in her plan, he must have pride of conquest. Anything less would make him ashamed, and consequently useless to her.

The bloating, misshapen ecstasy on his face—dangling above her like a grotesque mask on the Eve of Allhallows—was the signal that momentarily it would all be over. As yet, she had hardly been moved by, or in any fashion answered, his erratic rhythm. It would be a feat to pretend what was not there—she needed the stimulation of the damp flesh smell of sex, and what there was, and nothing more, was the soap odors of a scrubbed male body and the reek of camphor from the laboratory—but then she remembered, when there was no natural food, there must be a synthetic. Her arousal would have to be a chemical substitute, produced by the mind and not by nature. Desperation spurred her to action.

Any moment, she knew, and so, hastily, she implored her lethargic body to anticipate him. Once more, she closed her eyes tightly, and made her bound bosom heave, and she moaned and begged him not to torture her and begged him to be done with it or else she would die—wondering all through this if her performance was too theatrical, if he could sort the synthetic from the real—and at once, she knew that she was succeeding. Seeing that the climax of the play was upon them, she froze to his frame, then subsided into tiny helpless cries of pleasure, and clutched his elusive transported being as best she could, and when she was positive—for the expected thunder was merely a squeak—she acted a final heaving spasm of release, timed to match his own, but towering above his own to make her pride small and his pride large, and, *mon Dieu*, it was done.

He fell beside her, balancing precariously on the sofa to keep from dropping to the floor, and she placed an arm over her eyes—she had seen the pose once in a French film and had always thought it to mean the woman had been satisfied—and they both rested in silence.

At last, she removed her arm from her eyes. Her neck was stiff, and hurt from reclining without a pillow. She realized that he was looking at her, and that his features reflected growing shame—similar to those of a rough farm boy who had just learned that the female he had taken by force was none other than the Queen—and the enormity of his desecration was beginning to overwhelm him.

Denise moved at once to prevent this reaction. She did not want his protestations of guilt, his apologies, his humbleness, and, in the end, his frightened avoidance of her. He must know that he had not pillaged a holy temple.

"*Merci*, Oscar," she said softly. "*C'est beau*. I have never been loved better."

He blushed—that he could blush even now!—and sighed.

"It is true," she went on. "You satisfied me."

The Adam's apple skittered up and down, like a simian in a banana tree. "I am so glad," he was saying. "I was not sure."

"I am fulfilled, Oscar, and I thank you with all my heart." She glanced at her watch and sat up with dismay. "So late. It is difficult to leave you, Oscar—I do not know what I shall do—but I must hurry back to the hotel, before my husband returns." Her slip was still bunched at her waist, and quickly and chastely she drew it across her knees.

He had watched her. "You are beautiful, Denise."

"Do not be naughty—or you will tempt me again."

He pushed himself to a sitting position. "If only it were possible—"

She brushed his cheek with her lips. "It will be possible," she said, and then added, "You may as well know, I must see you every day I am here."

"I pray for that. When may I see you again?"

"Tomorrow—tomorrow night in my suite."

"But your husband—?"

"He is spending the evening in Uppsala, addressing the faculty. He will not return until long after midnight. You must come to me early—*à huit heures du soir*—I want to enjoy you in leisure. It will be heaven, I promise you." It will also, she thought, be the decisive turning point of my marriage.

When she had finished in the bathroom, had dressed, combed, made up her face, she returned to find that the blinds had been opened and that Lindblom, clothed, was regarding her possessively.

She was gratified. She had performed well.

"I was thinking how lucky I am," he said, "to have found—something besides algae—"

She went jauntily to him, and gave him a hasty off-to-work, married kiss. "It is not you who are lucky, but I. To think that I believed only France was the land of love. How provincial and insular we French become. But I am learning, and you are teaching me. *Au revoir,* dear Oscar, and thank you. Do not be late tomorrow night. Every moment with you is important to my life."

Although it was already two o'clock in the afternoon of December seventh, the double bed in the Nobel suite on the fourth floor of the Grand Hotel was still occupied by a laureate.

Except for several visits to the bathroom, John Garrett had not left his bed of pain all morning, or since. The major injury he had sustained in the Hammarlund garden was not corporeal but spiritual. His gut still ached from Farelli's fist, and his right eye had swollen slightly, although he had not been hit in the eye but on the jaw. But these were minor hurts, and would pass away. What would not leave him was the laceration of his self-respect.

The memory of what had happened to him was an affliction which no salve or pill could remedy. From the moment of wakefulness, early this morning, he had been reminded, by throbbing belly and jaw, of his humiliation, and morbidly he had relived the scene many times in the hours that were behind him.

Sometimes he thought that he had demeaned himself by his unusual behavior. He had not struck, or been struck by, a fellow human being since he had come of age. He was an intellectual, a man of medicine, not an outdoor brawler. Fists settled nothing, except whose biceps were larger and who took more exercise. He had not meant to fight. It was just that the sight of Farelli, so self-assured at the party, had incited Garrett beyond control. And the drinks had been his final downfall. He was not a drinking man, and so that was wrong. If he had not had the drinks, he might not have swung at his rival. On the other hand, if he had not had the drinks and had swung at Farelli, he would have been sober enough to have won the fight. The righteous always won the fight, didn't they? At any rate, he kept reminding himself, he had not meant to stoop so low, had only meant to put Farelli in his place with words, let him know that Garrett was no fool and had his number. He was sorry, too, that he had used the language he had used, and then, again, he was not sorry, for the charlatan deserved no better. But to have been knocked down, made to grovel at the criminal's feet, that was what really rankled. And, almost as bad, to have had an outsider, Craig, witness this miserable subjugation.

What had followed, he kept remembering, had not been too bad. His eye had not yet begun to puff, and, reinforced by more drink, he had survived the formal dinner. When Saralee had put him to bed, he had told her everything—his version, of course—and she had sympathized, wifely moved and upset, and had spoken darkly of putting the police after that unruly Italian hooligan.

Now it was morning—no, afternoon—and he was still in his bed, too distressed and heartsick to leave it and commune with the hostile world outside.

The door buzzer sounded, and he heard Saralee call from the sitting room, "That must be Dr. Öhman. I'll get it."

Garrett propped himself higher on the pillow, wondering why Öhman had come. Then, through the parted drapes, he saw that the visitor was not Öhman at all, but the white-coated room-service waiter who had called for the lunch tray.

When the waiter had gone, Saralee came to the foot of the bed.

"Are you feeling any better, John?"

"I'll live."

"Dr. Öhman should be here soon. Do you want to get out of your pajamas and dress?"

"No, I'll see him here."

After Saralee had returned to addressing her postcards, Garrett left his obsessive reliving of last night's horror, and tried to put his mind on Öhman. At eleven o'clock in the morning, Öhman had telephoned, and Saralee had taken the call. Öhman had sounded, she said afterwards, excited, bursting with some kind of news. He had inquired if Garrett would be free in the afternoon, because if he were free, there was something extremely important Öhman must tell him. Saralee had covered the mouthpiece and repeated this to her husband, and Garrett had waved his hand negatively, muttering that he wanted to see no one. But then he had said, "Ask him what it's about." Saralee had asked what it was about, listened, and said to her husband, "It's about Farelli." At once, Garrett had been curious, and eager to see an ally. "Tell him to come over at two." Now it was just past two, and Garrett was waiting and wondering. What he wondered the most about was whether Öhman had learned of the fight, and was coming to warn him of trouble. And again, obsessively, his mind relived the fight.

It was 2:10 when Dr. Erik Öhman, a thin leather briefcase under his arm, arrived. His pugilistic face was alive with good cheer, but at once sobered when he found his friend in bed, marked by recent combat.

The moment that Saralee had departed with Öhman's topcoat, the Swede pulled a chair up to the bed, studied Garrett's bruised profile, and clucked with concern. He scratched his short cropped reddish hair with stubby fingers.

"Uhhh—Dr. Garrett, my good friend, what has happened to you? Did you fall down some stairs—or bump into a door?"

"I was slugged by that drunken bastard Farelli," said Garrett with vehemence.

Öhman seemed confused. "He actually hit you?"

"Not once, but several times. And he kicked me when I was down."

"But Dr. Garrett, this is—uhhh—shocking, shocking!"

"Absolutely the truth. Last night, Saralee and I had dinner at Ragnar Hammarlund's—all the winners were there—and Farelli, of course. He was drinking, and so was I, and I'll admit I was sore as hell at him. I just couldn't get it out of my mind how he, knowing you were a friend of mine, put one over on me by using you and your good work for a publicity stunt. So, at one point, I decided to tell him that you and I knew what he was up to, and we didn't think he was being ethical. Well, we went outside, to talk privately in the garden, and one thing led to another, and he blurted out something insulting—I forget what—and I made some kind of innocent movement to warn him—maybe I waggled my finger under his nose—something like that—and without any chance for preparation on my part, he became violent—"

"He gave you that black eye?"

"Yes. Just out of nowhere—socked me in the stomach and then a couple of times in the face. I was off balance, not ready, and I tripped and went down. And then he kicked me. I would have killed him, I swear, only someone overheard us, saw us, and intervened."

"Anyone who can do you harm?" asked Öhman, worried.

"No, not at all. It was one of the other winners—Craig, the writer. He stopped Farelli from kicking me, and he kept me from fighting back."

"Just as well. It might have become uglier." He shook his head. "This—uhhh—this Farelli, I knew he was a bad one, after you told me the truth, but I could not have imagined he would resort to such a performance."

Garrett touched his discolored eye. "He is a man without morals, capable of anything."

"I see that," agreed Öhman. It grieved him to find his generous American mentor prone on his bed, so brutally victimized, and he became pensive. "Dr. Garrett, what will you do about this Farelli?"

Garrett shrugged helplessly. "I no longer know how to cope with him. I suppose you can say I am the martyr to my civilized Christian training. Men like you and me are taught to behave ourselves with dignity and forbearance —and, suddenly, when we are confronted with a barbarian who behaves like a pit viper, we are lost. I confess my failure—I do not know how to contend with this beast—this dangerous—"

"Dr. Garrett—"

There was something about Erik Öhman's expression, so set and avenging, that made Garrett halt his tirade in mid-sentence.

"—I have a way for you to contend with Carlo Farelli," said Öhman.

Öhman's statement, uttered like a sentence of doom from a bewigged justice on the bench, alerted Garrett's senses. He waited. Was there hope?

"Uhhh—at first—I was not sure if I should come to you with this." He had brought his thin leather briefcase to his lap. "It seemed to me too inconclusive. Yet, if it could be proved, your case would be won in a single stroke. You would not only silence Farelli, you would destroy him. He would vanish from the earth."

Garrett sat up straight, eyes burning fanatically. "What is it?"

"I will explain. Uhhh—after our meeting at the Caroline Institute—after you had convinced me that Farelli was taking credit for sharing a discovery that was not his but yours—and now even attempting to steal your credit, too—I decided to—uhhh—casually—uhhh—look into Farelli. If nothing more, at least to try to understand such a man being in medicine. As you know, as I explained at our meeting, the Royal Swedish Academy of Science appoints expert investigators to look into the cause of each candidate—I and another investigated you—and two of my colleagues at the Caroline—they had investigated Farelli. These studies are thorough. I had told you how, back as far as the turn of the century, our committee sent two men to St. Petersburg to —uhhh—see what they could see about Pavlov. To be confidential with you, our medical investigators—they not only verify a discovery and determine its importance, but—and this must remain in this room—they report on the—uhhh—character, responsible character, of the discoverer. Well, Dr. Garrett, such an investigation was made of Carlo Farelli."

All through this recital, excitement had mounted within Garrett. He could not be mistaken. Something of vital importance was coming. "You—you said on the phone you had something important. Is it about Farelli? Did you find out something about that dirty—?"

"Yes."

Garrett could not modulate his voice. "What did you find? Tell me—I've got to know!"

Öhman had slowly drawn the zipper back and opened his briefcase. He fingered through it, and removed two thin sheets of typescript.

"As you no doubt know," said Öhman, "Farelli's background is—uhhh—colorful."

"I don't know, except what's been in the papers." And then, he asked urgently, "What do you mean—colorful?"

Öhman tapped the typescript. "It is here. This is not the original investigation report. But one of the men who took part—an old friend and former schoolmate—a cardiac specialist like us—he told me from memory what he had found, and I took notes, and then I typed it myself. Of course, it might be possible to see the original report—through my friend—or someone. It is filed away, but I am sure it would be no different from what I have in hand. My friend has the memory of a bull elephant." Öhman examined the top sheet in his lap, and then looked up. "You know, of course, that in the last days of 1941, when Mussolini had already declared war on Russia and the

United States, Dr. Farelli was placed under arrest by OVRA, the Fascist Secret Police?"

"I don't know the details," said Garrett. "He bragged to me once that he was in prison during the war."

"Yes, that has been verified," said Öhman. "It must be admitted, on his behalf, that he has a long record as an anti-Fascist. Even as a student in medical school, Farelli opposed Mussolini's adventure against Haile Selassie in Africa. When the Second World War came, Farelli, along with several other young doctors, signed an open letter published in *Il Popolo di Roma* opposing it. Late in 1941, the OVRA learned, through an informer, that Farelli had acted as a physician giving comfort to *Il Duce's* underground enemies. At once, the *carabinieri* came and confined him to the Regina Coeli prison in Rome."

"What are you trying to do, make him out a hero?" said Garrett bitterly. "We were the heroes, if you want it that way. You were at least neutral and gave help to refugees, and I was in the landing on Iwo Jima—but, whatever you say, Farelli was an Italian—"

Öhman saw how troubled his friend was and forgave him his lack of objectivity. "I am only quoting our neutral report," said Öhman. "But, Dr. Garrett, I am leading up to something—of importance, as I promised you." He rattled the papers in his hand. "As I was saying, Farelli was confined to the Regina Coeli prison in Rome, and later, according to our records, he was shipped to another prison, near Parma, an old castle where political agitators were kept and sometimes shot. So far, all well and to the good for Farelli. But then our Academy investigator—the friend of whom I speak—found a mystifying, inexplicable piece of information."

"Yes?"

"Uhhh—hear this," said Öhman. "The next we know of Farelli, he turns up as a doctor—no longer a prisoner, but a doctor—in Nazi Germany."

The intake of Garrett's breath hissed through the silent bedroom. "Nazi Germany," he repeated, as if it were a blessing. Then quickly, "How do you know? Is there proof?"

"That is the point," said Öhman seriously. "By our standards, the evidence is flimsy, almost cryptic, but it *is* evidence. For a while, I was unsure, and was going to withhold it from you. It was so fragmentary. It could be misleading. On the other hand—"

"Read it to me."

"—I felt, in view of Farelli's behavior toward you, in view of our—uhhh—friendship, I owed it to you, in all fairness, as something you could think about and measure." He lifted the typescript from his lap, but still did not consult it. "As you know, Dr. Garrett, the German medical profession, which we esteemed so highly in the years before Hitler, which we showered with Nobel honors—the German medical profession disgraced itself in the Second World War."

Garrett remembered the stories from Nürnberg in 1947. "You mean the Nazi medical trial before our tribunal at Nürnberg?"

"I mean what led to it. Throughout the war, almost two hundred German physicians comported themselves in such a manner as to make the Marquis de Sade appear sweet and gentle by comparison. These German doctors employed helpless human beings—Jewish men and women, Polish and Russian prisoners of war, their own nationals who opposed Hitler—instead of guinea pigs and rats, for their sadistic experiments. I am—uhhh—it is sickening to know the truth of their record. Do you recollect the record?"

"It was so long ago," said Garrett. "And, anyway, I was in the Pacific."

"For their insane experiments, these long-worshiped doctors injected human prisoners with typhus, deadly typhus. They sterilized the sexual organs of Jews with X rays, and murdered most of them. They tried out synthetic hormones on defenseless homosexuals and killed some. They injected yellow fever into persons, not animals. They tried out poison gas on persons, not animals. They made artificial abscesses on persons, not animals, to study blood poisoning. They severed healthy limbs in order to experiment with transplants. The list is too nauseating—I will not go on."

He stared down at the typescript. "Then, one day, with the approval of Himmler and the Reich Air Ministry, they undertook a long series of horrible experiments—in the name of aviation medicine, and presumably designed to learn valuable information for their *Luftwaffe* pilots—with a decompression chamber, to study heart action at abnormally high altitudes. These tests were the ultimate in—uhhh—savagery. According to my notes, Dr. Sigmund Rascher had proposed the tests to Himmler, and Himmler had approved. The decompression chamber was moved into the Dachau concentration camp, and, one by one, these prisoners were led into the torture chamber—and the air was let out of the box—so that the prisoner, without oxygen or any equipment— the guinea pig—would reflect the human condition of a flyer in rapid ascent to an altitude of thirteen or fourteen miles. It was terrible, Dr. Garrett. I have heard the case histories. In the first minutes, perspiration and lack of control; in five minutes, spasms; in eight minutes, the dropping of respiration; in twelve minutes, boiling of the blood and rupturing of the lungs, with the human victim tearing out his hair in bunches and gouging out the flesh of his face to relieve his suffering, and attempt to find oxygen when there was no oxygen—and all this while, the—uhhh—doctors were studying the victim through an observation window, and checking their cardiographs, and later, making their calm autopsies on the corpses."

Öhman paused. He saw that Garrett had grown pale. Both men were silent. Only the ticking of Garrett's travel clock, on the bedstand, could be heard.

Öhman sighed. "The names of all the doctors participating in these high altitude experiments are known. One of them was Dr. Carlo Farelli."

"Farelli—" Even Garrett, who considered his enemy capable of any enormity, did not consider him capable of this. Garrett sat stunned. At last, he found words. "You have proof?"

"As I explained—inconclusive proof. I shall read it to you." He read from the typescript: " 'Report to German Experimental Institute for Aviation Medicine. Attention Dr. Siegfried Ruff. Lieutenant General Dr. Hippke. Subject: Experiment 203 of heart action at high altitudes. Place: Dachau altitude chamber. Test persons: Five criminals, volunteers. Test levels: 30,000 to 70,000 feet. (Results to be forwarded under separate cover.) Test effects: Two casualties. Physicians participating: Dr. A. Brand, Berlin; Dr. I. Gorecki, Warsaw; Dr. S. Brauer, Munich; Dr. J. Stirbey, Bucharest; Dr. C. Farelli, Rome. . . . Signed, Dr. S. Rascher, 3 April, 1944.' " Öhman stopped, looked up, and laid the paper aside. "There it is."

Garrett plucked at his blanket and stared at the opposite wall. "Dr. C. Farelli, Rome," he intoned, as if reading an epitaph. He shook his head in daze. "Incredible. Is there more?"

"That is all. There is nothing else."

"There can't be two C. Farellis in Rome, both heart specialists?"

"There were not two. There was only one. Our investigator checked."

Suddenly, Garrett turned on Öhman. "With that damning evidence, how could you let Farelli share the prize with me?"

"This evidence was weighed by my colleague with all else that was ninety-nine per cent favorable. He felt that this mere mention of Farelli's name was too little with which to disqualify him. He did not submit it to the Caroline staff of judges."

"Too little to disqualify him?" said Garrett sarcastically.

"Farelli's political record was otherwise good. He had been a prisoner through most of the war. This one blot, my colleague felt—uhhh—he felt Farelli might not have had a part in conducting the tests that day, might have only been a foreign observer."

"Is that what you think, Dr. Öhman?"

"To be honest with you, I do not know what to think. I can only guess that Farelli may have weakened under long confinement—possibly even punishment—and at last, to buy some freedom, some relief, abandoned his resistance and bent to Mussolini's will. In short, in those days, Il Duce was doing what he could to hold up his end with Hitler. There is evidence he offered some physicians to cooperate in various endeavors with Hitler's medical researchers. Farelli was a notable cardiac man, even that far back, and I suppose Mussolini offered him a parole if he would join with other Italian doctors in flying over to Germany and lending a hand in these—these—uhhh—experiments."

"It's no excuse," said Garrett relentlessly.

"I do not say it is. But it is the only explanation I can find for such hideous behavior."

"He should have been hung at Nürnberg with all the rest," said Garrett. "Instead, your weakling friend suppressed that and gave him the Nobel Prize."

For a moment, Öhman felt national pride and tried to defend his colleague. "He weighed this—this one indefinite mention—against Farelli's career before, and in all the years since. He felt Farelli's contribution to mankind was proved, but the one fragment of evidence of collaboration was unproved. That was the decisive factor."

Garrett's emotions had gone through many convolutions. At first, he had been revolted by the information—a description of an act of brutality and cowardice so low and foreign to his pedestrian nature and normal academic background that he had recoiled from the monstrosity and thought that he wanted no part of it. But gradually, as he became used to the evidence, as he again suffered the ache of his chin and stomach, his hatred for the Italian returned. Farelli had humbled him and humiliated him without mercy, in public and in private, the typical behavior of a man who would have assisted his German medical friends in butchery at Dachau. Here was evidence that the soft Swedes, ever fearful of trouble, had tried to suppress. And so, gradually, Garrett's mind substituted for petty revenge the soul-satisfying and loftier notion of moral indignation and retribution, in the name of all humanity. He had a duty to humanity, to God, to protect the world from this Roman Eichmann. In an hour's time, from groveling defeat, he had vaulted, using Öhman's pole, to a height of power and superiority. With Öhman's generous revelation, he could wipe Farelli from his life, from the lion's share of honors, and, at the same time, know saintliness for helping all unsuspecting fellow men.

He heard his voice. "Dr. Öhman, whatever your committee member thinks, I'm not going to stand by—I have too much conscience—and let this war criminal strut around Stockholm like a Caesar. I'm not going to let him sit on the same platform with me at the Ceremony."

Öhman scratched his scalp nervously. "What are you proposing?"

For the first time this day, Garrett smiled. "I have my ideas."

He threw off his blanket, and crawled off the bed, and stood up, a man rejuvenated, hitching and tightening his pajamas.

Öhman jumped to his feet. "I brought you this, because we are friends. I hoped you would take time to digest this, think about it, and then proceed with utmost care. I hoped, when you returned to America next week, you might bring this up—somehow—with—uhhh—friends in your Pentagon Building, and let them see if they could check further. In that way, you might learn every fact. If Farelli were then proved innocent, you could forget the matter. And if you truly found him guilty, it would become known—"

"No!"

"Dr. Garrett—"

"I'm not letting a war criminal escape. I'm not letting condemning information like this die in channels. Now is the time—now, when the whole world is here in Stockholm. Now is the time to make Farelli go on trial, before he makes fools of you and me and all of us."

"But the Nobel Committee will not support—"

"I don't need them. I have a better outlet, a far better transmitting agent."

"Who?"

"Sue Wiley of Consolidated Newspapers. I'm going to lay Farelli's infamy in her lap tomorrow. You won't have a part in it, and I won't. I'll just give her the tip, and let her run from there, and by tomorrow night—I guarantee you this—the whole world will know, and what I have promised will come true. At the Ceremony, I will sit on the stage by myself, and I, alone, will receive the Nobel Prize in physiology and medicine!"

Night had fallen on the city, and a damp fog laced the frosty polar darkness. It was five after six in the evening when Andrew Craig reached the shrouded waters of Nybroviken, some blocks behind the Grand Hotel. The portier had given him exact directions to the Royal Dramatic Theater, reminding him it covered an entire block near Strandvägen, on the icing bay of Nybroviken.

Now, in the fog, Craig was lost, and he waited for help. A Swedish youngster on a bicycle, whistling in the fun of the fog, bundled like a Lapp, approached the corner.

"Young man—" Craig called out.

The bicycle slowed.

"—please, where is the Dramatic Theater?"

The beet-colored face was puzzled, and suddenly it beamed. *"Dramatiska Teatern?"* He jerked his thumb behind him, and held up his forefinger—an improvement on Esperanto—and Craig understood that it was one block away.

He proceeded slowly, heading blindly into the blackness. His mind returned to—had really never left—the person of Emily Stratman. Her kiss, almost twenty-four hours old, was still on his lips. During the Hammarlund dinner, there had been no way to communicate with her, except with his eyes, nor had more been possible in the communal ride to the hotel afterwards.

This morning he had overslept, and had found her at lunch with her uncle and three Scandinavian physicists and their wives in the Winter Garden. He had joined the party, but there had been no opportunity to go further with Emily. Only afterwards, briefly, as they had all risen from the table, had he been able to ask when he might see her again. She did not know. In the afternoon, a social tea. And this evening, a performance of something or other—a pageant—at Drottningholm. Tomorrow then? She had hesitated, and worried, and he had perceived that she was again afraid, afraid she had gone too far on the Hammarlund terrace, afraid to be alone with him and take up from the last encounter. But he had been so pleading and kind that she had acceded, and almost with enthusiasm, finally. Tomorrow she was free for dinner, and so that would be it. He had not seen her since, and he wondered if she and her uncle had reached Drottningholm this evening safely in spite of the fog.

He found himself before a stone building piled high and stretching upward through the layers of mist. There were indistinct yellow lights, revealing ornate pillars and a statue, two figures, to the left. This was the Royal Dramatic Theater, he was sure, and he hastened up the steps and inside to keep his meeting with Märta Norberg.

In the lobby, a plump, bandy-legged cleaning woman was pushing a carpet sweeper.

He removed his hat. "Pardon me. Miss Märta Norberg is expecting me."

"Not inside," said the cleaning woman. "She finish rehearsal—go upstair with Nils Cronsten."

"Can you tell me where upstairs?"

"She go to—with young ones—Little Theater of Royal Training Academy. Fourth number floor."

"Thank you."

Craig took off his topcoat, and, carrying it over one arm, began the long climb up the staircase. When he reached the fourth floor, he was winded and overheated.

A big blonde, with the chubby aspect of an innocent milkmaid, and wearing a skintight red leotard that made her flaring hips and buttocks seem abnormally large, was hurrying down the corridor.

Craig intercepted her. Was it *fröken* or *fru? "Fröken—"*

"Yes, sir?" Her accent was clipped West End.

"—where can I find Miss Norberg or Mr. Cronsten?"

"The small theater down there." She pointed.

He considered the leotard. "May I ask—who are you?"

She dimpled. "Viola. *Twelfth Night.* William Shakespeare. I am overweight, but I am dieting."

With that, she hurried away, an Amazon in haste, and Craig enjoyed her as he walked to the theater and went inside.

It was, indeed, a small theater, ninety-eight red plush seats, footlights ablaze, and a fair-sized stage now displaying three performers in costume, a slender Olivia, veiled, a refined and dignified Malvolio, and a jester, all gaudily attired. Accustoming himself to the auditorium, Craig listened. Olivia was addressing the steward, her voice rising and falling: "O, you are sick of self-love, Malvolio, and taste with a distempered appetite. There is no slander in an allowed fool, though he do nothing but rail—" Craig thought of Gunnar Gottling, and tried to listen again.

"Are you Andrew Craig?"

Craig pivoted in the direction of the inquiry, and saw a stocky, conventional-looking gentleman of indeterminate but older years, a parted brown toupee, complacent respected banker's face, bow tie, pin-striped neat suit, rise from a seat.

"I am Nils Cronsten, Miss Norberg's director. She advised me earlier you were to be expected."

They shook hands in the aisle.

"I congratulate you, Mr. Craig, on your Nobel Prize. Indeed, I have admired your novels, and it is a pleasure to have you visit us. Please join me. I will send for Miss Norberg."

Craig took the second seat from the aisle, and Cronsten settled beside him, lifting his hand and loudly snapping his fingers. Immediately, a young man with tangled hair and padding beneath the abdomen of his costume leaped from the front row and came racing up the aisle.

"Sir Toby Belch," commanded Cronsten with mock severity, "an assignment for you."

"Yes, Mr. Cronsten."

"Go forth on winged feet to Miss Norberg's dressing room and summon the star of Sweden. Inform her that her caller from across the sea is present and waiting—the renowned Mr. Andrew Craig."

"Yes, *sir!*"

The young man was off, like a jack rabbit, and both Cronsten and Craig laughed. "Märta rehearsed a few hours late this afternoon," said Cronsten, "but then she tired of it—not in the mood—and we came up here to watch our future Norbergs. Don't ever repeat that to her, Mr. Craig. She can imagine no past or future Norbergs, only one, and that one touched with immortality anyway."

"I guessed it," said Craig good-naturedly.

"She finally went to the dressing room to make some long-distance call."

"Last night she told me that you were directing her in *Adrienne Lecouvreur*. It will be exciting news to the theater world. When will she open?"

"Never," said Cronsten. "I've rehearsed her in four plays these last years, but they never open. At the final moment, she always quits and goes into hiding again—searching for properties, she says, searching for the foolproof hit. She will never find it. You see, Mr. Craig, her malady is historic greatness. When you attain her summit, become not an actress but a legend, when you are so high, you cannot top it again. So you become overcautious. You must find the perfect vehicle for your perfect talent—there can be no possibility of failure—and, well, it is impossible to arrange such guarantees. So I play her fool—we have our little game of rehearsals. I delude myself over and over—maybe this time, maybe this time—but it will never be. I doubt if she will expose herself on the legitimate stage again. Someday, perhaps— just possibly—another film, but I would not wager on that. And so she goes on playing the enigma, the recluse, the unattainable—and since it is a better role than she will ever find, I suspect she will play it out for the rest of her days."

"What does she do with her time?" Craig wanted to know.

"She's not social, if that's what you mean," said Cronsten. "She busies herself with herself. When you are Norberg, you don't need anyone else. She devotes mornings to her appearance and health—she is a faddist, like so many actresses, so there is always something new. She spends afternoons reading properties or rehearsing. She gives evenings over to Hammarlund and his friends. Sometimes she travels incognito. She owns a villa in the hills behind Cannes and keeps an apartment in New York. Most of all, here or anywhere, she intrigues."

Craig's interest was piqued. "You say—she intrigues?"

"It is too complicated to explain. When you know her better, you'll understand." He looked off. "Here comes our runner with tidings."

The young man with tangled hair and stomach padding trotted toward them, and saluted them with the note in his hand. "Sir Toby Belch reporting. The Norberg has flown. In her place, she left with Viola a note addressed to Mr. Craig."

He handed the folded paper to Craig, waited for dismissal, and was dismissed by Cronsten.

Craig opened the note:

DEAR LAUREATE, Rushing off to be home for a call from New York. It is imperative I see you tonight. Can you come to dinner at seven? I will expect you. I am a mile beyond Hammarlund. You need only tell the taxi driver— NORBERG.

Craig saw that the director was inquisitive, so he explained. "She had to go, but she wants me to dine with her at seven."

"It's twenty-five to seven now. I'll tell you what we can do. Let's go to my office and have a drink, and then I'll drive you to Norberg's."

"I wouldn't think of imposing—"

"Not far out of my way, so I will insist."

They rose, and Craig followed the director into the corridor, and in a minute they were in Cronsten's tiny, spotless office, with its dark teak desk and contrasting pale beech-framed chairs, carefully padded with thick foam-rubber cushions.

Opening a wall cabinet, Cronsten asked, "What will it be?"

"No fuss. Plain Scotch. Don't bother about ice."

Cronsten poured, and brought the whiskey to Craig, who was facing the opposite wall, examining framed photographs of Greta Garbo, Ingrid Bergman, Signe Hasso, Viveca Lindfors, Mai Zetterling, and a half-dozen other Swedish actresses, all bearing affectionate autographs to the director. Above these, in solitary splendor, was a portrait of Märta Norberg. Across it was scrawled, "To Cronny—from his Trilby."

Craig took his drink. "You seem to have known them all."

"Yes. I've directed them. They all have three things in common—Sweden, talent, and the Royal Dramatic Training Academy. They are all products of our Socialist-supported school."

"You've got a remarkable record."

"I'm proud of it. Every summer, we print and circulate a poster. It says, 'Kungl. Dramatiska Teaterns Elevskola Prospekt.' It is an invitation to our young ladies, between sixteen and twenty-two, and young men, slightly older, to try out for our state Training Academy. After rejecting certain ones, we usually have over one hundred to judge. They all come to Stockholm, to the little theater here, in August, and do scenes for us. We have an elimination tournament. There are sixteen in the final round, and of these, we select eight to be trained for the stage."

"By what standards do you pick the eight?"

"When we watch a young girl, we think beauty is nice but only an extra asset. It is the least important factor. We do not watch for technique and tricks, either. We watch to see if the girl has emotional range, imagination, and courage. It will surprise you to know—I remember the very day—that when Garbo tried out, she was an extrovert, full of noisy confidence. The eight we select are given a three-year course here, tuition free, and the fifty teachers show them how to stand, sit, walk, move, train them in diction, Shakespeare, makeup, and the psychology of other peoples so that they will understand all roles, including those written by foreigners. For their third year, they each get a salary of two thousand kronor extra. After that, they are admitted to the Royal Theater repertory, but the best of them go on to the cinema in London or Hollywood."

"What school of acting do you follow?"

"We are still old-fashioned," said Cronsten. "We are still Stanislavsky. Norberg grew up with that method. I will never forget Norberg, when she came here over twenty years ago. She was gawky, strange, but she had inner beauty, burning ambition. Even then, we might have passed her over, except that Hammarlund had discovered her and recommended her, and he was already famous and one of the patrons of our Donor's Fund for needy students."

Craig swallowed the last of his drink. "How did Hammarlund find her?"

"She was an usher in a cinema house, and Hammarlund saw her, and liked her voice and fire. He became interested in her. I suppose we can assume that he slept with her. As Ellen Terry used to say, 'Men love unhealthy women.' When he found out that she wanted to become an actress, he arranged for some private coaching, and then entered her in our eliminations. Well, once she had the scholarship, she had her confidence, and she swept all before her. By her third year, she had the nerve to refuse to play the role of Queen Christina in a one-act play because—I remember her telling me— she felt that Christina was not a real woman. She would only play a real woman. You know what happened after that. We had her only one year on our big stage downstairs, and then she had that second lead on Broadway, and then Hollywood—and now, twenty years later, only one role is good enough for her—to play Märta Norberg." He glanced at his wristwatch. "I would invite you for another drink, but you'll be late."

They slipped into their heavy coats, descended the stairs, and went into the chilled, foggy night. Once in the Saab, Cronsten drove slowly. Every corner was camouflaged by murky vapor, and when they entered Djurgården, the mist enveloped them, and Cronsten slowed the Saab to a crawl.

They spoke little. Once Craig thought that he recognized Hammarlund's mansion. Five minutes later, Cronsten said, "Here we are."

He turned into a long circular driveway, and stopped, idling his engine, before a white two-story Georgian house.

"You will have an interesting time," said Cronsten with a riddle of a smile. "Not many men are invited here."

"Really?"

"Only the high and the mighty."

"I hardly think of myself as—"

"Do not think of yourself as you see yourself, but as Märta Norberg sees you. Did she tell you why she asked you out here?"

"No. Only that it was business and imperative."

411

Cronsten nodded as if he were knowledgeable of this and privy to some secret. "It was good to meet you, Mr. Craig. I wish you luck."

"I don't know how to thank you." He opened the car door.

"Do not thank me for the ride," said Cronsten, "but thank me for some advice I will give you, because you are a nice fellow."

Craig had left the car, but now he waited at the open door.

"Have you ever heard of the Coral Island clams found along Australia's Great Barrier Reef? They are the greatest clams in the world. They sometimes weigh one ton each, and are ten feet long, and they consume living things. An unsuspecting swimmer, coming upon such a clam, could easily be caught in it, have the shells close over him, and be devoured. It is a bit of natural history you may find valuable to remember in the next hour or two. Good night, Mr. Craig."

Craig remained standing in the driveway a few moments, until Cronsten's Saab had disappeared behind a bank of fog, and then he went thoughtfully to the huge door, touched the bell, and was admitted by a short, unsmiling Filipino houseboy.

"I'm Andrew Craig."

Entering the high-ceilinged vestibule, Craig gave his hat and topcoat to the houseboy.

"Right this way," the Filipino said in stilted English. "Miss Norberg is having her swim."

Craig did not comprehend. "In this weather?"

"The indoor pool in the *lanai*."

Going through the vast living room, across the muffling cropped-lambskin carpet, Craig took in the furniture. The pieces seemed definitely American and expensive, and Craig guessed that the actress had shipped her household effects from Bel Air or New York to this house in Stockholm. There was the flash of an elegant low sofa covered with yellow Venetian silk, fronted by a black lacquered table, and another sofa done in turquoise Thaibok, and scattered overstuffed chairs. On one wall, spotlighted from the ceiling, a towering, vivid oil of Norberg, full length, as Manon Lescaut. On a table, a piece of sculpture by Rodin, and another piece by Moore, and an eleven-by-fourteen Karsh photograph in a silver frame of Norberg as Héloïse, probably, but too resolute for that role.

The houseboy had pulled back a glass sliding door, and Craig went into the lanai and thought that, through a trick of time and space, he had landed in some primitive corner of Tahiti. He wished Emily were beside him to marvel with him at the sight of it. Three glass walls were almost entirely hidden by growing tropical plants and greenery the color of aquamarine. The swimming pool was not like any standard pool he had ever seen, but designed to resemble a South Sea water hole, clear as crystal except at the farthest end where an artificial waterfall cascaded into it.

And then he saw off to his right, lolling on a webbed lounge, wrapped in a silk Japanese kimono of Tyrian purple, Märta Norberg.

"I'm here, Craig."

412

He advanced toward her. She remained horizontal, not stirring, but arched a thin hand upward. Since the hand was not in a position to be shaken, but to be kissed in the Continental manner, Craig kissed the fingers somewhat self-consciously.

"I'm glad you could come, dear man." Lazily, her hand indicated the makings on the rosewood table near her. "Mix yourself whatever will make you happiest." She lifted her own drink from the artificial grass beneath her lounge. "I'm staying with vodka plain. You might freshen me up, while you're at it."

As Craig took her glass, and made the drinks, Norberg called off to the houseboy immobilized at the door. "That'll be all for tonight, Antonio. On the way, tell cook we'll dine at eight-thirty." When the houseboy left, sliding the door shut after him, Märta Norberg said, "Isn't Antonio a doll? Utterly unobtrusive and efficient. I brought him with me from Hollywood, brought most of them, Antonio, and my masseuse, and my secretary. The rest, the menials, are easy to find here. But Antonio's the one. My countrymen stare at him as if he's a zoo. A Filipino in Sweden. Well—why not?"

"He told me you were swimming. Were you?" Craig handed her the vodka, and sat sideways on the lounge beside her.

"Not yet. I was waiting for you. You swim, of course?"

"I used to. I haven't for several years."

"It's a must with me. Gives the muscles tone. I'm in the pool ten minutes every morning and for a half hour before dinner." She held up her drink. "I like vodka and water—separately."

Craig scanned the lanai. "I've never seen a room quite like this."

"Anyone can have one—for an extra forty thousand dollars."

"That much?"

Norberg shrugged. "Why not? If Lollia Paulina could have an evening gown for two million dollars, and Cleopatra have a goblet of vinegar wine worth a half-million—because she dissolved a pearl in it—surely Märta Norberg deserves this little bauble. Do you want to swim now?"

"After I finish my drink."

"Good. We can talk." She kicked off her fuzzy sandals, wiggled the painted toes of her bare feet, and then tucked her feet comfortably beneath her.

"Did you enjoy Ragnar's party?"

"It was an event. I'll use it one day."

"I suppose you will," she said. And then, she added casually, "I suppose you'll also use that ridiculous fight between Garrett and Farelli."

Craig's face did not betray his amazement, but he looked fixedly at Märta Norberg. "That's uncanny," he said. "I thought there were no witnesses besides myself. Did you see it?"

She shook her head, pleased with herself. "No, I did not see it. I heard it."

"Heard it?"

"That's right. Do you want to know more that I heard? Dr. Claude

Marceau is having an affair with a French mannequin named Gisèle Jordan. How's that? How am I doing?"

"You've got me baffled."

"More? The celebrated author, Andrew Craig, kissed someone's niece and whispered endearments—"

"Where in the hell did you hear that?"

Norberg teased him. "It's true, isn't it?"

Craig glowered at her and said nothing.

She threw back her head and laughed, and for a moment the bottom folds of her kimono separated, revealing her naked legs, and she primly covered them again. "Now you have something more to write about, don't you, Craig? Well, I'll relieve your mind. No sleight-of-hand, see, no mystic powers, no black magic. Ragnar Hammarlund has that Elysium of his bugged and tapped from top to bottom. Flush a toilet, and it goes on tape. Cough in the garden, and it's on tape. Kiss on the terrace, and it's for the ages."

"I never heard of anything more corrupt. The immoral son of a bitch."

Norberg laughed again. "That's what I said the first time I heard of it. But you know, from his point of view, it makes good sense and has a morality of its own. He's in business, and this is the age of communications. So why not go modern?"

"Recording the private conversations of guests isn't my idea of business."

"You'd be surprised, Craig. I'll give you an example so that you'll come off your high horse. Why do you think Ragnar gave that party last night? I'll tell you. He has his eye on the Marceaus. That's all he cares about. The rest of you were only window dressing. The Marceaus are the goods he is after. He once read an early paper of theirs on some synthetic food. He got the idea—and when he gets an idea, nothing can pry him loose from it—he got the idea that if he could lick the synthetic food problem, he could be the first to market it internationally, and treble his fortune. Don't ask why he'd want to do that. Empire builders are in the business of building empires. He's had this young Lindblom on the problem for several years, others too, but he wants the best. He figures if he can interest the Marceaus in it, the big minds, the Nobel winners, progress will be accelerated, and he'll see practical results in his lifetime. So he keeps plotting to see the Marceaus, propagandize them, use them. Well, now, give the devil his due, he's actually making inroads. He knows about Claude Marceau's affair. All to the good. He won't blackmail him, nothing so crude, but it gives him some advantage. I don't have his mind, so I don't know how he thinks. And he believes he's actually got Denise Marceau interested in Lindblom's work."

"I hope you don't condone that kind of thing?"

"Craig, I couldn't give less of a damn. The world is full of all sorts of people, and they include the warp-heads like Ragnar, and let them go merrily to Hades in their own ways. I'm interested in One World—mine."

"Why have you been telling me all this?"

"Because I've decided to double the population of my One World. I've

414

given you an entry visa. Behave, my good man, and you may become a naturalized citizen."

Craig considered her with wonder. There was some quality of unreality about her person. He could not divine it. His life, once, had been frequented by the self-absorbed and the egotistical, but never had he encountered another human being narcissistic to the point of total disinterest in general right or wrong.

"I would be flattered to be a citizen of Norberg," he said, to say something, "but I'm not exactly sure I know what you're driving at."

"Time will tell," she said cryptically. She squinted at his empty glass. "Now, what will it be—whiskey or water?"

"Hard to decide. I could use another drink. Hammarlund has left a bad taste in my mouth. At the same time, I'd like to cleanse myself entirely. I'd say water."

She pointed a limpid hand off. "Door behind the diving board. Built-in cabaña. There are drawers full of swim trunks. Take your choice."

"What'll you be doing?"

"Keeping the water warm for you."

He stood up and strode to the cabaña door, conscious of her wide, gray, amoral eyes upon his back, and then he went into the cabaña. He stripped down quickly, opened several wall drawers, tried various swimming shorts against his angular frame, and then pulled on a white jersey pair that appeared to have elasticity. They were cut high, and they were tight, and he still felt naked but did not care much. He wanted the water's refreshment—and to discover what business Märta Norberg had been withholding from him.

When he went out into the lanai, he saw that she was already in the pool, wearing a lemon-colored bathing cap and scant bikini, backstroking with the grace of a sea nymph across the pool. She bobbed up straight at the deep end, treading near the waterfall, and shouted deeply, "Come in, Craig, it's delicious."

He was inspired to do a dramatic jackknife off the short board, but knew that he was out of shape and would certainly strain muscles or break his neck, so he elected conservatism and went off the side in a flat, shallow, splashing dive. The water was tepid on his body, and as soothing as the lining of his old sheepskin coat left behind in Miller's Dam. Stroking and kicking in a modified crawl, he traversed the pool to Märta Norberg's side.

"You look mighty smart in those trunks, young man," she said, her long Swedish face sparkling with beads of water. "Like a tall Jantzen ad. What was your sport in school? Basketball?"

"Football. Left end."

"I never went to school—at least not much," she said. "My family was too poor. I had to drop out at the end of *realskola*—grammar school. I had my schooling later, when I could afford tutors. That's when I took up sports. Skiing for winter. Tennis for summer. And this all the time." She was almost girlish, and Craig liked her more. "Want to race?" she said.

"One, two, three—go," he said.

They went off churning to the opposite end, then touching and rolling, kicked off to reverse their course. She came in three yards ahead of him.

"You didn't tell me you were Gertrude Ederle," he said, gulping for air.

"Who she? Look, Craig, I'm not all *that* old."

After that they swam leisurely, no games, the backstroke, the Australian crawl, the breast stroke, a good deal of floating, and no conversation at all. After twenty minutes of this they found themselves facing each other, breathless, holding the rim of the pool at the shallow end alongside the metal ladder.

"You had enough, Craig?"

"Just about."

"So much for pleasure. You want to talk business?"

"I don't know what business—but you said there was some."

"Important business, important for both of us."

He held the rim of the pool, and splashed water on his chest. "Shoot."

"I won't waste words," said Märta Norberg. "I called my agent in New York. He called yours. My agent then called a studio in Hollywood. And minutes before you came, he called me."

"Alexander Graham Bell is the man in your life."

She ignored this. Her face was concentrated. All humor had fled, and even some femininity with it. "We have a deal to offer you, a firm deal, no ifs, no maybes. I want your new novel, *Return to Ithaca,* for a picture in which I'll star. Since you're still writing it, the studio has agreed I can offer you twenty thousand dollars down, against two hundred thousand when the novel is finished. That's fat, Craig, when your bank account is thin, and yours is, I know—I know from your sister-in-law and I know from your agent. I also know after you've paid up debts with your Nobel money, and lived it up a bit, you'll be lean again, scratching. What do you say?"

Craig was too taken aback by this news, and her offer, to say anything at first. His head spun. "How can you spend so much on a book that's hardly written and that you haven't read?"

"I know what it's about. Miss Decker told me the whole story last night. It's exactly what I've been looking for—for years—and, as you know, from the studio angle anyway, the fact that you've won the Nobel Prize enhances the property."

"You mean, Leah told you the whole story?" Inwardly, he cursed Leah and thanked her, simultaneously. Leah had typed and retyped those early pages, and outline notes, and knew the characters and plot as well as he. But she had no right to broadcast it, peddle it so naïvely, without his knowledge or approval. At the same time, it was a miracle that she had been so indiscreet. The timing was perfect. He could use the money. It was a windfall. He hardly bothered to consider if he was capable of finishing the book. Somehow, the freedom that the money would buy him made the creativity seem possible. That is, if he would not drink, if he would not flagellate himself with Harriet, if he could leave Stockholm an integrated man with a will for life.

Märta Norberg had replied, "Yes, I know the story forwards and backwards," and then had remained silent, allowing him his introspection.

Now a curious dark doubt crossed his brain and bothered him. "If you know the story," he said slowly, "then you must know there is no real part in it for you. The whole book is the hero, a man, one man. All the women have nothing more than episodes. There are six women in the book. They come and go. They have little bits and pieces. What would you do?"

"I would be Desmona, the bohemian girl he marries."

"But she's only in three chapters, and then she's killed. That's all there is of her, except what she is in his mind. You see, after she's killed—"

"I wouldn't let her be killed," said Märta Norberg simply. "I'd throw out the other five women—well, four anyway—and keep Desmona alive."

Craig frowned. "Miss Norberg, I respect your genius as an actress—indeed, I worship it. But you are not an author. I am an author. This is my book, and in it Desmona dies early. Without that, there's no point to the story line."

"Don't be so ridiculously inflexible. You can change it around. There are a hundred possibilities, based on the little I have heard. Why, you haven't even written her death scene yet. So all you have to do is not write it at all. You can make it an accident or something—she's injured—in fact, I think that improves your story a great deal. And then, you can reshape the rest."

Craig was appalled. He measured his words. "Let me get this straight. I want no semantic misunderstanding. Are you suggesting—actually suggesting —that you will buy my next novel if—only *if*—I change it to conform to your idea of what the heroine should be?"

Märta Norberg laughed, and lowered herself deeper in the water. "You make it sound like I'm threatening you. Don't be an arty boy, Craig—one of those too young, ever young, foolish New England boys, forever out of the Ivy—making believe they are tender Prousts, untouched by human hands or other minds, putting down their precious, puny, gilded words as if the heavens had rent asunder to inspire them. What nonsense, and you know it, and I know it. Dickens, Balzac, Dumas, the whole lot of them, wrote by the page, manufactured to please their printers or their public, and nothing was spoiled, because they were good. Well, you're good—and keeping one character alive to suit a customer and to keep your bank account in balance won't make you a hack or sell you out. It'll only teach you that you've grown up."

"What if I answer no, flatly no? Will you make the deal anyway?"

"Of course not. As you say, there would be nothing in it for me."

He hated to say the next, but he wanted the deal.

"You could change it around in Hollywood. I wouldn't give a damn about that."

"Impossible. The book itself will be widely read and known—serial, book clubs, trade edition, paper edition—and I want that heroine built up—talked about—loved—long before I give her life on the screen. Now, will you do it?" She smiled at him sweetly. He was about to speak, evidently in anger, for she quickly put her wet forefinger to his lips, sealing them. "Wait, Craig. Before you speak, there's another aspect of my offer that I've deliberately withheld from you. I was going to tell you about it later—under—under more favorable circumstances." She paused. "I see you're so male upset, I had better tell you now."

"All right—what?"

"The two hundred thousand was only a part of my offer. There is a richer part, and it's worth infinitely more. Do you know what that part is?"

"No."

"Me." She smiled at his bewildered reaction. "Me, Märta Norberg," she said simply. "I go with the deal."

At first he was puzzled, because what this innuendo suggested was possible between them had been so remote in his head, and then he pretended to be more puzzled than he really was, because if he had misunderstood her, he would be made to look a dunce. He studied her wet, celebrated, and mocking countenance beneath the rubber bathing cap, and held his silence.

"Did I shock you?" she asked.

"Are you saying what I think you're saying?"

"Bingo," she said cheerfully. "As the little girls with curls used to say, in silent pictures, I'm prepared for a fate worse than death. I don't have the cutes, Craig, and I don't have coyness. When I collaborate, it's all the way."

He was so dumbfounded, he wondered how he could offer any negative reaction without sounding less than adult, less than masculine. He decided to handle the offer as lightly as she had originally made it, and see what would come of their talk. "My dear, no man has ever been more flattered."

"Balls," she said.

The expletive was not coarse but businesslike, and he grimaced. "You mean it, then? How can you—?"

"It's easy," she said curtly. "I want what you have, and you want what I have. That's all that matters. I will add this. What makes the trade more agreeable is that I find you attractive, and I'm sure you find me so. Even if you weren't attractive, my offer would still stand." She read the lingering disbelief on his features, and solemnly took one hand from the ladder and patted his cheek. "Don't make a federal case of a simple proposition. You creative people are all the same. You think too much. You introspect every pleasure to death. Obey your real impulse, Craig, and you will look back on this night as the beginning of the most memorable deal—relationship—in your life."

With that, she turned back to the ladder and gracefully, sideways, in the way actresses are taught, climbed out of the pool. For a moment, she stood long and lean, high above him, water sliding down her concave breastbone and slight bosom and sleek flanks and dripping to the poolside. As she unclasped her bathing cap, and then shook her hair free, she was transformed into femininity once more, and he became aware of her, almost for the first time this evening, as a love object. The wetness of her, the brevity of her attire, the posture of her, the knowledge of her legend, gripped him. She wore two strips of peppermint bikini, one strip of material unfilled and pasted by water to her button breasts, and the other strip, stopping several inches below her navel, water-sogged and caught up and drawn up tightly between her legs to two bows on her naked hips.

Craig did not deceive himself. He felt desire for this person, but the desire he felt was not unadulterated lust for an inciting female but passion for Märta Norberg, a love object the whole world of men coveted and were denied.

If you thought about it—and now he did—the invitation was unbelievable, and because it was unbelievable, it was irresistible. Here now, looking down at him as she dried herself, was the most popularly desired woman on the surface of the earth, kept in the public eye by continuous reruns of her classic films. This moment, in darkened community houses girdling the earth, men in endless number, of every size, shape, complexion, morality—men who were Romanians, Bulgarians, Kurds, Afghans, Armenians, Siamese, Sudanese, Nigerians, Ecuadorians, Andorrans, and fellow Protestant Americans—sat glued to their theater seats and benches, staring up at the elongated, enlarged, flat and bright image of this enigmatic Swede projected on white sheets and screens before them. This night, they were united in a common admiration and indulgence. One and all were vicariously subjecting Märta Norberg to physical ravishment, and enjoying the bliss of their cinematic rape. Only when the lights went on, and the screen went blank, and they knew the image was all illusion, did they feel briefly cheated—but the fantasy of Norberg remained in their minds, and the elusive legend continued immortal.

And now, incredibly, the flesh and not the image of all this vicarious seduction was before him. She was his for a single word. Yet he could not utter it.

Having dried, she sat down at the edge of the pool, dangling her legs so that her toes touched the water. "Well, Craig, what were you thinking?"

"I was watching you."

"Yes, I know. Does it simplify your decision?"

"It makes it more complicated." He moved to the ladder. "I want you, you know."

"Of course you do. I want you, too. So what stands between us?"

"The deal. Do you really mean it?"

"Certainly, I mean it. Do you doubt me for one second? Say yes, and you shall have the preliminary letter to sign, and the down payment in the morning, with the rest of the money when you have finished the novel."

"No, I mean the other part."

"Me? That, too, of course, with pleasure."

"I'm dumb. Spell it out."

Her lips curled slightly in what he interpreted to mean a triumphant contempt for the inevitable weakness and surrender of all men. "What do you wish me to tell you, Craig?"

He grabbed the rails of the ladder, and pulled himself out of the water, and climbed the rungs to the poolside. He retrieved her towel and began to rub his skin under her gaze.

"I'm an amateur at these matters, and I admit it," said Craig, working the towel. "How do I get the bonus payment? And how do I deliver my work to your satisfaction?"

"It will all be quite natural."

"Natural?"

"You will see. You will remain in Sweden longer—you will move in here—we will work together on your outline until we are both satisfied." She saw his frown, and then amended her wish. "If you prefer, I will take you to my place on the Riviera, or even accompany you to New York, where I keep an apartment ready. In the day, we will work—and at night, we will love."

He threw the towel aside. "And that's all there is to it?"

"I will not intrude upon your work. I am an artist. Our minds are alike. When you are ready to be alone, resume creation, I will let you go your way. If you still prefer my presence, you may have it."

He squatted beside her, and then sat, wondering how he could reach a mind so foreign to his own. "Märta—I will call you that now—"

She smiled. "We're making progress."

"No, listen to me. I think—I really think—you believe this is possible. I want the money you offer. You know the facts. I can use it. And I think you believe that this novel I am writing, intend to write, my first since the Nobel Prize—a book that is a naked representation of me, of all I hold holy—can be falsely twisted and wrenched to satisfy your needs. Don't you see how wrong that is, how corrupting? You say we are both artists, our minds alike. If you were right, you would understand how I feel. What you mean is that you are the artist, and nothing else matters, and I am less an artist and should sublimate my individuality and craft in yours. When you made the offer to buy me, the cash offer, my answer was an automatic no. What made me hesitate—and you knew it would make me hesitate—was your added offer of an affair, of possessing someone every man on earth would give his soul to the devil to possess. So, indeed, I hesitated, because I was astonished, I was unnerved, and —I confess—I was curious and excited. But let us say this—let us pretend that this cold offer so dazzled me that I reversed myself and made the deal. What would happen? I would have my fun in bed, and you would have your book, your comeback property tailored by a name currently exploitable. But what would either of us have really? You would have a lousy book, it would have to be lousy. And I would have—what? memory of a virile conquest? How could I tell myself it was a conquest, when it was only a cold-blooded legal clause? Memory of an unforgettable love? Helen and Paris? Dante and Beatrice? Nelson and Emma? Or the memory of a mechanical, loveless union, dearly paid for, purchased, and in the end distasteful, because it was an extravagance I could not afford after all?"

She had listened, never removing her eyes from him, not attempting to interrupt, her features emotionless, her figure immobile. When he had talked himself out, she rippled the water with her toes.

"Make me a vodka, Craig," she said.

He lifted himself to his feet, grateful that she had not contended with him, and went to the table to pour the drink for her, and the whiskey he now needed more than ever for himself. When he turned around with the filled glasses, she was standing, waiting. He avoided looking at her bikini, her limbs, and handed her the drink.

"You can look at me," she said. "Why do you avoid it?"

"Why torture myself with something I can't have?" He tried to keep bitterness out of his tone, and made a lame attempt to be amusing. "I don't like to press my nose against shop windows."

"Craig, I want you to look at me, right now. How do I strike you?"

"Female. Quite the opposite of male."

"I'm more, don't you think?"

"Granted."

"Much more," she said definitely, "and the much more of me is the propaganda of me and the legend of me, and that is attractive. But don't be deceived. Even without all that, there is much more to me. Not merely my beauty, either. If I were to undo my bra right now and remove this strip of cloth down here—what would you see of me? First, two breasts. I'm realistic. There are better breasts to be seen in every half-dollar art magazine. Second, my nakedness below. No rare or exotic contour, no different down there from what you can see on any chippy you pick up for five dollars or fifty dollars. That's not the much more of me I speak of, Craig. What I speak of cannot be seen, must be intimately known. When you buy me, you are, it is true, paying a bigger price than ever before for lesser physical endowments than can be had at a fairer market price, but you are buying two marvelous things. One is, as you've guessed, the fame of me, the right to remember, when you are old and old memories are important, or when you are merely older and ribald with others, that once you possessed the flesh of Märta Norberg, yes, *the* Märta Norberg. That is important to men, of course. Imagine to be a man and to know that once you had enjoyed the favors of Ninon de Lenclos or Madame Du Barry or Eleanora Duse. That is the obvious pleasure you buy. But there is another that is better, far superior. Do I titillate you?"

"Go on," said Craig, drinking his whiskey, and keeping his gaze shoulder high, and wishing that they were dressed and elsewhere.

"Do I titillate you?" she repeated.

"Yes."

"Of course, I do. I have told you I am a good buy for two reasons. One is my desirability as a conversation piece. The other is this, Craig—my desirability as an experience. Do you know what that means?"

"I'm not sure."

"Do not regard what I am going to tell you as extraordinary vanity. I've simply equated myself against all others, I know my worth, and I am practical. When you come to bed with Märta Norberg, you eliminate the remembrance of every other woman you have known since adolescence. I will explain, Craig. Only a handful of others, in the world, know what I am to tell you.

The act of love is my other gift—the one I have brought along with my acting. Those are my two perfect skills. You have known experienced women, no doubt, active, intelligent amateurs, and prostitutes and call girls. Often such women have considerable knowledge of love, and are infinitely superior in their pleasure-giving to any housewife drab or dull-assed starlet. But the gifts of prostitutes are tarnished by their ready availability and the unspoken feeling of degradation. Nowhere can similar gifts be found untarnished, except in my bed. You will take my word when I say that I know more of love than any prostitute or courtesan or back-street Bovary. Your face tells me nothing now, but you may be secretly doubting me. I am sure you are. I pride myself on being a psychologist of men and their minds. You may be saying to yourself—what more can this boastful woman know of love than any other? How many ways can a woman lie with a man—on her back, on her side, on her stomach, sitting, standing, upside down, whatever you guess or know. You may be saying to yourself—how many erotic movements are there, and words, and pressures, and erogenous zones? All is limited and repetitious, and nothing can be new. You may even assure yourself that the ways of love, beyond intercourse, are restricted to six or sixteen. And so you will doubt me. And to that I can only say, Craig, say this—try me—find out."

She sipped her vodka.

Except for her profound, humorless sincerity, Craig would have been embarrassed. He did not know quite how to respond. "That's quite a sales talk," he said at last.

She smiled. "I'm rarely called upon to make it."

"But you have made it. And now I'll tell you something—I still don't believe it."

"Are you daring me? Is that what?"

"Nothing so childish. I simply will not accept your statement that you can please, entirely through physical skill, without one iota of emotion, passion, love given from the heart—"

"Save that fairy tale for your damn books," she interrupted, "and for all the empty women who read them and want to be deluded. Craig, *I know men*. Once you have a man between your thighs, you have his unconditional surrender on your terms, in exchange for whatever pleasures you wish to serve him. In intercourse, of whatever duration, a man is senseless, an absolute lower animal. His enjoyment derives not from the knowledge that his mate adores him—that may pertain before and after the act—but during the act he wants the primitive gluttony, and the better that is, the more voluptuous, sensuous, maddening, the more ecstatic he becomes." She paused and seemed to draw herself up, and the bikini bra filled. "I am honest, Craig. I don't barter my heart—only what is beneath it—and I have never had a complaint. On the contrary, my lovers have become beggars, debasing themselves with their pleas for more of me. Now, what do you think of that?"

"I think you have accomplished exactly what you set out to do—make me helplessly curious."

She tossed her hair. "Then we have a deal?"

"No—not on your terms."

"I see you still don't believe me." Her face had strangely darkened. "What will convince you? Do you want a preview tonight?"

"Not if you would consider it an option on my services."

"Don't be rude."

"I don't mean to be rude, Märta. I'm simply not on your wave-length. We're not communicating at all. You're speaking to me about a package you label sex, and I'm saying if it has no other name, it's a poor product. Haven't you ever been in love? What would happen if you fell in love?"

"I wouldn't be where I am," she said stiffly. "Craig, I have never and will never let myself be used."

"But you will use someone else."

"How am I to take that? Are you being sarcastic, chastising me?"

"I'm simply trying to believe you. I can't believe you. I'm appalled."

"Quit simpering at me. Don't be a sanctimonious child. And don't start categorizing me with your cheap writer's clichés—prefab characterization—Enter, the cold, calculating devourer of men, et cetera."

"I'm not judging you. I confine myself to observing, imagining, reporting. I'm trying to find out who you are. Do you know?"

"You're damn well sure I know," she said. "I'll tell you who I am, and who I am not. I am an actress, a great actress, the greatest in this century. That means one thing to me—my art comes first, and everything else can go merrily to hell. In this world, there are two kinds of actress. One is the actress-woman. She is schizoid. She is one-half public performer and one-half private human being. She is the one who winds up emotionally bankrupt, soon forgotten except for a fund-raising benefit and a ghostwritten memoir. The other is the actress-actress, who is not split in two halves, but is of a single indestructible piece, single, whole, self-sufficient, self-directed, devoted only to herself as celebrity and artist. Everything in her life, every judgment, decision, every choice and turning, must measure up to one standard—is it good for the actress that I am? This applies to homelife, leisure, children, finances—and above all, it applies to love."

She swallowed her drink, then, instead of asking Craig for another, she brushed past him to the table and began pouring her own.

"I was fortunate," she went on, "because I became an actress-actress early. The moment I was brought to America, I perceived how detestable and degrading the market place was. American show business, I found, was exactly like American sports and commerce and politics—a game of naked bartering. In Hollywood, on Broadway, what *they* had to offer was a good role with good money. But beauty, personality, talent were not necessarily enough to win the role. There were dozens of beautiful and trained young girls for every part. Then, on what would the choice be based? What could win such a role? The added offer of easy sex? No, not even that was enough. These dozens of girls were all too eager to divest themselves of pants and maidenheads. In fact, so eager were they, so uniformly accessible, that even I, as a young Swedish girl, was shocked. But then, because I was clever, I saw what extra was needed to win the role. Beauty was good, but too cheap. Nonconforming beauty was better. Acting talent was good, but too widespread. Overlaid on it there must be personality. Sexual availability was good, but there was a monotony to it, like raw steaks displayed in the meat market. But to offer something different with sexual availability—to offer fornication with skill, real skill—and once it be made known, to make the experience gradually more difficult to possess—that, and those, were the extra factors I understood and put into use."

She held her vodka before her, not drinking, and her earnestness was such that Craig felt she had forgotten his presence. But now she seemed to address him.

"Have you ever slept with a starlet? Groomed hair, cameo face, cherry lips, and figure always either forty, twenty-four, thirty-five or thirty-seven, twenty-four, thirty-five? If you've slept with one, you've slept with one hundred, one thousand. The same eagerness to oblige, the same tired endearments in accents of dramatic schools, the same practiced wigglings, the same superficial gamut of love play—warm pliable receptacles of love by rote, as if waiting in the wings for the cue, only waiting horizontally—until they can get the waiting done and be on with their real roles, the payoff. That was wrong, and it was not for me. At once, I knew that I would not be another pound— pounds—of easy flesh, to evaporate from memory by daybreak, to be paid off by some minor casting man with a bit part. I would be no starlet. I would be more, and I would be an experience. And so I went at this as I went at my public career. I schooled myself in the art of satisfying in bed as well as on stage. No matter how I did it, or how long I took. But I did it, and a night with Märta Norberg became not a passing physical release for a producer or director or banker, but an adventure in a new dimension of sensuality, and an enslavement and commitment. Soon, as I made my way, I was able to resist the cooky cutter in other ways. I would not let them coiffure my head like all the others. Or bob my nose. Or artificially inflate my breasts to the minimum expected size. Or learn the same carriage, and same, same diction. I stayed myself, and that made me unusual and different and remembered. And all the while, I remained a wonder in bed, and when this was known, and I was known, my roles grew larger, better, choicer, until they were the best, and exposure and publicity made me a household name. And when, at last, I was bigger than the spoiled men, the potbellied men, the sadistic men who had so often humiliated me—when they needed me, and I did not need them—I was able to become what I really was and am this day—remote, re- served, selective. My skills were less needed, but I had them when they were needed—a rivalry for the best play purchased, for the best director imported, for the great leading man, for a percentage of the gross. I kept my distance and gave sparingly, but when I gave, I gave well." She paused. "I still do, Craig."

In a curious way, her story had moved him. His perception had filled in so much that had not been told. Yet the story made her even more difficult to understand. "But now you can do as you please, Märta. You've spent a life trying to be yourself again. You've won. You are yourself. Why not love whom you wish and when you wish?"

"Because avarice never ceases," she said with a smile, "and mine is the avarice of the ego. My monument is in people's minds. To keep it there, I must continue building it. I have been idle too long. I must build again. And the materials I most urgently require are story properties. You have one such property, and I want it. Since I can't have it for cash alone, I am willing to return to the market place with my unique skills. But I am who I am, and I deserve to have what I want on my terms. Be sensible, Craig. I can dictate. You cannot. Despite this advantage, I am fair, because you are an artist as well as a man, and unless you are rightly rewarded you will not work happily, and I will suffer as well as you. So I offer you a fortune, and I offer you an experience, one that will be impressed upon your brain until it is senile, one that will mean more to your biographies than the silly prize. I am giving you all of me for a part of you. I'm leaning over backwards, and I don't want to go on like this any more. Simply say yes, and we'll seal the bargain with a kiss, and you'll stay the night. Now, are you happy—?"

"I'm revolted," he blurted out. The sympathy she had weaned from him had fled, as her cold bargaining had resumed. "For some money that can be earned elsewhere and some loveless convulsions in the hay, and a behind-the-hand conversation piece—you want a tooled novel, hammer and chisel and nails and plane, pounded and hacked out, slanted, a sham—"

"Goddammit," she cried suddenly, "I'm sick of your friggin' writer divinity—"

"No, wait, wait—I've got to finish. I'm not putting my art above anyone on earth who accomplishes an honest day of labor honestly done, so that life is earned and deserved. I make no pretense of being touched by a heavenly hand, singled out for special treatment, stand back because he's Muse-inspired —none of that. I'm not making myself out above a housewife who cooks a meal right and raises an infant well, or above a plumber who repairs the toilet efficiently, or the shoe clerk who gives you the right size. It's not a hallowed creation of work I defend—but destruction of myself as honest and decent and already in debt for my place on earth. If I grind out your untrue book as the pretense of a book truly mine, to be peddled far and wide with my name on it, my book is a lie, and I am a pervert before every reader who reads me, because he or she trusts me."

He caught his breath. "I am sorry, Märta, but I must write to please me, not you. That's why my answer is flatly no, Märta, flatly no. I'm not worried about you. You'll find fifty other properties, more suitable ones, or have them manufactured for you. And you'll find men you won't have to love to get them. And maybe someday you'll find men—a man—you honestly love, without this barter, far from the market place, although I doubt it. And as for me, I will keep my—I won't say integrity—but my nerve and my self-respect, always regretting that I had to let you keep your money and your dazzling skill. Yes, Märta, I have no doubt, no doubt at all, you will find other men who can afford, better afford, your money and skill, who have a backlog of integrity that can survive one small corruption, but I no longer have that backlog, and I can't afford you now. If I give you what little I have left, no reward of yours will help me survive as a man—because then, at last, I'll be totally bankrupt."

Where earlier had been her smile, he now saw her teeth bared. The drawn Nordic face gave him no satisfaction of emotion, but the teeth were bared, and she had never been more revealed.

"No man has ever spoken to me this way," she said, "and lest you think you'll get some satisfaction out of it, I'll tell you right now why you're turning me down—the real truth of it. I can tell—I can smell it—I always can."

He waited.

Her throaty voice was a bullwhip, and she lashed savagely at him. "You're quaking down to the crotch. You're the boy without balls, and we both know it. You're afraid of me, and that's the beginning and end of it. You're scared of sex, and you're scared of a real woman, and it's a thousand to one you're afraid of my bed and my body, because you can't get it up."

It was then that he did a foolish thing. He had been controlled, but now, like a high-school boy taking a dare, he lost control. "I wish I could save you face and say that's true, but the truth is I've done all right by myself, and right here in Sweden, and with a woman who has the decency to give love for love and for nothing else."

"You're a liar!" she shouted. "I wouldn't let you touch me now, if you were William Shakespeare and wanted to give me every word you ever wrote. I wouldn't let myself be touched by a puny, running weakling—who's got integrity instead of balls. Is that what you give your lady friend, your poor, starved lady friend, a hot injection of integrity? Get out of here, Craig, get out of my sight! Get your clothes and beat it, and stay out of my sight before I tell the whole world about their great masculine Nobel winner—the one man on earth who couldn't get it up with Märta Norberg!"

She spun away from him, seething so furiously that the contraction of the muscles in her shoulders and back was visible. He remained a moment, looking at her, at the disheveled hair no longer provocative, the slouched shoulders that would soon be old, the curved spine no longer lithe and slender but skinny and knobby, and the sparse folds of buttocks below the bikini strip no longer inciting but only grotesque and pitiful. The lofty, illusive female love symbol was, finally, only an embittered man-woman of the market place, and no more. Wordlessly, Craig turned away from her and went to the cabaña.

He changed slowly in the confined room, without anger, with only an inexplicable burden of sorrow, and when he was fully dressed, he emerged.

The lanai was vacant of life. She had gone. He went into the living room and found the yellow telephone. The number came to him at once. He dialed 22.00.00, and when the girl answered, he requested a taxi and told her where he was. As he hung up, his eyes caught the full-length oil of Märta Norberg on the far wall. As Manon Lescaut. The Trader, he thought—no, better—Trader in the Market Place.

His hat and coat lay across a bench in the vestibule. No one came to see him out. He opened the heavy door and went into the cold and fog to wait.

After he had lit his pipe, he felt better and wondered why. He had lost something tonight. In the eyes of the world, he had lost very much. Yet he was certain that he had gained infinitely more. For the first time since the Harriet years, he realized that he was not only a writer of integrity, but a human being of worth. The evaluation had a pomposity about it, and he considered rephrasing it, reworking it, and then he left it alone, because it was true, and because the feeling deep inside him, in that recess where the soul crouched and watched, the feeling was good, and it had not been that way for a long, long time.

He smoked his pipe, and enjoyed the fog, and waited for the taxi that would take him back to the living.

X

As each new day brought the climactic occasion of the Nobel Ceremony closer, the lobby and restaurants of the Grand Hotel became more and more crowded with new arrivals, largely journalists and dignitaries, from every part of Scandinavia and every corner of the world.

Now, at the noon hour of December eighth, with the Ceremony only two days off, the immense Winter Garden of the Grand was filled nearly to capacity. When Andrew Craig, wearing a knit tie, tweed sport jacket, and slacks, and carrying a folded airmail edition of *The New York Times* under an arm, entered the noisy indoor Garden, he found it difficult to make himself heard. The maître d'hôtel checked his reservation, then bowed across his folded arm and said, "Right this way, Mr. Craig."

Craig followed the dining room steward past a table of cultural delegates from Ghana, past another where American and English newspapermen conversed and several of these waved to him, past two tables joined to hold eight members of the Italian Embassy staff, and past yet another white-covered table at which Konrad Evang was in deep discussion with several Swedish business types. The variety of foreigners, like the variegated shifting patterns of color in a kaleidoscope, diverted Craig briefly from what had been uppermost in his mind, the scene with Leah just left behind and the scene with the Marceaus that lay immediately ahead.

The table that he had booked was on the carpeted higher level of the room, between two massive pillars. The maître d'hôtel removed the "Reserved" sign, pulled out a cane chair, dusted it briefly with a napkin, and offered it to Craig.

When Craig was seated, the maître d'hôtel inquired, "Does Monsieur wish to have a drink or to order now?"

"Neither one," said Craig. "I'd prefer to wait. I'm expecting guests."

When the maître d'hôtel left, Craig drew his chair closer to the table and spread open the newspaper before him. He had not read a newspaper carefully in days, but today, because he had slept late and soberly, and his eyes were rested, and because he had recaptured some interest in his contemporaries, he intended to resume following the serial story of his time.

But when he bent over the front page, he told himself that the light was too poor to read by. Through the enormous latticed glass dome above, he could see that even at noon, the day was sunless and somber. Then he realized that although the globular restaurant lamps on either side of him, and all about the room, were illuminated, the artificial lighting was diffused and yellow. Reading, he decided, would be a strain, and he knew that he was in no mood for it anyway. He closed his newspaper and slipped it under his chair. He tilted backwards, one hand fiddling absently with the table silver, and lost himself in thought.

In bed the night before, he had reviewed the astonishing encounter with Märta Norberg, had tried to remember what he could remember with emotional detachment, had sorted out one or two moments of it that he would have to relate to Lucius Mack once he was back in Miller's Dam, and then he had recalled something said earlier that evening that he had almost forgotten. What he had recalled was Norberg's bizarre revelation of Ragnar Hammarlund's machinations—the secret recordings, the information on Claude Marceau's affair with some mannequin, the plotting to snare the chemistry laureates into Hammarlund's industrial web.

In bed, Craig had considered all of this detestable scheming. Generally, he did not concern himself with individual morality. Most often, he preferred to play the onlooker, to live and to let live all the earth's cabbages and kings. Perhaps that had been his major defect as a human being. Last night, for once, he had determined to correct this defect in himself. He had detested Hammarlund for his cynicism, for his degrading of dignity by invasion of privacy. The Hammarlunds of the world, like the Sue Wileys of the world, he had told himself, must not go unchallenged. Moreover, Craig had identified himself not only with all victims of life, but, in this case, victims with whom he had a bond in common.

Somehow, he had seen that the Marceaus—like the hapless Garrett and distant Farelli and forever displaced Stratman—were, like himself, by chance, by circumstance, human targets. Through the prize, they had all become, with him, not only what Gottling had called democracy's elite, but also democracy's vulnerable ones. The six of them were, by birth and environment and interests, strangers before meeting in Stockholm, but with the awards, they had been pressed into eternal kinship. Forever after, they would be as one, the laureates of this year, and Craig had seen that if the Marceaus were harmed, so was he, and so were they all.

Once Craig had reasoned this out, and made his decision, he had acted. He had picked up the telephone and asked to speak to the Marceaus. There had been no answer in their room. This frustration had seemed to make the matter more imperative. Craig had left his bed, scrawled a note requesting Denise and Claude Marceau to meet him for lunch in the Winter Garden the next day, hinting at some private matter that would be of special interest to them, and had then summoned a bellboy and sent the message down to their letter box.

When he had awakened this morning, the luncheon invitation to the Marceaus had still seemed right, and he had not canceled it. After dressing, he had taken his coffee in the living room, alone, grateful that Leah had gone out earlier. After finishing the coffee, there had been more than an hour to spare before his date with the Marceaus. He had wanted to spend the time with Emily, and then remembered that she would be out, and that they were having dinner this evening. The anticipation of seeing Emily alone had heightened a desire, long dormant within him, to please and impress a member of the opposite sex. This had brought to mind a nagging duty—the formal acceptance speech that he was expected to deliver, after Ingrid Påhl's introduction of him, before the King and a large audience during the late afternoon Nobel Ceremony, in Concert Hall on the tenth.

Ordinarily, Jacobsson had previously explained, these laureate addresses were made following the Ceremony, in the evening, in the Golden Room of the Town Hall. But owing to the King's departure from the country immediately after the Ceremony, it had been decided to change the schedule and move the speeches up to the afternoon, out of respect for His Royal Highness. Because these addresses were widely quoted and read, Jacobsson had tried to convey to Craig the necessity of careful preparation. As a gentle reminder, and perhaps for use as guideposts, Jacobsson had mailed Craig several addresses made by earlier Nobel literary laureates. They had arrived the morning before, and Craig had merely glanced at them and thrown them aside, putting off the disagreeable task of composing a speech.

But this morning, after his coffee, thinking of Emily and of how she would be in the audience at the Ceremony and how much he wanted to command her respect, he had taken up the English copies of speeches by his predecessors and painstakingly read them through.

The Eugene O'Neill speech, prepared in 1936, Craig found interesting. A footnote explained that O'Neill, recuperating from a ruptured appendix, had been unable to attend the Ceremony in Stockholm, but had had his speech read for him. In it, O'Neill had given all credit for his career to the inspiration of August Strindberg. "If there is anything of lasting worth in my work," O'Neill had written, "it is due to that original impulse from him, which has continued as my inspiration down all the years since then—to the ambition I received then to follow in the footsteps of his genius as worthily as my talent might permit, and with the same integrity of purpose." The ring of sincerity was in this, Craig had believed. It could not have been a mere sop thrown the Swedes, since the Swedish Academy had ignored Strindberg and found his name an anathema to this day.

Next, Craig had studied the address made by Albert Camus in 1957. One paragraph he read and then read again. "Probably every generation sees itself as charged with remaking the world. Mine, however, knows that it will not remake the world. But its task is perhaps even greater, for it consists in keeping the world from destroying itself. As the heir of a corrupt history that blends blighted revolutions, misguided techniques, dead gods, and worn-out ideologies, in which second-rate powers can destroy everything today, but are unable to win anyone over, in which intelligence has stooped to becoming the servant of hatred and oppression, that generation, starting from nothing but its own negations, has had to re-establish both within and without itself a little of what constitutes the dignity of life and death. Faced with a world threatened with disintegration, in which our grand inquisitors may set up once and for all the kingdoms of death, that generation knows that, in a sort of mad race against time, it ought to re-establish among nations a peace not based on slavery, to reconcile labor and culture again, and to reconstruct with all men an Ark of the Covenant."

From the realistic splendor of Camus's phrases, Craig had turned to the courageous power of William Faulkner's uncharacteristic optimism in Stockholm during 1949. "I decline to accept the end of man," Faulkner had announced in his formal speech. "It is easy enough to say that man is immortal simply because he will endure; that when the last ding-dong of doom has clanged and faded from the last worthless rock hanging tideless in the last red and dying evening, that even then there will still be one more sound: that of his puny inexhaustible voice, still talking. I refuse to accept this. I believe that man will not merely endure: he will prevail. He is immortal, not because he alone among creatures has an inexhaustible voice but because he has a soul, a spirit capable of compassion and sacrifice and endurance. The poet's, the writer's, duty is to write about these things. It is his privilege to help man endure by lifting his heart, by reminding him of the courage and honor and hope and pride and compassion and pity and sacrifice which have been the glory of his past. . . ."

Long after Craig had laid Faulkner's speech aside, the majesty of his predecessor's words rang in his ears. He had remained motionless, moved by one who had possessed the strength to raise and shake a fist at Fate. Finally, because it must be done and because Emily would be there to judge it, Craig had tried to prepare his own speech. "Your Royal Highnesses," he had written, "Ladies and Gentlemen." That he had written, and then he had written no more. What cramped his hand had not been the literary brilliance of Camus and Faulkner, although their words had, indeed, been inhibiting, but rather their assurance and their authority. For all the progress that he himself had made since his arrival in this place, Craig still had no sure understanding of his role, his value, and his integration in his time. He still had not fully escaped Camus's "kingdoms of death." He had still the suspicion, as Faulkner had not, that man would be lucky to endure, let alone prevail.

And then, as he had attempted to explore what he did truly believe, he had heard the door open and seen Leah, arms filled with packages, come through it.

"It's about time you were up, Andrew," she had said, and had then stared at the pencil in his hand. "Don't tell me—let me guess—you're writing!"

He had thrown the pencil on the table and stretched. "Nothing like that. Just some notes."

She had dropped her packages in a chair. "I've got to rush, or I'll be late." She had started for her bedroom. "Märta Norberg invited me to lunch."

Immediately, Craig had been attentive. "Who? Did you say Norberg?"

"Yes. What's so unusual about that? She's very plain and friendly if you get to know her."

"Where did you get to know her?"

Leah had shown exasperation with him. "My God, Andrew, what a memory you've got. The night before last at the Hammarlund dinner. I spent a good deal of time with her."

"Oh, yes." He had almost added, "She told me," but had held his tongue in time.

"As a matter of fact," Leah had gone on, "we talked about you. She wanted to know what you were writing, and I mentioned the new book, and I think she's very interested in it for a movie or play. You may be hearing from her."

Craig had not replied to this. Instead, he had inquired, "When did she invite you to have lunch with her?"

"When? Why, at Hammarlund's. She said there's a wonderful restaurant called—it's a crazy name—Bacchi—Bacchi Wapen, and she wanted me to see it. I'm sure she really wants to talk about you. I think she's very impressed with you. Isn't it wonderful—all the excitement here—the people—" She had peered at her watch. "My God, the time. I'll be late. I wouldn't dare keep *Märta Norberg* waiting."

She had hurried into the bedroom, and ever since, Craig had felt a vague uneasiness. He had speculated on the outcome of this lunch. Originally, Norberg had probably made the date to learn more of his project, and had then taken the initiative to act faster and got in touch with New York. Now, she would have no use for Leah, yet she had not canceled the meeting. What did Norberg want? Would she mention to Leah, at all, the events of last night? And if so, how much would she reveal of them?

The questions had persisted inside him as he had gone down to the lobby in the elevator, and they persisted still as he sat at his table awaiting the Marceaus. His mind had strayed far from the Marceaus, the purpose of seeing them, and now he tried to recollect clearly what it was that he wished to pass on to them.

He had no more than a half minute to think, when he saw Denise Marceau, alone, looking less plump than usual in a smart charcoal suit, walking toward him. He leaped to his feet, welcoming her with a social smile, and she beamed at him cheerfully and took the chair that he held, and placed her purse and gloves on the table.

"How nice of you to invite us, Mr. Craig, but I hope you will not mind if it is me all by myself?"

Craig sat down. "I couldn't be more pleased."

"Poor Claude," she sighed. "He cannot say no to invitations. He had agreed for us to speak to the United Societies, and I prayed for any excuse to be out of it, and, mon Dieu, you gave me the excuse, so I thank you doubly, for that and for the invitation to lunch. Claude is off to his appearance, furious with me and sending you his regrets, and I am happy and festive. Would it be dreadful of me to ask you for a drink? A Bacardi *cocktail*, I think. Be sure to emphasize *cocktail*, or they always give you straight Bacardi."

Craig summoned the waiter and ordered a Bacardi *cocktail* and a double Scotch, and then lit Denise's cigarette.

"Well," she said, exhaling smoke, "here we are. I owe you an apology at once, Mr. Craig."

"For what?"

"I have never read a book of yours. Is that not shameful? Normally, I do not read novels, except the French classics. We have so many scientific papers to keep up with. But when I learned that you had won, and we would be together here, I determined to buy your novels and studiously read them so that if ever I was thrown in your company, I would have something intelligent to say about your work. But here we are, and I have nothing to say."

Her good humor surprised Craig. On the few occasions that he had seen her before, she had appeared high-strung and vexed. Now, at lunch, she seemed transformed and entirely at ease.

"You're forgiven," he told her. "After all, what do I know of spermatozoa?"

"Then we are equal," she said, as the waiter set the drinks before them. She lifted her Bacardi. *"Liberté, Égalité, Fraternité."*

He touched her glass with his. *"Entente cordiale,"* he said. They drank, and then he said, "Actually, we do have something to talk about. That was primarily why I invited you to lunch."

"Your note was very mysterious."

"I didn't mean it to be, but it is a private matter, and it does concern your husband and you."

For the first time, Denise was solemn, her brow wrinkling. "What is it you want to tell me?"

"This," he said. "Last night, I happened to be in the company of a woman who is a close friend of Ragnar Hammarlund. Her name is unimportant. What she had to say to me could be important. To begin with, whatever you may believe, Hammarlund is an unsavory character."

She shrugged. "But what else? Of course, he is evil. I would trust Judas Iscariot or Rasputin before I would trust Ragnar Hammarlund. What has he to do with this?"

"The friend of his I heard from—she is in his confidence—spoke of certain designs Hammarlund has—a scheme, if you will—to get you and your husband to work for him."

"How ridiculous."

"He's determined to make a major breakthrough in the synthetic food field, so that he can have it first, control it, and corner the world market."

"I have listened to his idiocy about synthetics. He makes no secret of it."

"Well," said Craig, "he seems confident he can win you and your husband over. I was led to believe that he already is sure you are interested in the findings of one of his chemists. And he seems to feel that he can—has the means to—how shall I put it?—convince, yes, convince your husband that he, too, both of you, must devote your next years to his work."

Denise laughed. "But that is impossible. We have not given him the slightest encouragement, neither my husband nor I. He has approached us, in his unsubtle way, but without success, I assure you. What on earth could make us collaborate with a horrible man like that?"

Craig bit his lip nervously. "Maybe I should tell you one more fact. That might be useful to you, throw a new light on what he's up to. I was told his entire house is wired to record anything spoken privately, between guests, in any room, and on the telephone. In short, every word any of us said at his party—every word is in his possession."

The merriment had again gone from Denise's face. *"Fils de putain,"* she said under her breath.

"My description of him exactly."

"So—now I know what you are trying to tell me. He has some information on my husband, is that so?"

"Well—"

"It is so. He knows about my husband's affair with that mannequin from Paris. Were you told that? Was it mentioned?"

"I'm afraid it was, Dr. Marceau. It's embarrassing, but I thought you should know, and since you know about your husband—hell, I wouldn't have brought that up—"

"The devil with my husband," said Denise suddenly. "There is me."

"I heard nothing about you."

"No," she said, thinking hard, "because the thing about me was too recent. You say every room of his house has a microphone?"

"So I was told."

"His private laboratory out in the rear. Was anything said of that?"

"Not that I remember."

"No matter. That would be wired, too. Well—" Suddenly, she grinned and looked at Craig. "I gave Mr. Hammarlund quite an earful yesterday. I do not mind telling you, since you already know about my husband. In fact, you can probably be of assistance to me. You are a famous author—you do know everything about plots—"

"My books do not always have happy endings, Dr. Marceau."

"I will take my chances. You see, Mr. Craig, I have worked out an intricate little plot of my own. I do not know if it will have a happy ending. It probably will not. But I am proud of my creative bent."

"Are you sure you want to tell me about it?"

"Of course, I do. If an enemy already knows, why should not a friend?" She sipped her Bacardi and then set it down. "My husband was at loose ends after our long years of work on our project. It was inevitable, at his age, that he would find some mischief. He met a Balenciaga mannequin, and she was clever and with loose morals, she saw a good thing, and she seduced Claude. Now, the affair has gone on a month or two—I know not how long— and it is still not resolved. The girl is flying here tomorrow, and Claude is meeting her. You can see that she is determined to take him from me. I am not sure that he is worth fighting for—but now I have become determined, too, to make the fight for him. How do I do it? What does a woman do? Nothing I have said has restrained him or made him give up this girl. Then,

I decided that there was only one hope left—and that is to fight fire with fire. Do you understand?"

"I'm not sure I do," said Craig.

"To do as he does, and try to make him jealous of me."

"I see."

"He has pride. He is possessive—or used to be—and so I am gambling on this. You remember Dr. Oscar Lindblom at the Hammarlund party?"

"I don't think—"

"Hammarlund's head chemist, a tall, thin Swedish boy."

"Yes, I know now."

"Yesterday, on the pretense of being interested in his synthetic work—I suppose that is why Hammarlund thinks I am interested—I called upon Dr. Lindblom in his laboratory. I was shameless. I seduced the poor boy. You may look amazed. I know I am not the temptress type."

Craig tried not to reflect either astonishment or disapproval. But he found it incredible to imagine this sedate, intellectual, almost matronly middle-aged chemist seducing anyone and committing adultery. "Why did you have to go to all that bother, unless you care for the young man?" asked Craig.

"He is nothing—a child—but I am trying to make him more, so that he will feel, and therefore appear to the world, to Claude especially, like a man deserving of my love. Otherwise, the plot would be a fiasco. Now, I will reveal the rest of my plot. If it has weaknesses, perhaps you will give me your professional advice. Tonight, Claude will be in Uppsala. I have invited Dr. Lindblom to my suite, to drink with me, to dine, to continue our passionate affair. What I plan is to do this. I will have drinks ready—I will make Dr. Lindblom consume more than usual, so that he is more, more—so that he is less afraid—and of course, before dinner, I will take him to my bed. After that, I will tell him not to dress—to put on Claude's pajamas—so that we can enjoy each other again after we dine. I will send for room service to see the menu. When the waiter comes, I will arrange that he clearly observes Dr. Lindblom, and after we have ordered, I will follow the waiter into the corridor and give him a large tip for a favor. I will tell him Dr. Lindblom is my husband, and tomorrow is his birthday, and I am eager to surprise him with a gift, a bottle of his favorite French champagne. I will give the waiter money, and ask him to buy the bottle and bring it back tomorrow and give it to no one but Dr. Lindblom. I will warn him that we may have visitors tomorrow, but he must ring and come in and give the gift only to Dr. Lindblom as a surprise. Do you see the outcome?"

"Tomorrow, the waiter will find your husband instead of Dr. Lindblom."

"Exactly. But he will think Claude is a visitor only, and that my husband is not there, and he will refuse to give the gift to Claude but say he will return to give it to the right man. What follows is almost mathematically predictable —I hope. Claude will collar the waiter or corner me to find out what other man has been with me. There will be a horrific scene. Because of violence, I will be forced to confess my infidelity. Then, one of two things will happen. If I have already lost Claude, this will merely hasten his leaving. Or, I will bring him to his senses, make him jealous, make him see how he has treated me—and maybe—there is a chance—maybe I will win him back to faithfulness. So, you see, Mr. Craig, Hammarlund holds no blackmail weapons over our heads. What can he do? Threaten to tell me of Claude or Claude of me? I already know about Claude—and, heavens, I *want* Claude to know about me. *Voilà*. There you have it." She sat back and brought her Bacardi to her lips. "There you have my precious plot. Do you see a flaw?"

Craig had been entirely disarmed by her easy candor. She spoke of herself, of her husband, her lover, his mistress, as if they were marionettes she was manipulating. It was difficult to take this seriously, it had so much the flavor of traditional Gallic sex comedies, and yet, Craig perceived, his confidante had suffered, and was deadly serious out of a desperation now repressed.

"A flaw?" he repeated. "Yes, possibly one."

She leaned forward intently. "You must tell me."

"No one can fight fire with fire," he said simply. "You are a scientist. You should know that. Fire feeds fire. It doesn't put it out. You may get your revenge and see destruction—that I won't deny—but you speak of salvaging your marriage. I can't believe this is the way. It's not a plot I would write, because it's psychologically wrong. You wanted my advice, Dr. Marceau, and I am giving it to you."

She had not expected this, and she was less assured, less gay. "What do you expect me to do? Just sit by, while he gets in deeper and deeper with this prostitute of his? I have tried that."

"I would suggest you try it longer. Sit by, go your own way with dignity, and that may make him more ashamed than anything else. But remain above him and make him less. Wait for him to tire of the other woman. The odds are heavily in your favor that he will come back to you, contrite, and with the single necessity to prove himself, hold his youth a day longer, a month longer, entirely out of his system."

"And what if he does not come back to me?"

"That is the chance, of course. But what you are doing now—I think it is a longer shot. Men are more moral than their women. Once he learns of your behavior, he will never be able to look at you in the same way again. And you won't be able to look at yourself in the same way. Not only will you have lowered yourself to his level, lost the one superiority you now possess, but you will have soiled yourself. You'll never feel quite the same just as he won't."

"You are not a woman, Mr. Craig."

"Indeed I am not. At the same time—"

"Men have an opposite view of it. I feel no differently now, and will feel no different later, than I ever have. It is only true love that changes one, that damages beyond repair, not a frivolous copulation."

"Perhaps that is the French attitude. I can only speak to you from my background and moral precepts, American and Calvinistic."

"Understand me, Mr. Craig. In all my marriage of so many years, I have never cheated or shown disrespect in this way for my husband. Before my marriage, before I ever knew there was anyone like Claude on earth, I had several earnest young student affairs. These were not mere indulgences of the flesh. For, whatever you have heard of the French, there are many of us brought up moral and constrained, and raised strictly French Catholic. Those student affairs were, you might say, part of the growing process, like menstruation and development of the bust. They were a process of maturing, seeking life's full potential, and a self-probing to learn if you could feel the way all the poets and novelists said you were supposed to feel. But when I was grown and I met Claude, there was never anyone else, no thought of it. Why should there have been? For me, the marriage was a contract, not to be lightly broken or ever broken. Furthermore, there was no need for infidelity, for I had nothing more to seek or prove. There was Claude, and there was our work, and that was enough for nine lifetimes. But when the work was done, and there was no Claude—what was there left for me, for the dull and serving wife, but a broken contract held in hand?"

She halted, and Craig struck a match and put it to her fresh cigarette.

"You mentioned your work," he said. "Wouldn't there be some absorption in finding new work and—"

"Find new work? Just like that? You should know better, Mr. Craig. Is an author so different from a scientist? One does not find work—the work finds one. Maybe, from now on, the work will never find me. And if that happens, and Claude leaves me, I will know widowhood twice and at the same time. Surely, that would be too much to bear. For this reason, in the only way I can think of, I am fighting to keep Claude." She drew steadily on her cigarette and then sat back. "So—you still do not like my plot?"

Craig threw up his hands. "What can I say? Criticism, without engagement, is not too easy to make accurately. It is just that I have the feeling, Dr. Marceau, that the plot, for better or worse, will resolve nothing. The solution must come by other means."

"Let it come by any means," she said. "Beggars are not choosers. But I cannot wait for happy accidents. I must go ahead."

"Then I wish you luck, believe me. If I can help in any way—"

"You have helped me enough. I *will* read your books. . . . Here, they have left the menu. Whatever is *Friterade sjötungsfileer med remouladesås?*"

Craig signaled for the waiter, and then, with his guidance, they studied the luncheon menu. Except for the pickled herring, salad, and mushrooms, they skipped the smorgasbord and ordered a filet of sole, to be accompanied by glasses of cold brännvin.

No sooner had the waiter gone than his place was filled by the figure of another man. Both Denise and Craig looked up as one to find Dr. John Garrett before them. His features wore their perpetual anxiety, even the purple bruise under his right eye seemed to jump, and he pinched nervously at his gray worsted suit.

"I thought I'd tell you, Dr. Marceau," he said, "they're paging you in the lobby. There's a phone call."

"Oh, thank you, Dr. Garrett." She rose and said to Craig, "Excuse me a minute," and then hurried off behind the pillar and through the tables.

Garrett remained standing, searching the busy room for someone. At last, he brought his attention back to Craig. "Do you happen to know Sue Wiley? She's the—"

"I know her," said Craig, and added, "unfortunately."

"Have you seen her around?"

"No, I haven't, and I don't want to."

"She was supposed to meet me here," said Garrett. "She has a lunch somewhere else, but she had an interview here in the morning and said she'd see me for a minute. Maybe she got tied up."

"I wouldn't concern myself about her," said Craig. "If you can help her, she'll be around."

Garrett seemed suddenly agitated. "What did you mean by that—if I could help her?"

"Why, nothing at all. Only you're a laureate, and she's doing a hatchet job on laureates, all of us and those in the past, and so she won't pass up a chance to see any one of us. Why don't you sit down? Keep us company until she comes around."

"If you don't mind?" Garrett took the chair facing the lobby entrance, peered off expectantly for a moment, and then turned to Craig. "You don't like Sue Wiley, do you?"

"I think I've made that clear."

"Would you trust her at all? I mean—I know about her sensationalism, but she has a reputation—a big organization behind her—and the press has some integrity."

"I wouldn't trust her under any circumstances," said Craig flatly.

This appeared to fluster Garrett. "But I mean—there are often special circumstances. For example, I'm always reading about reporters going to jail for a day or two, rather than divulge sources of their stories. Miss Wiley told me this once happened to her."

"I don't believe it. I don't think Wiley would go to jail an hour to protect her own mother."

"You're just sore at her."

"That's right," said Craig.

"There's good and bad in all of us," said Dr. Garrett.

"And some of us believe what we want to believe," said Craig. "I don't know what you're seeing her about, but you had better be prepared to explain that mouse under your eye."

Garrett touched the bruise. "Does it look bad?"

"On someone else, no, but on a Nobel Prize winner, it might provoke questions."

Garrett squirmed in his chair. "I guess you're right. I'll think of something." He hesitated, then went on. "I never got a chance—I mean—I guess I should give you my thanks for breaking up that fight the other night. It was foolish. I shouldn't drink."

"I'm glad I was there," said Craig. "He's a big man. He could have killed you."

Garrett said nothing, and then he said, "Maybe, but I would have killed him first."

"I won't ask you what started it, only I can't conceive of anything on earth that would make two—well, let's face it—famous men—make two of them risk their reputations—"

"Mr. Craig," Garrett interrupted, "there are times when you don't think of consequences. Self-preservation is man's first instinct. This was self-preservation—in a way, self-defense."

"I had the impression you started the fight."

"That night, yes, I plead guilty. But with moral justification. The original provocation came from Farelli. He stole my discovery, and if that wasn't enough, to get half my prize undeservedly—now, he's trying to get it all."

The waiter appeared with the two modified smorgasbord plates, and Garrett stopped speaking.

"The lady will be right back," Craig told the waiter. Then he asked Garrett, "Will you join us?"

Garrett shook his head. "Thanks, I'm not hungry." He spoke absently, as if his mind were elsewhere, and the moment that the waiter had gone, he addressed himself earnestly to Craig. "I suppose I can talk to you," he said. "I am desperate for some advice."

"I'm not sure I'm capable of helping myself, let alone anyone else," said Craig, and he picked at the salad with his fork.

"I mean, besides my wife, you're the only one who knows about Farelli and me."

Craig remembered Märta Norberg and Ragnar Hammarlund, but kept his silence.

"I have an awful problem, Mr. Craig. I make up my mind, and then I'm not positive about it. To tell the truth, and this is between us, I even telephoned my psychoanalyst in California last night—long distance. I've been overworked and upset this last year, and I've been in group therapy—and Dr. Keller has been extremely helpful, settling—"

"Well, I'm sure I couldn't give you better advice."

"Dr. Keller wasn't in. He's out of town for two days. And now I have to make this decision—in fact, right now. I had made it when I phoned Sue Wiley to meet me, but suddenly here I am, and I'm not sure."

Craig was reluctant to become involved in an intramural squabble, but the fact that Garrett was involving Sue Wiley made whatever it was sound more ominous. "What's the problem?" Craig asked. "Are you going to tell the Wiley woman that Farelli took a poke at you?"

"No, no, nothing like that. This is much more—"

"What is it then?"

Garrett dug a hand into his pocket and brought out a folded typewriter sheet. He unfolded it and handed it across the table to Craig. "Read that."

Casually at first, and then carefully, Craig perused what was entitled "Report to German Experimental Institute for Aviation Medicine" and signed "Dr. S. Rascher, 3 April, 1944." He almost missed Farelli's name in the first reading, and then he saw it plainly, and read the document a second time.

Craig looked up. "What is this supposed to be? Is it what I think it is—those doctors who were tried at Nürnberg and hung for experimenting on human beings?"

"Exactly. And all of Hitler's allies cooperated in supplying doctors, and Farelli was one of them. There it is—black and white."

Craig stared at the paper in his hand. "Where did you get hold of this?"

"It's authentic, all right. A friend of mine in the Caroline Institute made those notes from someone who had seen the photostat. When the Nobel people were investigating Farelli—they investigated me, too—they found this out, in tracing Farelli's war history."

"I read he was an anti-Fascist, arrested—"

"Only to a point," said Garrett excitedly, as if he were happy at his rival's weakness, "and then—well, there you see it—he decided to play ball and went to Dachau and collaborated with those medical murderers in torturing and putting helpless prisoners to death in experiments."

Craig dropped the paper to the table. "I can't believe it," he said.

"There it is," insisted Garrett doggedly.

Craig looked at Garrett's glowing, unnatural face, and was dismayed. "And this—this so-called evidence—is this what you are giving to Sue Wiley?"

"Well, I—I thought it seemed the right—"

"Is that your problem?" persisted Craig. "To do or not to do? Is that what you can't make up your mind about?"

"I've made up my mind—"

"But still you're not sure. Your conscience bothers you. And so you want someone else—your psychiatrist—me—anyone—to give our approval, so you're not alone."

"Well, not exactly."

"You want my advice?" asked Craig.

"Yes, that's why I showed you—"

"Don't do it," said Craig with all the firmness he could muster. "Tear this up and forget it."

"But—"

"I said forget the whole thing. What kind of revenge is this—to destroy an eminent physician, destroy him utterly, in return for a punch on the jaw?"

"It's not revenge at all," protested Garrett.

"What is it then—righteousness? Cut it out. Who appointed you supreme judge of all men? If a Nobel investigator, an informed and intelligent and balanced man, saw fit to weigh and reject this, why should you veto him and place your sole judgment, emotional and prejudiced, over an expert's? Who are you to do this?"

Garrett began to shake. "A criminal should be punished," he said too loudly, so that several at the next table turned to stare.

Craig lowered his own voice. "You're sentencing him to death without trial. Turning this unproved paragraph over to Sue Wiley is like giving a five-year-old boy a loaded Lüger and telling him to go out and play cowboy with the kids. She'll plaster this a mile high around the world. You'll ruin Farelli forever."

"If he deserves it—"

"And what if he doesn't deserve it? What if he can prove this is a mistake? Who'll remember or pay attention to the retractions? They're not worth headlines. For the rest of his life Farelli, no matter how innocent, will be the Nazi collaborator who helped kill at Dachau." Craig tried to reach the troubled man across from him with anything, even flattery. "Dr. Garrett, try to see yourself as others see you. Today you are world-famous, Farelli or no Farelli. You are known, respected, applauded—and deservedly. Your discovery is one of the most remarkable in history. You don't have to stoop to defamation of character to secure your own place. Can't you see that?"

"But letting a criminal—"

"Who says he's a criminal besides you?"

Garrett pointed to the sheet of paper between them. "The evidence is obvious."

"It's circumstantial," said Craig, biting the words. "Were you there? Did you see it? Have you found actual reliable witnesses? Have you heard Farelli's side of it? No, I'm sure not. All you have is a scrap of paper." He snatched up the paper and read the one line, " 'Dr. C. Farelli, Rome.' " He looked up sternly. "Is that enough, Dr. Garrett? Farelli is an Italian name, and so is Carlo, both common. There must be countless Carlo Farellis the length and breadth of Italy. And some of them physicians, and some of them with war records. Coincidences happen too often, and too often innocent men are injured for life because people refuse to believe in coincidences.

"I remember reading of a renowned criminal case, a lamentable true story —Adolf Beck, that was his name—he was the victim of circumstantial evidence and misinformation. Just before the turn of the century, a Dr. John Smith was arrested for swindling women out of jewelry. He was arrested, jailed, released. Years later, there occurred another series of similar swindles and a Norwegian chemist residing in London, one Adolf Beck, was arrested, identified by ten women, but what really convicted him was the old file on Dr. John Smith. This Beck's features, build, scars, handwriting were identical to those of Smith, and so the court decided that Beck was none other than Smith, and he was sentenced to six years in prison. He protested his innocence in sixteen petitions, to no avail. He was released from jail—in 1901, I think it was—and three years later, he was back in jail for swindling jewels a third time, although he pleaded that he was innocent and that it was all a case of mistaken identity. Then, after this long travail, two chance things happened to save Beck. An old identification of the original Smith, overlooked so long, was found, and it said that Smith was circumcised—and Beck was examined and he was *not* circumcised. And then a man named Thomas was arrested in the act of selling swindled jewels, and he turned out not only to resemble Beck, but to be the original Smith who was, indeed, circumcised. So after all those years in jail, his life ruined, Adolf Beck was freed. And all because of coincidence, hysteria, a mistake in identity."

Craig halted his impassioned account and glared at Garrett. "Do you want to take the risk of having an Adolf Beck on your conscience, Dr. Garrett?"

Garrett had grown pale and smaller, and Craig pressed his point harder. "It's not only that there may have been another C. Farelli at Dachau. What if there was none at all, and this was merely a diabolical trick, this insertion of the name of an anti-Fascist, by one of Farelli's blackshirt enemies, by Mussolini himself? At the worst, supposing Farelli had indeed been there, your Farelli, our Farelli. Maybe his attendance was enforced at the point of a gun—to obtain his diagnosis and advice. Maybe he was there and did not participate in the actual murders at all. There are all those possibilities, and more. Are you the one to say none of these is correct and only your angry indictment—Farelli capitulated, volunteered, killed others—is the true one? Will you accept that responsibility fully—and tonight, on thin evidence, see a valuable colleague ruined by unprincipled scandal? The decision is yours to make, Dr. Garrett, not mine—your own and no one else's."

Craig's appeal, so fervent, had depleted his reservoir of energy, and he fell back against the chair, exhausted, and waited.

Garrett stared down at the tablecloth, all dumb except for his hands in his lap, opening and closing.

"There you are, Dr. Garrett!" It was a young woman's voice that called out, and they both were startled and turned to find Sue Wiley, wearing her Robin Hood hat and a military coat, coming toward them. "I've been looking everywhere for you!"

Garrett, wraithlike, clambered to his feet, but Craig remained in his place.

Sue Wiley shook Garrett's hand and widened her eyes. "Boy, what a beaut. Where did you get the shiner?"

Garrett felt Craig's presence, and felt perspiration under his collar. "I—I was in the bathroom and turned around and the shower door was open—lucky I didn't lose an eye."

"I'll bet," said Sue Wiley cheerfully. "If that's your story—okay by me." She came around on one spiked heel. "Why, hallo, Mr. Craig. I didn't see you."

"Don't," said Craig.

"I heard that you had a divine night with my friend Mr. Gottling. Did you? He said he was too drunk to remember a thing, the beast."

Craig offered his silent thanks to Gunnar Gottling and hoped that it was true. "You can write that the alcoholic literary laureate was drunk too, and that he robbed the Royal Palace and raped a princess or two and that his mind is a blank."

"Thanks for nothing," said Sue Wiley with determined cheer, but her eyes blinked and blinked. She faced Garrett once more. "You wanted to see me about something? I have an important date, but if it's anything at all, I can call and put off—"

Garrett swallowed. "It—it's nothing—nothing at all—I'm sorry," he said. "I thought I would have some news for you, but—"

"About what?" demanded Sue Wiley.

"I—well, it was about the nature of my next—next work—experiments. But it involves others—an endowment—and there's been a delay, so I have no announcement to make yet."

Sue Wiley sniffed. "Anything is grist for the mill. Maybe you can tell me something?"

"I apologize for taking you out of your way, Miss Wiley, but what I wanted to tell you—it hasn't developed—and I'm not at liberty—"

"I understand," she said abruptly. "But if it happens, remember what I told you on the plane—I'm in your corner, and I want the beat."

"I promise you that."

"All right. See you before the Ceremony, I hope." She hiked her purse under her arm and turned to Craig. "You keep me in mind, too, Mr. Craig."

"You're never out of my mind for a second," said Craig.

"I know, I know. Well—happy skåling and *goddag* and *adjö*."

"The same to you," muttered Craig.

He watched her leave, stopping here and there to shake hands at various tables, until she had disappeared into the lobby.

Garrett sat down slowly, wiping his forehead with a handkerchief. After he had stuffed the handkerchief into his pocket, he took the sheet of paper from the table. He tore it into shreds, and crumpled the shreds, and shoved them into his pocket, too.

"Can I have a sip of whatever you're drinking?" he said, at last.

"Ice-cold brännvin," said Craig. "Have it all."

Garrett took the short glass in his unsteady hand and drank the brännvin down in one gulp. He grimaced, and then met Craig's eyes.

"Thanks," he said. And then he said, "I don't mean for the drink."

Craig nodded. "I know. You won't be sorry."

Garrett licked his lips. "I think you should know—this is only armistice—it isn't peace."

"Whatever you say."

After that, Garrett ordered another brännvin and smoked reindeer sandwiches, and by the time his order came, Denise Marceau was making her way back to their table.

"Have I held you up? Please do not stand." She slid into her chair, and beamed at Craig. "That was the party of the third part on the telephone. Everything is arranged."

"The plot thickens?" said Craig.

"Precisely," said Denise, opening her napkin. "Even though it isn't your play, wish me luck."

"Luck," said Craig.

And with that, they all bent to their food.

For his interview with Miss Sue Wiley, of America, Nicholas Daranyi had selected a distinguished restaurant several centuries old, the Bacchi Wapen, in Järntorgsgatan, not far from his residence in the Old Town.

In seeing established contacts, Daranyi made it a policy not to pamper them with lunch at all, at least not expensive lunches. For them, the money was enough. Gottling, although he had been sullen and uncooperative yesterday, in fact almost rude, had frequently been free with gossip for the price of a night of drinks. Mathews, the English correspondent, whose suits were threadbare, and Miss Björkman, Hammarlund's secretary, who was underpaid, were always valuable and dependable, as they had been last night, and never mde demands beyond the kronor offered. But Miss Wiley was a new one, of great promise, or so Krantz had suggested, and she was a highly paid American, and that meant that she might require being handled with considerable delicacy.

Bacchi Wapen was far too expensive for Daranyi's budget, but since he knew that he could not woo a rich American with his small funds, that he must entice her with other bait, a fine restaurant seemed an appropriate beginning. Daranyi had much faith in the seductiveness of expensive surroundings. For one thing, they gave him an air of solidity and prosperity. For another, they put his informants in his debt, in a subtle way, and wine of the best vintage and a fine cuisine more often than not made his guests drop their guards.

There was something to be said, too, for the enchantment of the surroundings. In Bacchi Wapen, a restaurant carved out of a rock, with its unique dining levels like so many descending cliffs, with its rare smorgasbord table, and the lovely young girl nearby at the piano, this somehow ennobled what otherwise might be regarded as a tawdry business. In surroundings such as this, the acquisition of odious calumnies took on the high purpose of a search for Truth.

At his table, enjoying the fragrance of his own body cologne, Daranyi nursed his dry martini and listened to the tinkling piano and wondered if Miss Wiley would prove a fruitful source. If she did, and Mathews delivered as he had promised, the few sources that remained would be inconsequential, the mere gilding of the lily. If Miss Wiley cooperated, he would surprise Krantz by presenting him with a thorough dossier on each laureate many hours before tomorrow evening's deadline. And for this, he would have a bonus besides his payment. Perhaps more, perhaps more. Daranyi would think about it when he was alone, and making his jottings, tonight.

He saw that the proprietor was directing a young lady—a surprisingly young lady, with a face like a gun dog, a pointer, wearing a costly soldier coat—toward his table. Daranyi shoved back his chair, to free his belly, and came to his feet.

"I'm Sue Wiley of Consolidated," she said, and offered her hand.

Daranyi clicked his heels and inclined his head. "Nicholas Daranyi," he announced, and quickly bent and kissed her hand.

After they had been seated, Daranyi inquired, "You will join me for a drink?"

"I don't drink," said Sue Wiley. "But I'm as hungry as ten wolves. What's the specialty?"

"I have studied the menu. Everything in Bacchi Wapen is delicious."

"What does Bacchi Wapen mean?"

"Bacchus Arms," said Daranyi.

"The names get sillier every day. All right, what were you suggesting?"

"In Sweden, for lunch, you can never go wrong with *köttbullar*."

"What in the devil is that?"

Her aggressive manner was disconcerting to Daranyi, but he retained his aplomb. "A superb form of meatballs with carrots in a thick sauce—"

"That's for me," said Sue Wiley. "I'm busy as all get out, so if you don't mind, let's be served and call the meeting to order."

"Certainly, whatever your pleasure," said Daranyi.

He snapped his fingers, and when the waitress came, he placed the orders, and added regretfully that they were in a hurry.

"What kind of accent have you got?" demanded Sue Wiley. "Romanian? Bulgarian? Hungarian?"

Daranyi was momentarily taken aback, for he did not know that he had an accent. "Hungarian," he said feebly.

"Oh, one of those." She fiddled with her purse, took out her compact, examined her face, then shapped it shut. "When you have a Hungarian for a friend, you don't need an enemy."

"I beg your pardon, Miss Wiley?"

"No offense. An American joke. There are hundreds about Hungarians. How does it feel to be a Hungarian?"

"I would not know. I have always considered myself a man of the whole world."

"Yes? Well, what are you doing then, hiding in Sweden? A duller place I've never seen."

"Oh, you must not be too critical, Miss Wiley. One becomes accustomed to the quiet, and after a while, one appreciates and enjoys it."

"There's enough quiet after you're dead."

"True, but for a historian, it is valuable in life, too." He had decided upon his role early this morning, when he had thought about Andrew Craig. "One requires solitude."

"You can have it." Her hand accidentally tipped over the salt-shaker, and she hastily retrieved a pinch of salt and cast it over her left shoulder. "Now, Mr. Daranyi, I'm not sure why I'm here, except you said on the phone you'd heard I was writing a Nobel series—"

"Yes, a correspondent from London so advised me."

"—and you might have some useful material for me, in return for a slight favor. What favor?"

"Before we go into that," said Daranyi suavely, "we must have at least a brief knowledge of one another, how I may be of assistance to you, and you to me. I am, as I have advised you, a historian. I have a contract with a British publisher to develop a thorough book on the Nobel Prize awards, and the personalities concerned, since 1901. However, much to my distress, the publisher has insisted that the history not be too—er, dry—that even, as regards the personalities, it be racy, and that emphasis be placed on the more recent laureates. Unfortunately, I am a scholar and not a journalist. I find it difficult to acquire such information on the current winners."

Sue Wiley's eyes blinked steadily. "So that's where I come in?"

"I had heard you were well acquainted with the current winners."

"You bet your life I am. I'm loaded. Are you? What's in it for me?"

"I have devoted two years to my researches, Miss Wiley. I have a mountain of important information on the past."

"My kind of information, Mr. Daranyi?"

"It depends. What exactly is your kind of information?"

"One paragraph'll do it for you. You want to know the lead to my opening article next week? Now, sit tight." She squeezed her eyes shut and recited: " 'Part I. Exploding the Nobel Myth. By Sue Wiley, CN's Special Correspondent in Stockholm. Paragraph, lead. That late gadfly, George Bernard Shaw, once stated, 'I can forgive Alfred Nobel for having invented dynamite, but only a fiend in human form could have invented the Nobel Prize!' Ditto, say I from the capital of Sweden, source of the world's greatest and most dangerous giveaway circus. Paragraph. I have been where few men or women have ever ventured, behind the scenes of last week's Nobel awards, and for months I have done firsthand spadework into past awards, and I am here to prove that the dignified, solemn prize-giving is, and always has been, an explosive, as deadly, as harmful, to giver and taker alike, and to the world, as the donor's invention of dynamite. Exclamation point.' " She opened her eyes. "How's that?"

"Provocative, to say the least."

"You can say that again. It'll be a sensation. Now then, I've laid it on the line. I'm not interested in any hifalutin scholarship. I'm interested in dirt, as one writer to another. Can you help me?"

Even Daranyi, who had been forced into many disagreeable relationships in the course of his work, was repelled by this young person. But he saw at once that she would have what he required for Krantz. Business is business, he reminded himself. "I believe I do have much that would be valuable to you, Miss Wiley."

"Okay, you come across and I'll come across. Your credentials first. For all I know, you may be a stringer for Associated Press."

"Credentials?"

"How do I know you're pounding out a book?"

"Yes, of course, I do not blame you." From inside his jacket, Daranyi withdrew a folded, blue-bound publishing contract which he had carefully prepared for this occasion. He handed it to Sue Wiley. "I anticipated that you might ask. There is my contract. I trust that you will not divulge the—er, financial—financial details to outsiders."

"What do you think I am?" She studied the first page of the contract, then riffled quickly through the other pages, then examined the last page.

She handed it back. "Kosher," she said. "You want to see my press pass?"

"That will not be necessary, Miss Wiley. I have been informed of your high standing."

"Okay, Mr. Daranyi, what do we do next?"

"We exchange information. You give me a fact. I give you a fact in return."

Sue Wiley blinked. "Not so fast, my friend. Let's have a preview first."

"What does that mean—preview?"

"Sorry—some samples. You throw me a couple of tidbits, so I know you've got the dope. I'll do likewise. If we're both satisfied, we can go on from there. You've got everything with you?"

Daranyi nodded. "In my head, yes. All can be verified."

"Bravo for you. I keep my notes under lock and key in my hotel. If I'm satisfied, we'll get this lunch over with fast, and you'll come back with me. We can make our exchange and take down the information in my room. Suit you?"

"Perfectly."

"Let's go, then. You first."

Daranyi found himself inhibited. "I do not know exactly what you want. There is so much."

"Anything off the cuff," said Sue Wiley, "but make it juicy and keep it factual."

He had prepared himself carefully, reviewing carbon copies of old assignments and writing down snatches of gossip overheard since his arrival in Sweden, and his knowledge had seemed formidable, but now, suddenly, he was less confident of pleasing her.

"Frans Eemil Sillanpää—" he began.

"Frans Eemil *who?*"

"Sillanpää," he repeated weakly, "the Finnish author. When he learned that he had won the Nobel Prize for literature in 1939, he immediately proposed marriage to his secretary and then went off on a fourteen-day drunk."

Sue Wiley scowled. "Is that all?"

Momentarily, Daranyi lost his composure. "I—I think it is amusing."

"If that had happened to Red Lewis or Pearl Buck, sure. But who in the hell gives a hoot about Frans Eemil Whatever-his-name-is?"

Grieved, Daranyi tried to save Sillanpää. "There is more to it, Miss Wiley. The Swedish Academy was prejudiced for Sillanpää, because he had tried to make Swedish the official language of Finland. Also, when the voting started in 1939, Russia was invading Finland, and by honoring a Finn, the judges were making a gesture against Communism."

Sue Wiley gave Daranyi no encouragement.

With quiet desperation, he slogged on. "Also—also—Sillanpää was a friend of Sibelius—no, I suppose that is not important. At any rate, he was poor and a widower with seven children, and when he heard that he had won the prize, he sent his seven children running through Helsinki shouting, 'Father's rich!'"

"Strike one," said Sue Wiley grimly.

"I do not understand?"

"It means you have one strike on you, and you'd better start swinging. Mr. Daranyi, I've got news for you—nobody, but nobody, in Kansas City or Denver or Seattle gives a damn what happened to Sillanpää. You'll have to do better than that. What else have you got in the hopper?"

"Sir Venkata Raman won the physics award in 1930—"

"Never heard of him."

"The Raman ray, Miss Wiley. He discovered it. He came from the University of Calcutta, wearing a turban, and he created the most embarrassing moment in the history of the Nobel Prize. When he made his speech, after the Ceremony, he accepted a toast to his award by glaring at the British Minister and saying, 'I accept not on my own behalf, but on behalf of my country and on behalf of those of my great colleagues who are now in jail.'"

Sue Wiley looked off with irritation. "Where are those meatballs? Are they growing them?"

"This Raman—" said Daranyi.

"You can keep him. That's two strikes. One more to go."

Daranyi, in disorderly retreat, scrambled through his memory, brushing past the great names he had waiting in line, until he found one and brought him forward. Andrew Craig. Andrew Craig and Lilly Hedqvist. He, alone, by lucky chance, knew of their love affair. What if he revealed it now? Ah, how Miss Wiley's mouth would water for every detail. This would win the day. But then, he saw, this act of revelation would make him as detestable as was Miss Wiley in his eyes. It would also make him a traitor to friendship, his only fatherland on earth. He had liked Craig enormously, and he regarded Lilly protectively, as a child of his own. Not Wiley, not Krantz, were worth losing her. Ashamed for having even considered the betrayal, aware of his guest's impatience he hastily located another author of the same nationality and led him to the assassin. It was all or nothing now. "Americans—" he said, and hesitated.

Sue Wiley was attentive. "Americans? What about them?"

"They were not always favored in the Swedish Academy. There was strong resistance to Sinclair Lewis, the first American author to—"

"I already heard that from Gunnar Gottling."

"Did you hear that Sinclair Lewis's publisher in New York, Alfred Harcourt, had been secretly promoting Lewis for a long time to win the prize?"

"You mean Harcourt was lobbying for him? In what way?"

"I do not know. It is only something I heard. I cannot prove it."

"Doesn't matter," said Sue Wiley. "That's good, that's more like it."

In that instant, Daranyi realized what she wanted of him, not bold human-interest sidelights but stupid slivers of modern gossip. Immediately, he consolidated his short gain. "There is the other one with a similar name—yes, Upton Sinclair. He was nominated for the Nobel Prize in 1932 by seven hundred and seventy famous people."

"I didn't know that."

"Oh, yes, Albert Einstein, Bertrand Russell, Harold Laski, they all nominated him, but he was defeated by John Galsworthy. And W. Somerset

Maugham, he was once nominated for the Nobel Prize, but he lost because a majority of the judges said that he was too popular."

Sue Wiley clapped her hands. "Wonderful. Home run, Mr. Daranyi. And you've got more where that came from?"

Daranyi felt the tension go out of his shoulders. "Much, much more, Miss Wiley."

"Good. We're in business."

His confidence came hobbling back. "Not quite, Miss Wiley. This is a two-way proposition. I have not yet heard what you have to offer."

His sudden lack of timidity surprised not only himself but Sue Wiley as well. "You don't have to worry about my end of it," she said. "I'm loaded. When we get back to the hotel—"

"I must know now," he said, more than ever pleased with himself. "I must have what you call the preview sample."

"All right," she said generously, "fair's fair. Let me see—"

He recalled the names on which Krantz had placed emphasis. "Dr. John Garrett?" he suggested.

"Garrett?" Sue Wiley nodded. "Sitting duck. He and Dr. Carlo Farelli hate each other."

"I know all about that, Miss Wiley."

"You do?" Her eyebrows had shot up, and now she was suddenly respectful.

"Indeed I do. They had an altercation at the Royal Banquet. And on another public occasion." He was pleased to retaliate in this way, and silently he thanked Hammarlund's secretary.

"Well, do you know that Garrett is in psychoanalysis in Los Angeles?"

"No, that I did not know. Most interesting. I would be pleased to hear more."

Sue Wiley glanced about her. "Not here. But soon enough. Are you satisfied?"

"What about Professor Max Stratman?"

"There's not too much new on him. You know about his background during the war?"

"I do."

"Mmm. But in Stockholm?"

"I know nothing."

"Well, then," said Sue Wiley, "for one thing, he's apparently got a heart condition, been seeing a heart specialist at the Southern Hospital. Also, he had lunch at Riche the other day with some big-shot German Commie—I don't know who yet, somebody who just checked in from East Berlin."

Daranyi's veins swelled in his temples. This was good, too good. He tried to think: was this armament for Krantz or against Krantz? He wondered. Then he remembered that he had his role. "Yes—yes—interesting, Miss Wiley. Of course, not exactly material of enduring quality for a staid historian—yet, one never knows. I think you will be a useful contributor. Indeed, I shall acknowledge your help in my book."

"Just leave me out of your book," said Sue Wiley. She observed the waitress coming with their tray, and beyond the waitress, just being seated, the famous actress, Märta Norberg, and a rather severe woman who resembled a governess and whom she suddenly identified as the writer Craig's sister-in-law. "Here's lunch," she said to the Hungarian. "About time. The place is getting too crowded. Let's make it fast and get back to the hotel. Our afternoon's work is cut out for us."

Emily Stratman hummed softly as she rode the elevator to the third floor of the Grand Hotel. Although she had long ago banished all that was German from her life, the tune that she now hummed, a stray wisp of recall from childhood, was *Du, du, liegst mir im Herzen, Du, du liegst mir im Sinn.*"

It was 4:10, and Emily's frame of mind was mellow and quietly happy. The late luncheon given by several members of the Nobel Committee for Physics, and their wives, in the large apartment on Ringvägen, had been more pleasant than she had expected. The wives had spoken so adoringly of their husbands, their children, their home lives, that Emily's desire to see Andrew Craig again, as she would in several hours for dinner, had been heightened. It was comforting, in a way she had always dreamed but never known, to have someone calling on her, attentive to her, protective even, someone with whom she felt safe and in whom she was emotionally absorbed.

Except for the brief exchange at noon the day before, Emily had not been alone with Craig since that natural embrace on the Hammarlund terrace, when he had kissed her. Or, in truth, had she really kissed him? She wondered what would have happened, been said, if they had not been interrupted by the summons to dinner. She wondered how he would behave tonight and what he might say and what she would say in return. Her constant devotion to him, in the privacy of her hidden fantasies, had at first alarmed her, but now if he was even briefly missing, she was bereft. In her world of make-believe, she had never been closer to any man. Her need for him, and trust in him, dominated her inner existence. How surprised he would be if he could know this! For she knew the reality of her presence in his presence, her withdrawn and withheld inarticulate presence, her aloof and cold untouchability. Well, she would try to represent to him her truer self tonight—that is, if there was a truer self.

Inexplicably, she found herself before the door of the suite, and still humming idiotically. She opened the door with the heavy hotel key, left it on the entry hall table, hung her coat neatly in the closet, then, fingers knitted together behind her head, through her hair, she stretched her shoulders and chest before the mirror, studied the fit of her new wool cardigan suit, and was satisfied.

A bath, she decided, a bubble bath. She would soak and soak, and dream a little, and perhaps nap briefly, before dressing for Andrew.

She strolled lazily into the sitting room, noticing that the maid had turned the lamps up—outside it was already dark—and then suddenly, turning fully into the room, she froze.

At the opposite end of the room, like a granite statue in a chair, sat Leah Decker.

Involuntary, Emily brought her hand to her mouth, and emitted a gasp. Her heart raced—the occupant had been so unexpected in a room that she had thought only her own—and then she closed her eyes, and animated herself with a shudder, and looked at Leah Decker.

Leah remained unmoving. "I'm sorry to have scared you, Miss Stratman," she said, but the voice was unusually hard and bore no inflection of apology.

Emily laughed nervously. "How silly of me. It was just that I didn't expect—"

"I know this is improper," Leah said. "I fetched the maid and told her who I was and asked her to let me in. It was important to see you. I wanted to take no chance of missing you."

Emily felt confusion at her visitor's conduct and her bitter tone. Her mind leaped to Craig. This was his relative. Emily moved a few tentative steps toward Leah. "Is there anything wrong, Miss Decker?"

"Should there be?" said Leah laconically. "As a matter of fact, yes, that's what brought me here. I think you'd better take a seat, Miss Stratman. You and I are going to have a short talk."

Leah Decker was totally in command, her voice so imperative (so familiarly Germanic to Emily's oldest memory), that Emily obeyed without question. Hastily, she took the chair nearest Leah, and gripped the arms, and waited in befuddlement.

"What is it?" she asked. "You seem so—you seem upset."

"I am upset." Leah's voice was nasal and imperious. "I have every right to be. Things have been going on behind my back, ugly things, and I want them out in the open."

"I have no idea what you are speaking about."

"You will, you will, indeed, in a minute. I had lunch today with Märta Norberg."

She said it as if it would mean something to Emily, but it meant nothing, and so Emily said nothing.

Leah resumed. "Märta and I had a long talk about my brother-in-law. And then we discussed you."

Emily was honestly astonished. "Me? I didn't know Miss Norberg was aware of my existence. What could you find to discuss about me?"

"You're very clever, Miss Stratman, but you will find I am no fool either, so you needn't try any of your tricks on me."

Leah's tone was offensive, and Emily was instantly affronted by it. "I beg your pardon, Miss Decker—"

"Never mind. You'll find I'm blunt and to the point, as I have a right to be. My brother-in-law called upon Miss Norberg last night at her residence. He was trying to sell her his next book for movies. According to Märta Norberg—and I do not know her to lie, and I do know my brother-in-law's weaknesses as no one ever will—Andrew behaved disgustingly. He was drunk, he was obnoxious, and he tried forcibly to seduce his hostess. He might have

452

criminally attacked her, had she not had a house filled with loyal servants. At last, she found it necessary to throw him out."

Emily felt the blood rushing to her head. "I don't believe a word of that, and I'm shocked that you believe it and dare repeat it. Everyone knows Märta Norberg's reputation. Why are you telling me this ridiculous story?"

"Because you are in it, my young lady, you are deeply in it, and I know Andrew's character, his irresponsibility, and it's my duty to see that he keeps out of trouble." She stared at Emily contemptuously. "I know all about you and Andrew. I heard it all from Märta Norberg. And she heard it from Andrew, yes, Andrew, your precious Andrew. He told her how he got you out on the Hammarlund terrace and kissed you—"

Emily sat stricken beyond the power of speech. A sinking ache lowered itself through her entire body. Leah's outburst could no longer be turned aside. Who but Andrew and herself knew of that moment on the terrace? How could Leah know of this, if Andrew had not humiliated her by telling it to that actress?

"—and that's the least of it," Leah was saying. "I know everything now. I know you've been sleeping with Andrew from the moment you met. I guessed it when I caught you two at the Royal Banquet, when he didn't come back to his room all night, not until morning."

Emily's body was stitched with pain, and her throat so constricted with dumbfounded indignation that she could hardly recover speech. "Sleeping with him!" she cried. "That's a filthy lie—and you're a filthy-minded liar, you and that actress—both of you—both of you!"

Leah sat unwavering. When Emily had spent her fury, Leah spoke once more with calm superiority. "Deny it if you wish. It'll do you no good. I have the facts. And I'm going to repeat one of them, exactly as Märta Norberg told it to me. When Andrew tried to seduce her last night, and she resisted, he began his drunken bragging, as he always does when he's had too much. These are his very words to Märta Norberg. 'I've done all right for myself right here in Sweden. I've been sleeping with a woman for sex and nothing else, so I don't need you, Märta.' Those were his words. That's what he told Märta, and she swears on the Bible he said them."

"I don't care what he says or does," said Emily, trying to keep her voice from breaking, "but he didn't tell that actress he was sleeping with me— he didn't say that—so how can you come here—"

"Does he have to spell it out? I told you I'm not a fool, and neither is Märta. If he behaves with you the way he does in public, what does he do with you in private? He said he's having an affair—"

"It's not me—it's not me—"

"Will you deny what happened on the terrace?"

"That's true—and I'll never forgive him—never—"

"And the rest is true, too, and you know it," said Leah relentlessly, "and I know it, and I'll believe it till the day I die."

"It's still a lie! No man has ever touched me."

"Please. We're not children."

"You are, with your foul mind. I'm not. If he said what he said—it's true about the kissing—but if he said the other also, it could have been some other woman he's having an affair with—it could be any of a thousand—"

"It's you, Emily Stratman."

"Believe what you want to, I don't give a damn!" Emily leaped to her feet, distraught and beyond restraint. "Now get out of here—get out of my room. What do I care what is in your sick mind?"

Leah rose slowly, the edges of her thin lips showing exultancy. "Of course, I shall leave. But first you're going to hear why I came here at all."

"I don't want to know! Get out!"

"You're going to know, and I'm going to tell you. I've watched you from the day we arrived here, watched you set your cap for my brother-in-law. I'm a woman, and I can tell when a woman makes up her mind—sets her sights—a handsome widower, tall, fascinating, free—a rich and famous author—a Nobel winner—well, why not? And how best to get him, this widower —the easy way, the way all crafty women trap and catch naïve men—by getting him below the belt, by giving their immoral, unclean bodies—"

Emily moaned at the shame of it, and began to sob piteously, eyes shut, shoulders shaking.

"—and so you think you have him, but I'll tell you what you have, Emily Stratman. If you want the truth or not, I'm going to tell you, and if you don't believe me you can ask him. You've got a murderer, yes, a murderer—a man who killed his wife, my sister—because he was a drunkard. Did you know that? I bet he didn't tell you that in bed. Ask him—ask him any time, see what he says. He killed Harriet. And that's not all. He lives like a pig. He is a pig. He's an alcoholic, drunk from morning to night, disgusting, every day drunk, every day and Sundays, drunk until he passes out. And as for being a writer? Ha! He's a fake, a hoax, and everyone in Miller's Dam knows it, but they don't know it in Stockholm, and you can bet your right arm Andrew's not telling them. He hasn't written a word in three years, and he never will again. And he hasn't got money, either. He's got nothing but mortgages and debts, and when the prize money pays for those, he'll be broke and drunk again. And sex—do you want to know about sex? Ask him about me, Leah Decker, ask him about when he was naked and I was naked, the two of us in his bed—see if he denies that either."

Emily had stumbled to the chair, and sunk down into it, head in her arms, her body heaving, her sobs wretched. Leah regarded her without pity, and stalked toward her.

"Why do I tell you all this?" she said. "I'll tell you why—because I'm all he has, and he's all I have—because even though he killed my sister, even though he's a wasted drunk, even though he hasn't done a day's work in years, even though he's behaving disreputably every night in Stockholm— he's still my charge, and I'm his guardian. He's my responsibility and I've devoted my last three years to him, and I'll devote the rest of my life if I have to, because it's what my sister would want, and I loved her in life, and I love her in death. When he marries, it'll be to me, if I'll have him, and I'll

454

do it for my sister. But I'm not letting him—not now when he's accomplished something, and even though he'll never accomplish another thing—I'm not letting him throw himself away on some foreign Nazi chippy."

She bent over Emily, shouting into her ear. "Do you hear me? If it is over my dead body—you are not going to get him!"

Slowly, Emily turned in the chair, hair tangled, eyes dulled, cheeks tear-blotched, gasping for breath, and then at last, she choked out her words.

"I don't want him—or anyone—no one. . . . Please leave me alone—please —please—"

Leah Decker straightened to full height. She could leave now, and she left.

When Andrew Craig, dressed for the evening, buoyant with anticipation, arrived at the door of the Stratman suite, it was a few minutes after seven o'clock. He rapped, waiting to hear Emily's quick step, but instead the door opened immediately, and there was Max Stratman buttoning his thick overcoat with his free hand.

"*Ach,* Mr. Craig—"

There was neither cordiality nor hostility in Stratman's demeanor, only sadness, as if he had aged too much overnight. He did not invite Craig inside, which Craig thought was surprising, but Craig wrote this off as an oversight due to self-absorption.

Craig crossed the threshold. Stratman avoided his eyes and stuffed his woolen scarf inside his coat.

"I should have telephoned you," he muttered. "Emily asked me to telephone you. She cannot go to dinner."

"Why not? What's the matter?"

"Since I have come back, she is lying on her bed in the dark room. She says she has a headache and wants to rest. I do not like the way she looks, but she has no fever."

Perplexed, Craig scratched his forehead. "I wonder what— May I see her?"

"She will not see you. What has happened, Mr. Craig? Did you two quarrel?"

"Of course not. I haven't seen her all day."

Stratman lifted his shoulders and then dropped them, as if to surrender the mystery as unsolved. "Then I give up. She will not have a doctor, and I do not think she needs one. She will not even have me around. 'Go out and have dinner, Uncle Max. I want to be by myself.' So I go out to dinner and let her be by herself."

"Well, I'd like to know what's the matter," said Craig. "I'm going in to see her anyway."

"Officially, no admittance. But if unofficially someone goes to her, what can I do? I look the other way. Have success, Mr. Craig, but do not aggravate her."

"Why should I? Of course not. You can trust me."

He waited until Max Stratman had gone, and then he tried to imagine what had gone wrong, and could think of nothing. He went into the sitting room, sailed his hat toward the sofa, yanked off his topcoat and dropped it on a chair, and opened the bedroom door.

He had expected it to be entirely dark inside, but it was not. The lamp beside the bed, which gave off a poor jaundiced-looking light, made visible only a portion of the bed and only a shoulder and arm that belonged to Emily. She was in the shadow of the light, and when Craig advanced to the foot of the bed, he could see that she had propped up a pillow and was settled back against it. She was fully clothed, except for her pumps, and her arms were folded across her bosom and her legs crossed before her. She seemed to be staring straight ahead of her, at some fixed point on the wall, and her eyes did not shift to Craig when he came into her field of vision. In no way did she acknowledge him.

He studied her delicate face, and it had the appearance of fragile china-ware accidentally broken and recently repaired.

"Emily—" he said.

She neither looked at him nor spoke to him.

"—your uncle said you weren't well and couldn't come to dinner."

"I heard," she said listlessly, and still did not acknowledge him.

"He said you wouldn't even see me. If you're not sick, it makes no sense. Has something happened?"

There was a movement of her head, and she acknowledged his concern at last. "I'm too tired to talk to you. Some other year, maybe. I'd prefer to be alone."

He did not like the hurt flatness of her voice. "I'm not leaving you alone, Emily, until I find out what's wrong."

She did not reply, but turned her face from him, toward the wall, and at once he knew that it was serious. He came softly around the bed. He sat on the corner of the bed.

"What is it, Emily? Is it something I've done—or not done? What? I'm completely mystified."

"Go away."

"Emily, what's got into you?"

"If you must know—" she said. She turned her face toward him. "—I'll tell you, and then I want you to go." She paused, and then she spoke. "Your sister-in-law was here this afternoon."

He did not hide his confusion. "Lee—here?"

"She came, and she had her picador sport, and she went. She said you and I were having an affair, and I was after you, and as proxy for your victimized wife, she would not permit it. She said you and I should not see each other again, and her arguments convinced me. That is all. My reserves are gone. I haven't the strength to go into it with you. It's too ugly, and I want you to go now."

He was taken unaware by this event, but he was not astounded. The logic of Leah, the predictability of this, he should have anticipated from the night that she had made Emily her enemy. Still, how far had she gone? What had she been capable of saying? He tried to visualize the scene that had transpired, and he shuddered. Leah and Emily: the cat and the canary.

"Emily, I'm sick at heart that you were subjected to this. But in all fairness, to both of us, I must know what Lee said to you."

"What does it matter? It means nothing now."

"Perhaps to you, but it means everything to me. I want to know."

"I don't feel I should tell you."

"Emily, for God's sake, this is no time for nice little games—sparing your tender feelings or my own. I'm as upset as you are, and I want the truth. I must have it."

"Very well, if you must. But I remind you, I don't care. I don't want a contest, no dispute, no more emotions. I just want to pay the price you are exacting to be rid of you." She seemed to steel herself, half turning toward him on her pillow. "Your sister-in-law was in my room when I came in. She had just had lunch with Märta Norberg—"

Craig nodded vigorously. He had been afraid of that lunch, and the detonation. One lunch, and two women scorned, and the inevitable fallout that maimed all at the periphery.

"—and Norberg had given her an earful about you," said Emily. "First off, you were supposed to have seen Märta Norberg at her place last night. True or false? Oh, I don't give a damn—"

"True," said Craig. "I saw her."

"You were drunk and tried to seduce la Norberg."

"False and false again. I was sober as I am now. I did not lay a hand on Her Majesty. Do you want the truth?"

"Don't bother."

"She tried to seduce me—it'll sound incredible—as part of a deal to make me write my next book to her specifications. I refused. Now she's being vindictive." He paused. "Is that all of it, Emily?"

"It's not even the preface of it."

"Oh, Christ. What else?"

"Must I?"

"You're damn right."

"I'll make it brief. I hate this. Leah Decker said you killed your wife."

He had feared this. What was there to say? "Yes and no," he said. "I'd had a few drinks, and we were driving, and I don't know what happened. Technically, I did not kill Harriet. But by some moral standard—and Lee is Morality—I am responsible, I am, because I was drinking."

"And you're a drunkard, she said."

"More or less, for three years, true. But since coming here—"

"And you've given up writing and gone to hell, and your sister-in-law nurses you—"

"Yes, I suppose you could say that. But I'm going to write again. I'm pulled together—if only you'll—"

Emily interrupted him. "And you were in bed with her naked."

Craig groaned. So this was how things were made to sound in a court of law, the half evidence, the half lies, the one-sided profile of truth? "Lee said that? Christ, the way it sounds!"

"Either it's true, or it's not true."

"It's true, but it's a lie. A truth can be a lie. Were we in bed together without clothes? Yes, we were—"

"Then—"

"Wait! But it was she who was the aggressor. She was jealous of you, and she thought she could keep me this way, and when I went to bed, I found her there, but I didn't—"

"I don't want to hear about it. I don't care."

Emily's controlled evenness, her lack of emotion, made Craig suspect the extent to which she was seething inside. He must attempt to reason with her. "Emily, can't you see that all this is the product of two angry, selfish women? I'm not worth all that devotion to distortion of truth. But here it is— and look what it's done to you. Without examining Lee's motives, you are swallowing it whole."

"Am I?" said Emily, with her first flare of temper. "Then maybe you're going to deny that you've merely been having fun with me, drunkenly dangling my scalp wherever it can be shown? How could Leah Decker know that we were out on the Hammarlund terrace—kissing?"

"She said that, too?"

"Norberg told her. Norberg said you bragged about it."

Then, it came to him. "The bitch, the goddam bitch. You know how Norberg knew that? In fact, she teased me with it. She knew that because that scum that walks like a man, Ragnar Hammarlund, has his whole house and outside bugged with hidden microphones—a business asset—and he's in on everything. If you don't believe me, ask Dr. Denise Marceau. I even warned her at lunch today."

"I'm not interested one way or the other," said Emily. "I don't care about any of that, but only one thing." For the first time emotion began to pluck at her face, and she turned it away, and then went on in a low, almost inaudible voice. "I can't stand that you made a public fool of me, that I behaved like a child. Maybe it could have happened to anyone, but I was the easiest to do this to because I'd never let my guard down before, never once, and now when I did, I did so entirely, and there was nothing to protect me, and now I'm so ashamed. It's so hard for me to understand, still. You were nice—kind—thoughtful—beyond reproach—and interesting—and the first man since I can't remember when—the first I wanted to hold me and to kiss—and it deceived me because I began to think—"

Her voice trailed off.

"Began to think what, Emily?" he said quietly. "That I might love you? I do love you, Emily. I am in love with you."

"No, I don't want to hear any more about that. I want only the truth about one thing. I know it's wrong of me, but I can't help it—because right now it's the only thing that matters. All the rest—I don't care—but this matters. While

458

you were with me—all the time you were with me—were you sleeping—having an affair—with another woman?"

Craig's chest constricted. It was known, and here it was. What could be said?

But Emily went on. "Märta Norberg told your sister-in-law you had boasted of it. I don't remember your exact words now, but something about —you were doing all right for yourself in Sweden, making love to some girl— woman—every night—something like that. Leah misunderstood this. She thought I was that woman. I told her I wasn't. She didn't believe me. But I didn't care about that. What I cared about—how can I put it? If you were having an affair with someone else—I don't mean pickups or prostitutes—but if you were making love to someone else, while leading me to believe you were—were—interested in me, giving me reason to trust you and have faith in you and pride in myself—if you were doing that—I'd be too humiliated to forgive you. And I've let you stay now because, I suppose, I had to know the truth. Be honest with me. That at least I deserve. Is what you told Märta Norberg the truth? Have you been making love to another woman while you've been seeing me?" She stared at him apprehensively. "Have you?"

"Yes, Emily, I have."

The breath she had held she now let go in a small sigh. She closed her eyes briefly. The timbre of her voice was that of a young woman turning from the open grave. "All right," she said, "all right." And then, "At least you're honest. I suppose it's the only virtue you have left."

"I have one more. I love you, Emily."

She moved suddenly into the yellow light, her glossy black hair reflecting the light and her green eyes flashing. "Stop saying that. I despise falsity. How can you say you love me, and how can I believe it? How can you pretend romance with one woman, and hours later—or before, for all I know—possess and make love to another? What kind of person are you anyway?"

"Emily, try to understand."

"I don't want to understand that kind of perfidy."

"Try to hear me out, Emily. I have a right to my side of it. You gave Lee hers, to my detriment, and now be generous enough to give me mine." He collected his thoughts, and then spoke with frank urgency. "On the way to Stockholm—no, it was first in Copenhagen on a tour, and then on the Malmö ferry—I met a pretty young Swedish girl, a good, decent girl, as good as you and more decent than I, but with standards somewhat different from our own. She never knew who I really was—doesn't know to this day. I had merely met her, had drinks with her, and charming conversation, and that was all there was to it. Then, the evening of the banquet in the Royal Palace—remember?—when I became so drunk, and you had properly turned me away— well, after the banquet, there I was, plastered and floating in self-pity—Lee told you my condition in Miller's Dam after Harriet died—so there I was, filled with guilts, loneliness, rejected—and I wanted someone to reassure me that I was a human being. Then, in my stupor, I thought of Lilly—not love or sex, because I was too far gone—I thought of a woman's warmth—hadn't thought of it for years, and I missed it—and then there was Lilly—that's her name, Lilly Hedqvist—and impulsively I went to her, and without a word, a question, the slightest hesitation, she took me in, a stranger, foreigner, a nobody as far as she was concerned. She put me to bed, and I slept it off. When I woke up in the morning, I tried to sneak out and let her be, but she wouldn't think of it. And so what happened—it just happened in a natural way."

"I don't want to hear of your disgusting amorous conquests," said Emily with bitterness.

"This was no conquest at all. I had a need to be wanted, and she had the gift of kindness. I don't know what was in her mind, if anything. Maybe she sensed my emptiness, my defeatism—there I was, brought down by drink, and exhaustion, and too many years—and so she gave her love and restored my belief in life. If there is one other soul on earth who thinks you have some worth, then life is possible. When I left that morning, I had no planned thought of seeing her again. But then, soon, the need came—it was after another bad evening. I had been drinking heavily with a well-known Swedish writer, and he had some inside information about how I'd got the prize." He paused, considered, but then it did not matter. "He had evidence that I didn't get the prize on merit, but because I was needed as a political pawn—my most popular novel was anti-Communist—and because I had so little that had been propping me up, this information shattered me. I wanted to go to you. But I was afraid of your own fragile sensitivity. So I went to Lilly because I had been there before and had come to believe she would not fail me. And she didn't. That's all there is to this great affair that Norberg goaded me into revealing—and I could kill myself for being so immature as to take her dare —but it was necessary, too. I won't say more or less about Lilly than I believe is true. I have affection for her, respect and affection—why shouldn't I have? —but what I have for you, Emily, is love."

"Please don't—"

"A man knows these contradictions are possible. On the one hand, I could accept one young girl's sympathetic tenderness and physical love—and on the other, at the very same time, give my heart to another woman who seemed unattainable." He stopped. Then he said, "There's my explanation. I can add nothing more to it, if you have no understanding of it."

Emily was gazing fixedly at the opposite wall once again. For some seconds she did not speak, and at last she spoke without looking at him.

"I wish I had such understanding, but I don't have it," she said. "I don't understand such things about men in general or you in particular. Maybe by some neutral judgment, you are in the right, and I am in the wrong, but this is what I am, and I have to live with my emotions and expectations." She paused, and now spoke with rising intensity. "I can't bear looking at you or being near you or being touched by you, when I know that for days I was being treated like a pitiable half-woman—which I may be—and being courted —if that is what you were doing—by the least part of you, and knowing that you only found even this possible because the most of you had to have and could enjoy a full woman in the night. I can't find the right words—it's all nerve ends—but it has to do, for me, with feeling inadequate and somehow cheapened."

She turned her head toward him. "You say you love me. I don't know how it is possible, and I don't know what the word love means to you, but I know what it means to me—and—and with me it is a different word altogether. But if you do have—let me say regard—if you do have regard for me, then the best thing you can do is to leave me alone." Her hurt green eyes had filled, and he had a sudden impulse to hold her—or shake her, or make love to her—but he could do nothing.

"Go away," she said. "Go to your Swedish friend, and let her fill your wants—let her love you again and again—but just don't come near me, not now and not ever."

She jerked her head away from him and buried her face in the pillow.

Craig lifted himself off the corner of the bed and dragged his feet across the carpet to the doorway and through it. He retrieved his hat and coat, all too slowly, hoping beyond hope that she had the inconsistency of all women —as Harriet had once had—and that she would recall him, because she loved him, too.

But no voice beckoned from the bedroom.

Craig went to the entry, and then into the hotel corridor, closing the door softly behind him.

He felt dislocated in time and purpose. He had no taste for dinner. His appetite was long gone. He had no interest in his room, where Leah might lie in wait, expecting his anger and relishing another opportunity to remind him of his debt. He had desire for nothing but oblivion.

He made his way to the elevator and descended to the bar.

He was lifted skyward in the triangular cage at Polhemsgatan 172C, and when it creaked to a halt at the sixth floor, he fumbled to open the cage and be out of it.

Only once he stumbled, which was not bad, not bad at all, he congratulated himself, for one who had been drinking steadily, alone, for over three hours.

He knocked on the door with the "C" and squinted at the window and fire escape nearby and he waited. It was important that she be in tonight, the most important thing in their lives.

And then came her voice through the panel. *"Ja?"*

"It's me."

The door flung open, and Lilly Hedqvist was his own, the cascade of golden hair, the welcome smile accentuating the beauty mark, the lavender robe.

"Mr. Craig, I am so happy to see you."

He directed himself in a straight line to the mosaic on the wall, and then sat clumsily on the hard, straight sofa beneath the mosaic.

"Lilly," he said, "I am loaded to the gills. Do you want to throw me out?"

461

"To have you run over by a car or maybe faint? Never. You will stay right here, until I say you are all right."

"And also I'm hungry. Haven't eaten since noon."

"I will cook for you," she said gaily.

"Only eggs. Scramble 'em. And black coffee black."

"You are so easy to please."

He had tried to find his pipe and tobacco, and did, and then dropped both. Quickly, Lilly picked them up.

"I will fix it," she said. She dipped the pipe into the pouch, and packed it, and gave it to him. Then she lighted it. "There. And do not burn my sofa."

"You'll make some man a good wife," he said.

She started for the kitchenette. "I hope so."

"But I won't let you," he said. "Because I want you to make me a good wife—me—not some man."

She had slowed with this, and then stood still, her back to him, and now she came around, forehead knitted, and looked at him.

"Are you making a joke, Mr. Craig?"

"I'm perfectly serious. I'm proposing, young lady. I'm asking for your hand in marriage."

"You mean it," she said. It was not a question but a statement of fact.

"Of course I mean it, Lilly. Never meant anything more. We can get married here, and then, you and your son, we can go back to the States, and—"

She moved toward him. "Mr. Craig, why do you ask to marry me?"

"I don't know why. You want to marry someone, and you ask them."

"But why—now—me?"

His mind dwelt on the incomprehensibility of all women, and he wanted a drink. "Because I care for you and need you, Lilly, and you can make me alive again." He was too sodden to concentrate in this serious vein. She liked fun. They had not often been serious. Fun. "I will buy you a Thunderbird and refrigerator and Bergdorf dress and nudist camp."

She had circled the coffee table and was now on the sofa beside him, rubbing the back of her neck beneath her golden hair, face too solemn.

"You do not want to marry me, Mr. Craig."

"Lilly, I know what I want. I'm asking you to be my wife."

"If you are asking so serious, it is bad then, because I must say no."

He prickled and sobered slightly. "You said no?"

"I do not wish to marry you."

He was too drunk to be depressed, but he had recognized her reply as a phenomenon. He had made up his mind while drinking, and had imagined her pleasure, a famous and wealthy American Lancelot, Galahad, to rescue her from insecurity, work, unwed motherhood. Yet she had said no.

"But I thought—" he began. "What's wrong with me? Am I too old?"

"Oh, no. That is all right."

"Don't you like me? I thought you liked me. We get along, and we have fun, and it would always be better." He narrowed his eyes. "Or is it that you have been sorry for me—the sad, middle-aged old man who is drunk and lonely—"

"Of course not—never!"

"Why did you let me love you, then?"

"Mr. Craig, you are making that too much, I have told you, and Daranyi has told you. Because a woman sleeps with a man in Sweden is not the same as America—is not to prove eternal love—is not a pledge for marriage. Maybe I was sorry for you, but not so much. And I would not give you body love for that reason. I offered my body love, because you are in many ways the kind of man I enjoy—you are serious and silly, and handsome and tall, and grown up—and, most of all, fun. I wanted to enjoy you, and you wanted me, and there was no more necessary. It is the most important thing, maybe, to have pleasure when you feel like it and not always look and wait for something that maybe does not come or comes too late. That is enough, what we have. Must I give you my heart too? Must there be a legal ceremony? Does that make us happier or better?

"We cannot marry together, because the fun is all right for a while—but a marriage is more practical and formal, and we do not have common things. You are too intelligent for my mind. You would tire of me. I am like a young girl who is always a young girl, who likes only the outdoors and to be frivolous, and you are not so, and I would tire of you."

A moment before he had ceased listening to her, because something else had entered his head. "Lilly, I know what is wrong. You know nothing about me, except I am a writer. You think I'm just another American tourist—a bad prospect—but that is not so. I could give you a fabulous life. Do you know who I am?"

It was like handing her an expensive birthday present, and he could not wait to open it for her.

But she was speaking. "You are Andrew Craig, the winner of this year's Nobel Prize in literature."

His mouth fell open. "You knew?"

"Not at first, but I have known. Daranyi told me."

"And you can still say no?"

"I respect you, Mr. Craig, and am proud to have been loved by someone so famous. But what has that to do with marriage? I cannot be happy because I have married a prize."

He felt maudlin and also depressed, at last. "Then it's no?"

"There is one more reason," she said at last, "and it is one more reason why you would not be happy with me forever."

He waited.

"You are in love with another girl, and you really want to marry her."

Lilly's knowledge was startling and eerie, and he kept staring at her. "What makes you think that?"

"Daranyi. He told me."

"How in the devil would he know?"

"He knows everything, Mr. Craig. It is his business. He is making an investigation now for somebody connected with the Nobel Prize—Dr. Krantz—a bad man, Daranyi says, because he is always liking the Germans—and now he wants to know all about you and the other winners, and Daranyi helps and finds out everything—"

"I don't give a damn about Krantz," said Craig. "I want to know about this thing you heard about me."

"It is because Daranyi is like my father—always protecting me—and that is why he told me about you and about Emily Stratman."

"You even know her name."

"Emily Stratman. Her uncle is Professor Stratman. She is born in Germany. She is now American. She is beautiful and strange and not married. You met her at the Royal Palace. You took her on a tour of the city. You were with her at Mr. Hammarlund's dinner. And Daranyi says maybe you love her like you did your wife."

"And that's why you won't marry me?"

"No, Mr. Craig, I assure you. It is for all the reasons I give. You do love her, do you not?"

He hesitated. Her face was so open, her honesty and strength so plain, that he could not lie to her. "Yes, I do, Lilly. And do you hate me?"

"Hate you? How foolish you are, Mr. Craig. Of course not. It is as always with us."

"Well, she hates me—because of you."

"I cannot believe it."

"All women are not like you, Lilly, and all are not Swedish."

And then he recited to her, as briefly as possible, sobering all the while, some of what had transpired with Emily several hours ago in her bedroom. Lilly listened enrapt, sometimes clucking with incredulity. When he had finished, he awaited her comment.

"She is most strange indeed," said Lilly.

"All women are different, different problems and neuroses, different heredity and upbringing, and many women are like Emily."

"No, I do not like it. I think she loves you and commits suicide. It is terrible wrong."

Craig shrugged. "There's nothing to be done."

"I am sad for her," said Lilly. "But you are the main one I worry about. It is no good for you alone. You can be so much and enjoy so much, but you cannot because you are alone. Emily Stratman pushes you away. Now, Lilly Hedqvist will not marry you. I am worried about you, Mr. Craig. Maybe I must marry you."

"Will you?"

"No. Still, I worry in my heart. What will happen to you when you leave us?"

"What will happen?" Craig snorted. "I think we both know. It was fated. I'll go back to Miller's Dam and answer fan mail when I'm not drunk—that'll be the writing I'll do—and I'll wind up with the inevitable—marrying my warden, Lee—the omnipresent Lee."

464

"Lee?"

"Leah Decker, my sister-in-law."

"The awful one we hid from on the ferry to Malmö? Oh, no, Mr. Craig, you must not—"

"There are worse things. At least, all my debts will be paid."

Lilly stood up. "Do not make deep decisions on an empty stomach. I will cook your eggs and heat coffee. After that, we will see how you feel."

"How do *you* feel?"

She wrinkled her nose. "Like my bed is too big for one person alone. And I want to remember the fun—because I do not think you will be here again, Mr. Craig, and I want to remember."

IX

For important business occasions, Nicholas Daranyi always wore the single-breasted, metallic-gray suit, of best English fabric, made for him via mail order by a Chinese tailor in Hong Kong. It was a suit which, had it been fashioned in London for one like the Duke of Windsor, might have cost between seventy and eighty pounds. By sending halfway around the world, and trusting the post, Daranyi had obtained the suit for twelve pounds, plus duty, plus the expense of a minor alteration across the shoulders.

Tonight, standing outside Carl Adolf Krantz's apartment door on the fourth floor of the fashionable orange building with white balconies and white flower boxes, located on the Norr Mälarstrand, Daranyi wore his Hong Kong suit. He had groomed himself carefully for the occasion, applying his favorite imported oil to his sparse, flat hair, and talcum and cologne to his smooth jowls. The suit draped beautifully, except for the right jacket pocket which held his folded sheaf of memoranda. He had taken care to look prosperous because, after tonight, he intended to be prosperous. Tonight, he reassured himself, would be his night of liberation from want.

Krantz had required the information by the evening of December the ninth, and now it was seven o'clock of the evening of December the ninth, and Daranyi had kept his pledge and met his deadline.

The door opened, and Krantz's maid, Ilsa, a broad peasant woman from Westphalia, a woman of indeterminate years but many, whose face had the appearance of a dried prune and whose upper lip bore down, bowed respectfully from the waist and admitted Daranyi to the vestibule. Daranyi gave her his hat, and the topcoat that he had been carrying on his arm since leaving the elevator, and then followed her through the parlor, with its embroidered lace doilies on every dark heavy mahogany piece, to the door of Krantz's study.

Ilsa pushed in this door, and stood back until Daranyi had entered, and then she closed it, and Daranyi was alone in the study. Only once before, during his long but erratic relationship with Krantz, had Daranyi ever been inside this study. He recalled that against one wall there had been a sixteenth-century German oak cupboard with ornate locks and hinges of iron that had once belonged to Krantz's father, and that over the oak cupboard had been a perfect square of framed photographs of Pope Pius XI, Fritz Thyssen, Franz von Papen, Paul von Hindenburg, Dr. Max Planck, and Hermann Göring, all autographed to Krantz. As if to prove his memory, Daranyi glanced at the right wall and was pleased to see the oak cupboard and the square of photographs above it.

He heard a rustling movement to his left, and realized that he was not alone, after all. Carl Adolf Krantz, more dwarfed than ever by his furniture, had turned from the lace curtains and potted palms before the glass doors of the balcony, and, hands clasped behind him, had spoken.

"I see you are on time, Daranyi."

"As I promised you, Dr. Krantz." Daranyi hastily went to his patron and took the perfunctory handshake. He observed that Krantz's mouth, wet between the mustache and goatee, was nervous, and this reinforced Daranyi's deduction that whatever he had obtained for the physicist was valuable and worth what he would eventually demand.

"I was looking out on the water," said Krantz. "It is pleasant at this hour."

Daranyi joined him, peering across the balcony at the Mälaren. The lights and silhouette of a freighter, going sluggishly toward the Baltic, could be seen, and then the reflection of a white ferryboat.

"You are fortunate to own an apartment with such a view," said Daranyi.

"Yes," said Krantz, but he did not seem happy. Suddenly, with effort, he brought himself away from the window. "Well, we must not waste our precious time with aesthetics. You said on the telephone that you have the dossier on each of our subjects?"

"I have."

"But did not have time to typewrite them for me?"

"That is correct, Dr. Krantz. With so much research to do and so little time—"

"Never mind," said Krantz. "I am prepared to register on my pad what you have to say. You will sit there."

He gestured to a squat leather chair that faced the great circumference of black coffee table. Daranyi sat down and admired the thick and lush green fern planted in a long iron antique basin, that dominated the far end of the table and all but obscured Krantz when he took the chair behind it.

"I trust you do not require alcoholic beverage before dinner," said Krantz. "I prefer you to keep a clear head. Ilsa has left a pot of tea."

Daranyi became aware of the tray, with its tea service and plate of cheese patties, on the table before the fern, and he nodded.

"Thank you. Perhaps later." He drew the folded sheaf of jottings from his pocket, and he saw Krantz match his action by taking up a yellow tablet and a pen. "I have been limited, by your deadline, to only the personal histories— as far as they were available—of the parties you are concerned with. I have omitted anything that might be known to you. I have pursued what might be useful to a committee fearful of a scandal before tomorrow."

"Excellent," said Krantz.

"I am proud to say that I not only have information of the laureates and their relatives up to today, but all through today. Besides the usual trusted informants, I employed several practiced operatives. I thought that the movements of the subjects, a day before the Ceremony, might lend some clues. I do not know. Perhaps I am overconscientious."

"We shall see," said Krantz, fidgeting restlessly behind the fern. "Please proceed, Daranyi. We do not have all night."

Daranyi examined his first page of scribblings. "Dr. John Garrett of Pasadena, California—"

"Speak up, speak up plainly," said Krantz with some testiness. "I must have everything accurate."

Daranyi cleared his throat. "Dr. John Garrett, the Nobel winner in medicine. His background, outside of his career, was singularly unproductive, except for one fact. For some months, Dr. Garrett has been having psychiatric treatment in the city of Los Angeles. His physician is Dr. L. D. Keller. His treatment is not individual, but as part of a group. There are seven persons in this group, including Dr. Garrett. Because I thought that it might be useful for you to have the names and some data on the others—in the event one might be linked with Dr. Garrett in some way—I went to the trouble of obtaining information on the other six, too."

With loving care, Daranyi read aloud the names of Miss Dudzinski, Mrs. Zane, Mrs. Perrin, Mr. Lovato, Mr. Ring, Mr. Armstrong, identifying each with a dry sentence or two. Daranyi went on to reveal facts concerning Dean Filbrick and several of Garrett's medical colleagues at the Rosenthal Medical Center in Pasadena. Daranyi admitted that he could locate nothing to show that Garrett and Dr. Carlo Farelli had known each other before Stockholm. There was evidence that they had first met at the Press Club, and several reporters then present had felt that the pair were not on friendly terms. This was corroborated by a brief quarrel between them at the King's banquet.

With true dramatic flair, Daranyi was saving his bombshell, acquired from Hammarlund's secretary, for the last. "As you doubtless know," Daranyi was saying, "Mr. Hammarlund gave a dinner for the laureates—Miss Märta Norberg was his hostess—on the evening of December sixth. There was a cocktail period before the dinner, and here the antagonism between Dr. Garrett and Dr. Farelli came to a head. They went into the garden, for privacy, and there Dr. Garrett accused Dr. Farelli of pirating his medical discovery. Harsh words—curses even—were exchanged. During the fracas, Dr. Farelli knocked Dr. Garrett down. Further violence was halted by the intervention of Mr. Craig, the literary laureate."

Daranyi stopped and looked up, pleased, expecting an exclamation of congratulations from Krantz for this deplorable and scandalous detail. Krantz was hunched over his pad, writing, and he said nothing. Daranyi's disappointment was keen.

"Interesting, is it not?" he asked hopefully.

Krantz glanced up with annoyance. "Yes—yes—what are you waiting for? Is there anything more on Garrett?"

Daranyi wanted to counter by saying: is this not enough? But he could not afford insolence. And then the thought struck him that Krantz's lack of enthusiasm about the Garrett and Farelli fight was an indication that Krantz either knew about it, or was not really interested in Garrett or Farelli. This was of some value to Daranyi. He could eliminate both of them, and he was closer to the truth of his assignment.

"More on Garrett?" repeated Daranyi. "Nothing significant, except his activity today. This morning at nine-twenty, he received a telephone call from your Foreign Office requesting him to appear in the Audience Chamber of the Royal Palace at eleven o'clock. I was unable to learn why he had been summoned or by whom." Daranyi looked up apologetically. "Reliable informants who are highly placed inside the Palace are, you will acknowledge, difficult to come by."

Krantz took out a handkerchief and blew his nose and scowled over the fern.

"Well—well—?"

Daranyi returned to his jottings. "At any rate, for whatever it means to you, Dr. Garrett arrived at the Palace at five minutes to eleven this morning, and was welcomed by the equerry . . ."

The equerry, impressive in his regimental uniform, had departed, and now, at 10:59 in the morning, John Garrett was briefly alone in the Audience Chamber of the Royal Palace, and gratified to the point of self-complacency. He wandered about the resplendent and baroque room, hearing his heels on the floor, and wishing that Dr. Keller and Adam Ring and his friends at the Medical Center and Carlo Farelli, above all Carlo Farelli, could see him now.

Garrett touched the magnificent tapestries on the walls, executed in Delft for Queen Christina, examined the oil portraits done by Franz Hals, gazed up at the angel above the dazzling chandelier, and then he stood on the carpet before the gold-and-velvet throne—an actual kingly throne!—and then he inspected the canopy high above the throne.

At His Majesty's request, the Foreign Office spokesman had told him earlier, on a matter of business personal to the King, could Dr. Garrett appear in the Audience Chamber for a private meeting at eleven o'clock? The meeting, the spokesman promised, would be of short duration, so as not to disturb Dr. Garrett's schedule, but it was on a matter of great concern to the King.

Garrett had been elated and was still elated. He was tempted to sit on the throne, for this was the way he felt, but he restrained himself for fear of being so discovered by the monarch. He wondered what the Swedish ruler wanted of him. It did not matter, actually. All that mattered—and this he had ascertained on the telephone—was that he, alone, had been called to the Audience Chamber at eleven o'clock, and now his ego puffed and strutted inside him. Poor, poor Farelli, he thought—to see the Italian's face when he read the story of this . . .

Lost, as he was, in his reverie, Garrett did not hear the heavy carved-oak door of the Audience Chamber as it was opened and closed, behind him. What he heard, after, were the footsteps, and he swung around, erect as possible, to meet the King man to man.

"Good morning, Dr. Garrett. It is gracious of you to come so promptly."

It was not the King of Sweden who spoke to him, and now approached him, but a shorter, stockier man, in his sixties, wearing a disappointing dark blue business suit.

He shook Garrett's hand. "I do not know if you remember me," he was saying. "I am the Baron Johan Stiernfeldt. We were introduced at Mr. Hammarlund's dinner."

"Yes, of course," said Garrett. "The Foreign Office phoned this morning—"

"At my urgent request," said the Baron. "I am really acting, as so often I do, on behalf of His Majesty. I will detain you but a minute or two. Shall we be seated?"

There were two low velvet stools, with crossed gold legs, against the tapestry that depicted a pastoral scene, several feet to the right of the throne. They walked to the stools and sat, the Baron Johan Stiernfeldt easily, Garrett uncomfortably and still chagrined by the absence of the one whom he had expected.

"It is my understanding," said the Baron, "that you are a close acquaintance of Dr. Erik Öhman, our cardiac specialist at the Caroline Institute, who has followed in your footsteps. He has spoken highly of you and gratefully of your contribution to his own work."

"I've been only too glad to be of some small assistance to him," said Garrett modestly, his ego rising once more.

"Perhaps it is presumptuous of us, then, when you are a guest of our nation and here on pleasure, to request your assistance in a personal matter. His Majesty was troubled about the propriety of this, and Dr. Öhman was consulted at length, and at last it was decided that we might take the liberty of hoping for one more favor from you."

Unconsciously, Garrett preened. "I certainly don't know what favor I can do for a King, but whatever is commanded, I am at His Majesty's service." He liked the gracious roll of his reply, and hoped that he would remember it for Sue Wiley.

"Excellent! In advance, we thank you," said the Baron. "Now to the favor. Dr. Öhman informs us that he has already spoken to you of his next transplantation case."

Garrett tried to remember. "There was a Count, if I recall—" He gave up. "I'm afraid you'll have to refresh my memory."

"The patient is Count Rolf Ramstedt, a distant relation to His Majesty and a relation for whom His Majesty has the deepest affection. Count Ramstedt is seventy-two, an athletic person of strong constitution and in the finest health—that is, until recently when he was stricken by an incurable heart ailment. I am a layman and cannot properly explain his illness, but I am told that it is grave and his situation critical. Perhaps you will remember the case from widespread newspaper accounts recently when Dr. Farelli, accompanied by an American newspaperwoman, visited the patient and gave an interview on the possibilities."

Garrett's face constricted. "Yes, I remember now."

"Dr. Öhman has been the soul of candor with His Majesty. For reasons beyond my comprehension, the case provides certain difficulties—"

"Yes, so Dr. Öhman told me."

"—but, nevertheless, Dr. Öhman feels, after numerous tests, that Count Ramstedt qualifies for transplantation surgery, that organ transplantation can be successfully effected because the patient's immunity mechanism will respond to the serum. With this assurance, the King has seen fit to allow Dr. Öhman to proceed with surgery tomorrow morning. However, His Majesty feels that as if by some kind fate, the world's two foremost authorities—the discoverers, in fact—of this heart transplantation happen to be in Stockholm to reap the rewards of their genius. The King would like to avail himself of the knowledge that you and Dr. Farelli possess. Since the operation is one that involves him emotionally, and beyond that will be widely reported in the world press, His Majesty feels a responsibility to see that the patient has every advantage. As much as he has faith in Dr. Öhman—and he has absolute faith in that young man—he would feel more secure if you could attend the surgery tomorrow morning, stand by, so to speak, in order that Dr. Öhman may draw upon your assistance and experience if necessary."

"Does Dr. Öhman know of this?"

"He has given his wholehearted approval," said the Baron, "and would be much relieved if you would share his responsibility."

"I will share it, of course," said Garrett. "I will be on hand."

"Capital!" exclaimed the Baron. "Surgery was originally scheduled for seven tomorrow morning. It will now be delayed until nine in the morning, so that Dr. Öhman may have time to go over his charts and plan with you."

Garrett saw, at once, the advantage of his participation, his collaboration, so dramatic, to save a relative of the King through the discovery that he had made. Before the entire world, he would be able to demonstrate why he had won the Nobel Prize and why he deserved it alone. It was this last that troubled him now. The Baron had said that the King wished Öhman to avail himself of the services of both himself and Farelli. That would not do, and he must be firm and make it a condition of his cooperation.

Baron Johan Stiernfeldt had risen, and that was when Garrett spoke his mind.

"There's just one thing," he heard himself saying. He came off the velvet stool and joined the aristocrat. "Few laymen are acquainted with the tension that accompanies this difficult surgery. Speed and precision are the saving virtues. I have found, in my long experience in heart transplantations, that two make for good surgery, but three is a crowd."

"I am afraid I do not understand, Dr. Garrett. What are you suggesting?"

"I assume you mean to confine the assistance given Dr. Öhman to myself alone. Since Dr. Öhman and I have exchanged notes on our work, and know each other, we will be able to perform at maximum efficiency together. A team of two—Dr. Öhman and I—will guarantee successful outcome. A third surgeon might make the undertaking extremely difficult."

472

Baron Johan Stiernfeldt's visage was stern. "Do you mean that you do not wish Dr. Carlo Farelli to attend the surgery?"

Garrett felt a wave of relief. It was understood. His victory was within his grasp. "Exactly, that is exactly what I mean."

"I am afraid that is impossible, Dr. Garrett."

The reply was unexpected. "Why is it impossible?" he wanted to know petulantly.

"Because at eight-thirty this morning, the King had Dr. Carlo Farelli in his private quarters for breakfast, and together, at some length, they discussed the details of the impending surgery. The King has already accepted Dr. Farelli's gracious offer to be of assistance."

Garrett stood aghast. "The King *himself* saw Farelli?"

"Oh, yes," said Baron Johan Stiernfeldt, "and quite relieved was His Majesty. You see, as I have explained, the King was reluctant to make any imposition upon your time and Dr. Farelli's time. Then, at last, he was convinced that the requests should be made. But before he could do so, Dr. Farelli relieved His Majesty of any embarrassment by voluntarily coming forward and offering his services to the King. You can imagine His Majesty's delight and appreciation. And—I suppose I can tell you this—it was Dr. Farelli's assurance at breakfast, that you would be as honored as he was himself to cooperate, that induced the King to have me meet with you forthwith. . . . Is anything the matter, Dr. Garrett? Are you having a dizzy spell?"

In Carl Adolf Krantz's apartment overlooking the Mälaren, fifteen minutes had passed since Daranyi's arrival, and now the Hungarian looked up once more from his memoranda and waited while his host finished his writing behind the obstructing fern.

"So much for Dr. Garrett and so much for Dr. Farelli," said Daranyi. "Next, I have the names of your chemistry laureates, Dr. Claude Marceau and Dr. Denise Marceau, of Paris. What I have learned of them, while not of considerable quantity, has quality, at least the quality I trust you will consider useful."

"Permit me to be the judge," said Krantz grouchily.

"Very well." He held up his sheaf of papers. "This is lurid enough to make one blush. The Marceaus seem to have led spotless lives, entirely dedicated to their investigations and experiments, until recently. Dr. Claude Marceau committed adultery in Paris, and his wife seems to have retaliated by having an illicit affair here in Stockholm."

"Decadent frogs," muttered Krantz from behind the greenery.

"I do not have the details, and so I will spare you that," said Daranyi, "but I do have in my possession certain facts. To begin with, Dr. Marceau's little amour . . ." With a fine sense of staging, Daranyi released his facts one by one, each like a gaudy helium balloon floating skyward. He covered Dr. Claude Marceau's indiscretions with the compliant Mlle Gisèle Jordan from their start in Paris to their forthcoming rendezvous this afternoon at the Hotel Malmen in Stockholm.

"I do not know for certain if Dr. Denise Marceau is aware of this rendezvous," admitted Daranyi, "but from the nature of her own behavior, I would suspect that she knows what is going on. In any case, she—and my source is unimpeachable—has committed two infidelities with one of your countrymen, Dr. Oscar Lindblom, a young chemist in the employ of Ragnar Hammarlund. One infidelity was performed in Hammarlund's private scientific laboratory three days ago, and the second was performed last night, on the occasion of Dr. Claude Marceau's absence from the city, when his wife received young Lindblom in her suite at the Grand."

"Disgusting," snarled Krantz, his pen busy.

"If you worry about a scandal," said Daranyi, "this may be it. I keep thinking Dr. Denise Marceau means for her husband to know of her own violation of the marital bed, and I keep wondering what Dr. Claude Marceau will do when he does find out. . . ."

At 1:02 in the afternoon, Claude Marceau had learned that his loyal spouse of ten years had become an adulteress.

At 1:08 Claude Marceau had extracted from her the name of her vile seducer.

At 1:29 Claude Marceau, linked in step with Hammarlund's butler, Motta, was striding over the forest path behind Åskslottet to the isolated laboratory, the den of sin in the Animal Park, where he would find the infamous, lustful, treacherous Swede, Oscar Lindblom, and give him the thrashing of his life.

Claude Marceau, protector of home and hearth, was boiling mad. Nor was his rage misdirected. Denise, ever timid and fearful of violence, had tried to protect her lover by protesting his innocence and presenting herself as a *femme fatale*. The gesture might have been laughable had it not been so transparent and pathetic. Claude had known his wife too long and too well to be fooled. Denise was essentially provincial, bourgeois, naïve, unworldly. There had been no doubt in Claude's mind where the blame must be put: the Swedish snake had taken vicious and caddish advantage of her distress, her weakness, and through his practiced wiles had hounded her into an infidelity.

Striding beside Motta, Claude reviewed the accident that had revealed all. He had returned from Uppsala after midnight, and immediately fallen into an exhausted sleep. He had awakened too late for breakfast and too early for lunch, to find Denise lounging in the sitting room, taking coffee and leafing through an imported Paris *Match*, and what had caught his eye was the flimsy pink negligee that he had not seen before and that ill became her, a married woman. She had been unaccountably vivacious, as she had been since the Hammarlund evening, and again he guessed that she had determined to show him her best side in order to woo him back.

Now, remembering: the door buzzer had sounded, and he had gone to see who it might be. The caller had proved to be a hotel servant, some relic fugitive escaped from Balzac's *La Comédie Humaine*, who held before him a bottle of something or other, gift-wrapped in red.

"I am one of the room-service help," the servant had announced. "I have the champagne Madame requested for her husband."

Claude had tried to think if it was his birthday. It was not. "I am Madame's husband. I will take it."

The servant had pulled the champagne away from the stranger's outstretched hand. Madame had been explicit, the night before, about this. "No —it is not for you. I have seen her husband."

Claude had then realized that this was a mistake. "I am sorry, but you have the wrong room."

"This is the right room," insisted the witless servant. "I spoke to Madame here last night."

Claude had become impatient with this tomfoolery. "What makes you think I am not her husband?"

"I saw *him* in there last night." He peered past Claude just as Denise rose from the sofa, and he recognized her. "Madame, here is the gift you ordered for your—"

Something had begun to penetrate Claude's head, and he wheeled about in time to see his wife desperately waving off the room-service relic.

"I—I—yes, it is the wrong room." The servant had begun to retreat when Claude was galvanized into action. He had gone after the man in the corridor and roughly collared him.

"You saw a man in the room with my wife last night?"

The servant had been struck speechless, but a severe shaking had rattled the truth out of him, quickly, stumblingly, even to the admission that the tall young man glimpsed with Denise had been in pajamas.

Claude had returned to the suite, slamming the door behind him, and advanced on Denise like the *procureur général* on a quaking defendant. The skirmish had been brief, and the defense had collapsed entirely. Foolishly, Denise had tried to take the whole burden of guilt upon herself, had even tried to transfer some of it to him. If she had not been so widowed and hurt by his affair, if she had not been so needful of love and reassurance, she would not have succumbed so easily to Oscar Lindblom's blandishments. There, the name was out—Lindblom! The betrayer, the traducer, the Nordic Casanova! For now, to absolve herself, the truer truths poured out—Lindblom's silken persuasion, his ardent whisperings and practiced hands, his strong and urgent body, his overwhelming and irresistible passion—Lindblom!

"There is the laboratory, Dr. Marceau," the butler was saying.

"Thank you," snapped Claude. "That will be all."

He left Motta behind, and strode vengefully to the door, gripping the knob with a strong hand that would, in seconds, bash in the face of the rapist. Since Count Axel von Fersen had played his little game with Marie Antoinette, every young Swede had fancied himself a Fersen. *Au revoir*, Lindblom, you will be the last of the line, Claude promised himself, and he burst into the large laboratory workroom.

At first, to his stinging disappointment, he thought the place vacant, and then, from behind the far row of beakers, he heard a voice.

"Who is it?"

Claude rushed around the counter, and then pulled up short.

Not Lindblom, but Ragnar Hammarlund, ridiculous in a one-piece suit of coveralls such as Winston Churchill had once affected, confronted him.

"Dr. Marceau—what a delightful surprise!"

"Where's this chemist—this Oscar Lindblom of yours?"

"Lindblom? Out. I sent him out on an errand. He should return shortly. May I be of service, Dr. Marceau?"

"No, it is this Lindblom I want," said Claude belligerently.

Hammarlund pretended not to notice his visitor's vexation. "Does he expect you?"

"I think not."

"He will be honored by your appearance, as am I. His admiration for you and your wife exceeds worship."

Claude was too irritable to enjoy insincerity. "You flatter us."

"Not enough," said Hammarlund, bringing a silk handkerchief from his hip pocket and brushing his forehead. "Dr. Lindblom is a shy, retiring young man of modest attainments who is well acquainted with your work, and for years you have been his idol."

This did not coincide with Claude's picture of a lecher. "I had a different impression of him at your dinner—a brash, overconfident fellow—"

"Surely you must be thinking of someone else," interrupted Hammarlund. "Why, when your wife came to visit the laboratory the other morning, Dr. Lindblom was incoherent with excitement."

"My wife came here?" Claude glanced coldly about the laboratory. So this was the sordid scene of the seduction. This was where it began—and the egotism of the lecher, to celebrate the insult further, in the husband's own hotel suite last night!

"Yes," Hammarlund went on, "your wife was intrigued by Dr. Lindblom's findings in the field of synthetic foods."

"I can imagine," said Claude bitterly. He looked about again, and a thought came to him: where had the seduction taken place? On the hard floor? Too incredible to conceive. "Is this the only room here?"

"No, by no means. We have what we call our 'think' room. Come, you can wait there for Dr. Lindblom. It will be more comfortable."

They walked into the adjoining office, and Claude stared at the offending sofa, and it all became clear.

"Have a seat," said Hammarlund. "May I order you something from the house?"

Although he had not yet eaten this day, Claude wanted no hospitality from a host whose employee he would momentarily reduce to minced sausage. "No, thank you." He sat stiffly on the sofa, and was somehow glad it did not squeak. He extracted an English cigarette from his silver case, and accepted the flame from Hammarlund's lighter.

"Have you come to see Dr. Lindblom on a matter of professional interest?" inquired Hammarlund, finding a place at the far end of the sofa.

Claude wished that the hideous man would remove himself from the premises, but then good reason reminded him these were, indeed, the hideous man's own premises, and that he would have to be answered. For a moment, Claude considered revealing to Hammarlund the real motive for his visit. But he wanted no forewarning, no bickering, no alarm. He wanted only one swift punch at Lindblom's leering superior blond face—one would do it—put him down whimpering, and salvage all pride and honor. Underlings simply did not cuckold Nobel laureates, he told himself, and the rebellious ones must be put in their places, even if by violence.

He tried to recall Hammarlund's question, and then he did. "Yes, you might say I have a professional interest in seeing your Lindblom."

"Stimulated by your wife's visit here, I hope?"

"You might put it that way," answered Claude wryly.

"Then she informed you of Dr. Lindblom's remarkable talent?"

"Only too well."

This was deteriorating, Claude saw, into one of those sex skits at the Concert Mayol all full of innocent questions and answers that had double meanings, and elicited from French audiences rollicking merriment. Although the immediacy of his anger had abated for lack of outlet, Claude was in no humor for this nonsense. He wanted to change the tenor of conversation. Now Hammarlund gave him the cue.

"Well, before Dr. Lindblom returns to speak of his work in person," Hammarlund was saying, "perhaps I could brief you on some aspects of it that might be of interest."

"By all means—do," said Claude, trying to display interest, but only eager to pass the time as quickly as possible.

At once, with the enthusiasm of a monomaniac, Ragnar Hammarlund began to expound on the necessity and value of discovering basic food synthetics. Edibles produced by chemical means would be healthier, would be cheaper, would bring an end to undernourishment, even to starvation, throughout the world. Once chemists could discover the synthesis for fats, proteins, carbohydrates, utopia would be on the earth.

"I am not alone in believing this," said Hammarlund. He jumped to his feet, went to the desk, ran a finger across a row of books and found what he was looking for. "Here is an American chemist, Jacob Rosin, who wrote a fine book on the subject, *The Road to Abundance*." Hammarlund was turning the pages, until he had what he sought. "Listen to him. 'Once the industrial synthesis of the carbohydrates, proteins, and fats is achieved, the bondage that chained mankind to the plant will be broken. The result will be the greatest revolution in history since man learned how to make fire. Hundreds of millions of hard-working farmers and farm workers will be replaced by chemical machinery. The surface of our earth will be freed from its dedication to food production. A new way of life will emerge.' " Hammarlund cast the book aside. "You see what is possible?"

At first, Claude had not listened carefully, but now Hammarlund's condescension as he assumed a pedagogue's lecture stance irritated him into a certain attentiveness. He was not, he reminded himself, a callow student. He was the winner of the Nobel Prize in chemistry. "I know the goal well enough, Mr. Hammarlund. There are always these dreamers' goals. The problem comes down to the obstacles—the hard obstacles we find in the laboratory—that usually make the end of the road unreachable."

Now that he had the laureate engaged, Hammarlund became more forceful. It was almost as if his invisible face had taken on human colorations of emotion. "Of course, Dr. Marceau, I am not so impractical as to ignore the obstacles. But what are these in the field of synthetic foods? First, we must overcome the belief of the public—coveted also by too many scientists—that the only healthy foods are nature's foods. You know that is rot, and so do I. Cauliflower, beans, peas, raw eggs, whole wheat, coffee are all hoaxes, filled with countless poisons that we have survived only because of restraint in our eating habits. Synthetic foods could be manufactured without these poisons. Second, we must sell the world the belief that chemical substitute nutriments can be as pleasurable as doctored meats and vegetables and bakery products, can look as attractive, smell as good, and taste as wonderful as the so-called natural foods. Third, we must prove to mankind that synthetic foods can be made to contain all the necessary values of known foods—carbohydrates, proteins, fats, water, vitamins, minerals."

What was annoying to Claude Marceau was that Hammarlund was making it all child's play. He was an industrialist and a superficial dabbler in the sciences. What did he know of the real problems of synthesis? For the first time in years, Claude began to recollect his early trials in the laboratory with Denise by his side, the days of toil, the weary nights of monotonous persistence, the tumbling into bed fatigued to the marrow, eyes bleary and neck constricted and bones almost arthritic, and in the brain, a chaotic spinning.

He was sorely tempted to expose Hammarlund to himself. He began to bait the millionaire, and to his surprise, Hammarlund delighted in the challenge and fought back with an amazing fund of case histories, facts, figures. It became evident, as the time passed, that while Hammarlund had no creative scientific imagination, he had sound knowledge of what had been done and what, indeed, might be done.

Gradually, without being fully aware of what was happening to him, Claude found himself locked in a rigorous debate with Hammarlund on the limitations of algae as a natural food substitute, on the degree to which synthetic edibles could be produced wholesomely and free of dangerous poisons, on the value of the findings in the synthesis of vitamins as they might be applied to foods as yet undiscovered, on the probability of breaking down the chemical structure of various proteins and inventing cheap man-made substitutes, on the usefulness of Chlorella and soybeans as springboards to other nutrients.

The minutes sped by, but so engaged and absorbed was Claude Marceau that he had no realization of the passage of time. It had been months since he had truly discussed a new field in biochemistry. After the discovery that he and Denise had made in the sperm field, their interest in that subject, already worn thin, had flagged. Lectures in France, and speeches and panels here in Sweden, had been undertaken as duties. The old subject had been discussed publicly as if by rote. For so many months now, it was as if Claude Marceau's scientific mind had been an arid desert, where nothing living could be seen, where nothing living stirred. And now, suddenly, so unpredictably, the desert was being populated by a clamoring mob, materialized divinely, from no-where, begging for the sustenance of life, dinning their desperation and their problem, an unknown civilization on the desert to be organized and led and saved.

And then, out of the anarchy of this new population, there appeared, lo, a leader with an Idea, and the leader was plainly Claude himself—he saw that it was he, himself, and no other—and the Idea was a way, an inspi-ration, a way to feed them and help them survive in a place so unnatural and antagonistic to life.

Hammarlund had gone on talking, but Claude no longer heard him, for he was thinking hard.

"Hammarlund," he said suddenly, "be quiet a moment."

The industrialist immediately fell silent, unoffended, for he observed the strange distant look on the laureate's face and acknowledged subservience to the mystique of the Idea.

"Hammarlund," Claude said slowly, almost to himself, "you and this fellow of yours, and all the people you have laboring for you in this syn-thetic field, are off on the wrong foot. Something so obvious occurs to me—I will tell you. Allow me to speak my mind aloud—feel my way. Do not in-terrupt. The mistake, I think, I am almost positive, is that you are attempting to imitate nature, all the processes of nature, in the invention of your sub-stitute foods. It would seem to me you must make a clean break from en-slavement to nature. If you do not, you will always run a poor second and get nowhere. Why try to improve on God? No. I should think it would be wiser to let God be and to go off on your own. I repeat, a clean break. Start from scratch. Do not make food in imitation of nature but as totally new and daring creations of your own, a chemical larder."

He lapsed into thought.

Awed, Hammarlund took the risk of intrusion. "I am not sure what you mean, Dr. Marceau. Do you mean—?"

"This," said Claude, not to Hammarlund but to himself. "Take the prob-lem of creating a synthesis of carbohydrates. Why do indoors what nature has already accomplished out of doors? Why bother to create artificial photosynthesis? Why try to create artificial atmosphere that plants require? Why not go directly to the source—glucose molecules—and from there build an entirely new chemical process that would lead to the discovery of man-made starches?" He paused. "And as to inventing the proteins we find in meat by imitating meat—why meat at all? Why not a new and improved type of product with the same protein values and unencumbered by wasteful sinews and bone?"

Through the haze of concentration, he became aware of Hammarlund, staring down at him, jaw slack. How he wished that Denise stood in Hammarlund's place, so that he could go on—on and on—throwing the Idea to her and catching it from her until they had their hypothesis. If Denise—Denise!

At once, he returned to his time and place, and remembered where he was and his mission.

"What is the time, Mr. Hammarlund?"

"The time? Why"—Hammarlund peered down at his wafer-thin gold wristwatch—"it is ten minutes to three."

"Mon Dieu!" Claude leaped to his feet. He had been here almost one hour and a half. He had completely forgotten his date with Gisèle. She had flown in from Copenhagen hours ago, and was awaiting his call and his person at the Hotel Malmen in South Stockholm. "I have a date—I must rush —I am late."

Hammarlund was beside him, apologetic. "What a pity. Your approach to the problem—the brilliance—"

"Never mind, I will know more when I discuss it with Denise. Call me a taxi."

"I can send you with my chauffeur—"

"No, a taxi. I will be out in front."

Hammarlund had gone to the telephone on the desk. "I do not know what has kept Dr. Lindblom—"

Claude stopped at the doorway. Lindblom. He had forgotten Lindblom, too. Of all things. He tried to summon forth the rancor that he had felt more than an hour ago. But it was no longer there. Lindblom was merely a bothersome beetle, one more minor disturbance with which the true scientist had always to cope. Still, as a matter of intellectual pride, Lindblom must not believe that he had not been found out.

"Yes, your Lindblom," Claude said to Hammarlund. "You can give him a message for me. You tell him that I came here to punch him in the nose, and that if I ever find him making advances to my wife again, I shall break his neck. Good day, Mr. Hammarlund!"

Denise Marceau, still in her pink negligee, examined her nicotine-stained fingers, and realized that she had smoked an entire pack of Dominos since Claude had stormed out of the suite in a frenzy of injured manhood.

The suspense, since, had been unbearable. She had paced, she had smoked, and she had wondered how her plot had unfolded at Åskslottet. She had made progress, of that she was certain. Claude's reaction to her affair had exceeded her fondest hopes, and for a while, she had believed that Craig's prognosis had been incorrect, and her own infallible. But now, with all this time gone, and no word of what had happened, she had begun to entertain serious doubts.

If her plot had worked, she would have known already. Claude would have salvaged his pride by knocking down Lindblom. After that, in a rage of righteous possession, he would have returned here, to the suite, and maybe knocked her down, too, and then would have regretted his fury and would have taken her to bed, and there would have been tender sweetness with all wounds repaired.

But he had not returned, and now she could only guess that he had behaved otherwise, after knocking down Lindblom. Duty performed, manhood restored, he had probably then regained his equilibrium, and determined that now it would be easier, more guiltless, to divorce her, and had gone on to enjoy his assignation with Gisèle Jordan, wherever that was taking place.

Grieved that Craig had likely been right, that her adultery had finally filled her husband with disgust rather than jealousy, Denise walked restlessly to the closet, located a fresh pack of cigarettes in her coat pocket, tore it open, and with pained sadness at the infinity of loneliness that confronted her, she lit a cigarette.

It was then that the telephone rang.

Her heart prayed: Claude.

She ran to the telephone, catching it before the third ring, and spoke into the mouthpiece with wariness.

"*Allô?*"

"Denise?" The high-strung voice was male, but it was not Claude's voice. "Are you alone?"

"*Qui est là*—who is there?"

"Oscar—Oscar Lindblom."

She sighed. Then he was alive. He would know her fate. "How are you, my dear? Of course, I am alone."

"Your husband—your husband has found out about us!"

"I know—I know. He found out by accident. Through the waiter who served us last night."

"He came to the laboratory to kill me."

"Apparently he did not succeed," said Denise dryly. "Well—what did he do to you?"

"Nothing. I was not there."

Denise's heart sank. He was not there. The third act had been a dud. "How do you know he went after you?"

"He found Hammarlund in the laboratory. He waited for me for about an hour and a half, and then he had to leave. He had a date."

Denise's heart sank further. A date? Gisèle. And for herself? Alimony.

Lindblom's voice continued tinnily through the receiver. "I missed your husband by ten minutes. Hammarlund was pleased as punch. He said that he and Dr. Marceau had the longest talk—"

"About us?"

"No—no—about synthetic food."

"*Synthetic food?*" Denise exploded. "That—that—that *worm!*"

"What—what did you say?"

"Nothing. Oscar, listen." She had lost, she knew, but she would not retreat without inflicting the greatest casualties possible upon the foe. The old plot had failed, but a fresh one had formed. "Tell me, where are you now?"

"About a mile from you. I had to return to—"

"Can you come right over?"

"But your husband—"

"He'll be out all afternoon—he will not be back until after dinner."

"Denise, please, it is dangerous. He might—"

"Oscar, I *know* where he is, and he will *not* be back. I am quite alone."

"But, Denise—as much as I want to see you—in fact, I was up all last night thinking about us—"

"I was too, darling."

"—it could be terrible, if he came on us. Hammarlund warned me."

"Warned you? Of what?"

"About seeing you again. Just as your husband was leaving, he told Hammarlund to tell me that he would break my neck if he ever found me with you again."

Denise's sunken heart lifted and soared. "He said that?"

"Exactly."

"Bravado, Oscar, mere bravado. He would not touch a flea. He knows that he is impotent, and that I cannot bear it—and he knows that I love you. I told him so."

"You told him?"

"Why not? It is true."

"Oh, Denise—"

"Darling, I am desolate without you. If I cannot have you here now—"

"Denise—Denise—" His voice broke off, and then was heard again. "Are you absolutely positive that he will not be back?"

"I swear to it on the Bible. You are safe, and so am I. Come at once. I must know everything that transpired at the laboratory. And I want you—do you hear? *I want you.*"

She could hear the choking emotion of Lindblom's voice. "I—I—I will be right there."

The moment that she returned the receiver to the cradle, she regretted the invitation. She had thought that last night would be the last of Lindblom's pitiful acrobatics. But on instinct, when she understood that all was lost, she had wanted to leave Claude with a picture that would haunt him the rest of his days. She had invited Lindblom with the intention of keeping him in the room, delaying him, and then going to bed with him at the time Claude would be returning. She did not consider what might happen after that. She considered only the humiliation to which he would be subjected. But now, that necessity seemed foolish, and worse, dangerous, especially if she still had the chance to save their marriage. For now, there was one ray of hope. Claude had, after all, displayed a flare-up of husbandly possessiveness in his last words to Hammarlund. This parting threat might have meant one of two things—a defense of pride or honest jealousy.

Why had she so blindly insisted on that child's coming to her room again, enticed him with the lure of one more fornication? It was some inexplicable intuition and nothing else, a yearning to know, firsthand, at length, what had taken place between Claude and Hammarlund. She could not believe that Claude, in such a wrath, could have coolly sat for an hour and a half and discussed synthetic food. There must have been more, and she would find out. She must trust her feelings and not her sensibility. She would learn if Claude had given any indication of a future for them. If he had not—well, the rest was clear—Gisèle the victor.

She trudged slowly to the bathroom, her slippers plopping against her heels. As to her promise to perform sexual intercourse with Lindblom, she would find a way out of that. She would be attractive, she would permit him to kiss her, even pet her, but beyond such innocence, she would have to say no. She would extract the information that she suspected he possessed, and bid him good-bye. With this last visit, his usefulness would come to an end.

In the bathroom, she discarded her negligee, and then, after giving the matter some thought, she decided on limited provocation. She unclasped her brassière, pulled it off, and allowed her full breasts to drop unhampered. With care, she washed and dried, improved her face bit by bit from eyebrow pencil and eye shadow to powder and lipstick. Then she doused herself with Arpège, behind the ears and neck, across her shoulders and collarbone, under her armpits, between her breasts and beneath them.

She had just pulled on her negligee, and was drawing it about the pink nylon pants, when she heard the door buzzer. Hastily, she secured the negligee, and went, in a trot, to the door.

The minute that Lindblom came into the room, hair disheveled and eyes too bright, and she closed the door and realized that he was staring at the movement of her breasts, she knew that she might not have everything her way.

"Denise—" he panted, and clutched at her, holding her so tightly to him that she could hardly breathe, pressing her bosom deep into his chest and running his hand down the arch of her back and across the curve of her buttocks.

In their previous two assignations, he had shown none of this impulsive aggressiveness, and now she tried to fathom it. Either she had aroused him to this pitch with her telephonic promise, or the combination of her attire and the dangers inherent in his visit had stimulated him beyond reason. Whatever lay behind his excitement, there was going to be a bout.

"Denise," he was whispering, "I could not come to you fast enough. I must have you at once."

She tried to push him away. "Oscar, what has got into you? Not so fast—"

"I must—I must—immediately. You do not know how it is!"

She was separated from him, and she saw his face and stance, that of an anemic Mellors who was a keeper of white mice, not game.

"Denise, you said you loved me."

"I do, silly boy, of course I do. It is just that I am no longer in the mood for—"

"Denise, on the telephone—"

"You have my affection, Oscar, but understand—I have been upset all day, so worried about you, what my husband might do to you—to you, my precious one, and no one else."

"Please, Denise—"

You give a teetotaler his first two drinks, thought Denise, and look what happens. She must put a stop to this. It was Claude who was on her mind. She must know about Claude. "Oscar, listen. I want to hear—"

"*Jag vill att du skall ligga med mig*—come to bed with me."

"I told you—I am not in the mood."

"A kiss at least—an embrace—"

"Very well. But first you must tell me everything that passed between my husband and Hammarlund."

"Anything."

"All right. No, wait—not here where the chambermaid may—" She squirmed out of his arms. "Come along. But remember—behave."

She went into the bedroom, and he hurried after her. She secured the door, wondering what he would have to say of Claude, but at once Lindblom was upon her, his hands on her negligee, his moist lips and short breath on her face. She favored him with a single kiss, then pushed at his arms, and slipped free.

"You must behave, Oscar—you promised," she said, distractedly. "Now, no more of this until you tell me what happened. Be a gentleman. Keep your distance." She began to pace the room, avoiding his hot eyes, his fervor, determined that he cool down, become rational, give her what information he could. She strode forth and back, still not looking at him. "Now, go ahead, Oscar," she said in her practical voice. "What did my husband say about me?"

"Only what I told you." Tie.

"Nothing more—you are certain?"

"Only that he would break my neck if he found me with you. Not another word." Shirt.

"I cannot believe it."

"I only tell you what Hammarlund told me. Dr. Marceau was there an hour and a half, and all he talked about was synthetic foods." Shoes.

"He does not care a bit about synthetics. Why should he spend an hour and a half—?"

"Because something Hammarlund was saying suddenly got him interested." Socks.

"What do you mean? I do not understand. Be more explicit."

"Denise, I cannot think!" Trousers.

"You must think. I have to know."

"Hammarlund said your husband got an inspiration—" Shorts.

"Inspiration about what? Synthetics?"

"What? I do not know. Yes. Please, Denise, stop running—stop ignoring —look at me." The compleat man.

"Oscar!"

"You see, Denise, I must—I am out of my mind." The compleat lover.

"I will not have it. . . . No, stop—you promised. Now, please, stop. Put on your clothes. Oscar, take your hands off—you will tear my beautiful new—" Sash.

"I have never desired you more. I will devour you. I will not live without you."

"You must. We cannot do this. Please behave. You promised to tell me, tell me—is Claude actually contemplating the beginning of actual research in—" Negligee.

"Ah, Denise, what divinity—your breasts—no woman on earth—"

"Oscar, wait. Oh, why did I let you in here? This is impossible. Let me off the bed. Will you stop? I refuse to let you take them off. No—no—" Nylon panties.

"Denise, my love—my only love—"

"Let go. . . . Are you mad? . . . I cannot breathe."

"Denise, be mine forever—leave Claude—"

"I will not leave Claude. I will not be so cruel. Oscar—Oscar—this is wrong."

"What?"

"This is wrong."

"It was not wrong last night, my love—not wrong in the laboratory. Love is never wrong."

"But this is different. Poor Claude . . . I cannot . . . no, we will talk. You have not finished telling me. You implied he has some new project. Has he, Oscar? Has he something—?"

"Something—what?"

"Do you think he has found something at last?"

"Oh, yes, of course he has—oh, Denise, I must—it is too painful."

"Contain yourself, Oscar—stop it."

"Live with me, Denise—leave him—forever us—like this."

"You say a project—a discovery? Could it be that—has he an idea about a new discovery—a hypothesis—?"

"What? I cannot hear you. Oh, Denise—"

"Oscar, wait. *Ralentiez*—let go, you are hurting me."

"It is my love—I cannot control—"

"I demand to know of my husband and his hypothesis."

"His hypothesis—?"

"Go on—go on—tell me."

"He and Hammarlund argued—synthetics—possibilities—everything—oh, Denise—debated all the while—your husband—fascinated—suddenly inspired with a concept on synthesis of foods—then—oh, Denise, my love, my love— *jag älskar dig*—I love you."

"You are nice, Oscar, yes. But talk—only talk."

"He kept saying we are all wrong—imitating nature—copying—must strike out to create new foods—not make substitutes for—"

"And you are sure he was sincere—completely absorbed—interested?"

"Hammarlund said he has never—seen—a scientist more excited—is sure—is sure—is sure—"

"What? What, my darling—?"

"Oh, Denise—yes, is sure your husband will embark on the greatest exploration of synthetics yet—yet—yet—"

"Go on, Oscar."

"—yet attempted by a science—scientist—in fact, he—Denise, I cannot—I must have you. Enough of this—"

"No, stop it, Oscar. I will not permit this—you are simply oversexed. You should be thinking of work, day and night, not this—"

"But in the laboratory you said—Denise, Denise—"

"Where is your honor? I am a married woman."

"You are body-starved. You are withering for love."

"Respect—respect. Release me. *I am a Nobel laureate.*"

"You are a woman—not embalmed in history books—not mummified by a prize. A woman—a woman."

"With a husband—with Claude."

"He is impotent—we are alive. He has his new inspiration. In fact, he—Denise, love me now—"

"You must tell me, Oscar. You were saying that 'In fact he'—"

"He was late for wherever he was going—for his date—he was so filled with his inspiration—"

"*No?* Is it true? Tell me—is it true?"

"Yes, for heaven's sake, Denise, I cannot talk. I cannot—"

"But—"

"He will explain it all—all to you—himself. He told Hammar—ah—lund he would discuss it with—"

"With me? With me?"

"Yesss—oh, Denise—"

"I adore you, Oscar! You have said so much. I am happy—I have never been happier."

"At last, at last—"

"*Oscar!* I only meant—"

"At last, at last—"

"*Mon Dieu!*"

"At last, at last—"

"*Voilà, c'est la guerre. . . . N'importe,* Oscar, only be quick. I think my husband may be coming back earlier than I thought. I am not sure, but there is a chance."

The Hotel Malmen, an imposing white square building on busy Götgatan, proudly advertised that its 250 guest rooms, equipped with bathtubs or showers and four-station radios, were among the most modern in all Sweden.

For many tourists, the only disadvantage to the hotel was that it was some distance removed from Stockholm's center. For Gisèle Jordan, out of consideration of her lover's position, and her relationship with him, this isolation was a major advantage, and once she learned of it, she had reserved a double room on the second floor for the afternoon of December ninth.

Now, in that double room on the second floor, Claude Marceau sat lost in thought, sipping an Armagnac that Gisèle had so considerately brought for him, and listening to the distant splash of the water from the faucet in the bathroom to which Gisèle had just retired.

Except for the first few minutes after his tardy arrival, Gisèle had been, he had to admit, admirable. In the first few minutes, when he had entered her room in a trance, after the mechanical embrace and kiss, she had pouted and shown dissatisfaction, rare in one so even-tempered.

"But so late?" she had said. "I did not fly all the way up here to the North Pole simply to sit for hours alone in some dreary hotel room. You had promised—the least you could have done was to call me, explain. I did not know what to think."

"I was tied up," Claude had said.

"With what? What could be more important than us?"

To explain to her what could be more important, or at least as important, was plainly an impossibility. Could he convince her that his brain, stultified, almost atrophied, these last months, had begun to grow, to burst forth with life this day? Could he tell her that until this afternoon he had been alive only from the neck down, and that this afternoon he had found his head? Could he tell her that one of the next great miracles of the chemistry laboratory would not be found in trying to synthesize carbohydrates through imitation of nature's sunlight, but by developing the photosynthesis process in glass tubes? Would his mannequin consider glucose molecules as more important than himself or herself?

It was no use, for this was the part of him that she had never known or even met. "Gisèle," he had said instead, "nothing is more important than we are, and I apologize once more. I tried to warn you on the long-distance telephone—this is Nobel Week, and people throughout Stockholm, from all over the world, are tearing at me, demanding my time, my opinion, my attention, and I—"

This had seemed to touch her, his fame and her petty demands, and she had immediately become contrite and gone into his arms. "Claude, I am the one who is sorry. I know how important you are, and how proud I am of it. I know you cannot belong to me alone. That is what bothers me always, I think, the realization that you are not all mine. I suppose that is part of what worries a woman when a man is late—that she does not matter enough—and so she becomes insecure." She had kissed him. "It is only that I have missed you so and looked forward to every minute of this. Do you still love me, Claude?"

He had kissed her gently, in return, and then had held her off, studying her, and for a moment the glucose molecules, the chain of them, had disintegrated before her beauty. Yes, he had almost forgotten her beauty—the beauty that had made him lose his head—in the finding of his head this afternoon. She had stood so tall and chic before him, pleased with this attention, her crocheted brown wool tweed displaying her lissome and supple showcase figure at its best.

She had taken his hand. "Come, Claude, let us sit and talk. You must tell me everything."

They had settled side by side, on the two-cushioned love seat, holding hands, fingers intertwined, and she had spoken of Paris, and of the preparations for Copenhagen, and of Copenhagen itself. And then she had asked him about the week in Stockholm, carefully avoiding any mention of his wife, and he had spoken of Stockholm, the officials that he had met, the other laureates, the sights he had visited, the appearances he had made, the dinner at the Royal Palace and the dinner at Ragnar Hammarlund's mansion, and he, too, had carefully avoided any mention of his wife.

As he spoke, he had retreated from her. It was as if he had addressed the room, and not her. Except for the play of her slender fingers between his own, he might have been unaware of her presence. And even when he had related an anecdote about Max Stratman, he had done so inattentively, with no conscious effort to please her and keep her by this sharing, so that their histories might become one. His deeper mind had churned with the entire protein question, the necessity of proteins at all in synthetics, the probability that development of chemically produced amino acids might be sufficient. Was this possible?

His consciousness of her presence had returned when he realized that his hand was empty, and he looked down and saw that she had removed her hand and was twisting the ruby on one finger. He had looked up, sheepishly, knowing her sensitivity to his every mood and to any withdrawal, and her pale blue eyes and usually emotionless mouth had offered him the briefest smile of understanding.

"You look so far away, Claude," she had said. "Let me change into something more comfortable. Maybe I can find a way to bring you back to me."

She had slid out of the seat with fluidity, and then, with her erect carriage, her lazy, teasing mannequin walk that had always aroused him, she had made her way to the bathroom and out of his sight.

Now he had finished two Armagnacs in his waiting, and poured a third, and wondered where they would begin—the experiments, that is—and had almost decided that, perhaps, to avoid discouragement, they should begin where advances had already been substantial—with fat acids, employing petroleum to develop a stearic acid that might be wedded to already synthesized glycerol.

He heard the bathroom door open, and when he lifted his head, she was standing in the middle of the room. She was staring at him curiously. He observed that she had brought the sheer peignoir from the rue du Bac, a street that now sounded unfamiliar, and that the flat moon breasts beneath the peignoir had been more promising when she had worn the crocheted tweed.

"Claude—" she said.

"Yes?"

"—you have not moved since I left you."

"What?"

She glided noiselessly toward him. "I thought you would be ready."

"Yes, that will take only a minute." He made as if to rise, but her hand touched his shoulder and kept him to his place, and she sat beside him and crossed her lean legs.

"Tell me—sitting here all this while—of what were you thinking?"

"Of you," he said.

"You have always been truthful with me."

He nodded, and then fell silent, and then, quietly, he tried to tell her. He had devoted so many years to vitrification of spermatozoa, and when that was done, there was nothing more, for he had been unable to consider another project seriously. What had saved him had been Gisèle, her love, her kindness. For a man, this was almost a great sufficiency, but there was always the parallel yearning. A job to do. An identity to be fulfilled. This had been missing, and yet he had not known its lack, because he had been so filled with Gisèle. But this afternoon, before their reunion, the miracle had taken place, and now he was filled with that, too. With rising intensity in his speech, he tried to clarify various aspects of the new miracle. He spoke of natural food and synthetic food, he spoke of carbohydrates and proteins and water and fats. He spoke of autoclaves and centrifuges and sublimation chambers. He spoke of freedom from want.

Gisèle listened diligently, hands in repose, the slightest curve of a set smile on her lips.

When she thought that he was finished, she said quietly. "I wish I had been born you."

"What an odd thing to remark."

"To be born you—and have many loves—equally loved—not one."

"You are mistaken, Gisèle, dearest. This is another matter, a different preoccupation. I have but one love, and that love is you."

The smile remained set, unchanged. "No, Claude," she said.

"But of course! What has got into you? I will prove it—you will see. Here, let me undress—"

Her hand darted out and restrained his hand. "No, Claude, not now. I do not feel you want to—to possess me now."

"But I do."

"You have no talent for deception. You are not in the mood, Claude. I can tell. Do not lie to me. And more important, do not insult what is between us by attempting to service me without love."

"Gisèle—"

"You are in another world."

"Well, I have been excited—and besides, this has been a week—"

489

"Claude, it requires no apology. You are exhausted—not from the week but from the new passion. You are forgiven."

"Gisèle, believe me from my heart—I would like nothing more than to lie down with you, but perhaps you are right—it would be best when my mind, when—it will be best when I am back in Paris again."

She had risen. "You had better go now. I think you will want to discuss your new miracle with—with ones who can appreciate it with you."

He rose quickly and took her hands. "It does not feel right."

"With me, it does. You must give me some time to myself now. I have never been here before. I want to shop, buy many things. There are only a few hours before plane time."

"I will go with you—carry your packages—"

She shook her head. Often, the bereaved prefer solitude. Could he know? "I would rather be alone."

"Well, if you insist—"

"I do insist."

"*Voilà.*" He released her hands and took up his hat and coat. He hesitated. "I will see you next week in Paris."

She walked to the door and opened it. "There will be no next week in Paris, Claude."

"Why do you say that?" He had reached her side.

"Because you are through with me. I know it. You know it. I am not a self-deluding youngster."

"I am not through with you. If you mean my wife—"

"You know what I mean, you know exactly what I mean. You have taken back your passion. You have now given it to your work. I knew it would happen, Claude. Of course, I knew from the start. My pleasure was that I did not know when. But now I know when. It is now."

She leaned forward and kissed him, and at once drew back.

"Thank you for everything. Now, go to your work. Some day—some year —between jobs—you might look me up." Her smile was bittersweet. "I just may be around—if I am unlucky."

He sighed and left, and she closed the door, and leaned against it. After a while, she went to the love seat, and saw his Armagnac, unfinished, and she finished it. Then she untied her peignoir and removed it, and walked in nudity—without provocation, for there was no audience—to the bathroom to clothe herself against the cheerless winter afternoon.

In the study of Carl Adolf Krantz's apartment, Daranyi had finished reading aloud from his dossier on Leah Decker, considerably less interesting than those he had read on the Marceaus, but necessary to show evidence of his thoroughgoing method. Because he had read swiftly, he knew that Krantz had fallen behind him in recording his report, and so he sat back in the leather chair for a respite.

The watch on his wrist told him that it was past 7:30. Well, only Andrew Craig, Professor Max Stratman, and Emily Stratman, and he would be done and have his reward by eight o'clock. Where to celebrate his riches? Perhaps a late dinner at Stallmästargården, near Hagaparken, with Lilly. He could almost smell the steaks on the charcoal grill. Then, reconsidering the gourmet indulgence, he knew that he had more vital uses for the money. Well, he would see. His throat and lungs felt parched. Ilsa's tea service still rested on the black table.

Daranyi pushed himself forward in the leather chair, and he poured the tea, now too dark and tepid, then took a cheese patty and munched it genteelly, and washed it down with some of the tea.

Krantz's head lifted from behind the green fern.

"I am ready for the next," he announced.

Daranyi put down his cup, and took up his sheaf of papers. "Next, we have Mr. Andrew Craig, your literary laureate."

"I will not require too much on him," said Krantz. "We have already investigated him. The high points will do."

Daranyi was grateful. The investigation of Craig had pained him, for Craig was Lilly and therefore of his own personal life. This was the area of loyalty, and he would not abuse it, at least not too severely. Lilly, he had decided from the first, must be kept out of the report. She must remain removed from this and unmarked.

"You will remember," said Daranyi, "the notice in one newspaper of an exchange between a female American reporter and Mr. Craig at the press conference? The reporter seemed to imply that Mr. Craig was a drunkard. I have checked this carefully. The reporter was inaccurate. Mr. Craig is by no means an alcoholic, but, at least before he came to Stockholm, was addicted to cycles of heavy drinking. A fine point, I know, but still, a difference."

"Go on," said Krantz.

"He was in an automobile crash with his wife three years ago. The place? In the southern part of the state of Wisconsin, which is unfamiliar to me. His wife—her maiden name was Harriet Decker—was instantly killed. Mr. Craig was injured and a convalescent for several months. His wife's younger sister, the Leah Decker of whom I spoke, has been his nurse and companion ever since."

"How has he comported himself this past week?"

"I was not able to obtain too much information that would have any value to you."

"Again, Daranyi, let me make the judgments, and you please confine yourself to the facts."

"Yes, Dr. Krantz," said Daranyi, chastened. "I am told that Mr. Craig spent one night drinking heavily with Gunnar Gottling."

Krantz made the ugly sound of spitting. "Gottling—pig!"

Daranyi waited respectfully, and then continued. "Mr. Craig spent another evening in the villa of Märta Norberg."

"He moves in high company."

"Indeed, he does. There is a rumor—I can find no verification—I give it to you as gossip—that Mr. Craig had an affair with Miss Norberg."

"Back to her old tricks, eh?"

"As I said, I cannot prove it. Moreover, there is better evidence that Mr. Craig has frequently been in the company of Professor Stratman's niece, Miss Emily Stratman, who—"

"How serious is that?"

"There is no way to know, at least not yet. They dined one evening at Den Gyldene Freden. Oh yes, and also—my scribbling is difficult to read here—but—here—Mr. Craig and Miss Stratman were off alone at the Hammarlund dinner, and he showed unrestrained affection for her."

Krantz chuckled in what Daranyi considered an evil way. "*Ach,* Daranyi, you poke your nose into everything, do you not? One second—" He began to write.

"It is my business," said Daranyi, offended.

"Your skin is thin," Krantz called up from his yellow pad. "I meant a compliment." He peered over the fern. "What is the latest on this Craig romance with Miss Stratman? Did he see her yesterday or today?"

"To my knowledge, no, not in public anyway. The last I have on Mr. Craig was as of four o'clock this afternoon. He was seen entering the building of the Nobel Foundation. I believe he had an appointment with Count Jacobsson. . . ."

Andrew Craig had been in no humor for this appointment with Count Bertil Jacobsson.

The riddle of Emily Stratman's personality, her unreasonable rejection of him, had left Craig almost destitute of will to live. The drinking of the evening before had not alleviated his desperation, and the enjoyment of Lilly's body in the night and the solace of her comforting extroversion had been all too brief.

In the morning, his resentment of Leah's meddling and her dangerous jealousy had hardened him, and he had returned to the hotel with every intention of a showdown. But Leah, no doubt anticipating his fury, had been too clever to present herself before him so soon. A flippant note, left on the stand beside his bed, advised him that, in the company of Margherita Farelli, and under the guidance of Mr. Manker, she was off for the day and the night to the province of Dalarna, north of Stockholm, to tour the Lake Siljan district. Her note begged Craig not to worry about her—this was the flippancy —for she would be back early the morning of the tenth, in time to help dress him for the Nobel Ceremony.

The day had been vacant, haunting, and he had read and wandered and avoided all bars, entertaining Emily constantly in his thoughts, resenting her and loving her and hating her responsibility for the resumption of his torment.

He had not been unmindful of his four o'clock appointment with Jacobsson, a date made several days before, and every hour he had considered canceling it on some pretext. Jacobsson had wanted Craig to visit his private apartment above the Foundation offices, and see his museum—whatever that was—and at the time, Craig had agreed, had even looked forward to the visit, assuming that Emily would accompany him. But, with circumstances as they were, it was a dull duty. What had made him keep the date, finally, was boredom—that, and no wish to disappoint the fine old gentleman.

Now, nearly a half hour had passed among the books and glass cases of Jacobsson's spacious library in his apartment at Sturegatan 14. To his surprise, Craig had not found the visit disagreeable. The tranquillity of the room, as removed from worldly cares as a station in space, the literacy of the host, had eased Craig's nerves and absorbed his attention.

They stood before the last of the glass cases. Jacobsson pointed his cane at a yellowed letter. "Romain Rolland wrote that on behalf of Carl Spitteler of Switzerland. More than anything, that helped Spitteler win the literary award in 1919. . . . Next to it, an 1882 first edition of *Det Nya Riket—The New Kingdom*—signed by Strindberg himself. Why is it here when Strindberg was never a laureate? Because of the book's association. In this nonfiction work, Strindberg used Wirsen badly—you recall, the chairman of the Swedish Academy—and it was one more reason why Wirsen kept Strindberg from getting the prize. . . . And here—look closely, Mr. Craig—the canceled Nobel Peace Prize check for $36,734 that was given to Theodore Roosevelt. It is signed by him. Do you know what he did with that check? Originally, he gave it to a special committee that was formed to further industrial peace in the United States. But, I am told, the committee dragged its heels, and your Rough Rider was not a patient man. Ten years later, Roosevelt demanded the money back and presented it to a fund for the comfort of the American soldiers fighting the First World War—the Peace Prize, mind you."

A cautious rapping on the door interrupted them, and Jacobsson excused himself and opened the door. His secretary, Astrid Steen, had a message, and she delivered it verbally, in an undertone. Jacobsson listened, frowning, and then considered the message a moment.

Turning suddenly to Craig, he said, "Miss Sue Wiley is outside. She has requested permission to see me for a moment, to authenticate some piece of information or other. Do you mind if I have her in here and get it over with?"

"Of course not," said Craig. "I'm inoculated against all Typhoid Marys."

Jacobsson chuckled and turned back to the door. "Very well, Mrs. Steen, show her in, but tell Miss Wiley it will be only for a moment."

He waited at the open door, and Craig occupied himself with kindling his pipe.

Sue Wiley entered breezily, thanking Jacobsson, and briefly disconcerted by Craig's unexpected presence. "Well, I didn't think I'd find you here," she said to Craig. "What's up? Counting your money?"

Craig kept his temper. She was not worth it, and she was too ridiculous in some kind of newly purchased fur Cossack hat, with a matching fur muff that she carried looped over one wrist. "If it's private, I'll step outside," said Craig.

"None of my comings and goings are private, Mr. Craig. Stay put. I'll be out in a flash." She pivoted on her spiked heels toward Jacobsson. "Just a point of information, Count. I'm becoming a historian—and I'm strictly contemporary—so every once in a while, I get shaky about a fact. This one concerns George Bernard Shaw. Remember him?"

"I certainly do," said Jacobsson courteously.

"Somebody told me he turned down the Nobel Prize flat. That's it. True or false?"

"I am afraid I must disappoint you, Miss Wiley. What is true is that we voted Mr. Shaw the prize in 1925. When the Swedish Minister in London notified him of the award, Mr. Shaw, who was often critical of prizes in general and our own prize in particular, replied in strongest terms, 'No, I do not want it. What do I need the money for?' The untrue part is your information that he actually turned it down. He did not. After giving the matter more mature consideration, for one week, he changed his mind and accepted the prize. I will add that he was most gracious about the money we gave him. He assigned it for use in the creation of an Anglo-Swedish Alliance that would encourage literary and artistic understanding between Great Britain and Sweden."

"Thank you," said Sue Wiley, "and, may I add, you are wrong to think I am disappointed. If I didn't know you were such a nice person, I'd believe you were letting people poison your mind against me. What do you think I'm after, Count Jacobsson—scandal and nothing else? I'm anything but an advocate of yellow journalism. I'm simply after the truth."

"Miss Wiley," said Jacobsson with infinite restraint, "in my experience I have found that truth has three faces—a whole truth, a half-truth, and a white lie that is barely truth." He paused. "As a matter of fact, I am glad you brought the word up. I have meant to invite you in for a little orientation talk. It has come to my attention—or would you prefer to converse at another time in private?"

"Not at all. Anything you have to say to me, you can say in front of Mr. Craig or anyone else."

"Then, what I have been meaning to say to you is this—and only the pressure of my responsibilities during this week of festivity has prevented my saying it sooner—it has come to my attention that you have been making numerous inquiries about the city concerning one type of information and one type only."

"What is that supposed to mean?"

"The inference has been, and I have heard it from several reliable sources, that you are attempting to acquire only such information as will be detrimental to the Nobel institutes."

"Says who?" snapped Sue Wiley, coloring. "That's ridiculous. I'm an objective reporter doing an objective job. I don't invent material. I take it as it comes. If it sometimes turns up black instead of white, well—as I said—truth." Suddenly, her eyes began to blink, and they narrowed. "You wouldn't be suggesting that I leave out some of the things I find, to conform to your ideas of—of censorship, would you?"

Craig found this unbearable, and shifted from one leg to the other, irked by her tone, her obvious attempt to force a censorship angle out of Jacobsson. But Jacobsson remained unruffled and diplomatic. "I am suggesting no such thing, Miss Wiley, and do not even dream of it. You are in a free country, among a free people, and we encourage you to write as you please. I only say that it distresses me to have our guests seek half-truths about us, and offer them to the world as whole truths."

"If that's all that is worrying you, have no fears about me. I'm sticking strictly to the facts. If you find lies or libel in my copy, you can sue. That's how sure I am."

A smile flickered across Jacobsson's wrinkled features. "The Nobel Foundation is a quasi-government institution, Miss Wiley. We approve or disapprove, but we do not sue."

"Then we understand each other. Well, I guess I've taken enough of your—"

"One moment, Miss Wiley. Something occurs to me. Since you have been gathering so much information from so great a variety of sources, perhaps it would be to your benefit to add one more story that comes to you straight from the headquarters of the awards."

Sue Wiley brightened. "A story! Any time!"

Jacobsson looked off. "If you do not mind, Mr. Craig—"

"I'm as interested as Miss Wiley."

"Please sit down, Miss Wiley. You too, Mr. Craig. I will make it as short as possible. Do you have a pencil, Miss Wiley?"

"I'm all set." She had seated herself across from Jacobsson's antique walnut desk, fishing pen and notebook from her purse. Craig stayed on his feet, lighting his pipe again. Jacobsson busied himself with the row of green ledgers on the shelf above his desk, removed a single ledger, and brought it down to the desk behind which he now seated himself. He leafed through the pages until he had located what he was after. He looked up.

"Miss Wiley," he said, "as you know, there are five Nobel Prize awards, and they have been given with some regularity almost every year since 1901. The world has come to look upon these awards as the highest achievement—highest honor on earth man can confer upon man. Therefore, the Nobel Prize awards have become a sacred cow. The temptation to journalists, every so often, to prove this sacred cow only a common bovine is irresistible. You will go around the city, and you will find it all too easy to learn our shortcomings—how many times in my too many years I have heard them repeated and broadcast with relish and glee—how we are anti-Russian, how we are pro-German, how we indulge ourselves in nepotism—above all, first and the worst of it, how we vote our prizes out of prejudices and politics and fears. Some of this is truth, and I am the very first to admit it. In fact, whenever I have the honor to take visiting laureates on tours of our academies, I always make it a point to let them know our worst side as well as our best, and Mr. Craig will confirm this. What bothers me, all of us here, the most, is that our visitors seize upon our worst side, and too often ignore our best side. I am going to take the liberty of giving you one instance, my favorite, of our best side. I promised you a story, did I not?"

"You did," said Sue Wiley, less brash than earlier.

"You came here this afternoon wondering if George Bernard Shaw had actually turned down the prize, and I told you he had not. Now, I will tell you the story of another man who was prevailed upon to turn down the prize, and did not, and of his prize that was by all logic and common sense not to be voted and given, and was voted and given. I will tell you about Carl von Ossietzky, and I will write the name down for you, because I want you to spell it right and not forget it and not let your readers forget it."

Unhurriedly, Jacobsson block-printed the name Carl von Ossietzky on a piece of notepaper and handed it to Sue Wiley, who accepted it and studied it with bewilderment. Hearing the name, Craig tried to remember where he had heard it before—either at the Royal Banquet or the Hammarlund dinner, one or the other—but still, the name was foreign to his ears, and he was curious about what Jacobsson might have to say of this unknown name.

Jacobsson gazed at his open green ledger, and then he resumed speaking. "There is an expression that has gained currency in our day that refers to 'the little man.' There are variations on this expression like 'the common man' or 'a member of the masses.' This is supposed to mean, I presume, the average man on earth who is not distinguished by wealth or fame or authority. From cradle to the grave, he eats and sleeps, does drone's labor, propagates the species, makes no policies or headlines or scandals, and when he dies, is mourned by none but relatives and a handful of friends, and disappears from the planet as casually and unmissed as the ant one inadvertently steps on every day. Such a man, for forty-two years, was Carl von Ossietzky, a German national who wrote mediocre articles for his bread, and whose one foible—we all of us have one foible—was that he hated militarism after having served four years in the Imperial German Army during the First World War. What lifted Ossietzky from the obscurity of the ranks of 'the little man' was his growing obsession that all soldiers were, in his words, 'murderers,' and that there was 'nothing heroic' about war. Most men know this and think it and hate any memory of killing, and most men live on, doing nothing about it. Ossietzky was the one who decided to do something about it, to eliminate the evil, to practice and preach what he believed."

Jacobsson looked up from the ledger at Craig, and then at Sue Wiley.

"His history is brief," said Jacobsson, "and his accomplishments few. He was a reporter on the *Berliner Volkszeitung*. He was an editor of *Weltbühne*. He was a secretary of the German Peace Society. He was one of the founders of the international No More War Society. He was an advocate of a new holiday to be called Anti-War Day. So far, admirable, yes, and obsessive, but not particularly meaningful. Then, one day in 1929, with more courage than common sense, he published an article in German exposing disarmed Germany's secret war budget, and telling the world that his Fatherland was breaking its treaty pledges by secretly building an army and an air force. For this, Ossietzky was charged with treason in 1931 and thrown into prison for almost two years. The confinement was shattering, not only because he had weak lungs and suffered from the early ravages of tuberculosis, but because he knew what evil was afoot and wanted freedom to shout a warning to the duped world.

"When he came out of prison, there was a new name and power on the land, and the name and power was that of Adolf Hitler. Ossietzky blindly resumed his pacifistic campaign. Friends reminded him of the consequences and begged him to flee across the border. To them Ossietzky replied, 'A man who speaks from across a border has a hollow voice.' He stayed in Germany. He hooted Hitler when others cheered him. He told his countrymen that 'German war spirit contains nothing but the desire for conquest.' He was a tiny thorn to Hitler, but a thorn, and he must be plucked.

"On the night of February 27, 1933—it is here in my Notes—the German Reichstag building in Berlin went up in flames, and out of the ashes rose the Third Reich. On that night the thorn was plucked, for on that night Carl von Ossietzky, among others, was arrested once more and imprisoned as an enemy of the state. For the first time, there were those who realized that a voice of sanity had been stilled. As Ossietzky suffered torture in the Sonnenburg concentration camp, the German League for the Rights of Man sent his name to Oslo as a nominee for the Nobel Peace Prize. But he was 'the little man,' and my colleagues ignored him. The following year, news of Ossietzky's suffering and martyrdom circled the globe, and suddenly the Nobel Peace Committee found itself inundated with official nominations of his name. Romain Rolland nominated him. Albert Einstein nominated him. Thomas Mann nominated him. Jane Addams nominated him. The National Assembly of Switzerland nominated him. The Labor Party of Norway nominated him. I could go on for hours with the nominations that poured into Oslo. No longer could 'the little man' be ignored.

"Now, Miss Wiley, you will see the difficulties that confront a Nobel Prize committee. On the one hand, the intellects of the world were urging the Norwegians to honor and reward a man who had defied the leader of the nation that was Norway's greatest threat to existence. On the other hand, the Nobel judges were being reminded of the possible outcome of such an award. Inside Norway itself, Knut Hamsun, who had become a Fascist, was writing against Ossietzky, and Vidkun Quisling was calling 'the little man' a traitor, in print. The League of Patriots in Norway were demanding that Hitler or Mussolini, not the detestable Ossietzky, receive the 1935 Peace Prize. And outside Norway, the pressure was as strong, stronger. Goebbels was cursing Ossietzky as Jew and Communist, although he was neither a Jew nor a Communist. Hitler's *Schwarzes Korps* was warning the Nobel judges that a vote for Ossietzky 'would be a slap in the face of the German people.' Göring, who knew the Nobel family through his first wife—the Swedish Baroness Karin Fock, who died of tuberculosis in 1932—put himself in touch with the Nobel heirs, and they allegedly advised the Nobel Peace Committee to turn down the Ossietzky nomination.

"Try to imagine, if you can, the state of mind of each of the five judges on the Nobel Peace Committee. One of the judges was Dr. Halvdan Koht, Foreign Minister of Norway. Another judge was Johan Ludwig Mowinckel, who had been Prime Minister of Norway and was the leader of the Left. Both were powerful men who favored Ossietzky, but both were practical politicians who knew that if they made Ossietzky a laureate, they were insulting Hitler and inviting him to break off diplomatic relations with their country. In its voting session, the five committeemen debated themselves hoarse. At last, the decision was made. It could not be Ossietzky. The survival of Norway came first. There was talk of giving the prize to Tomáš Masaryk, of Czechoslovakia, but even this seemed unsafe. At last, to squirm out of the trouble, the committee determined to give the prize to Prince Carl, of Sweden, for some Red Cross activities of his a decade and a half earlier. But before the vote, it was found that Prince Carl was ineligible, since his nomination had reached Oslo two days after the final deadline. And so the committee threw up its collective hands, and told the world there would be no Peace Prize in 1935—as there is none this year—because there was a war in Africa, and the time was 'inappropriate.' "

Throughout this recital, Sue Wiley and Craig had not moved from their places. Jacobsson stared at them meditatively.

"You wonder about Ossietzky himself, perhaps?" he went on. "Ossietzky was now in the Papenburg concentration camp. The Nazi tortures had ceased, but they did not matter. He was dying of tuberculosis. Had he died at once, the controversy would have been solved, and the world and ourselves the worse off for it. But he did not die yet. He was of indomitable spirit. He lived on, and so, quickly, it was the year 1936, and once more the Nobel Peace Committee was faced with his nomination. Again, it seemed that everyone outside Germany was presenting his name, and you will be happy to know that the names of United States citizens were among the foremost who nominated him. The Nobel Committee polled itself. Two were against Ossietzky, two were for him, and one judge was undecided. Then, overnight, the two who were against Ossietzky because of their political positions—Dr. Koht and Johan Mowinckel—resigned from the committee, and were replaced by substitute judges with no diplomatic entanglements. The day of November 23, 1936, as Germany shouted its threats, the final vote was taken. Yes, Miss Wiley, Carl von Ossietzky was awarded the Nobel Peace Prize for 1935.

"Our judges had shown their courage, and now the last act of courage was in the hands of the frail Ossietzky. What would he do? Because of his notoriety, Goebbels had moved him from the concentration camp to the West End Hospital in Berlin. There Göring called on him, stood over him, commanded him to turn down our prize. Ossietzky would not give Göring his answer, but he gave us and our colleagues in Oslo his answer. He smuggled out a cable thanking us and accepting the Nobel Peace award. Hitler's newspapers ranted, but Ossietzky was defiant to the end. When foreign correspondents, in the presence of the Gestapo, questioned him, he told them that he was proud and reminded them that the armaments race was 'insanity.' From his bed, he received a Nobel delegation which congratulated him.

His prize of $39,303 he never saw. He signed a power of attorney to have a man in Oslo, who represented a lawyer in Berlin, accept his money for him. It was transferred to a Berlin bank. It was embezzled. It did not matter to Ossietzky. He had won the greater prize. Because of 'the little man,' Hitler banned the Nobel awards from Germany and invented his own National State Prizes for the two leading Aryan scientists and a leading Aryan author. But still, Hitler was not satisfied. In 1940, when he marched into Norway and conquered that country, he arrested the entire Nobel committee. It did not matter, because by then the entire free world had been awakened and was fighting, and preparing to fight, for peace. By then, also, Ossietzky had been dead for two and a half years. But I like to think that he has never died."

Jacobsson paused, and gently closed his green ledger.

"We have had more famous laureates who have won our Nobel Peace Prize," he said. "So many more famous names. Jean Henri Dunant. Elihu Root. Woodrow Wilson. Fridtjof Nansen. Aristide Briand. Cordell Hull. Ralph Bunche. Albert Schweitzer. General George Marshall. Philip Noel-Baker. Yes, famous names. But I suspect that of them all, Carl von Ossietzky was the greatest. And because of him, this one moment in our history, our Nobel committees and judges knew greatness, too."

Jacobsson smiled an indulgent, wrinkled smile.

"Do spell his name right, Miss Wiley, please," he said.

She sat moved, but unmoving, features suffused by an embarrassment she could not understand and pen frozen to her fingers. Behind her, Craig stood where he had been standing from the beginning, cold pipe in his hand, touched and shaken at his deepest core.

Sue Wiley swallowed, and it could be heard, and then she emitted one word. "Whew," she said.

"If there are any questions—" Jacobsson began.

But then came the knocking at the door, and Jacobsson freed himself from his chair and opened the door, and it was Mrs. Steen once more. She whispered to him, and he turned to his two guests.

"I am wanted downstairs a moment," he apologized. "Always, before the final Ceremony, there are the invitation anglers. Please relax here as long as you—"

"Thank you, Count," said Craig, "but I had better be on my way."

"Thank you, Count Jacobsson," said Sue Wiley.

He was gone, and the two of them were alone in the high, quiet room. Craig walked to the clothes tree, and removed his hat and topcoat. He realized that Sue Wiley had not left her chair, but remained seated, watching him speculatively.

When he turned to depart, she spoke. "I suppose you think that story makes me look rotten, don't you?"

"Does it matter to you what the devil I think?"

This seemed important to her, and her eyelids palpitated nervously. "I have my job, Mr. Craig, can't you see that? I have my job to do."

"No one's stopping you from doing it."

"I don't like the way you and Jacobsson and some of the others look at me—like I'm some kind of reptile or adder or something crawly. Well, I don't like it, and neither would you. I'm a person the same as anybody. I know you're sore at me because of that question I asked at the press conference. I got a lead on you, and I wanted to know if it was true or not. Maybe I should have asked you personally, instead of in front of all the others—"

Craig stood beside the door. "I assure you, it doesn't matter, Miss Wiley."

"But it matters to me. I work from information that is picked up all over, from Consolidated's bureaus, just the way Associated Press and *Time* magazine and *Newsweek* magazine put together a story from leads they get from their bureaus. Before I saw Schweitzer, I didn't just depend on questions I might think of, or ones based on what I'd read, or just depend on anything we might talk about. All of our bureaus and stringers pitched in. They went digging in Kayserberg, in the German Alsace, where he was born—in Günsbach, Strasbourg, Berlin, Paris, Aspen, Colorado—wherever Schweitzer had lived, studied, worked, and then they shot me all the dope, some good, some not so good, and then I was able to get up my questions and go to Lambaréné and get the true story."

"The true story, Miss Wiley?"

"That's right. It comes in from all over—interviews, gossip, tips, leads, solid research—and I sift it, and check it out, and there's the true story. That's exactly the way I went about getting information on all you Nobel laureates. Take you. How do you think I got the idea that maybe you take a nip at the bottle now and then? Do you think I made it up? Not on your life. We put your name on the wire, and pretty soon our bureaus were spading up every day of your life—on the newspaper in St. Louis, London and Marseilles and New Jersey in the war, Long Island with your wife, and your honeymoon in Europe, and finally the whole rural bit in Wisconsin."

Although he would not admit it to her, Craig was impressed at the breadth of research. It was discomforting to know how much they must know, but yes, it was impressive.

Sue Wiley was going on compulsively. "Don't think our Chicago bureau didn't yell about having to send a reporter up to a tank town like Miller's Dam. You'd think we were sending someone to Tibet. But after you won the prize, there was this man of ours snooping around Miller's Dam for material to feed me—he got there a few days before you took off for Stockholm, and he stayed on through most of this week—and he was all over the county, casually asking questions, looking in here and there, searching back issues of newspapers and all kinds of documents. Mr. Craig, what I could tell you about yourself would make you blush. At least three people hinted that you got pickled to the gills every day, morning till night. At least one person tipped us that you visited a house of prostitution once in a while. I know your sister-in-law's shopping list at the grocery store, so I know what you eat, and I know who your friends are, and I have photostats of the mortgage on your house, and I know the words chiseled on your wife's tombstone. I even know how she got there—"

Craig's heart quickened, and he wished that he was out the door, so that he need not hear the sickening secret again, and from someone other than Leah. He waited.

"—because I know every detail of the accident," Sue Wiley went on, "and we dug it out because—painful as it is for you to be reminded—it's dramatic and will make good reading, and it is truth, and that's my business. I can reconstruct that accident better than you can remember it—tell you how many inches of rain there was that night, tell you how much time you spent at the Lawson Country Club, tell you how the birthday cake looked and how many presents your wife gave you, tell you the exact time you left the party, and the exact time your car smashed into that oak tree, and even how that tie rod dropped off under your car and put you in that skid—though I am no mechanic—and then I can tell you—"

Craig felt the chill from his knees and chest to his scalp. He could not have heard her right. It was a mistake. Automatically, he moved toward her, and the incredulous expression on his gaunt face made her words hang in the air.

"What's the matter?" she said, frightened. "Are you sore at me again or something?"

"Miss Wiley, repeat what you were just saying."

"About what? Repeat what?"

"The accident."

"Why, I was just saying I knew—"

"The car," said Craig. "What did you say about the car—your not being a mechanic—the skid—"

"Oh, that," said Sue Wiley with relief. "I was just showing off how thorough we are, and how I don't talk through my hat like maybe you think. You had lousy luck with the accident, that's all. When you came around the curve, your tie rod—you know, that *thing* underneath, under the front, that controls the wheels—"

"I know. I know—"

"It must've been defective or something, because when you came around the curve it broke—that happens to other people, too—and zing—one front wheel kind of buckles, goes out of control, you can't steer it—and if you're on a curve—well, I don't have to tell you, you know what can happen."

"Where did you hear this?" said Craig with agitation. "How do you know it's true?"

"How do I know? Well, don't you know? After all, it was *your* accident. Our man from Chicago went to the county sheriff's office, that's all, to find out about the crash and how your wife was killed—and there it was, with everything else—including their routine police report on your car after you smashed it up. The phrase on the report, as I remember, was 'accident due to mechanical failure,' and something about the tie rod snapping, and your inside wheel going flooey, and then the measurement of the skid marks on the wet road. I have the photostats right in my hotel. Also, the coroner's report waiving inquest, because there was no criminal liability, it was all open and shut, and they knew you anyway."

"Yes, we're all neighbors. I never bothered learning the details. I was laid up in the hospital—at home—a long time. And there was no reason to go into it afterwards. I think my sister-in-law handled everything."

"That's right," said Sue Wiley. "Somebody in the sheriff's office told our man that they called Miss Decker down there, after the funeral, while you were still half-conscious in the hospital, and gave her a copy of their police report on the case for you, to close it out." Sue Wiley stared at him. "Didn't you see it? What did you think caused the accident?"

"What?" he said vaguely. His mind was stumbling backwards, groping backwards through the months and the years, trying to remember every detail, and knowing with frigid certainty that Leah had hidden the truth from him, and in its place offered the guilt of his drunkenness and irresponsibility. The lie, half told him at first, then fully told him, then constantly told him, had been her hold on him and her insurance, and the enormity of her evil, and the depths of her unbalance and sickness, made the years a nightmare and made the memory of his self-hate a nightmare, and he knew his face was bloodless and the gorge was in his throat.

"I said—what did you think caused the accident?"

"This," said Craig weakly. "I guess I never thought about it, but I guess later I was told it was this. It—it was just—I don't know—strange the way you brought it all back to me today."

"I'm sorry if I threw you off."

"It's all right," he said, hardly aware of her. His mind was on Leah, and almost to himself, more to himself than to her, he said, "Yes, Leah, Leah took care of—of everything."

"What?"

"I said—" The shock was receding, and his surroundings were taking on their perspective, the walnut desk, and shelf of green ledgers, and the wall of books, and the glass cases, and Sue Wiley so confused with her eyes eternally blinking. "I forget what I said. I'd better be moving along. Thanks for everything. I hope you write as fairly as you research."

"I only wanted to show you how we work, so you'd understand—"

"I understand a lot now, Miss Wiley. Good day."

In the study of Carl Adolf Krantz's apartment on Norr Mälarstrand, Daranyi observed that the time was 7:41 and that he had only two more dossiers to report, and after that, one more odious task, and after that he would be free, free of the oppressive room with its crowded furniture and lukewarm tea and suddenly grubby fern, and its disgusting owner.

"So," said Daranyi, lowering his trouser belt to make his stomach more comfortable, and picking up his sheaf of memoranda once more. "If you are ready, we will proceed with the last of the two names on my list."

"I am ready," said Krantz. "Proceed."

"We come now to the redoubtable Professor Max Stratman, formerly of

Berlin, now resident of Atlanta, Georgia. By the biography you left with me, I see that you have already acquired most of the pertinent data on this great man."

"Yes. Our Nobel committee has researched the obvious facts, which are public, on his past. However, as to personal insights—"

Daranyi nodded. "I understand. I have done my best, but there was nothing I could find that bore the slightest hint of impending scandal. However, I will pass on to you the few items I have acquired. Only one of these, as I see it, might be of even passing interest. I refer to Professor Stratman's heart condition."

He waited, and was pleased with the instant heed that Krantz had given to this information.

"Heart condition? Do you mean he is ill? Are you certain?"

"I am certain," said Daranyi complacently. "I have my connections at our Southern Hospital, and that is where Professor Stratman has been to visit for examinations and shots. I do not know the particulars of his condition. I am informed there is an irregularity, but no immediate danger. I am told that if he takes care, he will have some useful years ahead."

Krantz was writing furiously. "Anything else on that?"

"I am sorry, but no more. Except this afternoon—this afternoon, Professor Stratman visited the Southern Hospital a third time. I can only presume this was for further treatment, necessitated by the excessive excitement of the week and tomorrow's Ceremony."

"What else?" demanded Krantz.

"Little else, I am afraid. His activities in this city have not been unusual. He is rarely without his niece beside him. I believe his affection for her is genuine, but there seems some indication that he feels a moral obligation to care for her, some debt he owes her father, his brother—"

"We know about that," said Krantz impatiently.

"With one exception," said Daranyi, "the people here whom Professor Stratman has seen are people well known to Scandinavian science or officials of the Academy. The exception is this. In the early afternoon of December fifth, Professor Stratman lunched at Riche with a Dr. Hans Eckart. I made an effort, in my limited time, to learn something of this Eckart, but current biographical dictionaries have nothing on him. A prewar dictionary listed him as a German physicist. I then checked the Bromma Airport and learned that he had disembarked from a Czech airplane that had taken off from East Berlin. I do not know if this has any value—"

"None," said Krantz sharply, massaging the back of his neck.

"I only mentioned it because this was the one person with whom Professor Stratman had met who was not known to me."

"Unimportant," said Krantz. "What else?"

"That is all I have on Professor Stratman."

Daranyi could see the flashing dip of disappointment on Krantz's features, through the leaves of the plant, and instinctively, he comprehended that the object of his entire assignment had been to research this one man. All the rest had been camouflage. One man: Stratman.

Daranyi reveled in his secret knowledge, and tried to retain his professional, noncommittal demeanor. "This brings us to the last name," he said. "Professor Stratman's niece, who is Miss Emily Stratman."

"Go on."

"The contact you suggested to me, Miss Sue Wiley, the American journalist, proved helpful in gathering this brief dossier. There is not much, of course." Daranyi had made the decision to withhold his most dramatic find for the very end. It would make his bargaining position the stronger.

He ran a finger down his jottings. "Miss Stratman resides with the Professor in a bungalow in the city of Atlanta. Several days a week, she works, as a nurse's aide, without salary, in the Lawson General Hospital, a government establishment where American war veterans are kept. This appears to be her principal outside interest, except an occasional film and the social affairs she sometimes attends with her uncle. You have seen her, so you know that she is beautiful. Yet, she has never been married. And she has not been engaged. She has not been seen alone in the company of men. It is Miss Wiley's opinion that she is a virgin."

"It takes one to know one," said Krantz grumpily. "How has this niece behaved in Stockholm?"

"Exactly as I told you when I discussed Mr. Craig. She has been seen in his company. Apparently, they do have interest in one another. She has seen no one else alone, to the best of my knowledge. I do not think Professor Stratman would permit it. As I have indicated, he is overprotective. In the case of Mr. Craig, I should imagine that Professor Stratman would trust a fellow laureate. This is her record here. I have been thorough, Dr. Krantz. I know of her movements up until a quarter to five of this very afternoon. That was when she left the hotel on foot, by herself, and walked across Kungsträdgården, and crossed Hamngatan, and went into Nordiska Kompaniet, along with all the other late shoppers. . . ."

Emily Stratman had been sitting at the table beside the window, in the fourth-floor grill of the Nordiska Kompaniet department store, for five minutes, waiting.

Suddenly, now, she had an impulse to run.

She could not go through with the embarrassment of this meeting, she told herself. She should not have agreed to it. Her mind was a turmoil. She had cried herself to sleep last night, and her eyes were a fright. And worst of all, she felt inadequate for the encounter.

Why had she consented?

Nervously, her hand kneaded the purse on the table, almost knocking off the menu, as she recalled the telephone call.

Only a few hours ago, she had lain listlessly on the sofa of the hotel sitting room, trying to read, when the telephone behind her rang. She had taken up the receiver, still reclining and still morose.

504

"Yes?"

"Miss Emily Stratman, please." The voice on the other end was young, female, possibly Swedish, and unfamiliar to Emily.

"This is she."

"I am Lilly Hedqvist," said the voice.

The name had already been branded distinctly in Emily's mind since Andrew Craig's confession, but the reality of hearing the name spoken aloud by its possessor was paralyzing.

So disconcerted that she was at a loss for words, Emily could not reply. Her knuckles whitened on the receiver, but her vocal chords were mute.

Apparently, her silence had disconcerted Lilly Hedqvist, too. "You know of me, I believe?" asked Lilly.

Emily's response was automatic, unsteered by thought. "Yes, I know about you."

"Mr. Craig came to me last night to speak of you, and to tell me what happened between you. You may believe it is none of my business, but it has been on my mind today, and I believe it is some of my business. This call is not easy for me to make, Miss Stratman, but my conscience tells me I must make it. I do not know you, but I do know Mr. Craig, and if he thinks highly of someone, then I tell myself that someone must be a good person. I would like to meet you for a few minutes today, Miss Stratman."

Emily did not know what to say. The voice sounded younger and cleaner and more simple than she had imagined it in her fantasies. After Craig's revelation, the name Lilly Hedqvist had become the name of all on earth who were abandoned and wanton and experienced. But this was not Lili Marlene or Cora Pearl or Märta Norberg. This was a girl.

"I—I don't know—I don't know if it's possible," said Emily. "I wouldn't know what to say to you."

"You do not have to say a thing," said Lilly. "I want you to see me. I want you to hear me. For a few minutes. And that is all."

At once, Emily was recklessly tempted. She did wish to set eyes on a girl who could give Andrew Craig kindness and love with nothing in return. She did want to see this girl and to hear her. But it was less these desires than another that was now influencing Emily. Above all, she wanted to find out about herself, why she still was as she was, and why yesterday had happened, and Lilly might be her fluoroscope. And then one more faint thought. If she said no to Lilly, that was the end of it forever. On the other hand, the Swedish girl was a part of Craig now, and to see her would be to see Craig one bitter time more.

"All right," she said suddenly, and it was as if another person had uttered the sentence on herself. "All right, I'll see you. Where and when?"

"I work in the Nordiska Kompaniet, the biggest department store, only a few blocks from your hotel. You turn to your right when you leave the hotel, and follow the sidewalk, and go across the park diagonally, and it is the seven-story store on the other side of the street. It is only a few blocks. If you are lost, ask someone for En Ko—that's how Swedes pronounce NK—

and they will direct you. Inside, there is an escalator in the center. It will take you to the eating grill—*lunchrummet.* You pick a table if you are there first, and I will come. Can you be there at ten minutes to five?"

"Yes."

"I will sneak off from my work at ten minutes to five, and we will have coffee and talk a little."

Emily began to panic. "I still don't know what we can possibly say—"

"Then we will say nothing," said Lilly. "But the meeting will be good. Good-bye, Miss—oh, wait—one thing I almost forgot. How do you look?"

"How do I look?"

"So I can find you."

"I—I'm a brunette—bobbed hair—and I don't know—I'll be wearing a jacket, a suede jacket."

"If I am first, you will see me with blond hair, also a white sweater and blue skirt. We will find each other."

"Yes."

"Good-bye then, until ten minutes to five."

All the interminable time after that, Emily had meant to call the store pronounced En Ko and ask for Miss Hedqvist and cancel the meeting, but in the end, she had not. And now, here she was in the half-filled grill, at the table beside the window, with her red eyes and suede jacket, and her desire to run from here, quickly and far away.

It was four minutes to five, and she told herself: I will give her one more minute and that is all.

"You are Miss Stratman?"

Emily's head tilted upward with genuine alarm, and there was a child of a girl, with golden hair, long and caught by a blue ribbon, and alive blue eyes, and a young mouth and attractive beauty mark above it. She wore a thin white sweater that hung straight down from her breast tips, and a pleated dark blue skirt, and low-heeled shoes, and she extended her hand and said, "I am Lilly Hedqvist."

Emily accepted the firm grip, but briefly, for this was the hand that had caressed Craig, and then watched with wonder as the Swedish girl, so fresh and flaxen and blue like the Swedish flag, matter-of-factly took the place opposite her.

"You have ordered?" inquired Lilly.

"No—"

"I will order. Is there anything with the coffee?"

"No."

Lilly waved to a passing waitress, who appeared to know her, and called *"Kaffe,"* holding up two fingers.

Now she returned her attention to Emily, leaning elbows on the table, cupping her chin with her hands. She considered Emily frankly. "You are very beautiful," she said.

"Well, I—well, thank you."

506

"It does not surprise me. I knew you would be beautiful, but I did not think in this way."

"In what way?"

"Like the lovely fawns I have seen in Värmland. They are delicate and withdrawn. And besides, you look like you are nice. I thought you would be more bold and sure."

Had she not been so tense, Emily might have been amused, remembering as she did, after the phone call, her first imagined image of Lilly as the one who might be bold and sure.

"Now it is easier to understand," Lilly went on, "because you are beautiful."

The irony of it came to Emily's mind—we are always, she thought, not what we are through our eyes, but only as we are to other eyes—for she felt anything but beautiful. In fact, she felt more inhibited than ever by Lilly's peach-colored natural freshness, and it seemed incredible that Craig could have been so attentive to her after spending time with this bursting, outdoor child, and suddenly she was glad that Craig could not see them together like this.

"Mr. Craig is beautiful, too," Lilly was saying, "in the same way. He is secretly shy. It is appealing. I do not know how you could send him away yesterday, when he loves you from the heart so much."

"What makes you think he loves me?"

"My eyes and ears and woman's sense."

The waitress had arrived with coffee, silver, and napkins, which she dispensed from a tray. Neither paid attention to her, and when she left, Lilly resumed.

"When Mr. Craig went away from you last night, he became very drunk, which is natural. Then he visited me and offered to marry me because that was like committing suicide." She had said the last with a twinkle, and then with tiny laughter. "He was not serious, and I knew he was not serious. I made him confess the truth, and he admitted how much he loved you, and he told me everything about that."

"I—I cannot believe he means it."

"Why, Miss Stratman? You cannot believe a man loves one woman from the heart, when he is also in another woman's bed?"

The naked question seemed to carry with it some implication of a personal failure in Emily, and she was less appalled by its asking than by this implication. "I wish I knew the right answer. I only know my answer. I was —yes, it upset me."

"You are now an American woman," said Lilly, "and I am a Swedish woman, and we are different. I must explain to you how I behave as I behave. On the outside, the Swedish girl is like the Swedish man—she is stiff, formal, with traditional manners. But with sex, she is open and free, because she is raised up with no prudishness. Education is honest about sex. In the country, we swim naked in summer. In the magazines, there is no censorship. And because there are so many women for so few men, it is a necessity not to make sex so difficult and rare—if you hold back the sex love, the man will find it easy in the next woman he meets. But that is not the main thing."

She paused and sipped her hot coffee, and Emily waited.

"In America, the heart love comes first, and if that is good, then you go until you have the sex love, which is last and made most important, and which the American woman saves for the final precious gift. In Sweden, it is the opposite way around. In Sweden, the sex love comes first, and if that is good, you wait to see if it grows to heart love, which is forever and to us the most important. Do I explain myself, Miss Stratman?"

"Yes, you explain yourself well," said Emily, envying her.

"I could so easy give Mr. Craig my sex love," said Lilly earnestly, "because it is not the important thing, and I think less of it, like kissing. The important thing, for me, was to see if our sleeping in bed would become more to us, would become heart love, so it would be a part of a greater love that would last always. But it did not grow and become more for Mr. Craig or for me, because he did not love me. He loved you."

For the first time, fully, Emily had grave doubts about her standards in relation to Craig.

"I tell you the truth, Miss Stratman," said Lilly. "If I had known that Mr. Craig loved me above the sleeping together, and if I had known my own love for him was more than that, we would not be here having coffee together, because he would be my husband forever. But I have told you, it did not happen and could not happen, because his real love was for you. I am telling you of myself, and I am telling you of Mr. Craig and myself, and now I will tell you of Mr. Craig and *yourself.*"

Emily waited outside Lilly, as if waiting outside the Oracle of Venus at ancient Paphos.

"Mr. Craig showed his heart love for you immediately, Miss Stratman. If you had welcomed this, and loved him back from the beginning, he would never have come to my bed to be warm with someone, because he would not have needed another woman. He would have had, for his heart and his manhood, all he wanted in the world. It is you who sent him to me. It is you who have had the power to send him or keep him."

"But I couldn't," said Emily wretchedly.

"You could not—what? Keep him with love?"

Emily was helpless. "That's right, Lilly."

"Why not? Is it because you are a virgin, or afraid to give your heart and life to someone's hands?"

"Neither and both. It is something more."

"Then I do not understand you."

Emily tried to smile gratefully. "How can you? I don't understand myself."

"You must change, or there will be no hope for you."

"I cannot change," said Emily simply.

She had gone beyond Lilly's depth, she knew, because she had guarded what was within her and had chosen to hide behind enigma, and now,

508

watching the wholesome Swedish girl finish her coffee and prepare to return to work, she felt the blackness of despair. For the conversation, so one-sided, open on Lilly's side, closed on her own, made it clear to her at last, the extent to which the fault was her own and not the fault of Andrew Craig. To have turned him away, when she had known that she loved him, and now, to keep him away, when she knew that he loved her, was the stark revelation of the illness within that had not been healed.

She had never believed that she would hear the final dooming toll of the death of the heart, but she heard it now. She listened. It was against her eardrums, heavy as the beat of her heart, and she surrendered to the knowledge that she was incurable, and she would not have Craig or any man, because the disease had eaten away her ability to love, and there was nothing more to give, because there was nothing left.

In Carl Adolf Krantz's apartment, it was now a few minutes before eight o'clock in the evening.

Daranyi had pretended to be finished with Emily Stratman, and then he had reported a few bits of scattered gossip on this one and that one, and then suddenly, as he folded his sheaf of papers, "Oh, there *is* one more thing."

Deliberately, he returned the sheets to his right-hand jacket pocket, and as deliberately, he tugged two large photostats and six smaller ones, folded and held together by a brass paper clip, from his left-hand pocket.

He held the photostats a moment, disliking this part of it and sorry for himself, and aware of Krantz's wondering face behind the fern.

"About Miss Stratman," said Daranyi. "I had almost forgotten. Your short biography of her interested me, the fact that she had been interned in Ravensbruck concentration camp during her adolescence. It occurred to me that it might be useful, on a long chance, to learn something of the people Miss Stratman had known in those years, and if any of her old associations had carried over, for her or Professor Stratman, to the present day. It occurred to me, also, that among the millions of old SS documents that had not been destroyed, that had been confiscated after the war, there might still exist one on Miss Stratman's history. Since I had a friend who has the proper connections in West Berlin, I suggested that he do what he could. His success was remarkable. Photostats of Miss Stratman's SS file came to my hands late this afternoon. The dossier may have no real value to you, but still, one never knows, and I thought it might be of certain interest."

"Let me have a look," said Krantz.

Daranyi half rose and handed the two large photostats and the six smaller ones across the top of the plant to his employer.

"You will note," explained Daranyi, "that there are two sets of photostats. The larger set is the copy of a summary of the report of Miss Stratman's military psychoanalyst. You may find something useful in several unfamiliar names referred to—Frau Hencke, Dr. Voegler, Colonel Schneider. I am sorry I had no time to trace their histories. The smaller sheaf of photostats represents a copy of an exchange of formal correspondence between departments of the Red Army and the American Army. Since the correspondence concerns Miss Stratman, it was also found in her file. Only one new name springs up in that correspondence—Dr. Kurt Lipski—not identified, but presumably a physician. I made a cursory check of my German library and found mention of three K. Lipskis of some importance in science today—one a naturalist, one a dermatologist, and one a bacteriologist. Nothing significant."

Now Daranyi sat back, fingertips touching, eyes never leaving Krantz, as the other read the documents to himself. Krantz's upper lip wriggled beneath his mustache, but his face betrayed no other reaction. At last, he looked up.

"Where did you get these?" he asked, and Daranyi detected that his tone was overcasual.

"You know, Dr. Krantz, I try to keep my sources—"

"It does not matter. Merely personal curiosity as to how authentic—"

Yes, Daranyi decided, overcasual, and therefore, it has value. "It is completely authentic," he said. "I will say this much. I have an English friend, a newspaperman now in Stockholm, who is down at the heels. He is underpaid and forever in debt. He, in turn, has a friend who works in British Intelligence in West Berlin—a Scotch girl—a file clerk. My newspaper friend offered to telephone her, and I supported this. When he advised me what was available, I agreed to give him—he must give half to her—nine hundred kronor of the expense money you gave me. That is steep for something that may have no value, but I thought I would risk the investment. I hoped you would find it illuminating in some way."

Krantz shrugged. "I cannot tell." And then—overcasual, overcasual—"by the way, has anyone else seen this?"

"No, of course not."

"Well, no matter. It really gives us nothing, but I will retain it as a curiosity."

"As you wish."

Krantz stood up, to indicate that the interview was terminated and the business of the evening was concluded. "For your part, Daranyi, you are to be congratulated, as ever, a thorough job well done. For our part, and I hate to say this, you have uncovered nothing of real value, nothing that can solve our little problem. Still, you have done what you could in a limited time, and for that, we on the committee concerned with this are grateful. I told you, the other day, your recompense would be generous. I believe you will be more than satisfied. I have discussed payment with my colleagues, and they have agreed with me that your services—considering the small amount of your time we have taken—are worth ten thousand kronor. I have the envelope—"

Daranyi had remained in the leather chair, and he remained seated still. "No," he said plainly.

Krantz had begun to move toward the mantelpiece, but now he halted and turned. "What was that?"

"I said no—meaning ten thousand kronor is insufficient for what I have done."

"What do you expect?"

This was the long-awaited moment at last. "Fifty thousand kronor," said Daranyi.

Krantz looked stricken. "Are you mad, Daranyi? You are pulling my leg."

"Your pocketbook, perhaps, but not your leg."

"You seriously think we would give you fifty thousand for that batch of prattle and pap?"

"I seriously think you will. I have a notion I have done well for you."

"You have done nothing. Fifty thousand kronor? Why, you will consider yourself fortunate if I can have your fee raised to fifteen thousand."

Daranyi sat Buddhalike, as immovable, as superior, on the chair. "The price is fifty thousand for my work"—he paused, and concluded—"and my discretion."

"Discretion, is it? I have never dreamed you would stoop so low as blackmail. Do you understand the position you are in? I could have you thrown out of this country in two minutes."

"I have counted on that. Eviction would coincide with my own plans. You see, the moment you have paid me, I will buy my air ticket to Switzerland. A second cousin of mine has taken residence there and plans to open a rare-book shop, and wants a partner. I think Lausanne will be more healthful than Stockholm. And I think there is more of a future today in rare books than in—research—and documents."

Krantz was livid. "Now you want to jew me out of the money to finance you?"

"Exactly."

"You are a greedy devil. Where is your sense of proportion and self-respect?"

"I have just regained both." He smelled his victory, and he came lightly to his feet. "I have done my part. Now you do yours. Fifty thousand."

Krantz stared at Daranyi with distaste. "You cannot be dissuaded from this crime?"

"No."

"I would have to talk to my friends first. It could not be fifty thousand in any case, perhaps closer to thirty thousand."

"Forty thousand is my bottom."

"I will not bargain like a tradesman," said Krantz. "All right then, forty thousand." He picked up a Spanish hand bell and shook it. "Ilsa will show you out."

Daranyi made no move. "When do I have my fee? Tomorrow is my deadline, tomorrow before the Ceremony." He would remind Krantz of the price of forfeit. "While the world press is still here."

"You will have your Judas money. I will send the cash in a plain envelope by messenger to your apartment. . . . You know this is our last meeting."

"I had hoped it would be. Good night to you, Dr. Krantz. And if ever you are in Lausanne, and in need of a rare edition—"

Daranyi permitted himself to smile, and Krantz glared and said, "Good night!"

Daranyi opened the door, took his coat and hat from Ilsa, and hurried out.

Krantz went to his study door and closed it and bolted it. Then he hastened across the room to the glass door and peered down into Norr Mälarstrand. Not until Daranyi was briefly visible, below, did he leave the point of vantage.

Hurrying on his short legs, he went to the sitting room door behind his chair and knocked three times. He heard the tumble of the lock, and stepped back. The door opened.

Briskly, polishing his monocle with a handkerchief, Dr. Hans Eckart came into the study.

"You heard everything?" Krantz asked anxiously.

"Every word." Eckart placed the handkerchief back in his pocket and adjusted his monocle.

"He kept staring at the plant," said Krantz. "I was nervous all the time that he would see the microphone."

"No one could see it," said Eckart.

Krantz danced closer to his patron, jittering. "You heard him about the money—"

"Never mind about the money. That Hungarian nincompoop's usefulness is ended anyway. I will see that he is paid."

"Was there anything in his information that—?"

"Yes," said Eckart, curtly. "The SS file on Emily Stratman. Let me see it at once."

XII

It had snowed all the night through, gusty flurries of large flat flakes, dry and adhering to where they fell, and on the early morning of December tenth, it was snowing still. The flurries had ceased, Count Jacobsson observed from his parlor window above the Foundation, and now the crystalline flakes floated lazily downward like confetti, and clung to every surface, and built one on the other, so that Sturegatan and the park below, and all the city of Stockholm encompassed by the eye, lay snug and white under a powdery blanket that rose and fell into the darkness beyond sight.

We are regally cloaked, thought Jacobsson, majestically covered by a royal cape of white to herald our climax day of Nobel Week.

He heard, behind him, the ponderous movements of his stout housekeeper, who came three times a week to clean his bachelor quarters, and listened as she set his breakfast on the oval table. He waited for her to leave, continuing to enjoy the snowfall, and when she was gone, he turned from the window and took his place at the table.

He had been too preoccupied with the problems of the big day ahead to think of breakfast, but now his appetite was whetted by the hot tiny sausages and scrambled eggs, the toast spread with red whortleberry jam, the *choklad*, and he began to eat ravenously. After he had devoured the sausages and eggs, and begun to sip the cocoa and munch the toast, he opened the three morning newspapers piled at his right hand. Each, he noticed, had picture spreads and long stories about the afternoon Ceremony, on its front page.

It was only after he had finished his cocoa that he opened the green ledger containing his Notes of a decade ago, now lying to the left side of his plate. Upon awakening, and welcoming the celebration of snow, he had remembered the entry he had made that decade ago. It had been made shortly after reading a memoir by Rudyard Kipling, and this morning had reminded him of that old entry.

Lovingly, he opened his ledger, scanning the endless waves made by his pen on every page—how firm his hand had once been!—flipping the pages, seeking what he had remembered, until he found it at last.

This entry in the Notes contained some reminiscences of King Oscar, who had awarded the prizes at the first six ceremonies held in the years just before his death, then touched upon his successor, King Gustaf V, with whom Jacobsson had become so friendly. Then the Notes continued:

I have finished reading Rudyard Kipling's recollection of his trip to Stockholm, of his arrival in our city immediately after King Oscar's death. I am setting down some of Kipling's impressions as he came here for his Nobel Prize in 1907. He wrote: "Even while we were on the sea, the old King of Sweden died. We reached the city, snow-white under sun, to find all the world in evening dress, the official mourning which is curiously impressive. Next afternoon, the prize-winners were taken to be presented to the new King. Winter darkness in those latitudes falls at three o'clock, and it was snowing. One half of the vast acreage of the Palace sat in darkness, for there lay the dead King's body. We were conveyed along interminable corridors looking out into black quadrangles, where snow whitened the cloaks of the sentries, the breeches of old-time cannons, and the shot piles alongside of them. Presently, we reached the living world of more corridors and suites all lighted up, but wrapped in that Court hush which is like no other silence on earth. Then in a lit room, the weary-eyed, over-worked, new King, saying to each the words appropriate to the occasion. Next, the Queen, in marvelous Mary Queen of Scots mourning; a few words, and the return piloted by soft-footed Court officials through a stillness so deep that one heard the click of the decorations on their uniforms. They said that the last words of the old King had been, 'Don't let them shut the theatres for me.' So Stockholm that night went soberly about her pleasures, all dumbed down under the snow."

Softly, Jacobsson closed his ledger, evoking his memory of the myopic, forty-two-year-old Kipling strolling through the Old Town in 1907, and conjuring up a picture of the city on the Ceremony day of that year, a field of snow then, as it was this day. But Jacobsson reminded himself that this day there was a difference. This day there was no mourning, except as men everywhere mourned the advent of the frightful nuclear age—in 1907, there had been reason to award a Peace Prize, and now there was no reason at all—but at least, this would be a better day, the city would not be "all dumbed down under the snow," and there would be festivity and formality and new fodder for his precious Notes.

Glancing at the time on his mantel clock—the numbers were Roman numerals and the clock had belonged to his grandfather—Jacobsson saw that the beginning of this long, ceremonious, climactic day was at hand. Pushing himself from the table, carefully, to avoid the twinge of pain that often came from his back, he regarded his person in the gilt mirror, and was satisfied that his tie was correct. Taking up his cane, he plodded out of the parlor to the chillier staircase, and then descended on foot to keep his meeting with the select members of the foreign press.

When he entered the conference room of the Royal Swedish Academy of Science, he observed, with satisfaction, that the response had been excellent. The oxhide chairs, used by the judges, were now filled by the press, the majority of those seated being ladies. The men, smoking and conversing, were standing all about the green room.

Jacobsson's entrance brought all fourteen occupants of the room to varied degrees of attention. Jacobsson accepted his manila folder from Astrid Steen, and as he passed the length of the green room, nodding courtly but vague greetings, he recognized Sue Wiley across the table before the marble ledge, and beside her an older Frenchwoman who represented a French periodical, and he recognized also correspondents from London and Manchester and New York and Hamburg and Barcelona and Tel-Aviv and Calcutta.

At the foot of the table, beneath the oil portrait of the donor, one painted in 1915, Jacobsson took his position and surveyed the gathering.

"The Nobel Foundation welcomes you to the final day of Nobel Week," said Jacobsson. "I trust you find the weather agreeable. You will see that of the three bronze busts that decorate this conference room, one is missing this morning. The bust of Alfred Nobel was moved, last night, to the stage of Concert Hall, so that he may, as ever, in spirit if not in fact, be present during the Ceremony late this afternoon."

He paused, opened his manila folder, and extracted a three-page, mimeographed schedule with the heading: "Memorandum. Dec. 10th."

"Before replying to any questions you may have," said Jacobsson, "I will read to you the official memorandum we have sent to each one of the six prize-winning laureates. Mrs. Steen has extra copies of this memorandum, and they will be available to you as you leave. I shall now read you the contents of the official memorandum."

Holding the mimeographed schedule close to his face, he read it aloud in a deliberate and dry monotone:

The festival ceremony in connection with the distribution of the Nobel Prizes will take place in Concert Hall—*Konserthuset*—beginning at 5 P.M. sharp. The persons invited have been asked to occupy their seats in the large assembly hall not later than 4:50 P.M.

The Nobel laureates with their families will please enter Concert Hall through the side entrance—Oxtorgsgatan 14—about 4:45 P.M. They will be escorted to the place from their hotel by two attendants, both attachés. Owing to the possible congestion of traffic around Concert Hall, it may be advisable to start from the hotel at 4:20 P.M.—not later. Autos will be reserved for the purpose and will be in waiting before the hotel at the fixed hour.

At 5 P.M. sharp His Majesty the King, with the members of the royal family accompanying him, is expected to leave the parlour reserved for them in Concert Hall and enter the large assembly hall. Their arrival will be announced by trumpet calls, thereafter they are to be greeted by the royal hymn.

When the King and the members of the royal family have occupied their seats, the Nobel Prize laureates will enter the platform of the assembly hall through the centre doors, conducted by the representatives of the various Nobel committees. This procession will be joined, as well, by the Nobel Prize laureates from previous years present at the Ceremony, and the other members of the Nobel committees which have proposed the award of the Nobel Prizes for this year, their arrival being likewise announced by trumpet calls. The members of the procession will please proceed in the following order—the Nobel Prize laureates to the right—Professor Max Stratman, Mr. Andrew Craig, Dr. Claude Marceau, Dr. Denise

Marceau, Dr. Carlo Farelli, Dr. John Garrett, with respective representatives of the matching Nobel committees to their left.

The laureates, after making their reverence to the King, will please occupy the seats reserved for them on the right-hand side of the platform, looking from their entrance door to the centre.

After the salutatory oration by Count Bertil Jacobsson of the Nobel Foundation, the proclamation of the laureates will take place in speeches held by one representative of each prize-giving academy. The speeches are to be held in Swedish but followed by a short address in the language of the respective laureates. The laureate thus addressed will please rise, and will be asked at the end of the short speech to step down from the platform in order to receive from the hands of H. M. the King the Nobel gold medal, the diploma and an assignation for the prize. Due to a change in schedule, the acceptance speeches of the laureates will be made upon their return to the platform, instead of at the banquet held afterwards in the City Hall, as had been customary.

After the ceremony the laureates may, before leaving the assembly hall, deliver their medals and diplomas to the head attendant, who brought them into the hands of H. M. the King and who will afterwards bring them to the City Hall, where they are to be exhibited during the evening. At the conclusion of the Ceremony, autos will be in waiting to convey the laureates and their families to the farewell banquet in the City Hall.

Having finished the official announcement uninterrupted, Jacobsson returned the mimeographed schedule to his manila folder. From the pitcher before him, he poured a glass of water, drank, then set down the glass.

"Now, if you have any questions concerning the afternoon Ceremony at Concert Hall—?"

A hand went up, and Jacobsson acknowledged it.

"Will the proceedings be televised?"

"Yes," said Jacobsson, unhappily, for he remembered better days and felt the modern monstrosity of the camera as intrusive as a circus act. "This is an innovation begun by the Swedish Broadcasting Company in 1957. The entire Ceremony will be shown on government television."

Another hand went up. "How many people have been invited to attend the Ceremony? To whom were the invitations sent?"

Jacobsson took another sip of water. "Besides His Royal Highness the King and his family, the laureates and their families, members of the Nobel academies and committees and their families, winners in previous years, invitations have been mailed to members of the diplomatic corps—with priority to those nations represented this afternoon by prize winners—and to accredited members of the press. That is the limit of the invitations. The general public is allowed to apply for tickets to extra seats on a first come, first served basis. By five o'clock this afternoon, there will be approximately twenty-one hundred persons in the assembly or auditorium of Concert Hall."

Sue Wiley was standing, one arm half lifted, and Jacobsson nodded in her direction and braced himself for a livelier question. He was not disappointed.

"Count Jacobsson," said Miss Wiley, "this is my first visit to a Nobel Ceremony. I am told, by those who have previously attended, that the occasion is always impressive but very stuffy and exact. Doesn't anything exciting ever happen?" A titter went through the conference room, and Sue Wiley smiled to those around her, and then added, "I mean, are there any embarrassing moments or any blunders or anything like that?"

Everyone waited now upon Jacobsson's reaction, and he, eager to have the friendliness of the press, ransacked his memory for something harmless and yet possessed of clolor.

"Well, Miss Wiley, there is never perfection," he said. "From time to time, we do have our—our trifling embarrassments. I do recall the time that our late beloved King Gustaf V, who had known Queen Victoria and was giving out Nobel medallions and diplomas when he was in his nineties, and who had become extremely nearsighted in his advanced years, gave a Nobel Prize to his own secretary instead of the laureate by mistake."

There was friendly laughter in the conference room, and Jacobsson felt encouraged. "King Gustaf—the Mr. G. of so many tennis tournaments—presented more Nobel medallions and diplomas than any other one of our monarchs. Every laureate left with admiration for his obvious nobility yet democratic bearing. I remember that Anatole France had just become a Communist when he met King Gustaf. It was thought that Anatole France might have some resentment for royalty. But King Gustaf's simplicity won the old laureate over completely. Afterwards, Anatole France said, 'The King of Sweden is a Bernadotte. He is accustomed to power. A President, on the other hand, always strikes one as a little new at the game.' As a sidelight, it may interest you to know that of all the many laureates that King Gustaf met and awarded prizes to, his favorite was the Irish poet, W. B. Yeats. On more than one occasion, I heard the King say that he admired Yeats the most because the poet had 'the manners of a courtier.'"

Jacobsson realized that Sue Wiley was still standing, and he addressed himself to her. "But you were inquiring about excitements and embarrassments, were you not, Miss Wiley? I can think of one excitement where embarrassment was cleverly avoided. You know, on Ceremony afternoon, this afternoon, it is protocol that a laureate, after receiving his award from the King, retire backwards from the orchestra and up the steps to his seat on the platform. I remember that Mrs. Pearl Buck was much concerned about this. Dr. Enrico Fermi had received his award before her, and had made his way backwards to his seat with no difficulty. Pearl Buck wore a gold evening gown with a long train, and was distinctly handicapped. Nevertheless, her backward march from the King was made successfully amid thunderous applause from the audience. She had managed it, she told a friend later, by memorizing the pattern of the Oriental rug at her feet and following the design to her chair on the platform. However, another embarrassing incident took place at one Ceremony when two British laureates—it would be improper to identify them—accepted their awards from the King, forgot protocol, and turned their backs on the King as they went back to their seats. The Swedish people in the audience were deeply offended. In surprising contrast to omissions by democratic laureates, the Russians have always been unfailingly correct, their courtesy impeccable, their bows to His Majesty the deepest. I recall distinctly that in 1958 the Soviet nuclear authority, Dr. Igor Tamm, who was one of the three physics laureates, bowed so deeply that he almost dropped all his awards. Beyond such trifles, I fear I have nothing else, Miss Wiley. Our Ceremony usually takes place without incident, as you shall see for yourself at five o'clock this afternoon." He looked about him. "Are there any more questions?"

A hand fluttered high. "Count Jacobsson—"

"Yes?"

"What about the laureates today? They must be nervous, waiting for the Ceremony. Do you know what they are doing with themselves?"

"I know what they should be doing," said Jacobsson. "They should be on their way to Concert Hall for a half hour's informal rehearsal of this afternoon's Ceremony. However, yesterday the rehearsal was canceled. So I am certain they are almost all resting at the Grand Hotel."

"Why was the rehearsal canceled?"

"Two laureates were unable to attend. There will be an announcement about this early in the afternoon from the Caroline Institute. I am permitted to say only this much—Dr. Farelli and Dr. Garrett are not resting—are engaged, this very moment, in an activity connected with their specialties. . . ."

It was 10:52 in the morning.

In this outskirt area of Stockholm, the structure weirdly framed behind the steadily falling snow—as if Seurat had pecked out a building in pointillism, white-dotted dabs on transparent glass instead of canvas—was the Caroline Hospital. Blending with the moving snow were the shimmering rows of yellow lights shining through the winter morning from the infirmary corridors and wards.

Inside the Caroline Hospital, inside the third-floor surgery room, the banks of lights were the brightest, not dull yellow like the corridor bulbs, not stark white like the falling snow, but silvery clear and steady as the luminosity of a summer's day in the early sunrise.

On the operating table, partially exposed but otherwise draped and shrouded, lay the unconscious patient, Count Rolf Ramstedt, seventy-two-year-old relative of H.R.H. the King of Sweden. Seconds ago, divested of the failing old heart that had been ravaged and weakened by atherosclerotic coronaries, he was being kept alive only by the five-thousand-dollar heart-lung bypass machine that supported his body tissues with oxygenated blood, while the gaping pericardium waited to be filled.

Bent over the patient now, in the disguise of the modern image of the Creator—gauze mask, gown, rubber gloves—was Dr. Erik Öhman, preparing to suture the living calf's heart to the great vessels of the host. Flanking Öhman, also masked, gowned, and gloved, were the three young Swedish nurses and the lanky anesthetist, now checking blood pressure.

Far away, the minute hand of the ivory clock ticked and jumped ahead. At the foot of the table, performing his role of observer, Dr. John Garrett exhaled tension through his mask and knew that the cardiac surgery, scheduled to last one and one-half hours (after the long interlude of hooking the patient to the bypass machine), was at the midway mark. Soon, all too soon, Garrett would be able to return his attention to the taller, bulkier gowned figure of Dr. Carlo Farelli beside him.

Earlier, in Öhman's office, in the dawn indistinguishable from the night, he and Farelli had met face to face without the exchange of a single cordial word. Öhman, sensitive to their animosity, had deftly come between them to seek their advice in charting the difficult cardiac transplantation. Except for two interruptions—one by a colleague on the telephone to discuss some youngster's congenital heart defect (cor triloculare bi-atriatum), and the other by another colleague, who had poked his head in, fretting, to report on the impending miscarriage, this morning, of the wife of a mutual friend —the team of three had worked steadily. Garrett had soon become absorbed in the preparations that had taken place, especially in the record of Antireactive Substance S administered.

They had debated all of the problems, so familiar and elementary to them, of the new surgical technique for removal and replacement of the heart, putting special emphasis on preventing clotting within the blood circuits, and on fastening of artificial materials to the blood vessels, so that there would be leakproof connections that would also discourage clotting. Garrett had brought up the possible discrepancy in the blood vessel sizes—those of the calf's heart might be smaller than the ones to which they must be attached— but Öhman had anticipated this and described his nonreactive adaptors. Farelli had brought up the advisability of a heterotopic transplant, but both Garrett and Öhman had supported locating the new heart in the normal anatomical position. Three mammalian hearts, only hours old, had been stored, and Öhman, Farelli, and Garrett had unanimously agreed upon the one to be grafted.

At last they had been summoned to surgery, and Count Ramstedt had been wheeled in. Everything had been efficiently readied. The patient had already been anesthetized, chest shaved and prepped, and merthiolate applied. The patient had received mild hypothermy to cool his system to 30° C. and he had received heparin intravenously to prevent clotting. The huge heart-lung machine stood ready, and the 4,000 c.c. of whole blood, crossmatched, awaited use in the event of emergency.

In his concern for the patient, Garrett had forgotten the presence of Farelli. At first, what was so well known to him—materials, procedure— seemed strange and otherworldly because of the quick singsong of the Swedish words that went from Öhman to his nurses and aides—*läkaren* and *hud* and *bröstkorg* and *blod* and *ådra* and *sköterska* and *bedöva*—and once, *pulsen är mycket oregelbunden,* which Garrett understood to mean that the pulse was irregular—and constantly, over and over, *hjärta, hjärta, hjärta,* which Garrett came to realize was heart, heart, heart.

But then, as Öhman flexed his fingers in the rubber gloves, and took the slap of the scalpel, complaining that there was a troublesome halation on the instrument and having one light adjusted, and then, as he performed the median sternotomy—the incision from the neck base down the middle of the sternum to the bottom of the breastbone—there was nothing any longer strange or otherworldly to Garrett.

As he observed what followed, Garrett's pride swelled. This was his discovery, his immortality. Critically, yet with continuing inflated ego, Garrett watched a son of Hippocrates attempt to raise a Lazarus from the dead. Garrett watched, his head involuntarily nodding its approval . . . the rubber-shod clamps . . . the open chest wall . . . the anticoagulant . . . the endless connecting of the plastic heart-lung apparatus to provide oxygenation of the blood and to remove carbon dioxide . . . the withdrawal of all blood from the major venous return before it reached the ailing heart, bypassing heart and lungs, diverting the blood through the pump and then returning it to the arterial circulation system . . . the crucial minutes of surgery with the delicate excavation of the old heart, transecting the pulmonary artery and the aorta beyond their valves and cutting across the region of the atria at the back portion. . . .

It was 10:52 in the morning.

The strain began to leave Garrett as his protégé inserted the cooled fresh calf's heart—two young mammalian auricles and two ventricles—and then sutured the walls of the atria together, avoiding separate anastomoses of the veins leading to the heart. Now, for the final suture by the Russian vessel instrument, woven dacron to hook up the aorta, the pulmonary artery, the four pulmonary veins, the superior *vena cava*, the inferior *vena cava*.

Garrett and Farelli looked on tightly, as Öhman completed the transplantation. With the new heart freed of air to avoid air embolism, Öhman released the aorta to permit fresh oxygenated blood from the great plastic outer machine to pass into the coronary vessels. The new mammalian heart warmed and was filled with fresh oxygenated blood. Gradually, gradually, the new heart began to contract, to take over circulation on its own, receiving and pumping plasma. The patient breathed on. Lazarus alive.

Garrett's gaze narrowed. Rhythm excellent. No electrical defibrillation necessary. He was about to speak up—there was another thing—he must remind Öhman to administer Polybrene to neutralize the heparin and to allow the resumption of normal blood clotting, but then he knew it was too soon and Öhman would not forget, anyway.

The lanky anesthesiologist spoke. "Oxygenation satisfactory. He is also maintaining satisfactory blood pressure."

Seventy beats a minute, thought Garrett, and 5,600 c.c. of blood pumping a minute—with a transplanted heart! His own private heart swelled once more.

"Go off bypass," said Öhman.

The glass cardiopulmonary heart-lung machine was disconnected. The new heart was on its own.

Only three times, in English made awkward by emergency, had Öhman consulted with Garrett and Farelli in the hour gone by, and three times they had confirmed what he had planned, once both supplementing his ideas with ideas of their own, and now, at last, the transplantation had been successfully accomplished. All that remained was the routine removal of clamps and catheters, the closing of the chest cavity, the addition of Polybrene, the injection of growth-inhibiting hormones to contain the calf's heart, and finally, the observation of life renewed and extended.

Öhman turned to the Nobel winners, and Garrett thought that he might be smiling wearily beneath the mask. "His Majesty will be relieved," said Öhman in an undertone. "It is done."

"Benissimo," said Farelli. *"Felicitazioni!"*

"Congratulations, Dr. Öhman," said Garrett.

"No—no—it is I who congratulate both of you for this," said Öhman. "I can handle the rest myself. Why do you not wash up and wait in the office? Nurse Nilsson will show you the way. I shall join you very soon."

He had already returned to the patient, and the tiniest of the three nurses came toward Farelli, and Garrett followed them out of surgery into the antiseptic, tile washroom of the Caroline Hospital. The nurse hung back as Garrett and Farelli worked free their rubber gloves and removed their surgical masks, and then, still unspeaking, bent over separate basins to scrub the starch from their hands with nylon brushes. Drying his hands, while Farelli still washed, Garrett was relieved by the presence of the nurse.

When they both were ready, the nurse said, "This way." They went with her into the corridor, and then into a small office, barren of all but a cigarette-scarred table holding several ashtrays and surrounded by five straight chairs.

But then, to Garrett's dismay, the nurse left, and he found himself alone with Farelli. He extracted a cigar, and made much of preparing it, and when he looked up, he saw that the Italian was already drawing deeply on a cigarette as he stood by the window.

"Still snowing," said Farelli.

Garrett said nothing. Now that the surgery was over, now that the worth of his discovery had been dramatized so remarkably and would soon be known around the world, the exhilaration had gone out of him. There could be no pleasure, he knew again, because Farelli existed, and somehow the transplantation would not be Öhman's or even Garrett's, but Farelli's own, just as the discovery itself and the Nobel Prize in physiology and medicine this afternoon would be Farelli's own.

As long as Farelli lived, Garrett's instinct told him, Farelli would be the savant and the man, and he, himself, would be the shadow. Yet what could be done about it? He had tried everything, and everything had failed. There was only one hope. Öhman had been against it. Craig had deterred him from it. Or perhaps what had restrained him, actually, had been neither one of them, but his own good conscience.

Yet now this conscience of his did not seem good, but a weakness that would relegate him to eternal obscurity. But for this conscience, he would not have to live out the remainder of his days as pretender to the throne. Except for this conscience, he would have the throne.

He studied Farelli's smug profile against the frosted window with undisguised contempt. There would never be another opportunity like this one. If he was not man enough to speak now, there would not be another chance. By late tomorrow, after they had their checks from the Foundation, Farelli would be off on a triumphal tour of the continent, gathering all the laurels from here to Rome, and he would go back to Pasadena with his limited success, and his grief that only Saralee and Dr. Keller and the group would know. If he attempted to expose his enemy next year, it would be too late, like pelting a Nobel idol with minute sour grapes. It would have to be now or not at all.

How to begin? Casually, he decided, cautiously. No blunt accusation. Rather, the responsibility of power. Toy with the mouse, do not destroy it with one swipe of the paw, but let it destroy itself in its consternation and fear.

To begin, then. "The King will be happy with the result," said Garrett.

Farelli came around from the window, surprised to hear Garrett's non-combative tone. "He will be extremely happy," said Farelli.

"I heard you had breakfast with him yesterday."

"I was extremely pleased. I had taken the liberty to volunteer our—"

"I know. I heard all about it." Garrett paused, wondering how the opening would come. "What did you find to talk about?"

"He was gravely concerned about Count Ramstedt. I tried to reassure him by explaining details of the surgery. I told him of our experiences with—"

"*Your* experiences," said Garrett. It was a small point. But Garrett wanted every point correct.

"No, *ours.* I had read your papers and had some knowledge of your specific cases. He was gracious enough to inquire about our medical backgrounds. Here, I could only speak of myself."

This was the opening, and blindly, his voice wavering, Garrett struck. "You told him about your—your visit to Dachau concentration camp, I presume? I mean, as part of your medical history?"

At once, Garrett saw that he had scored, and the thrill of impending mastery coursed through his veins.

Farelli's Latin face was fixed in an attitude of historic wonderment, the face of Julius Caesar in the Senate chamber beneath Pompey's statue, astonished by Tillius who had ripped the toga from him, the face of Caesar who saw Casca with the dagger of truth. Garrett waited on his lofty perch, almost expecting the Italian below to shout the classic "Casca, you madman, what are you doing?" Then, at last, he would show him the madman's full design.

But for all his wonderment, Farelli's first voice was mild. "Did you say Dachau? How do you know about that?"

"Oh, I just know it. Things get around."

"Something like that does not get around, as you say it. I have never spoken of that."

"I can't say I blame you. In your boots, I wouldn't speak of it either."

Farelli shrugged. "There are some moments of one's life one prefers to forget."

At last, Garrett had his dominance. He addressed Farelli with the complacent censure of the superior to the weak. "What I want to know is this— how could you go through with it?"

"How? Because I was forced to go through with it. I was a prisoner of the blackshirts in Regina Coeli, and I had no choice. It was a gamble to survive."

"But there are limits to what a man—"

"One does not weigh or examine, under the choice of life or death. It is easy now, so far away in time, to be logical about what is unreal. But when the OVRA gave me the immediate choice of the firing squad or the experiment at Dachau—well, Dachau was an unknown quantity. I had heard, I had read—but I did not know. The muskets of the firing squad, I heard every morning at daybreak. I told myself—say no to the OVRA, Farelli, and you are surely dead—but say yes, and who knows what waits at Dachau. I was promised it would only be temporary, several days, no more. So I went through with it." He paused. "I do not think of it often any more. They brought five of us to Dachau—"

"Yes, I know," said Garrett with scorn.

"You know? I still am puzzled how you know."

"Dr. Brand of Berlin, Dr. Gorecki of Warsaw, Dr. Brauer of Munich, Dr. Stirbey of Bucharest—and you."

Farelli's bewilderment showed. "You are correct. That is correct. Poor Brand and Brauer, they had the worst of it. They were Jews, and I believe they were meant to be killed anyway. They died—terribly."

"How long after the experiment?" asked Garrett. It was all coming out now, easier than he had expected, and Farelli was sealing his own doom.

"After the experiment? No, they both died during it, each in their first time. I was made to watch them through the window of the Sky Ride Wagon—that was what the high-altitude box was called, the Sky Ride Wagon —Brauer, such a decent young man, his lungs rupturing, and Brand choking, until his heart failed." Farelli had become excited. "You can imagine how I felt when they forced me into the high-altitude chamber. I thought I was the next victim—"

Garrett was positive that Farelli had made an error. He raised his voice, interrupting, voice cracking. "You—they—you say they put you *in* the experiment chamber—inside it?"

"Yes, of course," said Farelli. "What have you heard? I thought you knew the entire story."

"Some of it, but—"

"The Nazi Fascists had been using Jews, Polish and Russian prisoners for their guinea pigs, and one day Himmler wrote that instead of common prisoners, it might be wise to obtain five qualified doctors, heart specialists, who were also Jews or political prisoners, and try the experiments on them. The idea was that we would undergo fifteen-mile-altitude tests, without equipment, and be brought to the point of death, but not quite. Then we would be revived, and be made to set down our reactions and judgments, as physicians who had endured this, in medical papers, for the benefit of the Luftwaffe and the Medical Service of the Waffen-SS. I was the fourth one that day. Brand and Brauer had died, and they dragged out Stirbey half dead—he is in a sanitarium in Vienna still—and then, it was my turn—"

Garrett reached blindly for a chair, and found himself in it. God Almighty, God Almighty, he thought, and felt like a man who had slipped to the brink of the Grand Canyon, and been snatched from the fall by an unseen hand, and still had not recovered from what might have been.

He had missed some of what Farelli had been saying, and with effort he tried to hear the rest above the pounding in his ears.

"—and they kept pumping the air out of the chamber, and there I was, strapped in the pilot's seat with the electrocardiograph equipment attached to me, and the altitude gauge rising and rising, and—but what is the use to remember it now? At thirteen miles altitude, I gave up breathing and blacked out, as the aviators say—there was blood all over my face—and those animals carried me out, and I lived because I am a dray horse and will not die like that.

"I was in the Dachau infirmary three weeks, too ill to be of use to them, and when I recovered, I said I was still too weak to write their medical paper, but pledged to write it for Dr. Rascher and Himmler if they sent me back to my beloved prison in Rome. So they sent me back, but then everyone was busy with the landings, and I never wrote their paper. I also never recovered. I am still under medical care. Just as Dr. Stirbey and Dr. Gorecki are. I heard from old Gorecki the week before I came here, congratulating me, and recalling the horror of that day. He will write a book about it, he says. I hope he does. Someone should, to show the thin borderline that divides the doctors of Hippocrates from the sadist doctors of Satan. You know, I often think, it is not that men of our profession indulged in such bestialities that troubles me, but that not one man of our profession, in all of Germany, had the courage to raise his voice against these human experiments. Ah, well, it is past."

For Garrett, at first, his brain so long fastened to the obsession that Farelli had been the prosecutor of the evil and not its victim, the turnabout had been too dizzying to comprehend. But once comprehension came, there came with it the relief of self-preservation, that he had not leaked a falsehood, to be denied and disproved and to make of him an ostracized leper. Now that Farelli was through speaking, one last emotion gnawed through Garrett, and that emotion was shame.

Because he had to live with himself, he now tried to tell himself that even if he had been so wrong about this, his conscience—his conscience and Öhman and Craig—had not permitted him to go ahead with the canard. Too, the other irritations still existed—Farelli's use of his discovery, although his wrongness about Dachau made him doubt himself about this point—Farelli's self-promotion, although even here . . . but now, Garrett saw that these rationalizations were of no use. Shame sat fat and mocking on his head and shoulders. He had been a victim of himself. What would Dr. Keller call it? Paranoia. He knelt to the truth.

Raising his head, meaning to say something, anything, that might be placating to Farelli, he realized that Farelli had turned sideways from him and was staring at the door. He followed Farelli's gaze, and then he, too, saw Dr. Erik Öhman in the door.

He had never seen Öhman like this before. His picture of Öhman was of a reddish granite person of zeal and indestructibility, and now the picture was shattered. The reddish granite had been pulverized, and zeal had been crushed also, and what stood in the doorway was the representation of all anti-strength—in one person frailty, lassitude, bafflement, nullification, repudiation, and embodiment of every loss on earth.

"He's dying," Öhman croaked. He came unsteadily into the room, limply carrying his surgical mask. "Count Ramstedt is dying. The transplantation has failed."

He tripped slightly, and Farelli grabbed him, and helped lower him into a chair.

Garrett scrambled to his feet, beside Farelli at once.

"What do you mean?" Farelli was demanding. "What do you mean by that? Speak some sense to us!"

Öhman looked up blankly. "I cannot explain it. The immunity mechanism, the white cells and other agents, they are destroying the foreign tissue. There is activated rejection. All the signs—cyanosis—tachycardia—hypotension—"

"But you can't know so soon!" Garrett found himself shouting. "There must be a mistake—it takes three weeks to know!"

Öhman shook his head. "Dr. Garrett, you go in there—you can see—he will be dead by nightfall."

Garrett felt faint, and gripped Farelli's arm to right himself. Farelli alone stood strong, but the news had drained his countenance.

"Something must have been overlooked, something in administering the serum, or the surgery—" Farelli began.

Once more, Öhman shook his head. "No," he said. "If—uhhh—if I had performed this myself—uhhh—I would think so—my inexperience—but both of you were present—you witnessed every move—you supervised—you saw me —you assisted—"

Garrett tried to think, reviewing each step of the transplantation in his mind, but nothing had been omitted or been different, every move had conformed to the grafts he had made in the past. He realized that Farelli was reviewing the surgery, too, and that Farelli's conclusion coincided with his own. It had been perfect. The transplantation had been merely a routine extension of their own discovery and their own experiments and successes. Because they had proved its worth, they had won the Nobel Prize, and now suddenly, inexplicably, it had failed, and all that had come before or might be planned ahead was blackened by doubt. "Proved" had been stamped over by the old Scotch verdict "Not Proven"—meaning neither guilty nor innocent but simply Unknown (with Some Doubt).

"It can't be," murmured Garrett. "It doesn't make sense."

"There is always the exception one fears," said Farelli, more to himself than to anyone.

"We've got to do something!" cried Garrett. "Why, if this gets out—"

The same thought, and projection of it, seemed to strike Farelli at the same time, for he turned to Garrett, and their eyes met in a common bond of fear.

"It has got to get out," said Öhman helplessly. "Half the members of the royal family are in the waiting room. I must report to the King—"

Garrett articulated the common fear first. "But the prize," he said. "It'll discredit our prize."

"Uhhh—yes—yes, I have thought of that already. This will support the minority of the Nobel Medical Committee, who felt the vote for you was —uhhh—premature. The moment this is in the newspaper there will be controversy—a scandal, if you accept the prize this afternoon. You must—must turn it down—refuse the award before the Ceremony—send a joint note to the committee explaining more work will have to be done—but the prize is out of the question now."

"Are you crazy, Öhman? *Che diavolo!*" Farelli was in a temper, unreasoningly furious with the suggestion. "What about Dr. Garrett's years of experimentation and my own—our discovery—our proved successes?"

"Please—please—it is not in my hands," begged Öhman. "I am telling you what will happen. If your discovery had a hundred proved successes, and the hundred-and-first was a failure, by the same method, it would mean— in the eyes of the medical world—the public—your discovery is not infallible —not fully proved—is—uhhh—open to doubt. They will let you gracefully withdraw from accepting the prize—there will be talk about next year or the year after or someday—but if you refuse to withdraw, they will be forced to disgrace you by withholding the prize. They will do this, because they do not dare to have a repetition of the Dr. Koch fiasco."

Garrett leaned over Öhman. "Dr. Koch fiasco? What is that? What the devil are you talking about?"

"Uhhh—Dr. Garrett, my friend—we are friends, believe me—I owe what I am to you—I am not the prize-giving committee or the public, so do not blame me." Öhman rubbed his forehead. "I owe you the truth, before the world falls on your head, on both of your heads. Were there many medical discoverers in history greater than Dr. Robert Koch, of the Berlin Institute for Infectious Diseases? Consider his work with infections, anthrax bacilli, the solidifying media for bacteria—his discoveries, in eight years, of the tubercle bacillus, cholera bacillus, tuberculin. As you know so well, Dr. Koch found the bacillus that causes tuberculosis, and then he found the miracle drug, tuberculin, that might cure it. The whole world was in a fever of excitement, and the Kaiser commanded the nomination of Dr. Koch for the Nobel Prize, even though Dr. Koch wanted more time to experiment. So —in 1905 we made him a laureate, gave him the Nobel Prize in physiology and medicine 'for his investigations and discoveries in relation to tuberculosis'—which the world knew was for his discovery of tuberculin. Dr. Koch took his—uhhh—medal and diploma and money and went back in triumph to Berlin—and six months later his serum, hailed because it cured, suddenly began to kill. Hundreds of tuberculosis patients were killed by the serum, because tuberculin was not ready, except for cattle, and maybe Koch knew it. When he died, five years later, I am sure he died of—uhhh—of—uhhh— grief. And the Caroline Nobel committee was made to appear accomplices to murder, and scientific dunces, and since then, they have been conservative, always conservative. Now, this morning, the first time since 1905, what happened to Dr. Koch has happened again—a great discovery—my life is devoted to it—I believe in it—but now, there is an important patient in my surgery, expected to benefit from it, but now dying because of it—and soon, the truth of the failure will be everywhere."

Farelli had begun nodding during the last of this painful recital, and he was nodding still. "Yes, Dr. Öhman," he said, "you are trying to help us, you are a decent fellow. We will behave correctly, have no worry. If the patient is to die, we will die with him. We will know what to do. I am certain Dr. Garrett is as one with me."

"You are speaking for me," said Garrett quietly. "We're in this together."

"I do not want to lose the Nobel Prize, when I am hours from winning it," said Farelli fervently to Öhman. "Is it only the prize money and honor I will lose? No, it is a life of work, and every hope I have. I know what I say. If we take the prize, and the Count dies, it is a scandal, and if we do not take the prize, and he dies, it is a sensation. Either way we lose, because the world loves to prick bubbles, tear down idols, discredit. It is history. It is true. I know what awaits Dr. Garrett and myself—infamy—as if we had foisted on the public a hoax, a lie. We know better, but we will not convince mankind in a lifetime. Only when we are dead, and others live because of us, will we be honored again. No, I repeat, it is not the loss of the prize alone that troubles me. It is the loss of our standings, our grants, our cooperation, our future work. A generation will suffer for this one man's death. Dr. Garrett and I do not go down alone. Progress in medicine goes down with us." He halted and stared from Öhman to Garrett. "I want to prevent that regression. I want to fight for that one man—because that way, we fight for all men."

"I'm with you," said Garrett.

Farelli looked at him. "For the same reasons?"

"For none other."

Öhman had been observing the exchange with awe. He felt Farelli's hand on his arm.

"Dr. Öhman," said the Italian, "go back to the surgery where you belong. Keep an eye on the patient. Do what you can. Dr. Garrett and I wish to consult on this privately. Make no announcements. Show no white flag. Stand by your post. In a while, Dr. Garrett and I will come to you—for better or for worse."

Dazed, obedient, Öhman came out of the chair and left the room.

The second that the door closed, Farelli wheeled toward Garrett. "I meant every word I said to him."

"I know you did," said Garrett.

"I could not tell him everything, but to you I can reveal. I know very well what you have thought of me this past week—that I am an egotist, a promoter, a self-seeker who wishes too much credit for himself. It is not so, but it must appear that way to you, who are so quiet and self-effacing, an honest man of the laboratory. I was raised in Milan, Dr. Garrett. It is a busy and prosperous city, but not if you are poor and outside. My father sold spoiled fruit for what you call pennies. My mother scrubbed other people's dirty clothes. We lived in a shanty, six of us, wearing rags and sick from malnutrition. I robbed and cheated and procured for pimps, as a street boy, to go to school and escape and be better. The whole story is too long—but when you come from that, Dr. Garrett, you are always insecure, you want never to go back, you live in fright, and your body emits the stench of fear. I was so driven that I was made twice the man I was—and by perseverance and fright and a good Lord in the heaven, I made my discovery which is truly ours. But for all of this—and I swear it—I would willingly sink back to the past, if that one old man in that room could be made to live. It is because today I realize, maybe the first time, I am more a healer than an opportunist who wants self-survival above all else. That old man must live—and to devil with this prize and all prizes—because our work must not die. That is how I feel."

Garrett tried to smile his understanding but could not. "I have stopped thinking of two people—Farelli and Garrett—and begun thinking of only one —Count Ramstedt. My personal concerns have left me. They've been made too small to live on a morning like this."

"But now, what is to be done, Dr. Garrett? I told the Swede I want to fight for that one man. It was bravery without arms. I can think of nothing. I depend on you."

Garrett received Farelli's dependence upon him without feeling superiority, but with all the comfort that collaboration often produced. He had left the butt of his cigar in a tray, and now he retrieved it, and lit it, thinking all the while. His head had never been clearer.

"One idea keeps recurring," said Garrett, as he slowly circled the room. "Even though we have learned to neutralize the rejection mechanism with Antireactive Substance S, I have had my secret fears about potential steroid dangers—the side effects, that is. And so I always sought to improve it. I have never written this in a paper, but once, for a period, I experimented on dogs with another version of the serum, an antihistamine I called Antireactive Substance AH—and the early experiments were remarkably effective."

"Substance AH?"

"Yes. While it's been somewhat less reliable than the steroid version in blocking phlogistic response, it has been far superior in other respects—more selective—more effective in holding off the rejection, yet permitting immunity, strong immunity, against infection."

"Would it be possible?" Farelli wondered.

"I have never tried this mixture on a human being," said Garrett. "I intended to do more experiments on animal specimens when I returned to—"

"Dr. Garrett, I would be willing to take the chance here, now," said Farelli suddenly. "Can it be prepared here?"

"Easily," said Garrett, but his mind was elsewhere. "If only we had some insurance," he mused.

"What do you mean?"

"If there were something else in the event that this failed."

Farelli pursed his lips thoughtfully. "We could try a modified outside pump, a portable pump—"

Garrett shook his head. "Too impermanent. I am thinking—you know—possibly—" He halted, privately weighing something.

"Possibly what?"

"Something else is on my mind," said Garrett slowly, "something more permanent. I hesitated, because it is premature. Still—at a time like this—"

"Please—what is it, Dr. Garrett?"

"In this last year since our discovery, I have gone along on an entirely new offshoot, new tangent, of cardiac grafting. I have not published preliminary data, because I have not gone far—there has not been time—but I must openly confess what I have in mind. As you doubtless know, there is one tissue that can survive the rejection mechanism—I refer to living embryonic tissue. It is virtually nonreactive—it doesn't have any antigenic specificity. I confirmed this, to my satisfaction, with recent tests on rats. I determined to attempt a pancreas transplantation. I started by transferring a mature pancreas from one adult rat to another, and it wouldn't grow at all, it was rejected. Then I did something else. I typed a rat's estrogen cycle to find out when the rat was pregnant, and then—listen to this—at an early stage, I took pancreas tissue out of the fetus—although pancreatic tissue per se was not the object—and grafted this embryonic tissue into another rat, and, Dr. Farelli, it grew healthy and strong. It was not rejected at all. I kept wondering if the same could be undertaken, successfully, with an embryonic heart."

Farelli was staring at Garrett, his mind bounding ahead, his temples corded with concentration. "But why not?" he asked suddenly. "Let us say that a pregnant mother miscarries in the first trimester—"

"Remember the obstetrician who looked in on Öhman early this morning? He has a miscarriage he is handling, under this roof, in the fourth week of gestation."

Farelli could hardly contain himself. "We take this tiny four-week-old heart tissue and hook it up with an external circulation pump, induce speedy growth—even apply the new growth hormone those men down in—"

"Wait, Dr. Farelli, you've given me a better idea. Why develop this four-week embryonic heart externally? Why not internally? It won't be rejected. We graft this embryonic heart into Count Ramstedt's groin—the way kidney transplants have been placed in the neck—a heterotopic graft. We put the embryonic heart in the inguinal area, because the blood vessels there are twice as big as—don't you see? We hook it into the arteries and veins—we keep Count Ramstedt on Substance AH as well as Antireactive Substance S while the embryonic heart grows. Shortly after, as it develops, we—or Öhman, for that matter—begin to waltz it—move it into the abdominal area where it can work on bigger blood vessels."

Garrett flung his cigar aside, and paced a moment.

"Yes, Farelli, it is possible," he resumed. "There would be no discomfort. A woman's pelvic site accommodates a large mass in pregnancy, enough to hold a full-grown human heart in her twelfth week. A man with a stomach tumor suffers greater displacement. Why not an embryonic heart? Then we keep injecting the new growth hormone. In four or five months, the embryonic heart, unrejected, is full-grown. It is ready for a final transplantation. Now we have everything in our favor. We keep Ramstedt alive with the antireactives and booster pumps. If Antireactive Substance AH works, we let Ramstedt go on with the calf's heart Öhman put in this morning, plus the secondary human heart in his abdomen—they do not have to be synchronized in their beat—*but,* if Substance AH fails, we have this new heart—raised from an embryo—of sufficient size to transplant into the chest. It gives us our insurance—and a definitive experiment that can open an entire new avenue in the field of—"

Farelli had his big hands on Garrett's shoulders, rocking him with love. "Dr. Garrett, you are a genius, a genius! When everything is lost, there is nothing more to lose—but now, I can only think of what can be gained. We will work as we have never worked before. I will get hold of Öhman and obtain that embryonic heart tissue from the miscarriage—"

"And I'll start preparing the new antireactive serum."

For an instant, Garrett's mind was not on the serum, but on his recent past. He had the curious feeling that he would never know the end to Mrs. Zane's amorous dilemma. He was sorry for that—that, and the loss of Dr. Keller, crutch and friend—but suddenly he knew he did not care. For the first time in what seemed eternity, he felt released of the genetic shackles that had bound him to shadowed ancestors. He wanted to sing, but he did not, for he could never carry a tune. So he sang inside, ever so briefly, until Farelli's musical voice blended in to conduct him back to the present.

"We will do this wonderful experiment together," Farelli was saying, with enthusiasm.

"Yes," said Garrett, smiling at last, "for better or for worse."

It would not be until three hours later that the electric mimeograph machine in the clerical office of the Caroline Hospital began to revolve, imprinting Öhman's official release to the press:

> On behalf of His Royal Highness the King, the directors of the Stockholm Caroline Hospital are pleased to announce that a heart transplant has been successfully performed on Count Rolf Ramstedt, seventy-two. The

graft was dramatically accomplished by the two current Nobel Prize winners in medicine, Dr. John Garrett, of Pasadena, California, and Dr. Carlo Farelli, of Rome, assisted by Dr. Erik Öhman, of the Caroline staff. Early complications were overcome by the two brilliant visiting laureates, working side by side as a team, through improvisations based on their earlier experiments. As a result of the Ramstedt case, the directors of the Caroline Hospital believe that a new method, to supplement the Garrett-Farelli method that is being honored in Concert Hall this afternoon, has been found for cases where organ transplantation is rejected by the immunity mechanism which . . .

It was 11:14 in the morning.

Andrew Craig, one knee pressing his tan, lightweight valise to his bedroom floor, grunted as he tightened and fastened the straps of his luggage. Tired of awaiting Leah's return from Dalarna, Craig had begun to empty his drawers and closet ten minutes before, throwing his effects helter-skelter, without care or economy, into his luggage. Now the necessary task was finished. What remained was to telephone the portier downstairs and request a boy to move his bag, and the formal evening suit he had left out on its hanger for the afternoon Ceremony, to the single room he had arranged to have for his last night in Stockholm. After that, there were two pieces of writing required of him—the curt, decisive note to Leah, and the speech he must create before five o'clock.

He lifted himself off the valise, carried it into the sitting room, and then started back to his bedroom telephone, when the front door buzzer intercepted him. He expected it to be Leah, at last, and he would be spared writing the note to her. But it was a young bellboy, instead, offering him a sealed envelope on a silver tray.

Somewhat mystified, Craig took the envelope, and told the bellboy to wait a moment. Walking back to his bed, to find a one-krona tip in his sport jacket pocket, he tore open the envelope. On a single sheet of hotel stationery was hastily scrawled a brief message:

DEAR ANDREW, I have been thinking about everything, and I would like to see you once more, if you want to see me. I have something important to tell you. I'll be in my room at 12:30 sharp. Call me then. EMILY.

Craig came alive with hope. He read the message again, and then reread it a second time. Why had she put a boundary to their reunion—"would like to see you once more"? And what was the "something important" she had to tell him? His immediate elation now became earth-bound. Was this to be a courtesy farewell, a more sensible explanation as to why she would never see him after Stockholm? But then, he tried to see the brighter side of it. After an emotional breaking off, she had reconsidered. She would see him. The message was almost affectionate. She would see him, and that was all that mattered, and after that, it would be up to him.

He remembered the bellboy at the front door, quickly separated a one-krona coin from his copper and silver change, and hurried back to the bearer of good tidings.

Paying the bellboy, he inquired, "Who gave you this note to deliver?"

"A lady, sir."

"A pretty lady with dark hair and green eyes?"

"I did not notice her eyes, sir, but she was very pretty."

"Was she coming in or going out?"

"She was going out, sir."

"Thank you."

Craig closed the door, read the note a fourth time as he returned to his bedroom, and decided that there would be no use in trying to get in touch with Emily earlier than she had suggested. She was out, probably last-minute shopping, and hope would have to be deferred until 12:30. Then he realized that he had forgotten to ask the bellboy to move his valise and evening clothes.

Before he could reach the telephone, he heard the front door slam. He stopped short, listening. He heard footsteps. Someone was in the sitting room. Was it the chambermaid, or was it—?

He went into the sitting room.

Leah Decker was removing her hat and coat before the mirror, and when he emerged from the bedroom, she saw the reflection of him join her in the mirror.

"Andrew—"

She dropped coat and hat in the nearest chair, and turned toward him, her severely bunned hair glistening from dried snowflakes, and her face pinker and ruddier from the outdoors than he had ever known it to be.

She started toward him. "Andrew, it was divine up north. You simply haven't been to Sweden until you've seen Lake Siljan in the winter—everyone ice skating and skiing—and tobogganing—like back home—only so much more fun. I think we should—"

Her eyes had gone past the tan valise, bulging, strapped, traveled back to it, considered it, and then met his own gaze with puzzlement.

"You packed by yourself. Why the hurry? We aren't leaving until tomorrow night."

He knew that he would not be writing the note to her. "*You* are leaving tomorrow night—by yourself. *I* am leaving when I please—by myself. Starting right now. This is our last time together."

"Andrew! Have you been drinking or what?"

"Get off it, Lee."

Suddenly she made the pretense of understanding his motive. "Oh—I bet I know what's gotten into you. You tried to see your German girl friend, and she told you I—"

"I won't even bother about that," said Craig. "God knows, that was bad enough—but the other thing you've done is infinitely worse. You've behaved like an unbelievable weekend bitch in an old Broadway play. You've saddled me with a lie I never deserved. I won't forgive you for it, and I never want to set eyes on you again."

532

Leah was a study in confusion. "Andrew, I haven't the faintest idea what's—"

"You haven't? You really haven't? You can't think of one rotten thing you've done to me in the last—"

"No, of course not!"

"How convenient—Instant Amnesia," said Craig bitterly. "All right, maybe I can help refresh your memory. Ever since Harriet's death, you've led me to believe I was responsible. I had some drinks, and lost control of the car, and I killed my wife. That's been the canon, hasn't it?"

Leah's eyes had widened, and involuntarily her hand had gone to her cheek, elbow extended, as if ready to avert a blow.

Craig went on relentlessly. "All that time, you knew the truth. You had the report from the police. About the tie rod breaking under my car, and swerving us into the skid. All that time, you knew it was an accident, and that you were supposed to have reported it to me, and you didn't. The police thought you had told me—as any normal human being with compassion would —but you did not. You burdened me with a false guilt instead. You lied to Lucius and you lied to me. Why, Leah? Why didn't you tell me the truth?"

Leah's face had transformed before his eyes to something lame and hunted. "Who says that's the truth? Where did you hear that cock-and-bull story? It's not the truth at all. Ask Sheriff Hollinder if you don't—"

"Sheriff Hollinder," he said savagely, "Miller's Dam—what in the hell does he know? But I know who *does* know. We cracked up just over the line, in Marquette County. The record of the accident is in the police files in Pikestown. A photostat of the accident report you kept from me is right here in Stockholm."

"I don't believe you," she said, weakening, not believing herself.

"How could you be so stupid? Couldn't you know that nothing on earth is ever secret—no truth, no lie—as long as we are born in public, and live and die in public, as long as we are part of a community? And how could you be so vicious? That's the part I don't understand. Wasn't my loss, my grief, enough for one man to bear—without the added guilt you superimposed on these last three years? I might have drunk myself to death, shot myself."

"I knew you wouldn't. You have too much—" But then she stopped, for she had conceded his truth, and realized it, and had no more defense.

"I think I've understood you since I've learned the truth, but I've hated to face this insight into you. You were willing to sacrifice me for yourself. You wanted me in total servitude, didn't you? You wanted me entirely beholden to you—a prisoner to your commands and whims—or was it something else? Was it that you wanted security?"

Leah asserted her last claim to self-respect. "I didn't need you. I had Harry Beazley in Chicago all the time, and you know it."

"Well, you have him now, Leah, and you latch on to him while you still can. You go back to Chicago and marry that poor bastard, and put a ring in his nose and nag him and try to make him what you want him to be and drive him to drink—make him inadequate to make yourself—"

The last frame of her composure had crumpled, and she was bared to every thrust. "Oh, Andrew, please don't—"

He had no more stomach for this one-sided carnage. "I've taken another room. You can stay for the Ceremony. I'm changing our flight tickets. Your plane stops at Chicago. Don't bother to come to Miller's Dam. I'll send you your things."

"Andrew—?"

"I'm getting rid of the place—the house, furniture, guilts—one tidy package. I'll miss Harriet, but she's in my heart, not in Miller's Dam, and I'll miss Lucius—and for the rest, to hell with it."

"What are you going to do? You can't—"

"I'm going to do what I started to do before I met Harriet. I'm going to find a spot on a high hill over the Pacific—not an artists' colony, but a place —and I'm going to write."

"Write? That'll be the day. From inside a bottle—"

He stared at her and was sick of the sight of her. "Right now, I'm going to ring for a bellboy."

He strode into his bedroom, and she knew that it was the end, and was right behind him, trembling. "Andrew, listen—listen—"

"Listen?" He had whirled about to confront her one last time. "The way I've been listening for three years? The way Emily Stratman listened? You have no talent but for destruction."

"Andrew, hear me—don't be cruel. You're a writer, you're supposed to have understanding—try to understand me, let me live by understanding me."

He hated this, but sensed that he must endure it to be rid of her.

"You're wrong," she was saying, "so wrong about why—why I did what I did. I don't know why really—or maybe I do now—but it wasn't to make you my slave, owing me something, or to hold you down or keep you under my thumb. It was—it was something else—"

She choked, and had a spasm of coughing, and he waited.

"What was it, Leah?" And he realized that he had ceased to call her Lee. "What made you—?"

"From the beginning—with my father, my mother, the relatives—it was always Harriet—Harriet this, Harriet that—Harriet because she was older, smarter, better-looking, always being praised—when we were kids, when we went to school—and even boy friends and career—Harriet was the one—the shining one. And when she got married, I knew it would be that way again —she with somebody famous and rich—a professional man, a writer—and me scraping along in some hole with an underpaid, nobody schoolteacher—always the one they almost forgot to invite—or write—or think about. It would be poor Leah, let's not forget Leah, now remember Leah. And then—then—"

Her bosom heaved and settled, and she tried to go on.

"And then the horrible thing happened to Harriet—to my sister—and I felt shame for all my years of wishing her dead—for all my days of secret envy —and then, almost naturally, because there was an opening that fit me, and there was no one else, I was there in Miller's Dam, in her place, in her kitchen and closets and garden—and, I don't know how to explain it, it was like a dream—to be Harriet, have all her advantages, the position, the security, a husband whose name was in the papers—to overnight be Harriet, not poor Leah, it was like a miracle—like God giving me a chance to change my life over—and when you got well, when you recovered, it was like the clock striking midnight, and all my dreams falling away, because then I knew I wasn't Harriet but poor Leah, and the house wasn't mine, and Harriet's husband wasn't my husband—and I got scared—I was never more scared in my life. You'd leave, I kept thinking, go back to your kind of people, and someday find another Harriet—and I'd have no chance, because I wasn't in Harriet's class, I was an impostor, a fake Harriet, and you'd see it—and I couldn't bear the idea of having tasted what I had, what I'd dreamt of all my life, and then losing it forever.

"And then some kind of craziness came over me, because you weren't gone yet, and I began to imagine that maybe I could be Harriet—maybe I could show you—maybe it would work—and so—I don't know—at first, I didn't mind your drinking, because it made you depend on me like when you were convalescing and mourning—it made you need me—and then I started to hate the drinking, because it made you not you, not Harriet's you, and our life wasn't Harriet's life, and you didn't even know I existed as Harriet or Leah —and still, I would not let go—that's why I couldn't show you the accident report—I always meant to—but the lie slipped out, and then I couldn't take it back—maybe didn't want to—but this is why it all happened the way it did— for no other reason—and I'm sick with remorse—and I admit it—and I want your forgiveness, Andrew—your forgiveness, please, that's all."

This had gone beyond a cry for compassion and charity. This had been a plea for clemency of the soul. Craig recognized it as such, and knew that he could not condemn her to a lifetime in purgatory.

"I'm sorry, Lee, you know I am. I forgive you, of course. If I were a judge, I'd simply say—I sentence you to yourself. There are worse things." He paused. "You do know who you are now, don't you, Lee?"

"Yes, I know."

"It's not so bad being Leah Decker, person, if you will be true to her. Do as I've told you. Go to Chicago, and go to that man Beazley. He's waiting. Enjoy what he has to offer and what you can be. Yes, Lee, I forgive you and wish you well, I truly do. We've both lost Harriet, and we needn't forget her, but it's no use living any longer with a ghost. One day, when it is all forgotten, I think we might be friends."

"I want to be friends, Andrew. I'll need that."

"All right, then. We'll both say farewell to Harriet. She had her time on earth. Let's enjoy what is left of ours. I don't know if we can any more, but let's try. Shall we?"

"Yes, Andrew."

"Good-bye, Lee."

"Good-bye."

She backed off, and ran to her room. Craig sighed, lifted the receiver, and asked for the portier's desk.

It was 12:26 in the afternoon.

Emily Stratman, invigorated by the sharp, white winter's day, came back to her uncle's suite breathless. She had taken a taxi from Kungsgatan, repeatedly consulting her wristwatch. At the portier's desk, accepting her key, she had been impatient when the clerk delayed her to report that there had been three urgent telephone calls for her uncle in the last half hour, but no messages. "The party was most insistent," the portier had said. "He wanted to know when you or Professor Stratman would return." Emily had hesitated a moment. "Are you sure Professor Stratman isn't in? He intended to be." Then she had dismissed it, and started for the elevator, calling back, "I suppose something came up. Anyway, I'm here, so put his calls through to me." In the elevator, she had chafed at its slowness, then hurried down the corridor, fearful that she would miss Craig's telephone call.

But now she was here on time, in fact with several minutes to spare. She dropped her gift packages on the entry table, lifted a foot to push off one of the overshoes she had borrowed, and then the other, both still wet from the snow, and thinking all the time of what she had done and what might come of it.

She had sent the message to Craig this morning, on an impulse born of the meeting with Lilly at Nordiska Kompaniet. For hours in bed the night before, she had lain awake, examining what Lilly had told her, examining her own life and character, examining her feelings toward Craig. Eventually she had slept, but by breakfast, she had known that she must see Craig one more time. Nothing could come of it, she knew, but her affection for him was too great to allow their memories of each other to recall only the last meeting. He deserved more of her, and it was necessary that she explain herself to him. She would not reveal all of herself. That would be impossible. She never had to anyone, not even Uncle Max, and she never would in her life. But she would try to communicate something of it, some part, to Craig, so that he would know why she had acted as she had, and why she could never go on with him.

She had not sent for him immediately in the morning because she had wanted to be by herself, in the clear air, on the snow-lined sidewalks, to sort out her thoughts and decide what she must say to Craig. Shopping had been the lesser activity, the self-subterfuge, and so she had walked and absently shopped and given her memory rare freedom. Now she was ready.

Going into the sitting room, unbuttoning her coat, the possibility arose that Craig might not call her at all. Perhaps he had not received her message. Or, perhaps he wanted no more of her. The last could be, but she did not seriously believe it. In any case, his curiosity would make him respond. That, and also the fact that he was a gentleman.

For the first time, she saw the note propped against the lamp on the end

536

table, where the sitting room telephone also rested. The handwriting was familiar:

Had to suddenly go out to a business lunch. See you soon. Room service says your gown will be back at 3. Love, UNCLE MAX.

It surprised Emily that Uncle Max had gone out. When she had left to shop, he was still clumping about in his faded woolen robe and bedroom slippers. He intended, he had said, to spend the entire day resting and relaxing, so that he would have all his strength for carrying the medallion and diploma from the King. It was terrible, she decided now, the way the Swedes gave him no rest, a man of his years. But today was the last day of it, and then there would be fewer obligations.

Inevitably, her mind went out to Craig. Anxiety mounted. It was 12:29. He should be calling her any second.

And then the telephone on the end table rang.

She snatched up the receiver, but tried to keep her tone calm. "Hello?"

"Miss Emily Stratman, please?" It was not Craig's low, mellifluous voice, but a thin high Swedish voice.

"This is Miss Stratman—"

"Miss Stratman? Do not be alarmed. I call for Professor Max Stratman. At lunch, he suffered from the effects of a mild heart attack."

"Heart attack? Oh, no—"

"Do not worry, Miss Stratman. He is in the best hands. He is having medical attention this moment."

"What happened? How is he? Is it serious?"

"A mild coronary, Miss Stratman. He has asked—"

"Who is this? Where is he?"

"I am one of the attending physicians—Dr. Öhman—and Professor Stratman is now resting easily. He has asked to see you. I think it would be wise if you—"

"Where? Tell me where. I'll be right over."

"If you will be so kind as to write this down—"

"Wait—wait—"

Blindly, she sought for her pen in her coat, then remembered that it was in her purse, and she found it and returned to the phone.

"Go ahead—please hurry—"

"Take a taxi to Sahlins Sjukhuset. It is a small private clinic on the way to the Southern Hospital—two blocks before, on Ringvägen. Your driver will know exactly. I will be waiting for you."

"I'll leave immediately."

"Miss Stratman—one point more. Professor Stratman reminds me it is imperative that you mention this emergency to no one. He is most desirous of avoiding publicity. I believe you understand."

"Tell him not to worry!"

She hung up, tore off the bottom of Uncle Max's note, where she had written the name of the clinic, clasped her purse tightly, and rushed to the door.

As she reached it, the telephone began to ring again. She knew this was Craig, but could not wait to explain—and remembered that her uncle wanted no one to know—and she let the phone continue its monotonous peal, and kept going, half running, to the elevator.

When she emerged from the hotel lobby, almost falling on the slippery boardwalk, she started to call for a taxi, but at once a small Volvo with a meter drew up before her. She hurried inside it, as the uniformed doorman saluted her and closed the car door.

The driver, a gentle, elderly man wearing a chauffeur's cap and rimless spectacles, turned inquiringly.

"Sahlins Sjukhuset—a clinic before you reach the Southern Hospital—do you know?"

"Yes, fröken, I take you."

"Please hurry."

He bobbed his head, shifting the gears, and the car jostled and they were off.

The city sped by, white on white, the dim sun in the gray sky and the snowfall spent and the air blue-clean, but Emily was hardly aware of it. All that she could think was that Uncle Max had suffered a heart attack in this remote, faraway land, this foreign place, and that she was frightened for him and alone. Once she wondered if his visits to Dr. Ilman had been about his heart—she had always thought it strong and immortal—but none of that mattered, for now it had happened. She wondered if the Swedish doctor had told her the truth. Was the coronary a mild one? Was Uncle Max even alive? Yet he had sent for her. He must be conscious.

And then, before she realized it, the taxi had drawn up to a curb, and from the window she could see a narrow brick building, two pillars, two windows, a black door between. The elderly driver had come around to help her out, but she was through the snow and then on the sidewalk, before he reached her.

She fumbled for her change purse and gave him a five-kronor bill. "Never mind," she said.

"Thank you, thank you," he said, touching his cap visor. He pointed. "In that door, Miss Stratman."

She had already started toward the door, but she stopped now. "How did you know my name?"

The driver bowed. "The doorman of the Grand Hotel has pointed you out to us."

It did not seem odd, and Uncle Max was waiting. Hastily, she went into the clinic. She was not surprised to find a blond, brawny Swedish intern, with wrists of a mechanic, solicitude written on his features, waiting to meet her.

"Miss Stratman?"

She acknowledged her identity.

"I will take you to Professor Stratman."

He led her, bouncing lightly on the balls of his feet which were shod in white tennis shoes, to the end of the short hallway, then opened a door. She was in a reception room. The intern held open a second door.

"The doctor is waiting for you," he said.

She hurried into the office. The shutters had been drawn, and except for two lamps at the far end, the room was in shadows. She made out a chair before a glass-topped brown desk, and behind the desk, a tall swivel chair, and behind the swivel chair, his back to her, the doctor.

"Dr. Öhman—"

"Miss Stratman." He spoke before turning from the parted shutters. Unhurriedly, he reset the shutters, and at last, he turned to welcome her. "I am not Dr. Öhman," he said. "I am Dr. Hans Eckart. Please do sit down."

"My uncle—"

"Sit down."

She clutched at the chair arm and lowered herself to the chair edge. Eckart had come to the desk, and now he sat across from her, smiling reassuringly. She was not reassured. She had come into the office expecting a Swedish doctor, but the appearance of this doctor, unknown to her specifically, was known to her generally, had inhabited in many shapes her remembrance of times past, for the haircut, the monocle, the Prussian severity were all German, and she was repelled.

"Professor Stratman—my uncle—where is he?" she managed to ask. "How is he?"

"He is quite well, I should presume. For an old man with a cardiac irregularity, he appears wonderfully active," said Eckart. "As to where he is, I have no more idea than you. For the last hour, I have tried to locate him."

"But you called—you said he had a heart—"

"Yes, when I learned that he had not returned to the hotel, but that you had, I directed someone to telephone you. I am sincerely regretful it was necessary to frighten you with a fabrication. But it was necessary to bring you here on some pretext, so that I might speak to you. I had already spoken to your uncle some days ago. And I would have preferred to speak to your uncle again today. Since he was unavailable, it became important to have you here in his stead. As his proxy, so to speak." Eckart's fingers drummed the desk, and he seemed to consider her through the monocle. "Yes, I am sure you will do very well. In matters like this, I am sure you and your uncle can speak in one voice."

"In matters like what?"

Unaccountably, Emily dreaded to hear his reply. She sat straight in her chair. No facial muscle, no body or limb muscle, moved. Only the invisible antenna of her intuition now felt malignity and malevolence.

Eckart did not answer her question directly. It was as if he savored one more circumlocution. "If your uncle is ill at all," Eckart was saying suavely, "it is a moral illness that he suffers. You are here because I want you to assist us in curing him of this infirmity. I want you to assist us in making Professor Stratman recover his sense and his moral health."

She wanted to give him no satisfaction of weakness. She knew Germans. But, despite herself, her voice quavered. "You are not a doctor?"

"If you mean—medical doctor—you are correct, I am not. My doctorate is in physics. My acquaintance with Professor Stratman goes back to our early years in Berlin."

In the deepest pit of her stomach, she was terrified. "What do you—what do you want of me?"

"Little enough," said Eckart, as hospitable as if this were a lighthearted tête-à-tête. "We are not interested in you at all. We are interested in Professor Stratman. Your value to us is only as a means to an end."

"You still haven't said—"

"What we are after?" Eckart pressed his monocle into the ridges below his brow and above his cheekbone. "You are correct to be so businesslike. You want to have this—this unusual drama done—so that you may return to your author friend. Yes." He took a chained gold watch from his vest and studied it. "There is not much time from now to the Ceremony, so I will be as businesslike as you." He leaned back in the swivel chair, and the spring protested twice. "Your uncle is a German who turned his back on his Fatherland in its hour of most dire need, to lend his support to exploiters and capitalists, the warmonger clique, who are the masters of so-called democratic America. His genius, in a wrong cause, distresses us in East Berlin deeply. We have one object, and I have one assignment—to make Professor Stratman cease his dangerous tinkering—so harmful to world peace—for an irresponsible society, and to make him come to his senses and return to his beloved Fatherland. He is a German, and—"

"He is *not* a German!" Emily shouted.

Eckart scowled. "You think you can change your blood with a paper of naturalization? I did not take you for a foolish child. Your uncle himself, Professor Stratman—in the latter days of the war, when we were at the Kaiser Wilhelm Institute together—used to tell a story. I have not forgotten it. His story makes my point. One day, a wealthy American businessman was strolling with Professor Charles Steinmetz, the famous engineer who was deformed, past a synagogue in New York. 'You know, Steinmetz,' said the businessman, 'I used to be a Jew.' And Steinmetz said to him, 'Yes, and you know, I used to be a humpback.' There is the story. Your uncle is a German, and before the eyes of the world, he shall be again—when he defects from the decadent West."

Emily heard this out with smoldering anger. "Nothing—nothing on earth —would make him go back to you."

"I hope you are wrong, Miss Stratman. And I hope I am *not* wrong in judging that your good sense coincides with your uncle's good sense."

"About what? I still don't know what you're trying to say."

"I'm only trying to say in my diplomat's way—forgive the verbosity—that there just may be something on earth that might help Max Stratman make the change."

"No."

"If not something, then someone. For someone, to save someone, perhaps Max Stratman might reconsider."

Emily's mood of fearlessness, fanned by hatred and a feeling of unreality that isolated her from this improbable interview, persisted. "Am I the someone?" she asked, suddenly. "Are you threatening to hold me, abduct me? Is that what?"

Eckart removed his monocle, shaking his head as if genuinely offended. "My—my—Miss Stratman—America has spoiled you, too. I believe you are all victims of those glorifying gangster films on television and in the cinema. I promise you—we do not drop hostages in canals and such nonsense. We have more civilized means."

"There's nothing you can do to me to make me or my uncle—"

"Nothing, Miss Stratman? No barter at all? Are you so certain?"

Suddenly the self-righteous fury went out of her, and she was less certain. "I repeat it—nothing. You can kill me—"

"Please, Miss Stratman, do not offend me again. I am a scientist and a scholar, not a savage. You are my guest, and I am your host. In the end, you shall see, we will both benefit from this brief meeting. You have someone I want—your uncle—and I have someone you want."

Eckart had been leaning forward, but now he was erect in the chair, adjusting his monocle to its place. Deliberately, he rose, pulled his short suit coat straight, and slowly he came around the desk, ignoring Emily as he went to the door through which she had entered.

Emily's hands tightened on the arms of the chair, and the pulses of her wrists throbbed, as she turned to watch him.

He opened the door to the reception room, and he was nodding to someone out of sight. "All right," he was saying, "she is ready to see you."

Eckart stepped aside, almost deferentially (how curious), like a chamberlain about to announce the entry of nobility, and at once the figure of an elderly man filled the doorway. The light of the reception room was behind him, and the office was darkened, so that momentarily he was only an outline in black.

Slowly, he shuffled—was there a barely perceptible limp?—into the room, toward Emily, the colorless black of his outline giving way to human features and figure. He came past Emily, and then hesitantly around in front of her, and a few feet before her he halted, as if to inspect her and himself be inspected.

Now, at last, he was clearly visible to her troubled eyes, a stocky old man, slightly bent beneath time, attired in a heavy dark gray unfashionable worsted suit, the suit wrinkled and rumpled as if he had traveled steadily in it and had had no time to send for the valet. She stared without embarrassment, not because he was unusual, but because he was so usual, so almost known and faintly familiar, like one whose face you cannot quite place or whose name is almost at the tip of your tongue.

His head and face held her. The head was massive on a short thick column of neck. The hair was sparse but sufficient, shining white and carefully combed sideways from a wide part above one ear. The face was chapped rough red, all symmetrical and firm despite streaks of age, except for the prominently bulbous nose, which disconcerted her because it was known to her.

Still mystified and curiously detached, Emily could see that the kindly red face—so familiar, so once-known—was alive with emotion, the eyes watery and blinking, the bulbous nose sniffling, the lips trembling.

The familiar stranger swallowed and shook his head. "You do not recognize me, my little goose?"

That instant she recognized him, or thought she did, and even as her knotted fists pulled her to the edge of the chair, looking up at him, she rejected the possibility. Yet the bulbous nose, the timbre of his voice, the intangible cord between them that was drawing her out of the chair and unsteadily to her feet, could not be dismissed. Above all, the phrase of endearment this stranger had used so easily, so naturally, as if this was homecoming and they had simply resumed again. *My little goose.* Where had she heard it before and from whom? Where . . . back and back and backward the years . . . when he had carried her round and round the old, oak-lined living room, on his shoulders, aloft, propping her high, holding her, round and round, faster and faster, as she squealed and kicked, and he laughed and laughed . . . little goose, little goose . . . and again, again, leaving her, beribboned, groomed, starched, wide-eyed and pale, at the gymnasium with the frocked teacher . . . you are growing, a young lady now, my little goose . . . and once more, with pain, with wrenching . . . in the drizzle, at the door, down the steps to the street between the efficient, unsentimental brownshirts . . . I will write, Rebecca, I will have you out, soon, soon . . . soon, Rebecca . . . soon, my little goose . . .

His caress of love. Only his. No other.

She stood before him now, clamped immobile by a paralysis of disbelief. The massive, venerable face blurred an instant and then an instant stood in bold relief, as if cut from granite and now weather-beaten: the matted white hair, the tear-filled brown eyes, the working stubbled jaw.

Eckart's brisk voice was behind her, engulfing the incredible seconds and dim years, captioning the moment. "Miss Stratman—you must know him, of course—Walther Stratman, your father—"

"Papa." Her voice spoke, not she, to herself, not to the familiar stranger.

"—missing, but not dead, it turns out," Eckart went on behind her. "He's been alive all these years—in custody of the Russians after he helped your uncle escape—working for his captors. But now he is here in neutral Stockholm. It is a miracle I have managed for you—he is free at last."

The face of the old familiar stranger was nodding, nodding. "Yes, Emily, it is Walther—your papa. I know how you feel this minute—as I feel—the shock, the incredibility—but we are alive, my little goose—and together—the darkness gone, forgotten—from now on together, always. I am free, Emily."

"Papa," her voice said aloud.

And suddenly his rough red face slipped away, sucked slowly into the gaping vortex of the spinning room, and she felt herself moving into the vortex, too. Desperately, she tried to keep her balance, hold on to the something inside, the upright thing you held to keep straight, but she felt it crack beneath her, and she let go and abandoned herself to the airiness of the spinning room. For the eternity of a second, she hung suspended and legless, and then the carpet floated up into vision, and the coarse nap of the carpet was on her cheeks and mouth, and after that, the far voices and enormous shoes, and after that only blackness, star-peppered, and then blackness and blackness. . . .

It was two o'clock in the afternoon.

Seated on the side of the double bed, in the unfamiliar single room on the fifth floor that he had moved into, Andrew Craig dropped the telephone receiver back on the cradle in despair. For an hour and a half, every fifteen or twenty minutes, he had been ringing Emily's suite without getting a response. If she had been accidentally delayed, why had he not heard from her? The only answer was that she had regretted the message she had sent him, and was purposely avoiding the telephone.

He rose, jittery with frustration, and decided that some activity would calm him down. His valise stood on the baggage table, still not unpacked. He loosened the straps, set the suitcase flat, unlocked it, and began to throw his effects into a bureau drawer. He passed fifteen minutes in this way, and when the valise was empty, there was nothing more to do. There was, as a matter of fact, his acceptance speech to write, but he had no interest in it.

He filled his pipe, and considered phoning Emily one last time. But it seemed pointless. She knew where he was, or could find out by asking the operator, and if she wanted to see him, she would call.

Then, as he paced, worrying about Emily, troubled about the speech that must be written, something else occurred to him.

He strode to the telephone and asked to be connected with the portier's desk in the lobby.

"Yes? This is the portier."

"This is Andrew Craig. Tell me—the keys to the Stratman suite—Miss Emily Stratman—Professor Stratman—are both their keys in the box? I'm trying to find out if either one has returned to the hotel yet."

"One second, Mr. Craig."

Craig waited, holding the receiver to his ear, and then the portier was back on the line. "Both keys are missing, so they must both be in. I would— one second, please hold—" Craig heard indistinct voices, and then the portier again. "My colleague behind the desk tells me that Professor Stratman took his key and went up to his suite no more than ten minutes ago. And he says he believes that Miss Stratman came for her key about—it was shortly after the noon hour. So—"

"Thank you," said Craig.

He hung up. That was it, then. Emily had been in her room all this while, and returned to answer his call, and had then had a change of heart and stayed away from the telephone. The important thing she had to tell him would not be told. Their reunion was not to take place.

Suddenly Craig was weary of pursuit and disappointment. If she was this way, then it was this way she would always be, and there would be no making her over. He had not the energy for these ups and downs. He would forget her. That would be for the best.

He decided that he would go downstairs, have a few drinks and a snack in the Winter Garden, and after that, there might be time enough to outline some sort of acceptance speech—a brief, conversational speech larded with the literary clichés and double-talk (where man became Man) expected on these occasions, and then, at last, it would be time to dress for the final Ceremony.

But when Craig arrived at the elevator, and pressed the button, he knew that his destination was not the Winter Garden but the Stratman suite.

Quickly traversing the red-striped corridor carpet of the third floor, he reached her front door with every intention of buzzing and knocking until Emily was forced to make an appearance and engage in a showdown, but then he found that the front door was ajar. This was better, he decided at once. He would simply walk in on her and corner her, before she could temporize and equivocate, and he then would have it out with her. As he reached for the knob, the door moved away from his touch.

A stooped chambermaid, in clean but faded green, carrying a pail of suds and brushes, a mop clenched awkwardly, was opening the door to leave.

Craig stepped aside for her, nodding politely. "Miss Stratman is expecting me," he explained, because he felt that an explanation was needed.

The chambermaid muttered an incomprehensible phrase in Swedish, and waited for Craig to enter, and then she closed the door after him.

In the entry hall, Craig hesitated on the frontier of propriety. One did not barge into other people's private quarters unannounced, unless one was Leah, but then Craig justified his act by remembering that he had telephoned Emily often enough, and that she *had* wanted to see him. If she now suffered timidity or doubt, at least one of them should be the aggressor.

Nevertheless, he felt uncertain of his position as he went into the sitting room. He looked about. The room was vacant, and quiet except for the ticking of a clock. He moved past the sofa to what he recalled to be Emily's bedroom door, intending to call her or rap, when he was arrested by the torn note held upright between the telephone and lamp. The upper half of the note had been crossed out. It read:

Had to suddenly go out to a business lunch. See you soon. Room service says your gown will be back at 3. Love, UNCLE MAX.

Beneath these crossed out sentences was a later communiqué:

2:20. Liebchen—Have returned from lunch and want to rest. Do not let me oversleep. Wake me before 4 o'clock. UNCLE MAX.

Craig straightened. Emily was not in after all. He felt ashamed for having mistrusted her, and equally ashamed at this intrusion on her privacy. Whatever had detained her, he told himself, was her own business, and if she intended to telephone him, she would do so before the Ceremony. He felt better now. To hell with the Winter Garden. He would return to his room and outline the speech and wait for her.

Simultaneous with his decision came the sound of the front door buzzer. His first thought was: Emily, at last. Then his second thought corrected the first: she would not buzz, for she had a key. Well, he had no business here. He would see who it was—Emily's gown being returned by the valet, no doubt —he would accept it, hang it up, allow old Stratman his catnap, and then leave.

When he hurried into the entry to answer the buzzer, he noticed that a single sheet of white typing paper had been slipped through the crack at the bottom of the front door. He stooped to pick it up, not intending to invade privacy further by reading the typewritten message, intending only to place the message on the entry table, when Emily's name leaped out of the page at him.

He read the typed words set down entirely in capital letters:

PROF. STRATMAN: IF YOU WISH TO KNOW THE WHERE-ABOUTS OF YOUR NIECE EMILY STRATMAN THEN OPEN THE PACKAGE IMMEDIATELY AND LISTEN TO A FRIEND.

The cords in Craig's throat constricted. The words on the sheet in his hands were bland and harmless words, but the effect was ominous. Like all Americans, so isolated from the everyday intrigues of the Old World, Craig was conditioned by lurid fiction and film, to believe that such skulduggery was as extinct as history. To even project the possibility of conspiracy, on a level lower than unreal high government circles, was to cast aside maturity and sophistication. Automatically, to one raised as he had been, all machination was the façade of what was more familiar and innocent—the practical joke.

At once, Craig rejected menace and prepared for the unfolding of the joke. He opened the front door to admit the bellboy with his parcel. But there was no one there, which tended to confirm the joke. He poked his head into the corridor and searched off right and then left. The corridor was empty. And then his shoe bumped the package on the corridor floor.

Taking up the small, light package, meaning to place it with the ridiculous message on the entry table, he was nagged by an urgency to reread the message. Now he did so, and now he sensed jeopardy. What corroborated the threat of the message was Emily's actual absence. She had said that she would be back in her suite at 12:30, but it was past 2:30. The thing to do, he knew, was to awaken Professor Stratman—message and package were directed to him—and be reproved for interrupting an old man's rest with collegiate nonsense. His instinct was to obey the message himself, and, at worst, be accursed for a meddlesome fool. And if it was not a joke? His instinct was reinforced by a deep emotion: his stake in Emily was, by this time, as great as Stratman's stake.

Forgoing further vacillation, Craig tugged at the strand of twine around the gray package, tore it off, and then peeled away the paper.

When he was finished, he held in his hand a miniature tape recorder, no more than four by five inches, constructed of black plastic. To the lower left, in white lettering, were the words "Record . . . Play . . . Stop" with a tiny lever set at "Stop." A slot above revealed the miniscule tape inside. And next to that was a knob with lettering beneath that read "Manual Rewind." There was no trade name on the plastic machine. Craig turned it over. On the back, in a corner, imprinted black on black, were the words "Made in Stettin." And then Craig saw that a coil of wire was attached to the device, and at its end, a plastic earplug, which was the speaker.

Standing in the entry hall with this novelty, Craig decided that if it was a prank, it was an expensive prank. Somehow, he did not like this, whatever it was. Indecision had disappeared. He would follow the advice in the message. He would LISTEN TO A FRIEND.

Carefully, he placed the miniature tape machine on the table, unwound the wiring, pushed the plastic earplug into his left ear, and then he switched the tiny lever from "Stop" to "Play."

At first, there was the rubbing of the tape, and no other sound. Suddenly, piercing his eardrum, a disembodied male voice: "Max, this is your old friend, Hans Eckart, addressing you. I should have preferred communicating with you in person, and, in fact, tried to do so earlier today. Since I could not locate you, I took the liberty of arranging to meet with your niece. She is beside me now. Do not be alarmed in any way. She is well and the recipient of some extremely good news, which she will convey to you in a moment. Forgive my use of this melodramatic instrument, Max, but circumstances made it necessary. I might have sent Emily in person with the news, or had her telephone you, but she could have revealed our whereabouts, and that would have been troublesome. I thought to have her write you a note, but she is too excited, and moreover you might not have believed her news unless you heard it from her own lips."

There was the briefest pause. The clipped voice spoke perfect English, yet the cadence and inflection were unmistakably Teutonic. Craig, first tense and worried when he had begun to listen, then gradually disarmed by the speaker's informal reassurances to Max, tried to recall if he had ever heard the name of Hans Eckart. He could not remember, but before he could search his mind further, the same voice had resumed.

"Max, as I have already told you, your niece is understandably excited by the good news that has occurred. Before I put her on—and in order to prevent any misunderstanding of what she tells you—I had better present the news first. You must prepare yourself for a shock."

Once more, Eckart's voice paused, and now, for the first time since Craig had started listening, an intimation of benumbing horror ran through him. He did not like "good news" that had "excited" Emily and would "shock"

Stratman. He did not like "good news" that had to be transmitted in this fashion to conceal and protect the speaker's "whereabouts." He did not like or trust the "old friend" unknown to him. With desperate attentiveness, he listened to the rubbing of the tape, and then the Teutonic recorded voice came on again.

"Max, listen carefully. *Your brother Walther is alive.* Yes, I will repeat this for you, so there is no mistake. Walther Stratman is alive. He is here in Stockholm. He is with me in this room right now. He is seated beside Emily. They have had their reunion. I know you are stunned. I was no less amazed when I learned the good news yesterday. When you and I met for lunch previously, it was you who declared that you had heard he was dead, killed by the Russians at the end of the war. It was I who reminded you that he was known to be missing and only presumed dead. And it was I who had to tell you that only recently he was announced as legally dead. But the fact is—by what means is of no relevance at this time—I found Walther alive and healthy in Russia. What had deceived me, all of us in East Berlin, is that these many years he has lived and worked under the name of Dr. Kurt Lipski. The metamorphosis from Walther Stratman to Kurt Lipski had been engineered by Soviet authorities immediately after the war, for reasons of security. Once I was certain of this, I convinced the Soviets that a better use could be made of a Walther resurrected than a Walther supposedly dead. I also convinced them that Walther, under proper circumstances, deserved freedom of choice as to where he wished to live and work in the future. The Soviet authorities graciously permitted Walther to be flown to neutral Sweden. He arrived this morning. He has been with me since his arrival. The moment I had him, I tried to locate you. I knew you would want to see your brother at once. Because you were unavailable, I brought Emily here, in your place, to be reunited with her father. I will now permit your niece to confirm what I have said and to speak for herself. One moment."

Eckart's voice stopped, as if severed by a cleaver. The rubbing of the tape was the only sound. Except for pressing the earplug deeper, Craig had made no other movement during this recital, lest he lose a single word. Even his emotions had been frozen into unnatural attitudes of diligence. He was like one who, except for ear and brain, had been turned to stone by a dark force. Craig waited and listened. But as seconds passed, his mind began to admit thoughts of Walther alive, of Emily with him, of what this must mean to Emily, of what it would mean to Max Stratman, and, inevitably, of this Eckart's design and purpose.

The smooth passage of the tape in Craig's ear was suddenly disturbed by a loud click, and then a female voice, more distant, came through.

"Uncle Max, this is Emily." Craig was not sure. Was it Emily? He had anticipated an "excited" tone. The feminine voice was lackadaisical. Craig concentrated. The feminine voice resumed. "Uncle Max, it is Emily. They brought me here to meet Papa. At first I didn't recognize him, and then I did. It is Papa. Yes. There is no mistake or trick. He is well—he is—he is in good spirits, and wants to see you, too. It's all so sudden and surprising—I'm afraid I'm mixed up. Actually, when I saw him—"

The feminine voice stopped abruptly, edited out. Now Craig was sure, more than sure, positive. The tape was true. The voice, flat and low, oddly disinterested and heavy with sleep as if drugged, was the voice of Emily Stratman, and none other.

That moment, Emily's voice dragged through the earplug, verifying Craig's suspicion. "—but now, because of the way I am, so mixed up, they gave me sedation, and I must rest a little while. Uncle Max, I'm so confused I don't know what to say, I don't know what will happen." The blank tape took over, until Emily's tired voice rode it once more. "Uncle Max, Dr. Eckart says the Russians have agreed to let Papa go free and live in America if you will take the job that was offered to you—the job in the university in East Berlin. I don't know what to say. I can't think. Dr. Eckart will explain. I don't want you to do it. You can't do it. But I don't want them to take Papa back either." The slightest pause, and then Emily was saying, "They tell me to assure you I am not in danger, and whatever you decide, I will be released tonight after the Nobel Ceremony. At that time, they will either take Papa back or take you." Suddenly Emily's voice pitched higher, come alive in agitation, defying her sedation, and then broke. "Oh, Uncle Max, they want you, but please, please—" The next portion was edited out, and only the last of Emily's plea was retained. "—what is best for you." The tape rubbed on and on.

Shaken, Craig stared down at the miniature recorder. Through the upper slot, he could see that three-quarters of the tiny spool had run its course, and one quarter remained to be unreeled. He waited.

The Teutonic male voice had returned, but now, in some subtle way, changed, more clipped, more positive, more confident. "Max, you have just heard your niece address you without coercion. Everything she has told you —about your brother's presence, her own situation, your necessity to make a decision—is true. I will spell out our terms—let us say our offer to you—precisely. I ask you to listen with attention. It is our desire that you defect from the West and join the peace corps of scientists in East Berlin, capital of the Fatherland. You will be treated with the honors and care commensurate with your high position in the world. Between five and six o'clock this afternoon, after you have received your Nobel Prize from the King, you will make your acceptance speech. In this speech, you will announce your change of allegiance. It will be televised, and we will be watching and listening. If you agree to this, you will return from Concert Hall to your suite in the Grand Hotel after the program. You will be contacted there, and ultimately, sometime tonight, you will be brought to me. I, in turn, will take you to your brother and niece. Before midnight, the exchange will be effected. Walther and Emily will be released in Stockholm and be free to go to America. You will accompany me—the method of transport I cannot disclose—to your new and better life. Should you fail to agree to these terms, and persist in working as a tool of American capitalism, it will mean the rejection and loss of your brother, Walther Stratman. You will not see him again in your life, and he will be returned, against his wishes, to the custody of the Soviet Russians. Since you are a man of good will, and of good conscience, I have no doubt that your conscience will guide you correctly. You will not forget, I am certain, that it was Walther's sacrifice on your behalf in 1945 that allowed you the so-called freedom that he desired, and permitted you to gain the honors and comforts that are now yours. To forget this, to ignore the post we offer you, will condemn your brother to continued exile in a land he hates, and keep him from finishing his years with the beloved daughter he has longed for and loved."

There was the shortest pause, and then the voice concluded. "Max, we have made you a reasonable offer. Do not destroy it, or endanger those near and dear to you, by going to the Swedish security police. They will not find me. Nor will they find Walther or Emily. Act as I have suggested, one way or the other, but act on your own. Any other course will prove foolhardy. *Mit herzlichen Grüssen*, Max."

There was a click, the endless rubbing, and not another word in Craig's ear.

His hand darted to the machine, pulling the tiny lever to "Stop." He hesitated a moment, the torrent of information scrambled and dancing in his head. Had he heard it rightly? Had he missed anything important? He wanted to hear Emily's voice again, to test and judge the degree of her agitation and feeling. That, and to hear her. He gripped the rewind knob in his fingers and quickly reversed the tape. He edged the lever to "Play," cupped his hand over the earplug, and listening for eternal mute minutes. There was nothing, no voice, no sound of any kind, except the mocking rasp of the tape as it wound in its circle. Finally, he realized the recorded tape had been automatically erased after it had played, through use of some unusual device. All he had heard would never be heard again. The future of the three Stratmans was in his hands—in his head, really—their predicament and the condition surrounding their future. Craig stopped the playback and removed the plug from his ear.

He stood in the entry hall and tried to think. In his entire life, he had never heard anything more stupefying, unless it had been the first news of Harriet's death. And now, in a sense, he had tuned in on the death of a second human being, were he Max or Walther Stratman. He was overcome by an apathy induced by the impossible: to save Emily's father and yet save Max Stratman. But quickly the apathy passed, and necessity and responsibility mothered clarity.

To whom could he go? Where could he turn? What was right? What was wrong?

There was an easy but dreadful solution, of course. He need only awaken Max Stratman, soberly repeat every detail that had been on the incredible tape, and if Stratman believed him (and Craig thought that he would), Stratman himself could carry the burden of the decision into Concert Hall in two hours. It was tempting, dangerously tempting, this notion, to awaken Stratman and let him decide between his brother's freedom and his nation's need.

And then, at once, the notion of what he had been tempted to do sickened Craig, and gave him the old revulsion toward himself, which he now understood more clearly. If he performed in the old, smooth way—running from a shout of distress in the night, ducking away from an uneven gang beating in the street, hiding from reality and his debt to existence by the soft coma of drink and drug and self-pity and inaction and retreat—he would leave this northern place as he had come, a riven and dismembered man, lost to himself and his time, the eternal victim of all unseen fears. The test was finally the test of his bedrock character. Victory or failure was not the criterion of the test. Responsible action was the criterion. No, of one thing he was certain at last—he would not awaken poor old Stratman.

Yet, merely to prove something to himself, he could not be careless enough to accept a dare that would trifle with another's life. And it was more than that now, because now he knew that Emily's future was his own, and so this had come down to self-survival at last. To whom could he turn? The Swedish security police, of course. But even if they believed his wild story—and they might, because of his Nobel stature—what could they do? Eckart would evaporate, Walther would be whisked away, and Emily would long be a corpse in some narrow alley or a hostage in her hated Germany, before the police, without clues, could pick up her trail. The slow noisy wheels of officialdom, he decided, were to be ignored.

But then, what else? There was only himself, with his knowledge, and no other. He, himself, on the trail? It was ridiculous. He had created too many books not to know of what fiction was made. In books, most often, you knew the end result, the solution, and you tried, as credibly as possible, to manipulate your characters toward it. But this was awful life, where the end result, the solution, was unknown, and therefore the hero character, taking up the gauntlet, had to go forth aimlessly in a maze, toward a destination that had no existence and toward a climax that could not be predicted. If he were writing—and an old nostalgia for that happy hideout enclosed him—how simple it would be. His writer's mind revolved and wrote: a strange polar city blanketed in snow, a beautiful girl in hidden custody, a bizarre ransom note, two ideologies at war over the payment, and the attractive young man in the trench coat, treading his way through lonely foreign streets where dangers lurked, but always drawing nearer, as clue gave him clue, as—hell, and to hell with it!

He broke off the contrived fantasy and tried to think harder. There was no knowledge of international intrigue—euphemism for plain filthy blackmail —in the true experience of his life. Except for his reading of documented books, and hearing of occasional Communist fanatics, like the one Lilly's Hungarian, Nicholas Daranyi, had told him about—what was the name? Enbom, yes, Enbom, the Swede with Communist sympathies who had sold secrets to the Russians—except for such true . . .

Suddenly Craig stiffened. His mind leaped to one sound possibility. Daranyi, Nicholas Daranyi.

Craig tried to recollect what had brought him to Daranyi. A self-con-

confessed free-lance spy, yes, but that was as much foolishness as fiction. It was something else altogether that excited him now. It was something that Daranyi had once said of himself, and something, their last time, that Lilly had said of Daranyi. He racked his brain, and cursed himself for not having been a better listener. Daranyi had worked, was working—which?—for a Nobel committee judge—to investigate all the present laureates. He had hardly paid attention to it at the time, but now, in review, it had a foul smell. Had he himself been spied upon? And Stratman? Had someone been interested in Stratman for any reason—perhaps for the reasons that had been erased on the tape? Farfetched, and yet—Daranyi was a possibility. Even if he knew nothing of this matter, he, more than anyone, would likely know what to do about it. Suddenly, for the first time, Craig took Daranyi seriously.

He heard the clock, and he realized, painfully, that time was running out. He had less than an hour and three-quarters to act on his own. But now, for the first time, he had need to define his mission: to act on his own, yes, laudable—but to act how? And to what end? What was he after? He must reach Emily and Walther, of course. That was the goal. He must ascertain that Emily was alive and safe. He must look upon Walther with his own eyes and know that this sudden visitor was, indeed, Emily's father. If he was not her father, the cruel hoax needed to be exposed. If the tape was true, and Walther true—and Craig had little doubt about this—then Craig must reason and plead with Walther to withdraw from this drama and end the impossible dilemma.

Momentarily oblivious to his surroundings, Craig became aware that he had found the real motive for personal action. He reasoned the motive further; Walther, father, had come back into Emily's life as Walther, stranger. The accident of blood did not necessarily establish the sire. Rather, closeness and love and responsibility and sacrifice made the sire. By this standard, Max Stratman, not Walther Stratman, was Emily's male parent. If Max were snatched from her now, she would be condemned to life servitude with an utter stranger. Since she would not have Craig, and could not have Max, she would have no one but herself—and this self could not survive alone. For Emily, this emptiness would be the deeper death before dying.

Standing in the entry hall, thinking, Craig was vaguely dissatisfied and wanted to rationalize this action further. There was also, he told himself, the matter of the greater good: Walther was an unknown quantity, whereas the free world needed Max, dared not lose him. Ergo: reject Walther to save Max and Emily. Ergo: find Walther, and convince him that he should go back voluntarily to where he came from. If Walther truly loved Emily—more, if he was concerned with the future freedom of mankind—he would be persuaded.

But the pretentiousness and unfairness of this determination nagged at Craig. He tried to dismiss it, yet it was there, persistently begging a hearing. Reluctantly, Craig gave the defense its kangaroo hearing. Yes, in an ancient time, Walther had played Sydney Carton to his brother Max's Charles Darnay. Yes, Walther had suffered a long slavery under a system he abhorred, and deserved parole at any cost. Yes, Walther should be freed to enjoy his last years. That was justice. Nevertheless, for once, Craig looked upon justice as the baser choice. His emotions clung to the original impulse: go back, Walther.

Craig's quest was now clear. If he failed in it—failed to find Walther or, finding him, failed to convince him—there would be time enough to return to Max without imperiling Eckart's deal. The consequences of failure were automatic. He would have to return to this room and tell Max Stratman the truth and let him do what would have to be done. Max Stratman would offer himself to the exchange at once. He would offer himself because of brother love and Emily love and, most compelling of all, because of the old swollen guilt. He would do so, without second thought, if Craig returned helpless in an hour and three-quarters, and he would do so this moment, if Craig marched into his bedroom and woke him with Eckart's news. But not yet. Craig's passionate need for Emily, for her safety and her peace of mind and what he now knew was right for her, shook him. He was animated into action.

Pocketing the anonymous typewritten note, he hid the miniature tape recorder in the entry hall closet. Then, taking his pen, he added a thoughtful postscript to Max Stratman's note left for his niece: "Have taken Emily out on the town. We'll meet you at Concert Hall. Best, Craig." Now he lifted the receiver of the telephone and spoke to the operator. Did she have a number for one Nicholas Daranyi? He waited restlessly, and then the operator reported that there was no listing of any Daranyi in Stockholm.

Craig hung up, and promptly his mind went to Lilly. At this hour, she would be in the Nordiska Kompaniet. He would find her, and through her find Daranyi. It was the best that he could do, he told himself helplessly.

Swiftly, he strode out of the Stratman suite, hastened through the corridor, and rode the elevator down to the lobby.

The lobby was, as ever, crowded. Craig pushed through the circle of people trying to enter the elevator, jostled against the Marceaus, with no time to murmur a civil apology, and started toward the stairs leading to the revolving door and the outside.

As he reached the topmost step, he thought that he heard his name. He turned, and heard the stentorian voice again. "Craig!"

It was Gunnar Gottling, in his eccentric fur cap and mangy coat, his bloodshot eyes and drooping bushes of mustache, not this time hiding his outgoing affection, tramping toward Craig. "You old son of a bitch," he was bellowing, "I was just ringing your room. I wanted to tell you I reread all those crappy books of yours the last couple days and—"

Craig cut in. "Gottling, I've got no time for tea talk today. There's trouble, and I—"

"What trouble you in?" Gottling's face and manner had taken on the protective ferocity of a giant grizzly bear—*U. horribilis*—and there was no avoiding him. "You look pale as a specter, and you look sore as hell. What's eating you? Tell Gottling."

Craig became aware that Gottling's voice carried, and many eyes were on them. He lowered his own voice. "I'm not in trouble. Someone else is—and it's a matter of life and death—so—"

He started to go, when Gottling clamped his arm. "I am here to help, Craig. What can I do?"

Craig had started to say to Gottling that there was nothing he or anyone could do, and then, at once, he realized that Gottling could be of help. This was his city, this Stockholm, and he was a part of the best and the worst of it, and he was fearless. The question was his dependability.

"How much can I trust you?" asked Craig.

"Cut that crap," said Gottling angrily. "I won't fall in front of any trains for you—but I'll go damn far. What's your trouble? Abortion, blackmail, somebody's arm you want to break? Just say it. Since that night in the Wärdshus, I got to thinking—that tall drink of water isn't such a bad—"

"Have you got your car with you?"

"You bet your ass."

"I've got some mighty important calls to make, and I haven't got much time."

"Hop in," said Gottling.

And he thundered down the stairs after Craig, and through the spinning door behind him, and then caught up and pointed off to his compact Volvo station wagon alongside the quay. Craig had forgotten his topcoat, but the last of the setting sun was still visible, and the air was only slightly chilled.

They trudged through the low-packed snow, and Craig began to speak of what had happened and was happening in a sort of oral shorthand. With brevity, he filled Gottling in on his relationship with Emily Stratman.

Once inside the station wagon, Gottling looked at him questioningly.

"Just a few blocks for the first stop," said Craig. "Nordiska Kompaniet."

Gottling started the car, and crouched over the wheel in his nearsighted way, as Craig picked up his story. He related all he knew of Emily's tardiness which became absence, of his visit to her room, the typewritten sheet, and then he recited what he had heard on the miniature tape machine, feeling better to know that another shared the facts, should anything happen to him.

When he had finished, Gottling belched across the wheel, and cursed classically. "Those friggin' Commies," he said.

"We don't know—"

"The hell we don't," said Gottling. "Who wants the old man in East Berlin, anyway? Those little Prussky puppets? They're go-betweens. It's the big boys who want Stratman on their side. Goddammit, Craig, don't you ever read the papers any more? Every other week some fag Englishman or little American with goggles turns up in Moscow and says peace it's wonderful, and hands them a briefcase of discoveries. Do you think all the defectors do it just for love and money? Well, maybe most, because their heads are screwed on backwards, but dollars to doughnuts, every tenth man is blackmailed into crossing the line—they're holding a relative or somebody—and the poor bastard scientist or diplomat—what can he do?" They were on Hamngatan, and he swung the Volvo to the curb. "Here's your N.K. What gives here?"

Craig opened the door. Then, one foot still on the floorboard, and the other on the curb, he explained, in rapid-fire sentences, about Lilly Hedqvist and Nicholas Daranyi and himself.

"I know Daranyi," said Gottling. "Always nosing around for gossip. I'm one of the decadent little bastard's pet sources. I do it to let off steam. He knows it. But I like him. I like rabbits."

"Do you think I'm crazy to gamble Walther's freedom—maybe even Emily's life—on a longshot? Should I go to the police?"

"Police? Ha! Those crooks. For all we know, they pulled the job. Naw, play it like a one-man team, Craig, a decathlon entry—all by your lonesome and no bumbleheads with billy clubs. Go in and see that broad of yours, and find out where the slob Daranyi lives—I wish I knew, but I don't. Now, take off, and I'll keep my engine revved up."

Craig pushed through a glass entrance door, and once inside the cavern of the crowded store, he tried to take his bearings. His eyes fell on the information booth to his left, and he fought through the swarm of shoppers to the pert Swedish girl in the booth. It was imperative that he see one of the clerks, Miss Lilly Hedqvist, in ladies' wear, he pleaded. There had been an emergency in her family. The pert girl rang a bell. A slender young boy came on the run. There was an exchange in Swedish. The boy was gone. Craig was asked to wait. Ignoring the shoppers with bundles, who came and went before him, he waited, and he worried about Emily.

It was several minutes before Lilly arrived, blue eyes opened wide with concern. Craig drew her aside, to a corner near the doors.

"Lilly, I haven't much time. Emily Stratman is in trouble—"

"Trouble? In what trouble? I do not understand."

"I won't go into it now, but we're trying to stay away from the police to protect her and her father. It's all tied up with her uncle being here for the Nobel awards, and I remembered something—you told me Daranyi was investigating the Nobel laureates—"

"It is true."

"Where do I find Daranyi?"

"He should be home. I will take you there."

"I haven't got time. Just tell me—"

"No, it is better I take you. One minute. I will inform the manager my mother is very ill. Wait outside."

Craig went outside, shivered as the breeze nipped at him, signaled Gottling to wait, and then himself stalked back and forth before the wide entrance of Nordiska Kompaniet. Lilly had said one minute, and it was literally one minute later that she burst out of the store, tugging on a bright plaid coat.

Craig hustled her into the rear of the station wagon, and himself swung into the front seat beside Gottling, who had, as he had promised, kept his motor running. Craig blurted his introduction, and Gottling's dissipated face bore an expression of appreciation for Craig's taste.

"Tell him where to go, Lilly," said Craig.

She spoke in Swedish, Gottling nodding, and all Craig could make of it was Mårten Trotzig's Lane and Västerlånggatan. Gottling shifted, viewing the oncoming traffic through his rear mirror, and jolted the Volvo into a sudden skidding U turn. Now he straightened the car, and retraced their original course, heading toward the Strommen canal, and then over the bridge toward the looming Royal Palace and the Old Town.

Once, Gottling said in English, "I always thought Daranyi lived on handouts. He must be loaded to live in the Old Town."

"He is honest and works hard," said Lilly, defensively.

"I'm not criticizing, young lady, I'm envying," said Gottling. He glanced at Craig. "No use brooding, my friend. You're doing all you can. Don't try to outguess fate. That's the recipe for ulcers. Let's see what old Daranyi has to say."

Gottling now addressed himself to Lilly in Swedish as they drove on, and Craig lapsed deeply into himself. He was sickened with fear for Emily and Walther. Actually, less so for Walther, whom he had never seen, who had no existence in his memory, who was a wraith. It came down to Emily, actually. He tried to visualize her, her glossy dark hair and green eyes and virginal bearing, and he remembered how she shrank from men and violence. And now, despite Eckart's reassurances, the apprehension of where she was, who was with her, what was at stake, corroded Craig's insides like a bitter acid.

Gottling bumped his Volvo recklessly, twisting and turning through the crooked streets of the Old Town, and from the window Craig caught a name on a street sign that whisked past, and it was Västerlånggatan.

Lilly had moved forward to the edge of the back seat, and now her hand, pointing ahead like an aimed arrow, came between Craig and Gottling.

"It is there," she said, "right there past the lane where"—and then she caught her breath—"where the ambulance is parked."

Craig peered through the windshield. There was an ambulance—at first he had thought it a truck—against the sidewalk, and several dozen curious spectators, young and old, gathered around it in respectful attendance.

Gottling swerved to the curb across from Mårten Trotzig's Lane, braked, and the motor died.

"What has happened?" Lilly cried. "Do you think something has happened?"

The three of them were instantly out of the car and across the street, with Lilly running ahead to the ambulance. When Craig caught up to her, she was still conversing in an indistinct hum of Swedish with the white-coated driver and his assistant, who were leaning against the fender, smoking. A throng of spectators had pressed closer to Lilly and the ambulance men, to catch what they could of the talk.

Craig shoved his way roughly through the wall of people and was at Lilly's side. "Lilly—what is the matter?"

She was frantic. "It is terrible, Mr. Craig. I was always afraid this would happen. Daranyi has been stabbed many times, and he is inside, and the physician is with him."

"How did it happen?"

"Oh—they do not know."

"Is it very serious?"

"Come, quick, we must go inside."

Lilly took Craig's hand, and the crowd parted. As they hurried into the apartment building, Gottling called to them that he would wait. Craig waved gratefully, and stayed with Lilly.

Inside Daranyi's living room, so bachelor-neat and Middle European, Craig found four or five people seated in repose. They were mostly elderly, and obviously neighbors who were Daranyi's friends, and who had come to hear the worst. Lilly was addressing one squat old lady now—a shopkeeper, it turned out—and Lilly spoke in tearful Swedish, and the old lady's replies were almost inaudible.

"What is it, Lilly?"

"It is bad, Mr. Craig. He was attacked in the street—a half hour ago—and the physician is examining him now. I must see. I must find out the truth— poor Daranyi—"

She left Craig and went to the bedroom door, turning the handle gently, and then easing herself inside.

A voice from behind was directed at Craig. "Hiya, Mr. Craig." He spun about, and seated on a brown leather chair was Sue Wiley. "What are you doing here?" she asked.

"What are *you* doing here?"

"I'm dying by inches, I'm a wreck," she said, eyes blinking, hands fluttering. "Can you imagine such a thing? You want the morbid details?"

Craig pulled a chair toward her and sat sideways in it. "I didn't know you knew Nicholas Daranyi."

"We had a transaction," said Sue Wiley. "Never mind about that. Let's say we were both in the business of information, and we found each other. Anyway, I got to thinking about the Ceremony this afternoon, and I figured I could use some more dope on it—past performances, such—and since Daranyi is a historian—"

"Historian?"

She stared at Craig. "Isn't he?"

"Yes, I suppose so. What happened?"

"I decided to drop in on him for an interview a little while ago, before getting back to change for the Main Event. I took a taxi here, and kept it, and pounded on his door, but no one was home. So I started to leave, and just as I got outside—I happened to look off—and there he was, coming along the sidewalk. I started to call out to him, but before I could open my mouth— whambo!"

"Meaning?"

"Meaning two hoodlums pounced on him—in broad daylight, mind you— I guess they were hiding in that skinny little lane. They came out, one in front of him and one behind—and the bigger one in front clamped a hand over Daranyi's mouth, and the other one behind lifted a blade—some kind

556

of knife or dagger—and began punching it into Daranyi. Well—boy, oh boy —I stood on that sidewalk absolutely petrified. And then I started to yell, to scream bloody murder—and the hoodlums froze the way I'd been frozen— and then they just broke away and ran like crazy. And that little Hungarian, he flopped down in the street like a dead whale. Well, everybody was in the street by then, and my cabbie was calling the cops."

Craig asked himself: why Daranyi? Was this in some way a part of Eckart's intrigue? He was on the right trail, he felt, and then, sagging inside, he realized that he might be too late. "Did you recognize either of them?"

"No. Looked like a couple of delinquents, far as I could see. Wore those fat knit jazzed-up sweaters—one was turtleneck—I already told the police all I could see. The hawkshaws are checking the alley or lane or whatever for clues. So anyway, here I am—Sue Wiley, Ace Witness."

"Are you hanging around for a story?"

"What story? A down-at-the-heels historian gets mugged by a couple of kids who want his gold watch? Nuts. I've got to get out of here—this is the day—but those cops want me to wait a while. I'm sure sorry for the Hungarian. Hope he doesn't die. Sa-ay, Mr. Craig, you're a cute one, aren't you? I'm the interviewer, and you've got me doing all the talking. Who was that blond number you were holding hands with?"

"Daughter of friends of mine in Wisconsin," said Craig. "I met Daranyi briefly, through her."

"Likely story."

"That's right," said Craig, "likely story."

The bedroom door had opened without anyone's emerging as yet, but Craig was on his feet immediately. The doctor, prematurely gray and urbane, carrying his identity badge of a black bag, came out of the room, still speaking in Swedish to Lilly who followed him. As he spoke, Lilly hung on his every word, and then abruptly he broke away and went out the entrance door. Lilly's hand beckoned to Craig.

He joined her.

"They are going to bring the stretcher now," said Lilly. "You are permitted to have one minute with Daranyi."

"How is he?" Craig asked with concern.

"He will be all right. He was stabbed three times, but the physician says they are only flesh wounds, not so deep because Daranyi was wriggling and squirming when they tried to kill him. There may be minor surgery. I do not know."

She went back into the bedroom with Craig behind her, closing the door to shield them from Sue Wiley.

There was a fine old brass bed, worn but polished, and on the bed a mound of blanket, and this was Nicholas Daranyi. He was lying on his stomach, his arms up on the pillow and his head sideways within his arms, so that his face pointed toward Craig. His dazed eyes, with their sedated pupils, were on his visitors.

Quickly, Craig took the chair beside Daranyi.

Lilly knelt on the floor below the bed. Anxiously, she said to Craig, "Do not waste words. Even though it is not so serious, he is weak and in pain. Go to the point. I have already told him of Emily being with her father, and what is wanted of Professor Stratman. I am not sure Daranyi understood everything, but—"

Daranyi made a sound, from his pillow, halfway between protestation and groaning. "Lil-ly—I understand."

"He knows all about it, then," Lilly said to Craig excitedly.

Craig leaned toward the pained face on the pillow. "Daranyi, you can hear me—I have only an hour—a man named Eckart has Max Stratman's brother here. He—the brother—was supposed to have been killed long ago by the Russians, but he's alive—been brought here—somewhere in this city—in order to make Professor—"

"I—understand."

"Have you ever heard the name Hans Eckart?"

"Yes," Daranyi answered immediately, almost professionally. "A German physicist, East Berlin. He lunched with Professor Stratman on December fifth."

"Anything more?"

"No—nothing."

"Daranyi, once you told me that you had an assignment from someone connected with the Nobel Prize awards. And Lilly has told me you were supposed to dig up inside stuff on those of us who are laureates."

Daranyi closed his eyes and grunted into the pillows. "Yes. I had that assignment." His eyes remained closed, and the mound of blanket shuddered in a slight spasm of distress.

Immediately, Lilly reached out to touch him. "You are suffering too much. You have said enough. You must not—"

Daranyi's lids opened and his eyes were alert and angry. "Quiet, Lilly. Can I not have a gas pain like ordinary mortals!" He focused on Craig. "I have said little, but I am going to say much. Craig, these wounds of the flesh are nothing. The real injury that has occurred is to my professional pride. I have done this work for years. This you know. Always, I have been treated with dignity, with respect, like any competent workman should be. But this time I have been insulted—insulted. To have taken on this most difficult assignment—to have done so well, delivered so much, in good faith—and to be paid not in the salary I requested but in violence. This outrageous breach I shall not forgive. If I cannot have money, I will have revenge. Craig, I pray you can extract such payment for me."

"I'd like nothing better."

"Good." Daranyi tried to lift his head, groaned, and dropped his head to the pillow once more. He sucked his breath, and then he said, "Craig—what—what was on the tape? What did Eckart say? What did the girl say? Omit no detail."

Speaking with precision and haste, Craig repeated, to the best of his memory, the threat of the tape recording. When he was through, he thought that

Daranyi had not heard him, for the man appeared to be dozing or unconscious. Suddenly Daranyi spoke. "Walther Stratman was known as Kurt Lipski all these years—is that what the voice said?"

"Exactly."

The head on the pillow moved with some private understanding. The eyes opened fully. "Yes," said Daranyi quietly, "it is all one, then. I gave them the information about Lipski, the clue that Walther Stratman was that person and still alive. They had no idea about Lipski and his interest in Miss Stratman until I dug it out and gave it to them." He winced. "And you see how they paid me for—for giving them this information." His face showed anguish. "The pain they have given me—"

Lilly grabbed Craig's arm. "Mr. Craig, he is so white. He must not go on. He will faint. Please—"

"Wait," Craig snapped, pushing her hand away. He turned back to the bed. "Daranyi, for God's sake, while you can—to whom did you give this information? Whoever it was, that is the person at the bottom of it, the person responsible for bringing Walther here. Tell me *who?*"

Daranyi had vengeful strength for this. "Dr. Carl—Adolf—Krantz. He assigned—accepted—the information—paid me—this way. . . . I gave him the photostats—about—Emily Stratman—and—and—Ravensbruck—and about—the inquiries—from Lipski—from Russia and now—" The breathing from the pillow was heavier. "He—Krantz—Krantz—is—the—one—to—find—he—"

But the voice drifted off, as the lids folded over the eyes.

"Daranyi," pleaded Craig.

Lilly was touching Craig's arm. "You have what you want."

"Yes, but—"

The door had opened behind him, and the two stretcher bearers came in with the doctor.

"—I had just wanted to ask him," finished Craig lamely, "what he meant by Ravensbruck."

As Craig rose and backed off, the doctor replaced him and looked down at Daranyi. "The patient is unconscious," he said to no one in particular. "We must move him to the hospital. Do not be worried. The injuries are superficial." He considered Craig curiously. "You learned what you wanted from him?"

"I think so," said Craig. "Yes, I have what I want." Lost in thought, trying to fit together the puzzle, Craig walked through the living room with Lilly, ignored Sue Wiley, and went into the hall.

"Krantz?" said Lilly in an undertone.

Craig nodded. "Krantz."

"I must remain with Daranyi," she said. "You must find Krantz and Emily. Do not take bad chances—the police—"

Craig took Lilly's hands. "When you know about Daranyi, phone me at Concert Hall if it is before six-thirty. Otherwise—"

"You will hear from me, Mr. Craig."

Craig nodded, and hurried outside into the darkening cold. The spectators were still there, wondering, and the ambulance, waiting, its rear doors flung open, and across the street he could distinguish Gunnar Gottling behind the wheel of the station wagon.

When he slid in beside Gottling, he said, "I think we've got our man."

"Name him."

"Carl Adolf Krantz."

Even Gottling, whose features were too arrogant to concede surprise at any time, showed astonishment. "Krantz? I always knew that little rat was pro-German and anti the human race, but I always thought he was too proud of his position—a judge on two Nobel committees—to sink to this. So it's Krantz? Are you sure?"

"Daranyi was positive. Krantz hired him to do some espionage on the Nobel laureates—apparently Professor Stratman and Emily were the real targets—in order to get something on the Stratmans and force the Professor to come over to the other side. Daranyi dug up some information no one else but Krantz knew or could use—and the key part of that information was on the tape."

"I'll be goddamned, then it's true," said Gottling. "But I'll bet my britches it isn't Krantz alone. He's gutless. If a poodle barks, he goes up a tree. I called him a rat. That's too princely. He's a weasel, really. There must be others."

Craig chafed irritably. "I'm not interested in nit-picking. I don't care who in the hell is responsible. I just want to find Emily and her father. Daranyi says Krantz, so Krantz it is."

"Simmer down, pal. What time you got?"

"Ten after four."

"We'd better shake the lead out of our asses then. If I remember, everyone leaves for Concert Hall in ten or fifteen minutes." He started the station wagon. "Krantz is probably still in his apartment, getting ready to leave."

"Do you know where he lives?"

"Ha, who in Stockholm doesn't? It was the only balcony in the city, during the war, that was draped with a swastika!"

Gottling had said ten or fifteen minutes, but now he accelerated the Volvo through the Old Town, wheeling and careening, as if there were only one minute to make St. Peter's gate. They passed gay, open Christmas stalls and the municipal Christmas tree on Stortorget. They sped over the illuminated bridge, twisting away along the canal, and because Craig was still not used to the left-hand drive, with oncoming traffic approaching from the right, he had a mounting fear that he would never survive to see Krantz—or Emily.

There had been a sharp turning, and an attractive street stretched westward between the Mälaren canal and rows of expensive apartment buildings, the string of small cars parked before them shining under the high streetlights.

"Norr Mälarstrand," said Gottling.

As they drew nearer to their destination, Gottling slowed the progress of his station wagon, head ducked low, squinting past Craig and out the right-hand window, hunting for Krantz's apartment.

Craig's mind had gone to the Nobel judge they were seeking. Since his arrival in Stockholm, he had not seen much of Krantz. The Swedish physicist had been assigned to the Marceaus, Garrett, Farelli, Stratman, and Ingrid Påhl and Jacobsson had been assigned to the literary laureate. Nevertheless, Craig had a distinct image of Krantz—an ugly, stunted man with a hog's snout and a scrub mustache and goatee, and a repugnant personality. Craig had no specific plan of action in mind for when he came face to face with the vicious, misshapen hippogriff, but the rage in him was bursting now, and he knew that he would kill Krantz if necessary, to extract some word of Emily and Walther Stratman's whereabouts.

"We've caught him just in time," he heard Gottling mutter.

"Where?"

"The fifth apartment down. There's the rented limousine parked in front."

They had slowed to a crawl as they approached the limousine, and through the Volvo windshield Craig could see a portly figure in chauffeur's cap and uniform in the brighter area under the streetlight, gloved hands clasped behind, waiting for Krantz.

"You park," said Craig tightly, opening his door. "I'll grab Krantz."

"If you need help—"

"I won't need help," Craig called back.

He crossed the street, squeezed between bumpers of two parked cars, attained the sidewalk, and going fast, and then running, he approached the entrance of the orange apartment building, its shadowed balconies jutting above like military pillboxes.

At the entrance he slowed, became aware that the chauffeur was eying him inquisitively and with apprehension, as you observe anyone who is running in the night.

Craig stopped, and looked at the chauffeur. "Are you waiting for Dr. Krantz?"

The chauffeur came to loose attention. "Yes, sir."

"I must see him first. Which apartment?"

"Fourth floor, sir."

Inhaling deeply, Craig went inside. The modern elevator was at floor level. Taking it to the fourth floor, Craig tried to contain his impatience and temper, tried to rehearse an approach. Before he could do so, the elevator had whirred to a halt.

Almost blindly, Craig found himself at the apartment door, jamming his thumb at the buzzer, then rapping imperatively. In immediate response, the door was flung open. Between Craig and the one he must see, firmly planted, stood an annoyed housekeeper. Her width filled the doorway, and the hair on her upper lip momentarily distracted Craig.

"Yes?" she was demanding, crossly.

"I must see Dr. Krantz immediately."

She shook her head. "No—impossible. He is leaving for—"

"I've got to see him!" Craig bullied his way past her, ignoring an out-stretched arm, and entered the vestibule.

She snatched at his sleeve. "No—who are you?"

Roughly, Craig freed himself, trying to find the right door. "Where is he?"

"No—!" Nervously, she shouted off. "Dr. Krantz! Dr. Krantz! Please—!"

There were footsteps to Craig's left, and Krantz's harsh voice loud, "What the devil—what the devil—what is all the racket, Ilsa?"

He materialized, combatively, in the vestibule. For a moment, Craig was taken aback by his appearance, so ludicrous and pompous in silk top hat and formal overcoat with velvet lapels. Could this improbable figure be the spinner of plots, the formidable enemy?

Approaching, Krantz halted, recognition replacing annoyance on his face. "Why—it is Mr. Craig. What are you doing here? You should be at Concert Hall—"

"Never mind Concert Hall. We're going to have a little private talk first."

Craig's tone, the tremulous anger of it, seemed to surprise Krantz. Affability fought concern. He stood very still and when he spoke, it was past Craig. "That will be all, Ilsa."

The peasant woman brushed alongside Craig, with a shove of her body against his to display her displeasure at the rude intrusion, and then she disappeared into the maw of the apartment.

Krantz gestured off. "We will talk in the parlor. I have only a moment —my chauffeur—"

Craig had already gone into the room, to the center, and turned about to meet his host. His initial desire had been to seize Krantz by those velvet lapels and shake the information out of him. But somehow, the atmosphere of the homely old family room, the used squat mahogany pieces, the lace doilies (above all, the doilies), curbed violence. This was a man's home, and he the disturber of peace, and then, seeing Krantz come tentatively to-ward him, his mission became more real and his anger rose again.

Krantz offered no seat, and took none himself, as if to make it clear that the meeting was unwelcome and would be brief.

"You appear agitated, Mr. Craig. Is there anything—?"

"You're damn right," said Craig. "I'm here to tell you you're a son of a bitch and a blackmailer—and I've found you out."

The word assault hit Krantz like a physical blow. He stepped backwards, his tiny eyes terrified and his mustache and goatee opening and closing, and his top hat began to slide off his greased hair. Despite shock, he stayed his hat and tried to maintain dignity.

"Mr. Craig, I do not understand. What language is this to use—"

"I said you're a blackmailer, and you've been found out. There are no words for what I think of you—nothing low and filthy enough."

Krantz fought for poise, but his mustache and goatee still jumped. He had difficulty finding his voice. "What is this, Mr. Craig? A crude American joke? Are you drunk? I should have known this might happen—everyone knows about your drinking. I will not have such language under my roof."

562

Craig moved toward him, the muscles of his forearms prepared to lash out. "You're lucky I'm only using words—I should kill you!"

Krantz was in retreat against the wall. "Do not touch me! Go—or I will call Ilsa—I will call the police!"

"We'll both call the police," said Craig, restraining himself, "unless you tell me where you've got Emily and Walther Stratman."

A gush of air went out of Krantz, and he was smaller and very afraid. "You are ranting. What are you talking about?"

"I'm talking about the Stratmans, and what you've done to them, and you know it. It's all in the open, you bungler. It's all out. I intercepted the taped message you sent to Professor Stratman. I heard the whole rotten deal—how you exhumed Emily's father and brought him here, how you're holding him with Emily until you get your hands on Professor Stratman, and escort him behind the Curtain—"

"Fairy tales!" shrieked Krantz. "Crazy fairy tales! You are drunk! Where do you find such lies?"

"From your friend Eckart on the taped message, for one thing."

"Prove it. Show me this tape."

For the first time, Craig felt closer to truth. "Yes, Krantz, we both know I can't show you the tape. But I don't need it, you see. I have better evidence. I have Nicholas Daranyi."

Krantz straightened against the wall, and made a pretense of relief. "So that is it. You have been listening to that Hungarian simpleton. Well, you listen to me—"

Craig shook his head. "No, Krantz, you listen to me. This minute, Daranyi is on his way to the hospital. Instead of paying him, you sent some roughnecks to knife him. But you made one mistake. You counted on their killing him."

Krantz stood speechless, palms flattening against the wall behind him for support. His facial features revealed dumbfounded amazement at the news. "They—they tried to kill Daranyi?"

"In the street before his apartment. With knives. He's going into surgery. But the wounds are superficial. He'll live. He'll have much to say."

Krantz's disbelief was entire. "They attacked Daranyi? I cannot—I cannot believe it."

"You don't have to believe it, Krantz. You can see for yourself. Do you want to come along to the hospital and see for yourself? Then you and Daranyi can hold a joint conference with the authorities—"

Craig stopped. More was not necessary, he could see. It was as if Krantz had just swallowed Dr. Henry Jekyll's mixture of white powders and red liquid. The transformation on his face—from indignation and defiance to abdication and defeat—was immediate. "No, wait," he was saying, his voice a high whine. "You do not understand—I had nothing to do with Daranyi—the violence. I did not dream they would go to such lengths—it is terrible." Swiftly, he discarded old comrades for a better ally. "I had nothing to do with any of this—you must believe me!"

"I believe only one thing. Emily and Walther Stratman are stuck away some place—and Walther will be freed on the condition that Professor Stratman defects—and Daranyi says you're responsible."

"It's not true—mixing me in so deep. Daranyi knows only half of it. I would never go so far."

"You've gone far enough. You're smack in the middle."

"No—no." He wrung his hands, staring at Craig's feet, exhorting, explaining, cajoling in the cause of self-preservation. "Craig, have some leniency —know the circumstances. I would have had no part of this, if I had known they would resort to—" He lifted his obsequious eyes. "You must have compassion—try to know what happened to me."

Craig grimly waited.

Krantz went on quickly, a last plea to the jury. "I was *persona non grata* after the war, because I favored the losing side—you must always be with the winner here—and they passed me over for all the university jobs that I deserved—passed me over—me, their most valuable physicist, with so many honors, with my Nobel positions. Then Eckart came, in my blackest hour, and offered me—"

"I've heard Eckart. Tell me who he is."

"The one who engineered all this—the one who is a director of Humboldt University in East Berlin. He knew of my good work—and unfair persecution —and he offered me a brilliant post—but wanted a favor first. He said he would like to meet Stratman in Stockholm, get him away from the West for a week in Stockholm, in a neutral atmosphere, to offer him a job. By my influence, I helped Stratman win the award, to come here, and I brought him together with Eckart. But Stratman would have nothing to do with Germans or Communists. So Eckart dangled the post before me like bait, pulled me in deeper and deeper with harmless, small demands. He made me hire Daranyi to ferret out private information on Stratman and his niece. I never imagined how this information would be used. Only this morning did I have an inkling—but it was impossible—I would not permit myself to believe it."

"What happened this morning?"

"Dr. Eckart telephoned. He told me that, through the information I had gotten out of Daranyi, he had deduced Stratman's brother was alive in Russia. He had persuaded the Russians to send the brother here as an object to be traded for Stratman. I was upset. I had not known Eckart would use the information for such purpose. He had wanted it, he always pretended, as a civilized means of breaking down Stratman's resistance. I had no idea he would use it for blackmail. But there it was. So when Eckart asked me to get hold of Stratman and bring him to meet his brother, I refused to cooperate. I told him my standing was such, I could not endanger it by going further, not to such limits. I must say Eckart was reasonable. He said he would locate Stratman himself. Later, in person, he informed me that, to save time, he had found Emily instead and brought her to see her father. He introduced me to Walther. He said something of the tape. This I assure you, Craig—and there is no need for me to lie now—he promised me there would be no violence to the niece or Stratman or anyone involved. But Daranyi—the attempt to kill poor Daranyi—I swear I knew nothing of that until minutes ago when you told me. That is too much. It is not worth the contract for the university post. I was to go to the boat again tonight and sign—but not now, no."

Craig had been observing Krantz closely, to interpret his degree of sincerity, and now, much as he detested the cringing gnome, he believed him.

"The boat," said Craig. "Is that where they all are—on some boat in the canal?"

"Yes. Not all. Eckart is in the city with—with friends—to watch the television for Stratman's announcement of his defection, and to meet with Stratman after the Ceremony for the exchange."

"But Emily and Walther?"

"They are on the boat. It is guarded, of course."

Craig felt flushed at the nearness of his goal. He pressed harder. "Tell me where the boat is."

Krantz's pinhole eyes projected fear. He hesitated. "Why?" he asked.

"So I can inform the security police. They'll surround the boat, and we'll have Walther without any trade or—"

"No!" Krantz interrupted. "No—I cannot, Craig—not the police. It would be in the open—a scandal. It would be the end of me."

"If you don't tell me, it'll be the end of you anyway."

"I do not care. I will take my chance. My word against Daranyi's—but the police, no."

Craig's instinct about the human animal told him, at once, that even a beast at bay can be pushed only so far. He had gone the limit with Krantz, and he must take advantage of him within that boundary. He relented. "All right, then, not the police. You don't have to tell me where they are. But take me to them right now. So I can see that Emily is all right."

"She is all right."

"And Walther—I want to see him, speak to him, see if I can talk him out of this."

"Just that? Nothing more?"

"What more can there be? I'm alone. You say there are guards—if they'll let us through—"

Krantz nodded. "Yes, that would be no problem. But you understand, Craig, if I take you there, once you know the location, you will have to remain until late, when the exchange is effected—or perhaps the boat will be moved—so do not expect—"

"I only want a few minutes with Walther."

Krantz edged nervously from the wall. His top hat wobbled. His shrub-covered lips puckered. "And if I do this, you will not implicate me?"

Craig studied the crafty, servile thing with distaste. "I won't make any promises. I'll say simply that if you refuse, I'll take you to the authorities. If you direct me to the boat, well—we'll see. At least, there'll be one affirmative act in your favor."

Krantz hesitated no longer. "I shall take you."

He led Craig out of the apartment and to the elevator. On the way down, neither spoke. At the landing, as they emerged, Krantz seemed to have an afterthought. He broke the silence. "I must inquire—are you here alone?"

"No. Someone drove me. A friend."

"Dismiss him. There can be no one else. That is our bargain. The two of us."

Craig agreed at once. "Okay. But remember this. My friend may not know our destination, but if anything goes wrong, he'll know where to find you."

"Yes—yes—never mind about that."

They went through the building and outside into the cold of the Norr Mälarstrand. The portly chauffeur had opened the rear door of the limousine, and he stood beside it at attention. Craig looked off to his right, and then to the left he saw Gottling rise up out of the driver's seat of the station wagon and wave.

"One second," Craig told Krantz.

He hurried past four parked cars, and joined Gottling, waiting for him at the curb.

"What happened?" Gottling wanted to know.

"It's all settled, friend. He folded fast. He's agreed to take me where they are—but only if I'm alone."

Gottling scratched a shaggy eyebrow and squinted his bloodshot eyes in the direction of Krantz. "I don't like it, Craig," he said at last. "I don't trust that weasel."

"I've already warned him. If I'm delayed too long, you can spill the whole affair to Jacobsson."

"If you're not around to enjoy it, what fun'll it be?"

"Gottling, I'm only going somewhere to have a short talk with a nice old man, and then I'm leaving. If I get lucky, he'll be leaving too—in another direction. If I strike out, well—I'll have to tell Professor Stratman, and it'll be his turn at bat."

"Good luck with those bastards," said Gottling.

Craig started away, then stopped. "And don't get any crazy ideas about following us. You'll screw up the works."

"Do you think I'm a horse's ass? I'm going home where it's warm and where the whiskey is—and I'll be watching your empty chair on television."

Craig returned to the building entrance and found Krantz still waiting, blowing condensed air and apprehension.

"He will not follow?" Krantz demanded.

"No. You'll see for yourself."

"We must hurry. The Ceremony—"

Krantz started to enter the rear of the limousine, then withdrew, thoughtfully. He spoke to the chauffeur in Swedish. The chauffeur seemed to protest, but Krantz persisted. With a shrug, the chauffeur closed the rear door, and opened the front one.

566

"I must leave him behind," Krantz told Craig. "I will drive myself. You come in the front seat."

While Krantz got behind the wheel, Craig went around the long car, caught a glimpse of Gottling on the far curb ahead, and then he entered the limousine and sank into the deep seat. Krantz, barely able to sight over the wheel, had started the motor.

The car went around in a clumsy U turn, Krantz battling the wheel, and then the vehicle leaped forward. Ahead of them, Norr Mälarstrand stretched briefly free of traffic. Krantz jammed down the accelerator, and the limousine smoothly gained speed. Craig read the speedometer: ninety kilometers an hour. Automatically, he translated this: fifty-six miles an hour. Good, he told himself. Krantz was as anxious as he to conclude the business of the winter afternoon.

"Where are we headed?" Craig inquired.

Krantz's eyes darted at him, as if trying to detect trickery.

"Just in general," Craig added. "I wouldn't know exactly where that damn boat is anyway."

"Pålsundet," said Krantz.

"Is it far?"

"It is the section of canal across from us, between Södra bergen and Långholmen, about five or ten minutes from here, if the streets are clear—twenty minutes, maybe more, if there is heavy traffic on Västerbron—the bridge. Pålsundet is a fine part of our city. Many of the wealthiest families keep their cabin cruisers and small craft moored there."

Krantz stopped speaking and strained to feather the brake. A string of cars and a trolley loomed a block ahead, bisecting their path, crawling at snail's pace.

Krantz muttered into his goatee in Swedish. "That is our turning—we go left there over the Västerbron—and it is filled with traffic."

But by the time they reached the traffic, and Krantz imperiously took advantage of the limousine's size to force his way into it, Craig's mind had gone back to the events that had brought him to this moment.

"I'm still curious about something, Krantz," he said. "About Emily's father, Walther Stratman. He was thought to be dead. Of course, Eckart knew all the time that he was alive."

"No, that is not so," said Krantz from the wheel. "Dr. Eckart was puzzled always that Walther was missing, with no evidence of death, yet he accepted the legal verdict that he was dead. That is the way it was until yesterday."

"What happened yesterday?"

"Daranyi gave me the results of his investigation of the various laureates and their relatives. I, in turn, handed them over to Dr. Eckart. I must say, for all of his—his shortcomings—Dr. Eckart is very clever. He seized upon Miss Stratman's dossier—"

"Emily Stratman?"

"—yes, as most useful to his purposes. I repeat, I had no idea what was in his mind, certainly no belief he would do anything so diabolical. Emily Stratman's dossier contained the photostatic copy of an American army psychoanalyst's report on her. Attached to this were photostats of a curious correspondence between departments of the American military and the Russian military."

"Curious? In what way?"

"The first Russian inquiry was fairly routine. It requested to know if a Mrs. Rebecca Stratman or a Miss Emily Stratman had been found alive in any labor camp under American, British, or French jurisdiction. I say this was routine because there were many similar inquiries from the Russians to the West and vice versa. The second letter was a reply that Mrs. Rebecca Stratman had been—been sent—transferred to Auschwitz and been liquidated, and that Miss Emily Stratman had been found alive in Buchenwald and was being treated nearby. Now, there was a third letter in the dossier, a second inquiry from the Russians, specifically asking to see the reports of Miss Stratman's psychiatrist. This request was denied—as being highly personal and confidential—unless the Russians would explain who was making the request and for what reasons. Immediately, the Russians fulfilled this demand by explaining that their inquiry for the psychiatric report had come from a high medical official in the U.S.S.R., that his name was Dr. Kurt Lipski, and that his interest was personal. Upon receiving this, the American army psychiatrist had apparently gone to Emily Stratman and asked her if Dr. Kurt Lipski was a relation or friend or if she knew of him at all. She had never heard the name before, and so the Russian request for the psychiatric report was rejected. That was the final letter of the batch."

"And from this evidence Eckart decided that Lipski was Emily's father?"

"He was not certain. He had a suspicion. He reasoned, as he told me, that such interest in one specific young girl, a nonentity, could only come from a close relation. Also, this relation must be important, or the Russians would not have bothered. This tallied with Walther Stratman's relationship to Emily and his importance to the Russians. This morning, when Walther arrived, he confirmed Dr. Eckart's guess. When the Russians captured Walther in 1945, and tried to exploit his bacterial specialty, he refused to cooperate unless they helped him learn what had happened to his wife and daughter. And so, to pamper him, they undertook the correspondence that Daranyi found. In any case, once Dr. Eckart realized that Lipski might be Walther, he began to compare dates. He learned that the Lipski inquiries were made well after Walther was supposed to have been missing or died. If Lipski and Walther Stratman were one, then Dr. Eckart told himself that this person must be alive today—and, if he was alive, he would be useful as a hostage to be traded for Professor Stratman. Immediately, Eckart consulted with General Alexei Vasilkov, at the Russian Embassy here in Stockholm, and Vasilkov expedited contact with Moscow. There it was seen at once that Professor Max Stratman would be more valuable than his brother, and so the brother was flown overnight to this city."

Krantz paused, and glanced at Craig. "You see, I have told you all I know.

I want to be cooperative. You will make a mistake to associate me, in your mind, with the Russians."

"You were willing to do anything to go to East Berlin and work," said Craig dryly.

Krantz bridled. "That is Germany," he said, "the old Germany I have loved. That is not Russia."

They were midway across the Västerbron, snowbanks on either side, and the traffic began to move again, tires grinding and slithering on the slippery bridge.

"How far to go?" Craig wanted to know.

"Let me see." Krantz peered outside. "Not so far. That island right below us, on my side—Långholmen Park—and behind the hilly part is Pålsundet."

Craig felt the invisible band tighten across his chest. "Krantz, if anything has gone wrong—"

"Nothing is wrong. We are almost there."

Craig's nerves were raw with strain. He edged forward in his seat, leaning toward the dashboard, as they began to slow at the end of the bridge which ran into the intersection of Långholmsgatan and Söder Mälarstrand. The traffic signal was flickering from green to red.

They came to a full halt at the intersection, beneath Christmas lights and stars strung high above them. The headlights of home-going autos crisscrossed before them. The comfortable familiarity of the scene, cars carrying men to their families, to wives and children awaiting them in heated living rooms, with steaming food in dining rooms, enveloped Craig and heightened his sense of fantasy. Before him paraded the happy, relaxed, workaday world of ordinary living people. And here sat he, readying to meet a ghost.

"This is Pålsundet," he heard Krantz say.

"Where?"

"A block to the left."

"Where are they?"

"You will see shortly. We will park on Söder Mälarstrand."

The light had changed. Krantz drove the car forward, slowed, and then swung sharply to the left. They hugged to the outer left lane, along the quay, cruising beneath the holiday lights.

"We will put the car here," announced Krantz, easing the sleek sedan into an opening on the curb.

They quickly left the car, and Krantz preceded Craig into the unlighted recesses of a public park, empty of all life but their own, crowded with weeping willows. They crunched across the hard, snow-damp soil, into lowering darkness, as they left behind the row of apartment houses, and festive lights, and traffic.

"It is across this park and then down to the wharves," Krantz was saying. "The boat is moored—"

"Keep moving," ordered Craig.

They went on through the trees, descending and slipping often, until they reached the canal and the first wharf.

"We are near," said Krantz.

"Which boat?"

Krantz pointed to a large cabin cruiser moored to the next wharf. "There," he said. His hand shook as he pointed. "Emily and Walther Stratman are in there."

It was 4:57 in the afternoon.

Outside Concert Hall, which was ablaze with festive lighting, in the vast market place cleared of snow, several thousand Stockholmers, bundled against the weather, still stood waiting for a glimpse of late arrivals in their evening dress. There was civic pride in the air, and a spirit of lavish holiday fun, and for an hour, the mass of onlookers had been enjoying the smooth approach of Rolls-Royces, Cadillacs, Daimlers, Facel Vegas, and a dozen other foreign cars, many with Embassy and legation flags on the front fenders, and the native Saabs and Volvos, too, as they drew up before the stone steps of the auditorium, and discharged the men in formal coats and evening suits and the women in furs and long evening gowns.

A lesser crowd, but one more densely packed and contained by numerous police, had gathered at the side stage entrance on Oxtorgsgatan, where an illuminated "14" projected above the arched door. Through this door, the King and royal entourage had passed to cheers and applause, and through this the new laureates, and the old, and the members of the prize-giving academies had also passed. A sign outside read TYSTNAD!—which meant silence, but which one and all knew was observed on only minor days when concerts and symphonies were given, while for tonight there was no silence but a mass extroversion of pleasure.

The side entrance led, through a bewildering warren of passages and staircases, to the roomy backstage area of Concert Hall. There now the participants in the final Ceremony had assembled, and were being hastily formed into lines by Count Bertil Jacobsson—the representatives of the Nobel committees to the left, the laureates and former laureates to the right.

Jacobsson bustled among the laureates, directing and advising, setting each in his position, according to protocol.

He had reached Denise and Claude Marceau, to remind them of their seating, but they were absorbed in conversation, Denise's features earnest, Claude's contrite. Denise was saying, "*Oui,* I have your word about this one— but what about the next one? Will I ever be able to trust—" And Claude interrupted to divert her to their laboratory work that lay ahead. He was speaking of protein and glucose molecules when Jacobsson, embarrassed, backed off, and moved up the line.

He saw that Carlo Farelli and John Garrett were engaged in an animated colloquy. He wondered if he should disturb them, but before he could decide, he felt a hand on his elbow. Jacobsson turned to find Professor Max Stratman staring worriedly at him.

Jacobsson followed the physics laureate off to one side. "Count," Stratman

570

was saying, "I have a concern. I have not seen my niece since this morning."

"Surely, she is in the audience."

"No, I think not. I had a note this afternoon from Mr. Craig that he was taking her out—where I do not know—and that they would meet us here for the Ceremony. But where is Mr. Craig?"

"Why, I—" Jacobsson cast about. He had not counted noses. He had assumed that all were present. But now, he could not find Craig. "He must be somewhere around."

"I have not seen him, Count."

"He will be here, of that you may be certain." Yet now Jacobsson was worried, too.

Before he could make further inquiries, the trumpets began sounding from beyond the partition.

Jacobsson was cued into feverish activity. He clapped his hands for attention. "Everyone, hear me! In your places—the trumpets—the King is entering—we will follow."

In the gigantic auditorium of Concert Hall, like the building of a tidal wave, the 2,100 members of the audience, in the rear and side balconies above, in the rectangular first floor below, rose from their red-felt seats to honor the monarch of Sweden. The uniformed soldier and sailor were finishing their trumpet fanfare, and now they lowered their instruments and stood to attention.

The Royal March, and the pomp and pageantry, began.

One of the ten entry doors to the auditorium opened, and past a white pillar came the King from his private parlor, followed closely by the members of the royal family and palace household. The King took his place in the first orchestra row, off the center aisle, facing the flower-bedecked stage with its lectern and microphones, its four rows of empty chairs, its flags bowed forward from poles between the four alcoves of classical statuary. The moment that the King sat, and his entourage settled into their seats, the 2,100 members of the audience also sat.

Immediately, the center doors upstage swung wide, to the blast of trumpets, and through them, two by two, Nobel committeemen side by side with laureates paraded down to the platform. As the march swelled, committeemen taking chairs on one side, laureates on the other, the King rose to his feet—the rare occasion on which he stood first before his subjects and guests— because tonight he was greeting his equals, the royalty of intellect.

Jacobsson found his place on the stage nervously. Scanning Concert Hall, there was much to please him. He did not even mind the four detestable television cameras, two on the podium and two in the balconies. Every seat in the assembly room was taken, and the formality of the attire was gratifying. In the loges above, reserved for relatives of the laureates, he could make out Mrs. Saralee Garrett next to Signora Margherita Farelli, and beside them Miss Leah Decker. One chair was empty, and then he remembered Miss Emily Stratman.

The stage itself glittered beneath fern plants and great arrangements of white chrysanthemums. Covertly, Jacobsson examined the rows of chairs. All were filled save two, and now he no longer needed to count noses. Across the long steps, covered by Oriental carpets, that led down from the rear stage door, among the stiff committeemen, one hole gaped at him. Dr. Carl Adolf Krantz, who was to introduce Professor Max Stratman, was missing. This was disagreeable, but not serious.

What was serious was the empty chair next to his own. This was to have been occupied by Mr. Andrew Craig. Never, in the long history of the awards, had a laureate who had come to Stockholm failed to appear at the Ceremony. If Craig did not appear, it would become a national insult and an international scandal. The empty laureate chair became Gargantuan. Jacobsson gave silent thanks that the program was a long one, so that the chair might yet be filled.

Suddenly, Jacobsson realized that the opening moment of the Ceremony was upon them.

He rose to his feet and walked to the lectern where his salutatory oration lay waiting. He made his reverence to his King, and then gazed out at the audience. Could one of them know what was really in his head? Krantz was in his head. And Andrew Craig.

What possibly could have happened to them?

Krantz led the way, and Craig followed, until they arrived at the prow of a rakish, V-bottom cabin cruiser. It rolled evenly in its canal berth, and Craig, inspecting the white oak hull and mahogany planking and raised pilothouse in the semidarkness, judged it to be a forty-four-foot job with 110-horsepower engines.

"You go first," said Craig.

Gingerly, Krantz boarded the craft amidships, letting himself down the two steps to the white pine deck. Quickly, Craig was at his heels.

Before they could move farther, there were soft, hastening footsteps, and out of the night loomed a glowering, blond, athletic Swedish young man, attired in a navy-blue pea jacket and dungarees and white tennis shoes. His right hand was in his pocket. He recognized Krantz at once, and acknowledged him, and then glanced coldly at Craig.

Krantz spoke hastily, but with authority, in Swedish. The young man listened, then replied, also in Swedish, almost inaudibly.

Krantz turned. "It is all right," he said to Craig, "but he insists on searching you."

Craig shrugged. "He's wasting his time, but let him go ahead." Dutifully, he lifted his arms, and with expert speed the young Swede patted Craig's chest, hips, his coat pockets, and the pockets of his trousers.

Craig lowered his arms with satisfaction, as the young Swede addressed Krantz in Swedish.

Krantz said, "We can go ahead."

As they went on, Craig noticed that the young Swede was watching them, and that behind him, indistinct in the darkness, a taller figure had appeared.

"How many of them are there?" Craig inquired in an undertone.

"Two."

Crossing the deck, Craig noticed that the superstructure of the cruiser was polished natural mahogany. He speculated on the ownership of the expensive vessel, but decided that it did not matter. They reached the companionway. As they went belowdecks, Craig was aware of the nautical smells; burnished brass fittings and glazed mahogany trim, scrubbed decks and fresh paint, gasoline and oil, and the stimulating fragrance of salt water from the Baltic.

The corridor below was claustrophobic.

"Where are they?" Craig wanted to know.

"Walther Stratman is in the main stateroom. Miss Stratman is resting in the little bedroom adjoining it."

"Let me see her first."

Krantz, scrambling to oblige after his complete surrender, guided Craig past a locker, past the galley with its four-burner stove, to the gleaming knob of the bedroom door. "In here," said Krantz.

"How do you know she's in there?"

"They sedated her," said Krantz reluctantly. "The shock of seeing her father was so great, she fainted. They gave her something to quiet her down and let her rest."

"All right, let me see her."

They went inside.

The bedroom gave the impression of an elongated, well-lit wardrobe, furnished with a chair, bedstand, and single bed, and no more.

Emily lay curled on the bed, beneath a small oblong window that passed for a porthole, her back to the door. Because the heater was on, and the confined bedroom warm, she had pushed the thin white cotton sheet that covered her off her shoulders and down to her hips. She was attired in a light gray sweater and blue skirt, and the two pieces had separated, so that the curved ridge of her spine and a portion of her bare back and the elastic waistband of her pink panties showed. Her pumps were at the foot of the bed, and her heavy coat placed neatly on the chair.

Listening, Craig could hear her shallow breathing. Eckart's promise was confirmed: she was alive and apparently unharmed.

"You see," Krantz was saying eagerly, "nothing is wrong."

"No, not much," Craig said, ironically.

"You wait a moment," Krantz said. "I must go to the next room and explain to Walther Stratman."

There was a door to the left. Krantz went to it and disappeared. Alone with Emily, Craig quickly joined her, kneeling beside the bed. She had turned on her back, and now her hands were folded across her bosom. He took one hand, loosening it from the other, and his fingers felt her pulse at the wrist. The count was normal. He released her wrist, and then, gently, he shook her shoulder. At first she did not respond, and then she stirred, and he caressed her shoulder, and then, at last, she awakened.

Her head came around on the pillow, eyes sleepy, features reflecting confusion.

She recognized him. "Andrew—"

"Yes, darling, I'm here."

Her gaze shifted to the ceiling of the bedroom, then took in the rest of her surroundings. When she found her voice, it was caught low in her throat and thick. "Where am I?"

"Still in Stockholm. You were brought to your father."

"I remember—some of it—"

"Are you all right? Did they hurt you?"

She tried to think, but her mind and its answers were halting. "No," she said at last. "Only the shock and the—" Her eyes met Craig's. "Where is Uncle Max?"

"He's fine, better than ever. He's probably at the Ceremony now."

"I—I forgot—I'm mixed up."

"Rest."

"Andrew—why are you here? How did you—?"

"Never mind. I'll tell you later." He studied her. "You're sure they did nothing to you beyond the shot?"

"No, they—yes, I'm sure—nothing. Papa was so kind."

"Good." He stood up. "Try to sleep again, let the drug wear off. I'll be right back."

"Where are we?"

"Don't worry, Emily. You're in the bedroom of a motor cruiser—"

"I am?"

"—and you're safe now. I have to take care of something. I'll be back in a few minutes."

"But Uncle Max—Papa—what will—?"

He placed a finger on her dry lips. "It'll work out. Now—sleep."

When he withdrew his hand, her eyes were closed. With love, he remained standing over the innocent face, so much now a part of him, and when the rhythmic rise and fall of her breasts beneath the sweater told him that she was soundly asleep, he left her.

The door behind him had been softly opened, and the diminutive physicist, holding his top hat, gestured with it for Craig to come into the other room.

As Craig approached, Krantz said, "I have explained everything. Professor Walther Stratman will see you now."

Craig hung back for a second, trying to organize his thinking. He had struggled hard for this meeting, and now that it was here, he had no idea what he would say. He knew what he had intended to say, but at once it seemed less possible. All that he was positive of was that the meeting was in some way necessary and critically important. But then, as he started toward Krantz, he wondered: important for the sake of Emily and Walther and Max Stratman, or important, selfishly, for himself?

He passed before Krantz into the main stateroom.

It was a good-sized room, luxuriously furnished with a wardrobe that had

574

sliding doors, a dresser, a blond Swedish desk, a lavatory on the starboard side, and a brightly covered cot. Drawn up to the cot was a small round table, and behind the table, seated on the cot, was the hunched figure of a red-faced, big-headed elderly man with thin white hair neatly combed. He was in shirt-sleeves with old-fashioned armbands, the shirt striped, its collar open, with the stringy maroon tie knot drawn down. When he stood, bones cracking, his trousers, open at the belt, became baggier.

Krantz had guided Craig to him. "Professor Walther Stratman, this is Mr. Andrew Craig."

Walther's left hand held a half-filled glass, but his heavily veined right hand was extended. "So you are the formidable Nobel winner from America. I am proud to meet you."

Craid shook hands awkwardly. "I'm pleased to meet you, sir." He could see nothing of Emily in this weak old man with the prominent nose. Rebecca, he thought. Emily must be the image of her mother Rebecca.

"Draw a chair, sit down with me," Walther was saying, as he settled on the cot once more. He held up his glass—too rapidly, for some of the drink splashed and spilled on his trousers, and Craig, seasoned in such matters, guessed it was not his first drink—and then he pointed to the bottle on the table.

"I am celebrating my freedom," he said hoarsely. "Vodka. Not so potent as what I have known in captivity, but it will do. Have some, Mr. Craig—a little sunshine for the stomach, as my Russian friends like to say."

For some reason that he could not fathom, Craig was perturbed by the sight of the alcohol and the idea of drinking at a time as critical as this. Then, out of fairness, searching himself further, he realized that his disturbed reaction was based on his personal guilt. In his own life, there had been so many times of crisis in recent years, and he had always avoided them by burying his head in a bottle. Now, with more sympathy for Walther, he had the urge to warn the old man of the consequences of this weakness—like all reformed drunks, he told himself—and at once he felt easier and more understanding.

"No, thank you," Craig said to Walther. "I'm saving myself for the Nobel party tonight."

"Umm, party, yes." Walther looked up. "Dr. Krantz, do give our visitor a chair."

Krantz obliged instantly, and then melted into the bench at the dresser and occupied himself with a metal puzzle, pretending not to listen.

As Craig took his place across from Walther, the old man swallowed his drink, hiccuped, and said loudly, "So—it is a pleasure to meet the good friend of my brother and the suitor of my only child."

Something about this dismayed Craig slightly. Perhaps it was Walther's unexpected exuberance. He had envisioned meeting a beaten and hollow derelict of a man, a slave and sufferer, one long yoked and broken by the Soviets, and instead he found himself confronting a hale and boisterous hostage. Craig realized that the façade of weakness he saw was one he had built in his own mind and imposed upon Walther. It had no reality. Craig felt cheated.

"I'm not really a good friend of your brother's," he found himself saying, "but I would like to be. We've only met here in Stockholm."

"But my daughter—ah, you will not deny that." Walther Stratman winked, and poured himself a new vodka.

"No, I will not deny that, sir. I'm extremely fond of her."

"And she—what does she say to this?"

"I don't know."

Walther grinned in a conspiracy of his making. Two gold teeth shone. "Well, we shall see. Once we are all in America—we shall see—you will have a friend in court."

Walther's reference to America dismayed Craig further. It anticipated and smashed his line of attack before he could launch it. He was left without an alternative plan.

"—extremely pleased with her," he heard Walther saying. "She has developed as I hoped on that day we were torn apart. She is the pride of my old age."

Craig nodded. "Yes, I agree. Max has done a wonderful job."

Walther's head came up from his glass. "Max, you say?" He was about to make some comment, but appeared to recall it and alter it. "Max has done well, yes. But I hold heredity more dominant than environment. So—you will give me some of the credit?"

"I certainly will, sir." Craig paused, and determined not to continue in this fashion. He must make clear the object of his visit. "You must have been extremely surprised to be brought here from Moscow—"

"Leningrad."

"—from Leningrad, on such short notice."

"I was," agreed Walther. He stared at Craig, and at once his eyes filled and filmed, and his lower lip worked. "I had long ago given up hope of seeing Emily again. Or freedom, for that matter. I thought I would live out my years and die in that hell." He was thoughtful and sadder for quiet seconds. "How often, how constantly, my mind would go backwards to the happier days before the war, and then the miserable days when Max and I worked for the Nazis to keep Rebecca and Emily alive in Ravensbruck. Still, in the war days, there was always hope. But once the war was ended, all hope ended—there could be no hope. The decision I made, that night in 1945, to let Max go free—escape to the Americans, in my place—was both calculated and emotional. It was calculated because, at that time, Max was further advanced in his work than I was, and I knew he would offer more to the cause we both believed in. It was emotional, because Max was my younger brother, and I felt it my duty to see that he survived. After that, when the Russians had me, I thought they would punish me with death since they suspected I had aided Max. But then they had my records, and decided I would be more useful alive. They are a most pragmatical race, the Russians, with no emotional foolishness or waste as in America." Walther sipped his drink. "They sent me seventy miles away from Moscow to the place called Dubna, where they have their Nuclear Research Institute. It was their intention that I resume nuclear work, but then, in examining me, they learned of an early scientific paper on the bubonic plague that I had once published, and they demanded that I become a member of their biological warfare research unit under Dr. Viktor Glinko. I found this abhorrent, and at first I refused. I pleaded that I was a physicist, not a bacteriologist. I told them I had only an amateur's knowledge of bacteriology. They would not be put off. They said that I knew enough already, and that I would be taught more while I worked. I saw that I had no choice, so reluctantly I entered the project. During our first test, there was a tremendous accident, a blast, a fire, in the adjoining nuclear plant. Many on our project were killed or maimed. I was fortunate enough—as it turns out now—to survive. While I was hospitalized, the B.W. project was reactivated with greater funds. Once more, I saw that I would have to participate, but this time, shrewdly, I bargained with them. I agreed to do this work—cooperate, I said—if they, in turn, would bring me some news of Rebecca and Emily, my links to sanity. The Russians obliged, and I then cooperated, and have been forced to do the work ever since—despite my hatred of it—under the name of Dr. Lipski. The name was given me in the hospital, when we made our bargain—a political nonsense—so that those in the Western world, who knew of my old paper, could not put two and two together, and deduct that experiments were being made to develop a mutant type of disease." He stopped, and fell to reflecting on what had happened, and then he swallowed his vodka. "So—I have served my sentence, and here I am."

"Did you know exactly why you were being flown to Stockholm?" Craig inquired.

"Yes, yes, it was all made clear."

"The trade for your brother?"

"Of course. It is not a happy condition, but in some ways reasonable enough." Then he added defensively, "Max has had his milk and honey, thanks to me. Now it is my turn. I look forward with all my heart to this new freedom. I feel exactly like Edmond Dantès when he replaced the corpse of the Abbé Faria, and acquired freedom from the Château d'If and the riches of Monte Cristo. You understand?"

Craig felt traitorous to this old man, who did not know the purpose that had brought Craig to this stateroom. "I understand," said Craig. "Still, it must be difficult for you. I mean, you've been through enslavement, and now you know what you are sending your own brother into."

The blotches on Walther's cheeks seemed to deepen. "It is not so bad as all that," he said loudly. "Do not be deceived by propaganda. Do not be victimized by the reactionary press of the Morgans and Rockefellers. Max will be treated well in Russia."

"In East Germany, Walther," Krantz's voice piped from the rear.

"Yes, East Germany," agreed Walther. He faced Craig again. "But to return to the situation in the Soviet Union a moment. Our family lives well in Leningrad."

"Your family?"

Walther blinked at Craig. "That is what I said—our family of German scientists. They respect us as America or England would not. We are the elite."

A prick of annoyance—unfair, after all this old man had been through—urged Craig to a defense. "Scientists are as well respected in the United States. Your brother is a prime example."

"An exception—an exception," insisted Walther. "*Izvestia* ran a series of articles on the life of your scientists in America. It was enough to curl my hair." Suddenly, he laughed. "Or it would have, if I had had more hair." Then his face became solemn. "No, young man, I am not worried for Max. He may have more wealth and luxury in your country. But he does not have the proper respect and honors. In Leningrad, he will—"

"In East Berlin. He is coming to East Berlin," Krantz interrupted frantically.

Walther glowered at Krantz. "Stop with that sham, Dr. Krantz. East Berlin —Leningrad—Moscow—it is all as one for the Germans, and you know it." Walther returned his attention to Craig. "You see, I am not interested in artifices. Max is a Nobel winner today. He will have his free dacha, his free laboratory, his student apprentices, his preferred treatment from the Presidium, his place and extra rubles in the Academy of Sciences. If I know Max, he will love it, the fussing, to be treated like a Czar. And the work—it will not tax him—some solar experiments if he wishes—if not, they will use him as an academic showcase in Berlin, to attract the young ones. I have no guilts, Mr. Craig. I am not sending my brother to a Devil's Island or Alcatraz. It is a small price for the debt he owes me, to know I will be with my daughter again. And we can both be satisfied Max will be thriving, yes, thriving."

It was during this, as he half listened, that the thought entered Craig's mind: the pitiful old man is painting this pretty picture as a rationalization for taking part in the trade, as a necessity to shed the dreadful guilt of it.

"If it is all as you describe," said Craig gently, "so wonderful for Max, tell me—why are you leaving at all?"

This was impudent, but Walther appeared not to be sensitive to it. "For one thing, I am not Max," Walther said slowly. "He will be regarded as more useful, and treated accordingly. For another, I want to be with my daughter in a place where I can make riches and have the material things that Max has had. Surely, at my age, these desires are understandable."

"Certainly they are," said Craig. "Have you thought at all of what you will do in the United States?"

Walther smiled winningly. "I have not had much time for planning, as you know. But sitting here, relaxing, before you came, waiting for the evening and my freedom, I began to consider what is ahead. I am sure Max will cede me his savings and home, in exchange for mine, so I will have a start." He rubbed his watery eyes. "Of course, I would not live in the city of Atlanta in your Georgia as Max does. I am more conscious of inequities than Max. I will not live among people who club Negroes and lynch and incite riots. I will take Emily to New York or Detroit. I will work for the capitalists so that Emily and I can be capitalists."

"What work do you intend to do?" asked Craig.

"I will work for peace—if the capitalists will let me."

"You will continue your bacterial experiments?"

"Never."

"But you've been doing just that in Leningrad."

Walther's bleary eyes considered Craig as he might a precocious but errant student. "Young man, in Russia I did this work for peace—for nothing else—as a deterrent to war. That is one thing I trust. I must learn if, in America, there is the same good will."

"Perhaps you will resume your work in nuclear energy?"

"A possibility, if I am assured it is for peace."

"You can depend that it is for peace."

Walther set down his empty glass. "You mean like Hiroshima and Nagasaki?" Then, quickly, he smiled at the expression on Craig's face. "No, do not take me seriously. Those annihilations were political moves, I understand that, to exert influence in the East before we could. No—do not misunderstand me—I know your American people are peaceful, want to live, to let live, to have good relations, like plain common people everywhere. I know they are the tools of reactionary monopolists. I have only meant I would not sell myself to the house of Morgan, to help provoke and incite a total war. You can depend that Emily and I will work for the people."

During the last of that, a vagrant, teasing thought—which had entered Craig's mind earlier and been turned away—now possessed him. It was something astonishing and unacceptable before. But these seconds, his perceptions vibrated and wondered, and the vagrant thought grew, taking shape and identity. Craig hated to face the fact of it, yet the thought excited him. It was a hypothesis only, true, and there was no absolute proof of it, but proof might be possible to obtain. Suddenly his resolve was to test it for proof. He must gamble before time ran out, and all was lost.

"I am sure we can depend on you, sir," he said. His air was all guilelessness. He looked down at his watch. "I'm afraid I've overstayed. I've tired you—and I should be at the Nobel Ceremony."

"I am pleased you came," said Walther. "It was a good surprise, to find a friend."

Craig considered Walther. "Had you wondered, at all, why I came—why I forced Krantz to bring me here?"

"To see Emily. To know she is well."

"One part of it. The main part is—I came to see you."

"I cannot imagine why."

"I had some notion that I might persuade you not to go through with this terrible exchange. I know what you've been through, what Max owes you, but somehow I thought I could make you realize that your role in Emily's life ended long ago. Through adolescence and maturity, she has known only Max. In effect, he is her father and good to her. I thought I might make you see the trauma, for her, of replacing Max with yourself. Also, I thought you might be convinced of Max's importance in the free world—I do not denigrate your own—but Max is proved, looked up to, on the brink of greater work, for all the people, for our government, not private enterprise—and I thought—"

Walther's cheeks were ablaze. "You are an impertinent young man," he interrupted. He tried to control his voice, but it quaked with anger. All in his face that had seemed loose and flabby with age and drink now seemed to stretch and harden. "You are a meddling young man, and you have no feeling—"

Craig did not recoil, but sat immovable in his place. "I apologize then," he said. "I had no wish to offend you or—"

Walther's flat palm slapped the table like a plank of wood, and the bottle jumped. "What does any pampered young ignoramus like you know of life over here and what we go through? What do you know of discipline and sacrifice and suffering—you, all of you, with your belly softness and head softness—dancing puppets for the propertied class, educated by schools that will only cater to the wealthy, and learning all you know from newspapers and periodicals controlled by the rich? What do you know—and who are you to tell me what is right and what is wrong—to tell me to sacrifice more and more for a brother who has grown fat and fatheaded, usurping my place with my own flesh and blood?"

Krantz had rushed forward. "Please, Walther—please, please—Mr. Craig did not mean—"

Craig pushed back the chair and came to his feet. "No, Krantz, he is quite right. I should not try to live other people's lives and make their decisions. It is a disagreeable trait of authors. But I will make up for it now." He stared down at the angry Walther. "Yes, I will make up for it. There is no reason for you to go back—but there is no reason for Max to submit and go behind the Curtain, either. I don't intend to let Eckart pull off his filthy blackmail. There'll be no exchange tonight. You'll have your freedom, Walther, and Max will keep his. We're all leaving this boat right now."

Krantz darted to the table. "It is impossible, Mr. Craig—why—"

"Shut up, Krantz!" It was Walther. He addressed Craig with cool contempt. "I was mistaken. You are not merely a fool but a suicidal fool."

Craig contained himself. "It's possible if one wants freedom enough, as some Hungarians and some East Germans did," he said evenly.

"There are no odds to favor us," said Walther. "There are two guards out there, fully armed, young hoodlums who would enjoy the target practice. There are four of us—two of us old, and one a woman—with no arms but your nonsense."

"I'll take the major risk," persisted Craig. "I'll lead the way out. It's dark. I'll go toward the guards, block them, divert them, no matter what the consequences. There'll be time enough for the three of you to make the wharf—or, better, just leap overboard and begin to shout. The noise you make—the gun-fire at me—it'll bring people down in swarms."

"I am not going overboard," said Walther with deadly reserve. "I do not swim."

"You'll find cork jackets in the closet."

"And float there—sitting duck for those hoodlums? No. Why risk my life, after all I have been through, when my freedom without danger is only hours off?"

"But then we can save Max—not only you but Max."

"You are telling me how to think about Max?" Walther bawled, rearing to his feet, lurching against the table. The jolt of his agitated frame against the table overturned the glass and bottle, and sent both rolling to the cabin floor. As the vodka gurgled out of the bottle, Walther shouted, "Max is my business, not yours—not any of yours! I have had enough from you and all of your *provocateurs!* Now get out of here!"

Craig remained stolidly in his place. "I'm not getting out."

Walther strode noisily around the table. "Then I will have you thrown out, you capitalist scum—trying to tell me what to do—trying to tell me—a man honored, revered, looked up to, worshiped—in the most powerful nation on earth—"

Suddenly, Walther cut his heated outburst short. His eyes went from Craig to Krantz, and back to Craig, to the look of blank astonishment on Krantz's features, to the look of complete scorn on Craig's face. Except for their heavy breathing, the ticking of a clock, the creak of hinges off somewhere, the stateroom was a tomb of charged silence.

Craig spoke first. "You don't want to escape, do you, Walther? I never expected you would. But—why not? Because you don't give a damn about your brother or daughter? Or because you don't give a damn about freedom? You don't want freedom—do you, Walther?"

Rage covered Walther's face like a distorted hood. He reeled toward Craig, lifting a fist as if to hit him. But he did not strike. Instead, he bellowed, "Freedom? Freedom? What do you sheep know of freedom—of the true meaning of freedom? You with your holy false words—mouthings dictated by your capitalist hyenas—the provocateurs, the warmongers, and you no better, and Max no better—waiting with your ICBMs to destroy us, to protect your filthy green dollars."

They were only a few feet apart, but Craig did not flinch. Exultation swept upward through his veins. Reckless confidence, in knowledge of the truth, was his banner. "You speak like a Communist, Walther, exactly like a Communist. You're not even being cautious. You're one of them—not the decent people there—but the big ones, the cocky ones, so sure of your science and weapons—"

"You ignorant lout!" cried Walther. "What do you know of our science and our weapons? We are the fighters for peace—working day and night to save the world, keep it alive for you fools, to make one world—"

"Your world, Walther, not mine," interrupted Craig. "You want your world on your terms, and it has nothing to do with average people anywhere. You want your world. You've been brainwashed—indoctrinated—forgotten the old past—want the new future where you and your adopted comrades will be the royalty."

"The workers will be the royalty!" Walther shouted.

Craig studied the weaving old man, his pose lost, his stature taller, stronger, fanatical, and then Craig said, "You never intended to leave that world, Walther. I can see that now. You played along for the sake of the Party—it's the Party, isn't it, Walther? It's the parroting, brainless, robot Party."

"Another disrespect against the Party and you'll pay for it!" Walther swayed, unbalanced by vodka and outrage. "The Party is the best of us—all eight million of the CPSU—and we are the cream, the best, the most decent brains on earth, and your fate is in our hands—remember that, remember—"

"And so you played along for them, never intending to participate honorably even in blackmail? The bosses said go to Stockholm, suck in Max, get him back to East Berlin for us—so we can use him for evil—and then you come back to us, too. That was the game, wasn't it?"

Walther's mouth was strange, twisting, twisting, saliva-brimmed, with no word being uttered, until at last the hoarse words broke through. "Do you think I would come to you in a hundred years? I wanted to help them get Max on the right side, yes. And the girl—Emily—yes, if she would come. I owed it to her—after what I know of Ravensbruck, after what I guess of her life in America—to raise her under my roof, in a decent house, with my family. But to leave my family for the likes of Max or the lot of you? To leave a good Russian wife—my two young children? They are my life, they and my work and our cause."

He caught his breath, panting out of fever and fury.

"Dr. Krantz!" The voice, clear and assured, came from the rear of the stateroom, and it was Emily's voice.

All of them turned as one, startled, having forgotten her. She stood before the open door of the bedroom cabin, had apparently been standing there for some minutes. Now, shifting her coat from one arm to the other, head high, lips compressed, only her step uneven, she crossed to the group.

"Dr. Krantz," she repeated, "should you speak to Dr. Eckart once more, tell him this. Tell him there can be no trade—because there is no one for whom Uncle Max can be traded."

She considered Craig gravely, her countenance dry-eyed and composed. "Thank you, Andrew," she said.

Krantz was waiting at the stateroom door. He went first. Emily was the next to go. Then it was Craig who left.

Not one of them looked back at Professor Walther Stratman. . . .

When they had arrived at his single room on the fifth floor of the Grand Hotel, Craig helped Emily inside, switching on the lights as they entered. Emily was heavy against his supporting arm, and twice she stumbled. "I'm all right," she muttered, "I'll be all right."

They had emerged from the cabin cruiser at Pålsundet only fifteen minutes before, and the memory of it still hung over them. No sooner had Krantz led them up to the white pine deck than the athletic young Swedish guard had appeared, suspicious and edgy. Krantz had sternly rattled forth his explanation in Swedish, mentioning Walther once, invoking Eckart twice, and then the guard had conceded their passage.

Swiftly, they had made their way along the canal, waiting once when Emily had protested that she was weak. During that interlude, Craig had felt the cool white flakes of snow on his cheeks, as satisfying as Emily's warm presence leaning against him. Lingering thus, Craig had studied the dark waters of the canal and Långholmen island directly across, almost hidden behind the haze of the low mist, and then the snow came thicker. Where earlier it had seemed menacing, it now seemed a suspension in time, both cheerful and welcome.

After that, they had departed from the desolate embankment, and gone up through the hard, slippery park area, Krantz wheezing, and Craig concerned only for the one on his arm.

When they had come into the lights of Söder Mälarstrand, the traffic was still heavy in the packed snow, and the bright municipal decorations a proper jubilee. At the limousine, speckled with dry snow, Craig had asked Krantz to drive them to the hotel, and he had eagerly assented.

Inside the cozy automobile, as it slid into the traffic, Emily had sat straight and rigid a moment, staring ahead, then suddenly she had closed her eyes and choked forth a sob.

Craig had watched her with deep concern, aware of how depleted were her emotional resources. "I'm sorry, Emily. It must be shattering."

"No," she had said, shaking her head vigorously. "I—I almost cried because—only because I'm so relieved, at last. All afternoon, I did not know where I was, how to think, what should be done. Now it's solved. He—he's not my father at all—at least—not the father I knew. And the thought of having to give up Uncle Max for him or anyone—" She paused. "But thank God for you, Andrew, thank God for you."

She fumbled for his hand, and he met her hand with his own, and brought her close against him. She dropped her head on his shoulder, eyes wearily closing, and sighed like a little girl who had been lost and was now safely in her sheltering bed again.

"Andrew—" she had murmured, and the receding voice was shaded and troubled.

He waited, and he said, "Don't bother to talk. I'm here. I'll always be here."

"No," she had said, "no, Andrew—"

He had tried to understand this refusal to accept him, and had been about to contend with it, when he saw that she slept. He had sat all through the ride, arm about her, rocking with the motion of the limousine, wondering and wondering, until the time when they had drawn up before the canopy of the Grand Hotel.

"Here we are," he had whispered, disengaging himself, and rousing her. The doorman had opened the rear door, but it had been Krantz, skittering around from the driver's seat, who had shoved the doorman aside to assist Emily and Craig out of the car.

Going past the worried Krantz, Craig had remembered that he represented unfinished business. A decision must be made. Requesting Emily to wait, and the doorman to look after her, Craig had returned to Krantz. Wordlessly, they had walked several yards from the car.

Krantz, distractedly brushing the snowflakes from his face, had gazed up at Craig. "What are you going to do?"

Studying the servile physicist, Craig had known that there was only one thing he could do. From the beginning, when Daranyi had indicted the physicist, Craig had looked upon Krantz as Rumpelstilzchen, the evil dwarf, but now, hunched and drooping, he was only the pathetic dwarf. Craig could see how one so small had, in some way, to become big, and any witchery was worth it if the goal was reached. Craig could see that Nature had punished him from birth, punished him with lack of stature and discontent, and that more than this need not be done.

Craig had studied the pale little Swede. "I keep thinking of Jacobsson—Ingrid Påhl—the hundreds of others—decent people—who work hard to make the Nobel awards mean something—in a world where so little means anything—and I tell myself all that would be lost with one rotten scandal. Because you fear the scandal as much as I hate it, you've tried to make up for it. You took me to the boat. You took us off the boat. So—as long as I can know you'll never get caught up in anything like this again—"

"Never—never. My pledge—"

"—and as long as I know you'll square things with Daranyi—"

"At once—tomorrow."

"—I'm not going to say a thing, Krantz, only make a record of it, in case you should ever get out of line."

Krantz had been almost tearful. "Thank you—thank you."

"You don't have to thank me. You can be grateful to your colleagues. . . . Now beat it."

Briefly, he had watched Krantz hurry back to the limousine. Then, when the car was gone, he had returned to the canopy, where Emily rested against an upright. He could see that she was but half awake. He had grasped her firmly under the arch of the back, and led her up the stairs, and through the lobby to the elevator.

Now they were in his room. He removed her coat, and settled her on the double bed, and bent to pull off her pumps. As he did so, she forced her eyes open. "The sedation is wearing off, Andrew. But I'm still sort of—slowed down." She took in the room, disoriented. "This room. Is this your room?"

"Yes. . . . Now, stretch out. You'll be yourself in a little while."

She nodded, pushed herself to the center of the bed, falling backward to the pillow. She lifted her slim legs, making one gesture toward her skirt, trying, and failing, to cover her knees, then letting her arm drop limply to the quilt.

Craig turned down two of the three lamps, poked at his valise, removed his coat and tie, tried to busy himself in every way, hoping that she would sleep. At the telephone, he considered calling Concert Hall and leaving a message for Jacobsson, explaining that he would be late. But then, as he weighed the necessity of the call, he realized that Emily was still awake, her eyes following his every movement.

"Can't you sleep?" he asked.

"No." Feebly, she touched the bed beside her. "Come, sit close to me."

"Yes." He stood over her. Her silken black hair, and green eyes, and serious crimson lips, had never been more beautiful to his sight. He bent over her face, and she closed her eyes, and he kissed her.

At last, with one weak hand against his shoulder, she asked for release, and he granted it.

"Andrew—"

"Yes, darling."

"What are we going to do?"

"Very simple. We'll wait for the drug to wear off, and then we'll change and go."

"That's not what I meant," she said. "I meant—" But then it was difficult to know what she meant under the sedation, and her brain was slow. "How did you find me?"

He told her how hopeful he had been after receiving her message, and how he had waited for the telephone call and for her understanding. Then he related how he had gone to her suite, and received the tape recorder, and made up his mind not to burden her uncle with the terrible dilemma, but to see what he could do by himself. He told her about Gottling, and how they had gone to Daranyi, and what had happened there, and then he told her, in lesser detail, of his showdown with Krantz that had led him to the meeting with Walther in the stateroom.

She had listened without comment, but now she said, "You are good."

"I'm in love," he said simply.

She avoided the declaration. Instead, she said, "I keep thinking—what if it had been Uncle Max they had reached before you? He would have gone over to their side without hesitation—remembering my father only as he had last seen him in another age—forgetting, as we all do, people are different people at different times."

"That is true."

"Uncle Max would have been lost to me—and I'd be alone. How did you ever think you could—?"

"I didn't think, Emily," he said. "I felt. I felt, and I acted on feeling— something I have not done in years. That's all I did. I felt Max must not be given away. I felt your father must be reasoned with. Most of all, I felt alive —but for a while, as dead as before I met you—and I knew I could be alive again, and stay alive, only by being with you. . . . Emily, stop ignoring it, denying it. I love you, and accept this from me."

"I can't. Won't you understand? I'm unable to—I can't."

"But why not?" His mind went to a word, and he wondered if it might hold her secret. "Emily, I don't know what is wrong—I can only guess it must be something in your past. I've heard one word over and over again. From you. From your Uncle Max. From Daranyi. Even from your—from Walther." She was watching him with frightened eyes, but he went on. "The word is Ravensbruck," he said. "It's the only other thing I don't understand, besides your rejection of me. I know—you told me once—Ravensbruck was a women's concentration camp in Germany during the war. But I still don't understand its—"

"Andrew," she said, "I was going to tell you about that at noon—it was the important thing I had to tell you."

"Do you still want to tell me?"

"I don't know, except it is now all that matters again. It has never stopped mattering. I suppose if you know the truth about that, you will know me and have some understanding—of why I treated you the way I did that first night we met in the palace, of—of the way I've been withdrawn and strange, I'm sure you've seen that—of the real reason I sent you away." She paused. "It wasn't Lilly, you see. It was me." Her green eyes studied his features for long silent seconds. "And finally—finally—it's why I cannot marry you or see you again."

"Emily—"

"I want to talk," she persisted tiredly, and her speech had thickened. "I have to, sooner or later, so that you'll know why this is our last time together. You deserve to know, because of what you've expected of me. And besides —I guess—my poor brain—I'm so lightheaded now—besides, I think, for once I'm drugged enough to be uninhibited."

"Emily, I'd rather you rest, and then—"

"Now, Andrew, it's got to be now. It is more important to me than anything in the world."

"All right, Emily," he said, and he pondered what might come, and for some unknown reason he felt fear.

"You won't mind if I don't look at you while I talk?" For a moment, she was quiet again, as if rummaging through her opiate-scattered brain. "Ravensbruck," she said, "that is where it began and ended. They called it, in German, the woman's hell, but it was not nearly so pleasant as that."

Her thoughts had wandered again, but her determination was strong, and she went on. "My mother and I were sent there, you know, fifty miles north of Berlin, and were to be kept alive as long as my father and Uncle Max worked for the government in Berlin."

"I know," he said.

"I was thirteen and fourteen and fifteen in Ravensbruck. When I was first put there, I was a scrawny girl just out of puberty, but the next year I began to mature, and before my fifteenth birthday, I was a woman—much more attractive than I am today—a woman with a serious child's head. We lived like animals, deprived, ragged, filthy, and always in our fear of being Jews. But no one whipped or beat us or made us stand in the naked inspections, my mother and myself, because of my father and Uncle Max. And for me, most of the first two years, it was not such hell, because I had only then become a woman, and before I had been a child, and so this was almost the only life I knew well, and I had no real standard I would allow myself to compare it with. It seemed natural to me—as if it had always been—to wear a stinking and vermin-covered dress and underwear and to wear wooden shoes, to wake at five-thirty and have one cup of ersatz coffee for breakfast, and one tin can of cabbage soup for lunch, and one more for dinner, and to steal potato peelings from the garbage, to work eleven hours every day digging a road, to use a four-gallon drum for a toilet, to sleep with lice and my mother and one other on straw with one blanket for all three of us. I repeat, I refused to remember any other life, so I managed. It was my mother who suffered worse, but no matter about that. The real horror of the camp was not so much the indignities and punishments and suffering we saw—but the worse things we did not see. As the veterans in the Atlanta hospital where I work are often saying, there were constant latrine rumors. Some I could even verify, because I knew the French women and the Czech women. Our friends disappeared, and we knew it was true that fifty women a day were shot in the back of the neck and cremated. To speed up the liquidation, many of our friends were pressed to build a gas chamber, so we knew that existed. Then there were the scientific experiments, medical experiments—"

Craig thought of Dr. Farelli at Dachau, and then he listened again, still puzzled.

"—and one experiment I knew about," said Emily, words dragging, "was done on the Polish female prisoners among us—by Dr. Karl Gebhardt, a surgeon from the University of Berlin, and Dr. Schidlausky, our senior medical officer. They were trying to prove something about sulfa drugs—and instead of white mice they used the Polish women. They infected them in their legs —cut their legs and put tetanus germs, sometimes with ground glass, or made artificial gangrene in the incisions—to study the results. Most of the girls died in anguish. But that is not my story. My first time—"

Her eyes held absently on the hotel window, and after an interval, she continued.

"The Nazis were worried about their flyers who ditched in the water or navy sailors who had to jump in the water, when it was cold, in winter, and so they began experiments in freezing and heating of human beings. I don't know much about this, except what I saw and what happened. It was a bad winter night, and we were all huddled around the stove in the barracks after seven or eight, after the cabbage soup, and the highest woman supervisor, the *Aufseherin*, who was under Colonel Schneider, the commandant—her name was Frau Hencke—she came in with two men guards. She was wearing her gray uniform, with the holster and pistol, and black boots, and carrying the whip.

587

"She ordered all of us to stand in line, and then went down the line grumbling, flicking the whip, shaking her head, complaining of our dirtiness and ugliness and dead eyes, and when she came to me, she looked me over, up and down, and said, '*Ja*, this is the one—this one will do nicely.' Immediately, my mother was terrified and wanted to know what they would do with me, and Frau Hencke said it was to be an honor for me, to give assistance—I think she said clerical assistance—to their doctors in the scientific experiments. I would be busy, she said, tonight and in the morning, but I could rest the next day." Emily sighed. "The beginning," she said.

For a while, she lay still, and then, slowly, she resumed.

"It was ten below zero that night. It is hard now to remember how cold it was. I wore my sweater and my mother's coat and a shawl someone loaned me, and I went with Frau Hencke and the guards—the ground was like iron and there were icicles from all the barracks buildings—and I thought we were going to the *Revier,* the huts that were our hospital, but we went past it, and on and on, until we came to a small brick building I had never seen, and Frau Hencke said this was the science experiment building and infirmary.

"When we came near the entrance, I heard, over the wind, a man crying —it is wrenching to hear the sound of a man crying—and then a physician met us—Dr. Voegler, the assistant medical officer to Dr. Schidlausky—and he said that he would show me the experiment. They led me around the building to the side, and the man's crying was louder. Do you know what they showed me? A young Polish prisoner—a thin Jewish boy with curly black hair. He was on a stretcher on the hard ground, and he was all naked—and it was ten below zero.

"I wanted to run. I had never seen a grown man all naked, that was one thing, but the main thing was the bestiality—his wrists and ankles tied—helpless and naked on a stretcher. And then in front of me a guard poured a pail of ice water over him—and he screamed and cried. Dr. Voegler and Frau Hencke took me inside the infirmary and said that this was their freezing experiment, and it would be followed by a warming experiment. The idea was to see how frozen a subject could become and still be saved. They told me they must learn how they could save the glorious aviators of the Luftwaffe who went down in the channel. And now they said I had been chosen to help them prove that someone frozen like that boy could be saved. I remember I said, 'I will do anything to help that poor boy live.' And the doctor said, 'I am glad you are cooperative. You will have your chance in a few hours.'

"Frau Hencke took me into an empty room—it had windows around like a hospital nursery, but they were draped. There was nothing in the room but a double bed and a chair. Frau Hencke was friendly and said she would get me hot milk and rolls—I had not had such luxury in two years—and then I must nap, and they would wake me when it was time to work. I took my milk and rolls, and then took off my shoes and rested on the bed, with the lights off, but I couldn't sleep because I kept thinking of that poor freezing Jewish boy on the stretcher in that weather. Maybe I dozed off. I can no longer remember. But I suppose some hours passed, and suddenly the lights in the room were on and I was sitting up, and Dr. Voegler and Frau Hencke were standing there.

"Dr. Voegler said, 'Fräulein Stratman, now it is time. Our heating experiment begins. We are bringing in the test person—the boy you want to help—and now we want to find out if he can be unfrozen and warmed up with animal heat—the heat of the human body.' I had no idea what he was talking about. 'Take off your clothes, Fräulein,' he commanded. I wanted to know how much to take off, and he said every stitch, and I was not yet fifteen and ashamed of the size of my breasts, and how I was a woman, and I refused. The doctor then said the experiment could only be made by two people, one cold like the boy, and one warm like myself, and I was to nestle close to him, embrace him on the bed, to transmit my heat to him and see if it would bring him back to normal. I screamed that I couldn't, and then the doctor said that if I would not cooperate, they would go and bring my mother in my place, and I would watch. And so then I did not resist. Frau Hencke took off my patched sweater and the wool skirt, and she took off my cotton brassière and pulled down my pants, and I was naked, and I did what they told me. I stretched out on the bed, with one hand trying to cover my breasts and the other hand below. Then Dr. Voegler and Frau Hencke went out, and they carried in the poor, naked Jewish boy, unconscious, numbed like metal by the cold, and they threw him on the bed next to me. They left on one light in the room, and parted the drapes of a window halfway. The doctor demanded that I take the boy in my arms and hug him, and press him against my breasts and belly, and caress him, to see if this would revive him. The doctor said the boy's life was in my hands. And they would be watching, with others, from the window to see that I did what I must do.

"At first, alone with the boy, I was repelled—remember my age. I had never touched a man or seen one like this—but then I kept seeing they were watching me, and I looked at the boy, so unconscious, so suffering, and he was alive, I could tell, and then I didn't care, I only wanted him to live. I turned him sideways toward me—and pressed against his limp icy body—and I hugged him and stroked him. How can I tell you the rest? The witnesses knew it would happen—they had done this for weeks before—but I did not know. In an hour he was conscious, the boy, but weak, not knowing where he was or what was going on—and then Dr. Voegler came in and took his temperature, and it was eighty-four degrees—and then the doctor left, and the boy began to revive as I hugged him and ran my hands over him. And then he opened his eyes and kept looking at me, at my breasts, and suddenly —I can't tell you—he had an erection—and he was between my legs before I could prevent it, he was like some alley dog, and he broke my virginity and I was bleeding, and he sobbed that he was sorry, sorry, but he couldn't control himself, and he kept on until it was over, and then he fell back and slept. I had never known such a thing and was sickened, but Dr. Voegler and two other physicians and Frau Hencke came in and examined him and then congratulated me. They said his temperature had jumped to normal in coitus, faster than by any other means known except a hot bath, and that I would be rewarded with a fine breakfast, and he would live. I couldn't eat the breakfast, I had lost everything, but I told myself at least this was for something —to save a poor Polish boy's life.

"In the morning, I told my mother a lie about clerical work, and tried to live with myself, and a few days later, I found it was all a waste anyway. They had taken the same boy from his barracks and put him in a vat of ice water outside the infirmary, when it snowed, and then carried him in and put him between two naked Frenchwomen, but he died there between them."

She lay inert, gazing off, still not meeting his eyes.

He wanted to touch her. He wanted to take her to him and make her forget all that was dead in the past but so alive in her. But he knew that he could not.

He said, "And that was what happened in Ravensbruck?"

"The beginning," she said, "only the beginning, I told you. I will make less of the rest that followed, because that was the most of it. A week after the experiment—"

She faltered, briefly.

"Emily," he said, "I—"

"A week after," she persisted, "Frau Hencke, the woman supervisor, sent for me in her private quarters. It was dark, before dinner. I rapped on her door, and she called to come in. She was lying on the sofa of her small living room, covered to the neck with a blanket. She was a husky woman, not stout but big-boned, a woman of maybe thirty-five, with a deep voice that frightened all the inmates. She was a power in the camp. She told me to lock the door, and I did, and she told me to come to her, and I did. She asked me how old I was, and I said fifteen in a few weeks. She said she had been impressed with my behavior and courage the night of the experiment, and she had thought about me every day since. 'When I undressed you,' she said, 'I must admit I never saw a girl with a more wonderful figure.' I was scared, but I thanked her. She said she had suffered to see me on the bed letting that Jewish boy make love to me. If it had been in her hands, she would not have allowed any man to despoil such a lovely virgin. 'But we will forget that,' she said, 'because I have good news for you.' She told me that, aside from Colonel Schneider, she was the most important person in Ravensbruck. She was in a position to save lives, make life agreeable with comforts. She was prepared now to do this for my mother and myself. She would take me under her wing. I would be her protégée. But in a week I had become older, and I was suspicious. 'Why do you do this?' I wanted to know. And she said, 'Because, Emily, I am a foolish woman to have fallen in love with you.' "

From her pillow, almost oblivious of Craig, Emily seemed to consider the old scene.

"She kept telling me how she loved me," said Emily. "She promised that she would be kind to me, and I would never be sorry. Then, while she spoke, her tone became more—more excited. She said that she did not want to waste time in idle talk. She said I must take off all my clothes as I had at the experiment. I made no move to do this, and she asked me if I had heard of the douche room, and I said that I had. One French girl was sent there for punishment. The bidet—the douche—shot up water like a geyser, with pressure of a fire hose, and you squatted over it until you passed out. Frau Hencke said she would hate to have that douche disfigure me. Still I hesitated about undressing, and she saw I was obstinate, and then she said without meanness, 'Or do you wish your mother here in Ravensbruck with you or in Auschwitz where the crematorium buildings are? I am in charge of preparing the lists for Colonel Schneider.' One by one, as if in a dream, I removed my garments. When I was naked, she smiled. *'Wunderschön!'* she said. 'You are better than any I have seen. Now take the blanket off me.'

"Have you ever walked naked in front of a stranger? My legs were wooden sticks, and I tried to cover my—no matter—I went to her and took off the blanket, and there she was—with nothing on—so repulsive. I stood, shaking, and she told me to lie down with her. There was no choice. I sat down and —and—she stroked me and then again said, 'Now lie down.' It was ugly the way she was breathing—but I did what I was told, because I was so young and had only my mother, and I did not want my mother in the crematorium." Emily paused. "That was for three months—"

"Emily," Craig interrupted, "I don't have to hear any more. Don't—"

"Are you afraid to hear?" she asked without looking at him. "Is that it?"

"That is not it. I'm thinking of you." But then he knew that she must have her catharsis.

"I will finish," she said, and her words were not all distinct because of the sedative. "One night, as always, I went to Frau Hencke, and for the first time she was fully clothed. She said in her superintendent voice, 'There is too much talk in this camp. Not always the prisoners, but the foul-mouthed men, the guards. Colonel Schneider has called me in and said our meetings are known, and there is much jealousy. He thinks it is bad for morale. I am sorry, but this is ended.' I wanted to weep, and thank the Lord for ending the nightmare, for ridding me of that horrible Lesbian. But then she said, 'Colonel Schneider wishes to speak to you personally. After rations tonight, at eight o'clock, one of his guards will come for you. That is all, Emily.'

"The guard came at twenty after eight, I remember. I went to Colonel Schneider's bungalow. It was the best building at Ravensbruck. He was the commandant. I was shown into a study, and then the door was closed, and I saw him working at his desk. He was wearing a silk robe from occupied Paris. I stood a long time, and finally he turned around. I had never set eyes on him before. He had a fringe of hair with long sideburns, thick, and a broken flat nose, and he was middle height but big like a bull with no neck. He kept looking at me like—as if I were a prize heifer—and then he said, 'Walk—walk around the room.' I did. He said, 'You walk well. I wondered why Frau Hencke was so radiant these months. Now, I see why. Well, I will brook no perversion in my command.' Then he said, 'You will do. Go through that door to my bedroom. Disrobe. I will join you.' I was stunned.

I had expected anything but this. I knew if I was obstinate what I would hear, but I tried. I pleaded with him, I begged him. He would not listen. 'You are not a virgin,' he said. 'I have heard about you and the Jew boy. You brought him back to life, eh? Few females are so impressive. You will find a healthy Aryan better for you. Now into the bedroom. Worse things can happen to you—and your mother.' When he mentioned my mother, my resistance was gone. I went into the bedroom and undressed and waited on the bed. When he came to me, he was naked, also—a bull—"

"Emily, please—"

"I want you to know. I will spare you details. He did not even put a gentle hand on me. He treated me like something in a—in a breeding farm. He forced my legs, and he fell on me like a machine that pounds flat the pavement. A half hour later, he sent for Dr. Voegler, and I had four stitches and was told to rest ten days. I could hardly walk to the barracks—but I had a basket of food for my mother and the others—my mother never knew the truth.

"On the tenth day, the guard came, and Colonel Schneider was at his desk, and he didn't even speak to me, just waved me into the bedroom. After that, it was every night—except twice when he had to fly to Berlin for weekends—it was every night the same, for one month. Then, the second month, he said he was displeased with me. He said I came and lay like a stick and let him do what he wanted, but he was becoming bored, he did not have to endure such insolence from me. Henceforth, if my mother and I were to enjoy his favor, I must be demonstrative—pleasing—display love and genuine excitement."

She halted and was quiet for a painful interlude.

"I did all I was told to do," she said. "Apparently it was enough. I serviced Colonel Schneider four and five and six times a week, for as much as an hour at a time, for seven months—yes, seven months. It meant nothing to me any more. But then the gossip was that the Russians were near, and the war would be ending, and Colonel Schneider flew to Berlin to see Hitler and Himmler. He never came back—he was killed in an air raid—but he had told his junior officers about me, and a Major and two Captains of the Waffen-SS took me with them when they evacuated Ravensbruck, took me to their new post at Buchenwald, near Weimar, and for several weeks—my mother was gone and I didn't give a damn about life any more—I serviced the three of them in their quarters. I went like an automaton—Pavlov's response, I suppose. Night would fall, I would automatically go to the door, the guard would come, and the cot and the three of them would be waiting. And then, suddenly, one day they were gone—and no one called me to come in the night even though I was at the door—and it was April 11, 1945, and the Americans had arrived to liberate us. They checked our records—the documents, journals, whatnot—and they found mine—and the American psychiatric officer told me what a British psychoanalyst told me later—I was in a catatonic state. No one knew of what had happened to me except the doctors, until Uncle

Max found me, and they told him a little." She paused. "Ravensbruck," she said. "That is Ravensbruck."

"Emily—Emily—what can I possibly say? Except that—except now that you've—"

She would not listen. "Everyone thinks I am a virgin," she was saying. "Wouldn't their hair stand on end to hear this? Even you thought I was a virgin. I'm sorry, Andrew, but you had to know—your nun was a whore—a veteran of three hundred nights." Suddenly she covered her eyes and her voice broke. "God, oh God, how many times in the years after—how long I've wanted to die."

He reached for her wrists and pulled her hands from her tearful eyes, and he kissed her hands. "It has nothing to do with you, Emily, none of it. You were forced into that life—and now you are free—and it is gone."

She looked at him for the first time in all this long while. "Is it gone, Andrew? How can it ever be gone?"

"Because sadism and violence were inflicted upon you—and you confuse them with loving—when they have nothing to do with loving, because you have saved and preserved and never given your love. That is still untouched. In love, you are a virgin still."

"I know you want to be kind—you are kind—you pity me—"

"I'm sorry for what happened, but what I feel for you has nothing to do with pity."

"—and I want to believe you," said Emily. "But how can I? Ever since the day the war ended, and I came to America, no man has ever touched me. I would not allow it. It was as if I had to live in a sterile bottle, apart from human contact, doing penance for mortal sin—secretly knowing that I had been soiled beyond redemption—that below the waist I was unclean—and if I were ever with a man again, he would find it out and be revolted and cast me out—and if he didn't find out, he would be cheated and used, and I would be consigned to hell's fires. Then, in all the more than fifteen years since, I began to live a fantasy—this—that if enough years passed, that filthy part of me would rot away with time, and be replaced by new clean flesh—and I would become wholesome like any normal woman—and then I could allow myself to—to accept a man—or fall in love. You know, on the boat crossing, I tried once to see if any human contact was possible, and I couldn't—I couldn't go through with it. Then I met you—and I allowed myself to let go a little—to think it was possible—but then I knew. I met your Lilly, and I knew, seeing her, knowing me—that she was health, and I was an incurable emotional cripple—that what I fancied for you—to offer myself as young and cleansed and virginal—was unreal, and that you had suffered too much to be robbed by life again."

Suddenly she closed her eyes and shook her head, then opened her eyes wide, as if recognizing him as Andrew Craig, and then she pushed herself to a seated posture. "I think the drug is wearing off. I've talked too much. Did I tell you all the things . . . ?"

"Yes, Emily, thank God."

"I'm glad. Did I tell you—did I say anything about caring for you?"

"In a way."

"Then you know that, and you know why it can't ever be."

"I don't know any such thing," he said. "I'm going to love you, and I'm going to marry you."

"Don't talk like that. Have some respect for my feelings. We can't go on, and you know why. If we married, how would it be every night? You'd know what had been before—be reminded of all I told you—know that every move I made—the filth of it would corrupt your love—and in the end, you'd have only hate, and I couldn't bear it."

She patted her hair, and straightened her sweater, and began to move her legs off the bed. "It's no use, Andrew. Let me go back to my room."

He had her by the shoulder. "No," he said sharply.

The need for her to be a part of all his remaining years, the desire to possess and own her, had become an unbearable craving. "No, you're not going to leave me alone, not when I can't live without you, not when you want me equally as much." He took her hand. "Emily, think of it, Emily, I've heard the worst, and I love you more, and I'm not going to let you ruin my life by being no part of it. I won't think of all that happened, I don't now, I won't ever in our lives. It was a black planet, inhabited by inhuman creatures, but we are human beings of the light and the earth planet, and we deserve our time. And I mean what I've been saying—you have not been touched by any man, because you have not known a moment's love. And what is untouched is all that matters—and should belong to someone who must have you and care for you. Emily, I didn't think there could be another after Harriet. When she died, I thought I had died, too. But now there is another me, a different me, alive and yearning to belong to life once more —but not alone—only with you."

He took her in his arms, and her body relaxed in them, and he kissed her hair, her ear, her cheeks, her eyes.

"Andrew," she whispered against him, "Andrew—you do mean what—what you've been saying?"

"With all my heart and soul. I'd give my life for you. It would not be worth living without you."

"Yes," she said softly. She buried her head in his chest. Her voice was almost inaudible. "I believe you now. You showed that today." Then she said, "Lie down with me, dearest. Lie down and hold me and never let me go."

"Never in our lives," he said.

She had stretched out on the bed. He lowered himself alongside her, embracing her, at peace, with the contour of her warm breasts and smooth belly and supple hips as one with him, and safe at last. He kissed her face and kissed it and kissed it, and stroked her shoulders and hair, until the last of fright was exorcised, and the old past crept away into darkness.

"Andrew," she whispered, "now you can say it."

"I love you. Forever."

She lay in bliss, and she thought: welcome earth, warm earth, the sun-warm, the green-warm, the blue-warm, the singing earth of the living. She moved her face against his to tell him her secret, to tell him—yes—yes—now I can love, too—but then she knew that he knew, and so she kept her peace which was theirs, and they rested as one. . . .

It was 6:21 in the evening.

The majestic Ceremony in the auditorium of Concert Hall was drawing to a close. Dr. Claude Marceau and Dr. Denise Marceau had been introduced and extolled in Swedish, and greeted in French, and they had accepted their award from the King, and for both of them Dr. Claude Marceau had addressed the vast assemblage. Dr. Carlo Farelli and Dr. John Garrett had received their awards, and each spoke briefly, eloquently, in turn.

Now, Professor Max Stratman, having been honored, had tried to dismiss his apprehensions about Emily, and was at the lectern, reading the speech he had so carefully prepared, a plea for East-West understanding, a plea for eternal peace.

He had reached his last paragraph. "Every year, in my country, the United States of America, we sponsor a Nobel anniversary dinner in New York City, during the month following this night. On one such occasion, a giant whom I admired and was proud to know spoke in the role of scientist and pacifist, and fittingly, his concluding words must be my concluding words. In 1945, at the American Nobel anniversary dinner, Professor Albert Einstein said, 'May the spirit that prompted Alfred Nobel to create his great institution, the spirit of trust and confidence, of generosity and brotherhood among men, prevail in the minds of those upon whose decision our destiny rests. Otherwise human civilization will be doomed.' Thank you, and good evening."

Stratman bowed to the prolonged ovation, and he returned to his chair.

Ingrid Påhl, who was to introduce Andrew Craig, last of the laureates to be honored, had already taken the empty seat beside Jacobsson, and, tugging nervously at the corsage on her gown, she despaired of what to say.

"What has happened to him?" she asked. "It will be a disgrace. What excuse can I make to His Majesty, the audience?"

"You'll have to—" Jacobsson had begun to reply, when suddenly an outburst of applause, louder and louder, from the audience, crashed against the stage. Jacobsson saw all eyes on the platform directed to the rear, and he swung around.

Andrew Craig, resplendent in full dress, wing collar and white bow tie and patent-leather pumps, was marching slowly down the center steps of the stage to his place in the right front row.

Ingrid Påhl, pale with relief, leaped up to shake his hand and give him the seat so long vacant, and Craig bowed to her and settled next to Jacobsson.

Immediately, Ingrid Påhl walked to the lectern and began to deliver in Swedish the speech on Craig and his writings that she had memorized. As she spoke to the audience, Craig tried to pretend attention, but he spoke, too, in an undertone from the corner of his mouth to Jacobsson.

"Forgive me, I want to apologize," he said. "I was unavoidably detained—no discourtesy—there was some—some trouble—but it is solved. Perhaps one day I will be able to explain it to you."

Jacobsson stared at Craig with amazement, and then deep curiosity, wondering what had detained him, and Krantz, too, Krantz across the aisle, and it occurred to Jacobsson, with not a little sadness, that no matter what he heard and saw and read, his precious Notes would never be complete. But then, he consoled himself, no record of men can ever be complete, for what is inside them, the bottomless mysteries, are not meant to be known. And, at least, at least, he told himself with relief, Craig was here, and the Notes would not be forced to record a scandal. In all, in summary, it would be a quiet and pleasant account he could make of one more placid Nobel Week.

Craig tried to listen to Ingrid Påhl, but understanding no word of Swedish, again his attention drifted. He enjoyed the gala stage, and he oriented himself to the elegant audience, and he desperately tried to remember the protocol that must momentarily be observed.

In a loge high above, his eyes caught Lilly Hedqvist, Gunnar Gottling, and Emily, his own Emily, entering, standing, staring proudly down at him. And he smiled up toward them.

He remembered how he and Emily had left his bed, and dressed, and hurried downstairs to urge the taxi to speed them to Concert Hall. Backstage, Lilly and Gottling had been waiting for his cryptic reassurance that everything had worked out all right—and then Lilly, with her own news that Daranyi was watching television in the hospital and would be home tomorrow, and Gottling, with his news that "that flat-assed broad, Sue Wiley, has gotten suspicious, and is nosing around for the story, but I warned her if she made any more trouble, I'd bust into her room and deflower her, so I think she'll behave."

And as they had waited for Stratman's speech to end, listening backstage, Craig had taken Emily's hand, knowing that she had given herself to him for life, knowing that this life with her would not always be easy or uncomplicated, yet knowing, even as he left her to march into the glare of the stage, that it would work, because Humpty Dumpty had been put together again.

With a start, hearing his name and himself addressed, he realized that Ingrid Påhl had completed her speech in Swedish and was now speaking to him, briefly, in English, informing him of why he had been honored this night. And then this was done, and she advanced toward him, hand outstretched, a smile wreathing her face, and he was on his feet, accepting her hand, as the audience applauded.

She guided him now along the train of carpet to the railing and stairs that led down from the center stage. And there she remained, while he descended the stairs to the King who waited to shake his hand. They met again, clasped hands warmly.

"I congratulate you, Mr. Craig," said the King. He handed Craig a large tooled-calf portfolio. "Your citation—diploma," said the monarch. "And in this leather box, the gold medallion. Have a look at it." Craig accepted the box and opened it, and the medallion, bearing two classical figures, one with a lyre, sparkled, and he enjoyed it.

"Finally," the King was saying, "the envelope with the prize check, you may pick up in the morning. Once more, I congratulate you, Mr. Craig." The ruler's eyes twinkled. "And do not forget you have promised me your next work of fiction when it is done."

Craig smiled. "That will be sooner than you think, Your Majesty, and thank you."

He almost forgot, so many eyes upon him, and then he remembered what was expected. Bowing, he backed off from the King, and moving sideways but still facing the King and somehow Emily, he went backwards up the steps to his chair, as the audience rose en masse and clapped.

Craig handed his three awards to Jacobsson, and then, slowly, thoughtfully, he made his way to the lectern.

After applause overwhelmed him once more, a silence fell. He had no speech, but glancing up at the loge, he knew what he must say.

"Your Royal Highnesses, ladies and gentlemen. On this most memorable day of my thirty-nine years on earth, I do not wish to speak of creativity, of man the creator or man the politician, but rather, of man the individual. Not many years ago, a great countryman of mine, in my field, Mr. William Faulkner, spoke to you about the immortality of man, because man has a soul, a spirit capable of compassion, sacrifice, endurance. I wish to address you tonight on another facet of man—the obligation of man to his time on earth."

He paused, thinking about it, and realized that he was not speaking to the audience at all, not to these two thousand nor the thousands who were watching television, not to the millions who might ever read his words. He was speaking to himself, clarifying it all for himself, himself and Emily who were one, and thus, perhaps, secondarily to all humankind.

In each one of us, he reflected to himself in these fleeting moments, there were, like unused muscles and organs, resources of the spirit—courage and energy and responsibility—never employed in our time in the world. The blessed one was he who, confronted with a crisis in his life (as was all humanity this day), was driven to call upon these resources, to use them to survive, even triumph, over life itself. One so challenged and so triumphant had won the only prize that counted—the prize of the Maker of the spirit, the rebirth of a withering soul and, as such, a Homeric victory over life's disasters. In a lesser way, he had been so challenged, and had discovered the resources he had not known that he possessed, and was therefore, now at last, an entire man. This, indeed, was his prize. He wondered if all the others, before him, everywhere, could understand this victory and its honor. He must make them understand it. They must know the supreme value of challenge, and the eternal necessity to meet it as an individual and grow to fullest life.

"This is the foremost of earthly honors that you have offered me," he found himself saying aloud. "I am moved and grateful beyond inadequate words. But I believe Alfred Nobel would have understood what I will say next. It is this—that all man's honors to men are small beside the greatest prize to which he may and must aspire—the finding of his soul, his spirit, his divine strength and worth—the knowledge that he can and must live in freedom and dignity—the final realization that life is not a daily dying, not a pointless end, not an ashes-to-ashes and dust-to-dust, but a soaring and blinding gift snatched from eternity. The ultimate prize is to know that each new day's challenge is meaningful and offered for use, that it must be taken to the bosom, and it must be used—and to know this, to understand this, is the one prize worthy as man's goal and all mankind's summit."

He paused. He scanned the intent faces, the sea of faces, beneath him, and they came distinct, this one and that, as faces like his own, and at once he knew that they understood the urgency of his self-revelation, and that they waited to welcome him back to Ithaca.

Never, never in all his life, had he felt more reassured and more content. He knew where he was going. And so, at last, at last, he could go on. . . .

AN AFTERWORD

The gestation period of this novel was fifteen years.

I first conceived of doing a work of fiction laid against the background of the Nobel Prize Week on a Sunday noon in September of 1946, while I looked out from a window of a corner suite of the Grand Hotel in Stockholm and listened to the King's band play before the Royal Palace across the Strommen canal.

In that exciting autumn of 1946, I began the task of developing fictional characters and constructing a fictional story for what was to become this novel. Intermittently, through those fifteen years, I also devoted myself to the parallel job of researching the background of the story. During the month of July of 1960, in a hotel suite in Paris, I began the actual writing of The Prize, *and concluded the writing in October of 1961, in Los Angeles.*

In terms of story, this book is entirely a work of fiction, totally the product of the author's imagination. The characters who people these pages, and perform, are make-believe; and the entire plot or plots of the book are purest fabrication. If the characters or situations have, or have had, any counterparts in real life, the resemblance must be accepted as surprising coincidence.

What is factual in this novel is the following: with the exception of the characters' residences, almost every site and sight of Stockholm mentioned is a true one, visited by the author during the autumn of 1946 and again during the summer of 1960. Also, the history of the Nobel Prize awards, the descriptions of the academies, exterior and interior, the procedures and methods of nomination and voting and politicking and awarding of the prizes, the discussions about famous laureates, their names, their behavior, the information and gossip about them, the so-called inside stories about them, are all, to the best of my knowledge, true and accurate.

I have taken only a handful of liberties with the prize-giving procedure, and this to improve the dramatic aspects of the novel. The wording of the notification telegrams has been invented. These telegrams are usually sent off by the individual academies or the Swedish Foreign Office; I have preferred to have them originate in the Nobel Foundation. The innovation of simultaneous press conferences is my own creation. Usually, the press conferences are held at different times, although in 1959 the literary and chemistry press conferences overlapped. The King's Royal Banquet, which

I have placed early in my narrative, actually occurs the day following the award Ceremony at Concert Hall. This Banquet is never preceded by cocktails. But this seemed impossible to me, so I took the liberty of introducing a more convivial atmosphere. The laureates' speechmaking, which I have taking place at Concert Hall, actually most often takes place later in the evening at a Town Hall dinner. Finally, it would only be fair to mention that, while political conflicts and national antagonisms often permeate Nobel Week, there is no known instance of blackmail or criminal activity or major scandal in Nobel Prize history. The possibility always exists. But, to date, the Swedish security system has been faultless.

For the factual information woven through a work of fiction, I wish to acknowledge the cooperation of many persons during the years between 1946 and 1961. For personal interviews and unselfish correspondence, I owe much to the kindness of such Nobel laureates as Dr. Albert Einstein, Dr. Robert A. Millikan, Dr. Herman J. Muller, Mrs. Pearl Buck, Miss Sigrid Undset, Dr. Henry J. Cadbury (American Friends Service Committee), and several others who cannot be mentioned. For similar help, I must express gratefulness to such prominent Nobel officials as Sven L. Hammarskiöld, and Anders Österling, as well as the former and present executive directors of the Nobel Foundation, Nils K. Ståhle and Professor Arne Tiselius. My thanks also to members of the staff of employees at the Nobel Foundation, and especially Miss Margareta Delin.

For assistance inside Sweden, I want to acknowledge the help of Lakrederarc Norback, John Bergvall, Sven Gerjerstam, Rudolf Wendbladh, Mrs. Adele Heilborn, Ned Nordness, Dr. Nicholas Norlin, and Sven-Erik Bergh. For assistance in learning about Sweden, I owe thanks to Henry Goddard Leach, Allan Kastrup, Mac Lindahl, and several members of the Swedish press who prefer anonymity.

For general research assistance, I am indebted to E. J. Berman, M.D., of Indianapolis, Indiana; H. G. Harshbarger, M.D., of Riverside, California; Mrs. Luise Johnson, of Indianapolis, Indiana; Mrs. Esther Biederman, of Tarzana, California; Mrs. Elizebethe Kempthorne, of Arlington, California.

I am also deeply indebted to a number of lovely Swedish young ladies in Stockholm—who shall remain nameless—for generous and forthright interviews that acquainted me with the facts of life, as seen through the eyes of the typical unmarried Swedish female.

All these people, big and little in reputation, were selfless in offering of their time and knowledge. There is simply no way to thank them enough, except to tell the reader that—in what is factual of this fiction—these people bear absolutely no responsibility for the worst of it and deserve every accolade for the best of it.

Of books that went into the making of a book, I always find there seems no end. I tried to read everything ever printed in English in recent decades on the Nobel Prize awards and on Sweden. I found invaluable Nobel—The Man and His Prizes, *edited by the Nobel Foundation, 1951;* Alfred Nobel, *by Herta E. Pauli, 1942;* Nobel Foundation Calendar, *1960;* Alfred Nobel and the Nobel Prizes, *1960;* Nobel Prize Winners, *edited by L. J. Ludovici, 1957. My files are packed with clippings on the prizes and on Sweden from American and European periodicals and newspapers.*

As to the futuristic discoveries made by my science winners, these discoveries are, for now, as fictional as Andrew Craig's books. At the same time, a considerable amount of reading and research, as well as personal interviewing of physicists, chemists, physicians, was undertaken by me to acquire information that would root my discoveries in reality and probability. Needless to say, enormous advances are being made in the fields of organ transplantation, solar energy, and sperm vitrification. And, perhaps, someday, somebody from the Midwest will write a book entitled The Perfect State.

What is left to own and disown?

This: that, for the most, the opinions expressed in this novel are strictly those of the characters and do not necessarily reflect the opinions of their creator.

And this: that I owe, and wish now to pay, a debt of special thanks to my wife, Sylvia Wallace, for incredible tolerance in permitting all these characters, on all the preceding pages, to enter our home and become a part of our lives and our family for so long a time.

IRVING WALLACE

*Los Angeles
1962*

ABOUT THE AUTHOR

IRVING WALLACE *was born in Chicago and went to high school in Kenosha, Wisconsin. He won several scholarships in creative writing and accepted one from Williams Institute, in Berkeley, California, where he remained for a year, after which he quit to free-lance for magazines.*

Since Mr. Wallace sold his first magazine article (for $5.00) at the age of fifteen, he has written seven books, among them The Square Pegs, *a Book-of-the-Month Club recommendation;* The Fabulous Showman (*a life of P. T. Barnum*), *which was a Literary Guild selection;* The Chapman Report, *a best-selling novel which has now been made into a major motion picture; and* The Twenty-Seventh Wife (*a biography of Ann Eliza Young, last wife of Brigham Young, the Mormon Prophet*).

From 1942 to 1946 he served in the United States Army, writing scripts for orientation and propaganda films.

A tireless researcher, for his novels as well as his nonfiction, Mr. Wallace has traveled throughout the world, climbed a 17,000-foot mountain in Mexico, participated in an expedition into the Honduras jungles, and been barred from prewar Japan and Franco Spain. Mr. Wallace conceived the idea of The Prize *fifteen years ago in Stockholm. To guarantee its authenticity, he visited Sweden twice, conversed with Nobel officials and judges, received cooperation from such Nobel winners as Albert Einstein, Robert A. Millikan and Sigrid Undset, and made extensive trips to other scenes of the novel in Denmark, Germany, France and Italy.*

Mr. Wallace, his wife, Sylvia, a former magazine editor, and his two children, Amy and David, live in West Los Angeles, California. He is now working on a new novel, "The Three Sirens," the subject of which will be an anthropological team's study of a unique marriage system in Polynesia.